Katy of Catoctin

– OR –

THE CHAIN-BREAKERS

A National Romance

Katy of Catoctin

– OR –

THE CHAIN-BREAKERS

A National Romance

GEORGE ALFRED TOWNSEND

WILDSIDE PRESS
Doylestown, Pennsylvania

From the D. Appleton and Company (New York) edition of 1886.

Katy of Catoctin
A publication of
WILDSIDE PRESS
P.O. Box 301
Holicong, PA 18928–0301

www.wildsidepress.com

"Older than the Shenandoah mountains is love."

— EMERSON

To
COLONEL JOHN HAY
WHOSE ACQUAINTANCE I MADE IN THE WHITE HOUSE,
WHERE THE PRESIDENT AND EMANCIPATOR
LAY DEAD.

Preface

FROM the hour the author stood by the dead face of Abraham Lincoln, in the Executive Mansion at Washington, he has had the idea of writing a romance upon the conspiracy of Booth.

Like many such literary projects nursed by a journalist, this one had not only to be postponed, but finally to become a portion of a broader story, because too many of the actors in the tragedy still lived, and the mere crime presented no elevated moral to justify its embellishment.

Considering it, however, as one of a series of cumulative acts of violence committed upon or from the soil of Maryland during the conflict of Emancipation, the author felt not only an epic propriety to be in the theme, but it appealed to him as a descendant of Marylanders and one who had already, in his romance of "The Entailed Hat," pictured the twin lobe of Maryland and the rise of the slave interest.

The temptation to paint the more picturesque Western Shore, from the old Catholic tidewater counties and the metropolitan life of Washington and Baltimore to the German valleys and the mountain battlefields, was not to be dismissed, either by the sacrifice it would require, or from the delicacy of a generation still alive.

Experimenting with the subject, the author found such rapid changes taking place in all this region, in thought as well as in things, that he believed it would be next to impossible in twenty years more for anyone to realize the society which came first into national notice when Booth made his *hegira* through it. Besides, the author's stock of materials, made complete by visits and searches of nineteen years, required the interpretation of his own eye and hand.

He felt that, while to have written this book earlier would have been to speak too harshly and too narrowly of some agents in the crime, to postpone the composition longer would have been to remand it to mere antiquarian literature and lose the missionary use and the heartiness of adventure; for, when he knew Booth personally and saw his associates executed, the author was turning into twenty-five, and, when he unraveled the skein of Booth's concealment and flight after the crime, the author was turning forty-four years. Voters had grown up in the interim who had been but tottling babes when the mighty war ceased with this sacrificial mass, and the President's death ended the wild Maryland epic, of which the raid of John Brown, the Baltimore riots, Antietam battle, and the spy system in the old Potomac counties were elements.

Enough of all this was yet undiscovered to leave space for fancy to enliven the athletic game, and in one or two cases characters have been wholly invented, or rather made out of general types and conditions, to replace others not proper to be copied.

The author not only lived contemporary with the personages of his book, but he was an active traveler and sightseer with and among them. No natural scene is sketched in this book that did not dwell upon his sight, and he trusts that the impassioned scenes of action have been tinted in subordination to a national and human philosophy.

— GAPLAND, MD., 1886

Chapter I

MOUNTAINEERS

"MARYLAND is only a rim of shore, a shell of mountain, but all gold!"

So said Lloyd Quantrell, the gunner, looking down from the South Mountain upon Middletown or Catoctin Valley, an October Saturday in the year 1859.

The mellow light of afternoon touched or bathed the hundred farms, the bridges, barns, hamlets, stacks, corn-rows, brown woods, streams and stone walls, and with a fruity smell, as of cider-presses, seemed to come up the tone of bells ringing the Marylanders home from the labors of the week.

He saw the red and white spires of Middletown in the lap of the valley like its babe, and thought he saw, beyond its Catoctin Mountain knees, the father Frederick, the good old burgher, holding his devout fingers up, like index boards at the junction of his many pike roads.

Then fancy spread other terraces of Maryland, farther and farther on, like descending steps of gold and marble, beyond the hills of Sugarloaf and Linganore, to where Potomac and Patapsco blended their cascades and ocean-tides at the shrines of Washington and Baltimore.

Lloyd Quantrell's dog put his nose in the air silently, looking also downward, as if he scented, with the pheasants of the mountain, the sea-fowl of the Chesapeake.

A train of cars was crossing the mouth of Catoctin Valley from the dark chasm of Harper's Ferry, as the dog started back along the mountaintop, "pointing" for a bird; and when Lloyd had followed and fired at and missed the bird, he saw another view in the west, all flooded with the sunset — the plateau between the Antietam and Potomac, stretching in woodland or crystal to the North Mountain and the Conococheague.

Here, amid equal abundance, a wilder paradise extended, as if nature's ruggedness had somewhat delayed the gardener hands of man.

Beneath Quantrell's eye, to the left, a short, bold mountain intruded, which had begun a race with the South Mountain for the Pennsylvania line, but stopped in sight of the white clusters of settlement toward Hagerstown, discouraged at their beauty and multitude, like Balaam's stride arrested by the Hebrew camps.

Between this, Elk Ridge (or Maryland Heights) Mountain, and his own, and in the narrow peninsula beyond, where the Potomac begged a passage to the Shenandoah, a few wild farms found lodgment, as if poor, fugitive, and hermit men had clung there to a funnel, and now their white log and plaster houses and decayed black barns, in the midst of small mountain orchards, sent up to Quantrell light spirals of smoke, or flame of burning brushwood, or bells of milch-cows tinkling in alder-copses.

Where these wild homes and startled spurs of mountain halted, the basin of the great Cumberland Valley fell away indistinctly, and Keedysville lay in the foreground, like a bunch of the American flag.

The colors in the landscape were gold, purple, chrome, and all varieties of autumnal blue and gray, and, as if they were mixed in a cup, the young Baltimore sportsman drank them in and pined to understand the delight: for the love of scenery yearns to become an art.

In all this patriotic prospect there was no responsive heart, and Lloyd Quantrell was still unbeloved.

New pulses had beat of late in him, and, like the hair upon his lip, sentiment had begun to grow: the idea of woman followed him about — of no one woman but of womankind, and in this glowing Eden of his native State the scenery seemed to lack a sympathetic spirit to reach up her white arms from the vale and cry: "Come down, my love, appointed for me; and I will make thy soul at rest, to enjoy every prospect, which, lonely, thou never canst!"

Beautiful, detached time of life! when, like a mote of the Italian poplar's pollen blowing in the air to find the female cup, the souls of two young, destined people, yet unknown, solicit each other in the world.

The crude, destructive instincts of the young man were expressed aloud in his emotion between savagery and art:

"What would I do if all this was mine, on both sides of the mountain?" Lloyd Quantrell said. "Let me see! Why, I would clean out the whole region, like a Norman king, and make it a hunting park. All the wild beasts once here should return again — none but native American beasts, you bet! I would let them make their dens and shelters in these towns. The people would have to go — go West, I suppose — and then these stone, brick, and timber villages would decay, and we should have real American ruins in a few years. Too many Dutch are in this up-country for *me!* Instead of a lot of Dutchmen going to Baltimore market, we should have hunters sending down deer and bear. I would bring the buffaloes back from the West — for *they* used to herd here too, in the early day — and let them make dust, like an army, as they galloped before my hunters. The wolf should howl again, to make the mountains romantic. I would have grizzlies hug each other, panthers sneak away and prowl nearer again, and foxes should be protected, so that every day would be a morning chase. My castle I would put on the South Mountain, right here where I stand."

He stopped, thinking what would a castle be without a lady. But in a minute his mind ran along with the vision:

"I think," he resumed, "that I would not disturb the Dutch beauties, for I would need a few vassals, and, to reconcile these and give me society, I might marry one of them. Yes, she should be the rosiest of all. I would educate her and make her my baroness; Baroness of the Blue Ridge."

As his thoughts, like the predatory hawk, flew back to a domestic nest and mate, Lloyd basked a moment in the soft, languorous vision of a settlement in life, till the dog whined and pointed, and, looking where it indicated, the gunner saw, in the edge of the woods, a few steps distant, a strange, primitive old man, accompanied by two young companions, watching him.

The apparition was more lean than tall, and dressed in dark woolens, cut almost Quaker fashion, and his waistcoat was buttoned nearly up to a leather stock around the tough whip-cords in his throat, which were revealed when he took his bushy gray beard in one hand and drew it aside, looking meantime at young Quantrell with a pair of severe, gray-blue eyes.

The intruder's hair was brushed straight up from a rather low, receding forehead. He had a hawkish nose, and the beard which encircled his face, and would have fallen low upon his breast, stood outward at his chin like autumn brush against a rock.

"If this is your land, you don't mind my gunning on it?" spoke Quantrell.

"It is not my land, sir," answered the man, not finishing his searching look.

"Then I don't see why you look at me so hard, friend, unless I have stolen something."

"Are you from Virginia?" asked the man.

"No, I am from Maryland — from Baltimore."

"You have been walking around this country three days!"

"There's no law against that, old man. I have been shooting, what little there is, and picking a few fish out of the brooks. Have you been following me all the time?"

"I have seen you around my dwelling, sir, on two occasions, yesterday and the day before," continued the mountaineer, "and you are here still."

"Upon my word, friend, I don't see why I shouldn't pass your dwelling every day of my holiday here, particularly as I don't know where it is!"

An idea crossed Lloyd Quantrell's mind that there might be robbers in these mountains, and he gave a glance at the two other men.

They were young fellows, and, in appearance, were so nearly the same, that observing one, answered for both; of good height, spare-faced and sunburned, sallow, worn thin, and with long, dark hair and beards; mere rustics to look at, with some passing alertness of curiosity now, but too docile and gentle to retain a predatory purpose.

This time Lloyd Quantrell guessed that they might be an old preacher and his two sons, of Mennonite, or Dunker, or some mountain Dutch sect. But the nasal tone of the old man, and his bold, grave address, made Lloyd think again that he had seen such men bringing horses to Baltimore market from Ohio and the West.

The only sign of offensive warfare they possessed was a kind of spear of steel, like a broad, double-edged knife-blade, with a cross-piece or guard below, and carried upon a wooden pole by one of the younger persons.

"What have you there, my friend?" asked Quantrell, walking over freshly. "It looks like what we called at school 'a gig,' to spear suckers and pike."

"I calkelate you hit it right the first time," said the possessor, smiling agreeably.

"We live over beyond the Short Mountain there," explained the other young man; "down on the river road to the ferry. Since we've been here, so few well-dressed strangers have gone past, that father was a little surprised at you — that's all."

"Then we are all Marylanders," exclaimed Quantrell, "and I'm glad of that, because I have been lonesome for somebody to drink with me. Here's a flask of old Needwood whisky, I know I can recommend! Age before beauty, pop!"

He extended the flask to the old man and winked at the boys.

"It's something I never drank, sir, in my life," spoke the firm old man, shaking his head.

Lloyd then turned to the boys.

"We're not accustomed to it, friend," said the elder of these, "but don't let us interfere with *you.*"

Quantrell drank, and liked it so well that he drank twice, and then, laying down his gun and calling in his dog, he felt familiar and companionable with all men. He produced cigars and a fuse, and offered his cigar-case to the party.

"We're unfortunate," said the younger of the sons; "neither father nor we boys smoke, or use tobacco."

"Sit down, anyway," said the young man from the city; "there's the habit of talk, that is common to all. What is your name? — Smith will do; anything to begin on."

"You're a good guesser. Smith is what it is," spoke the old man, taking off his wool hat and stretching himself on the rocks and grass. *"Isaac Smith — and yours?"*

"Quantrell, of Baltimore."

"Ah!" exclaimed Mr. Smith, "that is the name of one of the slave-dealers there!"

"Yes," said Lloyd, reddening a little, "that's unfortunately an uncle of mine. He's managed, by the notoriety of the business, to have me identified pretty generally. It's a business I shouldn't go into — because it's not a gentleman's."

The young men, as if interested, now stretched themselves on the mountain-slope, and the older man, changing his look to one more neighborly, said, in an impressive yet kind voice:

"Hardly a good Christian business, Mr. Quantrell! A business has got to be good, I think, sir, to insure any prosperity. If nobody could be found to trade in slaves, the evils of slavery would be small, because they would not be sent to great distances and worked up on the plantations. It would then not be profitable. Slavery in Maryland, except in two or three counties, is a trifling matter."

"Yes," said Lloyd, "it's small, except in the tobacco counties, and they, as you have said, don't seem to prosper. But I hope you ain't an abolitionist, Mr. Smith?"

"Unfortunately, I am a slaveholder," said Smith, straightforwardly.

"How many Negroes have you got?"

"Six."

"Why, pop," answered Lloyd, familiarly, "you're a man of property! What are Negroes worth, up this way?"

"They're higher than they will be, I think," said Mr. Smith, reflectively.

Quantrell looked at the old man's Judaic nose and wrinkled bridge thereof, and wad of grizzly hair above his grizzled, updrawn eyebrows, with the gray-blue eyes wide apart, cool 'and deep as frozen springs, and that mouth, which was like a fissure in granite, and again it seemed to the young man that there was something wild in Mr. Smith.

"Yet," he reflected, "Smith is a man more substantial every way than he looks. Six Negroes and a farm, and reasoning so rationally against his interests — and with religious views, too!"

"What are your politics, Smith?" asked Lloyd. "I'll be frank with you, and tell you, *I'm an American.*"

"Why, so am I, Mr. Quantrell!"

"Shake hands on it, old fellow," cried Lloyd, while the sons laughed aloud to see the city stranger's open temperament pushing the acquaintance.

"I'm just keyed up on that," repeated Lloyd, clasping Mr. Smith's hands heartily, "for there are too many Dutch and Irish in this, our country. Down in Baltimore we have got them on the run. I'm a *cock-robin!*"

"I don't quite understand you, Mr. Quantrell. Is that a kind of fire company or political club?"

"You've got it, Smith! On every suitable occasion we turn out and have a parade, and go right through the foreign quarter, driving everything we see under cover. Our idea is that Americans are good enough to rule America!"

Mr. Smith reflected a minute, and said that good Americans ought to make the best rulers. "However," he added, "Senator Broderick, of California, was an Irishman, I believe, and he has just been murdered, in a duel."

"Well, he's an Irishman's *son,*" replied Lloyd; "he was born on the Potomac here, in the District of Columbia, and that's almost as good as Maryland."

"They killed him," figured up Mr. Smith, in his deliberate, nasal way," on the 18th of last month. It will be four weeks tomorrow night, Mr. Quantrell."

At this, the plain, independent old man, as Lloyd began to think him, looked at his two sons, and they raised their eyes to him.

"Next Sunday night will be four weeks," repeated Mr. Smith, still looking at his boys, "since David Broderick was killed by a judge, in a duel. The newspapers say his last dying words were, 'They killed me because I was opposed to the extension of slavery and a corrupt Administration.'"

There was a look of queer import, Lloyd Quantrell thought, between those plain people; for, as if forgetful of himself, they continued observing each other with a sense of some strong coincidence.

At this moment Quantrell's dog started and ran a little way down the mountain and "pointed" at some low saplings with his fine white and brown nose.

Lloyd took his gun and followed out of sight of his new companions, and finally saw a mourning-dove sitting in a leafless tree. He raised his piece and aimed, feeling it unworthy work to shoot a turtledove, but as he withdrew the gun his dog still "pointed," as if ravenous after the day's barren sport.

Quantrell waved his hand, intimating to the trained animal to seek to the right and farther on.

The dog, for a minute, obeyed the order, and then returned, and, with tail straight out and one leg lifted, "nosed" the solitary dove again and made a slight, whimpering entreaty.

"Well, Albion," thought his master, "I must either disappoint you or the dove," and he aimed again and shot the bird.

It was so soft-eyed and so harmless, and seemed to look with such love and suffering at him as it trembled in his hand in the convulsion of death, the red rill of blood making purpler its brown plumage — like the blood of Abel sinking in the ground — that Lloyd felt some self-accusation.

With the dead bird in his hand he walked back toward the place of conversation, where he was arrested at a cedar tree by the singular posture of Smith and his sons.

The old man was standing with his hands stretched straight out and their palms together, his body drawn up and his beard pointing upward, as his head was thrown back; while his sons, still seated, had crawled nearer their father, and had dropped their beards, as if assisting in prayer.

In the greatest wonder, Lloyd Quantrell looked at this scene, and for a minute doubted, as is natural with all men in a very practical land, seeing silent human marvels in lonely places, whether he saw anything at all; if the mountain at this point were not enchanted, and these three serious mountaineers only appearances or illusions.

But he heard articulated sounds proceeding from that old man's beard, and the word "Amen!" pronounced with respectful inclinations of their heads, by both his tough, grown sons.

A new feeling then suddenly rose upon young Quantrell's imagination; for the first time he had a sense of parental influence, something he had never known — confidence, consultation, and parental respect and discipline between a father and sons.

Before him was such a scene: absolute community of thought, directed by a strong-willed, plain-hearted father, who held his matured sons in the leash of his integrity and morality, till they loved his magistracy, and were like women to his counsel and authority.

"Such sons exist no more where I have been," thought Lloyd, "at least not in the life I have seen. There the restraint of sons is broken by their waywardness and rebellion in early boyhood, even if their fathers desire to control them, or are worthy to do so."

He thought of his own self-loving father, without moral restraints himself, or ever a rebuke for his son's indulgences.

At the crackle of his approaching feet, the old man, Smith, and his boys ceased their apparent devotion and turned their heads.

"Mr. Quantrell," spoke the old man, again examining Lloyd piercingly, "we do a little surveying on the mountains, and that is why we found you in this unexpected spot. They tell me, sir, who have lived here longer than I have, that General Washington was the first surveyor of these parts, and surveyed Harper's Ferry tract itself. But what have you been killing?"

He took in his hand the little bird, and looked at Lloyd as he had at first, with a severe, almost domineering examination, and tight jaws.

"I have no respect for any man who will shoot a little dove," he remarked, in a cold, reproving tone.

His sons also looked rebuke, and one of them said:

"Mr. Quantrell, that wasn't fair game!"

"No, I am ashamed of it," spoke Lloyd Quantrell, frankly. "My dog pointed so obstinately that I killed the poor thing against my better will."

"I will forgive you, young man," exclaimed Smith, the elder, "on condition that, if you ever see a man going to kill another dove, you will reprove him, sir."

"I will," said Lloyd, blushing, "unless he already feels as mean as I do."

"Father," interposed the younger Smith, "it was an accident, I calkelate. He's owned it like a man. Let us show him our favor*ite* view of the valleys."

They looked again over the Catoctin Valley, and also at the Hagerstown Valley, both softer, paler in the descending sunlight.

It seemed to Lloyd, when he recalled these scenes in later years, as if that sunset was the last vouchsafed the world of heavenly peace and blessing.

Chapter II
THE LOOKER

"FRIEND Smith," exclaimed Lloyd Quantrell, "I was thinking to myself, just before we met, that if this high country of the Cumberland Valley, and the apron of it off here to the east, were all my property, I would make it a great baronial park, and stock it with nothing but American game collected from every State and Territory — a sort of Forest of Ardennes."

Quantrell, who was a good singer, and of an unrestrained, hearty temperament, here recollected a bit of song, and without any ceremony raised his voice and sang, to the delight of Smith's boys:

> "'Under the greenwood tree,
>   Who loves to lie with me,
>   And tune his merry note
>   Unto the sweet bird's throat,
> Come hither, come hither, come hither:
>   Here shall he see
>   No enemy,
> But winter and rough weather.'

"Ha, ha, ha!" cried Lloyd, when he had ended, his melodious voice humanizing the place, and seeming to touch the younger son, whom the old man had addressed as Oliver, almost to tears, "that's a song a friend of mine, a great young actor, sings like a real hunter. Now, if you and I and the boys here had control of this, we'd live like banished dukes. Is that your sentiment, Oliver?"

The young man with the sallow face and modest, sunken eyes, and careless hair and beard, put his brown hand to his throat, where there was a rising swelling, and said: "I think it is beautiful as it is. One log-house and — and my wife, would be enough for me."

The old man, with a firm voice, interposed, glancing seriously at the son's evident susceptibility to the song and the question.

"This is pretty scenery, gentlemen, and rich country," he said, in a high, shrill tone, "and it delights the eye; but it fails to appeal to the mind, for the reason that history has not yet embellished it. Its great uses have not yet been perceived, I think. To grow grain and make butter and cheese, are agreeable to man; but even so fine a region as this can not compete with the great West in those respects — with Illinois, Iowa, and the Territory of Kansas. The political importance of the Allegheny Mountains far exceeds their agricultural importance. If I had been General Washington, and had his influence to locate the capital of the United States, I would have placed it behind the South Mountain, instead of in the clay gullies of the tidewater country."

"O friend Smith," cried Lloyd Quantrell, "there are too many Dutch up this way. They don't know anything in the Dutch country but saving and slaving, and that would never do."

"But hear father out, sir," exclaimed the elder son. "He's been a great reader and traveler. Father's been to Europe!"

It was not common in 1859 to have "been to Europe," and even the young Baltimorean looked at Smith with new interest.

The old man pointed over the valley with long fingers, his shoulders stooping a little, and his retreating forehead, hollow in the center, assisting the hawkness of his nose.

Lines of thought and an abstracted countenance marked his face while moving up and down and consulting the ground, but when he faced Lloyd Quantrell and his own sons, and gave them the full benefit of his steady and penetrating eyes, they felt that the narrow-shouldered, wiry old fellow must be a tall man.

He now took his beard in one hand, and with the other pointing over the autumnal-tinted plain and detached mountains, gazed out like some Hebrew seer.

"You want your political capital, gentlemen, where it has natural defenses against a military enemy, such as mountains interpose, and has population and agriculture enough to feed and defend it, and is also in a position to exert all its political influence with what I will call geographical directness on the country. The city of Washington can do nothing of that kind. It was easily taken and destroyed by a small army in the year 1814. Before it was established the people in its vicinity were getting their food from these German upland valleys. It has now no political influence at all, except a pernicious one, on the American people, having been governed for sixty years by the local ideas of two places — Richmond in Virginia and Baltimore in Maryland. Those cities were bound to influence it in the line of their very backward, or, as some say, conservative tendencies, because they received no other elements of population that lived around them in the old tidewater parts — people who continued to raise tobacco, catch herring, sell Negroes, and marry their cousins. On the other hand, the country above the South Mountain ridge could subsist a very large population, and feed a large army, during repeated years of war. This mountain, with its natural ramparts, could be easily held by a few troops at the passes. The great valley behind it is the line of emigration and of easy communication from the St. Lawrence to the Mississippi, and, gentlemen, the inevitable line of war!"

Without paying attention to anybody, Smith reached out his hand and took the spear instrument from his son, and, gesturing with it against the blue air, looked to Quantrell to be a colossal and seedy school-master, illustrating a lecture on an enormous blackboard.

"It will cost more fighting men than can be levied from all that tidewater country," he continued, "merely to protect the government and the public property located at the city of Washington. If the capital had been placed here, in the Cumberland Valley, it would have been able to launch armies against the enemy and protect itself from a perpetually flanking second army, moving up the valley and getting to the north of Washington. *Here* will the enemy invade once and again, and have the start in the race, and be deep in the resources and positions of your country before you can come up with him and make him turn and fight. I would remove the public effects from Washington. I would hold Baltimore to her allegiance by Fortress Monroe. I would take the valley of the Cumberland Mountains from them at the beginning, leaving them to scratch clay and eat fodder on the emaciated plains, and I would fight them from the west!"

"Crazy as a bedbug," thought Lloyd Quantrell, a little awed, "and on the subject of the Revolutionary War."

Sticking the fish-spear in the sward and apostrophizing it, Mr. Smith, now apparently aroused and in the depth of his subject, continued in the same plain, brief style of address:

"This is why God has established the Allegheny Mountains — for the refuge of his people! The geologist tells us that the first mountains in the world to be made were the Adirondacks. My schooling was all before these days of science, and I don't just quite get the idea. But if it be so, that the first land to rise above the sea and give the raven foothold after the deluge was *there*, where our household affections look today" (he glanced at his sons), "even upon that Ararat, I was always thinking of my boyhood, when I was a tanner on these Alleghenies.

"Yes," resumed Isaac Smith, after a pause, "in the year 1826 I was tanning leather near the spot where General Washington — at your ages now, and my age when I lived there — went on his long winter journey to stop the French at old Fort Le Bœuf. I used to look at the creek that supplied my vats, and wish I could follow it down to the Venango and the Allegheny, and ascend Washington's path by the Monongahela to the mountains and cross them to the Potomac. I married there, and the desire of money arrested my dreams; but every energy I put out in that direction failed. At times great fortunes seemed within my grasp, but slipped from me. In Europe, where I went for business, I found my mind led to battlefields and the study of war. I tried to drive the idea away, and regain my credit in the business of all my maturer life — grading and selling wool; for I could tell the difference in similar wools raised in different of our States if they were put in my hand in the dark! But the confused verses of Scripture would rise in my mind whenever I heard the military trumpets sound abroad: 'He seeketh wool and worketh willingly, but all his household are clothed in *scarlet!*'"

"And now, old man," exclaimed the irreverent Quantrell, "you think you are at last back in a good country!"

"Yes, Mr. Quantrell," said Isaac Smith, soberly, "I am in the country of my destiny. I love this country, and hope it may be loved for me and my children."

"You have made one mourner in advance, pop," answered Lloyd. "I think you only need to have been born in a military age to have reached the consideration of Sam Houston or General Jackson. But, unfortunately, you could no more get these Dutch, up this way, to fight than teach them style."

"We never can tell, gentlemen," said Smith, "when war is, as you may say, at our elbow. I have been a great reader of the history of wars, particularly in the Old Testament. Most of the wars there recorded, were made by Moses, acting out the will of God. He led the Hebrews out of their bondage in Egypt and toward a land of promise. The people in that land, we may understand, had done no harm to Moses or his people. They existed as peaceably as the people of Virginia and Maryland, that we see from this elevation — working for the dollar and expecting no enemy whatever. But Moses, who was keeping his flocks on the back side of the desert, as we read, 'went out on the mountain of God, even to Horeb,' say the Scriptures. Something took him there not in the way of interest, perhaps not his desire. But there he heard his name called aloud from a burning bush, or heap of brush — 'Moses, Moses!' And he said, 'Here am I!'"

Lloyd Quantrell was again convinced that the Smith family were crazy.

As he recited this old bit of Scripture, with a slow, shrill, nasal cry, Isaac Smith folded his arms, closed his eyes, and dropped his head upon his beard and breast, standing there a moment speechless, and his sons, also taking his attitude, looked to the ground as if all three were again to pray together.

"'Here am I, Lord, on thy mountain!'" repeated Isaac Smith with rising inflection, unfolding his arms and stretching them wide. His strong jaws closed a moment, as he slowly turned his head, and with a steady eye, looking into Lloyd's, finished the sentence: "These were the words of Moses."

Some picture of Moses that Lloyd had seen, probably in the old Bible of his mother's family, was revived by the appearance of Isaac Smith at this moment. His nose would have been quite the Jew's, but that it came to an end too bluntly. His eyes, at spells, turned inward, like a lost thinker's, and his manner varied from the hard, practical American to the introspective, tranceful Oriental.

"The poor man is crazy on religious subjects," thought Lloyd Quantrell, "but how in the deuce did he get the military lunacy there too? Why, out of Moses, of course!

"So, General Smith," interrupted the young hunter, pleasantly, "that was the way Moses got his military commission? He was made a general in the bush?"

"I was about to say, Mr. Quantrell, the general peace prevailing among many nations was broken — among the Canaanites, the Hittites, the Jebusites, the Philistines, and many others — who looked upon Moses, probably, as a sore disturber. They had not heard the voice he heard, nor seen the cause of war that lay among them. But in the deep prosperity of society often lies the live coal of war, as I have seen, at corn-harvest time, the fires break out in the woods and standing crops. One man might fail in this age — even one as obedient as Moses — to set in conflict the powers that now lie so tightly bound in cunning compromises that they can not draw back to strike each other. But the Power which sent the mysterious voice can bring the armies up, though the chosen captain look in vain to know how or where! He may excite only derision instead of war. He may be punished in a lunatic asylum. He may have the misery of utterly failing and involving others in destruction, but Moses thought all these things over, and they did not move him."

Lloyd Quantrell arose and whistled to his dog.

"General Smith," he said, "myself and your two sons have been greatly edified. To meet a man of your travel and intelligence on the top of the mountain is a refreshing surprise, sir. But the sun is getting low, and I have no shelter for the night. I would accept the hospitality of your house, if I knew just where it was."

"We are not going home, Mr. Quantrell," spoke one of the young men, "and there is nobody at our little cabin to entertain you. We are sorry, sir. You will do best to go down into the Catoctin Valley, here, where the settlements are close together. It is not very far to Middletown, where there is a tavern."

"Yes," said Isaac Smith, "we are out, Mr. Quantrell, on a night excursion to hunt minerals in the mountain. I use the divining-rod, sir, with much success. We expect to find lead in these hills, or iron, at least."

"Ah, General Smith, you have got a universal head there! So all-night luck to you, and good-bye. — Come, Albion."

The dog started ahead at the cry.

"God bless you, sir!" said Isaac Smith, taking Lloyd's hand in a large, fatherly palm. "Remember the queer old man's sermon on the mountain, and — never kill a dove again."

As the young man waved his hand and went on, he looked back once, and saw all three of the mountaineers watching him till he disappeared in the woods.

Chapter III

SOME OLD DUTCH

LLOYD QUANTRELL had still more than an hour of daylight; not enough to find his way back to Sandy Hook, where he had slept at the tavern, but abundant time to walk down the mountain into Catoctin or Middle Creek Valley.

He took the side-roads leading from the mountain pasture-lands, then crossed the steep fields, now stripped of their crops, and, finding plenty of chestnuts to fill his pockets, gnawed as he went along, and had a shot or two at some late-feeding partridges; and finally he jumped on a farmer's wagon, the farmer nodding assent pleasantly as he urged his horses, till, at a farm-gate near the creek, the wagon turned in.

Lloyd then jumped off and found himself at a covered bridge from which he could not see the white spires of Middletown. So he turned up a road at the creek's side, which looked cool and idling, and at a spring in the sandstone took a drink. Here his dog also drank, and then barked as if hungry.

Continuing half an hour on farther, a turn in the road brought to view a comfortable farm settlement on a slope of the sluggish, verdant-rimmed Catoctin, which, on alternate sides, as it wound through the deep-cloven fields, slid beneath the exposed layers of stone. Upon that side, opposite such an exposure, where the bank rounded down to a level lawn, in which a stone spring-house shaded a cool spring at the roots of a great, skyey sycamore, stood, above the spring-house, at the top of a path, one of the large log-houses, whitewashed, which make at once the cheapest and most wholesome residences in this part of Maryland.

There had originally been a square, stern stone house in place of this, and it still remained against the southern gable of the log portion like an ice-house, always cool and perhaps dampish, its small, deep-walled windows taking an expression upon them like one of the hard Scotch-

Irish race, who probably built it in the days when they needed such protection for their cruelties to Indians and each other.

But the peaceful German, in time crossing the Pennsylvania line, perhaps unconscious of a boundary, had bought his precursor out, sowed clover, reduced the stone to soil, and, as his family wants enlarged, became his own carpenter, calling his sons and neighbors together, and hewing in his own woods in winter, while farm-work languished, the native forest trunks to compose his addition. These, split in half and the faces smoothed, were called puncheons, and they were dragged to the side of the old stone block-house, and there fitted and framed together, and their chinks filled with plaster, while the family lived undisturbed in the stone castle.

This new and roomy dwelling, made of oak or chestnut, was set with its side to the road, propped on brick or stone foundations, and its roof, doors, and shutters were painted blue like winter cabbages.

These ideas went through Quantrell's brain as he caught sight of the long, homely farmer's dwelling standing on the hill, shaded there by maples and large willows, and to the north were a garden and small peach-orchard, and beyond that was a huge barn of logs, with a bridge leading to its main story, and cattle in the cow-yard and beneath its stone basement.

At sight of these cattle and of the dairy-house beneath the sycamore tree, Lloyd exclaimed to his dog:

"Albion, here! Milk, by George!"

Thus stimulated or encouraged, Albion darted in the open gate of the house-yard, and trotted briskly up the path to the dwelling. He was almost there, when a growl arrested him.

A dog of about the same size, of cross-breeds, but with mastiff in him, appeared on the top of the hill, directing his attention to both dog and gunner.

For an instant Albion appeared to be meditating an attack, and raised his hair and showed his row of white molars. But, without any ceremony, the country dog, seeing this, came down the hill with a steady trot, increasing it to a run, and then at a bound ran under the pointer, upset him, and rolled down hill, and then started back for a second wrestle and fight.

The pointer now lost all show of self-possession, and crouched down and looked rapidly for escape; but before he could conclude which way to fly, the ugly animal was upon him, and only Albion's agility, as he jumped high in the air, aided by his opponent's clumsiness, saved his fine ears from being torn. He turned and fled down the path to the spring-house, and, darting in there, upset a pan of warm milk as it was just being placed in the stone spring trough beside others by a little lady.

"Wass hut'm g'faild? Here, Fritz!" cried the milk fairy to her dog, and in an instant he plunged in at the door and turned over into the cold-water trough, upsetting two other pans of milk, and Albion crouched at the mistress's feet, trembling and whining for protection.

Lloyd Quantrell, who had hurried after his dog, peeped into the spring-house door in time to see a beautiful, dark-eyed girl, with her arms bare and a finely modeled foot, extricating her gown from the pointer's hysterical paws. As she saw Lloyd standing there with a gun, he heard her murmur:

"Waer is ar, anyhow? Down, Fritz!"

She menaced her own dog with a large wooden butter-ladle, and, as he came out of the dairy, Lloyd spoke firmly and candidly to him:

"Fritz, my brave fellow! Did we spill his darling mistress's milk? Well, Fritz, we must pay her father for it."

Admiration was instant and mutual in the young man and the girl. Her astonishment relaxed to the likeness of his ardent smile, and he said, without dropping his eyes:

"I thought it would be just my luck to stop where the prettiest girl in Frederick County lived!"

"You're sure you've found to right place, then?" spoke the girl, naturally, but blushing much.

"Won't you let me stop here and prove it?" said Lloyd. "What's your name? Mine's Lloyd."

"I'm Katy," said the girl, "Jake Bosler's Katy. I'm goin' on seventeen."

At this point the dog Albion, as if smarting under his recent discomfiture, grasped the situation: he saw Fritz being petted by his master, a thing to provoke his jealousy, and Fritz's mistress ready to apply the big wooden spoon to Fritz in case he violated any law of hospitality. Thought Albion, "It's a safe chance for intervention!"

So, with cool but, as it soon appeared, mistaken policy, Albion made a dart, after reconnaissance, upon Fritz's extended hinder leg, and, seizing it with his teeth, made an effort to hamstring his entertainer.

The rough country dog, suspecting no assault, was maddened by the pain, and springing backward and turning in the air he locked his teeth in the first flesh he came to, which happened to be Albion's ear, and both dogs rolled into the spring-house fighting, the one from courage and the other for life. Little Katy could not beat them apart, and Lloyd Quantrell rushed in to seize them, and, losing his footing in the dark interior of the dairy, fell full length into the water, and came out wet to the skin.

The noise of fighting and howling dogs brought down the inmates of the log and stone house: a large, barefooted man with a great black, wide-brimmed hat, and homespun clothes all of the same gray color;

and a younger man in a copy of the same dress; and a fine-looking blonde girl in brown homespun with flowers in her hat.

"Flint!?" exclaimed the farmer, looking at the gun; then looking at Lloyd, he added, *"Yingling!"* and cried out:

"Katy, wo fail's now?"

"Nothing's te matter, father," Katy replied, "but te dogs fought and te young man's wet his clothes."

As Lloyd came out, holding his fine dog up by main strength, they saw that one of the pointer's beautiful ears was gone. The humiliated beast, still in apprehension, ran to the feet of every person, cringing and whining with pain.

Lloyd Quantrell took a stick from the ground and whipped his dog till it seemed to lose all voice and spirit.

"There," finished the gunner, coolly, "he'll have just ear enough after this for good, big, right game, and no more doves!"

None interrupted the flogging but little Katy, who kept saying:

"Ganoonk! Enough! He won't do so anymore."

"No," remarked Lloyd, "not if it can be flogged out of him. — Farmer Bosler" — he addressed the man, with ready memory and frankness — "I've been gunning, and one of your talkative neighbors has kept me out late. Can't you give me a bed and a dry suit or a blanket, for love or money?"

"Yaw. Coom along!" the farmer said, asking no more questions, and the farmer's son took Lloyd's gun, saying:

"Take supper with us. It's a' ready."

Lloyd looked at the two girls, Katy with rich, dark eyes and dark hair, and small, supple figure, and the other girl, a full blonde, tall, large for her young age, and looking at Lloyd with bold, instant coquetry, as if she would not be anticipated in his conquest.

"Ha!" thought Lloyd, "it's well to have a choice, but I think that little Katy of Catoctin will do for me."

Katy, so happy and so startled that she did not know what she felt, replied to her female friend's suggestion, in the mountain Dutch *patois,* that Lloyd was *"orrick shtuls,"* or "very proud-looking," by saying:

"Sell is'n mistake; ar is orrick friendlich."

Lloyd grasped the meaning, and knew himself described as "very sociable."

The barefooted farmer walked up the steep grassy lawn to the establishment, which had three doors in its long front, one near each end of the log portion, and another in the older stone gable.

"Luter," he said to his son, "he sleeps py you."

Without anymore words, farmer Jake Bosler seized a rope which communicated with a large bell on the top of the log-house, and rang it loud and clear for the farm-hands to come in, saying:

"Soon-down! Bi'm-by!"

As the clear bell sounded in the cool amber mountain evening out of the perfect rest of this soft valley, it seemed that Sunday entered in and the lately savage dogs began to agree. Fritz licked the place where Albion's lost ear had been, and Albion, defeated everywhere, permitted the attention like one always in the right, yet sometimes put down. Lloyd Quantrell received the warm, admiring look of Katy's friend, but gave it back to little Katy.

"You sleeps py me," Luther Bosler said, leading the way upstairs by the door in the stone-gabled front.

They entered a bare room of good size with a fireplace in the end, and there Katy's brother had hardly put some wood on two stones, when her father brought up a shovel of coals and set the wood on fire.

"Here," said Luther Bosler, "git into tese clothes, Mister *Yager.*"

"No mister about me, Luther," answered the sociable Baltimorean, tenacious of a name; "my name's Lloyd Quantrell. You and Jake call me Lloyd!"

He looked audaciously at farmer Bosler, who, far from resenting the "Jake," now laughed.

"All right, Lloyd!" cried Jake. "Ha! ha! Luter, he's joost as plain as us ole Tunkers, ain't he? — Well, Lloyd, coom to supper. Bi'm-by!"

As father and son went down the stairs, Lloyd, slipping on the suit of coarse, clod-smelling clothes, and an old flannel shirt, lay on the bed, where he could find no cover but another feather-bed, and shut his eyes in the pleasurable tingle after a cold bath and by a now crackling fire. Night seemed to come and sit in the deep stone windows to warm at the fire, now brighter than the day.

"A Dutchman's guest!" he said to himself. "Well, well! The last Dutchman I met I stuck in the thigh with a shoemaker's awl for getting too near the polls. Can I ever respect a Dutchman? — even the father of little Katy of Catoctin?"

Chapter IV
KATY "P'INTED."

WHEN he came down to supper, several plain, uncultivated-looking men were already at the table, where Lloyd was accommodated with a place between Katy and her friend, who was introduced by Katy, saying:

"'Tis is Nelly Harbaugh; she's a Swisser."

"You're a Deitsher," replied Nelly Harbaugh to Katy.

"What's the difference, girls, between a Swisser and a Deitsher?" asked Lloyd of the two ladies alternately, looking his fondest. — "Jake, you tell me."

"Nay," said Jake, replying in kind. *"Ich wais's net,* Lloyd. Ask Andrew Atzerodt; he's quick."

"Te Swisser," spoke up one of the apparent serving-men — that only one whose face, as Lloyd now remarked it, seemed to have a little worldly restlessness — "te Swisser offers hisself for to pe bought. Te Deitsher gits sold and says *nix.* Dat's so, py Jing!"

He raised his voice at the end in a way to exasperate Lloyd, looking at Lloyd, too, as if to say, "I am always positive."

"Nelly," insinuated Lloyd, "when *you're* in the market, let me know, sweetness! — Katy, don't *you* get sold without giving me the first chance!"

"Ha, ha! Lloyd," Jake Bosler broke out, "you is a great feller for te girls."

"Do you mean it?" Nelly Harbaugh asked Lloyd, giving him the whole sunflower of her attention.

"I reckon so," Lloyd answered, but looking at little Katy.

"Py Jing!" exclaimed Atzerodt, across the table, fiercely at Lloyd, "Nelly, tare, is my gal, I haf you know!"

He looked to Lloyd now to have been drinking, or to be naturally a little drunk.

"There's nothing like being impressive, Andrew," replied Lloyd, looking straight at him, and mentally wishing he had him down the road.

"Are you a Swisser or a Deitsher?"

"Me? Py Jing, I'm a Swisser. I lif in te Valley of Fergeenia, where tey fights at te drop of te hat!"

"You better go down there and fight, then," Nelly Harbaugh said to Andrew. — "Luther Bosler, tell Lloyd about the mountain Dutch!"

"Te German-blood people," spoke up Luther Bosler, after hesitation, and in a still and somewhat dignified way, "come to Pennsylvany first. Amongst te first was us Tunkers. We been here hundred and forty year."

"You too, Katy?" interjected Lloyd. "A hundred and forty years here, and never sent for me?"

Everybody laughed loud. Andrew Atzerodt more boisterously than all, and Katy answered meekly at last:

"I'm going on seventeen."

Stopping till he was requested to continue, Luther Bosler, whose dark eyes were like Katy's, but his hair was coarser and of a deeper brown, said on:

"Yes, Lloyd, us Dutch is a hundred and fifty year in te United States. First off, te Germans come to New York, and didn't like that much, so most of tem moved to Pennsylvany. Te Tunker Dutch was Baptists, and they spread all over Pennsylvany and Maryland and down Virginia way. After they got to valleys, te Swiss come and took te hills dat wasn't good for much. So now we're all mixed up. Katy's got worldly; Nelly, she's no Tunker. Andrew, he's nothin' but a Dutch coach-maker."

"I'm te pest coach-maker in Fergeenia, don't you forgit it!" Andrew said, with rising inflection and want of equipoise.

"No, Andrew," put in Lloyd, "when Katy and I want our royal coach, we'll have you make it. — But, Luther, what do these Dunkers vote?"

"They don't vote in general," said Luther. "It's not religious. I voted three year ago."

"I hope you voted for Mr. Fillmore, Luther?"

"No, I didn't," said Luther.

"Oh! of couxse, you Dutch folks had to vote for old Buchanan. You couldn't go one of us Americans."

"Because I was an American, I thought," quietly remarked Luther, "I voted for Colonel Fremont. He got just two hundred and eighty-one out of 'most eighty-seven thousand votes in Maryland. So you can see my vote sticking up at te end, all by itself."

"Luter 'most got turned out of meetin' for votin'," exclaimed his father. "But dey took him back."

"Dat Fremont was a tam French abolitionist!" exclaimed the excitable Atzerodt. "I kill him, py Jing!"

"Go for him, Andrew," said Lloyd, grimly. "He's afraid of you, I know. But, pop" — to Jake Bosler — "can't you take me to meeting with you tomorrow?"

"O father, do!" spoke up Katy, impulsively, "it's *love*-feast!"

"We'll all go!" Nelly Harbaugh cried; "Luther must take me."

"Oh, you'll laugh at us poor Tunkers, Lloyd," Jake Bosler said.

"Nelly, you goes with me!" Andrew Atzerodt spluttered, hotly. "Didn't I come all to way from Port Tobacco to see you?"

"I have got better company," said the girl, negligently.

Py Jing!" raged Atzerodt, "I kill somebody!"

"Don't kill me," exclaimed Lloyd, with humor. "I'll run under the table if you look at me so."

Superior in worldly confidence and speech, and with unchecked humor and feelings, the city guest surpassed himself that evening as the candles were lighted and the wood-fire flamed, and the presuming Atzerodt also felt his influence as Lloyd jested light and complimentary.

Luther Bosler was a good listener, and whenever Lloyd looked his way, Luther, with a certain sluggish softness in his dark-lighted eyes, seemed watching him, but not with any dislike; for, once when Lloyd cried —

"Luther, I see you're a long-headed old sly-boots" —

"Oh!" said Luther, "my head, Lloyd, can't keep in my poots when *you're* a-talkin'!"

When they had partaken of the stewed chicken and smear case and cream, and what Jake called the "wedgable things" for vegetables, little Katy brought in pies for supper. Lloyd smiled to himself, thinking: "What heathens! pie for supper!"

"What kind of sweet things, Kate," he cried, "are you trying to sour us on with yourself?"

"Oh," said Katy, beaming joy, "here's peach snitz and elder, and some kickelins. I cooked tem."

Lloyd found the "kickelins" were sweet cakes fried in fat, and the "snitz" were dried peaches, and the queer pie was made of elder-berries. Said Katy, in their Dutch tongue, to Nelly:

"How I like to see him eat! He does it so easy."

"I should like to see him in love, Katy."

"Hush!" said Katy, trembling.

"Bedtime," Jake Bosler nodded, setting back his chair and glancing at the clock. "Bi'm-by!"

"Jake, your clock is fast," Lloyd observed, consulting his own gold watch, at which all the company looked, marveling.

"We keep it fast, Lloyd," Luther Bosler said; "it's te fashion up here, so we can go to work earlier."

"My goodness!" Katy cried, "te apples is cut and you men must snitz."

Two wash-tubs were brought into the whitewashed room, and sitting around them on wooden chairs all the men commenced to peel apples for drying, while Katy and Nelly produced two spinning-wheels and made them fly and hum on woolen yarn.

"We make all our own yarn," said Katy to Lloyd, "and send it to to weaver. He makes it into Dunker cloth."

Lloyd peeled apples awhile, till Nelly Harbaugh called him to unravel something at the wheel, and then he watched the two fine girls working on Saturday night, with a sense of reproof in his mind for so much avarice of time.

Nothing was here, he thought, but the physical beauty of these women to ornament life; no pictures on the wall but lithographs from Scripture, no books but the "Hagerstown Almanac" and Bausmann's travels in the Holy Land, and a Dutch Bible; no ornaments but some horns of deer and a robe of yellow panther-skins sewn together, with the eye-holes embroidered around the red lining. The very peace seemed, to the strong-willed American, heavy with unspiritual content; but it had brought to these young girls the perfection of everything but mind.

The face he understood the best, and which seemed also to understand him, was Nelly Harbaugh's; too open to his gaze, unretreating before him, ready to be admired whenever he turned toward it, and seeming to say, "You can make no mistake — I am ready to hear you."

Had Katy not been there to drop her eyes before his warm admiration, he might have paid closer regard to Nelly Harbaugh's sunny charms.

She was larger, fuller, taller than Katy, with a carriage erect yet indolent, as if Nature had given her such animal health that she could not droop, but like some strong-stemmed golden flower blinked not at the hottest sun, but took its color in every petal. Over Katy her influence might be strong, Lloyd thought, and he said:

"Nelly, I know I have seen your fine blue eyes in Baltimore."

"No, I have never been there," Nelly said, "except to market, and Luther made us come back as soon as we sold out."

She looked coquettish reproach, with the same searching directness, at Luther as he came over and, putting his hand upon her shoulder, looked at her with mild interest.

"Nelly," said Luther, "will you pe my girl if I drive you to Beaver Creek meeting?"

"I am always yours, Luther," answered Nelly, examining him with even more wistfulness than Lloyd. "But you don't want me."

"I do," said Luther, "but I want you all. I think you can not gif me all your heart. It is difided."

"It is not," said Nelly, "but you will not ask for it."

Lloyd Quantrell was arrested at both the deepened interest in Nelly's eyes and the finely contrasted animal perfection of her and of her admirer. Luther was dark and deep-voiced, and with a manly something in him, however rude. In her tall, well-rounded figure and long waist, which a bodice might adorn, and finely grained flesh and long braids of corn-colored hair, there seemed to be strength, fruitfulness, and power over man; yet in her undisguised ardor and will it seemed that she needed Luther's reality and slower though not stronger impulses of character. He looked at her with mild, almost devout, eyes, as if he kept love back by reason.

"Kiss her," said Katy. "I know you want to, Luther."

Luther passed his arm around Nelly, but did not kiss her.

With disappointment, yet pride, the girl turned on Lloyd Quantrell again the same penetrating and steady look.

Thought Lloyd, returning the gaze in kind, "That girl a man might dress to look like a queen, but even then she could take a lesson in nature from little Katy."

Katy had such large eyes, the pupils big and the eyeballs big too, that they turned in her head like poems, Lloyd thought, harmoniously rhyming in expression and so full of tender feeling that he said once, "Katy, I can almost see the water drip from those two buckets of your eyes as they rise on me a from the well of your fresh heart."

"Why," said Katy, "you're a poet, Lloyd. I can make rhymes too."

"*Singsht?*" Lloyd asked, having picked up a word.

"*Yaw,* Lloyd, and I play te accordion."

Modestly Katy went for the instrument, and bringing it back began to draw forth its sounds, opening her lips to breathe inward the harmony, and Lloyd saw that her teeth were full and white.

Sitting there a mere child, her long braid of chestnut hair hanging to her chair, her long, expressive fingers at the keys, and shyness and fervor playing in her countenance like trout in springs, she suddenly raised a little German idyll, and her brother joined in it with his untrained bass, and all the farm-hands turned their faces up to hear:

> "Oh was is shenner uf der welt
>   Os blimlin roat un weis?
> Un blo, un gail, im arble feld —
>   Wass sin de doch so neis!
> Ich wais noch goot in seller tzeit
>   Hob ich nix leevers du,
> Os in de wissa, long un breit
>   So blimlin g'soocht we du."*

Lloyd knew that it was a song about hunting bright flowers in the

---

*   By Tobias Witmer: "My Old Woman's Birthday."

fields, and almost understood the timid peep of Katy's eyes upon him, when she sang:

> "I know yet well that in that time
>   Naught would I rather do,
>   Than in the meadow long and wide
>   Such flow'rets seek as *you.*"

Jake Bosler, who had been nodding, awoke to hear the tune, and when it was done he wiped his eyes of some tears.

"Ich con's net helfa — I can't help it," he said: "I tink of my *olty* —"

"My mother who is dead," Katy explained, as Jake faltered; "she's been dead two years."

"Bettime — bi'm-by!" Jake Bosler managed to say at last, and Katy moved to the table and opened the old Dutch Bible. When she had read, in the sweetest tones, words intelligible to Lloyd only by their holiness, all present knelt and Jake Bosler prayed for his brood, for pure hearts and thoughts, and for the stranger within his gates. His daughter and son went up to kiss him.

"Goot-night, Lloyd," he said. "Soon-up, bi'm-by."

"Thinking of work even as he falls to sleep!" Lloyd exclaimed. "Now give old daddy a parting tune!"

He started up the little song by Samuel Woodworth:

> "The pride of the valley is lovely young Ellen,
>   Who dwells in a cottage enshrined by a thicket,
>   Sweet peace and content are the wealth of her dwelling,
>   And Truth is the porter that waits at the wicket."

Katy caught the air and kept the accompaniment with her accordion, and Lloyd changed "Ellen" into "Katy," and sang it to her with all his spirit, being in fine voice, and all the Dutch people listened with delight.

"Ah, Katy!" said Jake, going upstairs, "I guess you got a beau, Katy."

The serving-men took their departure too, and only Andrew Atzerodt remained.

"Luter," he said, "git me some of Jake's whisky. I hat a head on me yisterday."

"Here's some whisky we make ourselves, Lloyd," Luther said, producing it. "Te Tunkers keeps little still-houses and makes a few bar'ls a year."

The pure liquor soon brought a pleasurable glow to the men, Luther drinking sparingly, and for a while the influence was peculiar on Atzerodt, bringing out a vein of natural humor in him. Lloyd read him soon to be a man of such volatile nature that his forwardness was always getting him into predicaments. He challenged everybody, and probably had a brutal Hessian instinct, as Lloyd expressed it, but possessed no fortitude to carry it out. Seeing that Luther was now increasing his interest in Nelly Harbaugh, Andrew cried out:

"Now, py Jing! you haf been holting my gal's hand tare long enough!"

"Sit down!" commanded Nelly Harbaugh, "or I'll send you home to walk to Middletown in the dark."

"I'll go, den," Atzerodt cried, making a movement toward his hat.

"Behave, you fool!" cried Nelly, making Luther release her hand, however.

"She's got two fellows on the string," thought Lloyd Quantrell, "and is fishing for me too. — Ah! Andrew," Lloyd spoke out, "you are a courageous man. A desperate man, I call you. I have no doubt that you could take your hat and walk alone among these mountains all night, and not run from the ghost I saw today."

"Geisht!" exclaimed Andrew, looking behind him and turning pale, "I walk past a shpook and shust laugh at him — ha! ha!"

"Give me your hand, my brave fellow," cried Lloyd, standing up. "And you have got a strong grip too, Andrew."

"If I shqueeze you hard, py Jing," said the heedless mechanic, "you goes crazy."

"Don't squeeze me, Andrew," exclaimed Lloyd, with a wink to the rest. "Now you are doing of it. Ouch! Let me go!"

As he spoke, Lloyd, who was a powerful man, trained in athletic games, closed his great palm around the coachmaker's, and slowly tightened it. The poor fellow writhed and groveled in pain, but feared to cry out, since his oppressor kept saying:

"What nerve! what endurance! Don't squeeze me so! Oh, take him off! Have mercy, Andrew!"

Thus shouting, the tears came to Lloyd's eyes to see the poor braggart suffer, and all laughed but Katy, who cried:

"You're hurting one another, I know."

"Ah!" said Lloyd, looking at his own hand as if in misery, "never will I go into the lion's den again."

"Py Jing!" exclaimed the other, as soon as he could get breath and suppress his sobs, "you got a purty goot grip, too. But I'm a workin'-man. Better not tackle me, Lloyd!"

"Poor thing," said Katy, taking Lloyd's hand timidly, and looking at it. He raised her little fingers up as if to show her his wound, and kissed them.

"Don't," said Katy; "I been huskin' corn all day in te field."

"Do they work the women out in the fields?" asked Lloyd.

"Oh, yes," Katy answered simply, while Nelly Harbaugh made an effort to restrain her, which Katy did not understand; "father gives Nelly half a dollar a day for huskin' and plantin' corn. She must be rich."

"What ghost did you see on the mountain, Lloyd?" Nelly Harbaugh asked, evasively.

All seemed interested to hear this, and Lloyd, standing up to emphasize the story and test Andrew Atzerodt's nerve-powers, looked quite the necromancer in his farmer's suit and in a wide Dunker hat he now drew on.

"Andrew," spoke Lloyd, "only your splendid courage could have resisted the feeling that the old man I saw today was not mortal. He had a nose that seemed to curl like an elephant's trunk; his eyebrows stood up like a horse's mane; his beard fell below his breast-bone and had silver fire in it like old punk. He closed his big jaw, saying: 'Is this a dove you have been shooting? Agh-h-h!'"

"Stop! You lie! He wasn't tare!" cried Andrew, sinking at the knees, at the stranger's well-acted part.

"He was there, Andrew. I swear it! 'Is this a dove you have been killing?' the wild man said, his voice as cold as the October wind which blows that door open now — hoo-oo-oo!"

"Scat! Te wind is high," chattered Atzerodt, as the door to the kitchen opened a little way.

"'I have no respect,' the phantom said to me, 'for any man who will kill a little dove. No-o-o-o!'"

"You scare us, Lloyd!" murmured little Katy, leaving her chair and coming forward, as if to shut the creaking door. He held his hand out to detain her, and continued:

"'I did not mean to do it,' I said to that strange man; 'my pointer dog was obstinate, and nosed the harmless bird. Forgive me, mountain-wizard!' 'No!' pealed he, 'a dove! A little, little d-o-o-ve!'"

"Pooh!" said Atzerodt, "if dot was all, a little pit of a dove, you wasn't afeard."

Atzerodt took a stout drink of the whisky. The loose door obeyed the wind again and opened inward. Katy stepped forward, but Lloyd held her at an arm's length.

"'My dog *would* nose the dove.' I pleaded. ''Twas not my fault, indeed!' 'You killed a dove,' said he, 'a little, little d-o-o-ve.' 'Hist, Albion,' said I, 'seek farther on —'"

"Ha! what's dat? I hears a *kreisha!*" Andrew muttered, as a sort of wail came from the kitchen.

"*Albion!*" repeated Lloyd, himself disturbed by the noise and his own zeal, for he had involuntarily exceeded his joke.

As he mentioned the name of his dog, Albion himself, mechanically walking as if in sleep, came through the kitchen door that was ajar, and advancing near the middle of the large room, threw back his body and threw up his white and brown nose, and whimpered as on the mountaintop. His torn ear was turned toward them and showed bloody yet.

"The hoond p'ints something," muttered Luther Bosler. "What is it?"

"Ha! ha! ha!" Atzerodt replied, repeating his drink. "I tink it's Katy."

"Maybe it's the Black Dog!" shouted Nelly Harbaugh. "Say 'The Words,' Katy!"

As both girls started to mutter something like an incantation, Luther Bosler advanced to take his sister, but Lloyd Quantrell had assuaged her terror in his own arms, and as he drew her tenderly to him he threw Jake Bosler's big wool hat at the dog, which snapped at it and shrank back into the dark kitchen.

"Dear little dove," Lloyd Quantrell said, attempting to kiss Katy, but she pressed his head away, "that wasn't a black dog at all, only my English pointer."

"The Black Dog," said Nelly Harbaugh, "needn't be black. It's a spirit."

"Spirit of what?"

"Trouble," answered Nelly Harbaugh.

"Lloyd," murmured little Katy, "it p'inted at me and you. We must say 'Te Words' together."

"'The Words?'" Lloyd answered. "I don't know 'The Words,' Katy."

"O Lloyd! 'Te Words' keep off te Poltergeist. I say them when I see a bad sign and when I am too happy, for when we're happiest te bad man likes to come."

"Say them now, Katy," Lloyd whispered, pressing her close in his strong arms; "I'm very happy, for I love you!"

"Do you? Oh! you must tell to truth now; for I'm going to say 'Te Words,' and it's wicked to say them with a lie."

"I love you," Lloyd Quantrell replied, his arms trembling. "I'll say 'The Words' after you with joy, Katy."

"Call on te three Highest Names, my love," said Katy, in rapt awe.

As they said together in a country rhyme, he repeating after her, the dread names in the Trinity, they heard the dog howl in the kitchen.

"There," said Katy, "te Black Dog heard us and is gone. Lloyd, you may kiss me now."

"O blessed words," Lloyd Quantrell murmured, "which brought this kiss to me. Teach me from your pure heart all that it knows, dear child, and keep me happy as I am."

"You must peliev," said Katy, "pelieve in te Three Highest Names and say 'Te Words,' and then love will be beautiful."

"Who told you, Katy?"

"My dear mother, Lloyd, and my heart tells me, too."

"Did you ever love before?"

"No, but I often tried to. When you came to te spring house, Lloyd, I was saying to myself: 'I guess somebody is going to love me. But I wonder when he will come?' I knew he was somewheres."

"God bless you, darling! That very same was I thinking: that the country was beautiful, but I was lonely in it, for want of some gentle heart and glowing face. I have found you, Katy, and both of us are happy."

Again the stranger in the mountains pressed to his lips the simple and unresisting face which had floated to him like a sunny cloud in this high vale, and for a little while he forgot that she was "Dutch," hard as his native prejudices were against that humble race, longer in the land than his own name of Quantrell.

Chapter V

LOVE AMONG THE SPOOKS

W HEN they returned in consciousness to the whitewashed great room of Jacob Bosler, Nelly was sitting near the fire, which had burned low, with Luther on her right and Atzerodt on her left. Atzerodt was telling tales of spirits and frightening himself, and hence drew frequently upon the jug of whisky to give him what Lloyd called "Dutch courage."

He told of the snarley-yow and the were-wolf; the phantom soldier and the white woman which announced a death; of the big Indian's shade with a light in him; and of the fox-fire in the fields which lay on the meadow-grass at night and turned to silver, but like the fire-coals when stirred by avarice were silver only at night, but in the morning ashes.

Atzerodt's sallow, furtive, somewhat anxious face, like that of one intense yet animal, brightened up between the drink, the superstition, and his enjoyment of the others' fears; his voice was shrill and responsive to his emotions, his frame thickset and his movements were agile, his eyes a keen blue, and no repose was in his soul.

"He's one of the best coachmakers to be found," said Nelly to Lloyd. "If he'd be steady, he could marry any girl, and be a rich man."

"Can't you make him steady?"

"I don't want to be a mechanic's wife," said Nelly, "unless I must."

Looking at him again, as if trying to read him, Nelly Harbaugh said:

"Is your watch gold? Won't you give it to me? What do you do in Baltimore?"

"Spend money," said Lloyd, "run to the fires, turn out with the Grays, and guard the polls."

"The Grays? That's soldiers!"

"Yes, we're all Union men. Not a foreigner in the company. Our motto is, 'Put none but Americans on guard.'"

"I hope everybody is for te Union," Luther Bosler remarked; "we're all for it up this a-way."

"Katy," Lloyd said, "do you believe in ghosts?"

"Oh, yes, Lloyd."

"Tell me about one."

Katy shrank a little at being called upon to take so much attention, but her ready impulses carried her along.

"There was a girl over in Smoketown," Katy spoke, "who wanted to sell herself to te *divel*" — Katy here seemed to be saying "The Words" again an instant — "she wanted to pe rich and not to work; she thought she was a lady, and not a poor Dutch girl. So she asked her mother to let her sell herself to te little lame man. Her mother told her to go sit by te spring and say:

'I want clothes, and I want gold;
  I want nefer to pe old;
  I want peauty as long as I can —
  Gif it to me, little lame man!'"

"What a nice wish!" exclaimed Nelly Harbaugh.

"So te little lame man came right to te spring, and he said, 'Put your right hand on te top of your head.' She put it there. 'Put your left hand on the soles of your feet,' said he. She was sitting down, and she did that, too. 'Now,' said te lame man, 'you must say, *"All that is between my two hands belongs to te divel."*'" She started to say it, and had got to te last word, when her mother ran there and shouted *'God!'* so she lost the words and said, 'All that is between my two hands belongs to — God!' Te little lame man run back to Smoketown as fast as his legs could carry him."

"But didn't the girl get any nice clothes, or anything, for being so good?" asked Nelly.

"She got," said Katy, blushing, "a good husband, my mother told me, if he *was* a poor young man."

"Dot Shmoketown," cried Atzerodt, "is an ole Shpooktown, py Jing! I come along tare one night purty trunk, riding a horse, and joost as I crossed te leetle stream dis side of Shmoketown an begun to climb te mountain road dat comes dis way, and had got into de glen petween te Short Mountain and te Plue Ridge, I see pefore me a black man with a white face like a chiny plate. I said to myself, 'Py Jing, any company is petter dan none!' So I jined te black feller, and he was de nicest feller I ever did know; he was rale shentlemans.

"Says he: 'It's cold; we'll drink together!' He handed me a flask. When I got done trinkin', tere was another man riding with us.

"As we come up te mountain through te chestnut forest, te moon shined on te road, an efery time we took another trink, tere was another man on horsepack, till, py Jing! I counted apout nine men, and de last man was a woman.

"Tey all seemed to know te black man with te white face; he was a rale shentlemans.

"He made speeches out of pooks and drilled us like a solcher company, and we charged at a gallop, an rode company-face, an right-countermarch, an had a good time, py Jing! I guess I was purty trunk."

"You're not far from it now," said Nelly Harbaugh.

Atzerodt looked into the darker parts of the room apprehensively yet saucily, and continued:

"We got most to te top of te Plue Ridge, when te black man said, 'Who's dat long feller amongst te horses?'

"There was a man walkin' in te road. He was a long man in black clothes. He looked up and powed and said, 'Good-evening, friends; we're 'most home!' 'Te devil you are!' said te black man with te white face.

"We rode along awhile till te captain, as I'll call him, begun whisperin' to us an saying: 'Look at dat feller! He's eferywhere at once; he's on dat side, and on dis side, and petween our horses, and I pelieve he's joost a devil. Let's ride over him!'

"So we looked, an tere he was, right amongst te horses, dis side, dat side, not a pit afraid —"

"Oh, don't," spoke Katy, "don't tell us the rest unless it's good."

"Go to bed, Andrew, you desperate, brave man," Lloyd Quantrell said, drawing his arm tighter around Katy.

"Yes," Luther Bosler added, "it's late, and this story is too long."

"Go on," said Nelly Harbaugh; "I want to know what became of the black man with the white face."

"'Let's ride over him!' said te captain. 'All right, py Jing!' says I.

"'No,' says some, 'he's a nice ole man, and he says he's 'most home.'

"'Put it to vote!' says te black man with te white face.

"Py Jing! it was a tie; one half was one way and one half was te oder way.

"'Leave it to te woman!' says te captain."

"That was the right way," Lloyd Quantiell said. "The women are always for pity, Katy."

"Te woman," concluded Atzerodt, "looked a leetle queer an said nothing till te black an white man rode to her side and looked at her like a rale shentlemans. Den she leaned over an' kissed him, and she joost yelled, 'Charge!'"

Excited with the recital and the drink, Atzerodt had arisen unsteadily as he shouted this last word.

"'Charge!' yelled to woman, and on we put, py Jing! to trample dat long man in te road.

"The first ting I knowed, we was at te steep edge of te mountain, and te captain rode right over. Down, down he went, and efery feller after him, and I last of all, for my horse had stumpled —"

"Ah! ah! Andrew," spoke Lloyd, "surely, with your splendid courage, you were not in the rear?"

"I was pitched off te horse joost pefore he jumped over, and I was fallin', too, but I see te long man lyin' in te road, an' I took hold of his hand to save myself.

"Te moon showed him lyin' there dead, all cut with te horseshoes. Te hand I took was slippery with something, and I couldn't git a tight hold of it."

"Not with your stalwart fist, Andrew?" exclaimed Lloyd.

"I couldn't git hold of it," said Atzerodt, with a changed and lowered tone, "because his hand was bloody. So down I went, hundreds of feet, and next mornin' tere I was found underneath te mountain, and Nelly Harbaugh was py me. Py Jing! ain't it so, Nelly?"

"Yes," said Nelly, after a pause, "it was last April; he was coming to see me to make me marry him. I went out to hunt him, and there I found him asleep in the road, and his horse going loose. So I woke him up and sent him to the right-about."

"Py Jing!" exclaimed the tipsy man, tears of various origin coming to his eyes, "I'm come agin today, Nelly, to ask you to pe my wife. Don't say 'No.' You'll preak me all up. I have got a shop at Port Tobacco, and all te work I want, but I can't keep sober unless you marry me. Come, make me a home! You needn't work in te fields no more. I'll save you from want, and you'll save me from wickedness. Oh, I'll promise eferything!"

"It's worth considering, Nelly," Luther Bosler remarked, with grave emotion. "He's a good mechanic."

"Take the candle and go to bed," commanded Nelly Harbaugh, looking at Atzerodt; "if you intend to obey me, begin now. I will not give you an answer till you are sober."

She stood, beautiful and tall, with her blue eyes full of care yet spirit, like one with resources but in doubt.

"Oh, tonight," pleaded Atzerodt, "or I may dream agin!"

"Tomorrow," said Nelly Harbaugh, pointing to the door.

The common fellow, in whom seemed some real sensibility now, took the candle and staggered meekly toward the entrance.

"Kiss good-night!" he muttered unsteadily.

"You are not obeying me," answered Nelly Harbaugh.

He threw open the door leading into the night and stopped, with a trembling of the candle he held up, and the words, "It's dark, Nelly!"

"Now, now, Andrew!" Lloyd Quantrell cried, "I know you're not afraid to go to bed alone."

"You're a loafer," shouted Atzerodt in sudden rage, uttering an oath. "You'll pe no good to Katy!"

Lloyd made a push for the door, and Atzerodt fled, slamming it behind him.

"The cur!" exclaimed Lloyd Quantrell, throwing his arm around Katy, who had followed him. "You know he slanders me, Katy."

"Oh, he must," Katy said, "you are such a gentleman!"

Her brother's eyes followed Katy tenderly to the fire, as if to reassure her of their guest's good character; and then seeing her, without affront, caressed by the so recent acquaintance, Luther turned to Nelly Harbaugh, who had sunk into one of the wooden chairs.

"What will you answer Andrew tomorrow, Nelly?"

"Whatever you say."

"Do you love him?"

"Luther," exclaimed the girl, as a great sob escaped from her throat, "there is but one I love: you know it."

"If I could make you happy," Luther replied, "I would marry you. Your great beauty makes up for your poverty, Nelly. I haf a good farm next to father's. Could I tepend upon your opedience?"

"For life, Luther! You are the only man I would obey with joy."

"Girls nowadays, Nelly, looks at a man as a slave to gratify all their follies. My wife must do her part in toil and saving as our mothers did. Can you do that?"

"Luther, I can for you, I believe."

"I haf loved you a year," said Luther, deliberately. "Kiss me!"

Little Katy rose from her lover's side and came forward.

"Oh, what a night of happiness!" she cried. "*Hiresht se*, Luther? Marry and call Nelly 'wife.' I hoped you would, for Nelly is willful. But she is beautiful, too."

After Katy kissed them both, her friend, with a moment's care, exclaimed:

"Luther, will you hitch up your horse and buggy and drive me home?"

"Now?"

"Yes, I do not want to face that man tomorrow. He may be dangerous."

"Andrew? Why, stay and tell him. Be up and down about it."

"No," said Nelly, firmly, "I do not want to see him. He has once before threatened me, and, though he is a coward, he is unsafe. Tell him, Katy, from me, 'good-bye forever.'"

Her face expressed decision yet apprehension. Luther stepped out, and soon came to the door with the buggy.

"Nelly," he said, putting on his hat and big overjacket, "it looks as if I had pegun to obey you."

"Tomorrow, Katy," exclaimed Nelly, nervously, "we will meet you and Lloyd at the forks of the road this side of the mountain, going to meeting."

Lloyd Quantrell, as the door closed upon them, drew Katy to his heart again.

"Beloved," he murmured to her, "who would have thought it this morning? That my empty, hungry heart would now be full? That you, dear child, were waiting for me?"

"I love you, Lloyd," said Katy. "I hope te Lord sent you to me. Come, put your right hand on your head and this left hand under the sole of your foot, and say after me, 'All petween my two hands pelongs to God!'"

"All between my two hands belongs to God," Lloyd Quantrell repeated.

"Good-night, Lloyd."

She slipped from his ardent grasp.

As they gave the long, wistful kiss of faith and future, pain and gladness, life and love, a door opened and Jake Bosler poked his head down the stairs, and saw them clasped together, without reproof.

"Soon-up," Jake uttered, sleepily. "Bi'm-by."

Chapter VI

DOGS AND HOUNDS

LOOKING through the small stone windows of his sleeping-room, as soon as he was awakened by the big bell, Lloyd Quantrell saw the red and white spires of Middletown peeping low to the south, and the bounding profile of the Blue Ridge overlap itself like elephants marching, and the Catoctin Mountain to the east leap out of the plain like a boy's ball bouncing forward and falling again.

The Sunday morning dawn touched the high summits and crests of this double panorama with gilt as if it was the picture-frame, while between, just warming with the light, white farmhouses and gray barns, straight yellow-corn rows, sheep with brown backs, and next year's wheat just spearing above the pebbly swells, made the valley of the Catoctin seem itself another mountain, only kept down by its abundance.

Jake Bosler opened the latchless door without knocking, and entered with Lloyd's clothes dried and pressed.

"Soon-down. Bi'm-by!" Jake said, looking at Atzerodt asleep upon the floor.

"Who pressed these clothes so well, Jake? Katy, I think?"

"Yaw; she shtayed oop last *naucht,* Lloyd, to git tem purty."

"God bless her!" cried Lloyd. "And you, too, Jake, for being her father."

"Oh, yaw, Lloyd," Jake Bosler said, taking the proffered hand humbly. "Katy's my *letsht* — te last, I mean, Lloyd. Luter, he's engaged now to Nelly Harbaugh."

The man lying on the floor, in the second feather-bed, muttered here:

"I can't keep soper unless you marry me. Come, Nelly! make me a home."

"*T'zu shpoat,*" Jake murmured, "Nelly wanted Luter; Antrew wanted Nelly. When Antrew went to ped, Nelly took Luter. I don't knows not'ing about it."

"Nelly took *Luter!*" Atzerodt spoke, rising upon his elbow and looking through hot, dry eyes.

Jake Bosler looked still humbler, and, as he turned down the stairs, said compassionately:

"Soon-up! Bi'm-by!"

"Yes, poor fellow," Lloyd Quantrell answered for Jake, "wait for sun-up. Bi'm-by it will shine bright, Andrew, from another pair of eyes."

"Where is she?" whispered Atzerodt.

"Luther took her away last night. She thought it would distress both of you to see each other."

"O my Gott!" — the unhappy man threw his face into the gay feather quilt — she wrote to me to come and marry her. Dis is her letter."

He began to weep like a broken-hearted child. Lloyd reflected that even this unspiritual being had a heart.

"Don't be too hard on her, my lad," he spoke; "she's poor and ambitious. She thought well of you, but your coming has brought the man she loved most, to the popping-point at last."

Atzerodt finished his fit of weeping and rose up.

"Gif me a drink!" he pleaded, "I can't eat none. I'll git on te road an tramp agin."

"Pull at it light, Andrew," Lloyd interrupted, as he saw the deep draught the other took.

"She said she'd gif me her answer when I got soper," Atzerodt exclaimed, pulling his slouched hat over his brows; "she's run away from her promise. I'll never pe soper agin, so help me Gott!"

Again bursting into a wail and tears, he went down the steps and reappeared from the barn, riding a horse. Pausing a moment at the foot of the hill and looking fiercely back, he shook his fist and shouted:

"Gott tam dat house an eferypody in it!"

Then, with a cruel blow at his horse, and another sob and gush of tears, he galloped away.

"Dutch, Dutch!" Lloyd Quantrell said; "not fit to have a wife. Yet the fine Swisser did deceive him. She *is* a Dutch Venus; I might have won her instead of Katy. Dare I marry either? Well, I can be in love."

He took his gun and game-bag to carry them away. The dove was still in the game-bag, and he brought it out and looked at it again.

"By George!" he exclaimed, "Albion did point at little Katy, truly, just as he nosed this poor little bird. If I lived long among the Dutch I would get to believe in ghosts."

Katy was finishing the setting of the table, and she went up and kissed Lloyd before her father.

"I reckon you think I'm familiar for a stranger, Jake," Lloyd said.

"How else would you git acquainted?" queried Katy's father.

"I told *fadder* you was my peau," Katy said, blushing.

"Yaw," Jake said, "if Katy didn't tell her olt *dawdy* when she was happy, how could he pe glad?"

Katy spread her hands over the table and said the blessing in English, and Jake Bosler ended it with *Amen.*

"Lloyd," asked Jake, after Katy had helped them to coffee and ham and eggs, "what religion is you? Is you Baptist or not?"

"I'm a poor sinner, Jake. I was brought up a Catholic. That's how I was educated. My father is a convert; my mother was a Methodist."

"Any religion is petter dan none, Lloyd. Us Paptists was pefore Martin Luter. We asks all to come to te Lord's supper and to pe our friends."

A big wagon, with clean straw in the bottom, drawn by two great gray horses, Jake Bosler drove to the door and cried, "Git in, Lloyd." Little Katy had a bundle with her and a large basket, and Lloyd threw in his gun and kit.

"Stop," said Lloyd, as they started off; "won't you lock the house up?"

"Oh, no, Lloyd," replied Jake, "nobody steals up this a-way, pecause nobody is lazy, and the poor is a-welcome."

Jake Bosler's cattle in the bottoms looked up to see them go — those roan, red, white, and speckled cattle, calling "moo" so tenderly, and each with the great mild Bosler eyes; and the turkeys, now fattening, sat under the cherry trees in their white bodies with wings of gold and red and breasts of black, all agitated that Katy was going; the peacock spread his tail of eyes and fashions, and broke his heart in one long sob of protest; and pea fowls and Guinea-hens, cocks and pullets, came trooping from the barn to see the face which fed them smiles, as her hands had given them food, go away but for a day.

Along the row of cherry trees, by a little mill-race flowing in the clover, near hedges of the new Osage orange from the blood-red fields of Kansas, and where gum trees matched the sycamores in strength in some old sedgy pasture, they rolled in the reddish road, and now and then saw the Catoctin Mountain's purple-green sides, and black crest and yellowing foliage, bound up and fall.

At the first little hamlet they turned their backs upon the Catoctin range and faced the South Mountain to the northwest, and Katy at the little towns pointed out the United Brethren and the Lutheran churches ready for worship.

Going between the high, billowy corn-hills to cross the main Catoctin Creek, they rose upon a bold mound in their way, and only three miles ahead saw their road scale the Blue Ridge, which, like a giant child playing through the sky, showed dimples of turning foliage in his austere countenance, and grace and sweetness nursed by storm.

Near the foot of the mountain, at a road coming in from the north,

Luther Bosler and Nelly Harbaugh were waiting in a buggy.

Nelly now had a dress of bright colors and a straw hat of city jauntiness trimmed with natural flowers, and Lloyd smiled to see, as she put her straight foot from the buggy, that she wore hoops and flounces.

"Katy," he said to his little girl, who sat in a black Dunker hood and cape and gown, her hair plaited down her back, and her white Dunker cap transparent at her little ears, "why don't you dress like Nelly?"

"I am not so peautiful," Katy said, looking down at her dark gown and white apron, "and, Lloyd, I want to love God, who has let you love me."

"My child," Lloyd said, not repelling some tears which came to his eyes, "why do you not see the wicked fellow I am and turn away from me? I am not worthy of your pure heart, Katy!"

"Yes, you are," Katy said; "maybe I can pring you to God if I try hard. What else is woman for?"

The tears came again and yet again to the young man's eyes; at last they streamed upon his cheeks, and he felt them dropping like blood from a fresh wound into his hands, as he held his palms open and thought they would fill. It was the first mention of God, the first affection bestowed upon him, so hungry-hearted, since his Christian mother's death.

Katy threw her arms around him and drew his head upon her little neck.

"Tese is love-feast tears," she said. "Our Savior made tem holy, darling, at his last supper. Come, take it with me today and pe happy."

He sobbed so hard he could not speak: a past world of love now faded in the grave, another world of fatherly affection he had sought but could not find; recollections of prayers long taught but long unuttered, of gentle feelings brutalized by coarse city contacts, of the sense of home not yet obliterated but blunted, and of being at this moment too well, too nobly, if humbly beloved, stirred all the nature of the young man up and melted into rills of tears the ice in caverns long denied the air.

"My God!" he spoke at last, "can love do this? Was I experimenting with love, and finding such religion? — Katy," he suddenly looked up and pushed her from him, "you must let me go!"

"Nefer, now," said Katy, looking with all her heart and great deep eyes upon him. — "God, gif me this soul, and let it feed with me of thy supper and drink thy precious blood!"

Coming to the wagon to find Lloyd in tears and Katy clinging to him, Luther Bosler exclaimed:

"Wass treibsht olla weil? Are you two quarreling?"

"No, Luther," answered Lloyd, wiping his eyes; "Katy is trying to make something good out of me. Yonder mountains ought to be between us."

"'Faith,'" observed Luther, mildly, "'can remove mountains,' it says. Let us cross them together."

He took the reins, and Nelly Harbaugh sat by him, and so they slowly went up the pebbly mountain-road, old Jake going before in the buggy, with the parting words:

"Love-feast. Bi'm-by!"

Sitting with his arm around Katy, and with sweetly troubled feelings, yet manlier than he had ever known, Lloyd looked back into Catoctin Valley and remarked:

"Luther, why can't I see the houses and towns now?"

"Because te upper valley is hilly and tey puilt te houses py te springs petween te hills. But tey is all tere, Lloyd, and whoefer has pusiness with tem can find tem. When their country calls for tem, up will run te flag eferywheres and pe peautiful."

"We'll be there, Luther, won't we? This great, free Union is worth fighting for!"

"Yes, Lloyd. A pity it ain't free, too, and ten, I think, we should always have peace."

"What a singular Dutchman!" Lloyd thought to himself. "What he says seems eloquent, because he is so honest. How came he to be so grave and parental? I am not so. He is like a father to his father because, I suppose, he is so good a son. My father! Why will he not give me his confidence? Do I deserve it?"

"I live yonder where the hills are all rocky and wild, past Wolfsville," said Nelly Harbaugh, pointing north. "Mount Misery, where the counterfeiters had their cave in the Revolutionary War, is close by me. The Tories hid there, too, that were caught and hanged. I'm bad root, Lloyd," blushed Nelly, with a deep look on Luther.

"The heart is the true rest," Luther said. "Keep that steady, and your pad ancestors will not trouble you. But whose dogs are those?"

He pointed back, and coming together in the road were Fritz and Albion, the latter leading on, as if he had proposed the excursion; Fritz hanging back, yet looking at the carriage sturdily, as ready to take his reproof.

"Fritz, *wo gaesht hee?*" spoke Luther, without temper, to his dog, but looking serious, and stopping the horses on the mountaintop.

The Sugar-Loaf Mountain far away was peeping hazily over the giant ramparts of Catoctin, and up from the depths behind them followed the solemn green woods to where, upon this summit, lay ledges of sandstone, and the oak and chestnut trees shook with a coming tempest of wind and rain.

Fritz came straight up to the carriage, looked at Luther unhappily, and barked.

The city dog, with a vicious barking at Lloyd, took to the woodside and disappeared ahead in the road.

"Evil communications corrupt good manners, Luther," Lloyd said. "My dog has tempted yours away."

"Fritz," spoke Luther to his dog, shaking his head, "was not in the hapit of leafing home, where he is my friend and guard."

The dog came right up under the whip and barked with an excitement above apprehension, as if to say, "Whip me, but spare my pride!"

"Unfortunate dog!" exclaimed Luther, but more tenderly. "Can I do anything put send him home?"

The dog started back with head down, needing no further humiliation.

"Stop, Fritz!" Luther continued, his face lighting up, "does any person here speak for this tisopedient friend of mine, who has, perhaps, peen under pad atvice today?"

The dog had stopped, and when both Katy and Lloyd cried "Yes, do forgive him!" and Luther replied, "Very well, then," the dog took his place meekly under the wagon, and they entered the summit forest.

The winding road-track through the fallen chestnut-leaves and stone-heaps reminded them of Atzerodt's story, as they saw the pale, lemon-yellow leaves twirl in the rising gust like witches in a circle, and the squirrels run when mischievous lightning chased them from tree to tree. The clean trunks arose smoothly from stony ledges, and, ever young in form and foliage, though in their autumn days, the chestnut forest had an appearance pleasing even now in the grasp of coming storm. Something of the light and straight nature of the French was in it, tender in greenness, comely in maturity, engaging in the burr, and toothsome in the nut. However lofty the mighty shafts might rise, though monarchs of the forest, they had the complaisance and sentiment of kings in France.

Nothing crossed their way but wood-cutters' paths barely traceable through the translucent goldness of the trees and litter, and the rail-splitters' piles and chips seemed only larger yellow leaves and ferns that strewed the vistas. A cool, small cedar tree occasionally appeared, like a green parasol in the bright sunshine; but nothing of man or domestic beast broke the Sabbath stillness of the mountaintops — hardly the eagle yonder, so near overhead he almost touched the trees, like Jove taking his jealous watch and throwing from his eyes upon the woods below the citron glisten of Olympus.

"See!" whispered Nelly Harbaugh to Luther, "yonder are men — Negroes — runaway slaves. There's money for catching them, Luther! Quick!"

Across the road, not fifty yards before, passed two black men, one carrying the other.

The younger was barefooted and had no coat, and limped as he labored under the older man's weight.

The old man seemed in the palsy of fear, or age, or disease, and, as he saw the carriage coming and women in it, a habit of courtesy, too old to be forgotten, made him take off the old straw hat he wore and bow almost idiotically and make a chattering noise.

Attracted by the movement, the young man turned and saw the carriage, and at a run, still limping, he bore the old man into the woods, flying to the north.

"Oh!" cried Nelly, "they're gone; we might have caught them. Along this mountain they travel at nights. It's hardly thirty miles across Maryland to the free State. We have got people here who live by catching them and get hundreds of dollars reward."

"And a millstone it will pe around their necks," exclaimed Luther.

"I reckon so, too," Lloyd said. "Niggers oughtn't to run away, but let somebody else than me do the catching."

At this moment the pointer-dog, Albion, reappeared out of the place in the woods where the fugitives first emerged, and his delicate brown kid nose was trailing something.

"Hist!" cried Lloyd; "come here, Albion!"

Raising his head only to bark ill-naturedly, and striving to lick his torn ear once, the white and yellow pointer dropped to the scent again and darted into the opposite woods, barking.

"I hope he won't petray those poor fellows," Luther said, "but we can't stop for him, for te rain is coming hard, and tere's no shelter till we get to Smoketown."

"Oh," cried Nelly Harbaugh, "stop there at the fortune-teller's!"

The storm now burst in half-sunny nonchalance upon the mountain they were on, and yet, while its lightnings leaped vengefully here, the parallel mountain, beyond the gorge they were overhanging, seemed to be serene as Sabbath, and through the mist of sheet-rain, at pauses, they could see its happy countenance of chestnut woods and sulphur-tinted leaves, waiting like one beatified martyr for another to pass through his fires.

With cool, executionerlike method, the spirits of the storm whipped the longer mountain's back with rods of forked fire until it smoked, and the sound of riven trees beneath the thunderbolts seemed like the broken rods of Pilate's soldiery shivered upon the unanswering Pioneer. Yet, sometimes red as blood, the electric current flowed along the hairy woodlands till rain, like floods of tears from heaven, streamed down to cool the mountain's anguish, and groans, from none knew where, feebly or waillike accompanied the tempest.

The road grew black; the steady gray wagon-horses shrank as if they would crawl upon their bellies; dust and water, thunder and flame mutinied against each other in their common purpose, and fought together without proceeding, while the great dike of the Blue Ridge Mountain buried itself in mystery or melted away.

"Why, this is hell, or the portent of it!" Lloyd Quantrell spoke, covering Katy with his body and arms.

"Say 'Te Words,' Lloyd," he heard her whispering, "and we will pe happy."

"Steaty, Jim! Steaty, Sam! Holt steaty, poys!" Luther Bosler's voice spoke calmly; "it will soon pe ofer."

A scream from Nelly Harbaugh at this moment, and the horses leaping in their harness and striving to break from the driver's practiced hands, were occasioned by a sight in the road which seemed almost supernatural: a strange, half-transparent, rose-colored mist, like lava dissolved in wine, sprang up as if the lightning had been distilled and held a long moment in atmospheric solution, and through it were seen at the horses' heads two men and two large hounds, gazing up at the carriage, and themselves surprised as much as its occupants.

The men were burly, coarse-looking, neither good nor evil of countenance, and clearly people of this world.

While the occupants of the carriage gazed at them for a period of time measured only by its vividness upon the nerves and heart, blackness, as of a cloud, came down again like a mighty crow alighting in the road, and with it a silence that was the Sabbath of the dead.

Slowly this yielded to the influences of a gentle shower and returning sun, and soon they saw the road before them plainly open, and the freshly twisted and prostrate trees embarrassing the way.

"What made you scream, Nelly?" asked Luther, stooping to kiss her.

"The slave-catchers," cried Nelly. "Didn't you see them?"

"Did you know their faces?"

"Oh, yes — Lew and Ben Logan. They watch at nights and on all the stormy days; for then the slaves are running. They're rich, I reckon."

"Not in conscience, I think," mused Luther, getting down to examine his harness. "We must stop at te first house in Smoketown to tie up this breeching."

"Oh, I'm so glad!" Nelly Harbaugh exclaimed. "That's Hannah Ritner's, the fortune-teller."

"Lloyd," cried little Katy, "I wasn't frightened at all — you held me so close. And then you said 'Te Words' last night, and all your body was God's."

Chapter VII

WITCH OF SMOKETOWN

A LITTLE farther the South Mountain opened like an amphitheater, and showed some patches of fields and farms at the base of their broken mounds; but the landscape was yet ragged and almost uninhabited till, on the descending road before them, some small houses of a poor appearance were finally seen straggling along, each to itself, as if they came together by accident and had hardly discovered each other, so embowered were they, in fruit trees, weeds, gardens, and corn.

"There's Smoketown," Nelly Harbaugh cried; "some calls it Ginny Winders's town. Old Ginny keeps a groggery for the blackberry-pickers, chestnut-sellers, wood-choppers, charcoal-burners, and slave-catchers. Oh, it's a hard place!"

"I should think so," Lloyd Quantrell remarked, looking at the near mountains and at a deep gorge behind him, like the wide-open throat of a wild beast ready to devour the scattered place; "it seems to me to be running away, like the children in the Bible chased by Elisha's bears. Who is this Hannah Ritner?"

"She's a stranger, but I reckon she's lived here for years," Nelly replied; "she's religious, and teaches the poor children to spell and to sew. Some say she's crazy, and that's why they go to her to get their fortunes told. She tells them real true."

By this time they had come to the first house in the place on the right-hand side — a small, very neat, whitewashed cottage, with an old blackened roof, and with a little portico in front, the latter covered with a trained blackberry-vine.

The house stood in a small arbored garden, and the mock-orange and gourd vines could be seen dropping their yellow or roan-gold fruit from these small arbors, and also from the locust trees along the roadside paling. Yellow marigolds grew against the gable; bright flowers in white-washed flower-pots showed along the path leading back to the door from the gate; and a willow tree in the garden seemed to weep for an unmarked grave which was not there.

The fruit trees and bean-poles and shocked corn added a look of rankness and weediness in the midst of such providence and taste, and the forest coming down from the stony hills behind, in bits of chestnut thicket and brush, seemed to wrap the small cottage in.

An old stable was at the edge of this forest, and paths went back from it into the rain-raveled mountain-spurs.

Nothing else Lloyd Quantrell could see but a large preserving-kettle in the garden, hung on a wooden crane; and while he looked at this, a gray and yellow fox, licking his chops of sirup, leaped up from the kettle and ran into the woods, followed hotly by Fritz.

Nelly Harbaugh stepped out first, at the entrance of a little lane, deeply shaded with cherry and plum trees, which crept back almost mysteriously to the stable; a horse was tied here, and she had barely seen it when a man came through the garden and stopped her in the lane.

"Andrew!" she exclaimed, and started to run back.

"Nelly!" cried Atzerodt — for it was he — and he seized her by the wrist.

The girl, a moment shrinking, drew her graceful figure up haughtily and cried, "If you strike me, I'll have you repent in Hagerstown jail!"

"Going to haf your fortune told, Miss Nelly?" muttered the sallow, outcast man. "I'll tell it to you, py Jing!"

His lips trembled with excitement. The girl tore her arm away, and with a quick gesture she picked up a stick from a flower-pot, rending out the deep-red rose which grew upon it. Lloyd Quantrell had quickly come upon the scene, and he marked the fine beauty of the girl thus impassioned and defiant.

"I declare, Nelly," he said, "you're as splendid now as a great actress on the stage!"

The words seemed to have a power to arrest Nelly Harbaugh's attention even in her apprehensions.

"Am I, Lloyd?" she replied. "Oh, I would rather be that than anything in the world!"

"Dat is shoost what you are fit for, py Jing!" Atzerodt broke in. — "Luter Bosler, you got my girl; she'll pe no good to you."

"Come, Antrew, forget and forgive," Luther remarked, coming forward from the horses; "pad words putter no parsnips."

He reached out his hand, which the other repelled, and Atzerodt continued in a reckless yet suffering tone:

"Luter, she'll get you in love and preak your heart. She is false to eferypody."

"You lie!" exclaimed the girl, herself the dangerous person now, seeking to get past Quantrell and ply her stick on Atzerodt.

Lloyd interposed good-naturedly.

"She wants your money, Luter. She's a cold-hearted Swisser, you pet. She'll nefer marry you if somepody else will gif her petter clothes. Your poor heart will hang where mine is now, and den you'll feel for me."

He broke down in almost touching, though maudlin drunken misery, and the girl dropped her stake of wood and pushed past Lloyd Quantrell.

"I could not love you," she said to Atzerodt. "You earn nothing; you can not support a wife. Never do you come near me again, but say good-bye forever now."

He called her an ugly word, which he had barely done when Lloyd, with a flat-hand blow, struck him to the grass, and stood over him, saying:

"What do you say before Katy?"

"Dear Andrew," spoke Katy, coming forward, "come to church at Beaver Creek and be a petter man. If you don't like us Dunkers, there is te Luteran church, and te Mennese church and te Brethren too, all close together."

"Nelly Harbaugh," continued Atzerodt from the ground, cowed but still revengeful, "you'll nefer let me forgit you. Some day I'll be hung on te gallows for you, I tink."

He remained on the wet ground with his face in the weeds, and all left him there and went forward to the cottage.

As they approached it there was a sound of musical water, and across the embowered yard flowed a mountain stream so wide they could hardly step across it, and foaming now with the rain which no longer fell, but in the sky a rainbow took its place and spanned the mountain like an arch of beauty.

"My love," spoke Lloyd, taking Katy's arm, "the bow of promise is come already for us."

"Lloyd," she replied, "poor Andrew suffers so, it clouds my heart."

The cottage seemed to be empty, and consisted of only one room and a kitchen, the latter low as the ground, the main room higher and containing a bed, an open Franklin stove, and a large flag-bottomed rocking-chair painted green. There was no other chair, but in a corner a glass-faced cupboard contained Delft plates and coffee service, and many bottles of cordials and home-made wines, and a line of jars of preserves, and also several books.

A Bible was on the windowsill and a candlestick beside it, and on the wall was a print in colors of Hagar and Ishmael, showing a large hand, as of a man, protruding from a door, with the palm raised against the mother and son, who were thus shut out.

Everything in this room was clean as it was plain, the bed-quilt sewn by hand from little rag savings, the wood scrubbed white, the stove polished, and flowers in water, on a little shallow mantel, diffused a subtle perfume.

"Hannah Ritner keeps no servant," said Nelly Harbaugh. "See this beautiful candle! She makes it herself of bear's grease and beeswax, and they say her light never goes out the longest night."

Lloyd saw a movement at the stable in the rear of the house, and a tall woman came from it and walked at a dignified pace toward him.

She had coal-black hair, like the crow's wing, falling in combed tresses below her waist, so that her shoulders and fine, straight, matronly form were half covered with these splendid waves of hair, in which some silver threads made barely an impression.

She was one of the finest women Lloyd had ever seen, with something almost grand in her stature and bearing, unbent, and her skin of a clear, pure tint, as if its roses could be called back if she would only exercise the will.

Her face was rather large than long, the jaws being of fine, ample mold, and her hair was cut off between the tresses in front, and the short tassel of jet-black frontlet there half covered her forehead, or nearly meeting the rich black eyebrows, and under these were dark eyes, large, melting, sad, compassionate, and full of thought, with black lashes sweeping her cheeks, and a nose long and fine, but neither straight nor aquiline, and like an inverted bow.

She was dressed in a dark gown, with a dark apron tied round her waist. No ornament was in her ears or on her neck or hands.

As she approached, this woman, seeing Lloyd, opened her large eyes wider, but did not stop nor hesitate, yet continued to look straight at him till his own eyes sank down under the soul-searching gaze of this noble-seeming and mysterious being.

Still advancing upon him — for he stood in the door between the house and kitchen, looking outward through another door — the woman made a grave, sweet inclination of her head and countenance, and said, nearly like a question, yet with recognition:

"Quantrell!"

He started with astonishment.

"Lloyd, is it not?" she continued, with a slightly German accent, but in a voice of deep music, worthy of a prophetess.

"Lloyd Quantrell is what they named me," he exclaimed.

"Is your mother dead?"

"Yes, madam."

"I read so. Have you come to see the fortune-teller? That is a sweet child I see behind you. Do you pretend to love her?"

"Pretend, madam?" Lloyd answered with indignation, yet also with accusation and fear. "I hope you are not tempting me."

"God forbid!" she exclaimed, with stately reproof; "yet ye have golden tongues. What do you find to kill in these mountains like these simple birds of sex?"

She waved her hand toward the women.

At that moment Luther Bosler perceived the dog Albion come out of the woods and begin to scratch and whine around the little stable.

"Is that your dog?" the woman spoke, also looking toward the stable as if with some new interest. "Go bring him away, instantly!"

Luther, not Lloyd, started to do so. He found his own dog, Fritz, returned, and Fritz followed him obediently; but the English pointer was not tractable, and ran back into the chestnut and chinquapin brush, whither Luther followed, calling his name.

"Hannah," spoke Nelly Harbaugh to the woman, "the harness is a bit broke, and we stopped to mend it. Won't you tell our fortunes?"

"Idle request upon the Sabbath-day!" Hannah Ritner replied. "I have told one fortune for *you* today already. Is not your lover yonder?"

She pointed to where Atzerodt's horse was tied in the secluded path.

Lloyd Quantrell, looking there, saw Atzerodt standing up and looking intently toward the stable.

"Give me your hand!" the seer commanded, taking Nelly's in her own palm, and gazing with great candor and beauty of expression into her eyes.

Lloyd thought he had never seen together three more beautiful women than these.

Hannah Ritner then slowly spoke these lines, with such deep, distinct, and eloquent diction that Lloyd hoped she would speak more:

> *"Ebbes dunkel und weiss marrick ich,*
> *Mit dunkla soll's b'marricka dich!*
> *Gaed der roth-fogel uf 'n reis',*
> *Dann waersht net dunkel or net weiss!"*

Nelly Harbaugh muttered something Lloyd believed to be the protecting "Words," and dropped her fine blue eyes.

The fortune-teller, turning her own eyes to Lloyd, exclaimed:

"It is not my wont to tell on poor girls secrets that may smirch them in a man's eyes. Here is her fortune as I gave it, put in English words."

Still holding Nelly Harbaugh's hand, Hannah Ritner recited to Lloyd and little Katy as follows, studying Katy meanwhile, and only once looking at the hand:

> "Something dark and white I mark,
> It shall mark thee with the dark!

When the red-bird takes his flight,
Thou shalt not be dark or white!"

"Look out for the red-bird, Nelly," Lloyd exclaimed; "the dove is my warning."

Hannah Ritner caught the word and repeated it:

"*Die Dowb*: that was the bird of the Holy Spirit which descended on the baptizers, cooing as it flew from heaven, 'This is my beloved Son!' My well-beloved son!" she turned to Lloyd, with something very tender, yet sorrowful, in her great eyes, "you may be baptized with fire. Seek even in the fire for that immortal dove which bravely swept the Deluge with his tired pinions, and returned to the little ark of love at last. Why do you seek this simple maiden's eyes as if their luster was the window of that ark to you? — She trembles while I ask. — Fear not, my little peasant-maid! I'll tell your lover's fortune, and, if I tell it true, never need you fear to come to Hannah Ritner and ask her counsel. — Lloyd, give me your hand!"

She took Lloyd's hand, and little Katy, full of faith and yearning, took his other hand almost in stealth, and looked in Hannah Ritner's eyes with simple pleading.

At that moment, Lloyd Quantrell, cool and undisturbed, saw the stable-door unclose, and a Negro emerge, carrying an old man on his back, and, looking backward agonizingly, the Negro stole down the embowered lane.

Lloyd looked again in Hannah Ritner's eyes. He could not see them, for they were bent upon his hand, and, to his astonishment, some tears fell from somewhere on his palm.

"Why do you weep?" he asked; "I am nothing to you."

"This is a large, strong hand," answered Hannah Ritner, with deep feeling. "I see the marks of conflicts upon it, but not of toil. Oh, find some task to do, my son, and bless your Maker for sweet, constant occupation!"

"Tell my fortune!" spoke Lloyd. "I am not afraid to hear it. You will not hurt this little girl's feelings, I know; for she *is* dear to me, Mother Hannah!"

At this familiar salutation, tears fell from Hannah Ritner's eyes again, and she was unable to proceed for some time.

Throwing an arm around each, she drew both Lloyd and Katy to her breast, and, looking down on them, the silent tears fell from her splendid eyes all the more, and not like the tears of anguish, but of great commiseration.

Lloyd thought she was like the Virgin he had seen a picture of at the Catholic school, whose everlasting cause of love and woe was the successive ages of mankind, and their many sorrows, ever to recur.

Little Katy, also tearful and tender, reached up her lips and kissed the prophetess's mouth, saying:

"*Fergeb uns unser shoolda!* You must be good, I know."

"God bless you, my child, for those sweet words!" said Hannah Ritner, quieted and strong again.

Looking now at Lloyd with deep interest, she repeated what he could not understand, in her beautiful intonation, thus:

> "All's game's unna die Sunn Ich sae,
> Fer deina Flindt fleegt in die Höh;
> Und wann aw dodt sheest allum ort,
> Dann singt die Darddle-Daub doch fort!"

"Come, Mother Ritner!" Lloyd pleasantly entreated, yet feeling something remarkable to be in this person, and a slight sense of superstition in himself, "you will not leave my fate such a Dutch riddle as that? Tell my coming luck in English, too!"

The strange, stately woman tapped her forehead as if seeking to recollect or to compose, or, at least, to translate something.

"I have spent so much of my time, my children, among these mountain poor, teaching them in Dutch, that my English verse comes slowly back to me, and I am growing old, too, and memory and wit are weaker."

With the same slight German accent she then made the translation of Lloyd's fortune, not readily, yet with eloquence, like profound conviction:

> "All the game beneath the sun
> Shall rise up before thy gun;
> When thou killest everything,
> Still the turtle-dove will sing!

"Thank God for that, Katy!" Lloyd exclaimed. "Let the turtledove be heard, whatever happens to us. — And now, Mother Ritner, dear little Katy is waiting to have her fate told before she goes to church; for Luther, I reckon, has mended the harness by this time."

"I must be quick," Hannah Ritner said; "for I am strangely nervous this morning. It seems to me I hear the baying of dogs. Katy, let me see your hand! Why, my darling, the lines in it are almost like my own. I can tell your fortune easily."

As she repeated the following lines, Katy listened with deepening awe and final trembling, so that Lloyd kissed her to his heart, at the end:

"In dara hond sae Ich en Ring
  Ferleera, sollsht du's, schoenes ding!"

Katy heard with prayerful wonder and fear. The seer spoke to her
with deep and solemn tones the next couplet, as follows:

"Doch bawdst du fer's im krickly noof,
  Dan sollsht du's finna bei 'ma Buch!"*

As she spoke, Hannah Ritner accidentally laid her hand upon the
Bible.

"Now for the English, Mother Hannah!" Lloyd exclaimed seeing that
Katy Bosler looked pale and frightened.

"What noises are those?" Hannah Ritner whispered. "Surely it is the
blood-hound's bark I hear! Who is at my stable?"

She strode through the kitchen and shouted:

"What do you there? Stealers are ye of the souls and bodies of your
fellow-men!"

Lloyd, Katy, and Nelly following, they beheld come out of the small
chestnuts behind the stable, first the dog Albion, very animated and
frolicsome, and he threw himself into the attitude of pointing game a
few steps from the stable-door.

Next there bounded from the same thicket three dogs apparently
fighting, and one of these was engaged in a clinched struggle with
another, which bayed deep and loud; and the third dog, a great blood-
hound, rushed upon the stouter of these dogs and bit him terribly, while
Albion also barked as he "pointed," and so the air was full of fierce,
savage noises.

Luther Bosler, going to the relief of the injured dog, which was now
seen to be his own Fritz, was himself set upon by the two hounds, and
they seemed to be on the point of tearing him to pieces, when out of
the thicket rushed the two men already related to have crossed the
mountain during the thunderstorm, and both of these shouted loudly
to the blood-hounds and pulled them separate ways.

"It's the Logan boys," exclaimed Nelly Harbaugh; *"husht se g'sana?*
There must be runaway slaves hiding about Hannah Ritner's house."

"Go in there at your peril, hyenas!" shouted Hannah Ritner, throwing
herself between the stable and the pursuers. "This land is mine, and I
will defend it with my life!"

She had drawn upon her head a large leghorn hat, and as she spread

---

*   These predictions are all translated into Pennsylvania Dutch by Thomas
     C. Zimmerman, of Reading, Pa.

her arms across the stable-door and put her back against it and threw her fine white throat and strongly pointed chin up, the long elf-hair fell so wildly and so dead black down from her pallid face that both the men halted a moment irresolutely.

Lloyd Quantrell's ill-starred dog, however, dashed at Hannah and barked his ill-tempered and short, snappish dislike. Lloyd himself knocked the dog over with a stone, and it retired yelping a little distance, and again, with one fore-leg extended and the other lifted crookedly as if lame, raised its muzzle toward the stable, put its tail out straight, and cast its eyes trancefully sidewise like a somnambulist.

The long hounds bounded against the stable as if resolved to throw it down.

"Infernal dog!" thought Lloyd; "but a pointer's a hound, too, bred on a spaniel. – Open that door, Hannah!" Lloyd raised his voice. "If their niggers are not there, I'll fill both these loafers' hounds with shot."

"They shall not go in!" Hannah Ritner cried.

"Interfere with us at your peril, young man!" the taller of the ruffians said, but without any temper. "We've suspected this place a good while, and now we've got a warrant to search it. The dogs trailed right yer."

He produced his warrant, and, as he walked to Hannah Ritner and presented it, his companion slipped in at the rotten stable-side.

Hannah moved a little way to examine the warrant, and the stable-door, pushed open from within, showed nothing there but a lady's horse, all saddled, and nibbling at his fodder.

The two slave-catchers hastily examined the inside of the stable; their dogs, assisted by Albion, smelling and seeking everywhere, but in vain.

"We may be mistaken," said one of the men, a little pale, and hitching up his wet waterproof boots, "but we shall now search the house."

"There's nothing there," Lloyd Quantrell sternly interposed, "and now I'll pepper both your dogs with my gun, as I have promised."

Lloyd started at a quick stride toward the wagon at the end of the lane. He had walked but a step, however, when a voice was heard to cry:

"Coom on! Te niggers is here, poys, and te reward is mine, py Jing!"

At the end of the little lane, the black boy before observed, with the old Negro man upon his back, was receding and trembling before Lloyd Quantrell's gun cocked at Andrew Atzerodt's shoulder.

"I shoost found tis gun in te wagon," Atzerodt exclaimed, "and took it and headed off tese niggers after tey had walked ofer me in tis lane."

The hunters and their dogs dashed forward; the young man was overthrown and the old man fell heavily to the ground, and the wild dogs set upon them till dragged away.

When silence was restored after the baying thunder, the old black man still lay where he had fallen, and the younger man, bloody and nearly naked after struggling with the dogs, looked down upon him in despair.

"Father!" he cried, "is you hurt? Oh, speak to me, father!"

With a painful effort the old man turned from his side to his back, looked up into his son's face with a convulsive shudder of his lineaments, and saying, "Honey, I's mos' gone," straightened out, stone dead.

The young man knelt, clammy with the sweat for life and freedom, and raising his hands, clasped together, above his head, sobbed out the words:

"Father! Daddy! Don't die now, when I'se carried ye so fur. I'll go back to ole missis and take it all on me!"

The old man's jaw had fallen; his gray hairs only moved in the mountain zephyrs; he seemed worn out with age and terror, and very quiet in the light of God.

"Oh!" shouted the young man, turning toward the spectators of the scene, his hands still lifted prayerfully together, "kill me, won't you, and let me reign with daddy? — Reign, Lord!" he screamed with sudden, awful ecstasy, "and let me die and reign with father, too. I kin die under de whip if I kin reign!"

His streaming eyes were strained with this religious despair, till their gleaming pupils grew small upon the great white disks of his eyeballs. He was a sinewy, high-purposed young man, and the dogs came forward and glared at him as if he might be dangerous yet.

But as he prayed for human hands to give him death, his own long toil in night and storm, bramble and mountain, carrying that old man, and the excitement of his sorrow, threw him in a fit upon the earth — blind, silent, desolate.

The handcuffs of the Logans were fastened on his wrists, even before he fell, and while he appealed to human nature and to God.

"Off with him, while he's quiet!" spoke the elder Logan to his brother. "There's no reward for the older chap, and so we'll leave his body here for the neighbors, or the birds."

The two short, thickset men, tying the unconscious Negro's limbs, lifted him on their shoulders and started to go.

"Stop!" interposed Andrew Atzerodt; "I caught dat nigger, and want my money for him."

"The reward is three hundred dollars," replied the slave-dealer; "here is a hundred for your share, if you put in no further claim."

He passed a bank-note to the haggard man, who looked at it with fervor and accepted it, and then, turning to Nelly Harbaugh in a moment of revulsion and triumph, he cried:

"I earn nothing? Heigh? I can't support a wife? Heigh? Take it, Nelly, and I'll pecome a nigger-ketcher and make you rich, py Jing!"

The girl seemed attracted by so much money. She hesitated.

"Off with you!" hoarsely spoke Luther Bosler. "It is te Sabbath, and I would not fight. But this insult to a lady excites me. Plood-money to a woman engaged to be married to an honest man?"

His slow, intense exasperation was like some giant's aroused power — infectious, because so deep and real. Lloyd Quantrell felt it, and wresting his gun from Atzerodt's hand, he cried:

"Luther, I'm with you. We two can clean all three of these ruffians out."

He looked at his caps and raised the bright twisted barrel. The dogs perceived disorder near and growled ominously.

"You are too good a citizen, Bosler, to break the law," exclaimed the slave-taker. "Let us go in peace. We only do our duty under the compromise laws of the United States and the warrant of the State of Virginia."

"Put down that man!" Lloyd Quantrell said to the speaker, with the cool zest of collision in him.

"I'll put him down," the mountain ranger answered, "at the town of Harper's Ferry, and not before!"

The two girls became alarmed at the scene before them, and Atzerodt moved toward his horse.

"Go!" spoke Luther Bosler, with deadly calm. "God's vengeance hovers ofer tis guilty land!"

"It will come tonight!" pealed the deep tones of Hannah Ritner, as she walked forward. "Let me prophesy with head uncovered, as the Scripture commands woman to do!"

She threw her hat upon the ground and turned her face to the south. Her long, wild hair she threw behind her shoulders with sudden nervous energy, and her large dark eyes seemed inverted and gazing inward, and her tones were like a woman's who had never spoken with human people, but had wandered alone, talking loudly with herself.

"These are the two angels sent to Sodom" — she indicated the slave-catchers. "Turn in, my lords, and tarry in my house and wash your feet! For ye are compassed round. The mountain fires shall drown ye and yon city to which ye go. The cry of the poor, waxed great before God's face, calls for destruction, and it will not be put off. I see the chimneys reel, the hearth-stone shattered, the churches hollow, and the rivers flowing red. Escape? Ye can not! Brimstone and fire shall mingle this night, and the smoke of the country go up as the smoke of a furnace!"

She ceased, as if still talking to herself. The dogs whined, and the men looked at each other.

"She's crazy," said Lew Logan.

"Come, leave her," spoke his brother Ben; "we are twenty miles from Harper's Ferry."

They went at a rapid walk up the gorge, followed by Atzerodt.

A moment after they had disappeared from view, Hannah Ritner, resuming her natural tones, turned to the remaining persons and said:

"You will be late at love-feast. I thought to go there with you. But I must take a long ride."

As they were getting into the wagon, she went past on a nimble-footed saddle-horse, dropping them a courteous farewell.

"It seems to me I have seen a horse like that before," Lloyd Quantrell thought; "she's mounted like a huntress."

Chapter VIII

BEAVER CREEK DUNKERS

ALL made spasmodic remarks, with no great intelligibility of plan
or reflection, on the foregoing scene — the law to capture and return
fugitive slaves having been in recent years established by Congress with
the aid of all the great statesmen and the President of the United States,
for the purpose of composing the country, which seemed, indeed,
perfectly tranquil now, excepting many such agonizing episodes as that
just given, but which it was thought unpatriotic and disturbing to
describe or discuss.

"What was your fortune, Katy?" Lloyd asked as they came to the top
of a hill and saw before them a bounding prospect of fields uptilted,
and woods in plumes and crowns, giving every well-plowed farm a
human look like hair worn strong, yet comely.

"Hush, Lloyd!" Katy said, "it was not good; so let me be still and
think of the Lord's supper till we come to church."

"Yonder is Beaver Creek Dunker meeting-house," Nelly Harbaugh
spoke to Lloyd, indicating nearly two miles away a low white building
like a long school-house half sunken behind a moundy brown hill, and
defined against a higher crest of green. At the foot of the hills they
descended, woods and notches in the bottoms were signs of a stream
there, and the far eastern horizon rose up like a mighty rampart as if it
were an ocean's confines.

"That is the Antietam country," Luther exclaimed, "and Peaver Creek
is a part of it. Our mother, Nelly, was from Antietam, put she loved
Peaver Creek pecause she met father there one love-feast week. Tey slept
in te garret of te church, as us Tunkers do, and many a marriage, Nelly,
comes out of tese homely ways we haf of living like te tisciples, watching
with our Master, and eating of te Passover lamb."

"Passover!" exclaimed Lloyd; "that's a Jew jubilee of some kind, I
reckon?"

"Yes, and all te early Christians were Jews. When te Lord slew te first-born of all te Egyptians, te Jews in Egypt killed a lamb and marked teir doors, so te angel of death would see te lamb's plood-mark and go past. Tey always eat te Passover afterward, and so did te Christian Jews, and so do we. Tunkers and Moravians, I pelieve, is all that does it now. Te sacrament is not te love-feast, put te Lord's supper. *We* keep te feast; we kill a lamb, and Jew and Catholic is welcome. We don't drive te hungry away like Saint Paul; for it can't pe any harm in peing hungry."

"Ah! Luther," Lloyd exclaimed, "Judas was at the last supper, and got the sop above all the others. Money was what ailed him. Are not you good Dutch fond of money?"

"Luther worships it," Nelly Harbaugh exclaimed, patting her lover on the back. "He and his father want to be rich and nothing else. If I was rich I would want more than that: education, admiration, and splendor. But I can make Luther love them, too, and bring them to me."

"Money," Luther reflected aloud, "is te convenient result of industry and care. Whatever else we want, money fetches it. We Dutch puys land with it for our children."

Nelly blushed as he looked at her.

"Her first blush," Lloyd Quantrell thought, "since I have seen her. Then she loves that man! She will not blush for me."

"We can not spend our money, Lloyd," Luther continued, "if we keep diligent, pecause we have no fashions. Our clothes is te same from year to year. We do not take usury, so we do not take risks, and we do not go to law to maintain corrupting lawyers who create quarrels; Tunkers never sue one another. Te man who cheats, cheats only himself. We never fight, nor swear, nor shave our peards; so we require no barbers. Our women work and do not strain the men for their luxury. Children are plenty here, and we puy more land for tem. Education is good if it does not make people saucy and tisputatious and lazy; occupation is te only thing that peats education. Te world has plenty if people live simple and love their neighbor, who is their fellow-man. That was a fellowman tey carried back to slavery. No good can come of it."

Lloyd Quantrell had prejudices the stronger for his superficial good-humor, and he flushed as quickly as he spoke:

"You Dutch and Yankees — for I reckon you're the same breed — declare war on interest and property till you get some of it. I can say *that* from some experience," Lloyd remarked apologetically, for Katy had raised her large eyes at his suppressed tones, "because my father was a Yankee, and once had your ideas, but shaving notes and leasing *my* niggers are now his chief interests."

"You must be rich," Nelly Harbaugh exclaimed. "Have you got slaves, too?"

"Yes," said Lloyd, "fifty slaves, worth today thirty-five thousand dollars. That is, my father is my trustee for them. My mother left me her slaves. My father leases them in Charles County."

"Has your father slaves also?" Luther Bosler asked.

"No. He took my mother's land and personal property. The slaves are more salable. I suspect he took the less advantageous property because he had prejudices like yours, Luther."

Nelly Harbaugh stared at Lloyd with all her might, hearing he was so rich.

"Katy," she cried, with a breath from her fine aquiline nose, "your lover is the richest man you ever saw. Now make him marry you!"

This time the blush was Lloyd's. He glanced at Katy, whose face was turned toward her lap, and she, looking up, now showed her eyes all wet with tears.

"Darling," cried Lloyd, "Nelly has hurt your feelings. You do not love me for my money."

"Oh!" Katy murmured through her sobs, *"der auram mon hut koe haimat."*

"What does she say?" Lloyd asked of Nelly, drawing Katy's head into his hands.

"She says, 'That poor man has no home.' I guess she's thinking of that lazy, runaway slave."

"We can go to the feast," Katy sobbed convulsively, "to the Lord's feast. He must go back and be whipped. *Ich con sell net shtande.*"

"If he can stand it, you can, Kate," Nelly Harbaugh answered, gaily. "Lloyd has fifty slaves, he says. Did you hear that?"

"I wish," said Katy, "that he was poor. It's selfish, but I do. For now I see that the fortune-teller's verse is coming true."

"What was it, my gentle dove?" whispered Lloyd.

"I nefer saw so many doves, I think, as this morning," Luther Bosler remarked, overhearing the word. "See them flying down the pike before us!"

They all looked out, and behold! the doves were in the stony road, trotting across it or perching on the worm-fence rails at the sides, or flying like little living windmills straight before, picking sustenance in the grass, tame and trusting, coy and fluttered, and seeming to wonder why the dog Albion chased them so fiercely, while his companion, Fritz, kept demurely at the wagon's tail as if Fritz also had religious inclinations as he drew near church.

"Wild pigeons come by millions on the high Allegheny Mountains," Lloyd exclaimed. "These ring, and ground, and turtle doves are plentiful. They can't sing, and yet that fortune-teller thought so, for she ignorantly said to me:

'When thou killest everything,
  Still the turtle-dove will sing.'

Nonsense!" concluded Lloyd Quantrell, still looking at the flying doves with queer feelings at his heart.

"Here is Peaver Creek mills," Luther remarked, "where te Tunkers paptizes."

A large stone mill with low door and hoisting-gear in the gable stood on the right, and beyond it was a mill-pond falling across a stone dam, and bordered by thick willows and tall sycamores, and in the running waste below the dam were islets, over one of which a noble water-oak spread its branches.

Beyond the creek a large stone house and some barns clung between the water and the hill, and on the left of the road, by a store and post office, were a few other limestone dwellings and barns, giving the hidden hamlet that picturesqueness and mystic social drone in which old mills resemble old matrons with their spinning-wheels and family brood.

People were seen going to other churches off on the right in smart spring wagons or finer market carryalls.

Luther let down his bridle-reins and gave the lines to Nelly, who drove the horses into the creek to drink while he crossed by a foot-log. As the horses took their fill gratefully, the old mill seemed to sleep and snore; two kingfishers flashed over the mirror of the dam without a cry, and both dogs also drank, while still the gray and brown doves fed along the road as tame as chickens.

"Going to the Antietam?" Lloyd mused aloud, looking at the clear water. "That is a stream of which I never heard. How destitute is our country of history!"

Luther climbed in as Nelly drove the horses through Beaver Creek, hub-deep, and the Sabbath doves again led the way along toward the Dunker church, while in the fields were silent birds with green wings and scarlet heads, peeping up to see, and dropping into the blue clover again.

The church soon rose out of the ground, its limestone walls almost as white as marble, and the people and carriages and riding-horses were seen around it, and the graveyard appeared beyond with its delicate white tombstones in the grass.

Coming nearer, a large, open, grassy space or common bordered the road, and here Luther turned in, the low gable of the church extending toward them its end door and semicircular white window above. It stood a hundred rods back upon a little plateau, the slopes of which were covered with small fruit trees and a garden, and below the garden was the graveyard. A fence and gate divided the church from the common, and near the gate were hitching-racks, a shed, and water-trough.

Luther drove to the rack and tied his horses. A hundred or more worldly looking rustics saw the Dunker family descend and pass through the open gate, and gazed at Lloyd Quantrell's tall, city-clad figure with surprise, hardly dissembled by politeness.

Nelly Harbaugh, gathering up her hoops and flounces, spoke to several of these intruders as she passed through them. Little Katy, with her eyes to the ground, took her brother's arm and passed in.

The meeting-house was plain and long, and its low ceiling admitted no galleries. Wooden benches were stretched along its width, and faced that only side which had no door, while two aisles crossed each other at the middle of the church, entered by a door in each of the other three walls.

The door opposite the gable was open, and looking there Lloyd saw, to his astonishment, a great fireplace and an immense cook-stove before it, and in the fireplace something was roasting from a crane and hooks, while the stove was nearly red-hot, and large pots were steaming upon it and emitting the savor of animal food.

The kitchen door closed in a moment, and Lloyd looked in vain for the pulpit, but saw nothing resembling it, not even a platform.

A man came down a winding stairway in the corner of the church, and closed a cupboard door there behind him, and, passing to some naked tables at the blank side of the church, opened a little trap in the wall and took out a Bible and hymn-book. This man was dressed, like Jake Bosler and Luther, in a coat of dark drab color, or rather pepper-and-salt mixture, and vest and trousers of the same, the coat with tails to its square, jacketlike body, and the coat-collar standing up.

As the man lined out a hymn in English, Luther Bosler took the front seat on one side of the preacher, beside his father and other Dunker men, and Katy took the front seat on the other side of the aisle among the women, and, slipping off her sun-bonnet, sat in her white nightcap, as it seemed to be, corresponding to the dress of her companions.

Lloyd hesitated where to sit, till Nelly Harbaugh drew him into a long seat at right angles to the preacher and to Katy and to the congregation. Behind them was the cupboard door opening upon the garret stairs.

"The church will be full of the family," Nelly whispered — "they call the membership the 'family' — and there may be no room for us."

The singing had already commenced, and Katy's child's voice and Luther's strong tenor were heard in the strain, and without further delay Lloyd Quantrell, catching the tune, also dropped his bass notes in, and Katy thrilled to hear the bold, manly music, going to her heart.

The Dunker men and women turned their faces toward the church corner to see the brown-haired, broad-headed young man unaffectedly singing there, and then they looked at Katy, wondering.

Lloyd Quantrell was a large man, several inches more than six feet high, with a broad back, large hips, straight legs, and erect carriage. His hands and feet were large and strong, his neck was powerful; his eyes were a greenish gray, very clear-sighted, with large dark centers, and he had jaws full of strong, white, clean teeth, almost too large for a gentleman.

A boyish expression reduced the strength of his features, some of which, as his mouth and jaws and breadth of cheekbones, were indicative of high animal quality, but his nose was thick at the bridge and more solid than sensitive; his ears were too small for his face, and seemed to belong to a woman, and his forehead was a little beetling and rugged, as if things built their nests in it rather than bathed in a limpid brain near by.

Flexibility was in that countenance, however, despite the might of the features, but it seemed to be gayety and want of care rather than want of strength, and at instants something like an idea, or a purpose, halted a minute in the eyes, suffused with mischief, and then passed on.

Ready, joyous, mildly imaginative, voluptuous, nearly tender — one feared, while Lloyd smiled, that some day he might think and frown.

He was now looking with a Marylander's patriotism at a kind of worship he had never before heard of.

The preacher had prayed, and was saying something in broken English, and one by one the brethren first, and then the Dunker sisters, arose and passed by him and whispered, and he made for each a mark in a book.

"What is it?" Lloyd asked in a whisper.

"They're making a preacher," whispered Nelly Harbaugh. "After love-feast they'll tell his name."*

The window was open near Quantrell, and showed the Blue Ridge or South Mountain soft as a line of deep-green melons with some dull citron in their rind, lying along the horizon, but so near to the eye, it seemed as if they ripened on the windowsill.

So limpid was the air, so soft the mountain tints, Lloyd thought they were his morning thoughts reflected in the mirror of his conscience, and softly impelled onward by his delighted heart; yet, as he looked, shadows of clouds rippled those bars of mountain, like swans in lakes, and they seemed transparent and to reveal their dreams.

He watched them as if they were his own body and limbs reflected

---

*   A Dunker love-feast generally occupies two or more week-days. For purposes of narration it is here condensed into a Sunday.

there by the subtle medium of love, as it diffused from Katy's eyes.

Tingling, warming, ebbing, flowing, he felt his blood quicken to the love he encouraged yet forbade, and the mountains stretching across the pastoral upland flushed, cooled, sparkled, darkened, and thrilled with his own feelings.

He half closed his eyes and still more wondrous grew the illusion that, while his heart was here in the meeting, his form was extended yonder, walling up the Catoctin Valley, and in a blessed trance.

He saw the mountains breathe and expand, as he drank in their air; when he exhaled his breath, they seemed to fall like his own chest; he rubbed his eyes and challenged them with a look, and then they seemed to dimple and smile like a child asleep, on whom its mother looks and looks too near, so that her breath wakes playfulness in its oblivion.

"Why is everything so painfully distinct, so full of meaning and presentiment, so rapt, so haunted and so haunting?" Lloyd asked himself. "Is it love? I will not have it so, but so it is!"

The crowd outside the church increased in numbers and irreverence. They were playing games upon the slope, "Puss in the Corner" and kissing-games like "Copenhagen," and now and then loud laughter, or the scream of some hoyden, broke the quiet tones of the preacher and the singing.

Within the church nearly every seat was full of communicants: plain men in long, straight hair falling back upon their shoulders, and beards unshaved and unshorn except the mustache, which none wore; women in well-fitting black frocks with a little cape sewed upon them, and small white caps, almost transparent, tied beneath the chin and showing the smooth hair combed within.

Some of these women were comely to look upon, with skins of temperance and eyes of zest; others were fat and dull, and merely amiable; and others yet were old and wrinkled, and submissive, like women in whom beauty and life have ceased to strive, and God draws near as if he were no foe, but one as familiar in the house as once the baby had been in the cradle.

Katy sat there conscious, repentant, seeking, listening to the words with submission, fluttered by worldly passions, ready to cry out with pain, tender with gratitude.

Her beautiful head might have been the egg of the divine conception, waiting eternally to be born into life and goodness.

Her thick, dark hair left of her forehead only a narrow tablet, made whiter by the straight eyebrows; and, poised below, like moons upon the sea, her eyes gave night and glory to everything.

All the rest of her face seemed immature, but those great eyes to have been finished in her childhood, and, like large posies upon a slender stem, her delicate neck reached up to bear their weight. Her form was still a child's, barely budded; her sloping shoulders and long, thin arms, and apparent length above the waist, showed one still growing and aspiring to more stature. Her small white cap gave her the appearance of sitting up in bed. Lloyd saw her hymn-book in her hand, and thought of her belief in witches, strong as her faith in God; and his brain framed the words:

"The dear little Dutch darling!"

Turning to Nelly Harbaugh, he beheld a finer woman in everything but sensibility, to whose eagle strength Katy continued the similitude of the dove.

Nelly had a Roman nose, giving masculinity to her face, a nose which a man might have envied, so finely cut it was, and so like leadership. Beneath it was an upper lip of almost equal strength, and the blue eyes and heavy arched eyebrows equally became a resolute, ambitious man's face. But the lower lip and chin, however heroically modeled — the chin square — took the softness of maidenhood. The eyes also looked longing, as for love.

Her form was strong, her shoulders could bear burdens, her yellow hair was magnificent; in her rude flowers and bright print dress some of the style of her fine natural carriage was conveyed. The hand in her lap was large but fine, and the arm beside it, which Lloyd drew into his own, was modeled handsomely, and hard like ivory.

"Don't!" Nelly whispered, "you sly, *rich* man. They're going to make the preacher now."

There was already a commotion of some kind about the front of the congregation, and new arrivals pouring in forced the mere spectators from their benches, and, their places being demanded, Lloyd opened the stairway door, and he and Nelly went up a few steps and could see over the heads of all.

"My Lord!" Nelly Harbaugh whispered, "Luther is the new preacher!"

The elder minister or Bishop was standing by Luther Bosler, and little Katy was between them. The minister shook Katy's hand, and, putting his arm around Luther's neck, deliberately kissed him upon the bearded mouth.

Lloyd Quantrell pulled the door nearly fast, to hide his involuntary laughter.

"Don't mock us!" Nelly Harbaugh said, with a look of pain. "I shall have to stand there with him when we are married, and promise to do his work while he keeps the church together. They don't often make single men preachers. Katy takes my place today."

Opening the door, Lloyd saw a procession of the members, one by one rising and going toward the altar-space, and there each man kissed

Luther Bosler, each woman kissed Katy Bosler, the women shook Luther's hand, the men shook Katy's hand, and so they passed on, till Jake Bosler's turn came, and he fastened his wild, hairy face to his son's mouth and rich dark beard, and coming away full of tears and emotion, was heard to articulate:

"Luter – Himmel – mootter – Bi'm-by!"

Lloyd had to laugh again, and pulled the door upon his delight, never having seen in his life one man kiss another.

"Excuse me, Nelly," he sighed between his spasms of laughter, "but this grizzly-bear kissing really beats the Dutch!"

"You must kiss men, too," Nelly said, "when you become a Dunker. Oh, Katy will make you one! She never gives up anything."

This increased Lloyd's laughter. When he again widened the aperture, Luther Bosler was standing alone, and the brethren and sisters were in prayer. As they rose and burst into singing, the young Baltimorean again contributed his melodious voice, and Katy stole a glance to see her lover, as far in piety as music would advance him, singing straight toward her humble heart.

"Oh," thought Katy, "if he could only know how religion makes us love! He will love the world till God brings him to me."

She heard her brother commence to speak, and something almost like pride started in her mind, that she had a brother great and wise enough to be a minister.

Lloyd Quantrell also heard, in spite of the silly laughter and interruptions through the church-windows, the manly tones of Katy's brother, reading from the Bible the epistle old Saint Paul dispatched to them under the golden cornices of Corinth, in the day when, like a carrier-bird, the Christian carried the straw from the manger to build a nest in the acanthus capitals of the temple columns of the pagan gods.

With a slightly reproving look at the careless crowd without, Luther read:

"One is hungry and another is drunken. What! have ye not houses to eat and to drink in? Despise ye the church of God?

"As often as ye eat this bread and drink this cup, ye do shew the Lord's death till he come.

"Whosoever shall eat and drink unworthily shall be guilty of the body and blood of the Lord.

"Wherefore, my brethren, when ye come together to eat, tarry one for another.

"I would have ye know that the head of every man is Christ; and the head of the woman is the man."

Luther turned from the word and began to speak, plainly, slowly, modestly.

He told of the long struggle to extricate the Christian life from the pomp of ecclesiasticism and the caprices of theologians, and find in it the example of the disciples.

Princes and armies surrounded the Lutherans and kept them worldly; the Calvinists imitated their enemies, and wanted rebellion and conquest. Some found comfort in an intellectual formula like "justification by faith," or "the republic of the saints."

A few simple men like Menno and Landis, some of them Catholic priests, some students by prayer of the four Evangelists, resisted all conformity and formality, clinging to the holy life of the Son of woman.

Like a little thread from the land of Palestine trailing to the Alpine valleys, where the Waldenses lived in brotherhood, and thence to the springs of the Rhine and Danube, the tradition of the simple truth preceded the worldly Reformation which was irritated by its perseverance.

The spirit of St. Peter with the sword, the spirit of St. Paul with his dogma, resented the quiet faith of St. James, who was baptized again, and mirrored his brother Jesus in his calm heart.

Burned alive, banished, forbidden sepulture, exposed in cages to starve, torn between contending armies, the Baptist brethren, Swiss, Dutch, or German, bided their time till William Penn, at the end of one hundred and fifty years, heard of them, and opened the New World to those faithful sheep.

Non-resistants, submissionists, with an unpaid clergy, without other doctrine than what Christ *did,* they preserved in their Western vales the brotherhood of the disciples — not faith, not chiefly hope, but greatest of them all, love, which could die, but could not hate.

A tender intelligence and conviction spread from Luther's tones and eyes, and Lloyd forgot his uncouth dress and shaggy hair.

Luther was animated, by his engagement to Nelly, to dwell upon the family rest, where, at the table, every day, sat the almost visible Christ, saying, "Abide with me."

Quantrell turned to Nelly, and her eyes were wet with tears.

Chapter IX

THE SACRAMENT

A SUDDEN rising of the congregation, and clearing of certain benches, pressed the Dunker people back upon the spectators, and again the twain withdrew into the staircase, and this time they passed into the loft. It was lighted by the round window in the end, and, looking down into the yard, they saw the parasites of the love-feast eating bread, and meat, and pickles, and sweet things, as they came in procession from the kitchen door.

The loft was divided by pine planks across the middle, and the men's side, which they were in, was strewn with clean straw and some straw mattresses, for the lodgers at the love-feast.

"It will be full," Nelly said. "The Dunkers love to imagine themselves the disciples living together, like the Christian family. How can I ever be good enough for such a life?"

She seemed in real penitence and awe, and it occurred to Lloyd Quantrell to test the depth of her feeling. He took her hand and drew her to him, and in the low garret passed his arm around her.

"Do you love this obscure preacher," he asked, "so much that, if I were to tell you I admired you, you would refuse for him — *Baltimore?*"

Her eyes shone, and next they flashed. She pushed him away.

"Do not deceive yourself, Lloyd," she said, with dignity. "You can not deceive me. Katy is your passion. If she were not, I would prefer Luther Bosler to you."

"You are complimentary, queen!"

"You are rich, I suppose, but you have no ambition. He has — to be a good man. That is better than being a play-boy. Oh, how I love that man!" Nelly exclaimed, bursting into tears.

"Forgive me!" Lloyd spoke, in an impulse of respect and regret. "I had not given you credit for such feelings. Why do you cry?"

"Because I am so absolutely unworthy of him," answered the girl, permitting herself to be caressed. "He is peaceful and just; I am full of restless things, and know that I am beautiful. Am I not, Lloyd?" she asked, almost with eagerness, suddenly drying her tears. "You live in a great city: do I compare with the fine ladies there?"

"Few have such splendid style," Lloyd replied, slowly and with judgment. "But it is no place for you. Men who would marry you in Baltimore would not have the respect for you — they do not possess the sober merits — that Luther has."

"What can I do?" Nelly Harbaugh asked. "If I could make Luther an ambitious man, and turn his mind to the world, we might be made for each other. We *are* for each other. I love him with fear and rest. But out yonder" — she pointed beyond the mountains — is a life that often calls me. I think I have talent as well as beauty."

"Beware, Nelly," Lloyd spoke low and sagely; "you heard what Luther read, 'The head of the woman is the man' —"

"'And the head of the man' — my man — 'is Christ'; that condemns me to be buried in these mountains — a Dunker preacher's wife."

"But you are poor and he is prosperous. He has been indulgent to you. He knows it will be hard to reduce you to his image, but, in love, he takes the chance."

The girl's face softened in all its bold and spirited outlines, and she seemed profoundly moved.

"Why can't I feel religious?" she asked. "Why won't I submit? What makes me fear when I ought to be so happy? Last night I would have married Andrew Atzerodt. Today, engaged to the man I respect above all in the world, I want to tear him from his content and conscience."

She threw herself upon one of the freshly filled beds, with her head in her hands.

Her almost extravagant splendor of form, and straightness of neck, and spine, and limbs, and her length of tresses, in color like the straw, Lloyd Quantrell beheld, with rising dislike and dread of this woman continuing to be Katy's friend.

"Sis," spoke Lloyd, with cool familiarity, "you must be what they call an adventuress. It means a woman who would rather fool many men than not cheat herself. Be honest with this honest fellow Luther, and quarrel with him today!"

Nelly Harbaugh started up, and the spark of temper in her brain gave passionate character to her countenance, which Lloyd admired without losing his coolness.

"And you be honest with Luther's honest sister!" the girl exclaimed. "Take your advice to yourself. God knows I love Luther Bosler, and always shall!"

Jake Bosler's head appeared above the stairs looking at them, both in ill temper now, and he said:

"Nelly — Lloyd — love-feast — Bi'm-by!"

When they descended the wooden steps, the church had been darkened by closing all the shutters, and some tin lamps and candlesticks gave, with their flame, the aspect of night to the curious scene.

Every third bench had been turned over and made into a table upon the other two. The front benches remained full of worshipers, and the kitchen door, wide open, disclosed some beams of day, and also a pantry of dishes and of jars, and the stove and fireplace with diminished heat.

Through this door Dunker men were bringing white tablecloths, and piles of tin pans and plates, and iron spoons and knives and forks. All was clatter and decisive tread, yet with sobriety and respect.

After the tables were ready, large tubs were brought in, steaming with broth, and meat and pickles and apple-butter were placed up and down the table, and bread, in slices and quarter loaves.

Next two tubs were brought in and set one before the men and one before the women on the front line of benches.

"What's coming now?" Lloyd Quantrell inquired.

"The feet-washing," whispered Nelly Harbaugh.

By this time the tables, covering much of the church space, were occupied everywhere with waiting rows of Dunker brethren and sisters sitting neatly and by sexes. The dim light shone on the silver hairs of many, and here and there were sleeping babies at their mothers' breasts.

Suddenly the Dunker bishop began to read the story of the last supper, from St. John:

"Jesus riseth from supper and laid aside his garments."

At this two stalwart Dunkers arose and took off their coats, and two women arose on the women's side.

"And he took a towel and girded himself."

The attending Dunkers wrapped towels around their waists, and knelt by the tubs of clean water.

"After that he poureth water into a basin, and began to wash the disciples' feet and to wipe them with the towel wherewith he was girded. . . . Jesus said, 'If I wash thee not, thou hast no part with me.'"

The Dunker men and women on the front row were taking off their shoes and stockings.

Jake Bosler's feet seemed to stray around everywhere as they were disclosed under the lamp-light.

Little Katy's feet barely flashed a moment in the Dunker woman's hands, and the sound of splashing water was heard. An instant more, Lloyd saw the little girl's feet shine in the woman's towel as they were being wiped.

Then the Dunker quadrant went on washing and wiping others, till their own turn came, when they submitted to be also bathed and wiped.

The men kissed every man whose feet they washed; the women kissed every woman after wiping her feet.

A disposition to laugh was deterred by the solemn reading of the gospel — at times in Luther's deliberate voice:

"If I, then, your Lord and Master, have washed your feet, ye also ought to wash one another's feet. Now I have given you an example, that ye should do as I have done to you."

"Is that in the Bible?" Lloyd Quantrell asked himself. "Then perhaps these people are the only obedient disciples."

The feet-washing ended with a hymn, and then the love-feast began.

"Lloyd!" a resonant voice called. It was Luther Bosler, unable to press his way to where they stood.

"Come, sir," Nelly Harbaugh whispered, "or they will all be looking at us."

Hardly aware why, Lloyd followed the girl, for whom Katy had kept a seat beside herself.

"You sit over here, Lloyd; Katy wants you to do so," Luther Bosler spoke, showing Quantrell a place among the Dunker men.

These with kind countenances seemed to welcome him. In a minute the tin plates down the table were filled with hot mutton broth, and a man handed Lloyd a spoon and motioned to the full plate before him.

As the young man put his spoon into it, three other Dunker men did the same, all eating from the same dish.

With difficulty Lloyd refrained from choking himself with the savory mouthful, such laughter shook his stomach.

"By George! some Dutchman will kiss me next," Lloyd thought, "and then I must either laugh out, or hit him."

But the broth was good, and the four men continued to eat together; and one Dunker gave Lloyd some pickles, another handed him a slice of bread spread with meat and apple-butter, and a third pushed over a cup of coffee.

Quantrell adapted himself to the strange conditions easily, observing that all over the church, by fours, the men and women were eating; and he now remembered that it was at such primitive feasting when Christ had spoken to "one leaning on his bosom," saying, "He shall betray me to whom I shall give a sop when I have dipped it."

Quantrell had hardly thought of this, when a voice in broken English rang through the church:

"And after te sop, Satan entered into him. Den said Jesus, 'Dat tou doest, do quickly!' And Judas had te bag. He den, having received te sop, went immediately out, and it was night."

A sudden, strange fear fell upon the young hunter.

He wondered if this did not describe himself, who carried the game-bag, and had no right part in this solemn feast before the crucifixion of his Lord!

Old legends learned in the Catholic college, old ghosts and miracles and coincidences, came back to his mind. The dim candles and lamps seemed to be the same which shone upon the Last Supper, and these long-bearded, simple men were the real disciples, and yonder women were the friends of the Madonna and her gifted boy.

"Where, then, is Christ?" Lloyd Quantrell asked himself in scarce admitted awe — "the Christ I shall betray?"

He looked up, almost expecting to see the halo-lighted face and searching eyes.

The nearest to them in beauty and pity and glory, were those of Katy Bosler, looking at him!

A hymn was now lined out, as the love-feast was done, and some one handed Lloyd a great hymn-book in the old German language. He looked at the title with astonishment, as the translation had been penciled beneath the old black German text:

"The song of the solitary and abandoned Turtle-Dove."

He wondered if he could be dreaming.

No; the words were really there, and the date and printing-place of the book:

"EPHRATA, PENNA., 1747."

"Here, Lloyd," the voice of Luther Bosler said again, "Katy wants you at the communion!"

He found himself sitting on the front bench among the Dunker men. A cup was in his hand filled with grape-wine, strong and sweet, and in the other hand was a cake of curious bread. On each side of him the Dunker men sat with the very expressions he had seen in old engravings of the Lord's Supper.

"I haf desired to eat tis passover with you," spoke the resonant voice again, "pefore I suffer. . . . Dis is my pody which is gifen for you . . . . Dis cup is te New Testament in my plood, to pe shed for you . . . . Pehold! te hand of him dat petrayeth me, is with me on dis table!"

Lloyd gazed up again. It seemed to be Katy's illuminated eyes which had spoken.

He drank the wine, and the bread stuck in his throat.

Slowly there rose upon his mind a feeling of religious consecration.

He had been called to the Lord's Supper like other fishermen of old, and had dared to drink the blood of the Virgin and the divine Father, whose love had overshadowed her. This day he had taken part in the crucifixion of his Lord.

He thought his mother might be here, who had so fervently believed all this mystery, and dedicated him to Heaven with her dying breath. He looked among the women to see if one like her might not be happy now, in the wondrous accident of his coming to this supper and eating with these humble Christians.

Katy was all he saw, but the Dunker bishop was reading:

"'Lord, why can not I follow thee now? I will lay down my life for thy sake!'"

A sense of wishing to be a nobler, gentler man, followed the words, in the young man's heart.

"Verily, verily," continued the bishop, "the cock shall not crow till thou hast denied me!"

The cock did not crow, but a loud bark disturbed the worship.

It was Bosler's dog, Fritz, standing in the kitchen door of the church and barking for some one.

Lloyd's foot touched something soft.

Crouched at his feet, whither Albion had stealthily insinuated himself, that dog was lying and looking into Lloyd's face with an unsocial discontent.

The moment's serious feelings passed from the young man's mind.

Lloyd rose and motioned his dog to leave the church, and led the way.

The Dunkers had commenced to pray, and did not look up to see him go.

Mingling with the idle spectators in the churchyard, who had been fed like friends of the members, Lloyd fed the two dogs, and looked at his own with some dislike.

This dog was of full English pointer blood and valuable. Lloyd Quantrell's father, in a moment of unexpected generosity at the club, had allowed five hundred dollars to an English gentleman for his dog, said English gentleman having lost to Mr. Abel Quantrell one thousand pounds in a night's encounter at draw-poker, and therefore having no further use for the dog, which he had brought over to assist him in killing a vast vision of American game.

He had gone to the club, met Mr. Quantrell and party, liked their terrapin and wine, and, after an introduction to the pleasures of the city, relapsed to his normal love of game, and particularly of this rapid, bantering, bluffing, mettlesome American institution which had been till recently unknown east of Kentucky.

With a full knowledge of the game of poker, and but little of plover and partridge, the young man had obeyed a letter of instructions from his father — in answer to his own for a further remittance — by taking passage for Liverpool, leaving no lasting recollections of himself in Baltimore except this blooded pointer, which, in his honor, was called *Albion.*

Albion was trim-built like all the pointer class, and, except for his speed and activity, would have been a dandy among dogs. But his strength of loins and hips, and the powerful curve of his hind legs, and a certain blunt strength of neck as it solidly joined the more delicate head, indicated him further as a pugilist dandy, such as were not uncommon in those days, in Baltimore.

Withal, he was more alert than bold, and had his insinuating side.

Looking into his hazel, yellow eyes, soft yet with flame, as in the Kentucky beauty, their pupils almost black like deep wells in amber, one said, "What depth of sensibility!"

But closely watched, a sly, possibly sneaking management of those beautiful eyes, arrested the critical student. They did not like close watching, and would languidly close as if just dropping away to doze, but would open half-way and peep, and, if the spectator turned his head, would be found wide open, taking an inventory and laying away gossip.

Again, the high blood and careful inbreeding of Albion, though expressed in his warm head-colors and almost dainty white skin, could, in the observer's skeptical mood, be spotted with a certain manginess.

Superficially he was a beautiful white animal, with a small, delicate, lemon-colored bar on the back, and a head where the dark-brown hanging ear, like a loop of lady's hair, fell from reddish, deer-colored brows, whose warm tint extended around the eyes and to the top of the brain, and back a little way on the neck, opening to let a streak of white, with a diamond form between the brows, go down the profile and cover all the muzzle except the brown kid nose, so sensitive, familiar, yet precise, as if it were the organ of fastidious taste, and found sublimated odor in a lady's palm.

But that white muzzle was spotted with a dirty gray, as if obscurer tastes in the animal had led it to eat the bird it betrayed to the gunner.

Spots less objectionable, yet spots, like freckles on a gentleman, went all over the white back and flanks, slight yet visible to examination.

His flews just overhung the mouth without dropping, as in the lips of a man with no unclean habit except a mouth full of tobacco-juice.

And as for Albion's tail, it was like a cart-whip well flogged out, beginning as if it were meant to be grasped by a large hand, then dropping off to a mere string. It was still his courageous part, and, although his eyes looked mild and delicate, when another dog came along his tail would go out and up, like a wasp's sting, and, if that was not alarming enough, he would stiffen his back, lift his jowls, and show his row of grinders. Yet often he would affect sleep till the dog had passed.

He spared no birds, but seldom took up a challenge even from a terrier. It was generally remarked that he had a delicate barrel of a muzzle, and an intellectual, literary contour, but often it looked hollow as an exquisite's in consumption.

These defects in a valuable animal could have occurred to only censorious people. Almost everybody beheld the finest pointer in Maryland, soft yet with dignity, like a mistress, but a king's one.

At this moment his raveled ear, still raw and bloody, made the dog feverish and snappish.

"I have heard," thought Quantrell, "of the devil taking the form of a dog, and I begin to be afraid of mine."

Jake Bosler, when the congregation was dismissed, introduced Lloyd to many of the Dunker men, all of whom seemed to be neighborly and cordial, and asked Lloyd to come to see them.

Luther had received an order to attend some Dunker conference at another church such a considerable distance off, that he requested his party to get at once into the dearborn, and Jake Bosler took Lloyd by the hand, and saying —

"Coom twict — coom, Lloyd — Bi'm-by" — Jake executed the Dunker kiss upon the blushing Baltimorean.

They drove away to the south by a cross-road, and getting on the great National road, turned off to the west and crossed the Antietam Creek at a mill-town, by a bridge of such unconsciously beautiful stone arches that it seemed never to have been made by man, but to have condensed from the limestone mists, in the forms of those old mill-wheels which stirred the sluggish current.

Between sycamores and willows the green Antietam, like a veil, went winding among the corn-clad hills, and, at a cross-lane beyond it, Luther turned up a scarcely trodden track where ledges of limestone cropped out here and there and crumbled into clover.

Passing through some corn-fields whose long barrels and plumes were stacked in rusty lines, they saw at the side of another turnpike-road in a beautiful woods of hickory, oak, and chestnut, a square, chunky brick church with a steep roof. The clean, parklike woods revealed the limestone strata in parallel lines, and separate rocks and bowlders strewn about; and here, descending, Katy spread the lunch from her basket.

Nelly Harbaugh was very attentive to Luther, and when he went into the Dunker church she begged to go with him also.

"I am afraid to let you leave me an hour," sighed the girl; "there is such comfort, Luther, in being with you."

Then Lloyd and Katy strolled to a neighboring burial-ground, and, sitting there in sight of the mountains, felt all the tender joys of love compressed and ardent.

He told her all about himself, his temptations and his needs, the instincts for a purer life within him and the consolation of this great round day, hastening to its eve — the first eventful one in all his life.

"Lloyd," said Katy, "I feel all you say, too. But it is dangerous for a poor girl to trust a man like you. I haf been thinking about it, and I haf been warned."

"Katy," said Lloyd, "you have kept a secret from me. What evil thing did that fortune-teller say?"

"Here it is," answered Katy, "in English. I can make poetry a little."

"Read it, you timid little goose!"

Katy read, between shyness and a shudder, these lines:

"In this hand I see a ring:
  Thou shalt lose it, pretty thing!
  Wading for it down a brook,
  Thou shalt find it by a book."

"What do you make of it, Katy?" Lloyd asked.

"Some one will try to deceive me."

"I never will, my darling!"

"Do you mean to marry me, perhaps?" asked Katy, rallying all her courage to her eyes.

"Yes. I have my father's consent to get. He is a Catholic. But I will engage myself this day to make you my wife. Give me your dear little hand!"

She placed it in his with the excitement of delight and fear. He slipped a ring upon her finger which he had worn upon his watch-stem.

"Katy," said he, "that was my mother's mourning and wedding ring; her father, the foremost gentleman in Maryland, left it to her by his will. Take it with this kiss, and promise to be my wife."

"Whenefer you ask me, Lloyd," the girl replied with eyes gemmed with bright tears. "You haf taken of Christ's sacrament with me this day, and your heart is clean. We are near my mother's grave, who went to Antietam church."

He kissed her as purely as the fond young heart in passion can intend, and then, opening her basket, she brought out her accordion.

"I had nothing else I loved so much as this," said Katy, "and I fetched it to gif you. When you play it you will, I hope, think of me; for when you are gone, I can play it no more."

He felt the tears come to his own eyes as he touched the keys and valves, and played a little love-tune in the fields of Antietam.

"What's that?" Quantrell asked, when he had finished.

"Some other music, somewhere," Katy replied. "May pe it's on te canal; for te Potomac River is pack yonder through te woods."

"I thought I heard a drum and fife in the corn-field yonder," Lloyd spoke.

"I thought I heard soldiers' music too," Katy whispered. "Te dog hears it, Lloyd."

The big gray mastiff stood with his ears up. Albion was fairly gamboling, as if he danced to the mystic instruments.

The sound, if it were not the insects in the trees or crops, died away, and only the Dunkers were heard singing in their lowly meeting.

"Lloyd," Katy murmured, "let us go stand at mother's grave and say te Words."

Chapter X

ISAAC SMITH'S FARM

A SMALL town of limestone, log, and painted brick houses, with a sunny square in the middle, was near the Dunker church, and as Luther and Lloyd rode the uncoupled horses into an arched spring of water which gushed from the ground close by, a person came to ask them if they could deliver a letter on one of the mountain roads.

"It's to a Mr. Isaac Smith, who rents our farm there," said the letter-bearer. "We want him to send our cow up here to Sharpsburg."

"I don't go that road," Luther replied. "My horses will pe tired, and I shall cross te mountain at Crampton's Gap."

"I'll take the letter," Lloyd exclaimed, "for I shall leave you, Luther, at the road this side the mountain, and walk down to Harper's Ferry. I know Isaac Smith very well."

They crossed the Antietam by another blue-stone bridge of arches, hidden under the hills, and late in the afternoon reached a wild road which ran parallel with the Blue Ridge.

"I must save my horses, Lloyd, or I would trife you to te Ferry; put tey must plow pefore sunrise. Let me gif you a Tunker brother's kiss pefore you go."

Again the bearded mouth of Luther met Lloyd's nearly hairless lips. Nelly Harbaugh said, "Lloyd, we are friends: I forgive you, and shall disappoint your fears of me." Little Katy received the last kiss, and again the tears shone in her large eyes as Lloyd said, "I won't go home, my darling, till I see you again."

He stood waving his hat till the rattle of the disappearing wagon turned into that sound he had heard by the Antietam church — of a fife and a drum, in the distance, toward Crampton's Gap.

"These mountains are haunted everywhere," Lloyd Quantrell said, and turned down the stony road.

He had not walked far before his dog became suspicious and, growling, ran into the dogwood and alder brush. A woman on a single-footed racker came toward him, rapidly riding, and, glancing at him, reined her horse without stopping and pointed across the mountain.

"Yonder is your way tonight, Lloyd Quantrell," she cried — "to the Catoctin Valley. This road is rough and dangerous, and spirits are abroad upon it after dark."

"Let the spirits come, Mother Ritner! I have a dog and a gun, and have eaten the sacrament today."

"You will find that tonight," exclaimed the woman, "which will change your destiny!"

She was gone in a cloud of dust, and the sun, now sinking below the North Mountain, left a cool shadow on the Blue Ridge like billows on a sea. Lloyd walked rapidly, whistling for his dog, and when Albion reappeared the big mastiff Fritz was in his company. He stamped for Bosler's dog to go back, but the influence of the pointer was still greatest, and both dogs bounded down the road to the south and were soon out of sight.

"Dear little Katy!" exclaimed the traveler — "to give me her accordion and forget it was so heavy! I have more money, too, than it is safe to travel with — five hundred dollars — and Harper's Ferry has hard people in it — Poles, Dutch, Jews, Scotch, the scum of the earth!"

He reflected that this day had made him softer toward one Dutch family.

"Heigh-ho!" continued Quantrell, "we know not what a day may bring forth. I told my father, who called me a 'rowdy' before I left Baltimore, that I would marry any wife he would recommend. I hope he hasn't taken me at my word, but he is quick on the trigger. Let me see!"

He looked at his watch, and remembered that a train went through Harper's Ferry to Baltimore after midnight.

"I will stay up for that train," said Lloyd, "and go and tell my father I am caught and engaged. He believes in love-matches, he once told me, and my mother never thought she had his real heart, though he was kind to her. No, I must not waste a single day, for, next to Katy's affection, I want my father's."

The road seemed to get a peculiar, reflected light from the higher Elk Mountain as it kept well up on the lesser range, and every object dwelt in as much distinctness as the evening cowbells made distinctest music; yet everything startled the heart a little, while keeping it in a sunset tone of ecstasy.

The log-houses grew small and seldom, and the stony farms were dry. Sometimes small pines darkened the way, and made Lloyd, as he entered their defile, keep his gun cocked.

"I can't be far from Isaac Smith's," he thought. "If it's not the next clearing, I will get rid of this accordion, for my arm is sore, carrying the rough-shaped thing."

It was not the next clearing, nor the next, and he was resolved to hide the accordion somewhere or throw it away. Katy, he considered, would not miss it, or would take a better one for it. Darkness was settling upon the twilight, and he was thirsty for water.

The sound of a flowing stream soon tinkled in the cool evening. Lloyd knelt to drink of a blackish branch which crossed the road. As he arose, a voice, from the dusk somewhere, cried:

"Halt!"

"Isaac Smith's house — is it far?" Lloyd cocked his gun as he spoke.

"Yar it is," answered the voice, not very welcoming, nor yet confident.

"Thank St. Paul!" exclaimed the gunner, dropping his caution. "If you had said 'No,' I should have thrown poor Katy's accordion away. Now I can leave it here."

He stepped forward and saw a colored man standing in a kind of lane, and exclaimed:

"Ashby! who set *you?* free?"

"I don't know," answered the Negro — the same who had been carried back to slavery that morning from Smoketown; "somebody did it. Them yer!" He indicated, with a shining something in his hand, a sign of habitation up the lane.

"What's this?" Lloyd asked. "A spear? No, I see; it's Smith's fishing-gig. What are you doing with it, after dark? Robbing Smith?"

"No," answered the Negro, confused and uncertain. "I'se sot yer. I don't know what fur. If you know them yer, I s'posen you kin go in."

Lloyd's attention was now called to the dogs reappearing and lapping of the brook. As he called them to him, Albion snarled at the Negro, who awkwardly brought his singular weapon down to defend himself.

"Search on!" commanded the gunner, and Fritz led the way up the lane.

The moon and stars came out from some lowering clouds as he advanced, and showed upon a low ridge before him some scattered buildings, and he stopped upon a small bridge in the lane to listen to some human sounds he heard. The stream under his feet ran from an old log spring-house in a kind of bottom or hollow, and a torch moved under some oaks at this spring; and a torch, likewise, on the crest of the field, shone upon some forms of men around a little house. A metallic voice Lloyd was not unfamiliar with was speaking, and the stranger caught only these words:

"If it is necessary to take life in order to save your own, then make sure work of it. . . . And look to no dissolution of the Union, but simply to amendment and repeal; and our flag shall be the same that our fathers fought under in the Revolution!"

"Why, that's dear old Smith's voice!" exclaimed Lloyd. "Still crazy on the subject of the Revolutionary War! I'm glad he's home."

He continued up the rough, stony lane nearly to some low barns, and, turning in at the top, entered a little yard, in which were fruit trees. A small log-house was built against the hillside, with a high porch along its eaves, and, between this house and a Dutch oven, a small open space was filled with men. Advancing among these, Lloyd exclaimed, cheerfully:

"Mr. Smith — pop, I'm in luck again to find you here."

To his astonishment, a powerful hand immediately seized his collar and held him tight.

"Bring that torch here!" spoke the firm voice of Isaac Smith.

A torch came near, and, as it flashed upon Lloyd Quantrell's face, a person twisted his gun out of his hand and another person seized the accordion.

"Father, it's Mr. Quantrell," spoke up the voice of young Watson Smith.

"How did you pass the picket?" asked Oliver Smith, with a wondering face.

"Why, friends," Lloyd said, "a black fellow at the gate found I knew you. He wasn't as uncivil as this other nigger who has got my gun!"

Turning, Lloyd indicated a large, handsome mulatto man, who stood looking at him with an alert, undismayed eye, unlike that of any Negro Lloyd had ever seen.

"Newby," spoke Oliver Smith, "go away! Give me the gun."

It was good advice, for the laws of hospitality could hardly keep the white Marylander in check when treated disrespectfully by a slave.

"A man prowling through the mountains with a gun, on the Sabbath-night, must give an account of himself, sir," spoke Isaac Smith.

"Why, my dear old man, I came to bring you a letter from your landlord, who wants his cow. I think I wouldn't have taken the trouble, but that I was going to the Ferry to get the train. — Don't look at me so hard, men; the worst about me is — I'm hungry."

Isaac Smith took the letter, and, with a perplexed look, remarked:

"I don't want to treat you uncivil, sir, if you came upon an honest errand. — Stevens, you and Mr. Kagi get some of that pork for Mr. Quantrell, and take him to the spring-house and examine him."

Greatly puzzled to know what it could all mean, Lloyd, with a slavery-bred man's instinct for guessing wild, and being easily satisfied, considered that Smith might be a lunatic keeping a sort of mountain sanitarium for other lunatics.

The two men led him down the path to the old log dairy with its hooded roof, and, sitting there, looked at him intently and silently while he ate some lean pork and filled his flask-cup.

"We can get three drinks out of this old thing yet, if we divide fair," cried Lloyd.

"Take it all yourself," said the man addressed as Stevens, with a certain cool, bold self-reliance.

"*That* will be cleared off the earth too, some day, I calkelate," added the other man, who had been addressed as Kagi.

"You mean whisky?" laughed Quantrell, holding the glass up to the torch, which now illuminated the old spring-house till some bats or swallows there sailed out into the night; "it's cleared off the earth every rye-harvest now, and given, like man, to the *worm.*"

"Cool chap!" said Stevens, looking at Kagi.

"What's that about the worm?" asked Kagi, not informed about distilling processes.

"The *worm,*" replied Lloyd. "is what alcohol ascends to spirit through, and, so, another worm eats man before he can be a saint. So here's to the worm!"

As Quantrell raised the glass and emptied it, a look of dislike, and then of pallor, came over Kagi's face. The torch in his hand drooped nearly to the water, and oil or pitch ran out of it upon the bubbling spring.

"He is not safe," muttered Kagi to Stevens.

"He believes, like me, in the world of spirits," Stevens said. "Give me your glass, Quantrell! Here's to the Worm that distills us to the stars!"

As Stevens handed the cup back, Lloyd looked at these two with an interest always inspired by self-contained men.

Both were of fine, if uncultivated, appearance. Kagi seemed to be the more intelligent of the two, Stevens the more independent. Lloyd felt that he had not made an impression upon either of them, but Stevens seemed indifferent or careless to his approaches; Kagi was almost aggressive, yet disturbed.

Kagi was large, almost portly, with black beard, weather-exposed, and long black hair. Stevens was not so tall but more symmetrical and powerful, with military shoulders, straight, clean-made hands, a head poised in conscious strength of animal life, a skin soft as a woman's, dark-brown hair, beard over all his jaws, and hazel eyes which were both contumacious and keen.

"Did Pop Smith buy the dark fellow I passed at the gate?" Lloyd asked.

"Traded for him," Stevens replied.

"Give 'em a little something — to boot," put in Kagi, shaking off his heaviness.

Both men laughed.

"Well," said Lloyd, "that was my idea of Father Smith, that he was kind to people. That's why I can't understand his way of treating me tonight."

"Have you got any slaves to trade him?" asked Kagi, with interest.

"None I can control; mine won't come into my possession for more than a year."

"Quantrell," said Stevens, "Mr. Smith is about moving from the farm. You got here just as everything was packed. That's why you see so many people around; moving a neighbor, you know."

"Why, that's just it," exclaimed the young stranger, throwing away all offense. "Let's go up and make him apologize."

"No," said Stevens, "he's peculiar. Go up and bid him good-night — unless he makes you stay."

"Can't stay," laughed Lloyd, gaily; "I'm just in love today, and going to ask my governor's consent, by tonight's train."

They found comparatively few persons now at the dwelling, which was a miserable home for a man with six slaves — a long hut, half buried in the hill, so that there was a mere cellar under its high, rickety porch, and a small story and loft above. A candle assisted to reveal thus much, and boxes, trunks, and cheap valises, recently packed or emptied, were seen within this cellar. Not far behind the house the small pines grew dense and black, and clouds were hurrying in the sky as the winds rose and whistled.

"Is it correct, gentlemen?" asked Isaac Smith.

"Fuddled," said Stevens.

"Mysterious," said Kagi.

"Who is that young person making free with my girl's accordion?" spoke up Quantrell, hearing the instrument awkwardly played.

"That's Captain Cook," answered Isaac Smith. "He's quite a cultivated person and a teacher."

Chapter XI

KATY'S ACCORDION

A SMALL, stooping, light-haired lad came out with the accordion and looked at Lloyd through pale-blue eyes, which seemed to feel his accomplishments.

Lloyd took Katy's gift and put his fingers to the keys.

A little culture, if learned in engine-houses and partisan clubs, helps many a man through life.

Something about these people seemed still suspectful and forbidding. Quantrell had tried his temperament upon them in vain, and now he had only some rude tunes to lull them with.

He began to play "Home, Sweet Home."

After a few strains, other persons seemed to come in, as if from the barns and corn-cribs and pine thickets. At first sullen, next wondering, and soon affected tenderly, they lay in blankets upon the autumn earth, or stood around in curious groups, while he played the air that the simple and the cot-bred of the British races know everywhere.

Some of the people who ventured near were Negroes, strange-looking Negroes for Maryland or for the American States anywhere — so wanting in politeness or even hospitality; preoccupied, too, as if with the morrow's house-moving occupations; but these soon felt the infection of the tender tune, and one young, handsome white boy came up and sat by Lloyd upon an old hair-trunk and listening, filled with tears at his bright eyes. Lloyd sang the words in his own melodious voice:

"An exile from home, pleasure dazzles in vain,
  Ah! give me my lowly thatched cottage again;
  The birds singing sweetly that came to my call,
  Give them back, and my peace of mind, dearer than all."

As the song finished, a sob was heard at Quantrell's elbow. Watson

Smith came up and said to the young man sitting there:

"Ned, what ails you?"

"I've got people in Iowa and my own land there."

"*Isabel,*" was the answer, in a broken tone.

"Play something, Mr. Quantrell," spoke Isaac Smith, "which will remind us of the Sabbath and the heavenly rest; for here we have no abiding-place."

A camp-meeting tune, the favorite of his deceased mother, came to Quantrell's memory and art, and in the cool mountain air these simple strains ascended:

"I'm a pilgrim and I'm a stranger;
    I can tarry, I can tarry but a night;
Do not detain me, for I am going
    to where the streamlets are ever flowing;
I'm a pilgrim and I'm a stranger —
    I can tarry, I can tarry but a night!

"There the sunbeams are ever shining,
    and I'm longing, I am longing for the sight;
Within a country unknown and dreary,
    I have been wandering forlorn and weary;
I'm a pilgrim and I'm a stranger —
    I can tarry, I can tarry but a night.

"Of that country to which I'm going,
    my Redeemer, my Redeemer is the Light!
There is no sorrow nor any sighing,
    nor any sin there, nor any dying;
I'm a pilgrim and I'm a stranger —
    I can tarry, I can tarry but a night!"

During this singing a torch had been procured, which showed all the faces, even to the outer parts of the humble circle. There seemed to be at least twenty men present, and not a single woman. Of Smith's own sons there were manifestly three, resembling each other even in their differences; and two young men, addressed as Thompson, of very pleasing countenances, Lloyd found to be old Mr. Smith's sons-in-law. One of these, of a most cordial face and manly figure, was looking at the stranger as he finished the last tune, and Quantrell spoke up:

"Now, William — I heard friend Watson say '*Isabel*' just now. That's your sister, I reckon?"

"You're right, sir," the young man exclaimed; "my sister's married to him, and his sister Ruth's married to my brother."

Well, now, in honor of that union I'll play you one more tune before I say 'Good-night.'"

Mr. Thompson hesitated.

"Do you know 'America'?" he asked.

"Is this it, William?"

Lloyd found in his mind the measure and the words, and other voices joined in as he proceeded, till the last stanza pealed on the mountain night in trembling tones the player never forgot:

"My country! 'tis of thee,
  Sweet land of Liberty,
    Of thee I sing;
  Land where my fathers died,
  Land of the Pilgrim's pride,
  From every mountainside
    Let Freedom ring!

"Let music swell the breeze,
  And ring from all the trees
    Sweet Freedom's song!
  Let mortal tongues awake,
  Let all that breathe partake,
  Let rocks their silence break,
    The sound prolong!"

Whites sang it; blacks seemed singing, too; but it was not, to Lloyd's idea, a tune for blacks, though they might hear it.

At the resounding end, where "God, the author of Liberty," is appealed to, to keep us "in Freedom's holy light," and "protect us by his might," Isaac Smith made all rise.

"We will pray in the spirit of that hymn," he said, "and send each other on his way with God's blessing!"

Lloyd looked around, and the words of the prayer impressed him less than the manner of the listeners.

Stevens and Kagi were looking at Lloyd. Cook was stooping by the accordion as if he meditated a tune after the prayer which would put Lloyd's performances out of praise; nearly all the rest, whites and blacks, were standing or leaning with the expressions of people at a funeral where the dead was being re-hearsed by the preacher. Some had hands over their eyes; others with eyes closed seemed muttering responses; a few knelt on the ground and bowed low.

The imperfect light of torch and stars and fiery clouds showed chiefly the Mosaic old man in the midst, surrounded by his sons and sons-in-law, plainly praying, without the least excitement, in the practical tones he might have used to order his farm-work to be done. The words would have seemed full of feeling if the manner had not been so orderly and precise, and Lloyd remarked to himself:

"Pop Smith isn't the actor he was on the mountain yesterday. What can these people be so much interested for?"

He heard himself alluded to, toward the last, as "the young friend who, taking our hearts by music to home, admonishes us of them whose hearts and homes are never recognized. Those dear tunes of home, country, and heaven must be our only drum and fife, Lord! — as here we tarry but a night."

A sob seemed to go around somewhere in the dark, and there were sounds as of Negroes in convulsive prayer. Seeking to separate these mystic noises, Quantrell felt his hand grasped by long, bony fingers, and as if still praying, Isaac Smith was talking to him:

"Go, young man! The Lord bless you for the music you have brought and the pious mother, perhaps, who taught you tunes so comforting to these poor people! Keep off the streets! Don't expose yourself! Don't stand on the corners, particularly! — Captain Cook, go with him past the limits."

"I must be getting a reputation all over Maryland," Lloyd thought, "for standing at the street corners in Baltimore. My governor lectured me about it when he sent me off gunning. Well, now I am in love I shall stop loafing."

"Will you take the accordion along, Quantrell?" said Captain Cook, looking at it wistfully.

"I would like to leave my accordion here and my dog Fritz," Lloyd replied, looking around upon the people, who still watched him curiously; "but, if you are going to move, they won't be safe."

"Oh," said Stevens, "Mr. Smith is only going to move to his other house, across the road yonder."

Following the gesture, Lloyd saw a light a good way off, moving at some windows.

"Is this the dog?" old Isaac Smith asked, bringing Fritz forward. To Lloyd's admiration that sturdy mastiff made no resistance as Smith tied him fast to the railing of the little porch above.

"Copeland — Green," Smith spoke to two of the Negroes, "put food and water by Mr. Quantrell's dog. — You will be sure to find him here, sir, when you return."

As Fritz yielded to the gentle hand and firm control of Isaac Smith, the highly bred Albion, seeing the companion he had misled now tied fast and apparently in subjection, darted upon Fritz with treachery and fury, and seemed resolved to get an ear for an ear. He reckoned without his host, however, for Isaac Smith, kicking Albion almost without effort, caught him also by the muzzle and tail as he turned in pain, and threw him right over the railing. Half a dozen persons below kicked him along their line, and, frightened almost to death, the pointer fled down the lane.

"He'll go along with you meekly, now, Mr. Quantrell," Smith remarked, without apology. "You'll never get much pleasure from him, sir. The spaniel crossed on the cruel hound, however high he is bred, does not get the stability of such useful and faithful domestic mongrels as this!"

Putting his hand upon Fritz, that big creature set his head between Isaac Smith's knees and wagged his tail.

"Come," said little Captain Cook to Quantrell.

"Good-night, my mountain friends!" Lloyd Quantrell cried, cheerily, at the head of the lane. "You're rough, but ready, I know. We'll meet, I hope, again."

"Good-night!" rang out many voices; and still the sense of some dislike or doubt of himself seemed to linger in those sounds, and the last looks from the by-standers had something predatory in them.

He felt this so instinctively that he walked very slowly and cool-hearted down the lane, as if there might be an enemy behind him.

Near the gate stood a black man with the shining something still in his hand, and to him Cook dropped a word.

"Now, Quantrell," said Cook, after walking some distance along the road, "you'll find this accordion in the garret under the eaves, if they can't find it for you. You owe to it more than you at present know. If I hadn't my hands full now, I would learn to play it before you came back. Anyway, I know I'm a better *shot* than you. You'll be proud some day that you knew me. Good-night!"

"Good-night, Cook. With that good opinion of yourself I know you'll be heard from," spoke Lloyd, laughing — "Come, Albion!"

The dog now truckled low to Quantrell, and almost retarded his way, so obsequious was he after his late contemptuous chastisement; but his master was depressed in spirits from some unknown reason, and the animal's attentions did not compose the dangers of the road.

A slight sense of bodily fear which he had been ashamed to recognize in all these mountain wanderings, was over him tonight. Those strange, unclassifiable faces he had just parted from were the only ones he had been unable to reduce to fraternity; and even his music, while it touched them for its sentiments, had not softened them to himself.

He, somehow, felt that Katy's simple instrument had been his talisman.

Had they meant to rob him? Were they following him now with that intent? Lloyd stopped to listen, and on the disturbed air came the sound of the accordion, and a womanly voice to the old tune:

> "The season's in for partridges,
>   Let's take our guns and dogs;
>   It sha'n't be said that we're afraid
>   Of quagmires or of bogs,
>   When a shooting we do go, do go, do go,
>   When a shooting we do go."

"That fellow Cook's too simple to rob anybody," thought Lloyd. "No, they must have been honest mountaineers, too inexperienced not to stare at me. Besides, they all prayed — all but one or two. Yet old Smith was working on the Sabbath-day, spite of his religion. I reckon he's one of those Seventh-Day Baptists I've heard of, farther up the Antietam, who work Sundays and worship Saturdays. That would account for his praying more devoutly yesterday than today. Come to think of it," concluded Lloyd, "the Seventh-Day Baptists, Luther told me, did not believe in marriage. That may be why I saw no women on the farm. I would trust Isaac Smith anywhere. The fact is, I have seen so many queer things in the last twenty-four hours that everything looks queer to me. Two men have kissed me, and I have had my fortune told!"

As the dog came up with its insidious attentions now, the singular explicitness of Katy's fortune, and the vagueness of his own, as told by Hannah Ritner, occurred to his mind. How could all the game on earth rise before his gun?

Not unless the wilderness was restored here.

But the prediction that Katy should lose a ring?

Whatever that meant, it had for a moment — an evil, wicked moment, which he dispelled with indignation as a wanton idea tried to enter his mind — been verified in his own experience.

Last night he had gone to bed all fluttered and fickle-hearted after holding Katy in his arms.

Today her pure, religious nature had made him see the womanhood latent in her, and aroused a manhood higher than he thought he possessed.

"God protect her, and lay me dead ere I can do her harm!" Lloyd Quantrell fervently exclaimed, looking up at the agitated wind and rain-clouds which seemed seeking to overrun heaven.

The dog Albion barked.

It seemed to him strange that after such a passionate prayer his mind should again be suddenly possessed by worldly and selfish thoughts.

In a few minutes he suppressed them, but only to be attacked by other forebodings.

Now the recollection of Hannah Ritner's last prediction, that by taking this very road his destiny would be altered, oppressed his nerves.

The road was growing worse and worse as it wound down the plateau through the hills.

Sometimes the Elk Ridge, almost transparent, would ride through the night like a long, cylindrical billow, and seem to be rolling toward him in phosphoric sparklings; and then he would go down into depths like midnight, where some small stream could be heard hollow and distrustful, accompanying the road in some deep wash or gulf, and in the darkness the great grape-vines seemed to exhale a chill as they struggled up to the top branches of the basswood, or rank and giant wild-cherry trees.

In other ravines the rocks fairly grew across the way, as if planted in rows, and on the summits the gentle but melancholy locust trees shook in the wind which the angry and plunging moon seemed to blow from its lurid bag.

A pale-faced woman would peep from some occasional hut where the candlelight revealed her, and the turkeys roosting in the trees would cluck together, like people laughing in the ague's clutch; but on the glimmering wheat-stubble at the clearings the moon lay with a circling, partial light, like an insatiate sickle, which wanted next year's seedlings, too, before their birth, or Herod searching for the scarce-born babes.

Then mighty rocks would overhang the road, so big that they seemed masses of foliage, and for spaces the mullein-stalks stood up desolately, and no more bent to the wind than aged maidens to a smile.

At one level place a stream, winding through a kind of copse of alder and brake, came out of the thicket tunefully, and spread itself over sandy shallows, and compelled some soft grass to receive the subdued light twinkling through old sycamores which kept the clouds off with their speckled arms. Here, amid the willows, a little log school-house stood in a sort of fork of the road, and, as Lloyd rested on its sill, a screech-owl within, like the last schoolmaster, raised a dreary, quivering wail.

Repelled with superstition from the spot, Quantrell proceeded on, till at a summit there broke upon his view the lights of a town in the mountains.

Even this sense of relief was accompanied by superstition, since it seemed unnatural to find a town so high in the air as this manifestly was, and right in his road; but as he proceeded there opened between him and the lights a deep, black, glistening gulf or wilderness, which he soon recognized, by white riffles or dark rocks, and blacker heights hugging it round, to be the river Potomac.

Then he remembered that the town of Harper's Ferry hung around the base of an inhabited height, like the mountain he was descending, and that the town or suburb on the height was called Bolivar.

Hastening down a frightfully torn road, the music of a brook at its side was soon drowned in the roaring of the river, and a canal and locks were on the river's border, barely leaving space for Lloyd's road to creep beneath the mighty Elk Mountain that now began to tower almost perpendicularly, and become a buttress to the Blue Ridge which, two furlongs in advance, stepped across the river, leaving a ghastly rift between.

The dog in real companionship shrank close to Quantrell now, seeing the steeps above, amid the hurrying clouds, apparently falling down to close the chasm and bury them; while the wind, caught in this funnel, went wildly to and fro, shaking the trees in the crevices of the precipice, and rattling down roots and stones, and the river raised its thousand riffling voices as if birds and wolves in flocks dreaded to pass this storm-infested gap.

"Poor Albion!" Lloyd spoke sympathetically, "no wonder the dog's afraid! This place by moonlight is like the devil's throne, but, with storm threatening it, is like being swallowed by a sea-serpent."

He walked fast over the stony road till the great mountain was as directly over him — stepping from Maryland into Virginia — as if he had been between a giant's legs. Here, lying low to the water, a covered bridge, almost concealed in the mountain shadows, received at once the road and a railroad, which, meeting each other beneath the toppling mountain thirteen hundred feet above them, ran into the bridge and shivered there side by side.

A lock-house was near the bridge and a bargeman's tavern, and, across the wide flood, a thousand feet away, the railroad lights of red, and household candles of Harper's Ferry, shone and reflected in the water like jewels in an elephant's foot, whose great head and back supported the higher town.

Quantrell entered the solemn bridge, and the river beneath him seemed to sigh like the hurrying souls of all the Indian tribes drowned here, even in the whoop of war and chase.

He emerged at a place where the bridge had two outlets, like the letter Y, a railroad-track in each, and that to the left ended near another bridge which spanned a different river, not visible before, beneath the long Virginia mountain and the town. This river, the Shenandoah, was almost as fierce and wide as the Potomac, which it assisted to break through the mountain gate.

Lloyd took the other bridge outlet and came into the little inhabited strand or sill of Harper's Ferry, which lined two streets, one along either river-bank. The bridge was the key to the town, like a key to a trunk.

In the eye of the bridge and close by it was the gate of some stately institution, all noble with lines of lamps and walks and regular buildings, and between it and the bridge a hotel clung to the narrow railroad passage. Opposite this hotel was a detached part of the beautiful institution beyond, with similar walls of stone and fence panels of musket-barrels or spears.

It did not need a Marylander to tell that this was the great war-factory of the American Republic, where the muskets and rifles which equipped its little army had been made since the rule of President Washington.

The stately institution beneath the Potomac heights was the national armory; the detached buildings on the Shenandoah side were the arsenal; the two rivers meeting at the spot furnished unceasing water-power.

Leaving his gun and trappings at the hotel, Lloyd was directed to a saloon where a stealthy bar was open Sundays. It was a little place by the Shenandoah side, and, when he entered, it was quite full of men, some drinking, some drunk.

"Here's one of tem tam apolitionists, py Jing!" cried a voice, and a man came up to Lloyd sneeringly.

"You here, Andrew Atzerodt!" exclaimed Quantrell. "Spending your blood-money, I reckon."

"Tidn't I capture tat nigger, Lloyd?" the tipsy fellow inquired. "Tey want to take teir money back, pecause tey let him git away."

"You here, Logan?" Lloyd spoke up, seeing the two slave-hunters, also sullen with disappointment and drink. "Then your prey escaped you!"

"Why not," answered the man, "when this Dutch braggart stopped everybody in the road to proclaim he had tuk a nigger? We was waylaid and beat."

"Not me, py Jing!" shouted Atzerodt.

"No," said a Logan, "you took to your heels. We was licked, but we fought fur our nigger."

"Who did it?" asked Quantrell.

"That's what we'd give five hundred dollars to know."

"If I knew I wouldn't tell you," Lloyd replied. "Such fellows as you, without any interest in slavery, do its dirty work."

"Go fur him, poys!" screamed Atzerodt, getting behind the Logans. "He's a spy and a nigger-lover."

The larger Logan came up to Lloyd, while everybody stopped drinking at the bar and crowded around, hopeful of some "difficulty." His brother slipped around to Quantrell's side with a treacherous face.

"I think you're the man who wanted to take that slave, Ashby, from us at Smoketown," said Logan. "You wanted to fight me there. Take that!"

"Take that!" exclaimed the brother.

Both struck Quantrell in the head with their hard fists.

"Take this!" answered Lloyd, staggering but not falling, and without raising his voice, while he planted a blow in the face of each mountaineer, and followed them up with the rapidity of a pugilist, his countenance more smiling than angry, and his strength prodigious.

"Take this home to the children," Lloyd said as he struck again. "Take it carefully! Don't drop it and break it!"

The meaner Logan was down in a minute, crying anxiously, "Lew, he's armed!" The larger Logan fought well and tried to get in close and wrestle with Quantrell, whose skill kept him off and punished him terribly. In a few seconds he, too, was down and crying "Enough!"

The landlord had meantime drawn a long revolver pistol from the bar, but was too much interested in the fight to point it, and, before he could determine what to do, Quantrell twisted it out of his hand.

"Gentlemen," said the man, "my license will be taken away unless you all hurry out."

"Go out!" spoke Lloyd, indicating the Logans, the pistol in his hand. "Put that bridge between you and Harper's Ferry! This gun may kill better men."

As they slipped out gratefully, Quantrell turned to the landlord and spoke:

"Whoever is not ashamed to drink with a true American, is my guest!"

Silently, admiringly, everybody in sight came to the bar. As they waited for the champion to set the health, he deliberately raised his arms and shook them, wing-fashion, and crowed like a cock.

"Cock-Robin cock of the walk tonight!" exclaimed Quantrell merrily, emptying his glass.

They drank with even more quiet awe, for they recognized in "Cock-Robin" one of the dreaded Baltimore anti-foreign clubs.

When all had finished drinking, Andrew Atzerodt crawled out from behind a barrel and executed a crow with all Lloyd's nonchalance.

"Where's my drink, Lloyd?" he spoke, loudly; "tidn't we tackle 'em, py Jing!"

In the midst of the roar of laughter a stranger drew Lloyd away, saying:

"Come, sir, this place is beneath a man of your courage."

Handing the pistol back to the owner, Lloyd walked with the stranger to the hotel, and, giving him a cigar, drew chairs upon the railroad platform which extended on high trestles between the Potomac and the armory-yard. The tall brick edifices, plots of grass, high flag-staff, and chimneys, reposed among the lights beneath the profile of the upper town, where a great rock, like an anvil, overhung the Shenandoah, and the fiery-edged clouds seemed like red-hot horseshoes shifted upon it by the blacksmith of the Night.

"That is Jefferson's Rock, sir," said the stranger, in reserved tones; "I suppose you know it."

"No, my friend."

"Mr. Jefferson wrote his 'Notes on Virginia' sitting up there. My deceased father, who was a strong State-rights man, had a tradition that some day a child would come and push that rock over. It is nearly balanced, you see, by its own weight. Then, my father said, the State-rights of Jefferson would be no more."

"Your county here is called Jefferson, I think?"

"Yes. At the county-seat, a few miles south of this place. General Washington's brother Charles settled, and his descendant is my neighbor."

"Your name, my friend?"

"Beall — John Beall."

"Why, John, that's an old Maryland name around Washington city."

"Yes, sir," the young man, who was near Quantrell's own age, answered, with a subdued voice, like one naturally reticent; "I am of the McGruders and Bealls, Rob Roy's own blood."

Lloyd Quantrell put his hand on John Beall's shoulder affectionately, and could almost feel the young man's reserved countenance smile as Lloyd hummed the tune:

"'But doomed and devoted by vassal and lord,
  McGregor has still both his heart and his sword:
  Then courage, courage, courage, Grigalach!

"'Our signal for fight, which from monarchs we drew,
  Must be heard but by night in our vengeful halloo:
  Then halloo, halloo, halloo, Grigalach!'"

"You sing as well as you fight, sir. You must be a gentleman."

"Ah," said Quantrell, "that's the highest degree in Masonry. I'm afraid not. Lloyd Quantrell is my name, however."

"I'll take you for a gentleman, Mr. Quantrell. My grandfather was an Englishman; he lived most of his life in Virginia. He never would be naturalized here, though he was a Federalist and disliked Mr. Jefferson. I went to England with him to see him die there in his old Norman homestead. He said to me in his last illness, 'The man who can fight without hate and sing without invitation is a citizen anywhere.'"

"Well, John, I'll answer to being a citizen, then. With *you*, I'll be a Virginian. We can squeeze a small drink out of my flask."

"Thank you," Beall answered, accepting the Marylander's hand, "but I seldom drink. I went through the form at the saloon in compliment to your prowess. The fact is, I'm a communicant in our Episcopal Church. A large family — my widowed mother's — depend on me. I came here tonight for a poor neighbor who expected to recover her slave. She is a preacher's widow, and had an old Negro man. His son, to satisfy the old man's wife, who lived North, came down and stole the father. The son himself made his escape not long ago."

"John," said Quantrell, "the old man has got his freedom. He is dead."

"I'm not surprised to hear it," said Beall, unmoved. "He was too old to run away. But I considered it my religious duty to unite with others in offering a reward for his son Ashby, whose bold deed in coming into a slave State to make a capture shows a frightful demoralization in Negroes."

"What is he worth, John?"

"Probably not as much as the reward, since the extension of slavery has been defeated in Kansas. What an outrage on State-rights was that!"

With a warm invitation to come to his farm, Mr. Beall mounted his horse in the street below, and turned him up the hill through the middle of the town.

"A little inflexible," Quantrell reflected, "but a true-hearted Virginian all the same."

He took a room in the hotel, where only a very tall and very black Negro, probably six and a half feet high, seemed to be awake. The railroad agent, also a powerful man, was continually bantering this Negro, who seemed fully as independent.

"Ain't yo' nigger, noway," exclaimed this black giant, while looking for Lloyd's key. "Jess call myseff yo' nigger fo' convenience. Want a better-lookin' man than yo' to be my mossta!"

"So ho, now! so ho!" exclaimed the big white man, sleepily holding up his red lamp. "Ain't you 'shamed, Heywood? I'm 'shamed faw you. Anybody can see you're no Vurgeenian by your manners. Talkin' that a-way to a man o' my age!"

"Dat's what's de fack," said Heywood; "yo's too ole to be my mossta. Yo's a ole widower. Don't you 'so ho' me. I'm a free man, I am! Don't go nowhar for nobody if dey don't treat me right."

"I'm sorry faw you, Heywood. I hope your wife and childern won't hear how you talk to me. You may be a widowaw, too, Heywood."

As the big man walked up the platform as mechanically as he had been quarreling, swinging the red lamp, the gigantic Negro, paying no attention to Lloyd, seized a cloak and darted after him.

"Yer, squire, yo' ole dunce! Moss Beckham, you put on dis yer cloak. Do you hyar? Dat cole wind'll fall on to yo' kidneys. Den yo'll be 'busin' of me mo'."

"I won't have it, Heywood," Lloyd heard the squire say; "nobody can pet me aftaw spilin' of my feelin's. So ho, now! go ho, Heywood!"

"Dar!" exclaimed the Negro, "wrap it round yo' now and go to bed. Gi' me de lamp. You sha'n't stay up no mo' dis night."

Coming back with the lamp, the Negro selected a key and took Lloyd to an upper room overlooking the town, promising to call him for the Baltimore train.

"Does the squire own you, Heywood?" asked Lloyd.

"No. De prejudice ag'inst free colored men is so big heah, dat I's a kine of ward to him, to keep my property at Winchester. He's de bes' friend I got. Ef I didn't sass him a little, reckon he wouldn't like me!"

"Here," said Lloyd, giving the Negro a silver piece, "try, the next time he tempts you, to answer the squire kindly. We can't tell what word will be our last, Heywood, with them we love."

"Thank you, mossta. Reckon I will treat de squire better. Why, he'd die fur me!"

As the sound of the Negro's feet ceased in the bare halls and stairs, Lloyd drew off his boots and sat at the window, tired and bruised, looking sleepily out upon the great Loudoun Heights and the dark, riffle-fleeced Shenandoah, and the mill-races on both river-banks carrying strong water-power to State and private machinery. The sky was cloudy and windy, and brazen lights contended there with inky scud. The watchman at the granite gatepost below locked up the armory-yard, and Harper's Ferry expressed no sound but the hurrying, moaning rivers.

"Nothing has happened tonight to change my destiny," Lloyd remarked, nodding. "I got away with the two Logan brutes easily. I shall see my father at breakfast, and tell him, boldly, I am in love. Will he oppose me? No. I am my mother's bequest to him; and he does not despise beauty and virtue because they are poor."

A low whine rang through the room.

"Lie down, Albion!" Lloyd exclaimed. "I shall give you to little Katy of Catoctin. God bless her!"

He fell asleep, the highbred pointer at his feet. His mother came to him there in dreams, and seemed to say:

"Tired boy, sleep, for you have a long walk before you, and no shoes."

He did not know how long he had been sleeping when a shock, as if the Loudoun Heights had fallen, awoke him. A splitting, resounding, appalling noise thundered through the black village.

"Has a powder-magazine exploded?" asked Lloyd, gazing out and rubbing his eyes. "I couldn't have dreamed anything as real and loud as that! No, I see what it is now by yonder dim moon-rime reflected from the Virginia mountain — a part of Jefferson's Rock has fallen. Some infant must have been born here tonight and pushed it over."

Chapter XII

JAYHAWKERS

*H*IS watch showed that it was about eleven o'clock.

From the street below came up a sound of loose, creaking wheels and some footsteps, and the word:

"Halt!"

Lloyd Quantrell looked down from his window in the close yet damp night, and his sight slowly separated the objects in the little piece of street which has already been called the key of Harper's Ferry, and which led from the bridge to the armory-gate in a nearly straight line.

The saloon where Quantrell had been attacked, a little building of wood, confronted this street near the bridge, and was probably four hundred feet from the government gate. Between saloon and gate some small private offices and shops clung along the arsenal's wall, and the railroad tavern was a basement story lower on the street than upon the railroad.

Another street, at right angles, ran along the armory gate and yard, at the corner of which yard it sent off an oblique street, and a short block farther on, a steep street, both nearly parallel to the Potomac; while the first street, called Shenandoah, kept along between the houses and cliffs till, at a far distance, it ended at another armory, indistinctly seen by Lloyd, and called the Rifle-works.

Thus an armory closed up the town by either river, except for the passage of the two railways, and only the second or steep street led over the rough hill of Bolivar into the great upland Valley of Virginia.

Before the armory gate some things were moving and shining like steel, and suppressed voices spoke sententiously there:

"Open this gate!"

"Who is it?"

"Open this gate!"

"Where is the key?"

"You are a dead man!"

"Oh-h — mercy!"

"Make any noise, and you are a dead man!"

With this strange colloquy there seemed to be a jumping up on the wall, and a jumping down and a scuffle. Then came the words:

"That key, or you are —"

"Oh, don't! I'm the pore watchman!"

"Never mind him," spoke another voice, firm and cool. "Bring the crow-bar and the big hammer!"

A rattling, twisting, snapping sound followed, and the word —

"March!"

The wagon creaked again, the shining things in the streets moved within the gate, and the foliage of shade trees and the shadows of the armory buildings swallowed up the episode.

"What brutes these semi-military officials are!" Quantrell reflected. "Drunken superintendents and privileged political clerks, no doubt, who have lost their keys, and will conclude a Sunday's excursion by sleeping in 'Uncle Sam's' offices. But who could expect anything better with Wise Governor of Virginia, and his Dutch and Irish on top of true Americans?"

He had nearly fallen to sleep again when there came a sober sound from the open gate below.

"All's well!"

A voice replied, like a Negro's:

"All's well!"

"I'm glad of that," muttered Quantrell, "for I thought everything was sick. Why, they're coming away quick! Found the demijohn empty, I reckon!"

He was now able to perceive a small wagon drawn by one horse, and it seemed to be nearly full of men, though others walked by its side. They passed up Shenandoah Street, and seemed to divide at the second corner; and, at the gate below, there remained two other men standing still, with something shining in their hands.

"Close the gate," said a voice within, "and halt everybody now!"

"Having had the horse stolen," Quantrell mused, sleepily, "of course they lock the stable-door now. I think everybody hates the government."

He noted the sharp, black rim of Loudoun Heights again, like a ragged shell enclosing the oyster of the town, and the sighing, whispering rivers. As he dozed, voices in the still street seemed to say:

"Who goes there?"

"Prisoner! From the bridge."

"Who goes there?"

"Prisoner! From the rifle-works."

"All's well!"

"All's well!"

"Now," considered Quantrell, "these official parasites are concluding their spree by arresting all the sober men on duty! When I get to Baltimore I'll just describe in the 'Clipper' what sort of rule Buchanan and Floyd and Wise have clapped on Old Virginia, the mother of our Presidents. Meanwhile, I'll lie on the bed and not be disturbed."

He slept longer this time, and was awakened by a wheezing, grinding noise which made him leap to his feet and seize his gun and hunter's outfit and dash down the stairs. An engine and passenger train, pointed for Baltimore, stood at the station adjoining the tavern.

"You scoundrel!" Lloyd exclaimed to the Negro porter, "why didn't you call me?"

"Couldn't hyar from de train," answered the Negro; "telegraph wires all down somehow. Whar's dat ar' bridge watchman?"

"Where is anybody, responsible?" Lloyd exclaimed. "Everything seems left to one impudent nigger."

"Don' yo' say I ain't 'sponsible, now!" the porter vociferated, shaking his lamp. "I know my business! Squire Beckham, come out hyar! Nobody can't be foun', and I'm blamed by everybody."

The Negro continued toward the bridge, and Lloyd threw his dog into the smoking-caboose and climbed upon the train, which in a moment proceeded along the river-side, and the engine entered the bridge. He was settling down for a doze, when he heard clear voices in the hollow cavity of this long viaduct:

"Halt there, or you are a dead man!"

The engine had suddenly stopped, and continued to snore and tremble as if it dreamed all this indignity to the United States mail.

"What do you want?"

"Liberty. And we mean to have it!"

"What kind of liberty do you mean?"

"Like yours and mine. Go back!"

The train started back with a jerk, as if the lever had been pulled in panic. In a moment two or three persons came excitedly through the smoking-car, from the engine, running and ejaculating.

"What's ahead there?" Lloyd cried.

"Robbers, or lunatics, or Indians. Things with guns anyhow!" one of the railroad men replied, hastening on.

Qnantrell jumped into the aisle and ran to the front platform near the engine and looked ahead.

Three men, as they seemed to be, lined a railing in the bridge. Bright metal shone in their hands. The light was afforded by a lantern in the hands of a big colored man who had advanced beyond the engine and seemed more courageous or less impressionable than the whites.

"Halt! halt! halt!"

In rapid succession and with high nervous meaning had come these words from the obstruction ahead.

"Who's you?" hoarsely replied the great Negro Heywood, slightly moving back. "Who you a-haltin'? Free man, I am!"

"Halt! halt!"

"Sha'n't halt for no such damned rascals. Free man —"

"Boom!"

A loud report rang through the bridge, which made Lloyd turn and look at his own gun, to see if it had not been accidentally discharged.

Before he could look from the platform to the track again, a human cry, so piteous, so long, so profound, came from close beside him, that it rang in his ears for years after this night.

It was the cry extorted by a mortal wound in the first violent incursion into the house of life.

The Negro, still clinging to his lamp, was running over the bridge-ties in such terror as to put his late defiancé and tardy retirement to the blush. The train was also backing rapidly. As soon as the starlight came down upon the platform again, Quantrell leaped off.

"What is it, Heywood?" he called to the Negro, whose face expressed in outlines and dim eyeballs an agony insupportable.

"Death!" answered the Negro, staggering on.

"There — there's the man who shot him!" exclaimed the conductor of the train, indicating an agile figure which, between a walk and a slide, came out of the bridge and seemed to have some short weapon in the blanket he was wrapped in. As this figure went rapidly toward the armory-gate, Lloyd Quantrell raised his gun and fired upon it, yet with the want of aim which comes from an uncertain conviction. His mind was dazed, too, by a suspicion that he had seen that youthful figure before.

The moment Lloyd fired, two shots from the armory-gate replied to his own, and one of them cut a strand from his hair.

"At last!" Quantrell spoke, coolly, "I *have* seen something that came very near changing my destiny — for life!"

He put the railroad building and hotel between him and the armory. The passengers were now generally alarmed, and were peeping around the corner of the thin rim of buildings between the railroad platform and the armory-yard. A water-tank for the locomotives was at this corner, and some of the hotel people or passengers were exchanging shots from this cover with a group of people who stood in the armory-yard around a small low building near the gate. These people, whatever they might be, were distinctly heard loading their guns.

"Come away from that corner and tank!" Lloyd exclaimed. "Those robbers are firing rifle-balls that will go through these thin boards."

"You think they *are* robbers?" asked a very straight, clean-ribbed man with a thoughtful but not at all excited countenance, turning on Lloyd.

"Of course. Foreigners, I reckon, come to take the rest of our liberties. They can't be Indians, so they must be robbers!"

"O papa! robbers? Isn't it romantic! Such mountains, too! Such nature! Oh, let us stay here all night and see what they are."

A large, enthusiastic, handsome girl was sitting at the open window of a passenger-coach. She looked at Lloyd with a beaming countenance and a certain fine energy of impulse.

"Surely there is a hotel here, sir," she addressed Lloyd. "Can we not witness this unexpected tournament? Oh, it is so advantageous to be a man and see everything romantic!"

"Here is one poor man, dear miss, who will hardly agree with you," Quantrell replied. "Hear the railroad porter's dying groans!"

They listened, and sighs like a sick child's came from the little station, and the words:

"O Heywood! what will yo' wife say? A exposin' of yourself, Heywood, when I should have been the man! It 'twan't kyind of you, Heywood! It 'twan't thoughtful! What kin I do without you?"

"Po' friend," the Negro said, "look aftaw my chillen. Forgive me for my sassy tongue. It's got me in this trouble, mossta. Oh! kill me — I'm dyin' and I can't die!"

"There, Light!" exclaimed the lithe, quiet man, looking at the girl. "You hear the real tones of romance; the poor, sick notes of glory. It is the poor, helpless people, the women and the servants, who suffer for romantic ventures."

"Oh, that is dreadful!" said Miss Light; "I supposed they died fighting gloriously. But, senator — papa — may they not be Indians? We have seen the Indians in their beautiful eagles' feathers prepare for war. I suppose these robbers, as this gentleman says, must be foreigners — Italians, or Spaniards, or Garibaldians — in beautiful costumes!"

"Here is one, perhaps," replied the senator; "look at him, Light!"

A young man with a short gun in his hand, a rough, slouching hat on his head, coarse clothes, and a belt around him with weapons in it, appeared at the head of the train and called out, in a somewhat nasal tone:

"Conductor, bring on that train! Our commander has allowed you to cross the bridge and proceed."

"That a robber?" Miss Light remarked; "why, he's a mere boy. He must be fooling you."

"That's one of 'em," spoke the conductor; "I know that's one."

"Give me your gun!" exclaimed the aged railroad agent, running out and reaching for Lloyd's fowling-piece; "if that's one of those scoundrels, I want his life. He's killed my pore, faithful servant!"

The young man, who was not fully revealed in the imperfect light of the train's windows, half raised his piece and said negligently but frankly:

"Citizens are not allowed to carry guns! We are in possession of this town, and mean no harm to peaceable people. Put that gun down!"

Lloyd got on the train, out of the way.

"My friend," he said to the excited railroad agent, "I have shot my last load off. We must wait for daylight."

"Who are you?" cried the conductor again; "we can't understand you. What is your purpose in this town?"

"We want Liberty," spoke the young man, "and we intend to have it!"

"Oh, beautiful!" exclaimed the senator's daughter at the window. "So bold, and such a boy! If he only had some beautiful clothes!"

"He'd look well in a good long shroud!" Lloyd Quantrell exclaimed, grinding his teeth.

"I won't move my train," called the conductor; "one of the railroad's servants has been shot on that bridge. I am responsible for the lives of these passengers, and I am afraid to cross the bridge before daylight."

The young man retired into the shadows of night like an apparition.

The pointer-dog followed and indicated him with its instinct for an object doomed.

"Will you oblige me with your father's name?" Lloyd asked the communicative young lady.

"Oh! with pleasure. Mr. Edgar Pittson. We are just going to the capital for the first time. My father is a new senator from the West. I have never seen the East. If it continues as sublime and romantic as this, will it not be delightful? Such mountains! Such adventures! Are they always occurring like this, sir?"

"Ever since I have been in these mountains," replied Lloyd, between excitement and amusement, "something wonderful has been taking place. Perhaps they wanted to surprise *us*," concluded Lloyd.

The people on the train and the platform were all this while in the greatest agitation and wonder, while the town of Harper's Ferry was in absolute sleep. A doctor, whose office was at the station, alone had been aroused by the shooting, and he reported that the Negro was dying. The ball, entering his back, had passed entirely through the body near the heart.

"Gentlemen," whispered the doctor to Senator Pittson and Quantrell, "what can this midnight rebellion be? We who live here fear it is a bold and strong attempt to rob the armory of the treasure-chest. Mechanics of all countries live here, and some of them may be very desperate characters."

"Beautiful!" exclaimed Miss Light Pittson, overhearing the doctor; "what contrasts and heroes exist in the East! Washington city must be full of such revolutions. How else could it be *our* capital?"

"Young gentleman," said the senator to Lloyd, "I have been wondering if this *émeute* tonight can have anything to do with the Kansas troubles. I hope not, because the unjustifiable attempts to subjugate Kansas and give it to the slave system have entirely failed. She is on the threshold of the Union as a free State, and I hope one of my first duties at Washington will be to vote for her admission. It is for this reason that I would deprecate any such invasion of Virginia as some of our free-State bands have retaliated upon Missouri."

He conversed as quietly on this dread subject as if he had been in his Western settlement.

Lloyd wondered, and remarked:

"Have you seen anything to lead to that idea, sir? I am ignorant of the Kansas troubles. The slavery question is a bore to me. I am enlisted in the Native American question."

"I looked at that young man's gun just now. I think it is a Sharp's rifle, a new Philadelphia carbine, loading at the breech. A quantity of those rifles disappeared some time ago from one of our Western States and have not been found. The persons responsible for them fear some of the jayhawkers have got them."

"Jayhawkers? Are they something like our 'Blue Jays' in Baltimore?"

"Yes," said the senator, smiling; "they were free-State young men who got a taste of war and blood when the armed ruffians from Missouri and the South invaded Kansas, and they could not be composed to peace after the moral victory was won. They went hunting for an enemy. They felt that they had beaten both slavery and the United States Government which tried to foster it in Kansas. Some of them invaded Missouri and took slaves out and carried them to Canada."

"Who did that, Senator Pittson?" asked Lloyd, with a flushed face.

"I forget whether it was Montgomery or Brown. I rather think it was Brown. He had lost a son or two when the Missourians invaded Kansas. He won quite a battle out there at Ossawattomie. It seemed to bring out a latent pugnacity in him, entirely foreign to his long and steady life. Perhaps it unsettled a somewhat intense brain. Oh, my young friend! war is very close to human society everywhere. It is like the rats in the sewers of towns; whole armies of them are hidden under the gentlest homesteads. It is most unwise for our more warlike Southern countrymen to bring the argument of force into the comparatively tranquil North; for the war-rat is under every human skin, and at a pin's prick it may come forth in eruption."

They were walking up the platform as they spoke, and stopped to see the silent audacity of these unknown strangers, who guarded the two bridges, sentineled the street-corners, communicated with each other patrol-fashion, still held the armory gate and yard and the arsenal, and all this while the town of which they were masters slept, with its nearly five thousand people, in the funnel of the black mountains, like dumb animals in a stall.

"This is indeed wonderful," remarked the senator. "My daughter, you perceive, has read romantic novels; but what is taking place here is a little more curious than any such reading of mine. These strangers can not be a foreign enemy. Virginia can hardly have seized the General Government's armory. Mere thieves would not take such chances, for, when the brawny armorers in that town awaken, Death will keep a holiday here! Do you know what I think I shall do?"

Lloyd looked at him a moment by the variable lights of the environment, and saw something in the senator's long, fine, quiet face, which, in sympathy with Lloyd's own temperament, educed the reply:

"Yes, senator! You think you will go down to that gate with your life in your hand and ask the miscreants there for an explanation."

The young senator — he seemed hardly forty — looked also at Lloyd with mild-eyed penetration.

"How did you guess that?" he said. "But you were right. I am a fresh senator, without record or much ambition. I might save life by interposing here, while night and sleep keep this thing yet a nightmare dream. I can say, at least, I am a senator of the United States —"

A loud, long, heart-searching wail came from the dying Negro's agony.

"Sir, you shall not go to that gate!" spoke Quantrell. "Because you are a senator you shall not go. Because, also, you are a father! I will go myself. A prophecy is already on my head — that I shall see that tonight which will change my destiny."

"Magnificent!" exclaimed a voice at his elbow. "O papa, I could not stay and hear that poor man. So I have been fortunate to hear this gentleman's gallant offering. Isn't he a hero?"

"I fear, Light, he has been reading Monsieur Dumas and Mr. Ainsworth, like you, when he speaks of a prophecy and his destiny."

"I felt there was something like myself in him — like you, too, papa — when I spoke to him so unconventionally. Something quiet and unflinching. Something like Robin Hood and *Fra Diavolo*. Who does he resemble that we know? Of course he shall go and demand of the robbers, 'What ho!'"

Both Quantrell and the senator had to laugh heartily at the unaffected enthusiasm of this large, somewhat masculine-statured Western girl, who might have been eighteen, but was cast in that mold between the handsome and the noble that is commonly called "fine-looking."

"Miss Light," Lloyd said, joyously, "don't try to make an impression on me! You might succeed, and that would be wrong; for I have only this day engaged myself to the prettiest maid in these mountains."

"Splendid! Romantic! A hunter, a hero, a lover, everything noble in one! — Oh, he must go and challenge these robbers, papa!"

As they walked along, talking and speculating, and waiting for an opportunity, or for some decision, on the subject of these marauders, the sky gradually became overspread with clouds and it grew cold and chilling. The robbers within the gates had built a fire in the small square building there, and could be seen stooping before it, or counseling together.

"Are you an abolitionist?" Lloyd asked Senator Pittson.

"No, no; I am a Republican."

"A Black Republican?" asked Quantrell, suspiciously.

"That's a mere nickname. The few abolitionists also call us names, because we will not assault slavery in the old States, or break up the Union, so dear, I hope, to everybody. The Republicans merely reassert the doctrine of nature and of the founders of the republic, that slavery is a colonial thing, not in the blood and circulation of our system, and therefore not to be allowed in the external, new domain of the country. It has taken the noble empire of Texas, by colonizing there, and using American patriotic ambition to acquiesce in the evil. It shall not so colonize and pervert the noble empire of the Missouri. With pity for our countrymen tied up in old slavery, we shall not pity ourselves if we give it our Northern heritage."

"It seems to me, sir," Quantrell dubiously remarked, "that if slavery is so bad a thing, it is in danger from your people everywhere. Do you think a Northern man is as brave as a Southern one?"

"Not as fierce, but I think as brave. Not as decided, but I think more persevering. They are not as conscious of their principles as your friends are, because theirs are older and apparently forgotten, while the tremors of slavery have raised new and glittering doctrines which must perish if liberty is to live. When the great power of Britain was exerted to suppress the young American Republic, the only people they never overran were New England and the Allegheny mountaineers. King's Mountain echoed to Bunker Hill. Since that day, has come the West, the new power on this planet, I believe!"

They went in silence to watch the mysterious people again, and Light Pittson cried:

"Why, look! Papa, they are carrying spears. See how they flash against that firelight! This is glorious! — When are you going to challenge them, sir?"

"This is a good time," Quantrell replied; "I see the gate has been opened to admit wagons and horses. Please keep my gun and dog, Senator Pittson!"

People crowded around to see what Quantrell, who had become a man of leadership in the eyes of the passengers, meant now to do.

"I don't like to see you go down there alone," the senator said. "It appears too much like going vicariously for me, who suggested it."

"Let me tie this ribbon to your jacket, sir," Miss Light exclaimed. "I took it from my neck. Some lady always crowned the brave knight."

She tied the blue ribbon upon him in real admiration.

"A moment," called Senator Pittson, as Lloyd started down some rickety steps from the platform. "If anything happens to you, who is to receive your property?"

"My father, Abel Quantrell, in Baltimore."

"And you are —"

"Lloyd Quantrell, his only son."

"Stop! That man must not go. — I command you not to do my errand!"

The placid temperament of the senator was all lost now. He attempted to rush after Quantrell.

"Hold that man! He has a family upon the train. If he follows me and exposes himself, I shall lose my life for him," Quantrell replied.

The train-hands and passengers seized the senator and pressed him back.

Quantrell kissed his hand to Miss Light, and bounded down the steps.

"Oh, what a gentleman of romance!" she spoke.

"He *is* a gentleman," said Senator Pittson; "I had heard otherwise. Dear Light," he turned to his daughter, "do you say your prayers?"

"Oh, yes, papa."

"Pray for that young man as if he were my brother!"

Chapter XIII

LLOYD'S DESTINY CHANGED.

THE armory-gate was open wide, and a carriage drawn by two horses had already passed in, and four horses, pulling a large farmwagon, had stopped in the gateway.

"Jump out, you colored men, and take a spear apiece. We're short of hands for a spell yet, and want you to do guard duty. Be lively!"

Certain Negro men, impelled by others who carried guns, dropped clumsily out of the wagon and almost immediately were seen carrying sharp things on poles. The same nasal, military voice continued:

"Get out here, colonel! — You, too, old man! Fetch in your son! All report yonder, to the commander!"

Lloyd looked at the man, endeavoring in the moving crowd to distinguish him, but, before he could be satisfied, the same voice exclaimed at Quantrell's ear:

"What! You captured, too, minstrel?"

The young hunter turned, and, recognizing the face, he spoke in astonishment:

"Stevens?"

"Anything you like. Come right *to* me! Don't you put down your hands, or I'll tickle your heart!"

Stevens — the same he had drunk with at the spring-house, it seemed — thrust a pistol at Lloyd Quantrell's body. There was no doubt about his earnestness, and Quantrell walked at once to the pistol's muzzle, saying there:

"Then you're one of these robbers?"

"Anything you like. You're my prisoner. Go 'lang there, now!"

He pointed to some low buildings, and the gates behind him closed with a jangling sound. In the same direction had gone the other persons; and Lloyd, getting the instinct of obedience from his finely strung automatic captor, walked promptly up to the front of the nearest building.

It had three doors, and the farther door opened into a separate and smaller apartment, which contained only a bench and a stove, and some persons huddllng by the fire.

The larger room was nearly square, and contained two engines to suppress fires — low engines on wheels, with hand levers at the sides to be worked by double rows of men — and leather hose and a hose-cart; and also axes and other appurtenances of a fire company hung up under the open-beamed roof. The floor and walls were of brick, and were littered with arms, fagots, tools, and blankets, hastily distributed there.

Quantrell walked uninvited into the engine-house amid blacks and whites, all armed and standing listlessly or nervously about, and he picked up the fireman's horn:

"Put her right in now!" shouted Lloyd; "run her for all she's worth! *Liberty's* the bird!"

"That's the case tonight," grimly spoke Stevens, "but you'll cut no more loud capers like that, friend Quantrell! This engine-room is for the troops, white and black; you must go into the watchman's part with the prisoners."

Two fagots were burning in black men's hands in the engine-house.

"Hold on!" Lloyd exclaimed; "what are these things?"

The Negro he seized the fagot from gave it up with mouth ajar, and in the other hand held awkwardly a spear — the very fisherman's gig, as the burning fagot showed, that Quantrell had twice seen in the Maryland mountains.

"Ashby," he said, looking up at the Negro's face, "you here, and a robber?"

"I spec so," the Negro hoarsely urged; "dey say I'm one of 'em. I don't know."

The fagot was seen to be splints of hard and soft wood bound together; the fisherman's gig was the pattern of many spears seen in black men's hands or leaning against the wall of the engine-house — bright, glittering spears, too small, sharp, and narrow for display.

"Stevens," spoke Lloyd, "what does this mean? Spears — slaves? Are you arming Negroes?"

"Arming everybody!" cried Stevens, with a cool imprecation. "Slavery is war and everlasting captivity. We've armed the under dog in the fight. The boot shall be upon the other leg."

The blood left Quantrell's lips and head, to hear this hard avowal, which seemed to the Marylander like hollow blasphemy, unmeant and merely pretended.

"You will need an army, my indomitable friend, to carry out that idea."

"We have got it," Stevens exclaimed, in something between mockery and rapture; "see it hurrying yonder in the spirit realm — the cloud-bannered army of the Lord!"

As he raised his hand toward the small, wind-driven clouds trooping down the pallid gulf of sky between the black banks of mountains, Stevens seemed in a species of ecstasy, yet cold, like fishes disporting; and the weapons belted around him — pistols and a knife — shone coldly red in the flare of the fagots which burned, alarmed and drooping, like some of the Negro robbers; yet others of these Negroes had the appearance of boldness, like all the whites in the band, and, taking in the scene an instant as carefully as his stirred feelings would allow, Quantrell observed:

"Stevens, if you're a lunatic, you're a good one. And I suppose you are the commander of these people?"

"I?" Stevens answered, self-scornfully. "Why, our commander is a man so great, I am not fit to be his orderly sergeant! I happen, through want of better recruits, to be third in the command, but I'm willing to be the last."

"Who is your captain?"

"Come, you shall see him; for he is talking to the prisoners."

As they stepped out of the cold engine-room, the night wind came in a shriek down the long, grassy corridor between the great armories, bringing some autumnal leaves from the regular lines of trees, and, in the softened wind-wail which followed, was blended a dog's inquiring howl.

"Albion!" spoke Lloyd, as his dog came with obsequious gladness to his feet.

The narrow watch-room contained men standing and others sitting, and all trying to get some warmth from the stove, for the weather was unusually keen for October on the Potomac. A voice of somewhat nervous tension, and of metallic sounding in that brick-walled corridor, spoke up from among the group:

"Your name will be a help to me, sir. Are you his grandson?"

"Ah — great-grandson, captain; descended, sah, from his youngest brother, Charles, sah."

The person standing was a portly man who seemed endeavoring to rally his spirits into some complacency as he spoke these sentences in the nearly dark place.

"Lewis Washington, great-grand-nephew of General George Washington," repeated the voice of him sitting, which thrilled through Lloyd Quantrell and made him turn pale.

"And this is General Washington's sword, captain," spoke up a prompt little voice. "I had the tact, captain, to make him show it to me a month ago, and I said, 'We shall want that, for *prestige!*'"

"And don't forget, captain, that Frederick the Great gave it to old Washington," spoke up Stevens, over the heads of those standing; "he said it was from the oldest general in Europe to the greatest of the age. *We* think another great man can wear it again!"

"No flattery, Stevens!" exclaimed the metallic voice, low among the huddling people. – "Colonel Washington, I will exchange you as soon as it is daylight, and you can see to write an order, for any able-bodied Negro whatever. Your great ancestor's sword I will fight with for liberty again. Did you ever hear of me?"

"Ah, no, captain, sah," the voice of the portly man answered, quite subdued.

"Then, sir, you are not as familiar as General Washington with the great occurrences of your times. I have fought for American freedom in greater battles than Lexington and Concord. Tonight I have come to make Virginia free, and travel on this mountain-line as far as God will let me march, to startle slavery in the vales. I went to Kansas by the trail and sowed my children's blood there, and came away with a reward offered for my head. I shall go to Texas by the *pike*, or make my head a premium again. I am –"

The speaker had risen and come forward, and a way had been cleared for him.

"I know you now, old fox!" Lloyd Quantrell interposed, standing at the door by the light of one of the torches held by an armed Negro – "you are Isaac Smith!"

Quantrell had already identified the voice, and now he saw the gnarled and bearded visage of the mountaineer farmer stand in the watch-house door, dressed as before, except in two particulars: a great gray army overcoat with a cape attached dropped from his shoulders, and his head was covered with a heavy cap of wild-animal skin, rimmed with shining leather. In his hand was an uncocked carbine. He looked to be a rustic gunner or teamster out, betimes, for game or work before the break of day.

"I *was* Isaac Smith for a stratagem," the old man replied. "Now I am John Brown, and in that name I am come to cleanse with blood, if necessary, the crime of slavery from the land."

"You, Pop Smith – crazy Pop Smith – are you Brown of Kansas?"

"John Brown of Black Jack; Brown of Ossawattomie! I see you have more intelligence, Mr. Quantrell, than Colonel Washington and these gentlemen."

He pronounced the "John" long and nasal, like Jo-aw-en, dwelling upon it in that Indian guttural which abides in the resonant nomenclature of the land. A second torch held by a Negro revealed his Indian figure clearer.

Between his old army-cloak skirts a belt revealed pistols, and a knife in its sheath, and the dress-sword hilt of the great Frederick thrust in the belt.

"There he stands, Quantrell," Stevens exclaimed, "lighted up by two native citizens of Virginia, both of African descent, and I think you'll never forget him."

Quantrell had to look, for fascination and fear, and the plain, nearly aged figure he observed by the directions, was illuminated by the torches of that large mulatto man, who had seized his gun at the mountain farm, and the sad-cast countenance of Ashby, the fugitive.

The dog Albion, snarling once loudly at his recent chastiser, and crouching next to "point him" well, as if at some curious kind of game, finally leaped and gamboled, in the apparent idea that a gunning party was about to start and take him along.

"He sees doves," thought Quantrell, in a moment of horror, "and doves will be left to mourn this expedition."

Quantrell next saw at his elbow the small, stooping figure of Cook.

"Why, Captain Cook," Lloyd exclaimed, "are you a prisoner, too?"

"Ha! that's good!" answered the childish little man. "Don't you know I'm a captain in the provisional government? I took the slave census of this county for Captain Brown. I spotted all the big slaveholders, Washington and Allstadt, and now I'm going into Maryland to arrest our neighbor, Mr. Byrne."

"You treacherous spaniel!" Quantrell exclaimed, while his dog snapped at Cook's legs. "To think I let you play on Katy's accordion!"

"Take care!" spoke Cook, cocking his gun. "You make the mistake they made in Kansas about me — that I'm a little boy, and not a shooter. Sir, my brother-in-law is the Democratic Governor of Indiana, hating abolitionists like poison. But I'm a jayhawker to the heart!"

"What's this?" exclaimed a harsher voice, "prisoners quarreling with our officers? This gunner-spy here? — Go in there!"

It was the dark, raven-haired Kagi, the picture of a bandit, and he and Cook menaced Quantrell with their short rifles and urged him toward the watchman's chamber.

"Oliver! Watson! Captain Brown!" Lloyd called in the excitement of rage even more than fear, "are these cursed abolitionists to abuse and confine me?"

"We're all abolitionists, Mr. Quantrell," spoke Oliver Brown, at Quantrell's side.

"We glory in the name," said the voice of Watson Brown, at the other side.

"Pop Smith! Captain Brown!"

Lloyd had turned to the old Kansas chief, who was giving some directions at the wagon-side.

"Mr. Quantrell," observed that person, severely, looking up, "I let you go at the farm, when my officers wanted to take your life. You were instructed, sir, to keep off the streets. The first thing we hear of you is a shot from your fowling-piece at my son Watson, which I returned. The next shot I fire at you will be at closer quarters, sir! Then you walk into my headquarters and blow the fire-horn, sir. Let me have no more of your rowdy capers, but go in there among the prisoners!"

As John Brown spoke, the fagots flashed into his eyes, and something of a wild beast sparkled there.

Quantrell turned and fled into the narrow part of the engine-house.

For an instant the fickle torches shone upon the fresh, untarnished spears of moving Negroes, and low, firm, military commands were heard upon the night, and then the door closed and all was dark except the reddening clay of the little stove and dark sky coming in at a large round window above the watch-house door.

He heard a robber sentry pacing on the ground without, and the call of "Halt!" or "Who comes there?"

Lloyd leaned against the door in actual terror — not merely the fear of death, but the mental paralysis following these startling discoveries.

Not thirty-six hours had passed since he met this resolute bandit on the mountains. Now he realized everything.

The strange and mystic sermon of Isaac Smith on the mountaintop, upon war and military strategy, had been the personal cogitation of John Brown, the Border murderer, upon the campaign he meant next day to begin in Virginia.

The fisherman's "gig" carried in the mountains by Smith's sons was one of many spears, to arm Negro slaves, who would be unfamiliar with more complex weapons.

The boast of Isaac Smith, that he owned a certain number of Negroes, meant that John Brown controlled them for a war against their masters.

The reflections of Smith on Broderick's death were incitements of John Brown to his sons to revenge blood, shed by pro-slavery men.

The mountain farm of Isaac Smith and sons was the rendezvous for a vast recruitment of abolitionists and Negroes to drop upon Virginia in a single night from the great Northern State close by, and to aid John Brown, the fanatical bandit, to capture the tens of thousands of stands of muskets in Harper's Ferry, and arm a mighty insurrection!

Now Quantrell could understand the suspicious and even harsh treatment of himself at the rude mountain farm, his examination by Kagi and Stevens, and the deadly danger he had been in, as a supposed spy, entering their lair in the very instant of their descent upon a peaceful State.

He felt with agony and wonder that if he had discarded, before he came to that farm, Katy Bosler's poor little accordion, and had brought no music to be his intercessor, his body might now be lying in the upland thickets for the mountain crows to pick.

This dark and superstitious Kagi was, no doubt, the second to Ossawattomie Brown in command, and had power of life and death over Lloyd and every innocent prisoner.

As these coincidences and emotions rushed together, the young man felt not wholly a sense of despair, but of mental occupation too great and oppressive for his trifling and heedless mind, to which all his youth had been like a schoolboy's truant day, spent amid the wild haws and mountain plums, and by the rivulets, stoning the birds. In a day and a night he had come to the great crises of love, religious conviction, marriage engagement, fear of death, and prophecy.

Had he yet seen that which could change his destiny?

This question he asked himself slowly, and the sense of fear slowly dissipated from his clearing and cooling brain.

He felt again as he had in the saloon, but a few rods distant, when he measured physical strength and address with the "soul-drivers" and slave-catchers there, and at every blow had rejoiced and delighted in the perfect clairvoyance of his mind; yet, with this transference of purpose and returning courage, came also a cold, appetizing instinct, like the shark's, for human prey, and he almost smiled out of his late excitement, though he ground his teeth.

"If I ever get out of here," Lloyd Quantrell muttered, "death, death to all abolitionists!"

He felt so nonchalantly that he had found somebody to distinctly hate, that he softly, musically, forgetfully, uttered the rooster's crow of victory, as in the saloon when he smote the Logans down.

A dog barked at his feet.

"Ha, my faithful Albion, *you* here?" said Lloyd aloud, stooping and lifting his dog in his arms. "Bark again, and I will crow again, and they shall be our challenge. 'Death, death to abolitionists!'"

The dog replied right earnestly. The young man, with spirits fully recovered, crowed clear and loud.

In a minute the chanticleers of Harper's Ferry were heard responding, showing that it was nearly morn.

Chapter XIV

LEXINGTON, NOT CONCORD

*T*HE watch-house was about twenty-four feet deep and half as wide, and had windows on all sides except in the brick partition, which was a solid wall, and which left the engine-house portion nearly square. The windows in this structure were generally of an arched form, very high above the ground, being, indeed, segments of the brick arches which composed the walls, and the watch-house door was uniform with the two doors in the engine-house portion — a broad double door with a wicket in it.

These high windows showed the dark sky, and from the room-corners showed the blacker mountain shoulders and perhaps some few garrets of houses up the cliff. In one of these garrets a candle burned, and Lloyd wondered if there the infant was not being born whose baby hand had pushed down Jefferson's Rock and fulfilled the prophecy.

His mind reverted to the Dunker love-feast and that other babe which had been born in a stable like this; for the watch-house might have originally been the stall of horses to pull the fire-engine. Across the way was the inn of Nativity, perhaps, with travelers delayed, going up to their capital. "And here," concluded Quantrell, "may be Herod's soldiery seeking the young child's life."

A quiet awe fell upon him like the cold water of the Dunker baptism chilling the convert. He thought of Katy's prayer for his soul, and her solemn words inclined him to devotion now:

"God gif me this soul, and let it drink thy precious blood!"

He put his hand to his eyes and repeated the first prayer he had ever made with deep sincerity, though the words had been his task at school:

"Parce nobis, Jesu! Libera nos a malo!"

In asking mercy and deliverance from evil, he bowed his head and added, "God bless Katy!"

The dog began to scratch the door and to whine.

Quantrell touched something at his buttonhole — the ribbon of Miss Light Pittson.

At once the phantom of Katy Bosler seemed to disappear, and the ardent and noble youth of the lady whose admiration he had so candidly received, awoke a more worldly flutter in his breast.

"Something makes me want to see that fine girl once more," Quantrell thought; "she called me her knight. Her father is a senator!"

The pointer-dog leaped upon him fondly and touched his cold muzzle to Lloyd's face.

"If I had not seen Katy first, Albion," mused Lloyd, "I should have fallen in love with Light. But the *light* in Katy's eyes outshines hers."

He turned and walked back into the cell or corridor.

Talking in low tones together were several prisoners, awed and suspicious, and they looked up at Quantrell by the stove's poor light, and some greeted him with a thin laugh and others ceased to speak.

"Captain, ah — sah!" spoke a portly man whom Lloyd guessed to be Colonel Washington, and who had begun his sentence with courtly intentions, but judged it best to round up without saying anything.

"I'm *not* one of the captains," Lloyd answered; "my uncle Quantrell keeps a slave-pen at Baltimore, and I guess that ought to be guarantee for me, with you men, at least."

"Ah! yes — sah!" said the colonel, but hardly more considerate, as if his suspicions had been satisfied but not his scruples.

"What's yourn?" asked an old man who had been sitting, and who started up and looked at Lloyd unsteadily. "Bitters? Gin, did you say? Tansy? Fi'penny bit — fi'penny bit."

"Watty! Watty!" interposed another man of age, but less infirm, "you're not tending bar this morning. You're tuk, Watty! — He's a little off his *Americanus,* sir; I mean he's not just right in his head, since he's been tuk."

"Fi'penny bit! Come ag'in!" muttered the old bar-keeper, settling to his bench.

"And what are you, my friend?" Quantrell asked of the third person.

"Me? Oh, I'm the armory bell-ringer. I've rung that bell thirty-five year. I never missed but of a Sunday and a holiday. Dear me! ef Cap'n Brown don't let me go ring it at six o'clock, I'll go off of my *Americanus.* What'll old Ball say?"

"Oh, yes, what *will* old Ball say?" cried half a dozen voices. "Old Ball 'll come and git tuk."

"Ah! yes — sah!" coincided Colonel Washington, not yet settled that he ought to say something. In the pause, after waiting for him, the bar-keeper mumbled:

"Medford, Jamaikey, or Santycroo? He-he! All same bottle, gen'lemen.

Fi'penny bit — fi'penny bit! Come ag'in."

"Watty has to git up fur the airly trade at the bar," explained the bell-ringer. "You see they'll all git tuk — them airly birds — this mornin'; fur they'll come to git their drams, an' Cap'n Brown 'll git 'em all."

"An' git ole Ball, too — ha! ha!" shouted the great body of the prisoners.

"Dear me!" spoke the bell-ringer, again absently, "ef I can't ring the bell at the minute, may be I'll git discharged. That would set me clar off of my *Americanus.*"

The door opened, and three more prisoners were brought in, followed by three of the Kansas party, whom Lloyd identified to be Kagi, young Ned Coppock, from Iowa, and Newby, the handsome mulatto man who had been rude to Quantrell.

"Cold night for October," Kagi said.

"Colder morning for you!" Quantrell spoke up, with deep meaning and dislike.

"Blathering yet, are you?" Kagi replied, his cocked gun across his lap, leaning to the stove.

"That *worm* is crawling toward you," Quantrell said, remembering the man's pallor and superstition.

Kagi showed the same ghastly skin for a minute amid his long, dead hair, and then spoke in a tone of enforced quiet:

"Then that *star* is drawing near me."

He looked at Lloyd with a determination in which high fanaticism was blent, and without further anger.

"No quarrelin' in the bar, gen'lemen," old Watty, the bar-keeper, started up; "drink with the house! Whisky? Ahalt's or Horsey's? Lemon-peel? Fi'penny bit — fi'penny bit! Come ag'in."

"There, now, see what *you'll* come to!" Kagi observed, looking straight at Quantrell and indicating old Watty with his head. "Whisky will fetch you there. Slavery and whisky are distilled out of each other."

"Did you ever drink whisky?" asked Lloyd.

"No."

"Did you ever have a slave?"

"I'm not that kind of a serpent."

"That's just what I supposed," said Lloyd; "you're an ignorant fanatic."

"Ah, sah — sah!" put in Colonel Washington, a little apprehensive of a murder, and about to say something, but reconsidering it.

"Washington," spoke Kagi, "if you was worthy of the only celebrity in your family, you would have them pistols of Lafayette and the sword of the King of Prooshey, and be leading this expedeetion, instead of throwing it on to an old saint like Captain Brown. Freedom might build you up, as slavery has about buried you!"

"Ah, sah!" Colonel Washington exclaimed, with an instant's asperity, and then after a pause concluded with great docility — "indeed, sah, captain!"

"Solgers," spoke up the bell-ringer, "what 'll ole Ball do to me? what'll the sup'rintindon do? I must ring that bell, or I'll go off of my *Americanus* clar."

"Not this mornin'!" spoke up the bright-faced, negligently-dressed Coppock. "You and us and all can ring it, when slavery is over. Then, I calkelate, it'll be glad enough to ring itself."

"He-he!" chuckled a prisoner, "ole Ball — when he's tuk, what 'll he say?"

A low laugh, somewhat suppressed by awe, went around the humbler set of prisoners, and old Watty, who had been dozing, started up, saying:

"What's yourn? I'm gwyn to close the bar and git some sleep. Hollin? Ole Tom? Peppermint? Be quick! Fi'penny bit — fi'penny bit!"

"Ned," said Quantrell, familiarly, to young Coppock, "you're not a bad-looking fellow. Don't you know you'll be hanged for this freak tonight? What got you into it?"

"Common sense, I calkelate!" Coppock answered, amiably. "If I saw you working and spending the sweat of your brow for a man who stood over you with a whip and didn't pay you wages, wouldn't it be my duty to interfere? Wouldn't you interfere for me, oppressed like that? I think you would."

"Not for a nigger," answered Lloyd Quantrell.

"I didn't see no exceptions made against Negroes in my Bible," Coppock spoke, unexcitedly. "Nor in my Declaration of Independence, neither! Captain Brown — he was ready to throw his life in. So I throwed in mine!"

Coppock tightened his belt, full of arms, which he had loosened while warming, looked at the breech-loading of his gun, and started up.

"What do you think of my being heah?"

The voice was that of the fine-looking but fierce mulatto man, and he was looking right at Quantrell, who replied with indignation:

"I think you will *stay* here, when you get your deserts."

"Thank you," said the man, armed like a Turk, with pistols, dirk, and small, cunning rifle. "I know you mean I ought to die heah; but you never told as much truth in yo' life. Heah, in the county of Jefferson, I was born. So was Mr. Kagi's folks. The paymaster's clerk of this armory is in the family that owned me. I run away to be a free man! I left behind me a wife I love as much as you kin love yo' sweetheart, God knows that! She's had nine childern."

He stopped, still fierce, but trembling at the throat, as if agony was close behind his audacity.

"Don't cry, now," Lloyd said; "I can feel for you."

"I can't cry," spoke the man, with a proud intensity. "I come heah to fight, not to cry. These rocks around Harper's Ferry, I's seen so many years, is full of crows. Not a black crow that makes his nest in them rocks won't fight for his young against the eagles that tries to eat them. Do you think I could stay yonder in Ohio when my little childern called me heah, and Captain Brown called me, too? I had to be a man!"

"Oh, yes!" exclaimed Watty, the bar-keeper, starting up, "I reckon I'll sell a nigger a drink! Brandy? (good enough for you!) Tansy? Fi'penny bit — fi'penny bit."

"Where is your wife now?" Lloyd Quantrell inquired, interested, notwithstanding his repulsion.

Newby, the mulatto, hesitated, and a furious scowl came upon his brow.

"It's not my shame, nor hers," he continued; "it's the shame of this infamous slavery! She's got another family of childern by her master's son, and his and mine will both be slaves, unless I make them free."

Unable longer to suppress his sensibilities and excitement, the spirited mulatto arose and disappeared into the night.

"What do you think of that, Colonel Washington?" asked Kagi, turning his strong, almost gloomy countenance upon the chief prisoner. "Is that man merely an intruder in the land of his birth? Or has he here rights strengthened by wrongs — injuries which would make you die for shame, or fight for shame?"

"Captain, never did I hea' such rebellious and unconstitutional opinions advanced, sah — ah, sah!"

The legatee of the Father of his Country had reconsidered his reply before he made it.

Kagi also departed, and Quantrell asked Colonel Washington what he expected Smith, or Brown, would do with his prisoners.

"Sah," answered the colonel, with a deep outburst of feeling, "they'll sacrifice us all! Men with no respect, sah, for the Constitution, sah, can have no respect for human life or the ten commandments — ah, sah!"

The colonel was cut short by the entrance of William Thompson, the chief outlaw's connection.

"Mr. Quantrell," said this young man, "there's a lady on the train our chief has stopped, who wants to know why the cars can't proceed. Her father has took sick."

"Light Pittson!" exclaimed the prisoner; "she asked me to do her a service. William, you must get me permission to go. It is a woman, dear to me already."

"Some of our superior officers will have to give you leave, Mr.

Quantrell. I'm only a lieutenant."

"Go see Captain Brown for me, or Captain Stevens! You may want me, William Thompson, when you will have no other friend in the world. Do this, and then I will hear your call!"

"I should like to do anything right, sir. But here is Captain Stevens."

Stevens entered, and Quantrell addressed him with insinuating heartiness:

"Cap, why do you keep that train, full of innocent passengers, standing frightened and tired all night? It's got the mail. You might as well be robbing the mail as to be alarming all those females. The Government and the women will both resent it."

"It's not my idee," said Stevens, shaking his head. "It wa'n't in the plan of our campaign, neither. But here's the commander-in-chief!"

Isaac Smith, as Lloyd still named him, came in and looked around calmly, like one settled in mind by warlike responsibility.

"What are you debating, Stevens, with the prisoners?" he asked.

"There are passengers out yonder at the station," young Thompson spoke, "who have sent me here to speak to Mr. Quantrell and get them permission to proceed to their destination. They are hungry and some are sick. I don't see, father, why you keep them there. They'll only join against us."

"Hasn't that train proceeded?" the wiry, bearded bandit exclaimed; "I have been inspecting the posts, and supposed it had gone on. Who stopped it?"

"Watson Brown and Stuart Taylor. You told them to let nothing cross the bridge."

"It was my oversight and their mistake," the leader said, with a serious look. "All military orders ought to be obeyed, but with intelligence. I have been made to antagonize the Government."

"And to murder a railroad hand — a black man, too — I have seen him dying, Pop Smith," Quantrell spoke, clear and indignant. "You can not lose a moment in repairing a part of your offense. Senator Pittson is on that train with his family. He told me he suspected you to be the unknown marauder here. His daughter has sent for me to come to their relief. We'll go, old man, together!"

Concluding kindly, as he had commenced sternly, Quantrell's suggestion was accompanied by a stride forward and a hand upon the old leader's arm. They walked into the night, and Brown or Smith went up to his guards and spoke:

"Hazlett, Lehman, go find the conductor of that train — one of you; the other go order my son upon the bridge to let the train go safely past. I will myself guard it across the river. — Bring your light here, my man!"

The Negro Ashby, a little more at ease, came forward with the torch, and it shone upon a raw-boned, tall young man, ten years or more older than Quantrell, with red hair and dull, brown eyes. Quantrell remembered him long afterward by his name being descriptive of the color of those forbidding hazel eyes — Hazle-tt.

"The conductor was too scared to go on when we told him," Hazlett said, slipping his carbine under his blanket, which was wound around his body.

The other person, addressed as Lehman, was of black hair and bright, boyish face, hardly of citizen age. He measured Quantrell's strong form an instant and said:

"Captain Brown, you don't want this man. Put him on the train and send him off!"

He gave a significant look to Lloyd, who had the opportunity to say to Lehman, also, soon afterward, upon the bridge:

"I'll do you a good turn, my boy. Take your own advice, and never cross that bridge again."

"And leave my captain and comrades?" the boy replied; "I'll leave my body on one of them rocks first!" — pointing to the river.

This was after Quantrell had rejoined Senator Pittson's family upon the train, whither Brown or Smith allowed him to proceed, while looking for the conductor.

Chapter XV

DARK, LIGHT, AND KISS

THE train was nearly dark, as some of the passengers had blown out the candle and whale-oil lamps, so as not to attract the aim of rifles; and, feeling his way along, Quantrell softly called:

"Light!"

In an instant a woman met him and drew him to the vacant place upon her seat, and said:

"My hero! How noble of you! — Papa, mamma, here is Mr. Quantrell safe again."

Quantrell took her hand, and in the darkness placed his other hand around the large and glowing form of the senator's daughter.

"Speak quietly," he said, leaning toward the backs of her parents, on the bench before him, "or all the passengers will crowd here."

He felt the deceit he was doing, for it was to enjoy Light's society that he gave this counsel. She resented his endearment but a moment, and in the obscurity sat within his arm, he only the trembler.

The senator did not speak, but his wife inquired distantly of Quantrell what nature of men might have taken the town.

"Oh! sir, I know what you will say," Light Pittson exclaimed, bringing her form and face around to Quantrell; "I have considered it all. They are Mexicans. See their blankets, and wide sombrero hats, and flashing lances! Are they not *rancheros, caballeros,* patriots, who have come to repay our ungenerous invasion of their land?"

"Indeed," said Quantrell, "they have come from half-way toward Mexico. They are Kansas buccaneers. — Senator Pittson, the old man says he is John Brown."

"John Brown!" Light Pittson exclaimed; "that's a little plain. Not the Black Douglas! Nor Charles de Moor! Well, John Brown is simple heroism. And not Mexican? Why, all the more romantic, papa. He's our own American hero."

The senator did not speak immediately, nor turn his head. He remarked after a pause, in which the young couple sat bolt upright, enjoying the respectful flutter of their hearts:

"I feared some unbalanced, or overbalanced, man would stampede this nation, if violence in Kansas became chronic there. Our prairie-grass blows eastward in the season of prairie-fires. Brown has always trod a lonely and peculiar path, doing his own thinking, projecting comprehensive enterprises out of no resources at all, and self-confident enough to undertake the fulfillment of any forlorn hope or old Puritan dream."

"You knew him, then, papa?"

As she leaned ardently forward, Quantrell held her more tightly.

"Shame, sir!" Light Pittson whispered to him. "Where is your mountain beauty?"

"It was predicted," Quantrell whispered in her ear, "that my destiny should be changed tonight."

A slightly accelerated breathing was her response, and a stillness that was the bliss of pain.

"Yes," said the senator, reflectively, "I once visited John Brown in northeast Ohio, near the town where he was raised. His father was a pioneer of the great West, a poor man, a tanner, and a shoemaker. Yet this son, John Brown, was then aiming to control the wool-trade of all the West, and had a great flock of Estremadura sheep, and had mercantile aims which spanned two worlds."

"What did he look like, Mr. Pittson?" Lloyd asked, in the thrill of both beauty and political feeling.

"Why, sir" — the senator seemed more distant than upon their first acquaintance — "the scene he made that day to my boyish mind was so romantic I never can forget it."

"Ah! papa," Light said, "I get my romance legitimately."

"Yes, *that* legitimately, Light," the senator reflected, as if he was smiling, too. "John Brown was then about forty-five years of age. He had lost four of his children nearly at the same funeral. He was walking along on that high plain — the highest between the river Ohio and Lake Erie — with a large basket upon his arm full of newborn lambs. In his great white coat-pockets was a lamb in each. The mothers of the lambs were following him toward the fold, bleating. And what do you suppose he was thinking of, amid those bleating dams and lambkins?"

"Wool, I reckon," Quantrell spoke, sullenly — "black wool."

"Yes, sir, something like that," the senator rejoined. "He said to me, 'I was just thinking that if this Government did not do better, some day I would begin war upon human slavery and close it out.' Strange that I should have remembered it to this night, for I was myself a boy!"

"He has come," said Quantrell, "if this be the same man. His basket and his pockets are full of lambs. Their mothers will bleat tomorrow when we kill them, on the threshold of Virginia."

"I am not surprised that Brown should attempt anything, but that he could persuade enough men to follow him here within the lines of Baltimore, Richmond, and Washington, is a matter of profound wonder, and it shows, my dear," he addressed his wife, "how the anti-slavery agitation has caught the younger generation up. John Brown considers himself the executioner. He has an indifference about life, in the furtherance of any extreme proposition, that is particularly Puritan. I am not well, and yet I will try to speak to him, useless though it may be."

"I will go with you!" said Lloyd Quantrell, rising from Miss Light's side.

"No, sir!" the senator firmly spoke. — "Detain him here, my daughter. It is fit that I should risk my life for Abel Quantrell's son, and discharge my debt to him."

Mrs. Pittson, accompanying her husband down the aisle of the car, left Quantrell free to address her large, engaging, child-daughter according to the strange rebellion in his heart. He took Light's hand again, and said:

"It was to see you, Miss Light, that I risked returning from my prison, where I had intended to stay and see this outrage through. Do you understand why we became so soon interested in each other?"

"Romance — glorious, sincere romance!" Light Pittson spoke, with earnestness that was both eloquent and mirth-moving. "We met each other in danger! Among mountains! Going to the grand capital of our free country. You were brave and handsome, and became our herald to the bandits."

"Dear miss, it must have been something more than that. It was for your father, and not for you, I took my chances with the robbers. I did not want him to be exposed. And yet, since I have entered their prison, the thought of you, growing and growing in my head — I think it is not yet my heart — made me come back to see you again."

"Mr. Quantrell, you wore my ribbon, and it was your knighthood. You remember the knight who went down to the lion to bring his lady her glove she dropped there. He threw it into her face, because her intention was not romantic, and merely a bit of coquetry."

"Then you are no coquette?"

"Oh, no. A woman who would trifle with courage and danger, and expose another for less than true romance, is the unworthiest of her sex."

"Were you ever in love, Miss Light?"

"No, indeed. The man I love must have some fine romance in him, whether for good or evil. He must be true to his ideal, Mr. Quantrell. Papa is that kind of man: he admires candor, and says hypocrisy is the only enemy of freedom; that we need not apologize for nature's deviations in us, and if we err should do so frankly. Never to lie, nor conceal, nor evade; to take one's side in the battle of life, and let gallant conduct attest our honest motive."

"I believe with your father, Miss Light; with him and his family, I must disagree upon the subject of tonight's outrage. I shall take my part against the abolitionists with all my might."

"Splendid!" said Light Pittson. "Who can blame you for choosing your side? If not a Paladin, be a Saladin; and always chivalric."

"Let me wear your ribbon, and I will try to remember your father's motto. Does he know my father?"

"He must, I think. After you went down among the robbers, he was quite overcome. I heard him say, 'The right half of him is there!' He has been thinking about something ever since."

"Dear young lady — Light, let me call you —"

"Oh, do! We Western girls are never formal."

"There *is* a right half in me. There must be also a worser half. I have had no teacher. My aims are ignorant. I live by guess. May I have your smpathy?"

"Yes, but you must be true to your mountain damsel. No disloyalty, Mr. Lloyd."

"You mean Lloyd, Light."

"Well, Lloyd. It sounds like *loyalty.*"

"And your name sounds like *knowledge.* I can be loyal to my errors, but where shall I find *light* to show them to me?"

"Papa says that errors are the only lighthouses, and that dangerous coasts are lighted by the wrecks they caused."

"Do you feel any real interest in me?"

"I never was so attracted to a gentleman in my life. You must not feel complimented by the truth."

"If I had met you one day before yesterday," Lloyd Quantrell said earnestly, "I think I never could have loved any other woman."

She was not of the trembling kind of girls, her youthful body too precocious and substantial to yield to nervous rippling, but his ardent speech made her breathe audibly and be silent. A stranger had spoken the first avowal of love to her.

"Answer me," Lloyd Quantrell said.

"Oh, this beautiful Eastern land!" she replied. "In this, my first distant journey, I have found mountains and robbers, and had a gallant gentleman make love to me. What — what romance!"

"Add this to it," said Lloyd.

He kissed her.

She gave a scream, impetuous as her blushes.

"Don't be frightened, Light!" spoke the voice of her father at the car-door; "I'm not hurt, though I might have been."

Quantrell felt relieved that the scream had been passed to a false account.

"Never mind, my dear," Senator Edgar Pittson said to his wife, as they both came forward out of obscurity to more darkness. "He did threaten me, and his manner showed an indifference to life I had suspected of him when his self-righteous confidence is in commission."

"Who, papa — the brigand?"

"Yes, it is John Brown — grayer, graver, commoner, but peculiar yet, and walking tonight the loneliest of all his peculiar paths."

Mr. Pittson sank nervously into his seat, and wife and daughter soothed him, while Lloyd persuaded the interested passengers to give a sick gentleman privacy.

"I did not know I could be really scared so," the senator spoke, after taking breath. "He has a singular power over men's terrors."

"Indeed he has," Lloyd Quantrell added. "I have felt it tonight, senator; the maniac is dead in earnest."

"Wonderful romance!" Light exclaimed, and her mother reproved her. "What did General Brown say to you, papa?"

"He was at the side of the car, as Mr. Quantrell had intimated, and was commanding the unwilling conductor to cross the bridge with his train. I introduced myself, and remonstrated with him upon this extraordinary breach of the peace. He turned upon me and demanded my name and business. When he recognized me, he ordered me to get on the train and proceed, under pain of death."

"Afraid of your influence, Edgar?" Mrs. . Pittson observed, a lady large, like her daughter, as it seemed.

"Oh, no. He called me a temporizer and a compromiser, and said that if public men like me, from the free States, had done our duty, he and his lads need not be in arms upon slave soil tonight. 'Go to Washington,' said he, 'and tell Congress that John Brown has reopened the American Revolution!' His followers, like himself, were no respecters of my person. But, see! we are starting."

The train was really moving, slowly on squeaking wheels, like timid people going tiptoe up stairways, which creak the more for their indecision. Looking out of the window, Quantrell saw the mountain farmer walking by the conductor and his lamp — the conductor hesitating and downcast, the mountaineer with the step of one oblivious to danger.

"I could kill him now," spoke Quantrell, half aloud.

"Oh, no," the voice of Light Pittson answered at his ear. "Not while we are under his safe-conduct. What a simple old man! But, see, how venerable his beard is! How much he seems determined! How considerate, but not for himself! And this is Brown of Ossawattomie! Was there ever such a romance?"

The train passed the sentries and messenger; the sound of solid ground was beneath the wheels. Quantrell lighted one of the lamps. For a little while the speed was increased as if under fright, and then the engine lost self-control and everything was arrested.

"They need not be examining the wheels and gear," Mr. Pittson said; "if Brown designed harm to any here, he would not have hesitated to commit it."

"You think such a man can have any honor, senator?" Lloyd asked.

"Yes. It is the quality of the old Cromwellians to take life without much sensibility, but to stickle at any deceit, compromise, or false doctrine. This man Brown would have sat in Bradshaw's place to judge King Charles, and would not have masked his face when chopping off the king's head; but he would never throw a train from the track, to injure innocent people. His parole he never would violate."

"Much as I hate him," Quantrell said, "I will not be outdone by him. I was his prisoner, and am under some sense of parole. I will return to Harper's Ferry."

"Nonsense, Lloyd Quantrell! The parole John Brown intended for you, I suspect, was not to return. He told me that he wished there was not a citizen in Harper's Ferry; that he only came for arms, slaves, and slave-hostages."

"Nevertheless, I shall return," Quantrell said.

"Always my hero!" Light Pittson exclaimed. "Yes, return like Regulus, Lloyd, if they roll you down the mountains in a barrel of knives! I would always keep my word."

"My daughter," spoke Mrs. Pittson, a large, somewhat haughty lady, "you call Mr. Quantrell 'Lloyd.' That is not modest."

"Mamma, it is very natural to say 'Lloyd' to him. He calls me 'Light.' This is not romance, mamma. I feel it."

They were all standing in the car, which a brakeman had fully lighted. Lloyd observed that even under the late excited conditions some of the passengers were fast asleep. He also saw that Senator Pittson and wife were looking searchingly at him, with somewhat different expressions, and, unable to decipher these, Lloyd exclaimed:

"Mrs. Pittson, Light is as modest as any young lady in the land. That I would maintain with my life. Why we feel so near each other we can not tell. Let me come to see you in Washington if I live."

"My daughter is very young — too young for gentlemen's society yet," Mrs. Pittson coldly replied. "I think this chance acquaintance had better end."

"Mamma," pleaded Light Pittson, "it may be our destiny. Did we *seek* this precious opportunity of romance?"

"Romantic girl," answered Mrs. Pittson, "what will restrain you in Washington if you yield to these illusions of love upon a railroad-train?"

"Not love, but affection," Lloyd Quantrell spoke, taking Light's hand and seeking her father's eyes. "Mr. Pittson, in our short acquaintance we have both been in danger for each other. I like you all. Miss Light is dear to me as your daughter. I have a great favor to ask of you, sir; but I ask it boldly and in all the light of honor."

He glanced at the senator's daughter as he unconsciously played upon her name. The senator stood nearly rigid, slender, and, as it seemed, deadly pale.

"I know what you will ask," the senator said.

Lloyd Quantrell felt himself blushing, in spite of all his moral courage.

"If you know," he continued, "you must read me very deeply. I shall ask to repeat candidly what I have done covertly."

"Mabel," the senator turned to his distinguished-looking wife, "Mr. Quantrell wishes to kiss our daughter."

"This is going too far," exclaimed Mrs. Pittson, flushing and opening her dark, creole eyes.

"I do, madam; I wish to kiss my beautiful friend good-bye in sight of her parents."

"No, it should not be," Mrs. Pittson commanded. "I must forbid it."

The senator wore a strange yet touching smile as he contemplated the young man with something between wonder and affection. Almost automatically he spoke:

"It is the voice of nature, wife, and pure as nature ever must be in candor such as his. Yes —"

"Edgar!"

"Yes, Mabel — I say yes."

He made a motion with his foot a little imperious and turned to look at his wife.

"Is this prudent?" she whispered.

"No," said Senator Pittson, with a face made cheerful, as by his will. "It may not be prudent, but it is real. Let it come in its own way."

Lloyd took the youthful maiden's hand, her development so womanly, her expression so childlike, as she turned her face upward without fear.

"As I wear your ribbon, Light, take my kiss — openly, sincerely, heartily, before father and mother. God bless you!"

She stood looking at him in perfect admiration. Her mother took his proffered hand with a countenance indicative of pride and fear more than dislike. The senator wore a gentle smile, like one whose decision his mind approved, and said:

"You have everything, Lloyd, but what you will lose."

To the last Quantrell saw that superb flower of woman, yet in the age of the bud, giving him her whole romantic soul through her great gray eyes. The train moved eastward under the mountain-crags and cast its lights in the sluggish canal which wound beside it. Quantrell was standing alone, between road, railroad, canal, and the rocky gridiron of the river. He saw, a little way in the direction of the retreating red lantern of the train, the bars of houses at Sandy Hook.

"I'll wake my landlord up, and fill my flask, and tell him the news," Lloyd Quantrell said, carrying his gun and game-bag.

Chapter XVI
THE SUCK

"THEY'RE fighting at the Ferry," Lloyd said to the landlord, who arose half awake, and was not inquisitive.

"Always fightin' thar," the landlord replied, giving him some new country whisky.

"Abolitionists have taken the Ferry," Lloyd explained.

"Then they'll git tuk," the landlord observed, as if the Ferry was "tuk" every night. "Harper's Ferry is an ole suck."

"Suck?" repeated Quantrell, struck with the word; "how a suck?"

"That's the name of it. Injuns called it the Hole and the Suck. Nobody ever gits out that gits in thar. Railroad stuck thar for years. Gov'ment can't git out. It's the Suck."

"'Sucks people in,' you mean?"

"Yes; ole Bob Harper tuk it up from Pete Stevens over a hundered years ago. Pete had squatted thar years on Lord Fairfax and couldn't git out. Bob Harper left his bones thar. The floods gits it, the winds gits it, whisky gits it, and now, did you say, the abolitionists has got it? It'll be a suck."

"Old Isaac Smith and sons have took it," Lloyd said, falling into the syntax of the place. "They and a band of abolitionists. They're killing people there."

"Isaac Smith?" the landlord said. "And sons? Is them abolitionists? They stopped with me when they fust come yer. They come to Sandy Hook last July, an' said they was lookin' for minerals, an' sheep-lands an' farms. Well, well! Is them abolitionists? I thought they was Christians. They'll find Harper's Ferry a suck."

The landlord filled Quantrell's flask, put up his bottle, and went to bed. Having slept there two nights before, the gunner sought his own room mechanically, and stretching himself on the bed said, sleepily, "False to Katy! — not I"; and then, it seemed to him, the sun rose right into his eyes. He had fallen asleep, probably for hours.

Nobody was awake in the hotel. He strolled up the road leading from the river, and found himself in Pleasant Valley, between the two mountain-lines, in rugged farm-country. He retraced his road under Maryland Heights back toward Harper's Ferry, and soon saw that picturesque village standing like the nipple above "The Suck." The sun was just rising up the shining lap of the Potomac, and shooting silver arrows at the little city, which stood out like a target.

Harper's Ferry appeared between the two rivers, rising like a great green mound, with a road dividing it over the top through a ravine, and another road around the base of the mound; and for a little way up its scarp hung or clung the picturesque little town, which also raveled along the upland road among borders of shade trees till it disappeared over the summit. This hill was several hundred feet high, and three or four churches presented their gables from its grassy face, as if their pulpits had been buried in the earth. A spire or belfry or mountain graveyard added points of whiteness to the green background or clear gray sky, and some stone walls and terraces and bits of pasture — land where cows were quietly grazing in the airy tops gave a faint sense of inhabitancy. To the right over the Potomac the eastern portion of the mound terminated in a nearly perpendicular crag, out of which grew a pale-green thicket of trees and bushes, leaning almost horizontally. From near this abrupt headland to the low cape of the mound extended the stately line of low brick factories with high chimneys, and in the midst a lofty flag-mast. These buildings in their continuation also turned the cape and extended a little way up the other river, and below the factory line ran railroads coming down the sides of the two rivers and meeting at a covered bridge of wood which spanned the Potomac on arches of stone to the Maryland shore.

In overlapping rows of irregular heights the dormer-windowed houses and other dwellings, more detached, caught in their panes of glass the rising sun which shone through the rifted precipices up the broad, islet-sprinkled, rock-barred rivers, making them seem aisles of silver between borders of green and russet. A canal wound along the larger river like a silver cord under the bare crags of Maryland.

Another bridge, starting from near the commencement of the larger one, passed on slender abutments to the mountain above the Shenandoah. This mountain at the cape above the mingling of the rivers fell in perpendicular ledges or chimneys almost a thousand feet to the woodlands which grew from its *débris* and spread toward the eye in graceful wreaths of verdurous mountain, along whose sides could be seen the eagles, vultures, and crows circling as if around nests concealed in the rocks. For several miles these Virginia precipices curled over the

Potomac as if seeking courage to span it and connect with the bald, scarred wall of Maryland Mountain; but failing to do so till far below, a valley found place in Maryland to empty its creeks into the augmented Potomac between these hesitating ridges.

Thus the town of Harper's Ferry slumbered at the base of its own acclivity, between the jaws of grander mountains which threatened to fall upon it and drown it in a deluge, like that which had probably broken them asunder. There seemed wanting, to complete the subjugation of the town, some mighty castle of the feudal age to crown its dome of greenness. He who descends the Alpine torrents toward the great plain of Lombardy may see sublimer heights for the old Ghibelline castles which frown toward the Papal sees, but nowhere else could he see two such rivers meet and go forward like white-plumed cavalry to wash the old Catholic counties of the plain of Maryland.

An autumn russet lay inwoven with the green and gray scarps of the desolate mountains, like campfires which had gone out, in the awe of what had seized upon the usually whistling and hammering town in the vale. The crows and vultures chattered or circled in wondering gossip or augury about the steepling chimneys of Loudoun Heights, as on that morning when Romulus and Remus watched the birds of omen and spilled the first blood of brethren in cuddling Rome.

The little city hugging the heights, familiar with deluges, forging arms for battle, and often sheeted over by the thunderstorms, was on this day so commonplace amid its great besetments, that it stirred no more than the water-snakes upon the surface of the river rocks, which felt their cold blood grow torpid in the cloudy October air. The insensate and the superstitious, the vulgar and the rapt, lethargy and Nemesis, went together, as on that day when, at the walls of Troy, a wooden horse arose ridiculous, but in the sky a serpent shook the stout soul of the protesting priest.

The Shenandoah, in cool, green rapids and white ripples, came around a shoulder of wooded mountain in a stately curve, and a low stone dike, partly natural, held its current back, to guide the water-power into two milling canals which formed green islands under the mutilated heights of Jefferson's Rock. These islands were inhabited by artisans and by toilers in the tall grist-mills there, and the upper island was another Government armory, with a line of workshops enclosed by a wall and entered by a bridge across the mill-sluice. Within the wall, a cupola tower in the façade enclosed a bell and upheld a flag-staff, and behind the rifle-works, next to the river, a railway ran toward the great Valley of Virginia.

The sound of the Shenandoah churning among huge rocks and moaning over the low dam never was unheard here in the busiest days, and in the still dawn it seemed to speak a legend in the voice of sobbing, like the legend of bondage by the rivers of Babylon.

Upon the summits above Jefferson's Rock lived the chief officials of Harper's Ferry, in roomy mansions, and thus the double river-gorge and rocky redan of the upper town maintained a feudal appearance, and had that military air as of some castellated pass held for a distant emperor by his various mercenary bands.

A little passenger-packet lay in the canal, with steam up, ready to make her trip to Washington city through the many locks. Looking up at the telegraph-poles, Lloyd Quantrell saw that their wires had been torn and the broken strands hung near the bridge-entrance.

"Poor Heywood!" he said, thinking of the wounded Negro; "no wonder he could not apprise me of the coming train. Smith's band had severed communications. But by this time the night express is nearly at Baltimore, and all Maryland will be aroused."

Within the entrance of the Potomac bridge a form with a spear came out of the dark shadows and sternly ordered Quantrell to halt.

"Ashby! Is that your voice?"

"Halt! Ef you don't, I'll kill you!"

The Negro drove his spear close to Quantrell's throat.

"Kill me," said Quantrell. "Do! because I pitied you when your old father died. Because I was hated for taking your part. Because I fought and whipped your catchers. Come here and look at me, Ashby!"

The darkness, growing familiar, showed the Negro to drop his spear and gaze at his prisoner irresolutely. He wore the old straw hat his dead father had worn, but around his nearly naked body a blanket was tied, like the other abolitionists' uniform; his feet were naked, and he limped.

"Kill the only man who can save you from a horrible death, Ashby! By noon today you and the men who have seduced you will be howling on your backs for water to cool your wounds."

"What kin I do?" the escaped slave exclaimed. "I come for my daddy. Dey killed him and tuk me. De Kinsas men set on to 'em and give me freedom and told me to fight for my race. I must! I know I'll die, but I must fight. Come with me, or I'll call Cap'n Watson Brown yonder!"

He raised and clinched his spear again. In the perspective of the bridge-tube, Quantrell saw the forms of two more men. He spoke with quiet decision:

"Ashby, I am going to buy you and send you North to your mother. Mr. Beall has told me your story. Your mother never meant to have you mixed up in a rebellion like this. You have done your duty to your father, and I can pardon and pity you."

The kind tones brought down the Negro's pike again.

"Where is the man who owned you?"

"Over yer in Marylin."

"What are you sentinel for at this point?"

"I was goin' with Cap'n Cook and his party over to git de guns at de farm, but I limped so, dey leff me yer and tole me to take everybody prisoners an' march 'em to de engine-house."

"March me there, Ashby. Tell Captain Brown's officers and men that I was kind to you when your father died. You can help me out of danger, and I will try to save your life in return for it. Hide this piece of money to buy shelter, or food, or conveyance, if you need them. Keep me this day in your humble care and watch, and tomorrow I will not forget it."

"Mosster," the Negro said, "I'll do de best I kin for you, for your kindness. My heart's mos' broke."

"Halt! Who comes there?" cried a bold voice from the middle of the bridge as they advanced.

"Friend with a prisoner!"

"Advance, friend with the prisoner! Who is it?" spoke the voice of Watson Brown.

"*Isabell!*" resonantly answered Quantrell.

There was a startled motion, and the voice was not so bold, as it stammered:

"Isabel? What Isabel — not mine?"

"Watson," said Quantrell, coming closer, "it's Lloyd, whom you met on the mountains."

"Who answered 'Isabel,' sir?"

The young man was stern and excited.

"It must have been an echo," Quantrell replied, carelessly, but watching the young invader closely. "Your father let me out on my parole. I've seen my friends off, and I'm coming back."

"I know I heard my wife's name," repeated Watson Brown.

"It's probably an echo from the wind, my poor fellow — some premonition — some spirit, such as the spirits Captain Stevens sees."

"I never believed in such things before," the son of Ossawattomie Brown muttered. "'Isabel' is my wife. She has a little baby I never saw, sir. Where she lives, in the great North Woods, the snow drifts into our bedroom and the wind moans in sounds like that I heard, through the long winter soon to begin."

"You are cruel to Isabel, Watson. What are the moans of Negroes to the call of your wife and baby-child?"

"In God's ears they are the same, my soul tells me. I can't go home while things are done that I have seen, even in Maryland. Nine black men died and one killed himself near our mountain farm since we have lived there; all on slavery's cruel account. — Take Mr. Quantrell to headquarters!" he ended, speaking to the Negro.

"That was a home shot I gave him," thought the Baltimorean. "I heard him blubber 'Isabel' to Coppock at the mountain farm. What a fanatic! Does he expect retribution for every Negro mother's heart-ache? That would take too long."

Still, he was out of temper, spiteful but not afraid, and when he emerged from the bridge and saw Oliver Brown, hardly of man's age, standing there in blanket and gun, he cried, with cold gayety:

"Hallo, Oliver! I'm going to my prison. No wife have I to pine for me. I hope you haven't."

"Yes, Mr. Quantrell. I'm sorry to see you back. I *have* a wife that was with me in Maryland, and I took her and my little sister back to New York before we should be in danger: her next little boy will be a Marylander, I calkelate."

"Ah! Oliver, wasn't that selfish, to remove your women from danger, and start insurrection on ours?"

A young connection of the Smiths, named Dolph or Dauph Thompson, as Quantrell had observed, replied to this reproof:

"It was about this time of the morning, I calkelate, that the Border Ruffians moved on Lawrence in Kansas, eight hundred strong. It was only two or three years ago. Artillery with 'em, too! Mississippi rifles, you can calkelate. Georgians, Alabamians, Carolinians! They looked as if the pirates had took the poor-house. Jeff Thompson, of Harper's Ferry here, and now mayor of the city of Saint Joe, I calkelate was among 'em. United States Senator Atchison addressed 'em — drunk, you can bet! 'Boys,' says he, 'today I'm a Kickapoo ranger. If you find a woman armed as a soldier, trample her under foot as you would a snake.' A tiger was on their flag. They broke the printing-presses, robbed the people, pillaged from men and women, stole ladies' letters, blew up the buildings, and sacked the town. I calkelate I know, for my brother Henry shed his blood there."

"My brother Frederick," said Oliver Brown, "was shot in Kansas and killed. A preacher from Missouri murdered him. My brother John was drove crazy by chains and cruelty. Our wives was threatened with abuse and shame if we didn't leave free soil. Through the streets of Leavenworth the scalps of men were paraded on poles. In Bloomington a woman who spoke against slavery was outraged by a troop. Where women couldn't live, men didn't want to settle, and here we are, outlaws back from Kansas, starting the war at the right end!"

"Prospectin'like," added Dolph Thompson, almost merrily.

Quantrell passed on, bitter yet awed, as the dim recollection of past troubles in Kansas was made vivid by these survivors. He thought to himself, "Perhaps they do mean to put us all to death." As he meditated, the voice of Stevens was heard from the armory-gate. "No parley with prisoners. March your man right here! Shoot him if he hesitates!"

As Stevens spoke, his short rifle was in both hands. From both bridges blanketed guardsmen emerged, with rifles in poise. By the arsenal-gate Coppock was looking intently on, his belt full of weapons and his gun across his arm. The little wooden saloon in the eye of the vista was being opened by its proprietor within, and some of the band were watching it, also.

"March!" spoke the Negro Ashby, hoarsely, looking fear, yet fidelity, at his prisoner.

John Brown, or Isaac Smith, whichever he might truly be, came out to the gate and said to Quantrell:

"I allowed you to go away from here, sir. You will be in danger, and yet I warned you carefully. — Take him in there and see that he behaves himself," addressing the Negro. "He will not be discharged again."

"Still tender on the mourning-doves, Mr. Smith," Quantrell replied. "Listen!"

Two guns went off close by in the public street, and sounds of running or hustling feet were heard.

"What's that? Firing?" interestedly asked John Brown.

As they listened, another gun went off, from the arsenal-wall right opposite, and there was a loud cry of a man from up in the chasm of the hill street. Quantrell looked up where this street met the business street, and saw three of the blanketed men emerge, all three with smoking guns.

"Dat time I got him!" said a hoarse voice, as the Negro, Newby, quietly wiped his rifle-top with his blanket.

Another scream, or groan, floated from the railway-station, where the Negro porter had yet several hours to live.

These awful sounds in the still morning-time, blended by the two rivers in their plaintive wail, were followed by repeated whinings of a dog, and the pointer Albion made his appearance in the armory-yard, crouching or gamboling high in the air, as if the word "dove" had touched his soft and pliant ferocities.

"Spirits!" said the man Stevens. "They're never faraway! The men has found some citizens with arms, and sent them spirit-way. Now we'll get prisoners."

These sounds of war gave nervous impulse to the invaders in the streets: their heads were more erect, their vigilance was renewed. People came sauntering in and were halted and seized with a precision which paralyzed resistance or curiosity.

The evening bacchanal with a parched throat, going for his morning "cocktail," forgot his need when confronted by an open rifle-barrel and a stranger in the wild garb of blanket, slouched hat, and belted person, bristling with killing arms. The laborer coming toward work on river, store, canal, or farm, saw this apparition, and looking round in fear beheld its duplicate cutting off his retreat, and yielded, limp and docile. The saloons, half open, felt the absence of customers, and seeing these strange forms, both black and white, their keepers dodged within, or, walking forth, were taken from their bottles.

Occasionally some man and even woman would pass along and feel queer at the unexpected sights, yet be without the understanding to pause or inquire, carried onward by a simple instinct which preserved them from arrest. Again some fierce Caucasian laborer, seeing an armed Negro in his path, would raise the customary fist to strike the helot down, and, with astonishment that made him dumb, would find that Negro brave and deadly, and meekly receive from such a source his own favorite execration. The damning of black souls by fellow-men was impotent that day, because the white man's spirit had brooded over these black eggs and hatched them to armed men.

There was a sound of hoofs before Quantrell entered the gate, and a man with a pale face, whom he recognized as the village doctor, dashed past upon a horse and galloped up the hill street.

"Be firm but considerate, men," Quantrell heard John Brown say; "capture them who resist. Take no life unless your own is in peril! But we must hold our ground."

As he was marched toward the little engine-house, his guard, Ashby, muttered:

"Dat man up de street is dead; I heard 'em say so! Mosster Quantrell, what mus' I do?"

"Get across that bridge, Ashby, as soon as you can! Go past Sandy Hook and cross the big mountain into Catoctin Valley. Find Jake Bosler's farm, and say you came from me, and give my love to little Katy."

"Dey'll kill me, won't dey?"

"If you stay here, you are sure to be killed. This place is the Suck, and takes everything to the bottom."

Entering the watch-house again, Quantrell found it uncomfortably full, and some of the occupants were complaining of thirst and fatigue and hunger. Almost every moment some new prisoner was brought in, and those previously confined scanned the newcomer's person or timidly listened to the few who had volatility enough to talk.

"What do you think they mean to do with us, Colonel Washington?" asked the young Baltimorean.

"Ah — sah!" The gentleman spoke with such circumspection that Quantrell with asperity said:

"Sir, our situation levels distinctions. You should play the man here, and your suspicions of your fellow-prisoners are unworthy. It is your own State, your native county, that is invaded. I ask you for your ideas in our common emergency."

The gentleman replied, with subdued effort:

"Nothing in Brown's history is against my conviction that he will kill us all, sah. I have been searching my poor, breakfastless mind, to recollect what I can of his past in Kansas. I feel sure, sah, that this is the same man who, the day after the abolition settlement of Lawrence was destroyed, took four of his sons and one son-in-law, and grinding their sabers sharp as butcher-knives, they entered a slaveholder's dwelling, sah, and took a father and two sons out of there prisoners; and this old man shot the father dead, and his boys — the same, no doubt, whom we see around this engine-house — hacked the victim's sons to pieces with their sabers. The same night the old man set his sons upon two other men, who had been captured in their beds, and saw them cut down with as much indifference as a wolf. The very abolitionists in Kansas denounced such barbarity. Brown was then accused of meditating the massacre of the Kansas State Convention which was enacting a Constitution. He had previously fought two victorious actions with the slave-State settlers, and, being outlawed there, he invaded Missouri and ran off mules and slaves, sah. The mules he sold in Ohio at public auction, and the Yankees there, sah, bought them because stolen. The slaves he stole there, may be in this robber army tonight, sah."

No rage was in this statement, but a memory barely struggling above despair, and the revelation increased the doubt, and therefore the numb dread, in Lloyd Quantrell's mind. He asked himself if Watson and Oliver Brown could have done such wonders.

"Colonel," he whispered, "surely we can fight for our lives?"

"Ah — sah!" the inoffensive, hale, but broken man replied, "we are like butchers' calves, sah. What I saw when taken from my bed, sah, convinced me I was valuable for nothing but my slaves and the slaughter, sah."

"Nobody drinkin'?" spoke old Watty, the bar-keeper; among the crowd. "I reckon I'll turn the lights down. They has to be paid for! Sherry cobblaw? Brandy toddy? Fi'penny-bit! — fi'pennybit!"

"Watty! Watty! you forgit you're tuk. You're off of your *Americanus,* Watty! See all our neighbors comin' to call on us — all tuk!"

"All but ole Ball!" echoed a few faint and tired voices. "What will ole Ball say?"

"Ole Ball 'll say, 'Who didn't ring that bell accordin' to my orders?' That's what ole Ball 'll say. Then I'll be clar off my *Americanus!*"

There came floating down the gray and sharp October morning a sound like musical vibration. The whine of a dog seemed to protest against it.

"Hark!" spoke the bell-ringer. "Has Captain Brown dared to ring my bell? I've had the doin' of it so many years, to let another do it seems like as if I was dead and heard my funeral-bell."

With another hesitation and twanging, like some tender bird clearing its glottis of the mist, a bell directly above them began to ring, and through the vales its strong and steady tones went artlessly, in no imperious command, but mellow invitation, as if a cage of linnets had awakened full-throated and tried their hearts in song.

"It's the Catholic church," the bell-ringer said. "It's the *angelus* they're ringing for the workmen's early mass."

The sound of murmured prayers was heard among some of the humbler prisoners. Lloyd Quantrell called aloud the words of morning prayer as he remembered them at school:

"'*Gratiam tuam quæsumus Domine!* Pour down Thy grace into our souls!'"

"*Amen!*" in whispers filled the little place.

"'As we have known the incarnation of Christ Thy Son, by the message of an angel, so may we come to the glory of the resurrection. *Per eundem Christum dominum nostrum!*'"

"*Amen!*"

The bell hesitated again, continued on a stroke or more, and then a shot was fired.

The bell stopped, trembling; a dog stopped howling, too.

Watty, the bar-keeper, burst into tears.

Tears came to many others at his example. Their depressed feelings, violent superstitions, uncertainty, and fainting hunger, had prepared all for some sudden burst of agony, and the little Christian prayer had touched all hearts.

"Watty's off of his *Americanus,*" the bell-ringer cried, coming forward, a sob upon his voice. "Pore Watty! He wants his dram."

"I try to 'commodate you all," the old bar-keeper moaned; "sorry I can't please none of you! Pay me off and — let me go!"

His aged face and straggling hairs, vacant countenance, and inoffensive village ways, touched everybody. The bell-ringer wrapped him in his arms, shed his tears upon the old vagrant head, and seemed himself about to lose his homely self-restraint.

"Who broke the bell?" articulated Watty. "I can't hear none of 'em. They's a-callin' for orders, and I can't tell. Only let me hyur you, an' I'll do my juty. Fi'penny-bit! — fi'penny-bit!"

The bell-ringer, himself an aged man, but of some simple decision of character, here threw himself against the watch-house door.

"You le' me out!" he shouted. "I'm most off of my *Americanus,* and

I'm not desponsible. I don't own no slave. I ain't done no harm. Shoot, if you want to. But this pore man's got to have his dram!"

"Jimmy! Jimmy!" the bar-keeper muttered, nearly brought to reason by his friend's exposure. "Don't take no account at 'em. They fights as soon as they gets a little pizened. — Never mind yo' money, friends! Go out peaceable. Go, go!"

As the guard opened the door, Quantrell's dog rushed in, and with a yell of pain — for Smith or Brown, the bandit leader, kicked him, passing, and entered, himself looking poorly.

"Who is it making confusion here? Citizens, this is no child's play. Two men are dead already — one for not obeying orders, and the other for carrying a weapon."

"I ain't got no weapon, but I've got a heart!" — the bell-ringer alone had the courage to speak in his fierce captor's face. "Captain, there's men here who want their food. They ain't used to hollow stummicks."

"Every man who can send me a colored person for a recruit, I will discharge," the leader said, like one of business propositions, fixing one grayish-green eye upon the bell-ringer, and the other doing the summarizing.

The perfect daylight revealed him now, tired after the night's exertions, wiry, with one eye preoccupied and the other like a fisher-bird's, the nose vulturous, and the mouth as hard as intense opinionatedness and severe reflection could make it in man.

He had his arms beneath his old coat-tails, and his cap concealed there; and his unkempt hair flamed up like a beacon in ashes; and the fleece of gray and white beard made a blossom like a snow-ball to his breast-bone. Without an ornament but the dress sword-hilt of a king — no seals, no watch, no watch-guard, not even a pistol now — John Brown seemed terrible by his simplicity and indifference.

Unconstrained, natural, yet wild; not entirely sane in the expression of his eyes; deliberate but unfeeling, ready to become domestic or dreadful, like a house-cat to take a fit, he measured them all as if he was ransoming sheep.

All felt that he could toss them back like lambs to their pens if they sought to assail or evade him. His whole dress a slop-shop might have rejected; but the stringy frame within it, and lean, bushy head, at once patriarchal and animal, gave him the sense of some Calvinistic wolf — a savage qualified by theology.

"My blood," said this apparition, in a metallic, commercial voice, "is precious to me — tolerably so." He paused, as if reflecting just how much it might be worth. "Your blood I do not desire." They felt a dread come over them as if it were merely want of appetite that retarded his meal. "But you are my hostages for the offenses of your disobedient neighbors, who have broken the laws of God. This is war! I mean nothing but right. But I mean all I came here for."

Quantrell's chilled spirit recalled the curse of Hannah Ritner, not twenty hours elapsed: "I see the rivers flowing red. Escape ye can not!"

"You may be a great man," said the bell-ringer, not unimpressed, "and have your ideas, but an empty stummick is a cruel neighbor. It'll make a baby cry of a night. It'll make a wild beast go catch food for its young at any peril. It'll do more than that" — the bell-ringer dropped his voice to produce the full, pathetic effect — "it'll make a nateral being go off of his *Americanus!*"

He put his hand on Watty's forehead, and Watty advanced toward John Brown unsteadily and placating:

"Drink with the house!" he said. "Guarantee everything — to come out of the same bar'l. He-he! Medford rum! Parson's flip! Raw egg an' hell-fire! He-he!"

"There's a picture of slavery," said John Brown — "the slavery of alcohol."

"I'm one of 'em," another prisoner cried, coming forward. "Ef you doan le' me go git my dram, I'll take the rams an' git shot fightin' somebody."

His red eyes and unsteady hands told that his apprehensions were real.

"I can set slaves free and take them far from their masters," John Brown remarked, looking at the two men like a magistrate sentencing some vagrants; his great mouth was firm, but his eyes had a little thoughtful pity mixed with their contempt. "Slaves of vile habits no man can set free. The thing these two men serve" — he looked over the crowd — "whips and kicks them, even in their sleep, and then they go and whip and kick their unfortunate fellow-men! Go with him" — he addressed the bell-ringer — "and order breakfast for me for twenty men. I parole you to proceed to the hotel for that purpose. If the breakfasts are not sent, my army will hold you responsible when we take you again. — As for you," turning to the second toper, "go home, but do not stop to poison yourself anywhere on the way."

Quantrell had a peep of this proceeding, and saw the bell-ringer turn his eyes toward the bell-station and move that way, till a sentry turned him off. He shook his head disconsolately, but took old Watty's hand.

"Cap'n," Watty said to John Brown, "I'll mix you a Caner of Galilee: sodee an' hock an' ole Sassaurek! Then you'll feel so good, you won't shoot nobody. He-he!"

The lines of the invading "army," as Captain Brown had named it, were now perfectly formed. There was a guard on the armory green, another at the yard-top, a third at the gate, and men were upon the bridge. Brown himself went with the hostages to the public street and conferred with sentinels in the two arsenal buildings opposite. Shots were heard occasionally in the upper town, as if citizens might be firing old loads from their guns or making ready for resistance.

The breakfasts were brought over from the hotel, and Brown invited the prisoners to partake thereof in the engine-house; but some nervous skeptic whispered that it might be poisoned food, and only a few, among whom was Quantrell, took advantage of the request. John Brown bowed his head before he ate, and seemed to be asking a blessing upon his meal. Albion, seeking to steal a piece of fried ham, ran against the great bandit's claws, and was thrown toward the yard, but slipped over the old man's arm and ran beneath one of the engines, where he howled dismally.

His meal being done, Quantrell asked permission to remain in the engine-room, which contained no other prisoners. John Brown made no answer, but went off to inspect his posts.

Quantrell began to think of Katy in Catoctin Valley, of Light Pittson in Washington, of his mother in her grave, and of the new and solemn feelings which had impelled him to intone a portion of a public prayer.

"Am I infirm in my affections?" he asked himself. "I feel no guilt. Till Sunday I never was in love; no ladies' man have I ever been. Yet I seemed to make a conquest of the senator's daughter as easily as of Katy. What do I mean?"

He found the pointer-dog insidiously climbing upon him, and drowsiness was in his brain; so he drew the dog to a place beneath a fire-engine, and, crawling there upon some leather harness and blankets, fell asleep.

A loud discharge of guns, so close that they seemed to have been fired at the engine-house door, awoke Quantrell, and he rushed against the door and into the armory-yard, unconscious for a moment of his whereabout. Nobody paid any attention to him in the yard, and the guards there were crouching behind the stone gateposts and handling their pieces as if to kill some expected foe. Availing himself of the confusion, the young man ran across the open plaza and along the railroad side of the yard, until he could look over the iron railing and up into the town, by the Shenandoah street.

He saw nothing but blowing smoke in front of some high brick stores, and an object fallen in the street, and feebly moving. In another instant the object was still.

The smell of brimstone was in the air. The streets were perfectly deserted except by dogs, which were smelling and snapping at the fallen object — his own dog the most forward and conspicuous.

While Quantrell looked, a rifle sounded from one of the bridges he could not see, and a piece of brick, or lead, or splinter seemed to fly from the front of one of the tall houses in line with the armory-gate. In a moment the front of this house flashed smoke and fire, as if several guns had been shot off together. From the bridge and the stone gate-piers, shots went responsive against the concealed enemy in the house.

Quantrell distinctly noted a difference in the quality of sound of the opposing guns.

"Breech-loaders," he thought, "against the muskets of Harper's Ferry. The Virginians have got arms."

He noticed that no store in the village had opened its windows, though the sun was coming over the tall Loudoun Heights, some hours high. As he looked at this sun, the crows, flying around the chimneys of Loudoun Mountain, arrested his attention, and he thought of the black man Newby's saying, that not a black crow was in those rocks but would fight for its young.

"My God!" spoke Quantrell, slowly, seeking with his eyes the object fallen in the street again, "I know that man lying yonder. It is a mulatto. It is Newby himself!"

Obeying an impulse of mingled mercy and horror, Lloyd Quantrell vaulted over a broken angle in the brick wall, and, with both hands raised higher than his head, he ran along the public street, exposed to the concealed marksmen from either side, but barely conscious of their existence. A few shots, fired from the heights around the Catholic church, rattled along the limestone crossings and macadamized roadway and rebounded from the sloping traps of cellar-ways. The golden cross above the Roman chapel seemed also extending its arms in the truce of heavenly intercession and flaming with perturbed light.

He reached the fallen object; it was a human creature, tumbled with gun in hand, and belted round with other carnal weapons, but helpless as a turtle upon its back. Quantrell knelt and spoke the sufferer's name; a terrible wound was in his neck, out of which the blood was gushing.

"Newby, can't you get up?"

"Cap'n Brown called me," the pale lips muttered. "I had to be a man."

Feet and chin stiffened together, and the first victim on either side had been a black crow fighting for its young. Quantrell took up the Negro soldier's rifle:

"'Poor devil!'" he said; "Harper's Ferry is turning out to be a 'suck.'"

Chapter XVII
ASHBY'S GRATITUDE

WHISTLING bullets past Quantrell's head recalled him to some preserving fear. Looking down toward the armory-gate, he saw a Negro from the arsenal leveling a piece at him, and the ball grazed his hair.

Quantrell retreated up the hill street, called High Street, and while he turned his head to see if he was followed, his feet stumbled upon something soft, and he was thrown to the sidewalk beside a sleeping man. Scrambling up and seeing that the man did not move, Quantrell touched him and found him cold.

"Oh, bring him in!" a voice whispered from a neighboring grocery; "the Mexicans shot him there the matther of two hours ago, and we're afraid to walk in the strate; fur they fires at averybody."

A gun, thrown down in the shock of being wounded, lay beside this man, and showed that he had gone forth to kill. He looked to be a herculean Irishman.

"This is the man that yonder Newby killed, no doubt," thought Quantrell; and, as he sought to lift the bulky and heavy form, he felt himself seized and being dragged away.

Through an alley-way nearly opposite, which descended the slope into an almost unoccupied lane, right under the engine-house and wall, his captors bore him fiercely with firm hands and silent purpose, and he made no resistance whatever, considering that he had no arms and had sought to harm no man.

From various garrets, whose dormer windows partly commanded this lane, the popping of guns came momentarily and tore up the dirt around them, and scarred the long government wall. A church-bell somewhere up in the town began to ring an alarm, and over a broken place in the wall, some way ahead, a few men carrying something weighty emerged and fired their pistols at Quantrell's abductors. The latter shook Quantrell loose, but kept him between themselves and the enemy, and began to fire their short, breech-loading guns.

Lloyd saw that his captors were both Negroes, and under high excitement.

The fleeing white men made little response to the guns of these Negroes, but continued to bear off their burden; and among them Quantrell thought he recognized the young planter, Beall, and the pale and frowsy Atzerodt.

"Git ova yer, or we'll kill you in de road!" gasped one of these black men.

"Git over!" echoed the other, giving Quantrell a painful blow with the butt of his carbine.

They forced him across a picket-fence and up a slope, in a little garden or hog-yard, and near the top of this acclivity was a mighty rock which had been walled up below by human hands and made a cave or cellar for some adjacent house. Into this all three retreated from the bullets, which began to come from everywhere.

The Negroes, taking breath a moment, turned on Quantrell.

"Come," said a supple fellow named Green, "you got to die, man!"

He drew his gun and raised it.

"What?" cried Quantrell. "Kill me! What have I done?"

"You are a soul-buyer an' a slave-trader!"

"You keeps a slave-pen and sells men like me!" the other Negro, who had been called Copeland, exclaimed, with no less sullen ferocity. "We know you, an' you got to die for our brother Newby!"

Copeland raised his gun also. The despair of death fell upon Quantrell's soul.

"For Christ's dear sake, men, don't murder me! You are under a mistake. My uncle is in that business — not I."

He had literally fallen upon his knees. The sense of dying in that cave, of moldering in such a sty, of being hideously cut off in youth and bloom and happy love, made him beg like a child. The pugilist's bravado failed him in this test of death.

"De boot's on de oder leg," Copeland continued, while Quantrell grasped the carbine and turned it aside; "it's no harder fo' you to die than fo' Newby, shot fo' his childern!"

"I have never bought a slave, never sold one!" Quantrell gasped; "all my slaves are inherited, all well treated. Don't bring this blood upon your hands!"

"No man's well treated with his liberty and wages took away," the Negro Green exclaimed, his rifle at Quantrell's head. "We've all got to die here. Your life for Newby's! Say your prayers!"

"Nothin' kin save you," Copeland spoke, his gun at Quantrell's heart; "we made up our minds, when you said yo' family sold men, to kill you if one of us died, and Newby's gone to heaven. Come!"

At that cold word, so blank yet dreadful, 'Come!' Quantrell's heart and brain seemed to swoon. He said the Catholic names of "Jesus, Mary, and Joseph," and threw himself with arms outspread, like the cross he surrendered his life to, upon his face and on the floor of that foul cave.

The sound of both carbines exploding made him await in cold awe the torments of some wounds. He felt nothing; but feet were treading upon him, as if men were wrestling.

"I pushed yo' guns up. Is he dead? De Lord fo'give you!"

Raising his face at this strange voice, Quantrell saw a fourth man in the cave contending with his enemies.

This man had a Negro's face, but he seemed so bright and radiant in Quantrell's eyes, that the cry of Nebuchadnezzar appeared to be ringing in that rocky furnace: "Lo! I see four men loose, walking in the midst of the fire, and they have no hurt; and the form of the fourth is like the Son of God!"

"Dat man didn't do no black man harm," said a voice; "dat man's de black man's friend. He fought fo' me. He give me money to git away wid. He's a kine man!"

As this voice spoke, a piece of gold flashed in his hand — the evidence of Quantrell's kindness.

"He's gone dead," spoke the Negro Copeland. "O Green! may be we's killed a good friend."

"Ain't he no soul-seller?" answered Green. "It's a pity, then."

They gathered around Quantrell's outstretched form.

"Po' man!" said Ashby, the new arrival, feelingly; "de on'y kine words I got, in de lan' whaw I was raised, dis man said to me. Lord, raise him fo' me!"

Quantrell raised his head.

The colored men looked down wonderingly.

"Prayer, brother!" said Green to Ashby; "see how it's answered!"

"Raise him, Lord!" cried Ashby, loudly, in the ecstasy of religious superstition.

"Raise him! Raise him, Lord!" the late assassins repeated fervently.

Quantrell arose, pale as a ghost, and for a moment speechless. He leaned upon all their hands. They watched him like a spirit.

Nothing but gratitude was in his heart, and he felt like giving thanks even to his murderers, so violently had human power been transferred in a few hours from white man to Negro.

"Ashby, you turned their guns aside. I am not hurt."

"Come, den," Ashby shouted, "we's mos' surrounded. De gate's held open for us a minute. Come!"

Quantrell and the three Negroes dashed down the slope, and a wooden gate in the side-wall was held ajar. As they entered it, bullets came from old stone walls and hanging galleries, from garret-windows and from pig-pens.

They were in the armory-yard, and the gate shut fast behind them, before they had been well discovered.

"Here," said the voice of John Brown as they reached the engine-house, "you men are just in time. I want some loopholes picked in these brick walls."

As the sounds of the implements in the brick masonry and of guns of different kinds made the place far from tranquil, Quantrell asked himself how many of these bandits there might be; though he had hardly seen twenty in all, they acted as if they were an army.

"What is this thing of slavery?" Quantrell questioned of a somewhat depressed but not despairing man, whose only crime in John Brown's eyes had been slaves.

"You mean its value in property?"

"Yes, the strength or weakness of it. I never asked before, and now see, for the first time, that it is the question of questions."

"In Virginia," said the farmer, "we have about five hundred thousand slaves — half as many souls as the whites of Virginia."

"Souls," thought Quantrell, and added, "you mean that many *head,* not souls."

"*Wills,* anyway," the farmer replied, "if what we see tonight is representative. Maryland has ninety thousand slaves and nearly as many free blacks, or say two fifths of all her —"

"Souls," Quantrell finished; "we mean head."

"I had rather have souls into them today," the farmer remarked, "for their soul-fear is what may save our lives."

"That's true," Quantrell noted; "a nigger is a religious animal. But what is the extent of the slavery in all this American Republic which John Brown has rushed against?"

"Four millions at least."

"Worth — ?"

"Oh, a thousand million dollars, I reckon. Twice that, unless this fellow gets up a black insurrection."

"Has slavery been growing?"

"Yes; seventy years ago we hadn't but seven hundred thousand in the country. They're growing three quarters to a million every ten years. We're pore with 'em, and pore without 'em. Less than thirty year ago Virginia was half minded to give slavery up, but Missouri and Texas got into the Union as slave States, and it become too profitable to let the thing go. This man's raid today cuts down the value of my niggers from a thousand dollars apiece to six or seven hundred."

"Ditto!" Quantrell remarked. "Yet I have seen times in these few hours when it would have been cheap to me to give up every slave."

"Dreadful times!" the captive planter moaned. "I don't see why they may not as well kill us as outrage us in this way; my stomach is in torture."

"Here, drink from my flask," the young man said; "don't show it, for there's not enough to go round, and we may want it yet for —"

"Our wounds," replied the planter. "Sir, these men are demons. When they took me, they had studied my house till they knew every hole and corner of it."

"They come in hyur," spoke another person, "just befo' the armory watch changed, and so they tuk everybody. That little Cook sot it all up. We suspected him from the quare people that come to his mother-in-law's up yer on Union Street. He totched a school —"

"Taught it?" questioned Quantrell.

"Yes, totched our academy school up hyur by the Shinandoh, and, of cose, he picked out of the childern all about the comin' and goin'."

As this man ended, Lloyd observed that one of the late slaves of Mr. Washington had just opened daylight in the brick wall, and suddenly a leaden ball from outside struck this spot and came within a hair's breadth of Isaac Smith and dropped into Quantrell's hand, rebounding from the wall behind him.

"Here it is, Captain Brown," Quantrell said; "it's so hot I can't hold it."

"Yo' kin pick away fur yo'self!" exclaimed the frightened Negro, dropping his tool; "I'll do no mo' of it."

As the Negro slunk under the engine, his dreams of liberty departed, young Coppock took up the tool and began to widen the loophole. Two holes were thus made and manned, and balls came almost momentarily in the place. Some of the captives shrank, and others quietly looked at each other to give or take courage. The engine-house door was kept ajar, and just outside of it the young marksmen, black or white, replied with their rifles to every enemy. Quantrell now realized that Smith or Brown was at least twenty years the senior of every recruit he possessed.

"Is he a childish man to lead these boys," thought Quantrell, "or are these boys manful as himself, to seek such danger?"

Through the large round windows near the ceiling the balls would come, ever and anon, making the brick-dust fly, or glinting fire upon the metal of the engine; yet not a person within was struck, and old Brown paid no more attention to these balls than if they had been of paper and thrown at a schoolmaster. Sometimes his look was anxious, and he asked a subordinate once why his re-enforcements did not come. Finally, his son, Watson Brown, came in, with a blanched look, and sank down upon his hams, speechlessly.

"My son, are you wounded?" the old man questioned.

"I think I'm hit," said Watson Brown, whose skin had become the color of white dust in the street. "I feel queer, father."

Quantrell had already opened the young man's coat and removed his accoutrements. He found a perforation in his garment, and blood, and passed his hand around the lad's body. Watson Brown seemed to have swooned, for he said:

"Is that you, Bell? Oh, let me see the little fellow!"

"Wake up, Watson!" Quantrell spoke; "it's only a skin-wound. There's no hole in you. Taste this whisky and you'll be strong."

Watson Brown pushed the flask away. His face slowly flushed up.

"Not shot?" he spoke; "no bad wound? Give me my gun!"

He was up, the blood warm again in his hopeful face, and his belt of weapons in his hands.

"Go, my son!" his father said, in a sort of dry interest. "Stand by your companions! We have a great cause."

The young man fastened his belt around his body, looked at his gun and ammunition, and went cheerfully into the exposed yard.

"For all that," muttered Quantrell, sinking beside the planter, and himself sick with the sight of blood, "there's a hole in Watson Brown."

"Poor boy!" exclaimed the planter; "bad as he is, I pity him."

John Brown now walked into the armory-yard and began to listen to the sounds of shooting.

"I hear my guns," he said to Coppock. "They must be my re-enforcements. Or, perhaps, they have disarmed my men."

"Captain Brown," said Coppock, "why don't we hear from Captain Kagi? We're holding High Street corner open by sentineling the arsenal wall, but nobody comes down from the Rifle-works!"

"I ordered Kagi," said John Brown, "not to fire upon anybody; merely to hold his ground, and, if attacked, to retire upon us here. He could not defend himself there till re-enforced."

"I calkelate he's surrounded," said Coppock.

John Brown opened the engine-house door and called two men in from their posts:

"Hazlett, come here! Bring Lehman with you!"

The two men appeared, in military precision, belted, blanketed, alert, and armed to the teeth.

"I want you to proceed to the Rifle-works and find how matters go with Kagi. The citizens are behaving very badly, and you will need a hostage."

He looked around and his eye fell on Quantrell.

"Take that man," John Brown concluded. "He is intelligent, and will understand that your safety is also his."

"Come, march!" spoke Hazlett to Quantrell, his dull hazel eyes flashing unamiably.

"Go out in front," the bright-faced Lehman said, peeping at his gun-stock critically; "the man who can sing 'Home, Sweet Home' can find his way back to it, I guess."

Chapter XVIII

KAGI

*T*HEY went into the yard, and the watch-house was seen to now have an overflow of prisoners, so that some of them were loose and unarmed in the grounds. Stevens was in command here, striding to and fro in the beauty and regularity of manly form and accustomed soldiership. He glanced at Quantrell and spoke:

"Hostage, my boy? Well, if you've got a guardeen angel, no harm can come to you."

"Beautiful words!" thought Quantrell. "I know that I am guarded, from heaven and from this world, by my mother and by Katy's prayers!"

He saw that the two bridges were still guarded, by Oliver Brown and by William Thompson, and that the armory-gate was held. An ominous lull in the spluttering firing seemed to have taken place, and nothing stirred in the streets but hogs which had missed their breakfast, and dogs which discovered some evil abroad but could not locate it. Around the Loudoun Heights the crows were flocked together curiously, and their cawing and croaking came down through the chilly and spotted air like swallows' notes down a smoky chimney on a rainy day.

"Turn that way, Quantrell!" Lehman said, pointing up Shenandoah Street.

Quantrell looked back, and both men were watching him with all the calculation of self-protection.

"If you make one jump to escape," Hazlett spoke, divining Quantrell's mind, "I'll drop you in your shoes."

"He can't tell how to go, Albert," muttered Lehman, more generously; "I'll go ahead, and you bring up the rear."

Lehman led on, and soon they came to a yellow, plastered school-house of two stories, with a cupola and tin globe on the roof.

"No school today," Lehman cried back to Hazlett. "It makes me feel sorry that we've shut up the school. Here John Cook was teacher, but the teacher's played the truant today. And the little log school in Maryland — Will Thompson says they stopped that, too, and that the little children begin to cry to see John Cook bring in the arms and put 'em down by the desks."

As they looked at this shapely school, standing under the walls of rock upon a little shelf of grass, like a child's toy banking-house upon a cottage mantel, it seemed to Quantrell that there came out of its open door a sound of children's laughing.

"Stop!" he said. "Have the little ones had the simplicity to come to school this bloody day?"

Again, upon the air, or upon the haunted mind of Quantrell, came children's gleeful laughter through the parted door.

"I think I hear children," Lehman said. "Never before did it sound sad to me."

"Look in!" suggested Hazlett.

At that moment half a dozen shots from muskets poured down the street from sward, shelter, or steep ahead of them.

"Muskets!" exclaimed Hazlett, his gun at his eye, peering for an enemy. "They've got Harper's Ferry muskets from somewhere: I know the sound."

"You're right!" Quantrell spoke. "I saw them taking fixed ammunition out of the very armory you were guarding. Men who can be as bold as that, can fight you!"

Retreating from the fire, they had ascended to the school-house green, and in the pause their attenuated nerves seemed to tremble with the peal of play-yard laughter again.

"Surely there are children there!" Lehman exclaimed, his dark eyes in surprise dancing upon his boyish face.

"Guardian angels for you, my lad!" Quantrell thought to say.

"Then they are gone!"

Lehman had put his ear to the open door, and all was still.

"This school is open for the war," added Lehman, with a pallid smile. "If we have luck, we'll make a black folks' college on Jefferson's Rock!"

Across the road they were advancing up, a band of men appeared around a point of rock, and some signs of military trimmings were in their caps and coats.

"Soldiers!" exclaimed Lehman. "Albert, charge them!"

With Quantrell pushed before, these two men undauntedly marched on, firing rapidly as they proceeded. Hazlett felt a sharp pain in his foot and stopped: his shoe had been ripped by a bullet.

"Bill," he said, "look there! It's a whole company. We can't get to Kagi by this road."

A large company of armed men, indeed, filled the road and part of the bushy steeps in the *débris* of the mountain, but they had been frightened by the decision of the two marauders, whom they probably considered to be the skirmishers of a larger force.

Advancing with fine courage, the two men drove the company around a turn of the road, and then swiftly fell back to the shadow of the Catholic church, and, still driving Quantrell before them up the cliffs, attained a dizzy street of naked rocks which led them into the High Street and well into the upper town.

They kept along the sides of this street wherever open lots or paling gardens gave space, and so rose into the air till, at one point, they commanded the great amphitheater of rivers and yawning mountains.

"What's that?" asked Hazlett, looking up the Potomac. "Are they our re-enforcements?"

Following his eye, Quantrell saw men down by the shallow river as if intending to cross; and military accoutrements sparkled gaudily also there.

"I'm afraid the country is up against us," Lehman remarked, "but we've got our orders to obey and to reach Kagi, if he's alive!"

There was a sadness in Lehman's face which gave his resolution the beauty of courage. Hazlett, harsher, duller, without external grace, had no less courage, but his promptness was like ferocity, as if his nervous system could not carry in the tone of nature the strain of the occasion.

"Young men," spoke Quantrell, "don't deceive yourselves. I know, by the opportunities Captain Brown has given me, the smallness of your numbers. Around you are strong towns, and they have marched upon you from Martinsburg and from Cumberland, from Hagerstown and Frederick, from Charlestown and Winchester, from Lexington and Richmond! Yes, from Baltimore and from Washington! You look so lonely to me on this ragged mountain, like little sprats in the jaws of a whale, that I want to see you escape!"

"Here's John Cook's mother-in-law's," Hazlett said, pointing to a house in the cross-street, called by the name of The Union of the American States, so much imperiled this day; "John's safe across the river, anyway."

"It's just like him to return," the boyish Lehman answered; "but I hope he won't, and maybe he won't, because his wife's safe in Pennsylvania. I hope she'll draw him there."

"Lehman, were you ever in love?"

"A little; not enough to hurt. I'm glad no girl will break her heart for me when —"

"You die," finished Quantrell. "I'm afraid, Lehman, you will never see that lowering sun go down again."

"There's heaven, I calkelate," said Lehman, looking up; "and they say that's ever sunny. Mr. Quantrell, I wish we could get somewhere down here among the bushes and rocks and hear you sing 'Home, Sweet Home' again. It seems as if I wanted to hear it now. What is this music that it takes hold of people so? Do men make it up, or do they hear it from somewheres and remember it?"

The dark-eyed boy, with no tremor in his voice or steps, asked this question on the high plateau with the simplicity of innocence, though beleaguered round till there seemed no outlet for him but some miracle of wings by which he might fly into the gray and hungry heaven he had spoken of.

"O men, why did you come here?" Lloyd Quantrell asked, almost in bitterness, thinking of scenes of cruelty he might live to witness upon these men, as living and perceiving as himself.

"I heard a call," young Lehman simply said; "I thought it came from God. If it came from the devil, that's another sin of his'n to answer for."

"I heard an invitation," Hazlett said. "'Tain't often I wake to poetry or glory, but I thought this invitation was about right. I hefted of it, and it was jus' comfor'ble like."

As Hazlett spoke, he balanced his carbine in one hand, for practical examplification.

"How could John Cook marry a young wife here and become a father, while planning all this blood and insurrection? How could he teach children in Harper's Ferry, and be so treacherous?"

"Oh," Lehman answered, "God had his Hebrew spies. Love grows anywhere. John didn't come here to get in love, but he was lonesome, and love, I calkelate, peeped into the school-house. You are sent to school, maybe, to study and improve your time, but some day you look up from your book and see a little girl swinging her pretty feet as she hums, 'B-a ba; b-e be; b-i bi! ' The book flies out of your head; the girl slips into your heart, and next thing it's b-i *by*, and b-a *ba*, and *by-o-baby by!*"

Singing this like a lullaby, Lehman and his companions both laughed cordially, but not long, for Hazlett said, reflectively:

"There's no doubt about John Cook loving his wife. If he hadn't been a man of some 'sand' she'd have weaned him from his work. He did all the dangerous work: peddled books from farm to farm among the savage dogs, and finding where we had friends or foes. If any Negro had betrayed his talk, the white men here would have burned John alive. John Cook's vain, but he's a better spy than Major Andri ever was, and he never was trapped."

Thus talking, they descended open lots and fields between the officers' dwellings on the high upland and the raveling houses of Union Street, which continued toward the Shenandoah like another town, unaware of Harper's Ferry proper. Many thickets of cedar and pine, chestnut and brush, girted the hill-slopes between which this street picked its precarious way, and so they kept somewhat concealed until they reached an open rock right over the Shenandoah, and so close upon it that only the roofs of the Rifle-works beneath them could be seen; bell-tower and chimneys, foaming waste water, sycamore and willow trees, trim walls and comely grounds, and, beyond, the river singing its plaint to the stern mountains and captive town; and far away, to the southwest, this river ascended in light-green islets like an archipelago of moss in crystalline cascades, miles upward, as if the forests had opened for the blue horizon to melt through.

"What's that out yonder?" Hazlett exclaimed. "Is that Kagi? They're firing at him! He's not going without a shot?"

"Captain Brown told him not to use force," Lehman said; "only to hold the Rifle-works if he could."

Rattling musketry from unseen places below, and white smoke rising subsequently up the rocks, showed that a conflict of some kind was taking place.

Following Hazlett's eyes, Quantrell saw a few men in blankets and wool hats, and carrying short guns, run along from cover to cover, fired upon as they were exposed, but only pretending to fire back, and as they reached the Shenandoah shore one of them threw up his hands and fell into the river.

They all disappeared in a few minutes, and next were seen other men, with longer guns, following from cover to cover until they replaced the others near the river-brink, and there crouched down or found some shelter, and proceeded to load and fire with great energy and method.

In a little while there appeared at some distance in the river, men wading, with their short guns held above their heads. There were three of them whom Quantrell could see, and they sank deeper and deeper into the brawling but treacherous-bottomed stream, sometimes carried off their feet and swimming to a shallower part, where they found foothold again.

One was a Negro. Quantrell immediately identified him as the man Copeland who had threatened his life in the cave.

The bullets of the attacking parties on the shore cut the water all around these men, and the balls could be seen to strike and make jets of water fly, and in a little while one of the white men put his hand quickly to his breast, drew his gun, motioned as if to aim it, and fell over in the current, and floated down toward the low cascade or breast in the stream.

At this scene the Negro, who was also wading, lost self-control, and began to plunge and stumble in the river, making his way toward a rock nearly exposed above the current, and plainly seen from the shore by the ripple it made.

He climbed upon this rock, and, if he possessed a gun, it was not now visible; the bullets fell around him, and he faced the shore with a gesture of both rage and dread, grasping the stone with one hand.

It seemed to Quantrell, as he looked at that tired human being, with the open mouth and the eyeballs straining wide, that the wild roar of the river was Copeland's panting breath, full of the heartbeats of despair.

A gun exploded at Quantrell's side, and, as if obeying it, another gun immediately went off.

The people along the shore, who had meantime become bolder and bolder, hearing these shots, looked back and ran to shelter again, but there was one man, indifferent to danger, or inflamed by drink or rage, who deliberately waded in the water toward the Negro on the rock.

Hazlett and Lehman shot again at this pursuer, who turned his face toward the shore, and, still wading, raised his hand defiantly.

By the time they had made ready to fire again, the man was too close to the Negro for them to shoot one without imperiling both.

The man seized the Negro, pulled himself up on the same rock, struck the Negro in the face a blow so powerful that it seemed the spectators could hear it, and, as the mulatto, Copeland, came up from the water gasping and struggling, it was seen that his assailant had also seized his gun, and, pointing it at him, began to drive him ashore.

"I reckon you fellows have got your match in these Harper's Ferryers," Quantrell said, turning to look at his guards.

They were both deeply attentive, yet cool; Hazlett had fallen to his knee to aim, and Lehman was drawing his gun to his shoulder, and it seemed to Quantrell that his bright black eye at the barrel might set the powder off.

The black man was seized by strong and fierce hands as he arose from the stream, and it was plain that he was being knocked down and maltreated.

Into the huddle of men around him the rifle-balls of Lehman and Hazlett were poured; they took the ammunition from pouches at their sides, loaded at the breech with quick motion, and fired again and again.

The captors of Copeland broke and fled to the protection of the Rifle-works, carrying the Negro along.

"Come!" exclaimed Hazlett; "they will surround us in a minute."

"Stop!" said Lehman; "where's Kagi?"

"He's almost safe," Hazlett answered; "see, he's half-way over!"

Looking farther along the breast of the hurrying river, Lloyd saw a form floating upon its back, with face turned upward, and rapidly going down the current, yet by a method, so that it took advantage of the eddies and expanded the distance between itself and pursuit.

This man's arm held his gun aloft and paddled with one hand and the feet, and when it seemed that he was about to go over the falls he suddenly found a shoal, and stood up and looked at his gun carefully, as if now ready for action.

Quantrell divined this man before he saw the long black hair, portly figure, and manly proportions rise and be denoted.

It was Kagi, floating face upward, toward the unseen stars.

"He will not feed the worm just yet," Quantrell thought.

As Kagi stood up, he became the only remaining object of fire from the Rifle-works; the balls fell around him, but did not seem to strike near. He raised his gun to his shoulder, and the dark scowl of his countenance seemed to be interpreted by his fine, belted form, and elbows balanced beyond his hips, and the poise of his bearded and long-maned head and neck.

"Why don't he shoot?" muttered Hazlett, looking from under his red eyebrows with the greatest interest.

"Orders!" whispered Hazlett; "he's second in command, and the adjutant, and he's too good a soldier to break orders."

The fire on Kagi was now extraordinary. Not only did the concealed men in and about the Rifle-works make him a target, and aim with increasing coolness and care, but from the large island below and its mills and tenements other persons were trying their skill upon him and bringing him under a cross-fire, and from the heights nearly over Quantrell's head concealed persons were shooting; and, as he once looked up, he saw a woman of large frame, but almost girlish face, aiming a rifle, and as it flashed she disappeared.

The nearly perpendicular crags were fringed with little boys, some firing old horse-pistols, others throwing stones, and Kagi was the only living object of hate to engage their attention.

It was now later than midday, a Monday after Sabbath rest, when the energies of workmen were fresher than on other days, and all these energies were madly alert to find and destroy the purloiners of their wages, who kept the armories idle, and halted men and governments. Having had a taste of blood, the furious instincts of all were aroused for a full meal, and Kagi was the only game in plain sight.

As the bullets, passing over the intervening thousand or more feet of river, fretted the surface like hailstones, Kagi raised his hand and pointed toward the Loudoun Mountain, and shook his head as if to say, "I'm safe beyond the worm." Quantrell, remembering Kagi's apprehensions on past occasions, mentally translated his gesture of contempt and confidence in that figure of speech.

Beyond Kagi, who was within a few rods of the farther shore and its low strand of mountain *débris* and brush, there was a deep eddy among large rocks, where the current could be seen foaming mightily, and this he must cross to gain the wooded mountains and their lonely depths. No dwelling was on that farther shore except some fishermen's huts of drift-wood, and no clearing but a patch of wild garden exposed to the freshets; the solemn mountain reared its head among the crows and vultures like some prancing horse with insects flocking in its mane.

Kagi finally prepared himself for the endeavor; his companions were all dead or taken at the Rifle-works, and he drew his belt tight, raised his gun and blanket high above his head, and stepped into the boiling surface and went down, down, until he sank from view!

"He's drowned!" spoke Hazlett, breathlessly.

"No, he's come up," said Lehman, in a moment; "he's a good swimmer."

As Kagi rose it was seen that he was floating upon his back, his head thrown backward, and his rich beard raised with his chin into the air. His gun-barrel pointed upward. The river moaned loudly, because all had ceased firing.

In a moment more Kagi had reached a gentle ripple, where he could rise and stand.

"Thank God, he's beat them all!" spoke Lehman.

As Kagi stood and shook himself like a water-dog, he looked back no more, but straight upward, toward the ceiling of the day on the mountain cornice.

"He's thanking his star now!" said Quantrell, between his teeth; "it's served him well."

"Great man!" young Lehman remarked, reverently; "he's not as good a soldier, maybe, as Captain Stevens, but full of head and devotion. He's our statesman; we had a poet, too, but *he's* not reliable, I calkelate."

They saw Kagi fold his arms and look around him, like another William Tell, rejoicing in the freedom of the mountains. He gazed everywhere intently, on earth and shore, flowing water and cold gray sky, cloud and bird, and then raised up his arms and gun and entered the water again, where it flowed very deep against the rock-bound margin.

"Another minute," said Lloyd Quantrell, "and he'll vanish in the woods."

Suddenly, from the thick bushes which partly shut in the Loudoun shore, there burst a volley of sound and flame, so quick, so unexpected, that it turned every eye away.

Men were seen there firing again and again.

"He's cut off," Quantrell said; "the worm has inherited him."

Kagi had disappeared; the firing ceased.

"He's sunk!" young Lehman muttered. "Oh, Captain Brown has lost his best man!"

"Look there!" Hazlett gasped, with open mouth; "he's swimming again."

In the rapid current under the shore Kagi's body was floating, but not with the chin up; the rich beard had dropped upon the breast; the long hair floated like blackened weed in the eddies; the face was white as a silver coin, or the reflection of a belated star in Morning's countenance.

With agitation and a sick stomach, Quantrell had produced his flask of spirits.

"Poor soul!" he exclaimed as he drank the draught; "I drink to the worm that distills him to the stars."

Chapter XIX

FIRST CADET SLAIN

"COME!" exclaimed Hazlett to Quantrell, speaking with a pale face and eyes yet muddier in color, as if these were not both of the same hue. "Keep on before us, or we'll leave *you* with your worm."

"You must be our prisoner back to Captain Brown," said Lehman, also handling his gun, marksman-fashion.

"I've felt the fear of death myself today where I seemed to have no chance at all," Lloyd replied, "and I don't want to see you fellows murdered before my eyes."

He led the way up through the ravines and cedars; bullets came after them from the rifle-works, but they soon got into the grounds of the commandant on the hill-top; and, as the Potomac burst into view, soldiery were seen upon the Maryland shore, marching down behind the tow-path. Hazlett beheld them and turned pale.

"It looks like our bein' surrounded, Will," he spoke.

"I calkelate they're our re-enforcements," Lehman replied, his boyish countenance looking toward that shore with a gentle longing; "but I wish we was over there; for I grew to like Maryland. What do you think, Mr. Quantrell?"

"My lads, I shall see you all die before my eyes, like Kagi and Leary, unless you can cross that Potomac bridge before yonder men reach it. Your killing me won't save yourselves. Do, for mercy's sake, run for the bridge!"

"Not I," Lehman said, "without Captain Brown."

"He's got us into this," Hazlett spoke; "we'll try to get to him, and maybe we can cross the Shenandoah bridge."

They had now come on the flanks of High Street and were keeping down it, sheltering from observation wherever possible; Quantrell going ahead, and the other two concealing their short guns in their blankets and hiding their belts of knives and pistols.

Suddenly the sound of horse's hoofs was heard upon the turnpike's stones, and before they could secrete themselves a fine-looking, martial-riding man was right upon them, going at a gallop.

Both Hazlett and Lehman dropped a hand to their concealed revolvers and measured the man's body with an inner light of meaning in their eyes.

"Whaw aw they? Whaw aw they?" he cried. A rifle was over his shoulder.

"Whaw who?" Lehman exclaimed, with mischieflike innocence.

"The Arabs who have dragged my friend Colonel Washington from his bed."

"Down yonder." Quantrell waved his hand toward the lower town.

"I'll settle with them," hallooed the rider, "whawever they aw. I'll die fo' my friend, sah."

As he pricked his horse on, Hazlett raised his pistol.

"I'll drop him in the road," said Hazlett; "it's against orders for citizens to carry arms, and that man's a trained soldier. Look at his square, straight shoulders."

Quantrell struck the pistol down with his hand.

"Don't kill that man for risking his life for his friend," he entreated. "Every life you take will be reckoned against you. Kill me, if you want a life!"

While Hazlett stared muddily at Quantrell, as if going to cut him to pieces, a voice was heard calling:

"Come on! come on, heah!"

They saw the Negro Ashby, who had climbed the hills from the river, and all hastened toward him.

"De armory's mos' tuk," he said. "Dey got Thompson off'n de bridge. Dar's no way to git to Cap'n Brown now but by de big gate, an' solgers is stoppin' up boff de bridges. Cap'n Brown says come quick and bring Cap'n Kagi's comman' to him."

"Kagi's killed, Ashby," Quantrell spoke; "he and all his men but one — Copeland, the mulatto. What will happen to him the angels fear to know!"

"O my God!" the Negro sighed, in agony of fear and sorrow.

There trotted in their midst the pointer-dog Albion, insinuating and mysterious as ever. His muzzle was as straight out as his tail; his leg pawed with nothing, kittenlike; his fine white spots in the brown neck seemed like flies in stale liver at butchers' stalls; the outcast life of a single forenoon had gone thus far toward demoralizing animals and men.

Albion rather fawned upon all the party, and showed a suspicious recognition of their friendship, which may have led Lehman to say:

"Albert, I shall go by the upper yard. 'Twon't do for both of us to be took. You go by the town and take these two men along. One of us, I calkelate, if not both, will get to Captain Brown that way."

The two men clasped each other's hands.

"Fight, Will, and never be taken!" Hazlett said.

"I'll do my best, Albert. If the worst comes, we've got friends across the river — and friends up yonder, too!"

He looked to heaven, and a tear filled his bright eye.

"Forward now, both of you!" Hazlett exclaimed, as Lehman disappeared down the raveling face of the heights, and he drove Ashby and Quantrell down the road before him, his rifle and eye equally sentient and ready.

"Ashby," whispered Quantrell, "by hurrying, you may cross the Potomac Bridge before the troops in Maryland seize it. Remember my directions! Go to Bosler's, in Catoctin Valley. Here is all my money. Let Luther go and buy you, and hasten to me."

"Mosster," said the Negro, taking the gold pieces with fear, "what makes you trust me?"

"The fear of God!" said Quantrell. "Something in this world is wrong, and I want to lend to the Lord."

"God bless you, mosster!" said the Negro, huskily; "I'll try to git away, faw yo' sake!"

No sympathetic light was in the man Hazlett's eyes, and he watched them both with a merciless energy, the greater because he was now wholly self-dependent.

Quantrell remembered the acts of rowdyism he had assisted in toward unarmed and helpless foreigners, and wondered if it was in the remembrance of mercy to save his life. He remembered the contemptuous idea he had entertained of the courage of "Yankees," whom he had nearly included among the "foreigners," and asked himself if he dared, even with the Negro Ashby's neutrality, or possible help, to fall upon this hard, self-reliant, unadorned fellow in the rear, and contend with him to the death.

He turned twice, with this thought in his mind, and, steady as a common, regular soldier of the line, Hazlett was looking at him with his eyes, and, Lloyd thought, with his wrists too, so supple were those wrists with weapons and sensibility.

"He is a Western man," mused our hero; "all of them are Western men. What is this West I have heard so little of in my geography? When did it arise? And is it all for abolition?"

They now had entered the short, closely settled, down-hill portion of the street, where shops, sign-posts, small bay-windows, lower areas and ladders into back yards, upper verandas, mechanics' stalls, flights of stairs toward precipices, overhanging dormers, flaunting clothes on clothes-lines, and all the accompaniments of a disturbed or suddenly deserted town, closed around them tattered and grimy in the narrow throat of Harper's Ferry.

Guns and pistols and old blunderbusses began to rattle again in the hollow depths of the place, and the rain drizzled from the spotted sky above. At the foot of the street they saw the dog Albion, which had rushed on before, barking at a hog that was too familiar with the dead body of Newby, lying there.

No forms were to be seen in the street, but the heads of some men appeared, beneath the stoops or basements of porches, all turned down toward the dead Negro and the street which crossed that one Quantrell was descending. The reason for this was plain when, in a moment, two men, like Brown's followers, stepped out from the arsenal side there and fired up the street.

The men down in the intrenched and recessed basements of the shops returned the fire in another instant.

"This way!" Hazlett called, hoarsely, pointing up the hill to the right.

A scrap of street found lodgment in there, and, going the same way as the High Street, soon left it far below.

In the intensity of the moment Quantrell saw all things in the view — the chimneys, the chickens picking garbage in the street, carts uptilted at the curbs, plastered walls, and stone and brick escarpments on the roofs, uneven pavements of blue limestone, wild children yet without breakfast screaming or sleeping up the tenement halls and alleys; and, finally, the Catholic church at the cornice and ridge of everything, holding its pale golden cross to the moody heavens, and by its side the bell, suspended in a derrick of timber, seemed to be taking a second nap after having called in vain for others to arise.

Again the Shenandoah was seen beyond the mills and islands, cowering as it ran beneath the great gnarled mountain. Again, the mighty, scarred form of Maryland Heights reared back like a beheaded buffalo. The blended rivers, breaking in ripples over gridirons of rock, went down the mountain vistas like fugitive hosts of dead-faced people, flying from the wrath of Nature; or the volcano's lava-channel in the sheen of the moon.

But in this general awe there was indifference too — the indifference of the great to the little, of the torpid to the quick; the indifference of the basking crocodile to the bees upon his jaws; the inconsiderateness of mountains, after their convulsion, to the writhing of the birds that serpents in their bowels charm; the languor of old geology in its nap of cycles to the newsboy's darling revolution of some few people slain in riots.

John Brown had made no impression upon the trance of Nature. The hollow ear of heaven bending overhead considered him not — he, nor the perishing insects he had disciplined for another skirmish in the brief antiquity of freedom.

"Ashby, I see the men in Maryland yonder. You have time to cross the bridge — just time, not a moment to spare!"

"Come on, then, and go before!" cried Hazlett, descending the ragged natural steps from the church to the street.

As they crept down these steps, shot rattled in the High Street below, and Quantrell and Ashby hesitated.

"I'll take a shot," spoke Hazlett, with a deadly zest for combat in his heavy eyes; and, stepping down, he raised his gun and fired up the street.

"I left my mark that time," Hazlett said, surveying his work and opening his rifle-breech. "Now for the next slave-catcher!"

He had barely spoken when a ball or wad, or other instrument of percussion, struck his cartridge-box, and it began to explode, like Chinese fire-crackers. One by one the deadly projectiles broke forth, each with its cylinder of lead, and Hazlett sought in vain to throw it away from him, but the belt would not come loose. He danced in a frenzy of endeavor and apprehension, balls tearing his clothes, others whizzing near Quantrell's head; and the sight was so ludicrous that, as Lloyd threw himself down, he began to laugh till the tears came to his eyes.

"He's all fired out, I reckon, now," Ashby exclaimed, as the explosions ceased. "What mus' I do?"

"Run for the bridge! Tell him to run with you! Remember Crampton's Gap, the Catoctin Valley, and Jake Bosler's farm."

"I'm goin'," said the Negro. "Come, Mr. Hazlett, fo' yo' life!"

As Hazlett turned to look at Quantrell, the latter had a rock in his hand.

"I'll kill you if you come here!" Quantrell cried; "your carbine is empty and your cartridges are all gone. Keep off!"

Hazlett slipped across the street into the lane by the river. In a moment Lloyd saw him appear in the space before the armory-gate, where he hesitated, as if thinking to turn in. The Negro Ashby dashed past him and ran toward the bridge.

Being fired upon from the houses and hill-tops, Hazlett affected to be aiming his empty piece, and, stooping down and backing off, he finally disappeared behind the corner at the arsenal, and next was seen upon the bridge, running after Ashby at the top of his speed.

Both men ran, and Lloyd followed them with intense interest. He felt that the colored man's life had already been interposed for his, and might be his hostage with Destiny again.

The soldiers on the Maryland shore were very near the bridge, also,

     Katy of Catoctin

and now began to run toward it, firing their pieces.

It was a race for life with Hazlett and his dusky associate.

In another moment Quantrell saw both these men emerge from the distant end of the bridge, and steal along the base of the heights toward Pleasant Valley and the roofs of Sandy Hook.

"I've made a banker of a Negro, who has every inducement to run away," Lloyd Quantrell said, "and yet, I don't believe he will; for, queerly enough, I never heard of a Negro committing a breach of trust."

He peeped around the abutments of rock and houses at the foot of the stone steps.

Some townspeople were huddled beneath a low porch, looking down intently at an object they also sought to raise.

"That may be Hazlett's victim," Quantrell thought. "I'll see."

He came unarmed with raised hands among them, merely saying "Prisoner," and looked down at the form of an athletic, bleeding man on the stones of an old stoop or arcade.

Quantrell recognized the horseman who had been galloping to save his friend; he was shot in the shoulder and neck, and was already dead, yet warm.

"Lay him back, that-a-way, like a ossifer!" said one of the men, rifle in hand, seeking to see both the street-corner and the dead man. "He's a West-P'inter, an' they likes to die with their shoulders stiff."

Stretched out upon the stones of Harper's Ferry, the first graduate of the United States Military Academy, to perish in the conflict of slavery, lay trembling in the rich red chevron of his heart's blood.

"George Turner loved Lew Washington," spoke another man; "they was chums. They liked their juleps jess the same; one would mix for t'other, and t'other preferred his'n to he own. It's true he died tryin' to shoot, for he was, as you may say, a eddicated ossifer."

"Take him off the street, friends," Quantrell said. "Lay him in the house. Greater love hath no man than this — that he lay down his life for his friend!"

Chapter XX
GAULT HOUSE

"THREE citizens already killed; that is, two citizens and a nigger," Quantrell heard remarked, as he slipped across the Shenandoah Street to the railroad there, and, passing behind the arsenal, gained the exposed saloon on the railroad-track, where he had fought the Logans only sixteen hours before.

He now saw a sign over the door of this single-story frame saloon, "Gault House."

It was a cheap, perishable building, without social position or appearance, and yet, in the inconsistency of time, it remains down to the author's day, one of the three unimpaired monuments of ruined Harper's Ferry: these three monuments are the Catholic church on the hill, John Brown's Engine-House or "Fort" in the desolate armory-yard, and this saloon by the Shenandoah bridge — representatives of the three active principles of our century: Tradition, Revolution, and Alcohol — other words for Faith, Hope, and the Poor-House, or Charity; and now, as of old, the greatest of these is Alcohol or Charity.

"Let me in!" cried Quantrell, and, the door opening, he leaped in, and there was instant darkness.

"Who are you?" said a familiar voice.

"Why, Mr. Beall, I'm Mr. Quantrell, who made your acquaintance last night"; and there arose upon the dark the fine, natural tones of our hero, singing:

"Glenorchy's proud mountains, Coalchuirn and her towers,
  Glenstrae, and Glenlyon, no longer are ours:
  We're landless, landless, landless, Grigalach!"

The song brought admiration and low inquiries, "Who is he?" and John Beall vouched for Quantrell's courage; and when Lloyd told that he had been a prisoner, and what he had seen of Kagi's band falling, and of Turner's death but an instant before, all breathlessly listened, and then the back door was thrown open.

It was seen that a narrow and railed veranda ran along the back of the saloon, overhanging the foaming Shenandoah far below, and this veranda almost gave access to the Shenandoah bridge, whose rock abutment adjoined the saloon.

"Mr. Quantrell," spoke Beall, his face serious to the verge of gloom, "a few of us are holding this place with the greatest caution, because we believe it to be the key of the situation. We keep the front closed and have fired no shot from here because the enemy with his rifles, from the engine-house, can riddle this thin building. We expect to kill him — all that there is left of him — when he retreats across the Potomac bridge. He must pass right in front of this house to get to the bridge, and we want to kill every man he has!"

The suppressed energy of the speaker called Quantrell's attention.

"Why, John," he said, "you would pity the poor devils if you had seen them, as I have, falling in the river, lying in the streets, hungry, absurd, misled, weeded out."

"No," replied Beall, trembling, "I want to kill every man of them! We're lying low here, to shoot them down at their last chance! We let one scoundrel pass just now, lest we might draw every rifle in that engine-house upon us and spoil our full revenge, sir."

"Indeed, you're a Scotchman, John, and Highlander too, I reckon. But, of course, I'm with you. Where's William Thompson, the raider who guarded the Shenandoah bridge?"

"Taken. He's over in the hotel."

Beall's eyes smoldered, and his eyebrows and mouth were both drawn straight and hard.

"How did you capture the bridge?"

"From this saloon. We crept upon the guard, an unsuspecting fellow, and getting him fast, sent a detachment across the bridge to kill any who might escape from the Rifle-works."

Not a smile nor gratulation was in all this; a devout Indian, reciting the fate of the enemies he had doomed for the manes of his father, might have been less intense.

"I saw them die, John. It was a terrible scene."

"I should like to have witnessed it. But the leader is still yonder!"

He pointed to the engine-house, with a face drawn so hard together from the jaw to the skull, that every feature seemed to be a plain line. Reflective hate lay coldly there, incapable now of other joy.

Quantrell looked at the other occupants of the sinister place — at the saloon-keeper, with long, fox-red beard, who was continually stroking it, and with eyes wide apart.

"Forty drops," said the saloon-keeper. "Come up!"

He went behind the dusky bar and set the bottle out, and peeped through a hole in the shutter at the engine-house — laying hand, meanwhile, upon the long revolver there, which had been in Lloyd's custody the night before.

"They're all caged in the engine-house," the saloon-man said. "Hello! yonder's one coming down the yard."

They peeped successively at the hole, and, when Lloyd's turn came, he saw in the vista of the armory-yard two men, one with a gun, keeping the other man between him and a party of armed men, who now and then fired a shot, but, seeking not to injure the hostage, they did no execution.

"That's Lehman!" Quantrell exclaimed. "And, upon my word, the fellow running is Andrew Atzerodt!"

"Here, gentlemen," the warm-bearded saloon-keeper spoke; "we'll close the back door, and that will darken the room, so we may see, and be unseen, out of the glass door, by keeping back from the light a little."

He raised the blind, and they could all see.

The landlord brought out his pistol, which was nearly as long as one of the outlaws' rifles, and it had a skeleton breech which made it a veritable gun to rest against his shoulder. He rolled the great steel chamber, charged with six slugs like Minié balls, between his thumb and finger, to see if it was true and well oiled.

"I hope there's a dead man in every cartridge," he said. "That's my pious design."

They all gazed at the boy Lehman, skirmishing with twenty enemies. The balls from the hills and town would tear up the ground around him and cut twigs from the elm and maple trees, and Atzerodt would fall upon the ground till Lehman's rifle covered him, and then he would start up with wide, imploring arms, only to be paralyzed by the open muzzle of the rifle.

"That boy's dead game," the saloon-keeper said; "but our friends are shooting very poor."

"Lehman don't want to kill anybody," Quantrell said. "He can drop a man with every ball, if he wants to."

They now observed one man at the angle of a building behind Lehman, deliberately aiming at his back. The pistol exploded, but only Atzerodt fell down, and lay like one stone-dead.

Lehman turned upon the man, whose gun was now uncharged, and raised his rifle at him.

The man fell on his knees.

"Now he'll blow his head right off!" said the saloon-keeper.

As they looked, in the excitement of almost mortal suspense, they saw Lehman knock the pistol out of the man's hand and disappear behind the same angle of wall from which his assassination had been sought.

Atzerodt jumped up and ran at the top of his speed.

The man whose life had been spared, rose to his feet and quickly reloaded, rammed and capped his pistol, and started in the direction Lehman had gone.

"Forty drops," said the saloon-keeper. "Come up!"

Every man around the bar had a weapon of some kind, and they drank with the zest of hunters. Beall alone was abstinent and brooding.

"Will this insult upon Virginia ever be wiped off?" he said to Quantrell.

"We entertained your invaders in Maryland," Quantrell replied; "that must be atoned for."

All looked carefully at their weapons, like fishermen inspecting their tackle. The splutter of gunnery in the street was continued.

"Gentlemen," spoke Quantrell, "I want to see the fate of little Lehman, and, by your leave, I'll make a dash for the railway-station."

Before there could be objection, he had opened the door and closed it behind him.

A very few steps brought him upon the railroad bridge, and he looked in wonder at the changed scene around him.

Men were everywhere — upon both bridges, on the strands of the rivers, upon both shores opposite, and crowding the railway-station and fringing the hills; and from every safe place guns were shooting at the little engine-house in the armory-yard, which began to show the marks of a bombardment: its doors were ripped and splintered, the trees around it clipped of twigs and stems; and yet it was languidly returning fire from the fresh port-holes and from the partly open doors, where now a man could be seen crouching and another standing.

As Quantrell came to the station and hotel, he heard a voice cry:

"O Heywood, speak! What will yo' po' wife say to me. — He's gone. He's dead! Now get me a gun. I want a robber's life!"

Lloyd saw the Negro porter lying still, and felt his body, which was already partly cold.

"I know whaw I can find a pistol," spoke the mayor of the town and station agent; "I'll git it and return."

He dashed toward the Gault House saloon, and Quantrell swung down the railway trestle-work to the Potomac strand and crept along that churning river, stooping low. There were men lying flat upon their breasts from point to point, seeking to send a shot into the engine-house, and nearly every trestle-post had thus its revenger.

Running fast, the Baltimorean soon had passed most of the armory buildings, but was arrested by the whizzing of a ball within an inch, as it seemed, of his head.

He glanced across the river, in Maryland, and saw a puff of smoke rising from a place along the lower mountainside; beneath the smoke was a human form. Quantrell's eyes were keen, and he made out the person to be his late assailant, little Captain Cook.

If Cook it was, he had a fall in greatness, for shots from Harper's Ferry hills passed over Quantrell's head, and the person upon the mountain was seen in another instant to be rolling down the slope and then to lie quite still.

Lloyd's attention was immediately drawn to a man running from the upper end of the armory-yard right into the brawling and, at places, dangerous Potomac.

From pool to pool, and eddy to eddy, and from rock to rock, this man continued on, rapid, lithe, active, and manifestly meaning to ford the entire river or to perish in it.

The reason was soon manifest: a large body of armed men, in compact order, came across the armory mill-race and fired a volley at the fugitive.

He fell and lost his gun, but in a moment was up again, and he crawled upon a dry rock far out in the river and feebly held up his hands.

Quantrell could see, even then, a cheerful look, like a smile, upon his almost childlike face.

"Lehman!" was Lloyd's inward recognition; "I'm glad he surrenders — his eyes are so beautiful!"

The firing ceased; but one man was also rapidly wading the river toward Lehman, and something about him seemed familiar.

"Why, that's the man," Quantrell inwardly remarked, "whose life Will Lehman saved but a minute ago. It's natural that he should want to save the poor lad's life."

The man went on and did not hesitate, for Lehman continued to show the genial countenance of one submitting to capture, and to spread his hands apart in the hallowed way our common Savior died.

The man came right upon him but did not grapple with him.

Lehman seemed to speak to him, pleasantly, and Lloyd thought he could see the boy's large eyes bright with pain and gratitude.

The man suddenly pulled a pistol from his pocket, pointed it at Lehman's face, so close that he nearly touched it, and fired.

A cry of mixed exultation and horror burst from the soldiers on the shore.

Lehman fell upon the rock helpless, with a great hole in his face.

The man returned the pistol to his garments and drew a knife, and began to cut the skirts and pockets from Lehman's clothes.

By the stillness of the form upon the rock, Lloyd knew that Death, the invisible vulture, had as instantly alighted there.

The man now waded ashore, bearing papers and other things taken from the dead man.

"Fall in, Martinsburgers!" the command rang out; "we'll carry the engine-house next!"

They marched down the armory-yard, and Quantrell was left alone.

He also waded into the water and made his way toward Lehman.

The boy lay silent upon the stone, the roaring rapids being his lullaby. His head had fallen backward, and his hairs were toyed with by the cool waters.

"Will, look up! I'm your friend!"

The late tired legs of Lehman, which had walked all night and day upon a willful yet immortal errand — crossing the river to and from the farm three times in one night and morning — clasped the stone in the rigid manner of one who meant to hold fast and to bear testimony.

How solemn, how awful, seemed the sighing waters to Quantrell, waist-deep in them! No noise besides filled the air. It was as lonely as being drowned, to stand alone beside this uncomplaining man.

Quantrell bent over the rock, but only once.

What he saw there was too horrible for him ever to repeat.

Steadying himself upon the stone, Lloyd saved himself from swooning, though sick to the temples. He dipped his head into the waters, but, when he lifted it, some of Lehman's blood in the water fell down upon his hands.

"He asked me to sing, 'somewheres down among the bushes and rocks,' the words of 'Sweet Home.' I'll do it among the waters and rocks, for it will be his only Christian burial."

Quantrell raised his voice and sang:

"Home, home, sweet home!
  There's no place like home —
  There's no place like home."

"Poor lad!" he finished, "there's no home for him now but where he 'calculated' it was ever sunny."

With a tear in his eye, Quantrell turned to the shore, and when he gained it he looked back once, and Lehman lay there still, like one of nature's bowlders rolled in the deluges of time.

As Lloyd picked his way down the armory-yard he marked the powerful water accompanying the long line of shops, conducted behind them in a stone canal and, after driving wheels and cogs, grindstones and automatic turning-lathes, drills and trip-hammers, the mill-water then gushed beneath the ground, in arched places, to be used in a second line of shops, and then to fall back into the Potomac.

Here a gun-stock had fallen to perfection every eight seconds; every day of earnest labor manufactured sixty muskets; the doing of death was the soulful motive of the town; but today it was all distraught that barely two of its white men had been killed with arms in their hands.

As he drew near the little engine-house, our hero dropped behind the office-buildings just west of it; a lull had taken place in the firing, for the grimy operatives from the railway-shops of Martinsburg were to charge John Brown's little fort.

Quantrell saw them deployed to assail the nearest, or watch-house end, on three sides at once.

A man was slinking out of the column, and Quantrell recognized him.

"Contemptible assassin! Give me your gun."

It was the man whose life Lehman had saved, and who had returned the gift with death.

There was something queer about the gun he had wrested from the man; it came open at the breech, as if there was a hinge in the barrel.

"Pooh!" exclaimed Quantrell, "this is one of Hall's Harper Ferry rifles, a Yankee invention, thrown out by the regular army board."

He threw the gun down, yet lived to see the day when the *"breech* was more honored than the observance" of military boards; for by a similar needle-gun the winding-sheet of Napoleonism came to be sewed by Germany. America fought her great civil war loading muskets at the muzzle, when she could have been foremost of the nations with a Yankee breech-loader, thrown out of Harper's Ferry by military bigotry, twenty years before.

In the quick revulsions of a day of action and hunger, intemperance and fear, mystery and passion, Lloyd Quantrell had ripped a plank out of the porch of a small building labeled "Superintendent's Office," and crying, "Come on!" he dashed among the foremost of the militia, from whom a mighty yell went up.

To the yell the response was the throwing open of the engine-house doors.

Half a dozen boyish men, with John Brown at their head, stepped upon the sward and poured a little volley into these hundred herculean militia.

Among the defenders Quantrell could see the ashen face of Watson Brown, rallying up from death and standing by his rifle. His father waved the sword of King Frederick and called "Fire!"

It was but a minute that this startling picture of a handful of

                    Katy of Catoctin

farm-boys, directed by an old man's face in which was the very delight of battle, lasted upon the afternoon. The militia, after a broken fire, dispersed with groans and curses; and some, in the frenzy of fear, leaped the high brick wall behind the block-house, astonished at their own feat of strength.

As the defenders retired, they dragged one boyish form back with them, which had settled down upon its hands, as if the ligaments of the tough limbs had all at once given way: the face, of unspeakable emotion, was that of young Oliver Brown; he looked like one caught by some reptile and bitten in twain, while he was yet rejoicing.

Quantrell pushed in the round-topped windows of the watch-room end of the engine-house, with the plank he carried, and forced the plank over the window-frames.

"Break out!" he shouted, raising himself by the wrists to the window-level; "they won't fire on you!"

He also leaped over the tall brick wall and fell into the River Street, exhausted.

In a few minutes the released prisoners from the watch-house also came up.

"Where's Washington, and Alstadt, and — ole Ball?" Quantrell asked.

"Why, ole Isaac Smith — he picked all them big fish out half a hour ago and tuk 'em in the engine-house part. 'I want you,' he says. 'And you! And you!' He's got nine or ten, I reckon, in thar, yit."

Lloyd returned to the Gault House saloon around the arsenal wall, and at the alley there lay the dead Newby still, staring at eternity.

A strange quiet had fallen upon the town since the determined action of the bandits and their easy defeat of the burly Martinsburgers — several of whom had received wounds; a quiet partly induced, too, by the cold-blooded slaying of Lehman, which few had seen without compassion and awe. There were none in the streets but the dead, and all private attempts to storm John Brown's fort ceased from that time forward.

Entering the Gault House, a man escaping from the interior fell in the dark into Quantrell's arms.

"Let me go!" the stranger cried; "I've lost my poor black ward. I'll have a life for Heywood!"

The door closed upon him, and Quantrell breathlessly asked for liquor.

"Forty drops!" said the saloon-keeper. "Come up!"

It was now that Beall, the young Virginian, shook off a portion of his hard demeanor and commenced to ask Lloyd the particulars about Smith's or Brown's band: it seemed to have a charmed interest for him, less to appease his indignation than to awaken a latent thirst he betrayed for individual feats of danger, and to concentrate his mind upon the chief enemies of his State and neighborhood.

"Tell me, sir, as nearly as you can, who are the leaders in this foray. We must be sure to kill the right ones; the residue will do for the gallows."

"Next to Isaac Smith," replied Lloyd, "who calls himself Brown, was Kagi, who lies dead up the Shenandoah; but the best soldier of them all is the third in command, Captain Stevens."

"We'll mark him!" muttered Beall. "What is that coming yonder?"

They looked through the window, keeping well back in the dark, and saw four men coming out of the armory-gate; two of these were unarmed, and one hoisted a white cloth attached to a stick.

"That's Kitz," said one of the voices in the dark; "t'other's a citizen. It seems to be a flag of truce."

"I know the men behind," Quantrell added — "the two with rifles; the boyish figure is Ned Coppock. He's a handsome fellow, and good-natured. The stoutish, manly fellow is Aaron Stevens. He's a lion."

"Get your gun," Beall said. "The time's come for it!"

"All steady, now," remarked the saloon-keeper; "no one must speak. I want to let him have every ball."

He raised the skeleton-breeched revolver to his shoulder and took aim, the rest standing silently in the rear.

Right on walked the four men, the two hostages covering the two raiders in front, until they came abreast of the hotel beneath the station, when, at a word from Stevens, the hostages stepped upon the flanks, thus opening to the saloon-keeper's revolver the bodies of Stevens and Coppock.

Quantrell, in spite of his late vow of "Death to abolitionists!" felt that he would give the world to cry out and plead: "It is a flag of mercy. Do not kill them!"

Proud of bearing, full-bearded, his brown eyes keen but independent, his military shoulders carried erect without effort or stiffness, his dark-brown hair adding to the warmth of his bright skin and red, youthful lips, Stevens had his gun across his shoulder; he kept his eyes upon the bridge before him, and walked on as confidently as a regular soldier upon parade.

None in the saloon looked at any other person; this man was so strong, superior, and chieftainlike that the light of human eyes shone only upon him and seemed to glaze him into a Rembrandtish brightness and halo, and they could almost hear his broad lungs breathe.

The great pistol went off — once, twice, thrice! Quantrell shut his eyes.

Once, twice, thrice again, it spoke metallic decision, and with that regularity and interval of sound which showed the perfect nerve, deliberation, and aim of the firer.

The saloon was full of sulphur-smell, but of little smoke.

Quantrell opened his eyes.

There lay on the ground, a few paces from the door, an effigy or broken stalk of man, nothing of it moving but the broad chest, and that with a snarling, convulsive sound and struggle.

The hostages were not to be seen. Coppock was entering the armory-gate, and there a little band of the raiders poured out from the engine-house, and he and they fired with spirit, but only to draw upon themselves a roaring volley from near the bridge, like that of soldiery.

"Forty drops." said the saloon-keeper, wiping his piece with a yellow silk handkerchief. "Come up."

Amid exclamations of "Glorious!" "Grand!" and the sucking of liquids and the shaking of hands, Lloyd Quantrell opened the door and, despite the glancing of bullets over railroad-iron and street-gravel, he fell upon his hands and knees and crawled toward the prostrate form.

He saw in an instant what errand Stevens had walked forth upon. The Potomac bridge was full of soldiery just come from Maryland, and to these Stevens must have been sent with a proposition of surrender or truce, when the unrespecting assassin had emptied a revolver into his living frame.

"Now some other citizen will surely be killed," Quantrell reflected, "not only to avenge this dead comrade, but the raiders will kill to protect themselves from massacre. I reckon their blood is up."

A sound came from the large form stretched upon the ground.

"If you are a man and I am but a dog, come to me!"

There was in this sound something of involuntary woe, like mortal agony soliloquizing to its pain, or the "loud voice about the ninth hour" on Calvary, saying, *"Eli, Eli, lama sabachthani?"*

A woman from the hotel ran toward the prostrate man, careless of danger in the strong impulse of her pity, and Quantrell also rose to his feet.

They lifted the body up; it was limp, and had nothing whole to stand upon — shot in the members, the trunk, the head, and having received, like a target from a practiced hand, every ball where the marksman thought fit to deliver it.

"Save him!" screamed the woman; "he belongs to some home, maybe."

Quantrell raised the body to his shoulder and slung it there like a dead deer; and stalked away with it to the hotel where he had slept.

"Kill him! Drown him! Tear him to pieces!" yelled many voices, in the safe hiding of the station.

"Curs!" exclaimed Quantrell, facing them once, "go yonder and kill at the engine-house, where you are fifty to one!"

As he entered a room in the hotel where he was directed, another man came forward and said, cheerfully:

"Aaron, do you know me?"

"Good-bye, Thompson!" sighed the bleeding form.

"You are not going to die, Aaron?"

"Not me," Stevens muttered. "Oh, no! Good-bye to *you!*"

"Who tells you that, Aaron?"

"Spirits," whispered the man, swooning away.

The room filled up with drunken, excited, or cowardly individuals, uttering imprecations, insulting William Thompson, the prisoner, and threatening to throw the body of Stevens out of the window. Quantrell picked out a little guard of weak but better-meaning men, and by a doctor's aid cleared the room.

"Thompson," he, said, after this exertion, "what labor you have taken to make all this misery!"

"I didn't come, Mr. Quantrell, on any picnic. You and me will only die once. I'm just as ready to die for man now as I was yesterday."

"Don't you want to live?"

"Of course. Life never was as sweet to me as it is at this minute, because it's so uncertain now. But I brought my life along and put it in the cause; and, if it's wanted, I'll give it to Liberty."

"Nonsense!" exclaimed Quantrell. "Liberty to slaves, not one of whom has had the courage to fight for his own salvation!"

"No nonsense, Mr. Quantrell, to the many millions more still to be born, and to look back, perhaps, to this day's sorrows for their deliverance. Women don't fight for their freedom, neither, but still have men gone to women's rescue. It was because slaves didn't fight that we came to fight for them."

The door here burst open, and a young man entered with a gun. He looked around an instant, and approached the helpless man upon the bed.

"Villain!" he suddenly cried, "you've killed my kinsman, George Turner, and I'm going to kill you this minute!"

Before any person could interfere, he had pulled the trigger, with the muzzle of the gun at Stevens's throat.

The lock fell, but the cap did not explode.

Stevens had been stripped naked, for the doctor to dress his wounds. As Quantrell sprang forward, he observed the fine hazel eyes of Stevens to be wide open, and gazing with a most undaunted calmness into the assassin's face.

The other man blanched before that unshaken fortitude and almost eloquent contempt. Well he might have been alarmed, also, at the wounded man's athletic breast, solid arms, great shoulders, and Apollo-like strength in everything; his white body flawless except where torn by lead, and his soul reinhabiting that mangled frame, like an eagle returned suddenly to its nest.

"If I had a gun and could get off this bed," said Stevens, without an inflection, "you, and ten more like you, would jump out of that window!"

Quantrell sprang upon the intruder, who had already retreated before Stevens's steady gaze, and Lloyd put the door behind him.

"You're a great man, Stevens," Lloyd Quantrell said, looking down at the hero in admiration. "What made you wake just at that minute of danger?"

"My guardian angel," Stevens sighed, and closed his eyes in slumber again.

Quantrell locked the door and stretched himself upon the floor within it, and also slumbered a little while. He went to sleep, and he awoke to the continual spluttering explosions of fire-arms.

As he was relieved by other persons of the watch in this prisoner's place, he stepped out to the railroad platform in time to see an old, stout man peep around the water-tank, desperate to have a shot at the people in the engine-house.

The moment this man peeped, there came a sound of wood ripped by a ball.

"Tey've hit te tank!" exclaimed the voice of Atzerodt, at Quantrell's elbow.

"They've hit the man, too," Quantrell said; for he had seen the large form of the old gentleman pitch forward and fall upon his head, and there lie motionless upon the planks of the platform he so long commanded.

People dragged the old gentleman back by the legs and laid him beside his Negro servant, stone-dead; black and white man, loving each other in life, in death had not long been divided.

"The Mayor of Harper's Ferry," thought Quantrell, "pays for the violation of the flag of armistice. I believe Ned Coppock fired that shot for Captain Stevens."

It was now the middle of the afternoon, and whisky had done its work on many an empty stomach, while combat had made courageous men fierce, and cowardly men bloodthirsty.

A cry arose. "Kill that prisoner! Fountain Beckham's dead!"

If the utterer of this instigation had desired, in the same breath, to call it back, he would have been too late.

The dead mayor had been of a large family connection, and his cousins and nephews heard the cry of "revenge," in Virginia natures, where Scotch and pioneer traits and traditions lay ever near the passion for private feud and retaliation.

The hotel quickly filled up with young men who had not dared to expose their bodies, like the late rash and loving old man. The woman who had befriended Stevens threw herself before young William Thompson's body, and begged his life in vain. He was pushed and dragged toward the railway platform, and, for every hand which impelled him onward, another held a pistol to kill him. Voices derided him; and other voices raised the yell of battle, thousands of times repeated in after-years among these "blue-ridged hills."

"To the bridge! To the bridge with him! Kill him! Kill him!"

Lloyd Quantrell saw his pointer-dog leap joyfully among the murderers and bark with all his venom, and show his yellow eyes, and shake the flies from his blood-clotted ear. Lloyd saw the dirty visage of Atzerodt, crazed with the liquor his blood-money had procured, waving his fluttering hands and full of white-livered zeal, and heard him shout:

"Hang him! Hang him to te bridge!"

The crowd swayed and reeled forward, and the woman threw herself in its path only to be pulled aside. Toward the Potomac bridge it went, and skirmisher's before it, and stragglers behind, were seen to be picking the locks of rusty fire-arms, and trying flints and percussion-caps, in all the ardor for human prey. The black birds at the chimneys of Loudoun Mountain circled there, indifferent to the carcass that was being prepared for them by mankind.

Lloyd Quantrell determined to labor for that man's life. He caught a glimpse of Mr. Beall at the outskirts of the mob and called to him:

"Let us save his life for the law — and for shame!"

Beall shook his head, and muttered, with skull and chin pinched together at the thin lips:

"No, sir. He has dishonored Virginia!"

There were, however, some plaintive old Germanic faces there, ready to kindle to compassion when Quantrell raised the cry:

"Give him a chance! Don't murder him, gentlemen! Don't let us disgrace Virginia!"

"To hell mit him!" cried Atzerodt. "He kilt a good man."

"Revenge for Fountain Beckham!"

"Revenge for George Turner!"

"Revenge for Tom Boerly!"

These victims' names arose like tongues of fire amid the tiny streams of pity.

"Give him a trial!" shouted Quantrell. "You do not know who he is. His blood may splash you all."

"Oh, yes, take time!" said a tall old man. "The law will stretch his neck."

"Don't kill him here," cried the woman's voice; "the court will try him soon enough!"

William Thompson had not spoken; his face was pale but with manly submission in it, and yet the love of life rose to his temples in a great fervor, once or twice.

A man pointed a gun at him; Thompson put his arms around the man and held him close to his breast and spoke across his shoulder in the partial silence of the hard-breathing murderers:

"Let me say a word. Then kill me if you ought to! My blood will never put out the fire started here today. A thousand lives like mine won't do it — no, not a hundred thousand! Murder won't count in favor of sin. Let all your slaves go free! That's all we ask. It's cheaper in the end!"

"Down with the abolitionist!"

"Kill the blasphemer!"

"Shoot the vile fanatic!"

They tried to tear him fast from any other man. Severed from one, he grappled to himself another, in the piteous search for some one feeling breast. He spoke no more, except to cling to living frames and cover his own with living hearts. The contest drew tears from some, and others closed their eyes.

Finally, several men seized him by pinioning his arms, And then with their united power hurled him from them.

Half a dozen guns went off. He tottered and fell upon one hand. More guns were discharged.

"Father!" he cried, looking toward the engine-house, which was concealed by the hotel-building.

They fired upon him again and again.

His eyes, in pain of death, without a friend to call to, fell upon Lloyd Quantrell:

"Mr. Quantrell! Brother!"

"Drop! drop into the river!" Quantrell shouted, and pointed to the cool water below.

The dying man tottered to the edge of the planks and slipped through the hollow places there and fell into the roaring Potomac current.

"I'll carry the white flag this time!" Quantrell said. "Nobody can save him but John Brown!"

He raised his hat upon a rod and walked straight into the armory-gate and disappeared in the engine-house.

William Thompson floated down the current a little way and lodged against some stones.

A discharge of fire-arms from the bridge stilled his hopes and pains forever.

All the rest of the afternoon his body was used for a target-match between the gunners, shooting from the bridge.

Chapter XXI
ABEL QUANTRELL

MONDAY morning, at Jake Bosler's farm, found corn-shucking and fruit-drying, pickling and stewing sweets, the deep occupation of the women, of whom there were three, since Hannah Ritner had come over from Smoketown, uninvited, at an early hour, driven by Job Snowberger, the Baptist monk, whose Kloster (convent) name was Father Philodulus.

Job had grown up in the nunnery at Snow Hill, just over in Pennsylvania, and was nearly the last of the Monks of Seventh Day. He worked in the fields with threefold energy of Sundays, but his Saturdays were deeply religious ruminations, varied by the singing of Beissel's Ephrata music, of which he was believed to be the last living renderer.

To look at, Philodulus was a long, thin man with little peeping eyes, and one side of his baggy face seemed cunning and blushing, and the other side mystic and austere. He called Hannah Ritner "Shweshter (sister) Marcella," and paid great deference to her, while that large, considerate lady called him, according to her passing vein, "Job," "Job Snow," and "Philodulus."

At the sound of "Job!" uttered with Hannah Ritner's full decision, the hermit celibate would start up like a soldier to his arms; at the practical address of "Job Snow," he would look wise and reproved; when Hannah called him "Bruder (brother) Philodulus," blushes came to his froggy, loose skin, and he seemed about to fall upon his knees.

Job, the monk, was now sorely tempted, for Nelly Harbaugh, with mischief hardly delicate, had planted herself on one side of him and had pushed him back against the wall, while Katy Bosler was on Job's other flank, and the kitchen dresser kept her from moving farther, and just in front of Philodulus was a wash-tub into which they all were peeling fruit, and across the wash-tub from Job, holding him fast, was Hannah Ritner with her great Jewish eyes.

"Bruder," exclaimed Nelly Harbaugh, summoning Job's attention by hitting him with her knee, and then leaning over and taking his thin, furzy beard in her hand, "would you take me into the Siebentager and let me be your own little nun?"

"Nay, *unfershamed,* barefaced! you would possess the whole kloster soon."

The mystic and austere side of Job's face was, nevertheless, trembling a little, and he leaned toward Katy Bosler's large, modest eyes, and then the cunning and blushing side grew all dimpled as he piped in his high, falsetto voice:

"Sister Kate, you would not ask me that?"

Katy, full of laughter, cried:

"Oh, you would not invite me! I'm too little."

"Unshuldich," breathed the old bachelor, "sweet innocent, I do."

"Job *Snow!*" Hannah Ritner spoke, with recalling common sense.

"There is a difference," the brother said, throwing away the apple and dropping the apple-peeling in the tub; "te invitation of Nelly is to mock me. *Unshicklich!*" (Nelly had taken his hand with well-feigned rapture.) "I turn to Katy for to git purity. Te world will take advantage of so much goodness, and in our quiet convent we live like Him of old — like Yasus."

"Philodulus," Hannah Ritner spoke in her low, great voice, "when our sex is old and poor, then invite them to your rest; but the world would misunderstand young converts, like these maidens, appearing at Snow Hill."

"Nay, Sister Marcella, te first of te Vorsteher Beissel's tisciples was two married women, and one of those, Maria Sower, was very beautiful. It was her beauty he resisted with all his prayers, but half his psalms her beauty was te music of."

"Sing to my eyes, Job!" Nelly Harbaugh entreated. — "Hannah, he daresn't look at me without blushing."

"Oh, sing to my love!" Katy involuntarily added, "and I will play, Job, on te accordion."

"That is gone, Kate," said Nelly Harbaugh; "you've given all your music away."

"Nay," Job Snowberger said, "I'll sing for Katy te mourning-dove piece py Friedsam, when his soul was at peace, and love plagued it no more."

"Philodulus," Hannah Ritner sighed, "love plagues to the last. Often, in my girlhood, have I seen the Dunker nuns, at Ephrata and Snow Hill, carrying a lamb to which they gave the name of 'Yasus,' and dandled it upon their knees — it was the substitute for Nature's human babe, and they professed to be in a mystical union with its divine namesake. But while the women at the nunnery played the mother with these substitutes till themselves grew old and withered, how many of the monks fell away from grace and married, long after domestic happiness had passed its day!"

"I am te last," said Job Snowberger, "and I will persewere."

"Pure, good man! Kiss him, Katy, and encourage him to persewere."

Nelly Harbaugh, speaking, grasped Job Snowberger's head in both her strong hands, and kissed him down upon Katy, who sat imprisoned there; and she, seeing no escape, and somewhat in the mischief of the moment, also gave the monk of fifty-five a little timid kiss.

He looked from one to the other in rapid changes of austerity and weakness.

"Unshicklich — improper one!" he spoke to Nelly Harbaugh; and then, turning to Katy, his face melted in all its harsher lines as he gave back her kiss and piped high, *"Unshuldich!"* — the innocent.

"Job!" spoke Hannah Ritner.

He looked at her, thus in Saint Anthony's temptation, and burst into tears.

Katy was frightened. Nelly was studying Philodulus, the monk, with joyful analysis.

"My children," Hannah Ritner said, looking with tender humor on the scene, "whichever way you go with Love, or go without him, he makes you cry. His pleasantest mood is spring, with little showers of tears. His summer zest is thunderstorm among these mountains. If Love deserts you, it is winter and frozen tears. But if he never comes at all, you cry, you know not why."

She looked at the poor man and gave him some cider to drink, fresh from the press.

"Brother Philodulus, swallow your tears, as they drop into the cider; for they will come up many times again, and, after all, the tears of love are sweet — even those we shed to reject love."

He sat down at her counsel, and behaved like a little boy, doing whatever was requested of him; and while they continued to peel apples, pears, and quinces, a sound came in at the window —

"Ah-coo-roo-coo-roo!"

"It is te doves," Katy said. "It's most time, I think, for tem to go South. Tey are waiting for te young ones to pe smart enough to fly. Tey puilt te nest last April. Come see it, Job."

Job Snowberger's hand Katy confidingly took in hers, and led him out to a low apple tree nearly touching the house.

Upon a crotch of this tree, lower than their heads, sat, in an humble nest of dry grasses, two brown young doves. Above them, on the same bough, sat, side by side, the parent birds, unfluttered by visitors, and in brown and chestnut plumage and slate-colored crowns, cooing together.

"Ah-coo-roo-coo-roo!"

The little family had no brilliant marks upon them except a patch of bare pink skin under their chestnut-colored eyes, and toes of brownish red clinging to the boughs. A little purple warmed their breasts, which beat like Katy's little form beneath her brown gown.

"Ah,-coo-roo-coo-roo!" murmured both the old doves and the young ones, also, as Katy came near.

"Tey are full of love, Job," Katy said; "tey will fly down among te chickens and eat, and drink out of te trough py te horses. Tey are shy, but not suspicious. Two eggs is all te she-bird lays, and she hatches out of tem always a he-bird and a she:"

"What for?" Job Snowberger asked, with his austere side aggressive, after his late display of weakness.

"Job!" said Katy, "why, you know — to love one another!"

Job's half-shut eyes looked down at Katy with an idiotic smile as he murmured, half harshly:

"Unshuldich!"

"Oh no, Job. I'm not 'innocent' like I was yisterday; I'm in love, too."

"Unshicklich, Katy!"

"No, indeed. It can't be 'improper' if it comes like religion, dear Job. That's te way mine come to me."

"Ah-coo-roo-coo-roo," assented the she-dove from the tree, and si-dling down the bough toward Katy.

"Te she-dove never trifles with another he-bird," Katy said, "like so many other kinds of birds. I've set and watched those, ever since te 15th of April, when tey come here from te South. He's all attention to her, too, and cares for no bird else."

"Ah-coo-roo-coo-roo!" emphatically, from the tree, as the male bird trailed his wings, and puffed his breast up large, and paraded before his lady, and then fed her from his own bill.

"Unshicklich!," improper, intimated Brother Philodulus, with a femi-nine turn of his head. "Katy, I can do something tender, too. I can sing the turtle-dove psalm."

"Do, Job! My mate has taken my music with him, or I would help you a little."

Job Snowberger, with a straightening of his lean figure and an expression between ecstasy and childishness, piped in the German tongue a little psalm we may translate together:

SEVENTH-DAY DUNKER HYMN

"Coo-roo," the turtle-dove complains,
    Whose spouse comes never near,
And leaves her, with a mother's pains,
    Un-nested all the year:

"Coo-roo-ah-coo," the birdling true
    Doth with itself condole —
So does the dove of Yasus coo
    In every lonely soul.

"Coo-roo," the stricken monk or nun
    Within the kloster sighs,
By human sin or love undone,
    And hid from human eyes:
"Coo-roo-ah-coo!" that mate untrue
    Still fills dear Yasus' place,
And you can hear the turtle coo
    In her despairing face.

"Coo-roo," beside Ephrata's brooks
    And in Antietam's vale,
Comes in between the martyr-books
    The tender human tale:
"Coo-roo," to Peter Miller, too,
    To Beissel and to all —
The turtle-dove so soft will coo,
    It seems like Yasus' call!

"Coo-roo!" in vain we fly from Love,
    And world and flesh attack,
In vain we kill the human dove
    And set the Sabbath back;
"Coo-roo-ah-coo!" Love will undo
    The washing white of springs,
And only Yasus never knew
    How strong the turtle sings.

"Coo-roo!" in Zion's wooden house,
    In Kedar's shingled cells,
Softer than lowing of the cows
    The note of passion wells.
"Coo-roo-ah-coo!" like wood unto
 + Whereon was Yasus bound,
Our prison seems; and every coo
    Tears wide a bleeding wound.

"Coo-roo!" sing, more celestial Dove,
    In notes aye pure and clear,
To drown this strong, terrestrial love
    And help us persevere!

"Coo-roo-ah-coo!" dear Yasus, who
    No frailty turned aside,
Thy Dove set in the himmel blue,
    And keep our Church thy bride!

Job Snowberger's singing had method in it, and caused himself to weep. Katy saw him standing there in his coarse, home-woven and home-dyed clothes, sewn together by the hands of women who had no deeper interest in man than as a fellow-laborer, and she took her needle and pieced him together, saying —

"Dear Job, you have got nobody to love you."

"Unshicklich!" exploded Philodulus, referring to the needle-work, and then, raising his bashful eyes to Katy's face, he qualified the remark to *"Unshuldich."*

"Nobody will love me," Job exclaimed, "but Sister Marcella, and she only loves me to send me on arrands. I'm only one of her niggers, and she has many of tem. Katy, can't you jine the *kloster* and help me persewere?"

"Ah-coo-roo-coo-roo!" The doves had sidled together in the apple tree.

"Why, dear Job, I am in love already. I am engaged to a young man. See, his mother's ring is on my finger! And he has took my accordion. Oh, I am so happy!"

"Unshicklich! Unshuldich, too! No good will come of it, schwester Kate! Oh, come and jine the good *Siebentager* and help me persewere!"

Job had already burst open his late repairs; for, indeed, his clothes were too small for him, and his emotions had the effect of wind in the laden apple trees, bringing all their ripeness to the ground. He threw his arms around Katy, and, in ecstasy of groans and tears, piped high:

"Oh, can't we persewere together, Katy! It is so hard to persewere alone. I can't remember nothing: the music-writin' gits blotted; the saw-mill runs wrong; the fullin'-mill wants ile, the cider-press tastes of rotten apples. Come, come, schwester, to Schneeberg and te *heilich* life!"

"Ah-coo-roo-coo-roo!" very firmly, from the dove family in the tree.

"Don't kiss me so hard, Job!" Katy cried, fighting in vain against the tall man's impassioned caresses. "It's real *unshicklich* in you, for I'm going to marry another man."

"Oh, who is it? He must be some sinful one."

"No, indeed, Job; it's a Mr. Quantrell!"

"Hallo!" spoke a strange voice. "How do you know me, indeed? — And what rummaging are you engaged at, Snowberger? Fine hypocrite, you!"

"Persewerin'," Philodulus said, sheepishly; "we was persewerin' together."

"No doubt," said a strange lame man, standing before them; "persevering and perspiring, too! — Young woman, you're in a fair way to become a convert, unless your people look more carefully after you!"

"Who is it?" Katy spoke; "I do not understand."

"You ought to know me. You have just mentioned my name. I am Abel Quantrell, of Baltimore. And where is Hannah Ritner?"

"Here, master!" spoke an eloquent voice at the window; "I heard you were coming, and had you directed to this friend's retired farm; for I was all alone at Smoketown, and the time was full of portents. O master, if I ever needed help and a strong hand to lean upon, it is today!"

"Sho! Sho! Ninon, I see you are nervous today. Cube yourself! The root is the soul. Cube yourself! Some unusually Quixotic undertaking, perhaps? O child, I feel for you — extracting the cube-root of all this wrong, without the help of man!"

"Be tender with me, master. Oh, come and counsel me! The time is so short; the mountains are so dark; I can not read beyond them. I am so lonely!"

He led her toward the dairy, near the creek, and on the grass they talked together until Nelly Harbaugh took out chairs for them, and then they talked still on, till Luther came in, at dinner, hearing the sounding of the bell, and put up the strange gentleman's horse and buggy.

Mr. Abel Quantrell came in to dine, and looked at Katy and at Nelly with a sort of sardonic admiration. At Nelly he looked with bold favor; at Katy with no more interest than as at a hoyden child he had found in an old man's arms.

Katy was afraid of this strange man, and some great distress seemed overhanging in his wonderful appearance here, the very day after her lover had come and gone. She was too unworldly and ignorant to understand that she had been guilty of any error, or to know how to extricate herself, and be recommended in his eyes.

"I will leave it to God," said Katy, inwardly. "*He* must know what to do with me."

Nelly Harbaugh was soon in a running skirmish of merry and satirical talk with Abel Quantrell.

He was a man not to be forgotten nor confounded with any other, and even the splendid carriage of Hannah Ritner seemed to lose its superiority under Abel Quantrell's plain but strong address and countenance.

In the first place, he was a deformed man: one of his legs was shorter than the other, or the foot was clubbed; for he walked by the aid of a cane, without labor or any look of pain, and with a certain enforced erectness which had imparted a spirit of will, or defiance, or triumph, to the carriage of his head, the swell of his nostrils, the firm parallels of his eyebrows and lips, and even to the poise of a dark wig, younger in tone than the lights in his eyes, which were faded, spite of their fateful and inflexible cast.

His face was all shaved clean; a standing collar barely showed the gray hairs brushed beneath his throat upon the parchment-colored sinews there. At times, unconsciously, or from habit, he thrust his hand into the clean, starched, simple bosom of his shirt, and then he seemed, to those observing him, like one whose back was against a wall.

But for his lameness he would have been a man above the usual stature, and at this table he was easily the chief, as if a magistrate had come in, but not to depress anybody's spirits. His face was without any ruddy color, and the black wig gave it a certain pallor as if he were older than he seemed.

No Christian resignation was in Abel Quantrell's portrait — rather the heathen philosopher's stoic will and coolness. In repose, he seemed an orator with something in his bosom to defend, and covered there by his pallid hand; out of repose, his face assumed a certain earthiness and self-love, sometimes to the degree of coarseness, and this may have been why Nelly Harbaugh soonest grew upon easy terms with him and drew from him some particulars of his career.

"You seem at home among us Swiss and Dutch, and find your way about like an old *nochber?*"

"*Yaw, yung maidle,*" Abel Quantrell said, "I came among the old Dutch before your mother had a beau. I was the square root extracted from a small New England family of thirteen — the oldest, my little mother — and as I had kept them poor to send me to college, I needs must feed them all. 'Cube yourself, Abel,' said I; 'a few years at school-teaching will make you a lawyer, and then you can educate your little brothers and sisters, and set them on the way to love and independence.' Sho, sho! The Scotch-Irish bar, at the town where I taught their college, passed a rule, especially for me, that no school-teacher could enter at the law. They knew I was too poor to sit with my legs out of a lawyer's window studying for two years, and let my mother starve!"

"What did you do, sir?" Luther Bosler asked, sitting, like his father, at the table in his shirt-sleeves.

"I merely cubed the radius," Abel Quantrell said, with a firmer grip of his upper lip upon the lip below — that lip which seemed beaked, while his nose was straight as an index-board. "I rode over into Maryland and sat up with the bar of the nearest county there, judge and all, and played a good hand at cards, and staked my quarter's salary. They asked me a sleepy question or two at daylight and passed me into the law. So I extracted the square root of Pennsylvania smallness and moved my habitation to another Dutch county."

"Te Dunkers do not go to law," ventured Katy Bosler.

"Bi'm-by," Jake Bosler ejaculated, fearing that they had already leanings that way.

"No, bright eyes! And that was what took the square root out of my triumph. I could get love in too generous measure, but business never came. Here sits a pupil of mine: let Ninon tell the rest."

He turned to Hannah Ritner. She swept his pallid and volcano-scarred face with eyes of woe and pride, and answered:

"Master, you found your only client, after waiting long — in a murderer. He had taken a human life, but by his crime you and your mother's brood found food. His case was so bad that they gave him to you to defend him, in mockery of your hard condition, for you received not one penny for your toil."

"Sho, sho!" from Abel Quantrell; "I cubed myself, though."

"The eloquence of genius in the occasion of despair burst from you like a torrent. The murderer became, in your impetuosity, your only friend. His dark and stony nature poured forth the springs of fervent tears. The judge sat trembling, your rivals were astonished and abashed. All German-derived people, after that, went to you with their suits and cases, and found you just as God. You left us, then, for greater fields of use, and, by prosperity, you fell to be a man!"

"Nothin' but persewerin'," from the old-maidish face of Job Snowberger, with his sheepish and insinuating side still set on Katy.

"Job *Snow*," Hannah Ritner commanded, "be more respectful to my dear master!"

"Bi'm-by," meaninglessly from Jake Bosler, who executed the parental feat of throwing some corn "slappers" with his fingers into Katy's plate, a yard distant.

Only Nelly Harbaugh seemed to blush at this homely method of serving food.

"Teacher," Nelly said to Abel Quantrell, "which is best to live for — affection or greatness?"

"I have had all my happiness in career," replied the old man, with his pallid hand in his bosom, laid firmly on his heart. His eyes, ranging around the table, rested with some kindling embers of power upon Luther Bosler. "My career, for a quarter of a century, was to fight Power. Sometimes I fought it when it was rightful power — not often. For power, as I found it in my exile in these Middle States, was the power of old sociability, of cliques and lodges, of amiable ignorance and deadly prejudice resisting innovation. This dull majority had sat upon my heel; I turned and bruised its head."

"Soon-down, Luter. Bi'm-by!" from Jake Bosler, toward his son, glancing at the half-plowed fields.

Jake had taken off his shoe, and was examining his not very sightly foot with an eye to stone-bruises. No spirituality in the conversation bribed him from thrifty thinking on his crops.

"Retaliation is not the spirit our Lord changed this world in," Luther Bosler said, his dark eyes intelligently following Abel Quantrell.

Hannah Ritner's eyes shone with all their might of compassion, as she turned on Luther, before the old man could speak the repartee his folded lip concealed:

"Sir, Master Quantrell's retaliations were never upon the weak. He soared among the eagles in his indignations. We humble Germans he led by the hand as high as we could go, and there we saw him battling with the power enthroned in the sun. He defended slaves escaping over the free-State line. He assailed Freemasonry in its brutality toward a human life. He broke the power of ignorance in Pennsylvania and made Education one of the tyrants there, with the power to tax, like forked lightning in its hands. We sluggish Germans did not always understand him; we had not his mercurial sensitiveness to the injuries of simple multitudes — of women, of illiterate children, of poor, black slaves. But we felt that something of Messiah had come among us with righteousness in his hands, and we set him in the seats of power until —"

"The lower Yankee interest in his nature made him desert you," said Abel Quantrell, bitterly. "Yes, Ninon, I gave myself to career like the bright, impetuous waters of the Blue Mountains, which at last subside in the shallow and malarious estuaries of the bay. I laid down career, and I am dead. Look at me — whited, withered, wigged, and limping! Have I not thrown myself away?"

"No, master!" the woman answered in fervent eloquence. "The world has captured you, but not your principles, and, like our old German emperor, Barbarossa, you sleep in the cavern till the freedom of our land shall awaken you."

"I have a son," the old man said. "In him I may awake, but never again in my enfettered self."

Katy cried, before she could think: "Oh, he was here! We took Lloyd to love-feast. He eat with us Dunkers last Sunday."

"Sho, sho! No doubt he multiplied the base and height of himself together and the product by the breadth. The cube resulting is still a baby's block."

"He is a manly lad, master!" said Hannah Ritner, with her great eyes downcast. "Something of his father is there."

"Yes," said Abel Quantrell, languidly, "the complement of his father: he will be as rash to support power that is false, as I was to attack it. In my rowdy son, I see the compensation of my own self-indulgence."

"It is not true!" Katy cried; "Lloyd is a gentleman. He eat te Passover!"

"I guess he's purty bad, Katy," Job Snowberger said. "He ain't a-persewerin'."

"Job *Snow!*" from Hannah Ritner, "where is your charity?"

"Come, Ninon," said Abel Quantrell, with lessening interest in the subject; "I must have my game of cards."

Luther Bosler and his father went back to the field; Katy and Nelly and Job Snowberger went to fruit-peeling again; Hannah Ritner and Abel Quantrell had chairs under a tree near the creek, and a barrel-head furnished them a table; from the dwelling they could be seen playing for Spanish silver pieces.

Katy was still and troubled, Nelly Harbaugh no less preoccupied and silent, and Job Snowberger, the only talking quantity left, got no reply for his chance remarks.

"Katy," he said at last, "you is so still, I think you want to come to Kloster Schneeberg."

"Oh, you old fool!" Nelly Harbaugh spoke, "what does she want with your old stupid nunnery? We women want career."

She glanced at Katy, who looked up, her eyes full of tears, and said: "Nelly, what makes me so ignorant?"

"Goodness," Nelly Harbaugh answered.

Chapter XXII

THE YANKEE

*T*ILL late in the day Abel Quantrell played euchre with a spirit compounded of gain and hazard, his opponent sometimes requiring to be stirred from her abstraction, yet seeking to engage him with all her irregular solicitude.

Finally, the old man, as she studied a careful play, closed his eyes, and when she was ready, he did not respond.

The sun was growing low, and Hannah Ritner placed her chair so as to shield him from its glancing rays, as they were dandled on the South Mountain's crest.

"Oh, that this day would bring its result!" she sighed aloud.

A head was in her lap and a kiss upon her hand; she looked down, and Katy Bosler was kneeling on the ground.

"What is it, simple child?"

"My ring," whispered Katy. "He wants it."

She pointed at Abel Quantrell, sleeping.

Katy held up the mourning ring of Lloyd Quantrell's mother.

"Fortune-teller!" said Katy, "this ring Lloyd's mother was married with. Oh, must I lose it, as you told me I would? Can't nothing save it for me? It is all I haf, since I gif Lloyd my accordion."

Hannah Ritner looked at the ring.

"It is sanctified by death," she said. "Lord rest the soul who made this ring so dear!"

"Lord, let that soul be kind to me!" responded Katy, fervently. "I only want to gif myself to Lloyd, and nothing selfish haf I got but love — te first of love I ever felt. How strong it is, Mootter Hannah!"

"Drive it away, my child! Exert your mind to be free! Rings like this were never made to be worn by poor, ignorant girls. Give this ring to me, and I will wear it for you, and then it never may be lost."

"You, Mootter Hannah! Haf you got te power to keep it always for me? If I gif it to you now, maybe I will lose it, all py myself, and pe foolish."

"Hush, Katy!" Hannah Ritner pointed to the sleeping sire of Lloyd Quantrell. "Leave it with me to conjure with awhile."

She slipped the ring upon her hand, and Katy stole away.

Abel Quantrell opened his eyes and said:

"The square of self is but half selfish; but the cube of self has higher walls than angels ever scale. Plato, with all his divine reach, could never solve the problem which had baffled the oracle of Apollo."

"Dear master, what was that?"

"To start with one's self-indulgence and multiply it into a sacrifice; to double the cube. Geometry, no more than an oracle, can do it."

"Master, you have always defended the poor."

"Sho, sho! Too often from pugnacity, reasoning from them to my own fancied injuries. The humility of the Nazarene never was in me. He who seeks to save his life shall lose it, Ninon."

"Master, have I not been seeking to save my life by losing it? Are we ever all unselfish?"

"You have been, or sacrifice has no God, my child! If ever love was willful, suicidal, and martyr-minded, it was yours. I offered you myself, and you refused me: with every right to me, you sent me on my career and blessed me as another's bridegroom, and turned back with all your glorious powers of body and of heart to be, like Hagar, the bride of the wolf, and your habitation in the wilderness. What have you been recompensed in?"

"Career, my master. I saw a work to do."

"Sho, sho! I know what that has been: to take the place of danger on the Underground Road and save a slave or two, whose escape to freedom only aggravated the sorrows of the rest, and made the bloodhound Federal laws invade the North. A hundred Quakers have done as much, Ninon."

"Master," said the woman, "I have gained knowledge. I have predicted things which came to pass. I predict that, before you leave this humble farm, the brazen door of bondage will resound to the sledge-hammers of our daring smiths!"

As she spoke, fervidly, she seemed to swoon, and her long hair fell downward to the ground.

He placed his arm around her, and she pushed it away.

"No more of that, master! I am in the very labor of my lifework now, and my soul is in the depths of travail! Oh, be a just man to your son! He loves you."

"He is too brave to need my justice," Abel Quantrell said. "Like me, he will not bow the knee to man, and be ashamed of Nature — bountiful and wise in him. Justice is for the commonplace; freedom and independence are for heroes."

His face, being animated now, had lines of coarseness in it, as if he was of the satyr's type, and mocked conventionalities.

"Shall I be just to you, Ninon?" continued Abel Quantrell, when he had restored his hand to his bosom, and was restfully proud again.

"I have been just to myself, master."

"How?"

By my spiritual gift. I am your wife."

"Sho, sho!"

"See, sir! The dead deliver to me the rights I would not ask for. She who has sought to lose her life, has saved it."

His faded eyes fell upon the wedding-ring, which she had dropped into his palm, upon her hand.

"Magic!" said Abel Quantrell; "how came it here?"

"Wafted!" Hannah Ritner spoke; "the day of my agony, when my martyr-fires, perhaps, are lighted and my chain is forged, the ring I had refused slides down the rainbow to my feet."

"Are you one of those Spiritualist fanatics, Ninon? Sho, sho! There is no divination in geometry. Three times from the base is the cube. It was my son you got that ring from."

"No, master; but from the child he gave it to when he engaged himself."

"Sho! He had visited no lady when he left Baltimore six days ago. I have found a wife for him, and that brings me here."

"He has found love here, master. You may give him another wife, but not the one he loves."

"Who is it?"

"Little Katy, who sits in yonder house of log and stone; the Dunker farmer's child."

"Sho, sho! No need of marrying there. He can love in one place and marry in another —"

"And have remorse, like you, master?"

"How do you know that?"

"I heard you bring it from the woodlands of your sleep, saying that self-indulgence never could be expanded into a sacrifice."

The old man raised his club-foot and looked at it bitterly.

"There is a gnawing in my bosom, Ninon, but it is the decaying principle of life. I am sixty-seven. That self I accuse myself of is the selfishness of career. If I have sacrificed others, here and there, it was to keep the greater compassion in view, and change the systems by which wrong and tyranny were possible. I resigned most passionate love to plant myself in the domestic circle of border-State slavery, and to work its downfall by the social foothold I obtained. My son must marry to strengthen me in the same labor, and make Maryland a free State before I die."

"You will marry him to a religious woman?"

"Yes, to a Catholic. The strength of slavery in Maryland lies in the old Catholic counties and families, and in the increasing college and conventual institutions of that Church. There was a time when Carroll, of Carrollton, took me by the hand, when we Anti-masons came to Baltimore to overthrow the power of President Jackson. There lie latent in his church resentments against all forms of ruffianism, of which human bondage is the chief. I have sent my son to Catholic school and worship. For me all gates to heaven are too narrow; by freedom I will go in, or be the specter of Heaven's own injustice, agitating at the gate!"

He spoke with sardonic quietness, yet without quietness of soul.

"Master, is there not the Jesuit's method in your plan? 'The quality of mercy is not strained.' It passes no suffering human creature, to do some greater good, beyond. By Jesus came compassion in the world, and by politicians and by pontiffs came religious craft. The New World was given to tyrants, and its native millions thrown into slavery, that they might be saved from greater damnation. I predict, with truth in my soul, that one brave man this day, without scrip or raiment, and his life for the stone in his sling, will strike every false system down, and be the hero of the world."

"You wander, Ninon! Sho, sho! you were always wild of mind. Had there been such a man, he would have come to me."

"You were a politician, master, and he came to me. Oh, I fear I may have done wrong, that good may come of it!"

Abel Quantrell took her head upon his shoulder. She resisted a little moment, and was still.

"How much you have suffered, Ninon!"

"I have died, master, and am raised from the grave. When you married, I prayed for your wife, but all was death to me for days. I came to this world again, people thought a little crazy."

"Always a little above this world, child."

"That I might not be a burden and mockery to my great political relatives, I crossed the State line and lived in a little hut. The children came to me for curiosity, the mature to have me tell their fortunes; my cottage light was the polar star of a thousand slaves."

"All this time, Ninon, I was mismated. Disgrace followed me, also: my brother moved beside me, and became a Negro-trader; my son became a corner-lounger and a bully. Sho, sho! My heart sought you out in the dreams of sleep and in the nervous wakefulness of the night. Why did you not take the square root from our troubles and send for me?"

"You were married, master. A great thing had purified my heart."

"I know, my child. How noble you were, there! Behold my wretched residue of marital ambition! I am too old to love you now."

"Master, it was from you, in the days of our passion, that I drew the example to think on others' wrongs. The old Dutch sects — Quakers in other respects — felt no offense at human slavery. I took up the work when you relinquished it. My labors are almost ended. — What man is that yonder, master?"

As she arose, in all her strength and stature, Abell Quantrell saw that she was trembling.

"Sho! Joan d'Arc," he said, tenderly, "beneath your armor I see the poor child still."

A black man came forward with Nelly and with Katy; he was half naked, and nearly dead with fatigue.

"Speak, poor man!" called Hannah Ritner. "You were with Isaac Smith across the river?"

"Missy, dey's fout all day. Mos' all is tuck an' killed. Two of us got away — and what was leff in Maryland. Mosster Quantrell sent me."

He produced gold pieces.

"Good Lord!" cried Nelly Harbaugh; "this is the runaway nigger, and he must have stole the whole reward for himself."

"Missy, Lloyd tole me to come to Bosler's farm and give dis money to Luther to buy me with it. He wants to save my life and own me."

"Yes, do buy the pore man!" Katy cried. "He's known nothing but misery."

"I'll attend to the matter," Abel Quantrell observed. "Ninon, put yourself across the Pennsylvania line without delay! Has this weakness brought on a civil war?"

Hannah Ritner was the picture of one dying, yet struggling to live.

"Go with her," Abel Quantrell continued, speaking to the Negro Ashby. "I am anxious to gratify all my son's wishes at this moment, foolish as they may be."

"Why?" asked Katy Bosler.

"Because I have picked out a wife for him, little Dunker! and would persuade him to my will."

He called for his carriage and servant. Hannah Ritner and Job Snowberger drove away with the Negro Ashby.

Suddenly Nelly Harbaugh cried, as Abel Quantrell also passed from view:

"Katy, *fergesht!* where is your wedding-ring?"

Awakened from the stupor of several minutes, Katy looked at her hand and screamed.

She ran to the house and rang the bell loudly for the field-hands to come home, and then started up the stairs.

"Where are you going, Katy?"

"To git a-ready for Harper's Ferry and to see Lloyd."

Chapter XXIII

JOHN BROWN'S FORT.

AS Lloyd Quantrell entered the armory-yard with a signal of truce, his quickened apprehension took in the Washington family-carriage on the grass riddled with bullets, the engine-house doors splintered as if by lightning, and at least four short barrels of rifles pointing at himself from the door-crevices and the brick loopholes.

Expecting each instant to meet the fate of Stevens and wallow on the ground, a hulk of broken bones, he exerted his empty hand with an earnestness which enabled him to gain the door unshot.

"Captain Brown, they are killing your son-in-law, William Thompson! He cried to me for help. None but you can save him!"

At the moment he spoke a shower of balls made a circle around him, and the rod, on which had been his hat, was twisted out of his hand by a bullet which benumbed his whole arm, and from the wood and brick of the engine-house chips and brick-dust were struck. The door opened, and unseen hands pulled him in.

"Prospectin', heigh?" a merry voice said.

"Your brother, Dauph Thompson, is being murdered on the bridge. Listen!"

The sounds of many guns, a faint women's wail, and a cheer without a note of joy in it, followed by a sort of silence such as animals keep whose food has suddenly been thrown into their dens, related some horrible story.

Dauph Thompson turned pale, and still his voice was cheery:

"Willy murdered? They wouldn't do that!"

He threw open the engine-house door sufficiently to crouch in the sill, and said pleasantly, yet troubled:

"Prospectin'."

In a moment something appeared protruding on sticks and poles from the corner of the hotel and station, where the town mayor had exposed his life.

"That's something to draw your fire, men; don't be foolish!" John Brown's settled, metallic voice spoke from the top of a fire-engine, looking through an arched and shivered window.

Dauph Thompson stood up in the doorway and turned his face inward; it was pale, as if he had a mortal wound.

"Don't mind me!" he said, in mournful pleasantry. "I'm jess prospectin'."

"What is it, Dauph? Are you hurt?" Ned Coppock cried, throwing his arm around his comrade.

"Ned — it's Will's clothes they're showing — full — of his blood!"

"Murderers!" muttered Coppock. "Don't cry, Dauph. He give his all, and all is over now!"

"O Will! Never to see you more, my brother!"

"Yes, Dauph. This is not all the life that good men live."

Wiping the tears from his eyes, and shaking Coppock's hand, young Thompson turned his face to Captain Brown, and spoke pleasantly as before:

"Prospectin', father — jess once more."

He looked at his gun, closed his lips and opened his nostrils, and a slight flash of spirit, more sportsmanlike than serious, came from his eyes.

He stood erect in the crevice of the door, and raised his gun to his eye.

It went off, and with it he spun around, as if from its rebound, and fell upon his face on the brick floor.

Coppock turned him over, and called —

"Dauph!"

"Prospectin'," replied a faint voice, and his bosom filled with his heart's blood.

He had been shot, courting death, with a miner's phrase upon his lips, and had found the eternal treasure where the streets, they say, are paved with gold.

"O Isabel!" a moaning voice came from some muddy and travel-stained clothes upon the floor. "Oh, water, father!"

"Be composed, my son," spoke the steady voice of John Brown. "Your wife's brothers have both died like men. Die the man, like your brother Oliver!"

He gave the order to close the doors and risk no further lives, and to keep the prisoners back.

Quantrell would have been killed, to expose himself at the door, so he retired to the side of Watson Brown and leaned Watson's head upon the cold form of the dead Oliver.

"Drink of this flask, my lad."

This time the suffering man did not resist the life-infusing draught.

"Give some to Olly," muttered Watson Brown. "He is so cold."

Quantrell counted nine prisoners sitting around the edges of this nearly square room — which, as has been said, was some twenty-four feet upon a side; the watch-house, under the same roof, was now deserted by friend and foe.

The prisoners had nothing to do, but seek to get a little rest by sitting upon a narrow sill or coigne, like an abortive bench, which ran around the chamber a little above the damp floor. Some of them John Brown had permitted to shield themselves with the leather hose or any other fireman's traps which would divert a bullet. All the prisoners were tractable and worried; some nodded for a little while; others ventured a word occasionally with the chief raider or some of his men; and one or two had a thin, genial phrase to say, parrot-fashion, rather as formulae to keep up luck, than to court any popularity.

"Ole Ball" was seen to be a heavy, bacon-fed, middleaged man, probably of the large Virginia connection of George Washington's mother, and he paid great deference to "Cappen Smith," for, notwithstanding his own admissions, and the assurances of his men, the greatest bewilderment still existed as to the true name, location, or purpose of the bandit chief, and, with dogmatic loyalty to hearsay, the Virginians believed John Brown to be still Mr. Isaac Smith, carrying on some little game.

"Josephus!" Ball would say, when a bullet struck one of the engines and disported itself among the wooden girders above, "Cappen Smith, that was close, now!"

A Maryland man, with a little smiling shiver, would on such occasions add in a small, cowed voice:

"Zip! Be on your *qui vivy!*"

Mr. Washington had so far recovered from his melancholy as to make a suggestion at long intervals, directed ostensibly at Captain Smith's safety or comfort, but with a generous providence, also, which embraced himself.

"Ah, captain, sah!" he said, soon after Lloyd's entrance, "don't your son want a doctaw?"

"My son knows his duty, sir; and makes no complaint," John Brown remarked, inspecting his revolvers.

"But, ah, captain, sah! He did ask faw wataw, and captain — ah! we all want wataw greatly, captain."

"Your fellow-citizens, gentlemen, have killed my men sent on errands of our mutual benefit, and I will take no more risks till my re-enforcements come. — Here, men, back that fire-engine against the door, and stretch these ropes across the jambs! Put the engine-tongue so as to hold the door against a battering, and run the other cart forward! Wake up those recruits underneath the engine and let them earn their living!"

The recruits consisted of a few slaves gathered from neighboring "estates," as the farms were called; and these Negroes, debarred from any other excitements all their lives than Whitsuntide or "a licking," were now expected to take an intelligent, indeed, heroic view of their first opportunity, and the white prisoners faintly smiled at this proof of a natural incapacity for self-government.

"Cappen Brown," said the master-machinist of the armory, heretofore described as "Ole Ball," "don't you think it's an ongrateful time for these men and brethren to be a-snoozin' and leave you to earn their salvation? Josephus! cap."

A ball went whizzing among the men and peeled the rafters above.

"Zip!" said the Maryland man, in an awed voice; "be on the *qui vivy* now!"

"Ah — sah! Torturing — sah!" from Colonel Washington.

"The disciples," replied the gnarled old woodsman, in his shrill key, "went to sleep the night on Gethsemane, when their Master asked them to watch with him one little hour. They were continually sleeping, sir, until he requested them not to get up anymore, for, said he, 'the hour is at hand, and the Son of man is betrayed into the hands of sinners.'"

A piece of glass, sheared off neatly by a bullet, went sailing through the room. The four men able to stand by their arms returned the courtesy, and the place stank of sulphur, and every palate was coppery and hot.

"Zip! Be on the *qui vivy,*" the Maryland man was heard to say, and shudder in the smoke.

"Josephus! Cappen Brown, how you kin remember Scripter!"

"Nothing remarkable about that, sir, for I studied for the Christian ministry before I was of age, till an inflammation of the eyes, sir, sent me back to my tan-yard."

A nail came whistling through one of the sky-windows and played a little tune as it tingled on the levers of one of the engines. The Negroes, working there, fell on the brick floor again. The voice of John Brown was heard to say:

"No man is fit to fight for human nature who despairs of it. This world slept in trespasses and sins when the unwelcome Redeemer came. And why should these ignorant slaves, whose forefathers came to Virginia in bondage the same year my ancestor came to Massachusetts in the Mayflower, be awake, when we alone, of all the Mayflower's children, are awake to their injustice? That is why I am here, prisoners — to awake this land! I expected these slaves to awake *last.* If a thousand years to the

Lord are but as a day, may not these three hundred years of bondage be but as a night of sleep to *these?*"

"Bang!" "Bang!" "Bang!" "Bang!"

The four guns in the hands of Brown's surviving fighters went off sequentially, two at the port-holes, two at the doors.

"Josephus!" spoke Mr. Ball, "the place smells like a bad ror egg!"

Answering shots brought down a little shower of flattened lead upon everybody.

"Zip!" said the Marylander's quaver of a voice. "No use of bein' on the *qui vivy* yer!"

"Water! Father! O my God!" a breath sighed up from Watson Brown.

"Ah — captain. Your son! He is thirsty," Colonel Washington appealed.

"My son is a brave man," replied John Brown, firmly. "'I thirst,' gentlemen, was the cry that let the Christian era in. Your fellow-citizens, to whom we meant no wrong, but justice, give these dying soldiers of mine the hyssop and the sponge of vinegar to cool their thirst."

"Don't weaken for me, father!" gasped the ashen face of Watson Brown.

"O man!" Lloyd Quantrell cried, "are you, who rebuked me for killing a dove, so merciless as to hear your son howl like this? And quote your Bible, too!"

The usual momentary salute came tearing through the little fort.

Captain Brown peered out of the door, and the balls struck around his stiff hairs and stooping shoulders. He carried no gun, and returned like one who had merely been examining the weather-indications.

"Men," said he, "be careful now of your ammunition. My re-enforcements may be somewhat late. What you are to guard against is a sudden rush upon you, or the establishing of a rifle-pit, or a blind, within easy aiming distance of this building. That you must not permit."

"Captain," said one of his men named Stewart Taylor, a cool, freckled lad, "how many re-enforcements do you expect?"

"It is only a question of time, Taylor," Brown answered. "There may be thousands of them."

"We've got the promise of them," a taller man exclaimed; "and we're four good men yet, besides our commander."

"Yes, Anderson," the leader remarked, stroking his long beard; "we are in stout walls, well armed, and nothing but cannon can batter down our fort, and these prisoners forbid their using any cannon."

He looked around upon the nine or ten discomfited men, hanging or crouching there, like hams in a smoke-house when the bear family pay it a visit; and the free Negro, Green, the surviving one of the pair which had menaced Quantrell, remarked:

"Their lives, I guess, ain't worth no more than our'n!"

"No, Green," John Brown replied, "prisoners must take their chances; this is a war."

Ed Coppock gave a reassuring look at the prisoners and walked out upon the lawn, where his rifle was soon heard to crack. He returned, laughing, pursued by musketry which made the doors sound like rats gnawing through them.

"I gave that Gault House a shot," he said, "in remembrance of poor Stevens."

"Isabel, are you here, dearest? I can't see you!" — from the pale lips of Watson Brown.

"Drink, lad," said Quantrell.

"Oh, it comes out of my wounds!" the sufferer cried, putting his hand upon his stomach. "I can't hold anything."

"You have asked me a question, Mr. Quantrell," the indurated father observed, returning back along the course of the conversation — "why I could reprove the killing of a dove, and permit the killing of a man, even of my son?"

He came over and felt of Watson's bleeding abdomen, and covered Oliver's dead face with a blanket, and, regarding both with an interest which, in its very practicality, was pathetic, he continued:

"Blood is so precious that no man should take it for amusement; and it is the most wholesome sacrifice to the Lord. On Abel's bleeding altar came the approving fire from heaven, while Cain, whose sacrifice of sticks God did not respect, fell on his brother and slew him. The sole question of bloodshed is: 'In what spirit do you shed it? what is the motive of your sacrifice?'"

"Zip, cap'n! Be on the *qui vivy!*" from the Maryland man.

"Oh, kill me! O my Bell!" from the tortured Watson.

"Your cause is just, my son. Bear it like a man," John Brown proceeded. "Now, sir" (to Quantrell), "it is permitted to man to shed the blood of animals for his necessities. 'Have dominion over them,' said the Lord in the beginning. Yet every sparrow is counted, every lamb is measured out, and, in the dove's domestic love, is heaven made emblematic: the Holy Spirit's peace. As I have rebuked you for killing the inoffensive dove, I call this nation to account for its cruelty to our fellow-creatures. In either case, sir, the interference may have been gratuitous; but blood of mine, and of the humble doves of peace, in Kansas, was shed before I began."

"Josephus! Cappen Brown, you don't shoot us down yer, because out yonder in Kinsas there was a fight, do you?"

"Zip! Be on your *qui vivy!*"

Colonel Washington's hired black servant had a considerable wool-clip taken out of his head at this point.

"I want water, too," he exclaimed, in his terror. "I'm chokin' fo' it!"

"That fellow — ah!" Colonel Washington exclaimed, in a low voice, to Quantrell, "came to this resort too willingly when Cook and Stevens ordered him; it would be — ah! — retribution, sah — if he did lose his life, sah."

"Mus' we die heah of thirst, an' de rivers full of water?" exclaimed the Negro man, lying beside his abandoned spear.

"There is a river," sighed Watson Brown, "whose streams shall make glad the city of God. Oh, let me swim there — in the Au Sable! — Bell, Bell, bury me by the water, dear; I want to lap it, darling."

He opened his eyes, and recognizing Quantrell, added, manfully:

"Yes, bury me by my comrades, by the river-side, away from the cavalry."

"By the Au Sable, did you say, Watson? Where is that?"

"It's too far," spoke the boy, deathly sweat upon his forehead; "by the Kaw; that will do. Or by the Shenandoah. I fought by both streams — where father said it was right."

The evening came down upon this little scene — of the mysterious invader and his four remaining soldiers, standing by their guns against the assembling country. Toward night the firing became merely drunken about the streets, and Brown let a prisoner or two go out from his little ark, but neither dove nor raven returned again; and the whistling of trains, opposite and above the town, indicated the coming of more and more troops; but still John Brown believed, from time to time, that they were his "re-enforcements."

He evidently believed this, because he would confer with his men — Anderson and Coppock being the more intelligent of these — and he would, with the woodman-scout's carefulness of ear, compare the sounds of rifles in the distance, and say, "Surely *they* are my re-enforcements." His men had such entire trust in him that they offered no suggestions nor criticisms, and did the whole of the fighting self-directed. His only order, from time to time, was, "Don't lose your interest, men! Don't be surprised! My re-enforcements are not far off." A rifle was seldom in his hand; he sometimes drew the sword of King Frederick; but the Negro Green, alone of his men, was suspicious of the white prisoners. Quantrell counted these and sounded some of them upon the propriety of a *coup de main* — to grapple with this old man's three whites and one Negro, and throw open the doors and call for assistance: it was no longer practicable, for the prisoners, while not less apprehensive than in the morning, had become cowed in all their being, as from the short-learned habit of obedience.

"Why, friend," whispered Quantrell to one of these, "has one day made white men slaves? What would a hundred years not do, then?"

"Don't you feel cowed, too?" asked his fellow-prisoner.

"I must admit that I do, every time I reenter this place and fall under that old man's influence. But why are not his little band, enveloped by a world of our people, also made timid?"

"Crazy, I reckon!"

"Fanatics, yes," said Lloyd — "no doubt they are; but if they represent many abolitionists like them, what will be the fate of slavery? This old fellow has the self-deception of Mohammed; he is the prophet of God to all these boys: they pass, fighting, to his paradise."

"I can't be kept much longer!" from the dying Watson Brown; "I shall see Fred and Olly, over there, by the river. — Bell, let me kiss my little boy and go!"

"See there!" Quantrell said, "*he* is worse than a fatalist. Who paid him to come here? He would get none of our land and own none of our slaves, if he should prevail. Fanaticism in its purest, most ignorant and simple form, is behind and in these men. I never would have believed abolitionism could amount to this."

"Dreadful!" moaned the man; "I've leaned agin this yer brick wall till I'm damp as a goose, and my head's as sore with thinkin' as t'other end is of tryin' to soften this ar brick. I didn't never think I could think *so* much as I have this yer one day."

"How much thinking," said Lloyd, "has old Smith given to this thing? He began it when he was a young man."

"Oh, he's a smart old scoundrel. But if the Lord will let me out of yer, I'll promise him to think about nothing for the rest of *my* days!"

And so darkness fell upon the dead, upon them in bonds, and upon the living fanatics. Silence followed the darkness, except when Watson Brown cried out in pain and delirium.

At length there came to the door, after some parley, an officer of a company from Maryland, a plain-speaking, German-derived man, whom Brown had met in his rambles, perhaps, and he said:

"Cap'n Smith, I don't bear no malice to ye. Where in the world did ye come from? Who air ye? What did ye come *hyar* for? Now, Smith, surrender, and make no further trouble. Ye're agin the law — *you* must know that."

"If you knew who I was — what I have gone through against this thing of slavery — you could understand what brought me here, sir," the leader replied. "I have tried to send my proposition several times to them in command against me. Who is in command?"

"Why, Governor Wise, of Virginia; he's near by, they say, and the United States marines from Washington; they'll be yer soon. Jist at present thar ain't no commander, ezackly."

"Then, sir, I shall not surrender to a mob, to have my few men here massacred — before my re-enforcements come."

Later on, the same kindly disposed militia captain sent a doctor in, to see the suffering son of the bandit. He said he could not determine anything without a light. Brown would not permit a light; it would expose his position and the number of his command, and he might be taken unaware before his "re-enforcements" could arrive. It was agreed, however, to prevent, if possible, firing upon the engine-house for the night, lest the hostages might be injured. The doctor promised to send in some anodyne for Watson, but it never came.

A fear now seized the prisoners that, in the storming of the engine-house, they would have the double danger of being killed by their friends or massacred by their captors; and, this being mooted to Brown, he said:

"In war, prisoners are subject to all the dangers of the belligerents. I will send you to the rear as far as I can. Keep against the back wall there."

"Oh, can't I git a brick that ain't so much kiln-dried," from the man of sore body and soul — "a brick that's a leetle damp — outen the mold, like, and that would *give* just a leetle?"

"Have to be on the *qui vivy* to find that," another sore voice from the darkness.

"Josephus!" another voice, like a snore, "if the Government work is like this night's, I shall resign and settle as fur off as Kinsas."

"This night," expressed the voice of weary agony, "O darling, kiss me and say, 'Husband, go!' I am so burning! Water, Lord Jesus, water!"

"Patience, Watson!" the old man's voice. "Your father does not intend to sleep. — Keep ready, men! The enemy is treacherous and cruel."

All the night long they heard this old man, alone in his responsibilities, keeping up the weary vigilance of his men, and sure of his "re-enforcements."

Quantrell, busy with all chords of sensibility, from religion and the creeping dread of death to love and retaliation, asked himself, at last, the meaning of Hannah Ritner's prophecy:

"When thou *killest* everything."

He had killed nobody as yet, nor was like to do so.

He tried to nod, but his mind kept recurring to things of life — his father's half-withheld affection, Light Pittson's warm attractions and romantic admiration for himself, and Katy Bosler's nestling confidence and love.

The cool yet thirsty night passed away, and cloudy dawn came in at the hemispherical window-tops.

No food, no certainty, no solution.

Watson Brown had been rolling and vomiting and talking of his wife and baby all the night. His father was more of a satyr than ever, with spiky hair and matted beard, and powder-stains upon his long muzzle of a nose. No other apprehension than anxiety about his "re-enforcements" was in his cold, gray eyes, no tremor in those lean, muscle-jawed cheeks — nothing less than primeval, aboriginal, provincial, warlike purpose, from Hebrew to Scotch Highlander, was in his square mouth and stone-cut eyebrows.

Taking his rifle, he said to his men: "We will exact terms and be allowed to cross the river with our prisoners, or we will join our companions in the heaven of the merciful and the brave! Let no man be a craven now. You have been faithful soldiers. Sometimes re-enforcements fail, but ours must come. They are promised where it says: 'Strait is the gate and narrow is the way which leadeth unto life,' and 'he that findeth his life shall lose it; and he that loseth his life for the truth's sake shall find it.'"

Sounds of all kinds broke the early morning air — the crowing cocks, the soaring crows, the railroad's whistle, halloos, cries, and huzzas; and, finally, there came the sound of men marching past with solid, regular tread, upon the grass and graveled walks of the armory-yard.

The raiders were all looking through port-holes and doors ajar, and Stewart Taylor spoke:

"I never saw soldiers like them. What are they?"

"United States marines," said John Brown.

"We're not fighting against the United States," exclaimed the taller man, Anderson, "but against slavery."

"The United States," said John Brown, "protects slavery, and is protecting it now, with the marines we pay our taxes to support."

Directly afterward, while the earliest sun stood in the gateway down which the blended rivers rushed to extinguish it, a rap came on the engine-house door, and a voice, official, not loud, but with reserve in its tone, spoke:

"I want to see the commander here!"

"I am that man," John Brown spoke, promptly, coming forward with the sword in his hand and the rifle leaning beside him.

"I want you to surrender to the United States authority, of which I am an officer."

"What terms am I offered?"

"You will be protected from the populace, and handed over to the civil authorities of Virginia for trial."

"They would hang me and my men."

"With that I have nothing to do. Do you surrender?"

"I demand permission to cross the river on the bridge, and at the farther end of the bridge I will let my prisoners go, and we shall then have to fight for our lives. I consider this fair, lieutenant."

"It is inadmissible. You must surrender."

"I will not surrender. I will die here, resisting the United States!"

"Take the consequences, then."

"We are ready."

"Are you John Brown, who fought at Black Jack in Kansas?"

"Yes; I was there. Were you there, too?"

"I am Lieutenant James E. B. Stuart, of the First Regular Cavalry, which prevented you renewing the skirmish."

"Why, I know you, sir. And now you know, lieutenant, how I came to be here."

"You won't surrender, Brown?"

"Not on your conditions."

"Very well, sir" — in a tone of indifference.

"Stand to your arms, men!" the metallic voice of John Brown exclaimed. "Distribute yourselves to the best advantage. We shall not yield to such terms."

"Captain Brown," interposed Taylor, respectfully, "I did not come here to fight the United States."

"Nor I," said the other man, Anderson.

"We have fought well, Captain Brown, but we can't fight our country," Taylor continued. "Our Canadian constitution reads, 'Look to no dissolution of the Union, but simply to amendment and repeal.'"

"Yes, Captain Brown," added Anderson, "and further it says, 'Our flag shall be the same our fathers fought under in the Revolution.' I was the first man, captain, to come to Maryland with you; I helped you find the Kennedy farm for our headquarters. I have made war upon Virginia, but not upon the United States."

"Do as you please, men. I shall fight. In Kansas my son submitted to the regulars, and was marched in chains under the burning sun, fettered to a dragoon's horse, and he lost his mind."

The two men, Anderson and Taylor, unbuckled their belts of arms and threw them aside, set their rifles in a corner, and retired without fear or haste to a space within that corner, in line with the doors.

The dying son of John Brown sought to raise himself and take a gun; but his eyes glazed, and he could not see. Ned Coppock went to his relief, and put Watson's head upon his lap.

The Negro man Green, troubled but not dismayed, exclaimed:

"What will become of me? Colored men ain't got no country an' no flag."

"Stand by your gun, Shields," young Coppock replied. "I won't see you imposed on. — Captain Brown, we're three left."

He resigned Watson Brown's care to a colored man, and came forward with his rifle.

"We are three," said John Brown, firmly; "but we shall have re-enforcements."

As he spoke, the old man vaulted into the upper works of the engine, crouched there, and bent his eye to his rifle.

Green knelt at one side of the engine, and Coppock at the other side, each sheltered by a wheel.

The two dead men were used by some of the prisoners as defenses, among other articles.

In the intensity of that moment, John Brown turned to his prisoners and remarked, calmly:

"Your safety, gentlemen, is in not changing your positions during the assault."

Probably every prisoner there muttered or thought of some act of his own, or said some reverent word.

Lloyd Quantrell thought of the Negro man he had saved, and of the Dunker sacrament he had taken.

Regularly moving men were heard outside; their side-arms were heard to rattle to the decision of their tread, and the words —

"First file, forward! — second file, forward!"

These came close to the doors; their very breathing could be heard. The ragged port-hole revealed them to a few within. So could the prisoners be heard to breathe, and the shivering voice muttered like spell to its own fears:

"Be on the *qui vivy!*"

"Number one and two!" from outside.

In an instant fierce blows from great hammers were delivered upon the door, and the weight of those hammers expelled the breaths of the men who swung them through the air.

The door trembled with the weight of those blows, but was large enough to distribute their power, and ropes stretched within made the door recoil. Only some ragged parts of the door fell with the shock of the sledges.

Quantrell saw Brown looking down his rifle-breech, keen as a squirrel looking along a bough.

"The first eight from each file — forward!" spoke the same voice of high nervous energy, in tones low pitched.

In a moment a tremendous sound came from the door as if a cannon-ball had struck it. The very building seemed to quiver.

"Are you ready, men?" from the bushy, squirrel-eyed bandit leader.

"Ready, captain!" from two cool voices, of one black man and one white.

"Lord-a-mercy!" and groans from the fugitive Negroes of the neighborhood who were back among the prisoners.

"Back!" from the open air. "Forward, now — smart, and all together!"

The door seemed to split and to lose cohesion in all its bolts, yet hung by the upper hinge; and below, where it was unhinged, a bright flash of daylight came in, and the legs of men in blue were seen.

"In there, number one! Next man — file second! In with you! Use the bayonet!"

As the first marine came stooping through the fissure of the door, the colored man Green discharged his rifle; the man fell with a cry, and was dragged back from outside.

"In with you, number two!"

As the second marine came in, Coppock's gun went off; the man stumbled, but fell forward. Smoke, ascending from these rifles, filled the engine-house and slowly soared upward, and John Brown, lying along the top of the engine, was concealed in the smoke.

Lloyd Quantrell saw a small man in officer's dress creep in the broken space at the bottom of the door, and peer around like a rat, as the smoke arose.

Suddenly this man, by two switches of a sword in his hand, extorted loud cries from both Taylor and Anderson, who had ceased to fight.

"Murder! Oh!"

"Quarter! God!"

Quantrell saw this small officer's elbow and bright blade thrust vengefully again and right into the bodies of the same unresisting and unarmed companions, who fell howling to the brick floor.

His attention was for a moment diverted from this marine officer by a second one, possibly superior in rank to the first, who came half-way in and also peered around, and whose countenance was manly but unexcited.

The rifle of John Brown was leveled at this man; Quantrell looked to see him fall dead.

Brown kept the officer under his merciless aim a second, and then, seeing more marines come in, he put his rifle down and drew the sword of King Frederick.

His act was beheld by the first marine-officer, who had been looking everywhere, under strong excitement, as for the leader of this foray.

This officer drew his bloody blade, bounded upon the side of the engine, and with all his might slashed the old leader across the head, and then, by an upward blow, delivered with the whole fury of his feelings, he stabbed John Brown and felled him to the hard floor of the engine-house.

Hands seized one of the engines and hurled it forward. The door fell entirely outward, and the daylight shone upon the little prison and its huddling and furious or frightened beings: upon the smoke, the cries, the curses — the living, the groaning, and the dead.

The next thing Quantrell saw was the rush of a great multitude from the railroads and the river. They came with shrieks of —

"Hang them! hang them!"

While groping his way out, Quantrell saw the maddened lieutenant of marines, who had killed Anderson and Taylor and stabbed John Brown, strike one of his fellow-prisoners, a respectable old Virginia gentleman, with the flat of his sword.

"Shame, sir!" cried Quantrell.

The maniacal officer turned upon our hero and smote him, also, with the flat of the same sword.

Quantrell staggered backward and fell into a strong pair of arms.

"What! Bruder Lloyd. You here?"

It was Luther Bosler. He kissed Lloyd fervently in the Dunker fashion.

The next minute Lloyd Quantrell's bleeding face was passionately kissed also by Katy of Catoctin.

Chapter XXIV

THE FREE-STATE LINE

WHEN Luther Bosler and his father came in from plowing at the premature sounding of the bell, the news of an insurrection at Harper's Ferry had been confirmed, and Katy was almost distracted by her lover's danger and the loss of her ring; while Nelly Harbaugh, whose strong, worldly nature kindled at the great neighboring event, prodded Luther Bosler to take both the girls to Virginia.

"Nay," Father Jake Bosler entreated, *"wass is de use? Ich con's net goot afforde.* Te wheat-ground ain't a-ready, Luter. Stay away from worltly contintions. Trouble comes time enough. Bi'm-by."

"Fader," Katy spoke, "Lloyd's there: *sell is olles."*

Saying "That is all," she broke down, and Nelly Harbaugh cried:

"Dawdy Jake, you're hard on Katy: she's nervous; she's growing; it's a delicate time of life for Katy."

Jake Bosler took his child in his arms and called her *"leeb"* and *"dowb,"* while the turtle-doves at the window made their plaintive "ah-coo-roo-coo-roo!"

"Katy," he said, "you is too good for te city mans. Stay with fader, and pe te likeness of my Olty to my poor heart till — Bi'm-by."

His eyes were full of tears as he called her the only likeness of his dead wife. Katy threw her arms around his neck, crying:

"Oh, my heart pulls both-a-ways! But Lloyd pulls it the most!"

"Jake," spoke Luther Bosler, after reflection, to his father, "tese great events happens py us for some good purpose. We must not fly from te Lord's works. I'll put two hands in my place, and take te girls."

"No, Luter, stay home. I'm daddy, and I forbid you."

"I'm minister ofer you, Jake, and you must opey."

"Tere's your gal, sohn Luter — Nelly's giddy. Keep her at home and to work, and you'll haf her to enjoy. Take her into te world, and she'll find temptation. Bi'm-by."

Luther took up the Bible and called to prayers; he prayed for Nelly and for Katy, and for peace in the world.

"Now, girls," he said, arising, "we'll make some pusiness out of all this. Harper's Ferry is, maype, full of hungry strangers. You git to work and cook pies, chickens, ham, whatefer will sell, and I think I can pring home to fader more money than plowing prings."

Jake Bosler seemed placated at this business outlook, and went to the stable to give special bedding to the horses for the journey.

All night the girls and hands stayed up to cook, and before daylight the big wagon, with two seats in it, was moving down the South Mountain side. Climbing the mountain, they saw Burkettsville's spires come out of the valley mists, and in Crampton's Gap the early partridge cried "Bob White!" Katy slept in Nelly's lap.

"Pure child," said Nelly, "her worldly love is fresh, Luther, as a new-laid egg in the hen's nest; what will it hatch?"

"Experience, dear. If you are in love, it will be the same."

"Luther, you are too wise a merchant to be a Dunker preacher. You will get rich if you take to the world. Oh, take me to see a little of the world, before we settle into everlasting Sabbath! I want experience, too — what Lloyd's father called 'career.' There is no want of love for you, my darling, in my heart, but I am not made" — she blushed as she thought of her own vanity — "to be always unseen."

"No," said Luther, "you are peautiful, Nelly. You shall pe seen of children, healthy like yourself, and one of those is more career than any man can have. To be a mother, supreme ofer a family — it is experience only one man efer had, and that was Adam, from whose side the woman came."

She blushed at the moment's anticipation of purely brought motherhood; but suddenly men started up between the cross-roads in Crampton's Gap and seized the horses' bridles.

"Money!" exclaimed one — a slight, stooping youth, with pale blue eyes; "we want your money to buy subsistence."

Around them were seven men, one a Negro, and all the rest white — travel-worn, stern young men, and revolvers were in their hands.

"You are fugitives from Harper's Ferry," spoke Luther, looking at them out of his large, sluggish eyes. "We have food and plenty of it; take, and pay, if you can. But we carry no money in this country."

They ate like famished men, and inquired about all the roads to the free State.

"Walk on te mountain-ridge," said Luther; "it is wooded and not often steep, but you may get thirsty for water. When you descend to the springs, look well for enemies. Beware at te free-State line of te kidnappers, who are probably lying in wait for you. Get well into Pennsylvania before you descend te mountain — yes, twenty miles."

They apologized for rudeness, and went up into the mountain-ridge, northward, while Luther turned at the guide-post in the Gap to the south, and threaded the narrow Pleasant Valley by the winding cascades of Israel's Creek. They fed at the Dunker churchyard, at Brownsville, and as they drew near Harper's Ferry, before sunrise, the roads became crowded. All the country was up, and Sandy Hook was like the center of a great camp-meeting. Soldiery were waiting at the bridge, travel from everywhere stopped at this ragged point, and time continued to bring more and more crowds. The old man, Isaac Smith, had suspended the Western world to the wand of his mysterious will.

Luther sold out his load before he crossed the bridge, and awaited the preparations to storm the engine-house. They saw the marines formed, and the quiet Colonel Lee giving the signals to the marine-officers from a place in the armory-yard; and then the rush of thousands to the captured stronghold.

After Katy found her lover, they still paused to see the dying son of Brown led out, and Lloyd Quantrell gave him water, which ran through his wounds; and so, in time, Watson died in Coppock's arms, peacefully and unconscious.

Colonel Washington was the hero of the delivery, and his gestures, when returning felicitations, had the grandeur of his origin. The mob ran his hired Negro into the river Shenandoah and drowned him there, and desired to tear John Brown to pieces, also, but he, from his blood and bruises, exclaimed to the better officer of the marines:

"Sir, I had you covered with my rifle; I expect you to protect my life, as I protected yours."

The officer saluted the brave old man. "Captain Brown," said he, "I thank you; in return, I will protect you with my life."

Very soon the queer old captive was complacently conducting an argument with the Governor of Virginia, a man of great romantic sensibility, who had already planned, on this *émeute*, a political campaign to make him President of the United States; and the two delightfully vain characters were entertaining reporters, Congressmen, and militia-captains with their sallies: but around one lay his dead-sons, sons-in-law, and comrades; and his political campaign would lead to nothing but the scaffold, to which he had the task to give dignity, if possible.

He turned out to be poor as pauperdom itself, without the means to transport himself back from the slave States to the free States, had he ever repented, and he had begged the little money for this expedition as the last enterprise of a disappointed but once promising career.

The bodies of his sons and connections were either taken by surgeons to the dissecting-room at Winchester, or buried with their comrades in a pit across the Shenandoah, where they lie near the unending grief of the plaintive river — poor bones of boys assembled by a wizard, to be the last relics of a mastodon age, and ever curious to moral, mental, and political science.

Those followers of Brown who survived, fitted to his situation with the anatomical symmetry of his own ribs; they continued to accept the leadership of his dignity, philosophy, and consistency, as they had followed him upon that forlorn hope to which his sincerity had given infatuation and plausibility.

Ned Coppock, taken with his smoking gun, soon became a hero among his captors; Stevens was put together, like a bloody puzzle; and these two were sent to Charlestown jail, eight miles away, with Captain Brown, in a wagon, as also the Negroes, Green and Copeland, while the pursuit of the seven fugitives went on in the Maryland and Pennsylvania mountains.

The whole land was finally convinced that John Brown had made his insurrection with an "army" of only twenty-three men, of whom ten had died fighting.

It might have been possible to treat John Brown's raid as without full moral accountability, and thus to have remanded it, by the contempt of justice, to the silence of a lunatic asylum; but the politician at the head of Virginia became the instrument to connect this little affair with the mightiest revolution of the age.

Governor Wise summoned the military of Virginia to arms, upon the belief, or pretense, that Brown's was only a portion of a general insurrection and abolition invasion; and the little court-house place of Charlestown became, for five months, a garrisoned spot during the trials and executions of Brown and his survivors, while the example of Virginia led to the arming of every slave State, and thence proceeded the fomentation of the scheme of a separated republic, to assure the safety of slavery.

To Charlestown, therefore, let us soon proceed with our story-people.

Katy Bosler, after fondly receiving her lover, cried:

"Te accordion, Lloyd; where is it?"

"I left it at the old bandit's farm, Katy."

"Oh, goodness! And, Lloyd, te fortune-teller, who said I should lose my ring, has run away with it to Pennsylvania. O darling, what shall we do?"

"Go after them both, Kate, if your dear little heart is troubled. I have enlisted in one of the military companies to put down this insurrection, and we are ordered to cross the river and see if the enemy is at his stronghold."

"Come on, then," said Luther Bosler; "I'll trife by John Brown's farm, and go home by Solomon's Gap."

As they were setting out, the English pointer appeared, profuse in his gladness of rejoining friends; and to Katy he was ever a flatterer, cringing at her feet and licking her hand.

"The hound loves you, Kate," Lloyd Quantrell said; "I'll give him to you, to keep at the farm in remembrance of me."

At the school-house in the marsh, boxes of arms were found, ready to be transported to Virginia. At the little rugged farm, they found many evidences of the conspiracy: letters torn to pieces in the short, thick pines, and arms and lead in the tenement of logs across the road; discarded bundles, boxes, and bags; and on the porch the dog Fritz stood tied, and hardly disposed to permit intrusion.

Lloyd attempted to go by this dog, to look for Katy's accordion, and Fritz seized him by the garments and held him fast.

"Hallo!" Quantrell said; "why, here's the last of Captain Brown's recruits, and determined as all the rest."

"Fritz is a faithful friend," said Luther Bosler; "not as valuable a dog as yours, Lloyd, but more reliable. Katy will gif him to you."

"Yes, Lloyd, if I find you took good care of my accordion."

Quantrell disappeared into the loft of the small cabin, and there he found the humble instrument under the eaves.

"Here it is, Kate," he cried, returning; "you little goosey, what makes you fear?"

"Now go and find her ring," Nelly Harbaugh spoke; "it was your mother's; it will make Katy your wife. Hannah Ritner has gone to the Siebentager Nunnery, only a day's ride from here, in Pennsylvania."

"Shall I go, darling?" He turned to Katy.

"O Lloyd, do go! *De letsht naucht war's orrick dunkle.*"

"Dark was that night, also, to me, bright eyes, when I expected to be killed and never see you more."

"Lloyd, your father says he will marry you to a *Cordullish* — a Catholic, one *hochmoot un reich.* If you do not find my ring, I shall believe it."

"Dear old father! But he can no more make me love another than he can love me, dear. How does he know this strange Ritner woman? Why, now I see something!"

"What is it, Lloyd?"

"That pony she rides I have seen in my father's stable. He, like Hannah Ritner, is an abolitionist."

As they paused to let the horses blow on Elk Ridge Mountain summit, the vale of John Brown was seen behind them, stony and steep, and before them the verdurous Pleasant Valley, with its stone farmhouses and apple-orchards, and, like a great, green vine swung low, the South Mountain drooped to Crampton's Gap, to give admission to the Catoctin Valley.

"Katy, good-bye," Lloyd said; "don't ever fear for me, gentle child! Never in love before, I could not forget you now, if every interest declared against you."

"I shall nefer let you go," the child said, with a resolution he had not observed in her before. "Since you haf come, Love has took possession of me. I will pray; I will persevere. I don't see how I am to get you, Lloyd, but I don't dare to lose you."

"O Katy!" exclaimed Nelly Harbaugh, "the *difel* of love is striving in you as I never saw it before. I could not be so headstrong."

"Nelly," spoke Katy, in the tempest of her woe and courage, "you can never love like me!"

Procuring a horse from a Dunker farm, on Minister Luther Bosler's request, Quantrell made his way to Smoketown, and entered the garden of Hannah Ritner.

The cool mountain-brook gurgled through her lot; the gourds hung from the arbors; the bees were humming drowsily in the hive; but stable and dwelling were empty of furniture, and the mountain behind the house was streaked with the foot-tracks of escaping slaves.

The neighbors told him that the fortune-teller was a great traveler, especially into Pennsylvania, and was now reported to be in Chambersburg.

Quantrell put his horse in Hannah Ritner's stable, and lay down to sleep alone in the little hut. He was very tired, and not until he had slept off his burden of fatigue did he begin to dream.

He dreamed that his mother's lost wedding-ring was a great wheel or tire of mourning gold, with black enamel in its rich yellow, and he was trying to roll it like a hoop up the mountain; but it weighed heavily upon his sinews, and he felt it overthrowing him with its backward gravity; he cried for help, but all the response he could hear was a little baby's cry, until, when he had given up hope and resigned himself to be crushed by the black and gleaming cincture, a pike or spear was hurled from above, as if out of the sky, and it transfixed the mighty ring, like a dart ringed by a golden quoit; at once the ring was fractured, and the black enamel upon it was detached like a separate hoop, and went thundering down South Mountain with a sound like rolling fire, and he could hear it plunge into the Antietam Creek and sizz there, like the red-hot stones which, at hog-butchering time, the farmers boil their scalding hogsheads with.

Dart after dart came ringing from above — the very pikes, it seemed, that he had seen in boxes that day at the bandits' rendezvous — and each of these entered the other lucent rim of virgin gold remaining there, which, like a mirror, flashed the heavens back, and, becoming magnified to powerful proportions, this ring contained an inscription, "Pure Union."

Quantrell was afraid to look up and see what *valkyrias* or spirits had hurled those lances into the nuptial band; but, as the golden rim grew more and more distinct, he began to see faint faces reflected from the sky — faces with blood upon them: the ashen face of Watson Brown, the bloodless blue lips of Oliver Brown, the raven beard and wounds of Kagi, the hollow sphere of Lehman's skull, the mute, appealing countenance of William Thompson, and others he feared to pause and think on.

He awoke: at the little window of the cabin a golden-ringed light of a burning piece of pine illuminated a group of faces pressed against the panes. Quantrell raised a yell of dread.

The light was extinguished; steps were heard receding.

"This is a witch's den!" thought Quantrell, his heart bounding in his breast; "surely I saw the faces there of old John Brown, of Ned Coppock, and of Hazlett, Cook, and others of their band."

He entered Hagerstown next day, and found the whole population talking of the raid, and looking at himself and at all strangers with suspicion. Large rewards were out for Cook and others, guessed at or known, and Isaac Smith, or Brown, had been seen by half the people in the town, hauling away the boxes of arms he had received by rail from Chambersburg.

To that place Quantrell fearlessly proceeded, taking a roundabout course through a famous kidnappers' settlement called Leitersburg, within sight of the Pennsylvania boundary-line. Here the tavern was beset by wild-looking borderers, and Quantrell narrowly escaped being made to stop and fight, according to the chivalry of those times; he "treated" liberally at the bar, and was relieved to find that the Logan brothers, whose chief rendezvous this was, had gone off in the South Mountain to hunt for John Brown's fugitives.

Resolved to keep his word to Katy, the young man slowly continued on to Chambersburg, a flourishing shire town, twenty miles within Pennsylvania, and there, too, the excitement about the great abolition raid was universal.

Hundreds of people stood before an old, low warehouse with derrick windows, where John Brown had stored his Kansas rifles so long before employing them; and threatening groups molested a plain boarding-house on a back street, where the recruits for Brown, and that redoubtable captain himself, had been accommodated with Christian shelter.

The keeper of this dwelling bore the same family name as Hannah Ritner, and was said to be a daughter-in-law of a former Governor of Pennsylvania, but Lloyd found such apprehension and terror in the family that he could get no information of their mysterious connection, though he thought, when he said he was the son of Abel Quantrell, that they took a suspicious interest in him for a moment.

The Governor of Pennsylvania was a Democrat, of the same political party as the Governor of Virginia, and would manifestly deliver any of Brown's band up to the jurisdiction they had offended. The Pennsylvania public considered Brown's greatest offense to have been the purloining the sword of General Washington; and it was thought hardly less culpable to have provided a "nigger" with bed and board in a white family.

The person that all popular vengeance was now directed against was little Captain Cook, the forerunner and spy of the raiders, and he was believed to be in the very county of Scotch and Irish settlers where Quantrell was now wandering.

Considering that Hannah Ritner might be at the Seventh-Day Baptist kloster or nunnery, Lloyd, several days after the raid, turned his horse southward and began to approach the bright bounding hillocks of the South Mountain again. Toward evening he entered an old German hamlet called Funkstown, near the clove of the mountain, where the source of the Antietam Creek ran out, discolored with the ores of iron from an old furnace in the gorge. The aspect of the region was romantic, yet sinister, as if the near contact of slavery had caused premature decay and human degradation. He was eating his plain supper in the tavern, at the entrance to the little town, when he heard the sound of many feet in the small sitting room and bar, near by.

"Don't be afraid of me, boys; I won't do you any harm," he heard a not unfamiliar voice say.

Looking out, Quantrell saw a mob of little boys, trembling in the presence of one hardly bigger than the least of them.

This childish figure had his hands tied behind him, and was dirty and disordered, like one who had been living in the holes of foxes, or crawling on the earth like the serpents there.

"Eat your supper," spoke a practical voice; "we must have you in Chambersburg jail tonight, so be quick."

The speaker had a low, mercenary sparkle in his eyes. His victim's long-fringed orbs of blue shone out amid his dirt, and gave him some of the pathos and dignity of fate.

"Poor Captain Cook!" Quantrell exclaimed; "to think that he can be, in the eyes of any law, a worse being than his captor, that vile slave-taker!"

"If you mean Ben Logan," cried a plain man at the table, "I pray you not to speak so loud. He has his slave-pen close by us here, under the mountain, and in this clove the runaway slaves generally come down, thinking they are full ten miles inside of a free State. Logan takes them here, and gets his blood-money; and he has a band of lads he has demoralized, who would stop at no revenge."

Nevertheless, Quantrell made no concealment of his person; the slave-taker looked at him with some dislike, but it was now all subordinated to the avarice of a thousand dollars' reward.

"John," said Quantrell to the boy, who had washed his face and was eating like a famished wolf, as he stood before the drinking-bar, "what did you quit the safe mountain for?"

"Starvation!" replied Cook; "my companions were dying for food, and I quit them to find it."

"You might as well have sold life dear; you will surely be executed."

"They surprised me," said Cook, the food sticking in his throat, as his feelings rose. "But for their treachery, I would have taken a bloodhound's life for every ball in my revolver."

"Oh," said another captor of the boy, complimentarily, "he fought like a wild monkey. Four of us was atop of him at once, and the fattest feller had jest to fall on him and knock the breath out of him before he would give in."

"I pity you, Cook," Quantrell said; "though you, also, played a treacherous part."

"You may well pity me, sir," the frail little man said, with swimming eyes; "my comrades have no great friends, and can die with sincerity, while my distinguished relatives will ruin my fame to save my neck, and I shall be hanged all the same."

They took him to Chambersburg jail in the pleasant autumn afternoon. The news soon came that Hazlett, too, was recaptured at Carlisle; but the brother of Coppock, and another son of John Brown, and two other whites and a Negro, under the kind vigilance of Hannah Ritner's friends, escaped to Canada.

As Quantrell was walking up into the gorge at Mount Alto furnace, looking at the spot where Cook had been taken, after an exciting struggle, an employé at the ironworks said:

"Are you aware that the patron of John Brown is a relative of the chief captor of this Captain Cook?"

"How so?"

"The papers say that the great abolitionist, Gerrit Smith, gave the land in the Adirondack woods, where John Brown's family live. Now, Gerrit Smith married the daughter of Colonel Fitzhugh, of Hagerstown, and she is the aunt of that other man who, with Logan, took Cook away to claim the reward. So the aunt helps Brown and his band to come here, and her nephew sells him to Virginia."

"Strange," said Quantrell, "what coincidences lie in this short vale of the Antietam! We may be on the brink of a great strife, and, if so, the hurrying fates that have encamped in this small district may keep it still in their commemoration."

He next rode down the strong brook of the Antietam, to the old Seventh-Day Baptist nunnery.

It stood in a crevice of the mountain foot-lands, where a meadow bubbled up in copious springs which, fashioned into a bed, wound in a strong brook between the long brick monastery and the low, massive, white-plastered church, and then, caught up in a mill-race, turned two old Dunker mills. The dwelling, or kloster-house, was nearly a hundred and fifty feet long, and of a delightfully broken form, with a great-chimneyed, squatting kitchen in the middle, flanked by long conventional wings — on one side a cool porch and several doors, the other side more primitively German, with little lines of windows, and over the center dormers rose the naked cupola and bell. The gurgling brook, talking at its birthplace, described such gossipy rounds of flowing, that all the parts of this settlement seemed to be in a circle, and fruit sprang out of the earth as if here was some old corner of Paradise, neglected but uncursed. The humid spring meadow was tinted with blue sedge and flowers, and a pond in the midst was their looking-glass. Woods and rocks shut in the church, and its two doors that separated the vexing mystery of sex; cultivated hills hid the nunnery from the south; the cedar, fern, ailantus, catalpa, apple, and pear trees gave grateful shade; and milk and cider showed their butteries and presses to the covetous eye of the homeless tramp, for whose terror a sign was put on the door, which none of his brotherhood was ever known to heed. Close by, the graveyard showed the tombs of the Snowbergers, for whom Snow Hill (berg) was named, and of their Ephrata-reared friends; and the South Mountain, losing its coherence here in Pennsylvania, described great hillocks and cones near by, and in the south showed the blue promontory in which it crossed the free-State line, and then swerved irresolutely away.

Quantrell looked everywhere for some human being to speak to. Finally, he saw people — women and men — off in the fields reaping late hay and preparing winter ground. He remembered that it was the Sabbath, when the contrary zeal of sect impelled even the lazy Seventh-Dayers to exert themselves, lest they might be thought to respect the Sabbath they had discarded.

He spoke to some of the women, but they paid not the least attention to him — old, fat, dull women, like winter apples, never ripe nor mellow; they wore their hoods of figured brown or black calico, and plied their rakes, and seemed between a blush and contempt of man.

"Are you Job Snowberger?" he addressed the solitary man among these ancient pullets.

The man looked at him, with a countenance where gallantry had been suppressed and curiosity flagellated, an envious, simple smile, and proceeded to whet his scythe.

"Are you deaf, or only a fool?"

"*Unshicklich!*" exclaimed the man, with a piping cry, like a disappointed child's, and his mouth turned toward the women.

These came upon Quantrell with their field implements, all shouting German words together, and one or two looked as if desirous to fight a man, if merely for the novelty of encounter.

"I'm a-tryin' to persewere," cried the man, with tears of temper in his eyes, "and he calls me *Norr.*"

The women raised their rakes and hoes on Quantrell.

"Poor fellow!" Lloyd said; "the last rooster on the hill, and protected by the hens! But don't be violent, my beauties. I only want to find Hannah Ritner, for little Katy Bosler."

"*Wass!*" exclaimed the man, "is Katy persewerin'? *Unshuldich!* Does she seek te Kloster and te *heilich* life? O *yubelee!*"

"*Weck-gae!*" cried the old women, turning back to their work, as if disgusted with such enthusiasm.

"I'm Katy's beau — Lloyd — and I want to find Hannah Ritner, and get Katy's engagement-ring."

"*Weck-gae!* Depart!" cried Job Snowberger, again in tears. "Shweshter Marcella is in Ohio. Katy is in sin. You are in mischief, and you'll persewere in it. Te ring of Bosler's child is lost in te spring."

He pointed to an old dairy by the nunnery-kitchen, and, falling tearfully to his reaping, began to wail a piping psalm.

"Gone mad betwixt love and scorn of love, I reckon," Quantrell said, walking to the dairy-house.

Lying there on the floor was Andrew Atzerodt, beside the troughs of water, an empty bottle at his side. His snore was relieved by the falsetto of Job Snowberger in the meadow, sounding like a babe's complaint.

Quantrell bent over the spring, and in it the light, falling upon some tin or metal object, described a shining circle in the bubbles.

"That's what the poor lunatic meant by Katy's ring, I reckon," Quantrell said; "he's 'gone' on Katy, like myself."

Atzerodt aroused, and looked up wofully.

"Here, you vagrant fellow, come back with me to Virginia, and to your coach-maker's trade!"

"Never!" answered Atzerodt; "I'm doing nothing now but hunting niggers and apolitionists, and running petween te lines."

Chapter XXV
CHARLESTOWN

AS Atzerodt and Quantrell walked into Charlestown, Virginia, after many delays, they found it convenient to take one of the side streets, and avoid the herds of militia; for the entire State had knocked off work, and was making Brown's immortality with more than the directness of superior intelligence.

It had suited the prevailing opinion there to assume the gravity of a great injury, too deep to permit any other State to share it. The inhabitants, talking on the subject to strangers, adopted a reserve which showed how the sensitiveness of slaveholding had destroyed personal individuality, and banded into almost maudlin one-mindedness, like Niobe and her family, a society scarcely beyond its pioneer period; for a house where Atzerodt stopped to peep in was, like many others, composed of recently hewn forest logs. He drew back in a moment and exclaimed:

"Py Jing! tere's te black man with te white face!"

Quantrell approached the shutters ajar, and, at the first adjustment of the light within to his eyes, he cried:

"Why, that's John Booth, the actor, my friend and schoolmate!"

A young man with a large, intelligent face, given pale contrast by his rich, black mustache and curling black hair, was reciting in the middle of the floor, listened to by males and females with the greatest interest.

"It's te very picture of te man I rode with in my dream, py Jing!" Atzerodt continued.

The reciter within ended his task with these lines, given with robust and nearly impassioned vehemence:

> "Heroic matron!
> Now, now, the hour is come! By this one blow
> Her name's immortal and her country saved.
> Hail, dawn of glory! Hail, thou sacred weapon!

Virtue's deliverer, hail!"

"Look, Lloyd!" whispered Atzerodt. "Py Jing! he's got a knife in his hand, shoost like te black man with te white face!"

The young actor did shake above his head, and apostrophize it fervently, a glittering thing — continuing:

"Did not the Sibyl tell you
A fool should set Rome free? I am that fool! . . .

Hear me, great Jove! and thou, paternal Mars,
And spotless Vesta! To the death, I swear,
My burning vengeance shall pursue these Tarquins!
Valerius, Collatine, Lucretius — all —
Here I adjure ye by this fatal dagger,
All stained and reeking with her sacred blood,
Be partners in my oath-revenge her fall! . . .

Up to the forum! On! the least delay
May draw down ruin, and defeat our glory.
On, Romans, on! The fool shall set you free!"

Loud applause followed the reciter's tragedy-selection, from the same author whose piece of "Sweet Home" had been the battle-march of John Brown. In a moment the actor came out, followed by some of his more intimate admirers, and he called affectionately to Quantrell:

"My dear Lloyd, where did you come from?"

"Maryland, John. And you?"

"From Richmond. I threw up my engagement at the theater there when I heard of this outrage, and enlisted in the Grays; and I am here to stay till these myrmidons are hanged and Virginia avenged. Let me introduce you to my friends — Mr. Arnold, Mr. O'Laughlin, young Master Herold, and Mr. Fenwick, of the clergy."

Quantrell hesitated about introducing Atzerodt, who was unshaved and shabby, but he saw that Booth's following was hardly more genteel.

Arnold he had seen, as a Baltimore bread-baker's son of the old German stock; O'Laughlin, as a runner in that city, of the opposite political party. Herold was a mere lad from Washington, modest and wondering; and Fenwick, who wore a black suit neatly buttoned to the throat, and had a silver watch-guard, was a fresh, square-set blonde, with the dignity of the Catholic novitiate priest that he was.

"Who is your friend, Lloyd?" asked the actor. "We are all Virginians here."

"This is one also, I believe — Mr. Atzerodt."

Booth shook the common fellow's hand with such kindness that he stammered out:

"Say! Vere is dat womans dat said 'Sharge!' te night we rode up te Short Mountain?"

"What does he say?" asked Booth.

"Oh, he had a dream, when he was tipsy, and so he is tipsy now, and he thinks he saw you in that dream."

"Oh, some people are carried away by the acting," remarked Booth, considerately, as they walked along. "Now, do you know, I don't set much value on acting? This is what I like — real campaigning. Here is meat for your John Howard Paynes to write about — the coming of the Tarquins to this beautiful valley, their murdering of its yeomanry, and inciting servile insurrection; and who would not prefer to be Junius Brutus, to either the author or the player of his part? Think of the time when the hero of a convulsion like this will be the subject of poetry, and as he inflicts revenge for Virginia's injuries, he utters the motto Jefferson gave the shield of the insulted State, *Sic semper tyrannis!* 'Thus ever with tyrants!'"

Halting as he spoke, Mr. Booth put his foot upon a stone riding-step at the curb, as upon a tyrant's head, and again raised his white hand and eloquent face to the sunlight.

Quantrell now saw that Booth had been drinking a little, and was unusually aggressive.

"The stage," said the divinity student, Fenwick, much impressed by Mr. Booth's trained pulpit manner, "has never illustrated morals as it might do, Mr. Booth, in gentlemen bred for it, from religious homes like yours. That, perhaps, is why actors seldom realize in private life the affected virtues they delineate. Yet there is no reason why an actor may not be a hero, too."

"He can't be, Father Fenwick" (the "father" a deferential reference to the youthful priest's canonicals); "the actor is a closet-rat, a caged-up hawk. He must make so many paces to the rear, turn and fence, or strike, at such a distance from the foot-lights, go off by this or that numbered slide or exit; and all that preparation to deceive or impersonate is called 'study.' *Here* is the nobler theater of the roads, the cross-paths, the ravines, and the country maids. If I had been at Harper's Ferry, *there* would have been a chance: I am the best shot in the profession; I can jump like a circus-rider. My study has not been of dog-eared play-books, like my father's other sons: I have qualified myself for a soldier and a champion. With two or three good drinks in me, I would have been the man to give old Brown's party the start they wanted, and tell off an equal number of brave men with them, and chase them up the canal side of the river, killing as we went, or dying in our blood. What a death, or victory, would that have been!"

His animated, yet hardly egotistical manner, made its impression, and O'Laughlin said:

"Wilkes, I've seen you fence, and jump, and spar, too, and I know how you *parley vous* of it."

"And, John, I've seen you ride the devilishest horses in Harford or Howard Counties," Arnold added, "and you never got throwed neither."

"You ain't a bad man to be out with for a scrimmage, after midnight," added Quantrell, "as I have found out."

The recipient of these compliments took them with a good nature which had yet a manful health in it; he was not a tall man, but of strong-welded, equal bodily parts, the arms showing large muscle under his soldier-sleeves; and he was a little bowed in the legs, but this was only noticeable when one measured him for athletic utilities. His figure was so gentlemanly that he never would have been suspected of any physical affectations or prowess, but for his own reference to those subjects, which Quantrell, who knew him long, ascribed to his having drunk some liquor. The soldier-clothes and pompon hat he wore admirably became his trim figure and striking yet harmonious face, lighted by fine black eyes and in all its features clear and considerate.

"Py Jing!" exclaimed Atzerodt, "I played on te theater, too!"

"You?" from Quantrell.

"Yes, py Jing! I built the biggest band-wagon for te circus dat ever started from Fergeenia. It was shoost as long as dis street. It held most a hundert music-players. I trove it, py Jing —"

"And what then, old fellow?" Mr. Booth asked, with mischief in his eye, throwing an arm affectionately around the boy Herold.

"Why, I trove it into a ditch, py Jing, and proke te heads of tem tam horn-blowers! Hya, ya!"

All laughed loudly at Atzerodt's manner and terrier-bark of a laugh; and so they walked along, noting the straight, ridgy turnpike town, with its houses of brick, limestone, or logs, turned sidewise to the narrow sidewalks, and in the distance the Blue Ridge, or South Mountain, rising from the wooded *fosse* of the river Shenandoah.

In a depression of Charlestown stood the brick, porticoed court-house, opposite a tavern, and the stone-and-brick jail opposite another tavern, and diagonally opposite the court-house. At these corners was all the semblance of militia pomp — sentries, guardhouses, officers of the day, colonels, and generals; orderly sergeants riding, self-important, on errands of mighty insignificance; horses tied to racks, and warriors bowing and scraping, ogling and suspecting. There was apparently some Satanic plot, in the air or underground, to bewizard this sturdy, steady, demi-German population.

Rumors of coming abolitionists to rescue Brown and his six men were of daily and nightly verification: frenzied people came in who had seen marching columns; from the house-tops of Charlestown signal-lights and bale-fires had been distinctly noticed; anonymous letters threatening more insurrections came through the post; the United States Government was as fully suspended here as if Virginia meant to cast it off; and the mails — those nerves of healthy life or the torturing pins of political neuralgia — were manipulated, assorted, and controlled.

Thus, as the secret of a murder, extending through a large family connection, discolors the world to them, the cry of the unpaid laborers rang forever in the ears of those who had inherited the system, and two insurrections in one whole generation had been met somewhat as if expected — the injury was felt to be proportionate to the hazard of the institution.

Of all places in the world, except Mount Vernon, here was the spot to point the lesson of John Brown — the family settlement of General Washington's younger brethren, who had crossed the South Mountain barrier, not as the "Knights of the Golden Horseshoe," but as the knights of shoeless herds of slaves, to mix this degraded labor with the old German tide of voluntary labor, from Pennsylvania, and up the long valley, between the mountain parallels, to drive the discolored tide till, in the ignorant white race of the far Southwest and the hopeless black race there, phosphatic death seemed rich for the chemist of Revolution, to come, with his burning acids and hot retorts, and manure the New World with human bones.

The streets of Charlestown were labeled with the Washington family's *prenoms,* and in the churchyard there lay their dead; and the foremost of that name, which King George had put a bloody price upon, was but yesterday the captive of John Brown, the abolitionist, who desired to exchange him for "a nigger."

Was it this despair of pride, in a system as fleeting as the robber's booty, which occasioned all this military pomp? Or was it the self-deception of the Pharisee, which exalted to self-respect, and even to didactic and reasoning retort, the dying and impenitent thief beside the unfriended martyr?

This discrimination, which is the first of political crimes, is also the foundation of public hypocrisy — the classifying of men from the standard of one's own righteousness; and there was nothing so righteous in its own esteem, in all the nineteenth Christian century, as the insulted slavery of Virginia. Like Lucretia of old, it fain would die, in this instant of such perfect purity as to have become rapine's victim.

No face in Charlestown showed this expression of almost antique and fateful yet holy reverie like John Beall's, whom they met before the principal tavern, and whom Quantrell introduced to Mr. Booth. His settled features, straight lines of brow and mouth, and reserved address, were those of a man against whom, alone, the whole insult of Brown's raid had been directed.

He accompanied the party to a drinking-room, but would not partake; and, while they stood there, a tall, slim young person, straight as an Indian, and looking straight also as an Indian's arrow, walked up to Mr. Booth.

"May I speak to an actor?" he said. "I recognize you as Mr. Booth. I have never been to the theater but once in my life, and I shall never forget it. It would be such a pleasure to say, when I go home to Florida, that I shook the hand of the son of the great Booth, who must be, I think, a greater actor than his father."

"No offense, my young friend," answered Mr. Booth. "What did you say your name was?"

"Powell. I came to Virginia, sir, to attend a Baptist school, and be, like my father, a preacher; but I like excitement a little, like all the boys, and, as I peeped one night into the theater, and heard your grand — may I say, sir, your majestic acting? — so, also, I slipped off — with the money that was to do for me all next term at school — to see the great John Brown raid. I won't detain you, sir, after I have expressed my great appreciation of your acting."

"Oh, take a drink with us," said Booth; "here is another preacher — Father Fenwick. He's a Catholic, and you're a Baptist — and I'm part Jew. So we can't quarrel."

The respectable elements of this group soon found each other out; the Baltimore companions of Booth had been so attentive to him that their cause of interest was soon manifest: they wanted to borrow money to meet their expenses and get out of town. Atzerodt and little Herold struck up a friendship, and went off together; and Mr. Beall, the clerical student Fenwick, and Booth and Quantrell accepted an invitation to visit the prisoners in their cells.

The prison, on the public corner, seemed a respectable dwelling, with an extension of a more sinister appearance on the side street. A "reception-room" was within, and the partly open door thereof showed a boyish lad leaning upon his elbow at the window, and interrogated by one of several important-seeming men.

"That is said to be the Democratic Governor of Indiana," spoke Beall; "the boy is that infernal scoundrel Cook, his brother-in-law. Gentlemen, they are all abolitionists, or the same family would not turn out two kinds of professions."

Quantrell saw that Cook's face had the bitterness of death in it.

"John," the Governor was speaking, "why have you never written to your sisters in these two years?"

"Ashbel, events too exciting had occurred to me. There was nothing to write that you, or they, could have felt any sympathy for. I had been forced into this cause."

"John, your parents never brought you up to herd yourself with assassins."

"No, Ashbel, I went to Kansas to practice law. As I crossed the prairie with a youthful friend, strange horsemen rode up to us and asked us what State we hailed from. 'New York,' replied my innocent companion. At that, the challenger shot him dead. I had my rifle with me, and, as the cowards rode away, I emptied two of their saddles. For that a price was set upon my head, and I was hunted down, and I found John Brown's outlawed camp and joined his cause. Love came to me in my lonely and dangerous outpost at Harper's Ferry; like you, I have a wife and son."

He broke down in a sob which touched the Governor's heart. He sprang forward and cried:

"John, I have come to save your life. I will stand by you. But you must repudiate these ruffians who seduced you to this business."

They passed along and entered a comfortable cell. John Brown sat at a little table reading his Bible aloud to a man who reclined upon a bed.

The old woods-fighter was in discolored and rag-rent dress, having been too consistent to accept other clothes from those who lived by the toil of slaves; his wounds were healing, but his scalp was still bandaged up, and his face showed bruises.

The other man on the bed was a dreadful object, as the balls remained in his head and body, and between his gashes the pallid streaks of health were like the white stripes in the American flag.

"Captain Brown," Quantrell said, "here is a young priest who takes an interest in you."

John Brown looked up at Fenwick, while extending his hand to Quantrell.

"Of what persuasion, sir?"

"Roman Catholic. You would not reject my prayers for that, Captain Brown?"

"No, sir. But do you believe human slavery is right?"

"I think so, captain."

"Then you are a priest of the devil, sir, and need not bestow your prayers on me! Who is this fine-appearing young man?"

He turned from Fenwick, and looked up at Booth.

"That is an actor, the son of the great tragedian, Booth."

"An actor? I have never seen a play; life was too serious and engaged with me. — I hope, my young friend, that you may act your part, if occasion ever calls you to do so, with reference to eternal things. In my situation, with but a little while to live, it is my only comfort to feel that none of the poor and destitute consider me their enemy. Applause I have none; I am but little understood; yet here" — he touched the little Bible — "I do not find my condemnation."

Booth looked down at the old man with a respect which had no feeling in it, but he said, in a plausible tone:

"Captain, give me your autograph. Men like you do not live every day."

There was no paper, and Mr. Beall found a piece of a letter in his pocket, which he handed to Booth, and then subsided to his pinched brows and chin, and most hopeless face.

John Brown took up the pen, and slowly, silently wrote:

"I, John Brown, am now quite certain that the crimes of this guilty land will never be purged away but with blood. I had, as I now think, vainly flattered myself that, without very much bloodshed, it might be done."

As the four young men put their heads together to read this piece of writing, a resonant voice at the cell-door spoke in a slight German accent:

"Captain, your dinner is ready! This way, sir!"

They all looked up, and there met their gaze a large, black-eyed man, with a tray of victuals.

All looked down again but Quantrell; he stood, staring at this coarsely dressed servant in open-mouthed astonishment.

"Where — ?" he finally spoke, in a low tone.

The man raised his finger to his lip, and looked at Quantrell with the intensest meaning.

"I know you, surely," Quantrell said, almost breathless; "you are —"

"Silence!" whispered the man, with a stately motion, far above his roughly marked face and ignoble dress — "silence, by your mother's spirit! Let me pass."

John Brown took this person's arm and hobbled painfully from the cell.

When Quantrell turned again, with a countenance ghastly in its wonder, he found Booth and the nearly helpless fellow-prisoner of Brown conversing strongly:

"Spiritualist, are you?" sounded the voice of Booth. "Well, if I had you to do with, I would take you at your word, and, like the witches who dealt with spirits of old, I would burn you at a pile of fagots!"

The man, shot all to pieces, but cool as a red fall apple punctured by the wasps, answered, as well as he could talk:

"Kind fellow you are! Now, if I were to meet a bad, black eye like yours, going through a woods, I would give you a broom!"

"A broom!" said Booth, looking puzzled at Stevens, the disabled captive; "what would I want with a broom?"

"To get a-straddle of it," concluded Stevens, "like the witches you ride with, and go to hell!"

At these invincible sounds the young priest, Fenwick, crossed himself hastily, while Booth and Beall looked down at Stevens with strong hate.

"Keep out of such company, my boy," Stevens remarked to Quantrell; "they have no progress in them."

"Progress — what is that?"

"Heaven is nothing but progress," Stevens said; "my education was nothing: don't you suppose heaven will be a school to me? The spirits of my love will be around my desk; old angel friends will teach me music; I shall read, and know, and progress onward. That's my belief. My sweetheart left it to me when she passed away."

As they left the jail, Quantrell asked the kind-eyed jailer:

"Who serves the meals to Captain Brown?"

"An old Dutch baker out in the town; he sends the captain's meals in by his people."

Lloyd Quantrell was silent. He knew, however, that the person with the tray of victuals he had seen in the jail was either Hannah Ritner or her ghost.

He hastened to the baker's house, on a back street; they knew nothing of any person answering to the name, or description, or disguise, of Hannah Ritner.

Katy's ring was lost again: would she ever find it by "searching for it down a brook?"

Chapter XXVI

OATH-PLIGHT AND TROTH-PLIGHT

AT the south end of Charlestown a small limestone brook relieved the sunny situation and watered some Virginia lawns, and near its turnpike bridge and ford was a mill and tannery, agreeable to the sight and smell, with the dripping water-wheel and the cord-piled bark. Here, wandering together, Quantrell and his three companions came upon a large wagon, and in it were Luther and Katy Bosler, and Nelly Harbaugh.

Lloyd rushed upon the party, and his later friends were surprised to see him not only kiss the slight, childish, large-eyed lass, but also kiss her sluggish-eyed, bovine-moving brother.

"Dear Katy, where did you come from?"

Luther answered, as Katy sprang again to Lloyd's arms:

"Lloyd, we are huckstering a little. Te rules is against coming to Harper's Ferry from Maryland, so we cross te pridge at Berlin and cross te mountain at Keyes's Ferry, and we sell to te soldiers here."

"Breaking the laws, *bruder?* And you a minister!"

"Such laws as Fergeenia has on this occasion," replied Luther, dryly, "are te laws of insanity. Tere is no tariff petween te States of our Union, and I am an American citizen. If Fergeenia had petter laws, John Brown could have stayed at home."

"What, sir!" exclaimed Mr. Beall. "Is this your return for Virginia hospitality?"

"I am feeding Fergeenia, I think," replied Luther, plainly. "Terefore, I am not guilty of any inhospitality. What one thinks, he is responsible to himself and his Maker for."

"There are things thought," exclaimed Booth, sternly, "which are worse than bold crimes."

"Assuredly," answered Luther, "and that is why I have no tisguises. I do not come here and agree with everypody and pe a spy. I say te man who is in te jail, today, is truer to justice than te judge upon te bench! Te plood he shed I do not approve of — put we, Lloyd, haf seen innocent plood shed too. Remember te old daddy on te mountain, dying to get to freedom —"

"O Lloyd," cried Katy, "your fader has pought Ashby, and we've prought him to Charlestown; he's in a Tunker family's house, close py!"

"And here's a letter from your father, Lloyd," Nelly Harbaugh cried, returning a most respectful and admiring look Mr. Booth gave her. "We expected to find you, before long."

As Lloyd read the letter, Booth engaged Nelly Harbaugh in conversation, and Hugh Fenwick, the semi-fledged priest, talked, with deference, to Katy Bosler; while Mr. Beall interrogated Luther Bosler in his intense, unrelieved way, and with a fierceness his low tones just concealed. The letter said:

My son,

I have bought you another slave at your request. I present him to you, according to such law as there is for property in our fellow-kind. Your own money I keep for you. The cube of human bondage is Golgotha. Find that word in your dictionary, and don't forget it! I sincerely hope John Brown will be hanged as he is too valuable to live — like the prize steer. To spare his life would give Virginia another generation to patronize this Union. I hear that you are enlisted among the cavalier train-bands; I expected as much from you, my son, and I would rather see you walk promptly to your place, in the files of slavery and disunion, than to remain of an uncertain mind. The quicker every arms-bearing man is resolved, the speedier will be the issue. The request I make of you is, not to bestow your heart anywhere at present; and, as for your hand, remember that your mother's pride of family was her only sin.

Your father,
ABEL QUANTRELL

When Lloyd, with feelings of affection, anger, and distress, folded this letter, he was drawn to Luther Bosler's side, and to Mr. Beall, browbeating Luther. The words he heard were:

"I can have you whipped, and drummed across the river, for the sentiments you express!"

"Do so. Us Tunker brethren are numerous in this valley. They have never aroused to the voice of conscience upon this subject. Perhaps they might, if you would whip one of their ministers, like a slave."

Luther's countenance, as he spoke calmly before the pinched, pallid, and tortured arrogance of the Anglo-Celt, bore no ill resemblance to one of the rougher Christian disciples under the whip-master.

"Stop them!" commanded Nelly Harbaugh to Booth; "Luther is my friend, and shall not be imposed upon by that man."

"For you I will interfere," answered Booth; "your friend must be a gentleman."

By the aid of Fenwick, who saw Katy's anxiety, Booth and Quantrell appeased the combatants, and they went to see the Negro Ashby, whose unfortunate arrival had given Quantrell a new subject of annoyance.

He was at a Dunker family's humble house on an unfrequented cross-street, and, as they entered, an officer came close after to the door, to arrest a Negro suspected of having voluntarily given aid to John Brown, and borne arms under him, and accused also of invading the State of Virginia to carry off a person held to ceaseless servitude — to wit, the author of his own being. The penalty for the first of these offenses was death; of the second, imprisonment for life. The Negro Ashby, sustained by his religious ecstasy, heard of the fate awaiting him with a dignity surprising to Lloyd Quantrell.

"Mosster," he said to Lloyd, "I'm yours, and I don't want you to lose the money I'm bought with; but I'm tired of life. My ole mommy died when she heard of daddy's end. I wants to go in de cell with Green and Copeland and be hanged, and go to glory!"

"He ought to be hanged!" spoke Beall, with smothered fire of indignation. "He confesses to bearing arms."

"Oh," cried Katy Bosler, "hard man! He saved my dear Lloyd's life. When you come to die, maype a black man's love may pe your only friend!"

"Mr. Booth," cried Nelly Harbaugh, "you go to the door and deceive the constable, while Lloyd gets the Negro off. — He's worth all you paid for him, Lloyd; and, if he's hanged, the law won't pay you."

"You shall be obeyed," answered Booth; "if the constable persists, I'll throw him out of the house, and my Richmond company will stand by me!"

Quantrell started with the Negro through the back garden, and led him by the winding creek to the railway, and on toward the north; and, meantime, Katy Bosler threw herself upon Mr. John Beall, and by sighs and entreaties prevailed upon his modesty, until Booth came in and reported the officer to have been thrown off the scent. Luther Bosler had gone off to attend to his market collections, and Mr. Booth, seeing Mr. Beall's predicament with Katy, claimed a kiss for his good offices also, which Katy called on Nelly Harbaugh to bestow. In a little while Beall's sense of Virginia hospitality overcame his severity, and he took a gentle interest in Katy, whose merciful nature had also greatly affected

"Father" Hugh Fenwick.

Nelly Harbaugh, with a strong interest in these young worldly men, influenced Katy to prevail over Luther and let them both remain in Charlestown till his return with another load of provisions.

Luther's merchant instincts were now fully aroused, in view of this unexpected home-market and the calls of his approaching married life, and he kissed his affianced good-bye and started toward Harper's Ferry, with Beall and Booth in his wagon.

Lloyd and his new slave had walked two or three miles, and then they left the railroad near a mill, and continued through the autumn fields, Lloyd meditating how to get his dependent across the Potomac into Maryland. They finally came in sight of a peculiarly-shaped brick house in a grove of trees, secluded from the surrounding farms, but from its limestone swells could be seen the broad gateway of the rivers at Harper's Ferry, as they broke the mountain ramparts through.

"'Wide is the gate and broad is the way that leadeth to destruction,'" Quantrell said; "and yonder it seems to be."

"Dis is Walnut Grove, mosster," spoke Ashby, out of his desolate meditations, pointing to the house with the blood-red end and the cool white piazzas suspended in the middle; "de Bealls lives yer."

"Who are these Bealls," asked Lloyd — "so serious and intense?"

"I've heerd," replied the Negro, "dat de first of dem was a ole Scotch Covenanter, who come to America after killing a archbishop in Scotland — wasn't his name Sharp? He was a-tryin' to make de Scotch somethin' else dan Presbyterians. A few of 'em caught him at a bridge, and dragged him out of his carriage and murdered him. So de first Beall run away to de Potomac; he was one of de red Macgregors, dat is called in Merrylin Macgruders. Ever sence dar's been on deir faces a white look, an' a borrowin' of trouble, an' excitement about blood."

Ashby was bestowed in an out-house by a colored domestic girl, and, before Lloyd could call out the family, Beall and Booth drove up with Luther Bosler. The latter went to feed his horses, and Quantrell and the other two went into the house to partake of some liquor.

"Here is some of grandfather's port wine," Beall said; "he was the grandson of a baronet; I was his favorite among his daughter's children, and he gave me his name, John Yates. Today I feel troubled and excited, and I will try a glass with you, friends."

"You have behaved like a knight," Booth cried. "Let us drink together to some toast with a great purpose in it. What shall it be?"

"Virginia hospitality," Quantrell said. "Against his principles, Mr. Beall helped me in my personal desire to save my Negro's life, because he had saved my own. I shall never forget it."

"I accuse myself," said Beall, "of incivility in granting you so grudgingly what my natural impulses would have freely given. You were right to reward this disobedient servant for your life. Gentlemen, I have taken a real affection for you both; but the occurrence of this abolition invasion has strangely aroused me. Do you know that with all the hate I hold for this man, Brown, I have an admiration for him I can not control?"

"I admit it, too," Booth cried, unsteadily, for he had been drinking too much. "Monster as he is, I am fascinated by his dramatic crime."

"It was what we Scotch — we Bealls — call 'the bloody or deadly foray.' When one of these is made against us, we try in vain not to revenge it. My blood tingles now to take life for life."

He spoke with suppressed tones, jerkingly, and not a ray of cheerfulness was in his soul.

"Poor, insulted Virginia!" Booth exclaimed. "Lloyd, don't you feel for John here? It has bitterly humiliated him. Let us drink to this sentiment and swear to it, also — we three young men, nearly of the same age, devoted, determined, brave: 'The South, if trouble ever comes upon her, to revenge her; Virginia, if occasion ever offers, to invade her invaders!'"

They raised their glasses — those three, the two Marylanders and the Virginian. Said Quantrell, "My father has written to me, 'Walk promptly to your place, and do not be of an uncertain mind.'"

"Drink and swear!" spoke Booth; "'*Sic semper tyrannis!*' Virginia shall be avenged!"

As they drank with strong feeling, Luther Bosler appeared in the door.

"Resolutions taken in wine," he slowly remarked, "had best pe carefully considered. Lloyd, I will carry you to the cars at Berlin."

All present judged it prudent for Quantrell to go, while he could get the Negro off and be himself unsuspected.

As he disappeared in Luther's wagon, Mr. Beall said:

"I think Quantrell is a man of principle. I have seen how brave he is. Can he mean to marry that pretty Dutch child?"

"If he loves her, it is his own pleasure to consult."

"But she is quite ignorant; and that brother of hers is a huckstering Hessian."

"I have known Lloyd Quantrell since his childhood," Booth added; "my father, the tragedian, and my grandfather, who was an Englishman, like yours, were both present when Abel Quantrel came over from Pennsylvania to be admitted to the bar of my native county. They sat up all night at Belair to play cards. Years afterward, the father, who is a great man, but a voluptuous one, with remarkable power over women, became the idol of a lady of both fortune and descent, of one of the best families we have in older Maryland, and originally Quakers. Lloyd's father was a Yankee, with some Irish stock in him, making him poet and intriguer as well as Puritan; and that Quaker sweetness often breaks out in Lloyd's rough nature. It is said that Abel Quantrell never loved either his wife or his son, up to their warmth of affection for him. If the old man crosses Lloyd's love-affair, Lloyd may let the girl go, for he reveres his father."

"And break her heart?" asked Beall. "That won't be right."

"Why, John, you are very innocent of things of gallantry. Men's hearts sometimes break in love; women have little willful hearts, and adapt themselves to situations."

"We do not believe that of our mothers," said Beall; "as far as we can see, love is the whole of life to them."

Booth hesitated.

"You are right, John. But we do not see women — at least not in my way of livelihood — like our mothers. ." ..

Next day Lloyd Quantrell entered his father's house in Baltimore. It stood in Old Town, as that part of the city to the northeast was called, across the tumbling Jones's Falls, and as he approached it he passed the residence of the Booth family in the same part of the city — a broad, brick dwelling with marble base.

Quiet and comfort were the expression of this semi-neglected part of Baltimore, once the seat of fashion. The dwelling of Abel Quantrell had been the town-house of his wife's old colonial family, whose frequent relations with politics and finance brought them to Baltimore from across the bay, to live a portion of the year, and here, dazzled with the eloquence and independent nature of Lloyd's father, the heiress naturalized him into Maryland by a marriage, but found him half an alien to her heart.

The same longing with which she died, to have the full and absolute love of her husband, her athletic son had inherited; and now he came hungry to his father's door for a father's love, after all the mighty experiences of Harper's Ferry.

After he had bestowed the slave, Quantrell approached his father's library, and heard men's voices within. The first voice thrilled him well; it was that of the new Western senator, Edgar Pittson, saying:

"Depend upon it, they will force their convention early, and continue the excitement at Charlestown, Virginia, until the Southern heart comes all fired with passion to that convention, and they will hold it at Charleston in South Carolina. They will there demand a Southern presidential candidate as security for slavery, and break up the convention rather than take a Western man; and after having left everything in suspense, they will convene again in Baltimore, to capture this State by the alternative threat of breaking up the Union. Can Maryland be relied upon, Mr. Davis?"

"Yes," said a musical yet nervous voice, like a bass-violin's; "although the Native-American cause is gone, it will answer still in Maryland to compel the Democracy here to profess a Union spirit. This night we show our power in Monument Square. Come, and you will see how soiled is the outer fringe of slavery's garment. I must use the rowdy to save Baltimore to the Union; for Baltimore is Maryland."

"Anything, Davis," said the voice of Abel Quantrell. "Sho! use anything to keep the deluge back. The cube of the cutthroat may be the military genius, though I doubt it. The square of a riot may be a battle for the Union, though I fear not. But you are all there is of Maryland until the north star moves over Baltimore, and then you may throw off your dark-lantern mask and show the Know-nothing to be the Emancipator!"

"I am consuming for the hour," said Mr. Davis, in low, deep tones; "I saw no way to keep back the Loco-foco power in Baltimore but by catering to this Native-American prejudice. The naturalized foreigners always joined the Democracy, and for that I hated them. The devil shall have Maryland and me, before we shall be Democratic prey!"

"I sympathize with you, Mr. Davis," spoke Edgar Pittson; "your virtues are too great to classify you as the Artevelde of all these rough guilds and clubs; but the time a shifting one, and we need all the ground we can get to stand on. We shall nominate early, also — not later than next May — and our candidate, I think, will be Lincoln."

"Oh, no — Seward!"

"Sho!" said Abel Quantrell; "put not your new wine in old bottles; Seward has been too long in honors and office, Henry; he lives too far East. Go to the West, where John Brown lived and thought so long and undauntedly, until his old teeth fell out and grew up armed boys. The cube of old political success is compromise. We have had one Fillmore. I wish we could run Henry Winter Davis — or John Brown."

"Or Abel Quantrell," added Mr. Davis. "Old friend, you have been a great comfort to me in my lonely battle here, made under my semi-false position. Your son has been my devoted follower."

"My son," spoke Abel Quantrell; "what pride I take in my son! How brave he is — how indifferent to the world; how well he honors his father and his mother! Surely his days shall be long in the land which the Lord, the God of Freedom, will yet give to him. Oh, let me hear the sounding of his voice, like Isaac waiting for his Esau's tones!"

"Father, I am safe: God bless you, sir!" Lloyd Quantrell cried, his eyes all blind with tears as he threw himself at his father's feet.

Abel Quantrell, moved somewhat by the sudden onset, put his hands upon Lloyd's head, mechanically and coldly.

"The hair is the hair of Esau," he said, "but the voice is the voice of Jacob."

Chapter XXVII
KNOW-NOTHINGS

"FATHER, don't treat me so. I have been in great troubles, and the hope of seeing you, sir, made me want hard to live. I do want to lead a better life, and I have found a pure young woman who has promised to be my wife; and both of us require a father's blessing. Give me your heart, father!"

"Sho, sho!" the old man said, looking a little moved at his son; "the square of love is marriage; and the cube of love and marriage is incompatibility. Cube it — cube it! Look into the third production, son! You love: well enough! You marry: desperate step! You live long together: the cube is not one flesh, but wood or stone."

"I am your son; there can be no doubt of that," Lloyd spoke, looking around at the other witnesses, in wounded pride and challenge.

"None, Lloyd," spoke the kind tones of Senator Edgar Pittson; "your father called you his Jacob, the father of all true Israel's race. He did not mean to accuse you."

"If he had called me Esau," faltered the young man, "his words would not have seemed so cold. Some way, I can not get father to love me, gentlemen. I know I have taken to sad companions —"

"Have I ever rebuked you, my son? Sho!"

"No, sir. Why have you not? It was a father's privilege; and, had you done so, it would have been a proof of your affection for me. I wandered away because you never restrained me. It was too plain that you had no interest in me, father."

"Come, Lloyd!" spoke Congressman Davis, a little exasperated at the son's accusations. "Your father is as just as Heaven's viceroy here; and you know it."

"I wish he were not so just," the young man sobbed, with one long, soul-drawn sob; "then he might err into loving me, who have no mother!"

"Dear Lloyd!" the voice of Mr. Pittson said, with tender emotion in it — "to be motherless is the worst. My rugged, gentle brother, look out on Nature like your father, and take joy in her ceaseless maternities. There are love and grief and separation everywhere."

"Oh, if my mother was here now," Lloyd Quantrell spoke, "she would have encouraged me in my first pure affection since she died!"

"So will I, my son!" Abel Quantrell reflected aloud, with some curious sympathy. "Let me walk leaning upon your shoulder, for my old club-foot is numb. Come Edgar, too; since you young men have met, and liked each other so, I'll lean upon you both."

He stood upon his staff, and threw an arm around the shoulders of each, and paced the room to and fro. Henry Winter Davis, with his fine intellectual sight and handsome profile, looked up approvingly.

"I lean on Law and Nature, like Bacon of old," came the sardonic voice of the old man out of his lifeless countenance; "the support is all human aspiration can find; but where, my God! is Liberty?"

"Here," answered the young Senator Pittson, whose face was like that of Liberty's self upon a silver dollar, not warm with color but fine with ore — "here are three of us, and you can cube yourself! Do not regret, but feel God's providence to be wider than all the casualties and refractions of man's nature, and taking every aberration into his illimitable system of systems! You may have been the roving comet, crossing the orbits of the purest stars, or the rash meteorite flung upon Pleiades or earth; and still the scar on you will be greater than upon them, while in them the wonder of your falling is their incentive to a higher and wiser piety. We know God made you in his most subtle alembic, and that the material was better than gold; for we feel philanthropy and resistance to oppression to warm your setting sun and flash in the ashes of your lonely hearth-stone, like the dying prophet's face kindling in the radiance of the promised land."

Lloyd felt so rejoiced at this eloquent tribute to his father that he kissed both the speaker and Abel Quantrell. Mr. Davis was also showing the sympathy of fellow-genius upon his usually abstracted face, to hear the nearly chiseled words of Senator Pittson rising into such sculptured forms, yet ardent as life itself.

"Sho, Lloyd!" Abel Quantrell cried, "you have learned man-kissing among the Dunkers — woman-kissing as well, I compute. That's where I learned it, too, beneath the Dunker caps. Like father, like son! But you never imitate my better examples, Lloyd. I dare say you hate old John Brown, and the torch of insurrection he waved."

"I hate his cause with all my soul! I admire his courage. Wicked people set him on."

Abel Quantrell took one hand off Lloyd's shoulder, and, reaching for his stick, leaned only upon that, and upon Mr. Pittson.

"Edgar," said he, "resent that statement. I expect you to do it."

"No, sir" — Mr. Pittson took Lloyd's hand and continued to lead him in their chamber excursion — "Lloyd spoke with perfect honesty. Remember that your son may have the indignations of his birthplace, as you brought here others from the free Green Mountains. The incursion of John Brown was supported by no law whatever, except that which he and a few others made out of air. Time may excuse him; fanatical partisanship is preparing to do so now: but I am a senator under the law, and can take no part in such a rebellion, though it may have started, like Satan's, in heaven! I do not say all were wicked people who advised John Brown, but I do say that the calm and legal steps we Republicans were taking, to manœuvre slavery away from its respectable supports, have been pestered by John Brown's incursion, so that we are being manœuvred by slavery away from our own strong base, in the outraged conservatism of the country. How will John Brown's raid compensate us for the wrongs of Kansas? At this moment Mason, Davis, Bright, and others in the Senate, are preparing for an investigating committee upon John Brown's self-commissioned and gratuitous act, with the purpose of destroying the Republican party."

"They can't do it," Mr. Davis remarked, rising up. "The more stirring up the slavery-Democracy makes, the more Republicans there will be."

"Mr. Davis," spoke Lloyd Quantrell, with modesty yet directness — "often have I listened to your burning speeches with the feeling that you were sincere as truth itself. I never knew that the Native-American mask covered a Black Republican!"

"Then learn it of me" — Mr. Davis turned imperiously on Lloyd — "that I would rather wear the mask of the devil than lose my hold on Maryland, to help the Roger Taney Democracy to power! Yes, I would rather defend old Brown himself, for invading my own late home, Virginia, and support Horace Greeley for President here in Baltimore."

The impetuosity of Mr. Davis's reply showed that he had drunk at the well of Abel Quantrell's deep but boiling temperament. He was a Baltimorean in all respects — of well-nursed mustache, skin where the bright and sallow, the sanguine and bilious contended; aristocratic lines of countenance, a little pointed, perhaps hardened, by impulses which had turned to prejudices, and party combats which had soured to hate, and by a certain bluntness somewhere between volatility and sullenness; but, when his nature rose, a spirit of power and magnificence possessed him like the dark and gold of the oriole bird, whose yellow wings of flight flash from a sable breast.

Time and faculty, resistance and a somewhat false position, had muddied the springs of a generous nature, and kept him, with the instincts of liberty and refinement, a prince among brawlers, and he had come to recognize the omnipotence of events as above all reasonable endeavors to extricate himself from his momentary environment; and, therefore, the John Brown raid amused him, if it also perplexed him, because, while weaning young followers, like Lloyd Quantrell, from his side, it brought the terror of a general insurrection of the slaves to his political enemies.

Before Lloyd could excuse himself for rudeness within his father's walls, he, like Mr. Davis, was arrested by a strange and aggressive attitude of Abel Quantrell, his father, toward Senator Edgar Pittson.

The old man had concentrated the whole of his satyrlike attention upon this slender and shining-visaged guest; his mouth was set in the deepest scorn and resolution, and his hollow nostrils seemed breaking into articulate speech, so full of expression were they; and his faded eyes caught the dead, black shadow of his wig, and looked on Edgar Pittson as the ghost of Samuel from the tomb might have scowled on Saul.

One hand was upon his cane, his back against a table, and with the other hollow, almost transparent hand, he seemed holding something to throw into his visitor's face.

Mr. Pittson did not return the look of Abel Quantrell with either defiance or astonishment, but stood with his head slightly bowed and his countenance almost negative, like one receiving a sentence with resignation, or, as Lloyd Quantrell thought, like that passive respect with which the young Smiths on the mountains had heard the lecture of John Brown when our hero first made their acquaintance.

Abel Quantrell slowly lowered his menacing hand and put it into his bosom, and, after a moment's waiting, spoke:

"Do you dare hold those compromising sentiments in my presence! – you, from the unfettered, unconstraining West, which has honored you above your condition, and put the future of liberty and of labor in your trust?"

The young senator looked up and met that overbearing inquisition firmly, but without offense. His face had the beauty of a silver die, with every lineament fresh from the engraver's stroke: brown hair, flowing from a fine forehead to his low-set ears; beard prematurely silvered beneath his jaws, and hanging there in fringes like goat's fleece; mouth of cleanliness and courage, the upper lip almost too long, but the chiseled chin pendent to it with more delicacy, and in the nose was a faint tendency to match the eagle's beak; but, back of its bridge, the eyes drew far, like archers at the drawbridge bending all their strength – eyes of that same silver-gray which pervaded his complexion, the orbs of public life trained to think while shooting, and to have such nice relations with speech and hearing that every sense of man seemed in those clear gray eyes alone, placid under their brown-furred brows. His head was drawn a little back habitually as if receiving knowledge and attack; and above his slender, spare form, like the greyhound's, this kingly, harmonious head inhabited its own firmament:

"In the monarch Thought's dominion —
  It *stood* there!"

"Strange," said Senator Pittson, "that you radicals quarrel with every road but your own, which will lead to emancipation! John Brown showed more animosity to me than to any other person, as Lloyd Quantrell knows. He had taken offense at the lawful action of my party, and perhaps at its numbers also; for some men never can be right unless they are hermited and irregular, and there they show an incapacity to enjoy the fruits of freedom after those fruits are picked, because the people do not sanction agitations except for tangible results. The skirmish-line of life is the barbarian line; sometimes your skirmisher can bring on an action, but in that action itself he disappears. So will all you uncompromising abolitionists disappear if John Brown shall have brought on a war. Prudent men of the multitude, like Lincoln and Seward, accustomed to the training and restraints of legislatures and courts, will be required to save your country. Do you understand me now, sir?"

He turned with a respectful flash of his eyes upon Abel Quantrell.

"Whom have you stigmatized?" Abel Quantrell hissed.

"None, sir. I left off nicknaming when I became a man."

"'Satan's rebellion'; 'the wicked people who set Brown on' — you know what persons those stigmas include. You have defamed —"

"Not one," Senator Pittson replied; "none that you can mean, by word or thought. But, sir, you must not discharge one set of slaves, and create another. I claim for my reason all its responsibility and free course. Giving you honor, as is my duty, I shall in all public measures act as if my superior did not stand upon this globe!"

As the two men faced each other, the moral spirit of the younger rising and the physical rage of the older subsiding, both Mr. Davis and Lloyd were attracted by a something common to them both, as if between them was a place of fascination which could cause them to fight, like two duelists crossing an open but secluded spot which tempts their professional rivalry to the point of deadly onset.

"Come," said Mr. Davis, "we must not fall out on mere terms. Lloyd, go your way, if you mean to leave my fold, but keep my confidence!"

"Father," Lloyd spoke, "how can you treat Mr. Pittson so in your own house? Oh, he has a daughter that is so lovely! I could almost love Light

Pittson, father."

The old man sank into a seat, his late excitement gone.

"Mr. Pittson, when shall I see Light? Her face was before me in my danger and captivity, and it was a great comfort, too. It did not seem like any young lady's face that fluttered my heart; rather that rested me, and looked up to me for guidance."

"Sho, sho!" from Abel Quantrell; "you are on forbidden ground!"

"No," spoke Mr. Pittson; "come in that spirit, Lloyd, as to your child or sister, and Light will find you a blessing."

That evening Lloyd Quantrell strolled into a liquor-store in Baltimore, kept by one Martin, a companionable person from the old St. Mary's Peninsula of Maryland, and together they attended the great Native-American meeting in Monument Square. Such an outpouring of rude yet well-attired and solvent native men later times never knew; it was the apotheosis of the "rowdy," that culmination of physical spirit and national jealousy on the brink of ideal issues and against insoluble foreignisms.

The cold German, the mettlesome Irishman, had swarmed during ten years upon the settled land, and the power of their naturalization was already felt at the ballot-box. It was not in the nature of American boys to submit.

Great cities like New York had passed under the aggressive strangers' yoke, and Baltimore had been made the citadel of resistance. The mastering soul of slavery partly set this later contest on, but courage and patriotism were no less the instincts of the rowdy; his fathers had made a land, strangers were unmaking or remaking, and the very Jews of native stock were marching in the "American" lines; the Germans of eighteenth-century descent were deadly enemies of the nineteenth century's German importations; the latest Irishmen had taught fighting, and were getting the worst of it from Irishmen's native grandsons.

Toward the tall white pillar to General Washington the defiant and triumphant "Native Americans" moved in lines of sword and fire, in clubs, without any other purpose than battle, by fist or weapon, by steel or shot. The insignias on their transparent lanterns told the purpose and the degree of refinement of the time: "The Blood-Tubs," "The Red Necks," "The Pioneers," "The Regulators," "The Tigers," "The Ashlands," "The Spartans," "The Black Snakes," "The Gladiators," "The Rip-Raps," "The Eubolts," "The Plug-Uglies." With battle-axes, and in red shirts or grenadier hats, they marched as grim as executioners.

As these, soldiers in all but discipline, strode past Lloyd Quantrell, many a torch or awl-spear was brandished toward him, and the shout raised, "Come, Lloyd!" "Why ain't you marching, big one?"

He shook his head, and his heart was cold.

Finally came his own club, "The Cock Robins," marching from curb to curb, in broad lines of perfect form and step, sons of men of superior condition, and as confident of their righteous principles as guildsmen in cities ever have been, from Genoa to Ghent; their blazing sulphur and shooting rockets brought Washington's statue, on the summit of its candle, out into the prominence of a saint upon the Roman altar, and to every lad there he seemed giving them his benediction. This excess of light fell suddenly on the broad shoulders and rugged head of the idol of the club, Lloyd Quantrell, rising upon his long, straight limbs in sight of them all, the humanization of the cock they marched beneath.

A mighty cheer arose.

"Hip! hip!" from the captain.

"Hurrah!" roared the two hundred throats.

As these loud cheers, repeated thrice, seemed the very onset of battle, the young man's heart swelled high, and seemed to him to burst. Recollections of a hundred combats and sacrifices, of warlike friendships and assistances, of courage put to deadly tests, and convictions never till now disturbed, brought a feeling like exile and apostasy to Lloyd Quantrell's soul!

"Come! come! fall in!" the fierce command rang down the lines, addressed to him. The flaming column swayed and stopped; the fifes and drums were stilled.

He waved his arms, so that his elbows might hide his eyes, and, while the tears streamed down his cheeks, he called in broken but loud and manly tones:

"No! never — anymore — old boys!"

The latest form of prig may smile at pathos here, unconscious of his own father's service in just these associations, the rudest and most ingenuous of his life, perhaps, when his country was no more to be reasoned about and sublimated than his sweetheart or his mother, but its profanation by skeptical philosopher or foreign savage, alike, brought down the swift clinched hand, and armed young organizations, like the call in the Marseillaise song.

"What! what do you say?" hoarse, excited words broke from the ranks.

"I say, 'No!' No Henry Winter Davis! No John Brown abolitionists for me!"

The lines were broken; the clubsmen rushed upon their refractory member and seized him with rude affection; a torch was forced into his hand, and he was pushed into the ranks.

Amid a wild huzza the music and the march started up, and before Quantrell could dry his eyes or find an initial point of rebellion, he was in front of the great square base of the monument; and when he looked up to see Washington at the summit, resigning his commission at Annapolis, he saw his father, Abel Quantrell, cutting off the view, and introducing Henry Winter Davis as "the Samuel Chase of Maryland today!"

The orator stood forth in the August of life, barely turned his forty-second year, and pride and preoccupation worked together in his countenance till it seemed to have caught the Voltairelike mischief of old Quantrell's wigged and upholstered face, as the latter leaned near, like a statue in wax, with his bloodless palm in his shirt-bosom. The Governor of Maryland, Mr. Hicks, of the Eastern Shore, stood wonderingly by; the Mayor of Baltimore, Mr. Swann, a Virginian by birth, looked on approvingly; the senator from Maryland, Mr. Kennedy, educated in that Virginia town where John Brown now lay in jail, presided at the meeting. Over their heads was suspended a shoemaker's awl as long as a sword.

The awl was the favorite symbol of the monster meeting. Near by was a blacksmith's forge upon a wagon, hammering out awls; transparencies bore signs like "Third Ward — awl right"; "Seventh Ward — the awl is useful in the hand of an artist"; "Eleventh Ward — the votes *awl* counted."

What was this awl, the peaceful tool of the cobbler, doing at this fierce political meeting?

It was the stealthy and convenient weapon to punch intrusive foreigners with, as they crowded upon the polling-places; and by that instrument, here publicly recognized in the presence of Governor, mayor, senator, and congressman, the city of Baltimore had been governed several years. The slavery question had broken up the old national Whig party, and out of its ruins an irresolute local majority had turned their fury upon the foreign opposition.

Mr. Davis addressed himself to the connection between the Governor of Virginia and the foreigners; for that Governor had checked Native-Americanism by his election, raising the slavery question to the forefront. A man no less dogmatic had put the slavery question under his nose at the point of a pike.

"Pikes and awls, Lloyd!" spoke the liquor-dealer, Martin, at Quantrell's elbow. "Won't it be guns next?"

"The awl must make shoes for soldiers soon, I fear," Quantrell replied.

Never had Mr. Davis spoken as he did that night, his seat in Congress being at issue, and the accusation of covert abolitionism already raised against him. He denounced the opposite party as "hoping to retain power by the fears of one half the people for the existence of slavery, and of the other half for the existence of the Union. . . . False to their mission," said he, "as the portress of hell to hers, and ready for the purpose of retaining their hold on power to let loose on this blessed land the Satan of demoniacal passion! . . . I am stronger in my district," he exclaimed, "and in the State of Maryland, in any appeal I may see fit to make to the people, than all the banded power of the Legislature bound into one man."

Robust, scornful, fierce, magnificent, his oratory and temper were the exact mirror of the meeting he addressed, and proved the dangerous power of the public platform or "stump" to educate crowds. Had he ordered those men to demolish any public or private-building, they would have done so after a few sentences from Henry Winter Davis; and yet this man, in what he was truly aiming at, was as lonely before those masses as Galileo with his convictions of science before the superstitious priests. He could abuse his enemies, but never advocate freedom and opportunity for black men.

It was this sense of moral impotence in Baltimore which made his sentences fall like the lash of flagellation upon himself; and, when he had done, he looked at the electrified thousands as if he would like to kick them out of his sight, and nothing delighted them like that expression.

As Lloyd Quantrell, with his sensibilities all disturbed and his enthusiasm frozen, passed along that night into the Old Town quarter, a man addressed him in a foreign accent:

"I do not beg. I give you zis ring."

A priestly-looking man, in shabby priestly dress, was speaking. A little ring was on his finger, and he held it under a street-lamp, continuing:

"I tell you why I do zis: I starve for bread."

"Foreigner!" thought Quantrell, his Native-American repulsions not all gone. "Why do you come here, friend, to live on us?"

"I came for justeece," exclaimed the man; "I want justeece for my mothair; my fathair's name for me!"

The man's black eyes shone; his face was thin and haggard. He pressed the little ring into Quantrell's hand.

"Only two dollair," he said; "not to sell it you, but to borrow on it. I know you, sare; you live there."

He pointed to Abel Quantrell's house.

"Let's see," said Lloyd; "two dollars. I have only got one, but I can borrow another here, for I see June Booth at the window."

He stood opposite Booth's residence, and at the open window thereof sat the very likeness of the noted dead tragedian, smoking a cigar. As he stepped toward this person, the stranger cried:

"No, no! Not one cent from there! Nevair!"

He was gone, with Lloyd's dollar in his hand, and the ring left in Lloyd's palm.

As Quantrell looked at the ring that night, he found the letters chased
within it:

"J.B.B. TO HIS WIFE, CHRISTINE, *1814.*"

Chapter XXVIII

NEW FACES IN THE VALLEY

HAVING sent his new slave Ashby out of harm's way, to be the foreman of his other slaves in the lower Potomac country — forwarding him thither, with Katy's dog Fritz, through Lloyd's man-dealing uncle — Quantrell returned to Charlestown and witnessed the conclusion of John Brown's small, wide-surging act. Nothing had happened in the history of English America to produce the same profound impression, except the defeat of Braddock and the treason of Arnold; and John Brown's work had the mystery and subtlety of the last and was followed by the panic of the first.

The magnitude of slavery's interest — hardly less than four thousand million dollars — the sophistical statesmanship and political economy created about it, which involved the ridicule and self-respect of leaders long self-deluded; the peace and safety of white society, and the patriotism of compromises, this beggar-man had treated as common obstructions and idolatries, like some captain of Mohammed bursting into an old religion and state, cimeter in hand.

Beggar he was, by all the evidence, having begged from town to town the few dollars for his expedition, and procured his arms by a misapprehension almost like deceit; with neither scrip nor raiment for his intrepid journey, no change of clothes, no provision for his needy family in the cold mountains of New York on winter's brink; and recruiting chiefly from the children of his loins, and holding none of them to be better than any vagrant Negro in his command.

Lloyd Quantrell had followed John Brown so closely that he, almost alone, with his Vermont father's business eye, discerned the reality of this naked martyr.

His friends, Booth and Beall, adopted the current view — that a great conspiracy existed, of which Brown's band was only the courageous tail, and therefore they held the North responsible for a private deed.

Quantrell saw in John Brown's lonely act the isolation and exposure of slavery, which could incite the poor Northern whites against it — those who, possessing the vote-power, would compel the Northern rich to follow them speedily; he began dimly to discern the meaning of the distant Kansas contest — wage-labor against forced labor — he saw that his father's work was bearing seed, and that abolitionists were no longer the philosophers and the idealists only, but the simple, the deadly farmers of the North and West.

He resigned himself to the universal fear, and resolved, for his property, his prejudices, and his indignation, to act with that Democrafic party he had so long hated, and to proselytize for it among his Native-American friends.

He felt the clearer to do this because his father had written: "I expected as much of you, my son; and I would rather see you walk promptly to your place in the files of slavery and disunion than to remain of an uncertain mind."

"Dear father!" Lloyd thought, "nothing he has ever said to me seemed so warm with compliment! We can differ and respect each other more."

Then there came the kind desire of his father, added to the same letter, with the confidence of a chivalric opponent:

"The request I make of you is not to bestow your heart, and, for your hand, remember your mother's pride of family."

No other command had Abel Quantrell ever laid upon his son, who had many a time longed for a father's warm commands.

While other sons had chafed under parental restriction, this son, deeply affectionate and consciously his father's mental inferior, had pined for obligations and for the love which imposes them upon a son.

The first command his father had given him, in proud respect, had been to go to battle for his convictions.

The next — a request so kind that his tears came to read it twice — was the great old father's desire that Lloyd should withhold his heart and hand.

"My heart," cried Lloyd in the depths of his soul, "is gone beyond my reach. Can I give my hand to Katy and break my dear old father's sole injunction? No, I must wait. I will not disobey him. He asks me, too, in my dead mother's name!"

This conclusion was enjoined on him by another parental confidence: his father had named to him the lady of his choice.

The disturbance effected by John Brown's raid in the old settled lines and communities near by, hardly the local scandal-monger could enumerate or follow. It created an imperial theme where, for a hundred years, the torpor of slavery and the milking of cows had blended with each other's patriarchal thoughts, as when the herds and herdmen of

Lot and Abraham once looked up and saw rising from the plain of Jordan the alluring mirage of the sinful cities of the plain.

New, willful people came and camped by the Shenandoah. The girls saw finer and bolder men than had filled the measure of their ambition. Soldier-clothes invaded homes of piety and humility, and, while the women yielded to the trance of idleness and compliment, their fathers and brothers grew fuddled with strangers, and heard new doctrines of morals and disloyalty.

What a temptation for Nelly Harbaugh when she found her society desired by the actor Booth!

Luther had arranged with Nelly to baptize her into his church, and his loving mastership had already begun to soothe her soul to peace, when here appeared a wiser admirer yet, all eloquent with youth, beauty, and worldliness.

By Luther's sunburned and unshaved face and rough Dunker cloth the form and countenance of Booth seemed like a prince's in military uniform beside some giant peasant-recruit of his hereditary subjects.

The large, tender eyes of Luther were worth all Mr. Booth's refinements, but too often of late they had worn the dull coin light of avarice. He had seen a great, neighboring opportunity to make money, and his heavy Bavarian-French nature had kindled to it like his military forefathers to the stranger's *loot*.

"Miss Nelly," spoke Booth, as he was giving the girls a supper at the principal hotel, with ale and wine among its fall birds and new venison, "do you think I would go away to make five dollars a load huckstering, and leave for a single day a noble face like this, fit for Queen Semiramis? No, I would be too proud and jealous!"

"Hush!" said Nelly, as Booth looked with all his serious and insinuating interest into her face. "Not one word against my lover. You do not know how hard it is to make five dollars."

"Tell me," said Booth; "I feel such an interest in you. It is the interest I would feel in a noble treasure hidden for years in the mountains!"

"It took me," Nelly answered, with a cold blush of modesty, like one at last looked down, "six whole months to make five dollars, when I wanted it to buy a pair of shoes!"

"Oh, shame!" said Booth; "and I was making my three dollars a day as second walking-gentleman!"

"Your father left you that rich chance; I have heard of him. But I could only make thirty cents a day, and could only find work at seeding and harvest, hardly four weeks in all; and rain, or too many laborers, or woman's ailing, would throw me out a day here and a day there, so it was winter before I had my shoes."

"And dress becomes you so wonderfully! I have paid much attention to dress for ladies. Nelly, I could make you the sensation of Richmond or Washington — yes, of Baltimore!"

As his eye roved over her fine throat and commanding profile, her abundant length of hair and length of trunk, Booth clasped his hands and seemed to tremble.

"You actor!" Nelly spoke low, with her eye on tender Katy, to whom Mr. Fenwick was modestly attentive — "am not to be carried off my feet by your artful praise, for in my own land and station I have been courted by many."

"Let me see your native region," Booth appealed; "I hear it is not far from here. Though you are engaged, and to a real good fellow, who will take all the care of you he knows, perhaps I may find your counterpart in the Catoctin Valley, and not go away all broken up. What lovers have you had? You almost tempt me to turn farmer."

"I have had all the poor young men around to come to see me and propose; nearly all the widowers of a marriageable turn; several mechanics; a preacher out of nearly every sect. The merchants' drummers from the city generally want to run away with me. More than one married man has offered to be divorced to get me."

"And temptations often?" Booth spoke, with the gentlest respect.

"No; insults, but no temptations. I always knew my value; I know it now, sir!"

She turned to her admirer with the reserve and bodily self-respect of a greater person than one in a half-cotton print. He did not flinch, however, but distended his eyes in the greater rapture, slowly saying:

"No woman on the American stage can do that!"

"What?"

"Give the expression to language that you can do, Miss Harbaugh. There is a fortune for you, and a world-wide fame as an actress!"

"Oh, do not tell me that!" the woman said, fighting down another rapture in her own face — "do not be a devil to me! I tell you, sir, nothing can separate me from that child's brother, to whom I am engaged!"

She pointed to Katy Bosler.

"I know it," said Mr. Booth, with a shadow of deep regret; "not even your duty to the talents which nature gave you for a mighty life!"

Katy, no prude in the joy of her new love, readily yielded to the invitation of the two young men to visit her home, in which her pride and hospitality were innocently excited; and Lloyd's absence she did not weigh in her duty to his friends. Mr. Booth obtained two buggies through Mr. Beall's good offices, who had been much taken with Katy's goodness and beauty; Hugh Fenwick driving Katy, and John Booth driving Nelly, they left Charlestown the day Quantrell spent in Baltimore.

Eight miles to Harper's Ferry and eight to Crampton's Gap let them down over the mountain rim into the brown and gold bowl of Catoctin Valley; and, as they moved toward Jake Bosler's farm in the exhilarating air and restful sceneries, the young priest-student spoke to Katy of religious life, and love made benevolent to human creatures.

"Are you, too, of te old Dutch like us, Mr. Fenwick?"

"Say 'Father Fenwick' — it's more agreeable to me from you, Katy; you are so like a dear child. If you can't say that, say 'Hugh'; for I must be either your spiritual or your familiar friend, and 'Mister' is neither."

"Oh, then, I'll say 'Father Fenwick.' Tell me about marrying people and about wedding-rings."

"Dear Kate! marriage never was sanctified till after Luther's death."

He crossed himself, speaking of Luther, and Katy cried:

"Luter dead! Our Luter?"

"Martin Luther, the apostate, Katy."

"Oh, I guess I didn't know him, Father Fenwick."

"Marriage was first celebrated in the church by Innocent III, having been a mere civil contract before that; but the Council of Trent, meeting while Friar Luther" — crossing himself again — "passed to his flames, ordered and fixed it fast."

"Oh, it did?" observed Katy; "I'm glad of that."

"Then, my child, marriage was made one of the seven sacraments, conferring grace, and forbidden to clerics; and all clandestine marriage, also, was forbid."

"Seven sacraments?" observed Katy; "not all at once, I hope! Not wine seven times of a Sunday?"

"No, little Pope Innocent; marriage was then taken into the church, like the dove taken back into the ark, and made one of seven holy things, like Penance and Holy Order."

"I learned a little penance at school one winter," thoughtfully added Katy; "but our Luter he's a penmans that's wonderful! Luter can shade letters like a sign-painter. Gracious! don't you squeeze me that-a way!"

"Kate, you are such virgin mold and mind, I would like to educate you. No flower transplanted would grow more nobly. Oh, if I had you at old Saint Thomas's Manor, far down the Potomac, I at the Jesuits' old palace there and you in the pretty school right by, my studies would be relaxed by the care of your education, and, like the Carmelite sisters who lie buried in the garden, I could lean above you, my sweet sister, and guide your soul and mind!"

"Eferypody wants to make a nun of me, Father Fenwick; Job Snowberger is crazy for me to come to Snow Hill, and you want me to go to Saint Thomas's; but I want to marry Lloyd."

The broad-chested, fresh-skinned, hale young novitiate looked at Katy pityingly:

"We are forbidden to interfere in courtships, but Lloyd, my Katy, is dreadfully robust for your gentle nature! I grant his open temper, but are you a being prepared for him, to wear with him in the long round of life?"

"Oh, maype I can learn some time, Father Fenwick! Maype you might help me. My gracious! tere is a horseshoe in te road."

Before Hugh Fenwick could stop, Kate was over the buggywheel and back again with the cast shoe.

"*Hoofeisa!* That's good luck always," she cried, "and now, maype, I'll find my wedding-ring."

A growl and loud bark came from under the buggy-seat, and the pointer-dog Albion burst from under Katy's gown and jumped into the road and ran after Mr. Booth's carriage, into which Nelly Harbaugh had him taken.

Hugh Fenwick now displayed his prying scholarship on the subject of finger-rings, mixing his traditions and science superstitiously, like the young Jesuit he would be.

"The ring, my mountain flower, is in our church *fidei sacramentum,* the badge of fidelity. Levinus Leminus held, and so did Gellius, a holy philosopher, that an artery or vital nerve stretched from the ring-finger to the heart."

"My heart's empty," sobbed Katy, "ever since I took it off."

"That was a grave error, little penitent; many married women will never remove their betrothal ring even to wash their hands. In Spain the giving of a ring is a legal claim to a husband in her who can show the ring. The Holy Father wears the fisherman's ring, and seals his letters with it."

"Yes," cried Katy, "and a wedding-ring cures fits and a sty on the eye, and fetches up girls out of a swoon. No girl without a ring-finger, to put te ring on, can marry safe. Te fortune-teller told me I should lose my ring, and then she took it from me herself. I can only find it py te Bible now, and I must find te Bible in a water-brook where there never was any books, Father Fenwick."

Katy's head leaned convulsively upon the gentle divinity student, who told her of the solemn beauty of his church's ceremony, the priest in rich pontificals, the clerks in surplices carrying the holy water pot, the basin, and the sprinkler to bless the golden marriage-ring.

"*'Ego conjungo vos in matrimonium.* Our help is in the name of the Lord. Lord bless this ring, which we bless in thy name, that she who shall wear it, keeping true faith unto her spouse, may abide in thy peace and will!'"

Hugh Fenwick made of a silver ring he wore a circle around Katy's finger as he pronounced this copy of the ceremony, and, blessing it with his finger, he kissed the bruised little hand and then the lips of Katy, trembling himself.

The pious nature of the child was swayed to the strange, strong words, and, seeking about her for additional help, she found the horseshoe at her feet, and held it above both their heads.

"Father Hugh, you'll marry me to Lloyd, won't you, if nobody else will?"

Katy clung to him in the emotions of fierce will and fear alike. He felt her large, swimming eyes shine in on him with power.

"Why me, Katy? I am a Roman Catholic — a Jesuit to be — and not of your mountain sects."

"Lloyd is a Catholic. I will pe what he wants me. I'm nopody, and God gif him to me. Oh, promise me you will pe our friend!"

He hesitated as the carriage stopped at Jake Bosler's gate.

"Ha, Fenwick! What's this — a conquest?"

It was Booth who spoke, seeing Katy with her arm around Fenwick's neck.

"Promise me!" cried Katy, indifferent to who looked on. "I will not let you go."

"Yes, yes; if it ever becomes my duty I will be your ghostly friend."

Luther Bosler and his father had just come in from the field, and Luther's wagon was loaded for another huckstering trip to Charlestown. Nelly Harbaugh saw that her affianced was worn and haggard with his double labors, and she took him in her long, strong arms with real affection, sharpened by almost maternal compunction.

"My poor, willing slave, are you laboring so hard for me? I am not worthy of it, darling. But I have thought of you with a full heart. Oh, I love you so painfully, so fearfully, so selfishly!"

Fenwick and Booth looked on with surprise at the exhibition of devotion and tears from this late worldly beauty of the country, and Booth said to Fenwick, so that Nelly heard him:

"Every attitude she takes shows the natural artist."

"Well it may, sir," cried Nelly, turning on Booth, with tears like rage as well as pity in her telling eyes; "if Nature ever taught me well, it was to love this man!"

She threw her arms around him again, and, standing almost to his own height, kissed him and still wept.

"Dearest," Luther said, tenderly, "why do you cry? We have not parted many hours, but in an hour more I must go away again. Tere is money to be made, and Decemper is almost here, when we will pecome man and wife."

"December? Oh, my love, my teacher, it is too far away! I am afraid something will happen. We are not what we were in peace and content, before all these strangers came."

"Not what we were, Nelly? Revolutions could not alter me when I have started out. Tisturbance is love's mutuality, driving us together, like when te Indians infaded our Dutch forefathers, and te women and men tefended each other. This revolution is for our good. Men will see te danger of slavery, and times will grow better when it is gone."

"Who wants to go?" pleaded Nelly Harbaugh. "I have been a slave, too, working in the corn-fields among the men. It was my joy and independence, and I would be your slave, also, for all the hard and steady life of the farmer's wife. But do not leave me so much! Do not love money more than you love me! Take me to Virginia with you today!"

"What, Nelly! Are you so impulsive? I thought you was keen and worldly. Time prings good discipline. Waiting is surely not hard for genuine love. Here are visitors, and we owe tem hospitality."

He indicated Booth, who was looking critically on, and the dog Albion snapped at Nelly's feet like another mentor. Jake Bosler remarked, vaguely:

"Eferyting coom right, maype. Bi'm-by."

Booth spoke to Luther with manly equality, just cordial and no more; but to Luther's father he was attentive and respectful, and he soon became the attractive personage of the farm. Hugh Fenwick hung the horseshoe over the dove's nest, and heard the doves' "coo-roo," and remarked that the young doves were big enough to fly.

While Nelly and Katy went to make some special dessert dishes for the distinguished guests, Mr. Booth challenged Luther and Fenwick to gymnastic feats upon the lawn at the tree where the doves roosted.

He bared his arms, and the white muscles there seemed like blue-veined marble, and each great globe of sinews swelled like a human brain, as if the thinking culture of this young gladiator was in his arms, and not within his skull.

He raised himself upon the limb of the apple tree, and, by alternate arms, singly, until his chin was higher than the bough; and he vaulted over a stone wall by one hand and wrist without running, and raised a grindstone to the level of his shoulders, none of the others being able to do the same; and he also outleaped them both upon the level — and so Nelly Harbaugh found him, with coat off and sleeves rolled up, the hair black and strong upon his arms and breast-bone, so that it might almost have been combed, and his knees slightly bowed, though not sufficient to affect his erect, compact stature.

"Why, sir," cried Nelly Harbaugh, "you are training for the circus, and not for the theater."

"O Queen Nelly! I am training in the athletic school, like my father.

He and Kean drove classical acting off by the splendor of their combats, dying all slashed to pieces and with broken blades, but fencing yet with hand and foot and tooth and nail."

For the first time at Bosler's farm the girls were taken into dinner, society-fashion, on the arms of Booth and Fenwick, to the blushing confusion of these twain; and Nelly and Katy saw with curiosity the strangers eating nimbly with their forks. Katy had always been told that it was politeness to eat with the back of her knife, instead of with the blade to the mouth, as Jake Bosler did. Jake, however, took no note of methods, except the method of the clock and of the sun-dial; and, passing up his plate for animal fuel, whereby to plow and sow, uttered the suggestion —

"Bi'm-by."

Fenwick asked the blessing at Luther's request, sectarianism being only superficial in this region, and the girls watched the intellectual play between the young men — the Jesuit, the Protestant pietist, and the Oriental-looking type of Booth, where may have been a distant trace of Jew. Luther and Booth were seeking to draw each other out, and Fenwick was the moderator between them — too prone to agree with both, as if some moral weakness remained in the fixed intentions of his clerical career.

Luther, on the whole, furnished the strong meat of the discourse, unsuspecting of Mr. Booth's persuasive line of inquiry.

"You think, then, friend Luther, that John Brown was not altogether inexcusable?"

"Not excusable; for in our faith no man can do war and pe right, neither offering nor resenting violence. We submit, considering oppression the least of evils. But few do submit on principle, like us, and in human nature John Brown was te least selfish of soldiers. He had no interests at stake, no chance; nothing but te moral example of his failure and tespair."

"A strait-jacket and lifetime in the lunatic asylum would suit him!" suggested Booth.

"He is too proud to take that refuge," Luther said. "He resented it when te Ohio lawyers came to his help. That would be the meanest of all, and Governor Wise is too honoraple a man to put a sound head like John Brown's among te maniacs. Te Scribes and Pharisees in their spite nefer offered to treat Jesus so."

Hugh Fenwick was prompt to make the pious sign, and he exclaimed:

"Compare John Brown to Jesus?"

"But for Jesus no man would be in John Brown's shoes now, saying over te words: 'Take no thought for your life; for te morrow shall take thought for te things of itself, and sufficient unto te day is te evil thereof.'"

"Oh," said Fenwick, "authority, not caprice, must order these things — Washington or Rome!"

"But tey never do. King George nefer ordered General Washington. Te authority that counts te sparrow's fall said also, 'Beware of men, for tey will deliver you up to te councils, and ye shall pe prought pefore governors and kings for My sake.'"

"O Luther," Nelly Harbaugh sighed, "why don't you choose a public life? It is so comforting to hear you talk."

"Indeed it is," said Mr. Booth; "he's up in the lines, too! — But, Luther, wasn't it great conceit for Captain Brown to take this stupendous task upon himself?"

"Ah!" exclaimed Fenwick, "the Puritan never goes to a confessor to assure his intentions. He is a secretive, treacherous mover!"

"Whoever does anything original is conceited, te dull and envious think. Columpus had no pusiness to find te New World. John Brown had no pusiness to cut at this tumor in our society. I haf been accused in our Tunker body of te conceit that I could preach, pecause I haf been elected. Only te greatest kind of man sees te universal, daily necessity; what eferypody else ought to have seen, but nefer did see — steam to save toil, lightning to save time, liberty to save sorrow. I wonder at John Brown, but te great conceit was his. These mountains will not hold his name!"

"Soon-down — Bi'm-by!" Jake Bosler spoke, rising and kissing Katy welcome home.

"Wait!" said Mr. Booth; "let me give you a recitation, Luther, before you leave us."

As Booth arose, the doves beyond the windows rose also, from the crotches in the apple tree, and took their migration to the South.

Mr. Booth repeated Hood's "Bridge of Sighs," standing at his place in the plain low room, with its cheap paint-grained cupboards and white plaster; and first he explained that it was the story of a poor girl abandoned by her lover, and found self-drowned in the muddy river.

Bending over the table, as over the drowned one, with his manful manner and serious white face, the actor delivered this, his favorite recitation, with a fervor and pathos that drew tears and sobs from Katy; and, between the stanzas, Jake Bosler could be heard to whinny, and to say, with reference either to temporal or everlasting things, and perhaps both:

"Temmerlich!" (pitiful). "Bi'm-by! — Bi'm-by!"

Luther Bosler listened with a drop of dew in his eyes, like cloudy amethyst, and still kept his judgment upon the words; and Nelly Harbaugh came around and leaned on him, watching Booth with colder emotion:

"Fashioned so slenderly, young and so fair!" the victim of love and trust betrayed was raised in dumb show by the actor, and all her mutiny and disobedience, her dripping clothes like cerements, and water-oozing lips, her past dishonor and her residue of what was "pure womanly," he revealed with delicate and tender respect.

Then, bending over his plate, Mr. Booth asked in intelligent wonderment, solicitously:

"Where was her home?
  Who was her father?
  Who was her mother?
  Had she a sister?
  Had she a brother?
  Or was there a dearer one
  Still, and a nearer one
  Yet, than all other?"

Nobly modulated, punctuated by his black-eyed glances, every pain of meaning opened wide like a wound held open till it could bleed, the poetry stuck in every throat but Booth's, who next descended into speculations not less pathetic, because analyzing to the very nerves and household chords the causes of the outcast's suicide. Her

"Feelings had changed —
  Love, by harsh evidence,
  Thrown from its eminence;
  Even God's providence
  Seeming estranged. . . .

  She stood with amazement,
  Houseless by night — . . .

  Swift to be hurled —
  Anywhere, anywhere
  Out of the world!"

Here, rising to a wail, with eyes of simulated despair and arms describing the fateful leap from the bridge's parapet, Booth saw Nelly Harbaugh, without a tear in her eyes, gazing at him in rapture. He knew that there was no art of betraying woman like reciting with sympathy woman's betrayal, but this fine peasant-girl's eyes showed none but intellectual sympathy with his effort, and the passion to enact like him.

He changed his tactics and assumed the more heroic form of recitation, giving his robust voice and chest their volume and power; but the sense in her warm, blue eyes soon reproved this exuberance, and with astonishment, amid his corrected cadences, Booth discerned in this cool auditor a capable and unexcited critic, not to be affected by his sentiment, but only through her own ambition. She rose in his respect the more, though now he saw the route to her weakness.

"Yaw, Katy, take her sinds to her Savior, *hera Heilond!* — Bi'm-by!" Jake Bosler sobbed at the conclusion, drawing his little daughter to his breast.

"Fader, she was dead in te water-brook!" Katy cried, kissing him.

"Yaw, my child. Proke her old daudy's heart for some young city man's," Jake sighed, "and couldn't look her fader in te face. Dat's te way with some girls up dis-a-way. Te *leeb,* te courtin,' is everyting, till — Bi'm-by."

"This is a gift of God, right used," Luther Bosler said to Mr. Booth, as he took his whip in hand and the team came to the door; "but te tears we pring by eloquence must not pe idle tears; for tears should come from deep, pure places, Mr. Booth. As I go around among te Tunkers to pray at pedsides, where te old ones die and te pabes are born, I feel what loads of sorrow make one tear. — Nelly, you shall see it for yourself when we are both believers!"

He kissed his affianced devoutly; but Booth saw that something had broken Luther's spell over her, and she said:

"Luther, may I have your buggy? Mr. Booth has a foolish desire to see my home."

"Oh, surely," Luther answered, hospitably; "anything here, friends, is yours. Pe welcome!"

As Luther Bosler drove southward that afternoon, he crossed the great blue mountain at the old Sharpsburg hauling-road, at which the backbone was depressed, and left Turner's Gap above a mile to his right, where the National road found an almost hidden clove to go through. In the wild brush and pine-grown gullies of the former deserted way he suddenly came upon two women riding easy-racking mares.

"Whoa!" cried Luther, pulling his four horses in. "I think I know you, madam. What have you done with my sister Katy's engagement-ring?"

His unerring country eye had seen, through her Dunker hood and smock-frock, the stature of Hannah Ritner.

"Ah, Luther!" she spoke, with frank and strong articulation. — "Come here, Light, and see my young Dunker pastor! Is he not a handsome bachelor?"

"A Dunker pastor! And so fine-looking, too! Perpetual romance, Hannah, your beautiful mountains hold!"

Luther looked up into a beautiful, sincere, attractive child-woman's face. He did not remove his hat, but wondered what such a lady, in plain, long riding-dress, was riding through these lonely ways for.

"You had no right to take my sister's gift," he said to Hannah Ritner. "Its loss has caused her innocent credulity tears."

"Luther, it was Lloyd Quantrell's mother's ring. He had no right to use it to trifle with a child. I took it to his father. Let Katy seek it there, and ask for Abel Quantrell's consent."

"Will he give it back, Hannah?"

"I keep the ring," spoke Hannah Ritner, with unconscious austerity; "I did not ask it, but it has become mine. When Abel Quantrell refuses his son to her, let Katy come to me at the nunnery of Snow Hill."

"Very well, Hannah. It is better that all shall pe understood, and there pe no deceit."

"The old German spirit is in these hills," Light Pittson cried; "the ring of betrothal, the enchanted maids, the bearded men, like Odin, doing justice! Hannah, tell this gentleman's fortune before we go to Frederick, and you send me back to papa!"

The weird elder woman gazed earnestly in Luther's face, and, obedient to Hannah Ritner's command, he removed his wool hat, and looked with mild pleasure in Light Pittson's ardent eyes.

Hannah Ritner's dark orbs roved over Luther's countenance carefully; and then, with eyes closed under her long black lashes, she muttered like one with wits scattered and evasive, till finally she cried:

"Bosler, do not see! Be blind till I am done."

He closed his eyes, in gallantry more than interest, and soon the low sounds pierced his ear of the improvisatrice's poetry, sighed forth with passion:

"The yellow star will fade some morn —
  Yellow tassels leave good corn!
  Then attend the bugle-horn,
    And all thy merit see!
  Though in the church they censure some,
  Pain and duty keep thee dumb:
  To hollow heart the hollow drum
    Beats peace and victory!"

Luther kept his eyes closed, waiting for Hannah Ritner to speak again.

When he opened them, he was alone on the mountain with his wagon and horses, and the two female apparitions were nowhere in sight.

"Amen!" sighed Luther, shaking his horses up; "if Hannah raised that spirit by her side, it was a lovely one!"

Chapter XXIX

THE ACTOR

MR. BOOTH asked Nelly Harbaugh if she would not prefer horse-back-riding to Luther Bosler's buggy; and there being only one saddle, though horses to spare, Nelly, with country character, mounted herself on a folded blanket and forced Booth to take the saddle and stirrups. Leaving Hugh Fenwick to keep Katy company, the other two started off in the middle of the afternoon for a ride of several miles, toward the upper portion of the Catoctin Valley.

They passed through one small town, and then crossed between the two branches of Catoctin Creek, which drained the opposite parallel mountains that gradually converged and pushed the hillocks between them higher and higher, until, at Wolfsville, a clean and tidy village, they forded the clear green mountain-run and began to ascend a steep and rugged road, nearly on the mountain-plane.

"There is no Maryland place north of us now," said Nelly Harbaugh, "but one little store and old tavern at the edge of the wilderness, in the stone-heaps of Hunting Creeks. There the waters run off to the Monacacy River and the Antietam through the gorges of the mountains, and the people are woodsmen and berry-pickers. I have never been in those wilds."

Booth seemed to enjoy the increasing loneliness of the way. He chose parts of the road to charge his horse and gallop up and down the steeps; and, although Nelly rode firmly and fearlessly, she was no match for her companion's dashing horsemanship, and soon he drew from his hip-pocket a revolving pistol, and began to terrify his steed by shooting it at trees and stones while riding at full speed.

The unsophisticated horse, finding so wild a rider on his back, attempted to run away; but Booth was still his master, and, by mingled skill and strength, would throw the animal's head out of its purpose and relation, or force him to stumble and collect himself at the sacrifice of his fury. Then, with the rough, honest steed all covered with foam and trembling, Booth would awaken him to terror anew by firing the pistol right between his ears, and let him run into exhaustion again and check him as before.

The horse was conquered at last, but not composed nor quieted to his fitful rider's way.

"Please do not misuse Luther's horse," Nelly Harbaugh said, catching up. "His horses are steady as himself, and some of the neighbors may see and report us to him. Don't fire that pistol again! It will alarm this quiet valley."

"I was merely chasing John Brown and his men, experimentally," answered Booth, laughing. "I dare say, too, that such conduct as mine would not reflect credit on the Dunker preacher's affianced?"

"I am watched as never before. So is Luther. His learning is not to his credit in his sect, which regards eloquence and fame as evil vanities, and his intention to marry me is already the subject of their muttered talk."

"Perhaps they will turn him out of the church?"

"Oh, if they only would, and he consent to it! But it would ruin his peace, and that I could not see. His interest in that church is stronger than ever now, and the Dunkers, I fear, will never trust me."

"Why, Nelly?"

"Because I am ambitious. The vanities they hate are life and religion to me. My love for that man is greater than everything, but I shall marry him like a girl entering the nunnery on account of her love."

"O Nelly!" cried Booth, "he never could shine in any other world. You can!"

"But to shine and have no heart left: that is just as bad! Luther Bosler is a great man. He sees everything for himself. He loved me with slow, steady strength till the quiet time came to declare it, and, ever since, I have been a child before him, yielding up everything. I am to be baptized, to put away my bright clothes, and become the example of people who will not have a musical instrument in their houses, nor even hear Katy Bosler's accordion without dislike."

"Oh, shame! It would be ingratitude to God. The best families in this valley are not your superiors. Look at that profile — that upturned eye like Medea's accusing the Fates, the eagle curve of the nose, and the strong, placid mouth that could speak one's doom as quietly as the Empress Catharine on the Russian throne! No wonder, my great girl, you have some aspirations beyond a Dunker meeting-house!"

He saw her countenance flush to this praise, and, riding by her side, had put his hand upon her chin, to give her profile the proper lines.

"I love praise," said Nelly Harbaugh, hardly repulsing his hand. "I believe all you say, though I don't know who the people are you compare me to. If my Luther would only speak to me like that, I could fall off this horse in the dust and worship him."

"Oh, cutting compliment, Nelly! To be compared to a fanatic like that! Are you an abolitionist, too?"

"No. I have no politics. Negroes I look upon like all us poor whites — with dislike. Luther's views on this and many subjects I do not understand. Please take your hand down from my neck, sir! But if Luther Bosler was to compliment me I should feel that love and justice had crowned me, like religion itself. He is so much a man!"

Booth drew his hand away from Nelly somewhat testily, but interested in this girl with all the zest of a hunter of fierce animals.

"You don't think me of a man's growth, then?"

"You interest me very much. You are a handsome man. I never saw a more agreeable and distinguished young gentleman. Once in my life I went to the theater, and never since have I forgotten anything in the performance. To have an actor for a friend seems wonderful to me — so wonderful that I can't find composure to flatter you. You are not settled, like Luther. He never would ride a horse furiously for no purpose at all. Therefore, when he says 'Love me,' it is like the command in the Scriptures — the voice of his natural, undivided heart."

"How do you know my heart has ever been occupied before?"

"It may never be fully occupied hereafter," Nelly answered; "the heart adapted for love has the sound of love before love enters in it. Many a voice has uttered love to me, and I know all the tones. Lloyd Quantrell is in love: he talks to Katy in love's tremble. You make me like you by the self-love you start in me; Luther draws me to him by his full-grown character."

"What has he got to recommend him in any worldly view?"

"Substantial property — farms, horses, standing in his county, a whole sect at his back, a gentle, steady nature, relatives over a wide country — all that a poor girl here wants, and more than enough."

Booth listened with an affable countenance whose very politeness exasperated the woman engaged to share these benefits.

"Are you rich?" she demanded.

He started, as if not quite prepared for the question.

"How much land have *you* got, sir?"

"Not an acre."

"Have you any city houses, or bonds, or stocks, or insurance, or even furniture?"

"Not yet, Nelly."

"Your friend Lloyd says that actors spend everything upon their own vanity and appetites. I hope you don't. And yet you rode Luther's horse like a man who never owned his own horse."

"I possess no horse," admitted Booth; "I am only beginning."

"There's Katy Bosler; her daddy will give her a farm and stock. And here, sir, is my farm. I am not ashamed of it, because it is everything I have got, and every weed in it seems dear to me."

A capacity she had for rapid fluctuations of feeling was instanced in this turn from challenge to sensibility, and her throat filled up with emotion as she pulled her horse toward him at her own gate, and pleaded:

"You won't despise my little home, John?"

"With you, Nelly, it would be fair Rosamond's bower."

She leaned forward in gratitude and apprehension, as if she knew no other way, and kissed him welcome.

Nelly's place was a patch of ground a few acres in extent on the foreland of a high, sliding knoll, with a queer, low, rough-plastered house set at a spot where she could look off into the far distance at the diverging mountain-walls of the Catoctin Valley; and the spire of Wolfsville Lutheran church was just visible over the nearer hills, while underneath her wild perch the ravines yawned full of rocks; and beyond them the Catoctin Mountain was piled up in lonesome walls of woods just feeling the teeth of autumn. Some great rocks still stood like shepherd-dogs above the well-picked fields; a cowbell tinkled in the unknown bottoms; a dog ran out, half civil, and watched Booth fiercely.

"Who lives here besides you, Nelly?"

"Not one. My mother died a year ago, and is buried by that church-steeple."

"Your father?"

"He is dead, or gone. I may as well tell you, so that you can ask no further: He was a sergeant in the regular army, who came to Frederick recruiting before the Mexican War, and married my mother. He said one day, when I was a little thing, that he must go see his kin in the North, and he never came back. Mother took her old family name again, and I built her this home. Come in it!"

The structure was simple, of refuse lumber, but made neat by vines, pots of flowers, an arbor, rude fences, and stone walls.

"I plastered this house myself," Nelly said. "A beau of mine lent me the tools. I hauled the lime in a borrowed wagon. The cow-hair a love-sick butcher gave me. Luther Bosler brought me the lath. I sifted the sand from a gully; and so I kept out the cold."

There were pictures on the wall, taken generally from labels of cotton prints or from illustrated newspapers.

"There," cried Nelly, "is evidence to you, John" — she had fallen easily at her own home into this familiar address — "that I always loved the actors!"

It was a show-poster in colors, representing a fine blonde female, and entitled "Laura Keene, in 'The American Cousin.'"

"This seems to be good land, Nelly?"

"It was a stone-heap when I came here. While others picked berries I and mother picked stones, from week to week and from year to year. Sometimes I would pet a susceptible farmer to come with his team and chain of an evening and pull out a few big rocks. I live here all alone; do you wonder that Luther Bosler is a rich man to me?"

He flattered her less, because he began to feel that she had self-reliance as he had seldom heard of it in a worldly woman.

"Do you not require help for some things?" he asked; "some things disagreeable to women?"

"I had to do without it. Winter was before me, and I made ready to butcher myself, for bacon and ham do not grow; but a neighbor relieved me of the killing. I have tended my cow, and been its only doctor at calving; and have run the plow in my field rather than incur the obligation of a lover. In this exposed place one has to be careful about multiplying equals. Dangerous men might get access here through my indiscretion —"

"If they did — ?" said Booth.

"I should then shoot off my pistol, too; but powder and shot are dear."

She drew down an old single-barrel gun from above the door, and raised it to her shoulder with a flash of the eye that took sight at the lock like yellow fire.

"This was all my father left my mother," Nelly said. "More than once I have taken it down to kill an insolent man, and marched him past my gate!"

"Great God!" exclaimed Booth, watching her thoughtfully; "the women of Daniel Boone were no greater. Nelly, I came here with you for pleasure only. I know that I can not deceive you. You are a revelation to me of wonder and of wealth, and you have reason to love old John Brown that he invaded your country and brought me to your side — yes, Miss Nelly Harbaugh, to your feet!"

He had taken her hands in his, and he knelt before her, doing homage, with an actor's cleverness, to a playing queen. She watched his manner, or actor's "business," with serious rapture.

"Not one point am I richer than you in," continued Booth, softly and soothingly. "This little land you possess is more than I have saved — more shame to me that it is so, for I have been better salaried than my superiors these two years! With strong body and willful tastes I have followed pleasure and been a spendthrift, knowing no woman of kin-dred ambition to lead me forward by love and emulation in my profession. I have *found* that woman. I can give you, Miss Nelly Harbaugh, the one chance of a hundred years on the stage my father's name is still our passport to!"

She looked at him severely, sadly, but with a longing, and her eyes roved through her lowly window to the sun retiring over the South Mountain and flooding the haze of the valley with golden cloud.

"Get up," she said. "and let me set you some supper. I am not to be taken by surprise."

He saw her take down her father's fowling-piece, and for a moment he was frightened, as he considered her positive and hardening face, all strong in nervous reflection.

"Perhaps," thought Booth, "she is going to spurn the temptation, and march me to the gate with that gun!"

She set before him an earthen jug of Bosler's whisky and clear water from her spring, and lighted her fire at the oven. He followed her out and began to cut some wood for the oven, and he soon heard her gun discharged in her buckwheat patch, and she reappeared with a partridge.

"Why, Nelly," he cried, assisting her at the fire, "these seem to be brook-trout frying!"

"They are. An old lover of mine has been fishing today in Little Hunting Creek, and his devotion comes in time for you. Since Brown's raid nobody much in Catoctin Valley has worked."

She observed that a single glass of the liquor changed his temperament, and made him less considerate and less gently negative.

"You are not ignorant of farm-life, I see," Nelly remarked, as Booth ate heartily of the trout and baked bird.

"I should think not. Every child of my father was born on a Maryland farm, and he had a morbid dread for years of our going to the cities or the theaters. It was thirty-seven years ago, when he had been only a year in America, and was hardly older than I am now — for he had gone upon the stage at eighteen — that he bought a wild patch of ground like yours, and put my patient mother upon it. For company for her he brought out his penniless old father, a graduate of the radical spout-shops of London. What a place for two people who had lived abreast of Napoleon and Wellington in the greatest city of the world! The rank woods grew around us, full of wild animals and poisonous snakes. The nearest town was a rude court-house place, and there we went to school three miles and back of a day, while father roved all over the country acting till he would be discharged, or wander away disgusted; and then he came home to turn the satyr side of his nature upon us. He had a dread of final poverty, and if we wanted money we had to work for it. So I have planted corn for three levies a day, and picked stone off the neighbors' fields for a quarter of a dollar."

"I am glad of that, my friend. Then you know what humility is?"

She reached out her hand to shake his with sympathy.

"No, Nelly. Humility only our mother knew. We had derived a terrible ambition from that seedy old ruined grandfather, who claimed relationship with a Lord Mayor of London, for whom I am namesake — John Wilkes! One by one we departed, all for the same assertive vocation. I was the last."

He had retained her hand, and, holding it warmly, concluded:

"I can feel for you, my girl! and the bright spirit of art has sent me to break the spell that walls your beauty in with these dragon mountains. Think of these fair, long hands, whose silver sinews Apollo might have driven the stallions of yonder setting sun with, growing misshapen and warty at the plow and the hoe, when Heaven intended them for rings of precious stones, and to be kissed by merchant princes kneeling for your regard!"

He kissed her hand, but she asked with a still, steady voice, amid her flushing:

"What were you paid when you became an actor first?"

"My father wandered off and died seven years ago upon a Western river. I was the only son at home, in Baltimore, and tired of school and dependence; so my brother-in-law, a manager, gave me eight dollars a week to act small parts in Philadelphia. I despised such employment, and a Virginia manager next offered me three times that salary, and in Richmond I have become a great favorite. This volunteering I have done, to defend Virginia, has made me a hero in the South. Look, Nelly, at these newspaper clippings!"

With a nervous avarice of praise he read to her, in an accentuated, professional style, the unqualified fulsomeness of Southern writing in the provincial days of State rights: "The gallant Booth," "The successor of Brutus in name and deed," "The South's defender," "Virginia's champion," etc.

Soldiering had not been required for so long in America that Brown's raid had obtained all the importance of a war, and every private in it received the notoriety of a general, while a Marylander volunteering in aid of invaded Virginia, seemed in the strained State "sovereignty" distinctions of those times like Lafayette assisting another country.

"Mark me, Nelly!" declaimed Booth, feeding his excitement at the whisky-glass — "this coming of mine to Charlestown, with the devotion of a patriot, makes my fortune as an actor!"

"You mean in the South?"

"In the South and the West, too, for half the West is Southern. We are three brothers, and we are to divide our father's raiment by taking his name in three great sections separately — Junius on the Pacific, Edwin in the North, and I am to have the cotton States and the Mississippi Valley. It makes no difference whether I act good or bad, since I have joined the forces against John Brown, and am become a Virginian. I shall be a 'star' next year, traveling with my own manager and company. Now I am only 'Mr. John Wilkes' on the bills, but then I shall be 'Mr. Booth, the tragedian,' and half the receipts will be my share. I shall make twenty thousand dollars in three months!"

"My Lord!" exclaimed Nelly Harbaugh, "what can you do with the money?"

"Give it," replied Booth, "to the woman I love, and whom I will make my leading lady — to pay her a salary worthy of her beauty, and to encourage her talent by noble dressing and cultivation."

"To me?" she cried. "I won't believe you!"

"No, the surprise is too great, my honest girl. You have set your mind no higher than keeping a Dunker farmer's milk-cans, and can not grasp the sum of your value to me."

The girl's eyes sought her father's gun above the door with weak temper, and she started from her seat at the table and retreated from Booth.

"I was prepared to be flattered by you," she exclaimed, trembling. "I thought I was armed against you everywhere. Why can you tempt me like that? If I am strong and alone, I am only a woman."

A flood of actual tears came out upon the bursting of a sob. He endeavored to break this instant of weakness upon his compassionate breast, but her arms were thrown outward, instinctive as her cry, to ward him off.

"Where is my man?" she moaned, laying her golden-tinted neck and unbound wave of hair upon the clay chimney-place; "the man I am promised to, and who should be my shepherd now when I am asked to stray from the fold? Gone, and I am left with a beautiful devil and this temptation!"

"Pardon me!" said Booth, also rising. "Your ingratitude wounds me, too. I thought I interpreted your wishes, or I would not have expressed my own. Your sensibility, Nelly, convinces me the more that you can reform the evil in me, and make me a man. Young as I am, a woman's influence is already my necessity. If not as an artist, help me as a *wife!*"

He took the old gun from the place above the door, and walked out into the fields noiselessly, but she knew that he was gone.

Her dog was growling suspiciously to see her cry, when she looked up, and she walked to her cheap, gilt looking-glass, and took it from its peg and sat with it, under her arbor, looking alternately at her great, reddened, expressive blue eyes and at the falling of sunset upon the receding billows of the Catoctin Valley.

She had lost the joy of this home, the humble monument of her hands, and lost, also, the solace of her marriage engagement, so dearly invited and full of sacred whisperings — mutuality, trust, children, worship, and widening good name; the opportunity of charity, the manna of improvement, the self-respect the world can not take away. A superficial man, full of strong will, hardly her senior in years, and unscrupulous in friendship, had crossed the gentle vista of her domestic settlement like the shadow of a croaking crow she saw go across her white buckwheat-blossoms — a winged appetite. With superstitious memory she recalled the fortune-teller's lines:

"Something dark and white I mark,
 It shall mark thee with the dark!"

She heard the gun of Booth go off, and the crow dropped out of his driving career, limp and nondescript.

Deeper helplessness settled upon her as she thought how her very thoughts were countered by this stranger's casualty.

Glancing at her looking glass, something of her mother's piteous expression there, whom she had seen so often cry at Nelly's waywardness, brought real tears again; this time she let them come like steam from the scalding kettle, grateful with relief.

That mother, the flower of the valley, culled by a bold, effusive stranger, and briefly worn with a devotion above constancy, had died with one faith and prayer alone — the preservation of her child's pure soul in wifely custody to some native, unranging man. Her prayers were now answered, for Luther Bosler had been that mother's choice, though she might never knew his and Heaven's condescension in this world.

"Oh, speak, mother!" the soldier's orphan sighed; "let Nature somewhere break this chain that drags me down like the hewed tree to the mill in the valley! I feel the high wheels take one down; I hear the saw scream for me in the long coffin of the saw-mill; my body is on the trundle, and I am going forward in the grooves. Oh, pray — pray — pray!"

Booth heard these words, and they made him superstitious. Thrice in that way had his father spoken when he died, a poor, old, lonely man in the state-room of a Western steamboat, saying with strangling breath, "Pray — pray — pray!"

The son felt the admonition of conscience, and he answered Nelly's prayer:

"I withdraw my offer, Nelly. You are too good a girl."

"What?" She had arisen from her struggle, like one made the subject of a miracle.

"This independence you live in, is better than the dependence and uncertainty of the stage. The man you have promised is better for you than I could be. Come, be my friend, and God bless you!"

His better nature had prevailed; the game had vexed him, and he abandoned it.

"O John! I will always be your friend, for now I see the whiteness and the darkness fall apart in your nature."

With friendship made up of gratitude and relief, she took him in her arms like a brother long wished for, and on her ardent kiss the gypsy in his blood flamed in an instant again. He reached for the jug of whisky, but she interposed:

"Oh, do not drink again! It changes your nature so."

"You know me already," spoke Booth. "What an angel you can be, throwing worldly ambition away! It was not made for woman."

"I confess that sin, John. Am I cured of it?"

"I never would have robbed you of this independence, Nelly. It is the dream of my own life to stand above and away from vulgar contact. If I had made you my pupil, I would not have advanced you beyond your growth. First I would have put you in the chorus, and let you find your own level. Your courage and perseverance would have brought you out."

Again her imagination hearkened to the revelations of that glittering mimic world, but he had assuaged her fears. She listened to him now without suspicion, since he had redeemed himself. He talked long and sensibly, with most instructive *minutiæ*, of information about the chances and rewards of actress-life.

"Why, Nelly," he cried at last, "it is past eight o'clock. You must not be compromised by staying alone with me in this house. To horse, my Dunker cavalier!"

As they stood in her little stable together, making the horses ready, he murmured, taking her hand:

"Am I trusted?"

"Always."

"Then you can kiss me."

"This is the last, dear John."

It was late when they reached Bosler's farm, and the great dog Fritz being absent there, no barking announced them. They put the horses in the stable quietly, and, guided back to the house by a candle in a window, paused there to look within. Katy was asleep, with her accordion still in her hands.

Gazing down at her, with his Catholic breviary in his lap, Hugh Fenwick looked in more than image-worship.

The spotted pointer, Albion, took in the scene with one eye, as consonantly mischievous with his own general intentions.

"My gracious!" cried Katy, as the door opened and the dog snapped; "is it you, Nelly? Why, I dreamed you had pecome an actor at te teatre."

Jake Bosler, too, had been aroused, and his shaggy hair and beard were seen at the stairway-door, and he remarked:

"Soun-up. Bi'm-by!"

Chapter XXX

JOHN BROWN EXECUTED

A WARM Friday within the brink of December — like the climate of the better world let down to temper an old man's winter — saw the lean, long body of John Brown turning, with the breezes from the Shenandoah, at the end of a cord.

There hung the unprefaced one, amid two thousand soldiers, the captain of the greatest episode in time.

The gallows tree was framed about with lines of chivalry; but something odd, and moral, and pitiful, hung there on a hempen string, which made the imposing military display seem moderate, and no volunteer in it felt the occasion not to be dignified.

Nearest the gallows was the company in which stood to his musket John Wilkes Booth — stern, handsome, and classical. Quantrell was a substitute in a more distant command; John Yates Beall was also in the gay-vestured field — each of these young men taking a lot in the old man's bloody raiment, here raffled in the chief gateway to the slave States.

It was the dress rehearsal of the mightiest war since the courts of Europe had repressed and imbibed republicanism.

Stuart and Lee, Wise and Vallandigham, had rehearsed at the old man's capture. Stonewall Jackson at the head of his school of cadets, Turner Ashby commanding the pickets, Israel Green, the marine-officer who had cut John Brown down, and Jeff Thompson from far-off Missouri, were some of the pawns at the scaffold. The gray uniforms from Richmond, the light blue from Alexandria, the buff and yellow from Winchester, and the crimson from Appomattox, stood in the great hollow square of troops, to which the militia from Petersburg had guarded this one old man from jail, as he rode upon his coffin. The guidon-flags to designate the positions these and others were to take, prophesied the name, also, on each, of some unborn battle.

No gambler ever paid the odds of life which these neighborhoods paid John Brown — a thousand, at least, to one. No Valkyria of Odin and the Northern gods ever marked more surely the sites of devastation: Gettysburg, Chambersburg, Hagerstown, Winchester, Richmond, Knoxville, and Chattanooga, had all been spied out for the strategy that John Brown appeared at this moment to have brought to such a small and personal conclusion.

Short had been his shrift — tried in seven days, sentenced in six days more, executed in another month — not seven weeks in all; but in that time he rounded life with the accuracy and completeness of a comet predicted and fulfilled. His foolishness ended at his taking, and his greatness began in his failure. The letters he answered, the speech he made in court, his consistency and simplicity, had a moral influence feebly prefigured by the reckless Samson pulling the heathen temple down. Of Samson had remained only strength; of Brown, no strength — only testimony.

The abolitionist — that unseen terror — had at last been captured and displayed in the slave States, and probably the only perfect specimen. Nearly every one of the same genus who had been privy to his plans retreated from the responsibility, and left him on the enemy's side, a deadly hostage, subtle as wisdom itself.

Quantrell, Booth, and Beall, the youthful trio we are to carry through our narrative, all heard John Brown when he rose in court to answer why sentence should not be passed upon him.

His head still ringing with sword-strokes, and his side and kidneys wounded, he was able, by long absorption of his theme, to preach upon it without preparation, and to the most modest and wondrous effect.

He rose from his blanket and cot, like Lazarus from the dead, all bandaged and feeble, and said that he had come to Virginia to set free slaves:

"Had I so interfered in behalf of the rich, the powerful, the intelligent, the so-called great," said John Brown, "and suffered and sacrificed what I have in this interference, it would have been all right, and every man in this court would have deemed it an act worthy of reward rather than punishment."

His tones were almost hesitating, and therefore the quiet meaning felt its way along the heart-strings as art could never do. Glancing, in need of an idea, at the little Bible by the judge, the old man, touching sixty years of age and looking seventy, raised his mighty plaint again:

"I see a book kissed in this court which I suppose to be the New Testament, which teaches me that all things whatsoever I would that men should do to me I should do even so to them. It teaches me further to remember them that are in bonds as bound with them. I endeavored to act up to that instruction; for I am yet too young to understand that God is any respecter of persons. I believe that to have interfered, as I have done, in behalf of his despised poor, is no wrong, but right."

Those high words had been a felony spoken anywhere in Virginia except in court, and for the first time in thirty years they were now legally proclaimed. The judge was presiding at an abolition meeting, and was powerless to arrest an orator who came shod in the supernal light of martyrdom. Poor men without slaves heard the gospel where no misinterpretation could distort the preacher's nature, and the great slaveholders would feign have cried out in chagrin, as in a noble poem, contemporary with John Brown, "Hadst thou sought the whole State over, there was no one place so secret — no high place nor lowly place where thou couldst have escaped me — save on this very scaffold."*

He continued, and they felt it was a gentleman who now spoke, whatever he may have been before:

"Now, if it is deemed necessary that I should forfeit my life for the furtherance of the ends of justice, and mingle my blood further with the blood of my children, and with the blood of millions, in this slave country, whose rights are disregarded by the wicked, cruel, and unjust enactments, I say, let it be done!"

Quantrell's eyes filled with tears at the recollection of Brown's dying sons, who had gone in bloody testimony before him. He heard other sobs, also, in that long, deep court-room, with people standing in windowsills, and oil-lamps feebly lighting the packed enclosure; but the voice of Booth rebuked those symptoms, audibly saying:

"The damned, black-hearted villain!"

"Heart black as a stove-pipe!" muttered the tight-shut skull of young Mr. Beall.

The old man now thanked the court, the neighboring society, and the jury courteously, and those who had prematurely muttered against him grew small in their own esteem. He disclaimed any design of treason or general insurrection, merely desiring to take people out to liberty. Nor had he misled any, many of his volunteers having been strangers to him, and most of them had paid their own expenses to death.

Thus he disposed of the impression sought to be made by some Northern lawyers, afraid to defend freedom from freedom's side, and destroyed the stigma that he, an old, wise man, had decoyed some boys to danger. The little army of fanaticism was made to stand equal everywhere upon the high ground of principle.

Only one man applauded when he was sentenced, and him the judge severely rebuked, so that in after-years he was afraid to shout at all, and grew timid of his own natural emotions.

---

*   "The Scarlet Letter."

Little Ned Coppock had been tried, as John Brown came up for sentence, and when they sentenced him, who was almost a favorite with the populace, so fair and young he was, Ned also spoke:

"I never committed murder. When I escaped to the engine-house and found the captain and his prisoners surrounded there, I saw no way of deliverance but by fighting a little. If anybody was killed on that occasion, it was in a fair fight."

Coppock had been a poor orphan boy, but the Quaker who raised him found somewhere in him the spirit of the wild *copack,* or Russian lanceman, whence may have come his name; and when John Brown discovered him in Iowa he entered the crusade cordially, and it was not to his disparagement in Virginia that he had fought bravely. He stood up to be sentenced with his arms behind him, abreast of John Cook, whose arms were folded; and between them stood two Negroes, Green, the South Carolinian, and Copeland from Oberlin — a college which educated blacks with whites.

Green was from Charleston — the city which was to begin the war — a runaway slave, and he had fought revengefully. Copeland had been raised of Virginia seed in Ohio. These two, the least culpable in motive there, were the most friendless; but Virginia took distinction that day that she, alone of the slave States, probably, would do no more than punish them equally like the white invaders. Farther south they would have died by torture.

John E. Cook, the most befriended of any by relatives and power, and he alone dressed newly and well, was the most unhappy person in the band. The rest had put life behind them, and were resigned to die, while he had been tempted to confess upon his comrades, as he had also been the Hebrew spy upon Virginia, and therefore his intelligence did him no credit, being unaccompanied with constancy. A thread of self-love and glorifying went through his natural courage and left him unsupported in despondency, but, as his life was taken at last, he died manfully, and might have left a noble figure with his delicate outlines and better mental organization than the rest. It would seem from John Brown's final rebuke of him that Cook had proceeded to Harper's Ferry in advance, upon his own motion chiefly, liking the adventure even better than the cause.

Stevens was tried reclining on the court-room floor, with his back against a mattressed chair, old slippers on his feet, and his head in a kerchief. He accepted no favors, looked with contempt on court and foe, regarded Ned John Brown as less of a military genius than he had supposed, and for the rest cared nothing; since he joyously believed in spirit-people, and meant his death to be a visitation.

Hazlett, who had also been recaptured, was a plain, dull Pennsylvanian; for the little roster of Brown's daring lads covered many States — Maine, Massachusetts, Connecticut, New York, Ohio, Indiana, Iowa, Pennsylvania, Virginia, and South Carolina; and Kansas had been their military academy.

In spite of their injury to Jefferson County, Virginia, its people were seldom harsh with these strangers. The Teutonic wave rippling through that region was mild and laving, and in many a farmhouse lay Kercheval's old "History of the Valley," saying: "Twenty-four hours never pass during which my imagination does not present me with the afflicting view of the slave; and my consolation was that the master would receive the punishment due to his cruelty, while the slave should find rest from his toils and sufferings in the kingdom of heaven!"

This conscience ran through all grades in Virginia, from the Governor of the State, at Richmond, to the jailer at Charlestown. "I am in charge of a jailer," the old man wrote to his family, "like the one who took charge of Paul and Silas, and kind hearts and kind faces are more or less about me, while thousands are thirsting for my blood!"

He was a multiform study indeed, with prismatic lights and sides. Now he was Cromwell, and now John Bunyan; now Presbyterian, and now Independent, but no preacher would John Brown have, since all who came to pray with him justified slavery. He had skeptical or infidel sons, some of whom had died with Christian devotion fighting for his political cause, but he averred that his expedition and defeat had been predestined in the eternal decrees of God. He disclaimed having ever had the spirit of retaliation, yet admitted advising acts of deadly reprisal, such as friendship, to this day, feels bashful to defend; and, indeed, he was an Old Testament pupil, possessed with the complacency of Heaven's headsman and hewer-down. Discerning people said he was partly insane, but he remarked acutely: "I must be very insane, if insane at all; but if that be so, insanity is like a very pleasant dream to me." There seemed an unfeeling side to him, as when he advised his wife not to come to him, and to have all the bodies of her slain sons and sons-in-law burned; yet his letters home were tender as a daughter's, and from Maryland came proof that he would never kill a pig nor cut open a watermelon without dividing with the poor people around him there.

Death seemed to John Brown a mere incident in justice, and wrong-doers or wrong systems to be under the sentence of Moses and Joshua. That terrible book which waked the Calvinist and Baptist to civil war and cut off the English king's head, John Brown had balanced over the Anglo-Saxon republic, and made terrible again by his willful reading of it. The democracy of the saints seemed still his religion, and he wrote to a merchant: "I go joyfully in behalf of millions that have no rights, and I look forward to other changes to take place, believing that 'the fashion of this world passeth away.'" "Let me be spared," he said to another Joseph of Arimathea, "any weak or hypocritical prayers made over me when I am publicly murdered, and let my only religious attendants be poor, little, dirty, ragged, bareheaded and barefooted slave-boys and slave-girls, led by some old, gray-headed slave-mother!"

Quantrell took Katy in to see him one day when Lloyd was on guard and Katy in the town. The tears came to Katy's eyes to hear his chains rattle.

"Tears for me?" the spiky-haired old borderer said; "I will turn them, my children, into songs. At my little farm in Maryland, twelve miles from here, was a nest of wrens under the rude porch, and one day the old birds flew right into the room where my daughter Anne was sewing, and I reading my Bible. 'What can be the matter, father?' Anne said to me. The wrens were flying and trembling, and twittering, as they had never done before. I took up a pike that one of my black volunteers had brought in, and went out on the porch. Nothing seemed to be there. The brooks and copses, and wild hills were glad with sound and silence, and shadow and light. ' Nothing is here, Anne,' said I; 'the young birds are in their nests. It is a false alarm.' 'O father,' she answered, 'look at that snake!' I then saw twined round the post, below the nest in the eaves, a black snake, all ready to devour the young, so helpless and unknowing in the nest. My child" (to Katy), "I killed the snake, and such a song as those old birds gave me, sitting on the rail of the porch, never will be sung till the chains fall off and the young birds are free!" He rattled his chains. "You may be lovers, children, and your young will be some day in the cradle, and slavery, if twined around the pillar of our system, will choke their life and chance away. Sing to the old man's pike when slavery is no more! for you are all my children, Southern as well as Northern, though the snake will strangle me, and leave my young wrens to starve!"

Katy had not blushed, pity starting in her maiden's milk; and, while she strained her eyes in earnest woe, Lloyd tapped his foot and they sang, and John Brown knew the piece and joined in:

"Carol, brothers, carol; carol joyfully!
　Carol the good tidings; carol merrily!
　And pray a gladsome Christmas
　For all good Christian men.
　　Carol, brothers, carol —
　Christmas-day again!

"Hearing angel-music,
　Discord sure must cease:
　Who dare hate his brother

> On this day of peace?
> While the heavens are telling
> To mankind good-will,
> Only love and kindness
> Every bosom fill!

> "Carol, brothers, carol;
> Carol joyfully!" etc.*

The unwonted singing raised a great commotion. The general, Taliaferro — whom usage degraded to Tolliver, and whom some dubbed Tolable — had been at the guard-house across the way, taking his nap on the veranda, heavy with epaulets and juleps, and ridden by the nightmare of responsibility. He heard this singing, and took it superstitiously. Some abolition angels might have rolled the stone away from John Brown's tomb, and celebrated his escape with Yankee hosannas.

He came tearing up the jail-porch, his mighty sword raising echoes down the silent afternoon street, and his spurs catching in his trousers' stripes.

"Campbell — Avis, what's to pay?" roared the general. "Who's a-doin' this breakdown? Is this a time faw levity?"

The sheriff and the jailer, thus addressed, entered the condemned man's cell, and the general followed, cunningly, lest some black art might be at work.

"Cappen Brown," asked the doughty general, "am I to understand that you, sah, desire, sah, of this saranadin', sah? It's not in military usage, cappen, but we consult yo' wishes, sah."

"I do, general. The young people sing at my request."

"Cappen Brown," exclaimed the general of militia, saluting for the third time, "yo' desiah shall be complied with, sah, in spite of regulations."

Hereupon the general turned, at such a military right angle that he ran into six of his staff, who had come to rescue him, and an inextricable confusion of sabers, chapeaux, epaulets, spurs, salutes, oaths, and apologies ensued, ending by a strewing of the place with fallen magnanimity. Some one ran to the cannon under the court-house portico to fire it off, and the Negroes at the two hotels rang the big dinner-bells in the trees, and fell down their respective cellars, to anticipate a bombardment.

Keenly alive to the humors of the siege of Charlestown by a phantom abolition army, Quantrell and Booth put up tricks on the Virginia

---

*   By Rev. W. A. Muhlenberg, of the family of General Muhlenberg, the Lutheran pastor in the Valley, whose gown covered his Continental uniform.

militia, including John Beall, who regarded everything with a lowering and serious temperament. But the culmination of burlesque and pathos was in the reception of John Brown's wife.

The subject of her visit had been made a diplomatic matter, and was the occasion of more telegraphing between the old pagan Capitol at Richmond and the seat of war in the Valley than all the Virginia press required for news.

Would she bring, concealed about her person, the plot for his rescue or escape? Did the art of war show an instance of a woman entering the picket-lines? Could the reception of Mrs. Brown give a pretext for the Federal courts to interfere?

Chivalry prevailed at last, and word was passed to bring Mrs. Brown from Harper's Ferry to Charlestown, not by rail, but by private conveyance and military escort.

The carriage-cushions were carefully taken out to see if they concealed any Northern newspaper correspondents, and an escort of cavalry formed around the ancient vehicle, that had apparently been used in the Shakespearean age by Captain John Smith, and was at least as old and as decrepit as the American Constitution, which was soon to furnish old lumber and leather enough for two governments.

A file of Virginia dragoons in the uniform of Marlborough's age surrounded this crazy State vehicle; the poor lady's friends were not allowed to ride with her; but the Virginia militia officers, instead, inflicted their preposterous eighteenth-century sympathy and compliment upon a woman simple and native in her life and ways as Pocahontas.

Up the long, dry turnpike stretches, like causeways to the top and bottom of the world, dragoons and coach came rattling, pistols and sabers ready; and Negroes peeped from knot-holes in toll-house and barn, and white families turned out at lanes and blacksmiths' corners, to see this ogress, who had been the bandit's bride and maternal font of bandit sons.

Alas! She had hunted for twenty-four hours at Harper's Ferry to get a wandering bone or shoe of her lost babes killed there in the foray; and one had been the sport of a dissecting-table, and the other clapped into a dead Negro's arms and buried indistinguishably.

So she reached the hill-top of Charlestown, marked by the stumpy-towered Episcopal church and the prosecuting attorney's mansion, and there the great review was taking place to prepare for the execution on the morrow. The poor lady, worn out with the silly chatter she had been subjected to, took little note of the glittering bayonets and loud comments — each yelled with special reference to "Madame" Brown; or of the churchyard filled with rabble and the church itself a barrack; of the absence of black people from the streets, and the curiosity of women. She heard the sharp echoes on the stones, felt the sharp pain in her heart, and realized where glory and philanthropy left the blasted home.

The street at the jail corners was so crowded that the military had to clear a way and form a square; but all their ostentation was wasted on the plain, large woman who had learned patience in Northern winters and unintermittent child-births, and who had dealt above a quarter of a century with a husband impracticable and persevering as the wild steer.

They gazed on her with hardly recognition, thinking she had not yet come when she was gone; for they expected they knew not what, but something dazzling, like Taliaferro's aides, some of whom had their hair plaited double behind and brought around to the front and tied in a bow-knot between their eyes!

The general himself was an entire review, as he stood in the upholstery of militia regalia, with a staff never afterward equaled in numbers and pomatum in the New World.

Leather thighings, prodigious boots, loops of dyed horse-hair, epaulets which seemed to clank, and sabers which seemed to titter, spurs pointing upward, swords pointing forward, scabbards getting awry, mustaches twisted, beards like breastplates, dignity and vanity mixed, like the quid of tobacco under the martial jaw, and the solemnity of an historical occasion attempted to be preserved coincident with the gallantry due a lady.

"General Tollivaw" (the scene seemed to give it the sound of Bolivaw), "pawmit me, general, saw, to present Madame Brown, saw, of the State, saw, of New Yawk — ah! saw."

Solemn silence, punctuated by an officer letting fly his tobacco-expectoration over his helmet-chain without moving his countenance from its austerity.

"Welcome, welcome to Vahgeenia, madame," spoke the general, vast hat in hand, and describing the radius of a great circle on the floor. "Pawmit me to shake yo' hand. Pawmit me to wish yo' health is faw. Pawmit me to intojuce the offisaws of my staff."

Severally, to this unabashed, unrelaxing, stalwart mother and pioneer, the well-meaning but inconsiderate sons of Mars were introduced, each in sentiment surrendering his personality to "Virginia," while, in fact, with a whetted self-consciousness provincial patriotism alone could so deform. Some assured her of "true Virginia hospitality" if she should ever visit their respective counties — she who was to know upon the morrow the pang of widowhood and want, and in whose life, for years past, the acquisition of a calico dress was an historical period!

But of that fantastic staff how many were to fall and clutch the turf, crying on God and mother, and forgetting that Virginia ever was!

It seemed a comfort to her, after a quarter of an hour of ill-timed smirks and inanities, to be taken aside by Mrs. Avis, the jailer's wife, and searched for implements of suicide; but Mrs. Avis knew John Brown would never take his own life, and her hands had the tenderness of caresses. There was the real and memorable hospitality of Virginia, in that shoemaker-jailer's family, facing the roar of merciless millions, who called for severity to Brown's men, but saying back, "These are my captives and my guests." Such jailers, a little later, might have made prison-pens also pitiful.

The jailer alone remained in the little parlor with the condemned man and his wife, although Taliaferro broke in once, to say that they could only have two hours, and then gave them four, for he was a kinder man than his wind.

The resolute woman of forest stature and manual labor's mold went up to John Brown and called him "father." He was the only father she knew; for, marrying him at half his age, when she was of only sixteen years, she paid the penalty childhood, like Ruth, pays to old Boaz and his prospects and intellect.

He was then postmaster, surveyor, tanner, and town-maker, with the dogmatic will of one predestined to be restless all his days. He led her continually into the deserts, and left her there, and went off on some inspired freak of ruin, leaving little babes around her, and even a babe to come; and when she gave him her destiny and tenderness in charge, he already had been the father of seven children, five of them alive.

He gave her the life of a poor white, aggravated by the splendid illusions of a schemer and a dreamer, and the end of the dream had come.

He had levied upon her sons, the support of her mountain-patch of land, and taken them to death, with their widows to be left upon her care. Thirteen children had she borne this old man, the sire of twenty; and tomorrow he was to die, and bequeath her only his body.

He took her in his arms, and in his white beard lay her face, as often she had thrown it into the fleece she spun for his clothing in his absence, wondering if he could be dead. The spasm of her broad shoulders showed that she was weeping, and the gurgle of the spirit within, breaking over this last flinty barrier, sobbed forth a few times; but he stood like a rock used to the flood and full of its moss and lichens; the tears that wet his face were the splashings of hers. He was pitying her and Nature, but not himself.

She looked up, and saw him so natural and strong, and dried her tears, still leaning on his mouth; for she looked like his buxom daughter, and only his shaftlike head made him higher than hers.

"Father," she said, "they let me come to see you at last."

He kissed her, and asked for the widows he had made and the children he was never to see.

"Mary," said he, "is grandfather's old granite tombstone set up by the big rock at North Elby?"

"Yes, father, with son Freddy's name under your grandfather's, who fit in the Revolution."

"I value it highly," said John Brown, "for I am the first of my family ever put in jail; and, Mary, I want my name to go by Grandfather John Brown's. A revolutionary soldier, too, I hope I was."

"Papa, we don't accuse you. You thought it was right. We think so, too."

"Three of my sons, killed in this war for liberty, I want remembered by an inscription on that stone. Grandfather and me will make two more. I have loved this life, wife, so much, I want to leave a line upon a stone."

His ambition was greater than the expectations of religion, for he had found that tombstone the day he ordered his deadly pikes from the blacksmith, by his grandfather's grave.

The tombstone being discharged from his mind, Captain Brown settled into a contented mood, and sat down to the meal the good jailer furnished, eating sparingly, and with business references to small matters of property; for he adhered to the idea, and his wife also, that he was a great master of affairs, and had always failed through the incompetence of the times, seasons, and agents. He asked if his wife could not remain with him that night and depart with his mold next day, instead of retiring, as if she were a whole army, to Harper's Ferry, eight miles away, and there await his dumb remains. The request was denied; for the rabble clamored about the jail, and the moral pulse of the State was in a high fever.

So Brown settled down to read his will, which the jailer witnessed.

It was a will of souvenirs, and not property: the tombstone, his surveyor's compass, a silver watch, a glass, a lost gun, Bibles, and debts. He wanted all his little debts paid, even to people whose names he had forgotten. When this was ended, the old man looked quite comfortable and commercial; for his ideas never had failed to impress his family, and the departure he was to take on the morrow seemed only a larger journey and with no traveling expenses to provide. Strange that he had read the Bible every day of his life, and forgot it now! We all think we shall die anticipating, but we die retrospecting, and preparing for this world. It was, probably, with an insight into his high, ambitious, Puritan nature, that Mary Anne Brown inquired:

"Father, wasn't you disappointed at being took so soon?"

"My dear," the old man said, with a nervous twitch, his hairy forehead wrinkled speculatively, and his gray eyes preoccupied, "the errors of my plan were decreed before the world was made, and I had no more to do with the course I pursued than the shot leaving a cannon has to do with the spot where it shall fall."

"Pappy," she said, the last word being a cry that struck the jailer's heart, "didn't you suffer when Olly died, and our oldest boy, Watty?"

"No pain is like our offspring's death," the old man said, with his right shoulder pushed forward as if to lean upon some spirit unseen; "I loved my children, Mary; you have seen me nurse them weeks at a time. But I saw them die without tears, they were so brave."

All trembling, the large child-woman rose and meant to say something proudly, but it would not articulate.

"I have no boy left," she meant to say, "and you will be taken, too."

"Courage, wife! We have made our mark on this world by our failure. Death is the incident of a great purpose. There is a bright morning and a glorious day. Moderate circumstances, Mary, is the best blessing of this life. By poverty and failure I have been preserved to do this work. It is done; and I shall see our sons and daughters who have gone before — the three babes who were buried in one grave, the three grown ones who died for liberty. The blessing of our offered blood will follow you for all the remainder of your days.* See this, Mary!"

He took up a newspaper and read a message from the Governor of South Carolina, which had just come to hand, threatening secession in the event of a "Black Republican" being elected President, and also a legislative act, as follows:

"*Resolved,* That the State of South Carolina is ready to enter, together with the other slaveholding States, or such as desire present action, into the formation of a Southern Confederacy."

She did not understand it, or was in grief too profound to try; but he explained to her that he had forced slavery to become revolutionary, and made the Union of the American States the national cause, and involved it with the fall of slavery.

She listened with interest at last, and so he absorbed the time till she was commanded to go, and his failure took the light in her loyal nature of a postponed success.

Proudly she repulsed the insinuations of the smirker who assured her, returning to Harper's Ferry, that slavery was a gentle boon to white and black.

"Every child of John Brown believes he died for the greatest cause in this world," she retorted, "and so do I."

---

*   She survived John Brown twenty-five years, and lived to see a statue of him voted by Kansas to the national capital, and his scaffold sold in pieces valuable as their weight in silver.

Having had his way and will to the last, John Brown went forth to die next day, taking no pains with his toilet, and wearing the same clothes in which he had fought, and an old slouched hat. He gave what silver change he possessed to his fellow-prisoners, and admonished them to die like men, and never spoke to Hazlett, lest the identification might be testimony against him.

Stepping forth in the public street of Charlestown with cords upon his arms, the old man was indifferent to his coffin in the little wagon and to the movements of the military; but when the young wheat in the winter fields met his gaze, and the fodder-rows of russet maize, and the winding mountains in the near east, he felt the farmer in his blood again, and not the radical.

"This is a beautiful country. It is the first time I have seen it just here."

Life swelled in his nostrils, and the sense of beauty that is the joy forever. He looked on those blue and mellow mountains to the last, thinking of nothing else, except that the boys and citizens ought not to have been kept from the execution-field.

It was a privilege to see him die, beyond the death of any man yet known in America who had chosen the gallows for his deathbed. Some who had looked into his genealogy thought they saw in his face and works signs of all the races that were united in him: English Puritan, Holland Dutchman, Welsh — the stocks of Hampden, De Ruyter, and Jefferson.

He climbed the scaffold first, shook off his hat, thanked all for favors, and over his kindly smile the death-cap was drawn.

"I can't see, gentlemen. You must lead me," the muffled voice petitioned — to be led to the death-trap.

He did not desire to publicly speak, though it had been forbidden. The only inhumanity he suffered was the delay of the militia, who were made to march, countermarch, face outward and inward, and repel an invisible attack. There was one side of the hollow square left open, where the sun was shining overhead.

"I am ready at any time," was extorted from his lips at last; "do not keep me waiting!"

The scaffold-trap then opened beneath his feet, like the wicket of heaven on golden hinges turning, and all that was erratic in the old man's life straightened on the silver cord that let him down into the bosom of the Valley.

In after-years the armies there faced every way, to repel insidious Liberty seeking to come in, but it was let down from a side they had not thought to guard.

Chapter XXXI

DISINTEGRATION

LUTHER BOSLER had learned, by the John Brown raid, a lesson nearly forgotten among the Maryland Germans, with their other Pennsylvania Dutch antecedents — of which was their dialect, fast turning into unadorned English — namely, the ready money of going to market.

He and his father would now rise by the moon and get the wagon ready, and when all strangers were shut out of Virginia, in the season of the executions there, Luther bethought him of the market at Baltimore, and he took Nelly and Katy along.

It was at least forty miles, but the way seemed grand, over the old National road, with its remaining wagoners' taverns, the hollow tavern-yards of Frederick City, the turbid Monocacy River, Sugar-Loaf Mountain in the south, the Patapsco winding in its wooded hills among mills and convents, and Ellicott's Town, so stately with factories.

They stopped part of the night at a tavern near St. Charles College, fifteen miles out of Baltimore, and Father Hugh Fenwick, teaching there, showed them by moonlight the park and mansion of Doughoragan Manor, right opposite the college; and there, where he had lived, the last survivor of the signers of the Declaration of Independence, Charles Carroll, of Carrollton, lay buried in his family chapel.

The long, yellow-coated mansion, trimmed with white, its architectural balustrades and projecting wings, great servants' quarters and many slave-cabins, its terraces of flowers and winding walks and mighty trees, formed a real palace amid an estate that would have been belittled by calling it baronial.

Katy walked with Hugh Fenwick, and a young pupil at the college opposite, named Surratt — a tall, slender, modest person — accompanied them. The manor-house was perhaps an eighth of a mile in circuit, and a friendly gardener led them close enough to the windows to see the portraits within, and hear the various company there engaged with music, dance, or conversation. They started at one place to hear Lloyd Quantrell's name mentioned.

"Hush! listen!" Nelly Harbaugh whispered.

"Isn't he dissipated?" asked a woman's voice within.

"A little, but his father says marriage will end all that," another lady was replying; "and he is remarkably fine-looking, shy of ladies, and has a fair property in Charles County. Abel Quantrell told cousin that she was the only maid in Maryland beautiful enough to marry his son, who was a Lloyd, you know!"

"When is the marriage to take place?"

"He is with the soldiers in Virginia now, but both families are agreeable. Cousin fell in love with Mr. Lloyd at first sight, and he is so affectionate toward his father that no opposition is expected."

Katy Bosler's eyes shone so wildly in her suddenly paled face that Hugh Fenwick reached out to support her, but her brother already held her in his arms, murmuring:

"Katy, it may not pe true. Tere are other men, Katy, petter for my peautiful sister!"

The girl straightened up, and spirit flashed from her eyes.

"I am going to see Lloyd's father in Paltimore," she said, "and get back my wedding-ring!"

She listened a little to the consolations of Hugh Fenwick as he took them all through the old Sulpician College, which Mr. Carroll had founded in his ninety-fifth year of life. Katy thought only of her lover, who had attended this school; and, standing in the chapel before the great crucifix, she saw her priestly friend cross himself and mutter.

"Tell me what to say!" spoke Katy, in trembling, nervous energy. "I want to pray like Lloyd!"

"Say after me," Hugh Fenwick answered; and Katy repeated:

"'O all ye saints of paradise, men and women! obtain for me these graces —' These graces?" Katy hesitated. "My gracious! what is graces? Is 'graces' what I must get, to get Lloyd's love?"

"'To love God alone,'" Hugh Fenwick quoted from the service.

"I can't say it now!" Katy burst out. "It would be a sin. I love Lloyd alone, this wicked minute!"

"Love *me!*" Hugh Fenwick whispered, with trembling passion on his tongue; "I am to be the priest of God, and will teach you the way of his will."

"And all tem graces, too?" Katy entreated. "Oh, I am ignorant, and te fine people in te palace won't have me amongst tem!"

She reached her hands up to her learned friend in helplessness and great solicitation, and hardly knew that he was kissing her in the very moment of his own invocation to love the highest One alone.

"I do not understand all tese names, Mr. Priest," Luther Bosler observed, as they looked over the great stone building, and heard the owls call. "What is Sulpician and what is Jesuit? And which are you?"

"I am not yet ordained," Fenwick replied. "I admire the Jesuits for their worldly learning, and the Sulpicians for their theological learning. Washington city, or rather Georgetown, is the university and headquarters of the Jesuits; by a miracle it was directed that the American capital should be located at its gates, for the college preceded the capital."

"So, if us Luterans and Reformed people had got tere first, it wouldn't pe a miracle?" suggested Luther, controversially.

"The Jesuits and Sulpicians always assisted each other, and the Sulpicians had the first theological seminary. They put it in Baltimore, and put their college near Gettysburg, in Pennsylvania; but it did not flourish among those old Germans; and, after the Irish began to emigrate in 1849 strongly to America, the Sulpicians removed to this, their only college now. I am Irish and German, Mr. Bosler, and my choice is not yet fully made."

"Do not waver," Luther spoke; "pe not of two opinions! Love and religion pegin in single-mindedness."

He looked at Nelly Harbaugh tenderly, and added:

"Like our love, Nelly!"

"Oh, always believe I loved you," Nelly answered, as she put her hand in Luther's. "Two ways there may be to walk in, dear, but two loves never!"

If Katy Bosler really meant to go and see Abel Quantrell, she was spared a journey. As she stood with her brother in the market-square, in Baltimore — Nelly Harbaugh reading theater-bills on the bill-boards — she heard a voice say:

"Sho! Light. Cube all your romance and it is four walls — the same as a prison!"

"'Stone walls can not a dungeon be,
    Nor prison-bars a cage,'

where love and romance live within them," Light Pittson replied. "See this beautiful group of Germans, sir. What rosy girls! What a bisonlike, great-eyed young man!"

"Young squabs, Mister Quantrell! Winter spring-chickens! Egg-plants never frosted! New-laid eggs! Putter! Putter-peans! And a Frederick County capon as pig as a goose!"

"No scrapel, Bosler? Sho! You Dutch forget your Pennsylvania fare. No Moravian *case*? No Crefeldt sausage? What's the price of pepperhash? — Light, will you like some of their mountain honey?"

He looked down from his wig, with his mouth turned down at the corners, and his sardonic smile, like the last red coals in ashes, fell upon the two girls. — "Ho!" he spoke; "here are peaches and cream! How much for such marketing as this?"

"I'll sell out," cried Katy, leaning against the wagon-tail, "for te ring you took from Hannah Ritner. It's mine. You sha'n't cheat me out of it!"

"Sho! Rings were superfluous for love-matches when I was a boy in York and Adams Counties. They put a ring on the bull and a lawsuit on the bridegroom. They had the herd first, and the herd-book afterward. I wish I was a boy again!"

"You can pe a petter poy than I guess you ever was," replied Katy, "py letting your son pe honest, as he wants to pe, and marry me!"

"What!" spoke Light Pittson; "Lloyd in love with this child? He said he had a mountain beauty; and isn't it romantic, father, that I should find her here, and exclaim that she was beautiful!"

"It is a compliment for Katy," Luther Bosler bluntly said; "pecause you are right lovely yourself, if you may pe a little wild!"

"Hallo!" exclaimed Abel Quantrell, putting his hand into his shirt-bosom, his market basket at his feet, and his black boy attending him — "we are cubing compliments, and I'll complete the square by saying that yonder is Miss Amazon herself!"

He gazed on Nelly Harbaugh, who was nettled at Luther's unconscious compliment to another woman, and she replied:

"When you got to be a right old man, I reckon there was one rogue the less."

"Why, this is Hannah Ritner's friend, the Dunker pastor!" Light Pittson said. "She told his fortune, Mr. Quantrell. Can't you see Philip Melanchthon in his soft eyes? And Zwingrus in his soldier-port? Oh, how the East is embellished!"

"Ho! sho!" said Abel Quantrell, "I see we shall buy nothing here. I'll cube the matter. — Bosler, send all you have to sell, to my house; my boy will show you the way. And bring your girls along, and dine with us. Sho! never mind the expense. I want some information from you."

As these mountain people went through the street of Old Town, Baltimore, they saw against the great shot-tower there the theater bill of Edwin Booth, brilliant young son of the historic tragedian, announcing that he was to play that night.

"O Katy!" Nelly whispered, "make Luther take us there."

"No," said Katy; "Luther is a preacher; I'm a preacher's sister, and my heart's too full for te theater, Nelly."

"I'll ask Luther!" Nelly said, impulsively. "If he loves me he'll give me one chance. If he won't — I'm not afraid of men!"

When they were all seated in Abel Quantrell's library, among the law books and card-tables there, after a wonderful day, Nelly asked to be taken to the theater. Her spirit was feverish, and she felt out of place in a rich man's home before that Miss Pittson, whom Luther had complimented; and she observed that Katy Bosler, with less intelligence, absorbed the surroundings without fear.

"Nelly," Luther answered, "I think you do not know what te theater is. It is a place where they play life, and do not work it out. I have come from te Plue Mountain to make a little money, and take it home. We are in te house of a great man, who has achieved education, justice, and real things; so let us look around and grow wise, and save our money te theater would get from us."

"Mr. Booth said I had talent for the stage. I want to see a real city play. It is the call of my nature, and, if you love me, you will take me."

"Yes, Luther, take her," Light Pittson interposed; "if it is the call of her inspiration, you must respect it."

"It is not te call of love, I know," said Luther; "it is not te inspiration of your mountain home and poor, deserted mother, but of te sergeant who deserted both te army and te wife. It is te spirit of restlessness and change."

"It is no worse, Luther, than your restlessness for money, that sends you all over the country before the chickens can crow."

Luther replied, gently: "If I seek a little money too sinfully I shall be punished for it; but te life we are to enter on, my dear, has all te joys of both te worlds to me — of heaven and love besides. It has a mystery te theater tale can not have: two hearts united in te family, two dispositions to be yoked together, one pelief to cultivate, and a grave also mutual at te end of days."

"That is not all," the girl exclaimed; "if some of my father's spirit is in me, I came by it naturally. You have refused the most earnest request of my life."

"Nelly, darling, I must be consistent. I am our preacher."

"Yes, Luther. You obey the call of your inspiration, but if I have one it must be smothered in my heart."

"Nelly," the large, bearded young man spoke, tenderly, "we have only one inspiration, and that is love."

She accepted his hand, but her soul was wayward, and she said to Light Pittson when they walked aside:

"I have asked him, and been refused. Now I can go by myself."

Abel Quantrell asked Luther Bosler all about the effect of John Brown's raid in mountain Maryland, and what vote the Republican candidate would draw there the next autumn, saying that Hannah Ritner, a trusted friend of liberty, had recommended Luther as a firm and just man. Luther heard, thoughtfully, until the fierce spirit of the old man suggested war as a possibility, and sought to incite Luther to resistance.

"Abel Quantrell," Luther spoke at last, "there you go too far, like te disciple of our Lord, who drew his sword and cut off te high priest's ear; and ever since St. Peter's spirit has been in te Christian church, till Christ is everywhere in sound and symbol, and nowhere in te soul. We Baptists had our St. Peter, too, in John of Leyden, who took a city like John Brown, and prought upon his brethren generations of persecution. But Menno Simons, a former priest of Rome, died peaceful in his cabbage-garden with thousands thirsting for his plood, pecause he would not meet evil with evil. He is te father of all te non-resistants, Quakers and Baptists, and te first of all rebukers of man-holding was us."

"Sho, sho! Old Brown has cut off the high priest's ear this time, and the priest must needs hear everything. Go preach to your people that Christ is for liberty."

Katy came in at this place, and Abel Quantrell looked at her with steady curiosity, ending with something like approval.

"No wonder Lloyd fell captive to your eyes, young plover; I could have taken them once to my dreams, too. Are you a Dunker, like Brother Luther here?"

"I promised to be, mister."

"You do not believe in rebellion, then, but obey the laws and seek the spirit of peace and submission?"

"I want to pe happy," said Katy, "and to have God bless me and —"

"And Lloyd. You are a child yet. There is time enough for affection to try itself. Your brother will tell you that what I am to say is right."

He came to her and sat by her side, and put his bleached hand upon her head, and, turning back the small forehead, her radiant eyes, that would be his daughter's, looked at him with the dew of prayer in them.

"Are you afraid of me, Kate?"

"No. But you are going to preak my heart."

"Kiss me forgiveness before I do."

She raised her chin and kissed him, and suddenly a thought, like coincidence, rushed through her ardent brain:

"God gif me this soul," she cried aloud, "and let it feed with me of thy supper!"

"Amen, *shweshter!*" from Luther Bosler.

Her arms were around Abel Quantrell with all the strength and affection she showed his son that love-feast Sunday, and tender kisses thawed his frosty lips. The magnetism of life and childhood entered the cold portals where once was the throne-room of a conqueror's mind.

He could not arrest her attack; it came like Indian summer and its thunderstorm upon the fading head of winter. Luther Bosler looked on with the sensibility of brother and of priest.

"Gif back that ring where it pelongs," sighed Katy. "Then God will bless you, old man, and, till you love somepody, he never will."

"'All hearts in all places under the blessed light of youth say it, each in its own language,'"* the old man repeated and explained.

"Had I the merry devil's trick to be young Faust again, my son would wonder at my gallantry! You can not kiss, my child, the warm blood back where it has flowed, nor by a ring revive the golden passion of my prime. What justice is a wasted frame, presented at the altar, and love's signet, falsified by a ceremony no nuptials will attend! Sho, sho! how few there be who work for the bettering of this world! how many work to people it!"

"Nothing," said Luther, "can be more acceptable to our Creator than te sight of a well-replenished earth. If he preferred Abel's sacrifice of a lamb's life more than te insensible fruits of Cain, will he not approve te offering of a human life prought forth in all te piety of love and te sacrifice of pain?"

"That has been my lamb upon the altar. I have rendered it," urged Abel Quantrell. "I will not be a hollow hypocrite, and raise another altar to the world."

"Mister," said Katy, "you seem to pe fighting love away. I know you love something, pecause it troubles you. Te ring is not love, I know, but it is comfortable to have, and to look at it and say, 'It's mine.' What made you gif my ring of love, that made me so happy, to Hannah Ritner? She told me I must git a ring and nefer lose it, and, when I lost it, always hunt it back."

"You can lie, I see," the old man said, austerely. "She never was so weak — to hunger for what she never was refused."

"I won't let you hate me," Katy cried; "you know I don't tell lies, mister. Look at me! And this minute I would rather die and pe took home to my old fader dead than to lie apout my love and Lloyd. He loved me pefore we efer thought of any ring. Te Lord put te ring upon his jacket, and he found it there, and it was his mother's. When he gif it to me he didn't love me more than we both loved a'ready, but it made me happier."

"Dunce!" said Abel Quantrell. "Why?"

"Pecause — pecause —"

"Cube it! Because what?"

Katy blushed, and then looked up again, all beaming:

"Pecause, mister, his love respected me, and wasn't going to hurt me."

---

*   Goethe.

"How could you know that? He meant to cheat you."

"Not with his mother's ring — that was too holy. If his mother had nefer had a wedding-ring, he might not haf cared."

Abel Quantrell was now excited, and the blood that would not start to beauty's caresses, ran to his temples at the stern alarum of his intellectual indignations. He rose and placed his wrinkled hand in the scarce whiter folds of his bosom, and paced the room in the spirited tread of that pagan who defied the lightnings; yet Luther Bosler saw that his face was not now spiritually refined, and that the cane on which his lame foot relieved its burden nearly trembled in his grasp.

"I will witness before every God," he said, "how false that imputation is — that a child of love is lawless to his mother's sex, and only to be humanized by form and hypocrisy! The mighty races of the bond and poor are thus to be tainted by the public opinion which refused them marriage, and the wedding-ring is to be a higher test of love and interest than the fond homage of separated hearts and offspring noble as the stag!"

As he stopped and stood, with erect head and trembling nostrils, a magnetism as of some old, gallant husband to his young bride, flowed toward the Dunker girl. Katy went up to him with her nature aroused by his words:

"Yes," she said, "I think I know what you mean — that if people lose te wedding-ring, God will still let love make tem happy. I love your Lloyd. I can try to forget him, but God will teach me."

"Abel," Luther Bosler said, reflectively, falling into the simple speech of his sect, "nobody blames te slave-people that can not marry and own their children, anymore than them who lived without te knowledge of te law of Christ had to pe judged by it. But all them who knew te law by te law were judged. Te slaves seek decently to pe married. After tey are free, some day te licentiousness got from living without marriage will pe their accusation. Marriage is te sign of a man's respect over te world, and te due of woman, who is judged by her relations with man. It is te tyrant, in his self-love, who refuses te woman te ring, and pleads te tyranny of marriage for refusing it."

The old man looked at Luther's mild brown eyes and shaggy beard. The rage of intellect, still uncurbed, was about to break forth, when he was arrested by the calm yet clerical look of his plain guest, firm as priestly authority:

"I am a pastor of te Tunkers," Luther said; "I speak God's will and not man's. So much in you is good, so much is fierce and troubled like te storm, that I claim te privilege of a guest and of te Holy Spirit, to pray with you, my brother!"

Katy reached up to Abel Quantrell and kissed him fervently, saying:

"Come. It is te priest."

He hardly knew how to yield, yet he was yielding. He had but little experience in kneeling, yet he was kneeling. To the melting word of "brother" from Luther Bosler had been added the whisper of "father" from the Dunker girl.

It was a Dunker girl, perchance, the old man once had loved; a Dunker priest he might have been married by. Who knew but Abel Quantrell?

The prayer flowed over him like a waft from the hemlocks in the Green Mountains with scents of childhood; like the purl of Pennsylvania brooks, bearing away a hidden scene of love and tenderness. The words he hardly heard; but the chastening spirit in them was balm in his nostrils and well-springs in his heart.

As they arose, others were in the library silently — Edgar Pittson and his daughter, and Nelly Harbaugh, and Lloyd Quantrell.

Katy looked at her lover but did not move, feeling that judgment was suspended over them and the parental law.

Luther Bosler stood among the statesman's books and prints, in his wool coat and rough boots, and long hair and beard; he drew his sister to his heart and looked around upon them all — senator and reformer, son and heir.

"Friends," he proceeded, "we are poor Germans who try to make no trouble. We have as little ampition as we can. Lloyd came a-gunning and stopped with us a bit. We didn't enfy him anything he had — his watch, nor gun, nor fine clothes, nor money — but he and sister fell a-loving. It's not te rule of our church; but love is a sheep that jumps efery fence. Lloyd has a manly, loving nature, and Katy couldn't help hearing what he said, down in her pig child's heart. Her heart-strings are tender yet; and I must take her away pefore tey get sore for life. I am her pastor and her brother. She will do what Lloyd's father temands. — Abel, tell her!"

Lloyd looked worn and wretched. His eyes were turned on Katy, and she looked at him with woe and submission and pity greater than for herself.

"Sho, sho! young sparrows," Abel Quantrell spoke, looking at both like the judge who is to divorce the mismated, "take out the square root of small figures and the surgery is safe. Sixteen and Twenty-two are not fit for life's responsibilities. I have laid on my son the injunction, and he has given me the promise Miss Katy will respect, I know — to wait one year from spring. In that time you are not to communicate with each other! Lloyd has given no attention to ladies, and must look around him and cultivate the sex. You can not cube life blindly."

There was a pause. The sentence had been less severe than Katy expected. The promise was only for a year, and not forever; but Nelly Harbaugh, alert to the subject of woman's equality, spoke out:

"I suppose Katy is to look around, too. She doesn't go a-begging up our way."

Lloyd grew pale to hear this; but Katy, never taking her eyes from him, cried:

"I wasn't a-begging when Lloyd come first, neither; but I guess he didn't have much trouble finding me a-ready. I'm only goin' on seventeen."

"Father," Lloyd Quantrell spoke, "I have waited years for your commands. The first one cuts me deep, but I obey you, sir. I will spend the time trying to find some career; and if my heart is changeable, some one may take Katy's place. I will not be stubborn; but the past two months have been the first I ever knew of love, and they may never be effaced from my life."

He stopped with a long, inhaled breath, on which there rolled a groan toward his heart.

"Lloyd!" sobbed Katy, answering the painful sound with its echo and a flood of tears.

Nelly Harbaugh took Katy's head into her embrace, and wiping Katy's eyes, muttered:

"Heartless old man!"

Luther Bosler did not move; but his eyes were filmed with sympathy, and Light Pittson went to his side impulsively.

Lloyd Quantrell was too strong-natured to express his pain more than an instant, and, rallying with some pride, he addressed his father, while Senator Edgar Pittson held his hand:

"Father, to complete my obedience to my parents, I must remember my mother's pride of family, that you have already reminded me of, as her only sin. There is a spot, I hear — an old one, some generations back — upon the family where you have picked me a wife."

"Beware, Lloyd!" said Abel Quantrell, instantly moved.

"I recognize your right, my dear father, to say where I shall not marry. I would die, sir, rather than put a stigma upon your noble name. Not a word you have ever spoken of your early trials, poverty, and humble family, but has been cherished in my brain as testimony of the pure fountain that flows down to me. I am so jealous of that, sir, I can not permit even you to say where I shall marry, if it mixes my mother's blood with the remotest suspicion of illegitimacy."

"Be silent, ruffian!" the father commanded, in terrible excitement. Lloyd hesitated, not knowing where he had offended.

"Let him explain," Senator Pittson quietly said.

"Yes; he shall express the chivalry that is in him, and that I feel all through me, also, papa!" Light Pittson cried.

"Surely I can tell what my mother would have turned her face against," Lloyd continued. — "Dear Light, here, will forgive the story, if Katy's pure heart does. It is related in Maryland that in one generation the father and the mother did not marry till their son, more sensitive to their situation than themselves, refused to return to his country and accept their boundless wealth, until they would give him, also, the marriage rite. It was very long ago. Proud generations have intervened, with earls, and dukes, and kings for sons and sons-in-law; but I am so proud to be the son of Abel Quantrell and his honest wife that I refuse, father, to take that blemish into our house, though the best blood in the world may have washed it out!"

He finished, all flushed and stalwart, the powerful moral antithesis and physical reminder of that Faulconbridge in Shakespeare who rejoiced in the blemish of his birth. Republican self-respect, which is the greatest aristocracy in the world, frowned now from his small gladiator's brow, and his strong jaws were shut, and his gray-green eyes looked as bold and greedy as some rude Bayard or other unlettered knight in the days of setting-to.

"I glory in his principles!" Light Pittson cried.

"You, too?" old Abel Quantrell spoke, turning on Light Pittson. "You know not what you say!"

"Sir," Light answered, spiritedly, "you have not your son's sensibility. Surely I can understand the pride of pure descent and unstained pedigree! My father is a gentleman, too."

They were all attracted and alarmed now, by the exceeding pallor and lifelessness of countenance on old Abel Quantrell. He stood beneath his dead-black wig, like the fabled pillar of salt, looking back and stricken into stone. He seemed to seek to articulate, but could not. Pride faded in his face, while yet most obdurate and firm-set.

"Go, friends! — Go, Lloyd, also!" Edgar Pittson spoke. "He has nothing more to say."

They left the room wondering, and Edgar Pittson closed the door.

The old man still stood there, as if he had died upon his feet, his under lip folded hard upon the square lip above, his hand in his bosom, his long, straight nose like the stem of a galley in the storm of fate.

"Sit down," said Edgar Pittson, kindly. "There — be composed! We can not afford to lose you yet."

The old man breathed, and all his countenance broke in its fixed lines like the shivering of glass. There remained a panting, failing, broken-spirited man.

"You have a fine son there," Edgar Pittson said, soothingly. "I fear you did wrong not to let Nature do her work in that young couple.

What is it, after all, but the replenishing instinct of life, which gives color and romance to everything, and takes a thousand aberrations?"

"Edgar, I can not hear you say *that word* to me. Do you accuse me?"

"I? Why, never! God has blessed us, and will bless us more. Thou strong fountain of my life and parent of all my best emotions! take wine and oil from my unworthy youth, and feel I love and honor you forever, O my Father!"

Chapter XXXII

STRAY ENDS

*L*UTHER BOSLER was very tired, and, having to drive the girls home all the next day, he went early to bed.

Nelly Harbaugh had been comforting Katy, and Luther had given Light Pittson an account of the romantic Dunkers, who never went to law, and were the detestation of lawyers and constables. Nelly was no more appeased by her betrothed taking notice of this stranger, than by his making no further reference to her curiosity about the theater.

She was piqued in her own nature that this established city society did not interest her, nor yet put her at ease. Wild and rebellious promptings came to her, and received instigation from the settled fact that Lloyd Quantrell and his friends were not to come to Catoctin Valley anymore. She had bantered Lloyd upon the hollowness of his pledge to his father, and his indignant loyalty to that pledge, satisfied her that the city people were to leave Catoctin Valley to its quietude and routine, its corn-planting and wood-hauling, manuring and liming, cattle-fattening and distilling, hoeing and harvesting.

She shrank from the recollection of her lonely patch of ground, the consciousness that all her meaner, worldlier suitors had been dismissed, and from the shadow of that Dunker life closing in upon her, with regular attendance on church, responsibility in the "family," or Dunker congregation, and loss of all admiration, coquetry, and adventure.

"Oh," she thought, "if I had the temptation here in Baltimore that pressed me so hard in my little cottage but a few nights past, what might I not do — where might I not go?"

Yet what oppressed her most was love. That plain, deep-slumbering man in the next room, had power over her self-reliant nature. If he would only break away from his dull, unambitious, progress-stunting sect, and lead her to the theater now, and tomorrow to the great capital city, hardly two hours' journey away, and bathe his strong sense in the dyes of illusion and cultivation, what stuffs and scarlets might the shuttle of their union not weave in a busy future, where wealth, activity, and following would be traced across their children's prospects, like the marvelous checkered quilt at Bosler's farm, that was to be the regalia of her wedding-bed!

These thoughts, and the growing darkness of evening, frightened her. Maidenhood, independence, admiration, self-love, temptations, were all to end within another fortnight; and they had already purchased, that day, the preparations for their housekeeping.

She started up and looked in Luther's door. He had lain down in his clothes, to be the earlier ready for the long-aching ride of the morrow.

She went downstairs. In one room Senator Pittson and Abel Quantrell were playing cards, and took no notice of her; in another, Katy Bosler was enjoying the last night before their separation, with Lloyd Quantrell — strengthening him, who was the weaker one.

Nelly found in the library Light Pittson, reading a book called "Shakespeare."

"Medicine?" asked Nelly, concerning the subject of the book, "or what Luther calls The Holler Gee?"

"No," Light Pittson laughed again and again. "This, Miss Harbaugh, is neither the holler gee nor the holler whoa, but the plays of a Mr. William Shakespeare."

The country girl looked resentment at this reminder of her ignorance.

"Oh!" said she, "now I remember my dear friend, John Wilkes Booth — the great actor, you know — did mention a name like Shakespeare."

"I am just reading 'The Merchant of Venice,' that Mr. Edwin Booth is to play here tonight," Light said. "I have never seen Shakespeare well acted, and they say this young man is the greatest genius of his time."

"Read some to me," Nelly Harbaugh asked, her curiosity triumphing over a certain hostility to the younger woman, who had the promise of stature like Nelly's own, with a roundness and maternal endowment the mountain-girl had not.

"With delight," Miss Pittson replied; "the stage is a favorite pleasure I anticipate in Washington, and I should like so much to know a great actor."

Miss Light read, with schoolgirl eloquence and gusto, the interesting text, where she selected it, at Jessica's flight from her father. The style of elocution Nelly critically noted, reflecting how much better she could do than the senator's daughter, as Light recited:

> "In such a night
> Did Jessica steal from the wealthy Jew;
> And with an unthrift love did run from Venice."

"Give me that book," Nelly called, overbearingly. "I can read it better."

She glanced over the lines which succeeded, and, standing up, recited, with strong energy:

> "In such a night
> Did young Lorenzo swear he loved her well;
> Stealing her soul with many vows of faith,
> And ne'er a true one."

"Why, that is wonderful!" cried Light. "I think you might make an actress. Where did you learn to read?"

"In the plow-field," replied Nelly, bitterly, "hollering at a borrowed horse that would not *gee.*"

Light burst out laughing, and laughed against her will.

"Won't you excuse me?" she pleaded. "I was thinking of something."

"What?"

"Oh, never mind it."

"You was thinking of The Holler Gee, I reckon, miss?" Nelly questioned, grimly. "Well, that theolergy is all I am to read, if I marry the preacher upstairs. He won't read plays. Come, let us go to the theater alone, and see this piece!"

"Alone! why, it is dangerous. Surely, you dare not do that!"

"You will see," Nelly Harbaugh replied; and left the room, all flushed with Light Pittson's praise of her reading.

In a few minutes she came down in her manifestly country dress, almost absurdly and cheaply flounced; her gay bonnet trimmed with bright berries and "loud" common flowers, her blanket shawl and a peddler's mixing of winter and summer, that would have made a caricature of less than her fine height, bright skin, and her expression of reserve and decision.

"I can pay my admission," the girl said; "I won't pay yours, but you can come along."

"You are dreadful, Miss Nelly! Surely, you have some acquaintance there."

"You can keep my secret, if you want to!" the girl said, defiantly. "I may come back."

She had never been to other than a strolling company's performance, or that of amateurs, at Harper's Ferry or Frederick, and was innocent of the bold act she was to do, at that demoralized date, of taking a cheap seat in the highest tier of a city theater. She stopped to look at the Booth dwelling in Exeter Street, turned the corner, and followed the tide of people up a parallel street to a great, lighted building, with its back against a dark sluice or sewer running through the city. Her money was gripped tightly in her hand, and she was confused by the number of entrances and the files of people going to the ticket-boxes.

"Where is the cheap place?" she asked a policeman, who was eying her at the curbstone.

"The Third tier. You don't mean that?"

"Yes, the cheapest place."

He took her along the side of the building toward the smelling sewer or creek, where only one lamp split the almost solid mist with its rays.

"I haven't seen you before," the officer said, still looking at her closely. "When did you turn out?"

"I just came this morning," Nelly answered; "I wanted to see Mr. Booth play. I'm acquainted with his brother."

"Johnny? Ah! now I see."

She paid the quarter of a dollar for a ticket, and began to climb dimly lighted stairs, where troops of wild boys went past her hallooing, and she wondered if she would ever reach the top. Her heart failed a little, but she persevered, saying to herself that she could at least look a little while, and slip back to Luther and the snug comfort of her bedroom, and never be found out.

When she reached the top she looked down upon a great depth of seats in tiers — thousands in number as it seemed to her — and at gilded galleries and carved side-boxes in faded gold, and at the green curtain hanging there like the window-blind of another land and world, so suggestive in its blankness, so large to be so unadorned, all faces directed toward it like an oracle of the antique nations, and silent in its green eye as the stagnant lake that harbors the crocodile.

So was it, and so it was to be: that mimic world between this world and both the worlds to come, so seductive and so deadly: joy of the senses, rest of the inquests of toil and intellect, framework of folly and of grandeur, home of genius and of deceit. It lifted the mind to heaven, and sunk the habits to the shadows of hell. It made shame and ignorance look angelic, like peddler's jewels in pinchbeck gold, and gave subtlety and witchcraft their inspiration and reward; raining on the gypsy plaudits from the purest, and tingeing with some gloss of scholarship and chivalry the mere bully and Alsatian.

There, behind the mystic baize, the school-boy conspirators were conning their little tasks and painting their faces now, trying on their greasy wigs, lacing their paper bodices, making ready their fickle furniture and wooden fruit and food, and shifting their coarse scenery to where the lamps and reflectors would make it cheat like nature's sheen of dew and sunshine.

And there, in a not distant morrow, in this same theater where Nelly looked, the ruling conspiracy of government, the great Democratic party, was to play its last scene, and divide like Cæsar's assassins; and, in four years more, the actors of the opposite and succeeding party were, in this theater in Baltimore, to give the sword of war and peace a second time to the ruler as yet unknown, who was to be and to be not, walking like Enoch with the ideal, and by this ideal treacherously taken.*

Nelly looked around her, and she was astonished and alarmed. The bare, steep-pitched, low-roofed tier she sat in, was a dense mass of boys and men, huddled together, peering over, exchanging oaths and nicknames, some intoxicated, some already asleep, some full of street wit, others ravenous as if they could gnaw the wooden benches, so spasmodic and fierce were they in everything. Some were without coats, many had not been combed; police of some kind, also common and fierce, disciplined the most disorderly; and Nelly looked for some place where a woman might have privacy in vain.

There were also women there, the strangest people in the tier. For a brief moment Nelly thought they were extravagantly dressed ladies. Their "loud" feathers and velvet trains, powder and rouge, and freedom of manners and of charms, appeared to the mountain orphan the very splendor of society; but a second look, a burst of laughter, and a word that seemed from women's public lips to invite God's lightnings down, froze Nelly's blood!

Where was she? What were these? Dare she stay one moment longer here?

"Hush!" a loud whispered command came; "get down, all of you! The curtain is up."

She found a place to crouch down at the top of the tier. The next person to her was an old Eastern Shoreman, with a chin which seemed to run down his collar, and be a mere wrinkle of his loose neck; and he was asleep, and said occasionally: "Luff off! luff! P'int on the beam!" In course of time this melancholy man would droop his head on Nelly's shoulder, but she felt protected by his honest obliviousness, and all her soul was in the play.

The first words met her sensibility like tones of sympathy:

"In sooth, I know not why I am so sad
It wearies me; you say it wearies you."

So spoke the merchant Antonio, soon joined by his noble friends all

---

*   In Front Street Theater, Baltimore, 1860, met the Democratic National Convention; in the same theater, 1864, Abraham Lincoln was renominated by the Republican National Convention.

dressed in rich attires with comely hose.

"Your mind is tossing on the ocean,"

one of them says, and so was Nelly's. Then Bassanio, the lover, borrows the merchant's money to wed Portia, and Nelly felt the description to be her complement:

"Her sunny locks
   Hang on her temples like a golden fleece."

Portia and her maid, and the caskets of gold, silver, and lead, Nelly saw like wondrous apparitions; and then came in the piercing eyes and pointed face, like jewels set in flesh, of Edwin Booth, as the Jew usurer, at only twenty-six years of age, his youth revealed in his fine limbs and crafty ankles, his head alert and manly everywhere, life set in him on silken nerves, and character inlaid with strange translucencies like gold and tortoise-shell.

He had decision like the wasp's in rage, and grace like the young cock at morning striding the poultry world. Something subtle was woven in his manliness like guile in the pagan gods.

Beauty and terror seized the country girl as this disguised Apollo spun his deadly mesh around Antonio, and bound him in a pound of flesh to repay the loan of friendship.

"P'int on the beam! Luff hard!" the oysterman at her side muttered, looking at Nelly idiotically, and asking:

"Whair we dropped anchor? P'inted whair?"

He gazed at her awhile, and was again asleep, nodding, and now the curtain rose once more upon the Jew's abode and most unfilial daughter Jessica.

Nelly's sensitive excitement, seeking everywhere for her excuse and rebellion, made Jessica in her mind the likeness of herself, and Shylock's avarice her lover's disposition. She heard the Jew's servant say:

"'Launcelot, budge not!' 'Budge'! says the fiend; 'budge not,' says my conscience. . . . To run away from the Jew, I should be ruled by the fiend."

Who was Nelly thinking of as "the fiend?" She stared at the play as if it were another work of Hannah Ritner, the conjurer.

Now came "the fiend" of Jessica in — beautiful Lorenzo; and at first Nelly thought it was Mr. John Booth, so much alike, to unpracticed eyes, do actors look in their mediæval clothes and dazzling powdered and penciled faces, and she was not soon convinced of the contrary, as Lorenzo took Jessica's secret letter, saying she would rob her father and fly with the actor, who thus excused her:

"And never dare misfortune cross her foot,
   Unless she do it under this excuse —
   That she is issue to a faithless Jew."

Why did Nelly recall her recreant father, and accuse herself of his wayward blood? Alas! the well-deserving never stigmatize their ancestors, but in the crimes of these the willful seek incentive!

Then Shylock's penurious soul and habits in his household seemed to comfort the country girl:

"What, Jessica! thou shalt not gormandize,
   And sleep and snore and rend apparel out,
   Nor thrust your head into the public street.
   Let not the sound of shallow foppery enter
   My sober house! By Jacob's staff, I swear, . . .
'Fast bind! fast find!'

All this seemed Luther Bosler's early rising, rebuke of morning sleep and worldly apparel and of holiday joys, while "By Jacob" seemed to mean Jake Bosler, with his everlasting "Bi'm-by." Yet Nelly's rage had the heart-burn in it, and she wondered why Jessica could sing:

"Let me, then, in wanton play
   Sigh and gaze my soul away?

The daughter of Shylock slipped down from the casement with her father's plunder and fell into Lorenzo's arms, who protested for her the compliment so soothing to Nelly:

"For she is wise,
   And fair she is,
   And true she is;
   And therefore, like herself, wise, fair, and true,
   Shall she be placed in my constant soul."

"Why," Nelly thought, as the curtain rolled down upon this praise of deceit, "the people applaud that girl's ingratitude, though she dishonors her old father! And so do I! So does her lover reward her with his constancy!"

"Luff!" the Eastern Shoreman muttered, awakened by the applause. "What! not slipped anchor yit?" He stared at her in a melancholy way a while, and then began to pucker and to cry.

"What's the matter, sir?" Nelly asked.

"I got a darter big as you," the man replied. "If she was hyar, I'd cry.

I'll cry fur you. I'll give you her quarter. Take it, pooty, an' luff off."

He had a quarter of a dollar in his hand. She was about to repel it, when she saw men and women looking on, and, to stop his sniveling, she took the silver and put it in her pocket. Avarice rose up at that moment, and she thought, "I have seen the show for nothing."

The rising curtain showed young Edwin Booth, all fired to his mettle, cursing his daughter's flight till Nelly's blood ran cold, and thanking God for Antonio's losses and shipwrecks; yet in the crude girl's ear the glory of the actor's art put down the human interest, and started the wild passion, too often impelled on slippery virtue, to be an actress like Portia, who next took the scene as custodian of her dead father's casket, in which her husband and her fortune lay for her suitors to choose. "Of course," thought Nelly, "Bassanio will choose the gold casket, as it is worth the most." He chose the leaden one, and made Nelly reflect, "Is that my dull lover, with the leaden eyes and sure instinct of right?" But Portia's speech again inspired Nelly's ambition, and seemed to reason with her country fears, as Portia declaimed:

> "I, an unlessoned girl, unschooled, unpracticed,
>   Happy in this, she is not yet so old
>   But she may learn."

The ring which Portia gives her engaged lover awoke the country girl's superstitions as resembling Katy Bosler's lost pledge; and next she saw the chaste Portia, too, take secret flight, fresh from her marriage vows, and treacherous Jessica installed in Portia's palace. The play-maker in his sectarian uncharity was rewarding evil-doing, and confirming a worldly course in at least one of his auditors.

"What time is it, sir?" asked Nelly, as the curtain fell on act the third.

"Ten; but I sha'n't go. Luff away from me now. I'm o' family!"

He raised his voice, and half the people of the tier looked where they sat.

"I must go if it's ten o'clock. Don't cry out so!" Nelly said.

"She won't luff," loudly whined the tipsy oysterman. "She'll run me down, and I've sot my lanterns by the law. I've got my own family, but she'll run me down!"

Nelly gazed at the man in wonder and alarm. Her intuitions were quick as her necessity; for people were running over the benches and crowding down the steep, narrow aisles to see the occasion for an altercation, and she saw among these overwilling witnesses some women unescorted, and giggling childishly. It thus occurred to Nelly that this poor man had mistaken her for such as those female frequenters of the place, and was under the temptation of her beauty, which his conscience was resisting in the shouting Methodist way, general to his peninsula.

"Let me pass! The man is crazy!" Nelly called in the tempered boldness of her fear and indignation.

"She took my money," piped the man's high, quavering voice, "but she won't luff off!"

A terrible word began to sound through that high, steaming, whispering loft:

"Thief!" "She's a thief!" "He says she took his money!"

A thousand eyes seemed to stare at the girl; she could discern the people below turning their backs to the curtain and throwing their faces upward to look for the commotion, and opera-glasses from the boxes and front stalls were pointed toward her.

Despair was fast freezing her tongue to her throat. She saw herself the subject of a police item in the morning, the inhabitant all night of a police station, rejected of her lover and his family, and flung back into the mountains like a crippled bird, never to fly nor renew its plumage again.

In this appalling instant a person, about whom something seemed familiar, though Nelly in her excitement took no heed of him, pushed right through the motley people to Nelly's side, and seized the Eastern shoreman and hurled him up the aisle, and sat down by Nelly, exclaiming loudly:

"It's nothin' but a drunken man with the delirium tremens."

The fickle crowd set on the Eastern Shoreman, and chased him down the stairs into the street.

"Silence, there, all of you! The curtain's rung up," an officer cried, looking down on Nelly and her deliverer.

She determined to go the moment she was unobserved, and breathed a kind of prayer to God and her mother that, if they would only let her depart in safety, she would join the Dunker fold, and grudge the world its snares and excitements no more: but something in the splendid act below held her spellbound: the Jew with scales and knife confronted the merchant to cut his heart's flesh out at the award of the duke of the country. Young Edwin Booth was now in the nervous exaltation of his art, and spoke this unintended picture of the slave system of America:

> "You have among you many a purchased slave
>   Which, like your asses and your dogs and mules,
>   You use in abject and in slavish parts
>   Because you bought them; shall I say to you,
> 'Let them be free, marry them to your heirs;
>   Why sweat they under their burdens?'
>   You will answer,
> 'The slaves are ours'; so do I answer you:

'The pound of flesh is mine!'"

Thus Shakespeare, universal as the sun, had thrown his prophetic glance upon the Dred-Scott decision, made in young Booth's generation by a Marylander as chief justice of the whole republic, that slaves "had no rights which the white man was bound to respect." Emphatic applause shook the great theater, for Shylock had been confirmed by nearly a full American bench.

How Nelly's heart bounded in ecstasy and envy to hear Portia, the woman, in the disguise of a lawyer, plead for the stay of such insensate law:

> "Mercy is above the sceptered sway,
>   It is enthroned in the hearts of kings."

So was it, for the audience loudly approved this sentiment, also, and most eminently where the poorest people sat; and they, being the majority, were the "enthroned." Nelly forgot her prayer, the time, her fears, and everything but that most vivid scene of one law-authorized usurer whetting his knife to cut the bankrupt's heart out, and nothing but woman's wit and skill to stay the murderer.

The woman-lawyer triumphed. The butcher departed, foiled and beaten and broken-hearted, and his wealth confiscated to his false child.

The gallant actor wrung from every condition in that theater a meed of approbation subtle as his own art, some approving of Shylock's fate and some of the artist's skill to make him hateful yet imposing. The act closed with the surrendering of Portia's ring to the lawyer, in whose part her husband had not known her:

> "You swore to me, when I did give it you,
>   That you would wear it till the hour of death,
>   And that it should lie with you in the grave;
>   Even so void is your false heart of truth."

No ring had Nelly Harbaugh of Luther Bosler but the ring of loving arms and his rugged kiss. She thought on Katy's lost ring, and on her own mutiny and loss of honorable faith, and started, pale-faced, to retrieve her husband.

It was too late.

The new person who had taken the seat by her side whispered to her. What he said was so low and familiar that it drove from her mind every safeguard of forethought or prudence, and awakened the spirit which was wont to draw down the old gun in her cabin and march insulters to her gate.

She looked at the man.

It was one of the Logans, the slave-hunters of the mountains.

He repeated his insinuation, having, no doubt, recognized her as from his own neighborhood, where she enjoyed more than a local fame for beauty.

The spirit of the poor white race, that always disdained the slave-buyer, sprang to Nelly's temples.

"You think you're talking to a nigger, I reckon," she exclaimed, in uncontrollable rage. "Take your change!"

She slapped his mouth with all that strength manual labor sometimes gives to women. The blow resounded like a pistol-shot.

The coward, smarting with the pain, struck her with his fist.

The gallery-gods raised the cry of "fight," and the officer present arrested both Nelly and her degraded neighbor, and passed them over to the same policeman who had shown Nelly to the gallery-door.

They were marched to a station-house, followed by a motley crowd.

Indifference and despair now seized upon the orphan girl — the transitional emotion from her combativeness. She gave up the future and the past, cunning and repentance, love and hope, and stood before the committing clerk or sergeant, pale, beautiful, and cold.

They took from a cell the poor old melancholy Eastern Shoreman, now sobered by mortification, and he testified that she had neither robbed him nor addressed him, and he wished to pay her fine, with tears in his eyes.

Nelly refused his kindness with contempt.

"I don't want to keep you here all night," the committing official said, "nor do I want to turn you out, lest you might do worse. This seems to have been your first appearance in that part of the theater. Give your name!"

"Never," replied Nelly Harbaugh. "I have only gone to the theater and protected myself. This exposure is ruin enough. I will answer nothing."

The police people began to feel interested; but the girl saw that their pity was not for one they supposed to be respectable. Her motive to go alone to the theater was above their understanding, she perceived; and thus the purest motive which could inspire so bold and ignorant a step — the motive of pure intellect — had brought her to the inexplicable depths of a false position.

The brilliant scene at the theater an instant before, the splendid adventure of woman in Portia, to take a lawyer's part, the late elation of spirits and of ambition in Nelly, had been like the lightning at the precipice, hurling woman deeper down.

A sense of universal injustice swept over the poor stranger. Her lover had refused to consider her intellectual nature; her father had abandoned her; her very name was not her own, but her poor mother's maiden legacy.

"If you will not tell your name you must stand committed for disorderly conduct. I do not insist what name you shall give," the kindly official said.

The rough, real interest in his tones, and other compassionate eyes looking on, swayed her fierce feelings, and she could neither advance nor recede.

"Oh! cowards, men everywhere!" she cried, in a gush of tears and passion, and throwing her head upon the rail that barred her from the clerk, her hair fell to the floor like Jupiter's insidious shower of gold.

Strong, firm steps came up the bare floor.

A voice spoke to the magistrate: "Here is a mistake, or an outrage! What charge is against this lady?"

"I have offered to release her if she will give her name. She will not give even a false name."

"I will answer for her. It is a respectable girl from the country, unacquainted with the city's spoiled places, and desiring nothing worse than to see a play at my invitation. Take down the name of Miss Nelly Starr, of Belair, Harford county."

She turned and saw the fine, intrepid face, and graceful, genteel figure of John Booth.

"My deliverer! My only friend!" cried Nelly, held in his muscular arms and respectfully drawn to his breast, like Jessica to Lorenzo, and kissed once in manly compassion with the barest tremor of affection.

"Enter Miss Starr's name. Discharged on Mr. John Wilkes Booth's recognizance! Take this man Logan's fine, and throw him out of the building!"

As Logan passed Nelly and Mr. Booth on the street, his chagrin of animal and social expectations vented itself in one unfortunate remark:

"Run away with a fancy actor, heigh?"

Booth had knocked him into the street before his sentence was well finished.

"Kill him! kill him!" commanded the girl, her intense feelings breaking in the fierce shout for blood and reparation.

The slave-catcher was followed up by the actor's cool, enjoying, and skilled pugilism, tumbled over every time he arose, headed off at every point of escape, and finally he ran back into the station-house for protection.

"Do you know that he has bruised your face — the coward!" Booth said, panting, as he walked along. "Your friends can't see you for a week with that scar. The officer at the theater had sent for me, suspecting that you had made a mistake in going into that vile gallery, Nelly, and he said you mentioned my name to him. How natural that you should think of me; for you have been in my mind all day! Come in!"

He led the way into an oyster-house, and to a private room up the stairs. She thanked him with gratitude and pride.

"You, John — to think of me with all your prospects and acquaintances? Oh, is it true, or made believe?"

"I love you," replied the actor, in tones low and firm, articulated like chimes of steel, and his dark eyes shining the eloquence of passion. "I feel my fate in your untrained and strong maturity. You can not evade me, Nelly. I demand that you feel my will and love me, now."

He took her hands in his, and held her off, and looked his strength and gentleness together, and slowly drew her to him.

"I have earned a kiss of real affection. I must have it."

He clasped her to his athletic frame, still in the manly tingling of the conflict with her enemy, and ardent with victory and invincible masculine resolution.

The old gun of her father was not above the door; her strength of citadel and rural independence was gone. He kissed her in her betrothed one's place and with a betrothed one's confidence.

"Your name is Nelly Starr hereafter; for you are to be my *star*, and play such parts as *Portia* to me. I am going to Belair to study, and you shall be my pupil there; and so I gave your residence to the police as at that haunt of my childhood where our family grew up. All arrangements are made. I am to be the only Booth in the Southern States, and make my fortune there. — Waiter, some wine and terrapin!"

"You do admire me, John? Can you even love me?"

"I swear, Nelly, to be devoted to you alone — to lay my youth before your beauty, and to cherish and worship you! All that you can learn shall be taught you. All the career I can reach, you shall share and conquer in; but my admiration is not equal to my love. Your stalwart beauty has been walking in my dreams like the long shadow you cast upon the valley as you walk at sunrise on your mountains. Begin the world anew, with people worthy of your queenly endowments and a gentleman for your lord and knight; and that the disgraceful past may be forever behind you, come to my arms and heart at once, with faith and perfect love!"

*I*t was not yet day at Abel Quantrell's residence when Luther Bosler came down the stairs with Katy, his to-be-banished sister, and wondering where Nelly could be.

Light Pittson came out of the library to meet them.

"Has she not returned?" Light queried. "I have waited all night to let her in. There is some one knocking now."

She opened the door, and a boy appeared with a letter for Miss Kate Bosler.

"Oh, gracious! read it, Miss Light," spoke Katy; "I can't read writing fery well. It must be from Lloyd."

Light turned up the lamp, and Katy read these blurred, misspelled lines:

"Darling, good-bye! I expect some day to be your sister, when Luther loves me more than money and his Dunker dunces. Tell him he can not become so ambitious, but I will try to rise worthy of him in mind; for God knows I shall love him forever, whether I be good or evil. NELLY."

Luther stood with his whip in hand and robe across his arm, staggering and pale against the door.

"She has gone," he said; "I am punished for loving money too sinfully. Hannah Ritner predicted te yellow star would fade at morn. It is just morning, Katy. I feel my heart is proken!"

He was comforted in the arms of Katy and of Light Pittson.

"I will kiss you a better morning, dear friend," Light Pittson said, "and a wife more worthy of your sincere nature."

With that kiss upon his brow, Luther drove out of Baltimore, silent and resigned, yet with a great emptiness in his breast.

He did not know that from an upper window, as he went by, Nelly Harbaugh was gazing down, at hollow dawn, with streaming eyes and misery unrelieved by resignation.

Chapter XXXIII

LOVE'S FIERCE PROBATION.

*T*HE executions at Charlestown ended in the middle of March, 1860, with Stevens and Hazlett going manfully to death. Three months before this, four of Brown's men were executed in one day — the two Negroes, Green and Copeland, an hour earlier than Cook and Ned Coppock. These latter, the night before death, made an attempt to escape, which might have been successful but for the accident of Quantrell, Booth, and Atzerodt being in an office across the way, amusing some friends.

Quantrell had Katy Bosler's accordion, playing airs, and Booth recited ballads and scraps from plays, while Atzerodt was the cup-bearer, and ran errands to the tavern. He came upstairs, crying:

"Py Jing! I saw a man's head git on te jail-wall!"

Booth, who had made the punishment of these men a fierce if gratuitous duty, at once ran down and notified the guard. A watch was set, and this time two heads instead of one appeared, and a man, identified by all as Cook, leaped on the wall, and was menaced by the guard below with his bayonet.

"Jump on him, John, and bear him to the ground!" the whisper of Coppock came up from the jail-yard.

Cook hesitated, and the guard also seemed dazed.

"Let them escape, boys," Quantrell whispered, where he and his companions crouched together; "think how young they are, like ourselves! That guard may have been tampered with."

"No, sir," Booth retorted, "no mercy to them!" but, before he could raise the alarm, Atzerodt, with the avarice for a reward, sprang up and shouted:

"You tam guard, why don't you fire?"

"Murder! Escape! Treason!" cried Booth.

The guard now threatened the prisoners, and they dropped behind the wall, while Charlestown streets filled with excited soldiery and civilians.

It was reported that these two lads had used their knives and forks to dig through the jail-wall; but Quantrell suspected otherwise, from an incident which took place after the execution.

Certain women from the North, in spite of all precautions, by patience and refined address, had obtained communication with the prisoners. Among these had been Hannah Ritner, and Quantrell met her the night after the executions, when vigilance was relaxed and conviviality had succeeded the panic. She was at one of the hotels in Harper's Ferry, and had assisted to reclaim the forfeited bodies. Her name was a fictitious one upon the register; but Lloyd, who had endeavored to understand her in vain, took Booth to call on her after a horseback-ride past Mr. Beall's.

She was sad and troubled. The errand she had come upon was not these poor, staring dead, but their living forms, and malice had intervened. She heard the tale — how Cook and Coppock had reached on the gallows for each other's hands, and said good-bye affectionately on the brink of the dark unknown; and she heard, trembling, how Booth and Atzerodt had discovered their attempt to escape, while Quantrell "weakened," and desired not to intercept them.

At this moment Atzerodt, who had become an intolerable parasite of the two young men, made his way to the room, and stood confounded to see, in the full dress of a Quaker lady, the prophetess of the mountains.

"Py Jing!" he muttered — "te witch of Shmoketown!"

"You have asked me more than once to tell your fortune, Andrew Atzerodt," the dark and passion-possessed woman exclaimed, rising. "I never supposed, till cruelty took possession of your frail and prating nature, that Fate had the least concern in you. Hold out your hand, sir! — And you two gentlemen as well! The opportunity is condign."

She meant Booth, Beall, and Quantrell.

They extended their hands. She looked the palms over, and the faces as well, and labored within herself like a Pythoness in pain. Then, beginning with Quantrell, she spoke these lines, at the outset tenderly, but, in the sequel, to Lloyd's companions, with a haughty power above all plays and players:

> "He whose heart to pity swells,
>   In his fever shall spring wells!
>   Who their tears ungenerous stop,
>   Shall feel, burning, but *one drop!*
> 'Water! water!' cry they, 'Lord!' —
>   In the fire and on the cord!"

She ended with her dark hair raveling through her distraught fingers, and her arms spread wide, as if she implored the vision she described in rhyme.

"Come away!" muttered Atzerodt, in terror; "she has fits, and pites beople!"

"Truly a nice, comforting hostess," added Booth, undisturbed; "but I never did like above a drop of water, and, as for the cord, we'll ring it for a bottle of whisky."

Edgar Pittson had been almost as true a prophet as Hannah Ritner. Scarcely had the last man been hanged in Virginia, when the Democratic party convention of all the Union was held at Charleston in South Carolina, and the slave States withdrew, because they could not make a President to force slavery into Kansas, whence John Brown and his sons had expelled it. This convention adjourned to Baltimore, but, before it reconvened, Abraham Lincoln had been nominated by the young Republican party in the nearly as obscure city of Chicago.

Another world had grown up beyond the termination of the old Maryland National Road, and all the presidential candidates, four in number — of whom three received their nominations in Baltimore — were from this West — Lincoln, Douglas, Breckenridge, Bell. The loins of free labor made such increase, that counting slaves as votes had ceased to be a counterpoise.

Ever since Presidents of the United States had been nominated by delegate or popular conventions, Baltimore city had been the party focus of the Union, and the seat of nearly all such conventions. The day of its prestige was over when, at the theater where Nelly lost her content, the slave States again seceded from the convention there, by whose verdict they had agreed honorably to abide, and there the majority set up a Western man.

Maryland cast her electoral vote for the extension of slavery into the free public domain, the great remainder of her votes going to the candidate of parleying and powwowing on the subject, and only twenty-two hundred and ninety-four votes, out of above ninety-two thousand, being cast in Maryland for Lincoln, the victor.

Maryland, indeed, had always lacked a coherent public character, and was a fortuitous settlement rather than a moral undertaking, and no general fact had disturbed her monotony in two centuries, but Baltimore.

This powerful new city, lying across the gateway to the Federal capital, had consulted its momentary interests and decided against drawing the line of freedom down a little way, so as to stand upon it; and only one great and passionate citizen of Baltimore, educated at a college of the far West, saw where his native State should take her place.

Mr. Henry Winter Davis, who has already appeared in this story, advocated the union of his party with Mr. Lincoln's party, and sneered at the decision of the Maryland chief justice, who had argued out the pro-slavery tenet of the Supreme Court, as "a ridiculous farrago of bad history, worse law, and low partisanship."

If there was the equal of Henry Winter Davis on the other side, he is not to be found among Maryland's public men. The nearest approach to him in self-contained purpose, deep and silent passion, mental courage, and haughty ambition, was John Wilkes Booth.

As Mr. Davis had learned in the West the forgotten realities of freedom, Mr. Booth had learned in the South the spirit that stood ready to reopen the African slave-trade, as Henry Winter Davis had declared, months before the raid of John Brown, saying: "The preparation of men's minds for the grand end has already begun, either consciously or unconsciously. The great English experiment of emancipation is loudly proclaimed a failure. The party of the South is ready to make the issue: repeal of the laws against the slave-trade, or Rebellion!"

Booth had no training nor regular profession, was a very young man, and his intellectual nature was narrow; but he possessed more than the average maturity of persons of his traditions, and, to use the expression of one who knew him from childhood, "he was all man from the child, and the feet, up."*

If his knowledge of the world and of civilized principles was no greater than the constraints and illusions of an actor and an actor's son, they were as real as the understanding of any of those who expected to return America to Asiatic conditions, and then bully Europe out of her attitude toward slavery. Booth's habits were as good as the young men's around him, his manners were generally better, his loyalty to friendship and to locality unquestioned, indeed, reputed; and he had those powers valued by savage and statesman — still confidence, and "the still hunt."

He had not only kept Nelly Harbaugh's confidence, but Lloyd Quantrell was convinced that he did not know where she had gone, and no imputing of the girl's principle or virtue would extract from Booth a retort.

"He can not be her lover," Lloyd reasoned, "and not resent things said against her, at least by his looks."

In like silence and still-craft, Booth took Lloyd during that spring to the village of Belair, half a day's ride by horse to the north, where Booth essayed to study his father's old parts — in order to "star" them in the South — at a long, quaint tavern with a swinging sign in a retired corner of the court-house square. Nelly Starr, as she is henceforth to be known, was looking down on Lloyd Quantrell from her play-book, and he never

---

*   John E. Owen, comedian.

suspected her to be near.

Precocious in his coolness and in his trespasses, Booth listened more than he spoke; yet, when he was gone, his friend always felt lonesome.

His moral standard was purely traditional: to hate "meanness," to defend women, to resent insult, to stand by all his own family; and yet, he was not open in his nature as he appeared, coveted the pearl of woman's honor, seldom elevated any companion's nature, in his appetites was predatory, and often low in his affiliations. He seldom tolerated his equals from the stage, but would take mere vagrants up and use them for his willful rides and strolls. He had joined a volunteer company, of anti-national bias, at Belair, and was full of warlike thoughts and feats of prowess.

He took Quantrell to his birthplace, on the road to the Susquehanna — a clearing in a dry forest, with a ditch for scenery, and no other improvements than a small Gothic cottage, itself erected by a filial-minded son, and not by Booth's erratic father; yet John Booth was deeply attached to this spot, and he carried Quantrell to the Priest's Ford of Deer Creek, to look at the massive-walled ancient priest's house on a hill-top, and to the Bald Friar's view of the great Susquehanna River falling in miles of rocks and foam to the pale lagoon of the Chesapeake. The bandit haunt, as it seemed, of the rock Pass of Deer Creek, the young men visited; and in their company were the two Baltimore friends of Booth, Sam Arnold and Mike O'Laughlin, impecunious, common-place followers, quite below Booth's fine appearance, emulousness, and reserve.

Lloyd asked his father to account for some of the contrarieties in his friend. Abel Quantrell said:

"I have known three generations of these Booths — old Richard, the grandfather; Junius Brutus, the immigrant; and the present boys. You can see, my son, from the swelling name of the second Booth, that the vagary was in old Dick, his father. He was full of brooding self-esteem, and seldom spoke to anybody here, but left a bombastic diary behind him. He claimed to be kin of John Wilkes, of London; and so the young fellow whom you affect is named for that first of modern blackguards, who created a political reputation by the worst vices of the press. The square root of his endeavor was self-indulgence and the love of notoriety. The cube of the personalities he invented in Anglo-Saxon politics is the discouragement and degradation of public life."

"Why, father, Johnny says he was a great patriot and friend of America."

"Sho! We are not so weak that we must be grateful to every foreign vaporer. I will tell you, Lloyd, how John Wilkes became our friend. Aspiring to aristocratic place and society, his domestic cruelty and licentiousness disqualified him. He was a *parvenu* distiller's son, and he set up a press, subsidized by the discharged ministers of a young king, to attack their successor. How did he do it? Let the outraged republic of human nature answer! He accused the king's widowed mother of being the minister's mistress; and the minister being a Scotchman, he harangued the vulgar intolerance of the English against the Scotch. From that hour disgusting personality has been the favorite dagger of the political assassin."

Abel Quantrell arose and put his hand in his bosom, and leaned with the other whitened hand upon his stick, while resentment against oppression made the line of his firm-shut mouth against the straight lines of his nose and chin the skyey cross of chivalry.

"Lloyd," he said, "beware how you impute evil to the domestic misunderstandings of your fellow-man! It is deadly homicide, and God will punish it. The eagle flies in heaven unchallenged and admired; the warhorse bears his rider in the good fight, and no inquisition is ever made into the secrets of his stall; but man in full career, nobly serving his species, finds his nest invaded in his absence by the weasel and the crow. A crime is contrived out of some aberration of love or nuptial confidence, and the scandal-subsisting world rejoices until its own turn comes, when Heaven's great Drummond-light will prove, at last, the widest tyranny to be hypocrisy."

"Father," said the son, "you believe that love should be pure?"

"Pure as this earth can yield it. It comes like the seed from the ground — in the act of life distilling its corruption. But Jesus could not preach without some imputation on his birth, nor Mohammed marry Zeinab without the reflections of his guests. There is no boundary to prurient and idle curiosity. It spins into its daily web the heart-strings of the wounded, and the wickedest of its torture-chambers is the modern scandal-press, founded by John Wilkes and his fellow-debauchees. Mixing in his quarrel the cause of America, I fear his bad example is in our types and presses. From Britain came the vituperative Jacobin writers who made public life unendurable to Washington himself — the Paines and Callenders, who could not worship liberty without private hate and mercenary defamation."

"But, father, was this Richard Booth a brilliant writer, too?"

"Sho! No. He allowed his son to support him, and his only talent was his reticence. The theatrical life is no help to an unbalanced intellect, as old Booth, the actor, proved. He was an imitator of Kean, who was, like many on the English stage, the progeny of the lawless nobleman and the actress. The pride of the aristocrat and the assumption of his favorite is in many an earlier Booth and Wilkes, whose records run back to the triumphs of Nell Gwynn.* The actor, Junius Brutus Booth, aspired to rival the gypsy genius of Edmund Kean in England, and came to America to forestall him. They arrived nearly at the same time — both little men, greedy of fame, both wrecked by appetites, and each left one son to distinguish the name and walk highly. Young Ned, our neighbor, has seen his father's errors of life and art, and imitated neither; but, by study and hardship, has made a bright and original name. John Wilkes, your chum, expects to out-Herod his father, and vault to celebrity as he vaults the bars at his gymnasium."

"Father, you are too harsh. John Booth has an affectionate heart."

"That he drew from a martyr mother, one of the best of neighbors; but the son's affection is in the sequel, and we shall see what his precocious obduracy and indulgence will leave her in the residue of days. The cube of a childlike nature is manhood; the cube of the premature man must be either angel or fiend."

The old man hesitated.

"Speak; father; it is pleasant to obey you."

A tear ran down Lloyd's face.

"I know the price you are paying, my son," Abel Quantrell said, "and I will lay no further commands upon you; not even" — his voice broke and his eye glazed a moment — "to hear the call of your country, when mere locality and reaction beat the drum in your native streets! But, Lloyd, you have sinister companions, who will invite you to conduct irregular and partisan warfare. Never do it! Go join the open enemy, if you will, but never lurk within the lines, in Maryland, and be a spy and a villain."

"Father, do you approve of John Brown's methods?"

"No. Senator Pittson was right. I antagonized him because I took a woman's part."

"Father, who is Hannah Ritner?"

"My son, she is a woman in politics. But she is also a woman in mercy."

Had Abel Quantrell permitted his son to love, he would have let politics alone in that critical year of 1860; but, kept from Katy, and sent into influential society, he imbibed the violent feelings of social Maryland, where free speech was confined to the mountain counties, and a

---

†   It is not known that Robert Wilkes and Barton Booth were of the stock of John Wilkes and Richard Booth. The former actor, grandson of a Cavalier judge, flourished about 1700, in London; and Barton Booth claimed to be of the Earl of Warrington's stock, and was the hero in Addison's "Cato," about 1713. His first wife was a baronet's daughter, and his second a dancer. Edmund Kean, if not a duke's son by an actress, was the illegitimate descendant of another nobleman. Richard Booth applied to Arthur Lee for a commission in the American army, at the age of twenty; and his father, John Booth, called John Wilkes "the sacred protector of freedom."

convention of the Republican party could not be held.

Two such local conventions, four years apart, were mobbed — the last of them assembled by the subsequent Maryland member of Mr. Lincoln's Cabinet; and when Mr. Lincoln's wife and young children came through Baltimore, "an immense crowd with groans and hootings"* received the Chief Magistrate-elect of their country, as they supposed, but he, advised by wisdom, had passed through Baltimore at night, a matter of infinite jest to the ignorant scribblers there; but the murderous spirit that followed him to Washington and used the hospitality of a Baltimorean's theater to destroy him, was in that same hooting crowd he had avoided.

It was the murder of free speech and the slavery of opinion which took Maryland into the vortex of loss and folly; for had meetings and debate been free during the few years of inquiry, the paltry two thousand slaves held in Baltimore would never have been the masters of the city.

Negro-traders, like Abel Quantrell's brother, dictated the reasoning of jurists and the consciences of theologians. All heaven, in that most gentle atmosphere, displayed of eve the Star-spangled Banner in the skies of the Chesapeake, but the sons of them for whom the national anthem had been made, tolerated in their streets the paroquet colors of South Carolina, and received her "embassador" when the heir of Washington had not where to lay his head.

The Eastern Shore, more loyal to its plain ancestry, had furnished the Governor of Maryland in that perilous time, and he, guided by Henry Winter Davis, refused to convene the State Legislature — the conspirators' method of capturing unwilling States — first to draw Joseph away from home, and next to sell him to Egypt, and last, to show his bloody and ravished garment of bright colors at the desolate door of his fathers.

In this way Virginia was betrayed by beleaguering her Legislature and convention around with murderers, like those who had gone to Islamize Kansas; and when Virginia surrendered, the war passed on to her soil, and left Maryland a sullen or frightened hostage in the Union, with brave soldiers here and there, but many a chronic Thersites or Caliban.

Lloyd Quantrell's year of banishment from Katy expired as Virginia gave up the ghost. With a hungry and troubled heart he took the railway for the Catoctin country, hearing, as he left Baltimore, the insensate salutes on the Federal Hill for the secession of Virginia, and the capture of Fort Sumter by South Carolina.

Uncertain where to find a conveyance among the little towns along the Potomac, Lloyd continued on to Harper's Ferry, and found everything there in confusion; the people were for the Government which employed them, but the Government superintendent had gone off to

---

*   A rebel history of Maryland, 1879.

Richmond and assisted to vote for secession, and rival sentinels were patrolling the place.

At midnight the State troops were entering Harper's Ferry from Charlestown, when the small guard of the armories crossed the bridge to Maryland, and an explosion echoed along the hollow mountains and lighted their gloomy countenances with the glow of the resurrection-day; the splendid workshops were riven to pieces, and, as the flames climbed the Rifle-works, the bell in the falling tower was heard to ring as it went down into the ruins.

"There, there! Do you hear it?" a voice said at Quantrell's elbow. "It's a-waiting for me. It's a-ringing for me. I can't git to it. Oh, I'm gone clar off of my *Americanus!*"

Leaving this old "suck" of a ruin on foot, Quantrell walked to Middletown. Excitement over the destruction of the country, and the probable invasion of their border realm, stopped all the usual facilities and conveyances, and it was evening before Lloyd reached Bosler's farm.

The spotted setter he had given to Katy came out and attacked him vehemently at the gate, but Katy appeared herself, and was lifted and carried in his mighty arms.

How splendid she looked! How more grown and child-womanly!

"Did you expect me, darling?"

"Of course I did. Luter and fader have gone away and left te house to us. Nopody is here but Fader Fenwick."

A sudden thrill ran through Lloyd at this information.

"Katy," he whispered, drawing the yielding form deeply inward, "he shall marry us. *Now,* darling — or it may be never!"

A scream from Katy was hushed in a kiss of man's decision.

"Lloyd, he won't marry us."

"Katy, he shall! When I demand it, you must insist. I know he is fond of you."

"And of you, too, Lloyd. Oh, what shall I do?"

"Get us refreshment, darling, and listen, and obey. Today we are free to marry. Tomorrow, another promise may send us apart through the tumultuous years that have come."

"O Lloyd, my fader! — and Luter, who is my pastor! What will tey say?"

"Katy, we are past everybody's saying. It is love alone with us — the desire of our hearts, the trembling heaven above; or cruel pain and cowardice attending upon that world's consent which does not know love's desperation. Take the step with me! All our parents have taken it, and the world is still happy; birds singing, and children everywhere. The priest is here. God may have sent him. We are here —"

"Te ring!" whispered Katy, with superstitious awe. "We have not got one."

"We shall find one, if I must make it out of the clasp of your mother's old Dutch Bible with the fire-tongs!"

He took her in. Hugh Fenwick was reading his *Directorium Sacerdotale,* and Lloyd took it up and read of the "vain cleric," who "gives way to thoughts of self-complacency," etc. The suggestion was not lost on Quantrell's alert thought, resolving to take this man unawares.

"Hugh," he said, as they sat at the table, and some of the Dunker still's liquor had warmed their blood, "you must be a full priest now — no make-believe? And I know you will be a smart one!"

"Oh!" replied Fenwick, maturely, "I am hardly a seminarist now. The fathers consult me on the rubrics and grave matters of that kind."

"Have you got an outfit, Father Hugh? I mean the gown, and stole, and all that?"

"Oh, yes; I've brought a surplice with me and a stole. One never knows when he may be called on for unction, or baptism —"

"Or marriage, too, I guess!" cried Katy, deadly pale.

"Pshaw!" said Lloyd. "He can't marry people. That's above Hugh!"

"Oh, yes; I'm qualified," said Fenwick, blushing; "that's the easiest of our duties."

"Great Heaven! You? Can you be what that noble old Friar Laurence was to Romeo and Juliet when secretly he married them at his cell, as they pleaded —

'Both our remedies
Within thy help and holy physic lies.
I'll tell thee as we pass; but this I pray,
That thou consent to marry us this day'?"

The complacent Hugh allowed Quantrell to praise his robes when they were put on, and heard, with gratified vanity, compliments upon his pulpit impressiveness.

"Hugh, our dear, proved friend, I am enrolled, and sworn to go to the war. Our company leaves for Virginia, probably this week. Give me that silver ring I see on your finger as a keepsake of you!"

Katy was listening, with her great eyes on the rim of her pallid face.

"Friend Lloyd, it is a poor little thing; take it!"

"Hugh, it is the greatest friendship you can do in this world but one — and that you are to do now. This ring must unite Katy and me this hour!"

"Sir," remarked the seminarist, with indignation, "this is an impertinence — a trick!"

"No, our friend and tried young father, it is anything but that. It is what churches and marriages were made for — to sanctify the love that is so universal. I have but a night to tarry here. — The time has come, Katy, when I, too, am a pilgrim and a stranger. Will this man prove himself our friend, or forsake us when we need him first?"

"Fader Hugh," Katy cried, with the impulsiveness of despair, "you said if it efer was your duty, you would pe te minister to us. Lloyd asks you!"

"And you, child! Dare you take this step?"

"Yes," cried the girl, in a burst of tears; "if Lloyd's going away, I want him to pe happy. He is te man, and I guess he knows if I'm doing right."

The dog Albion, observing some commotion, barked vigorously, and gamboled in hysterical delight.

"I fear," faltered Fenwick, "that to marry you is beyond my powers."

"No more of that!" Lloyd Quantrell cried; "you have boasted of your authority to marry. Marry us; or be a false priest and a false friend! Love's heavy necessities are above all your churches, and this is our moment of anguish. I shall leave my wife in your charge. If to marry us embarrasses you now, we can all keep the secret till better times."

"It is absolutely necessary to do that," Hugh Fenwick said. "Promise, both of you, never to reveal this ceremony till we all agree to do so!"

Katy seemed to protest. Her lover kissed her to peace.

In deep embarrassment the priest performed his office; and Albion howling thereat, Lloyd fastened around his neck the horseshoe on the tree.

"Katy," said he, coming in, "the doves have come back from the South, and have got the old nest in the tree."

*D*awn had not come on the dark Catoctin hills that had gamboled the night away, and rested now in outlines of slumber, when Luther Bosler, going to the barn, was met by Lloyd Quantrell.

"Brother," said Lloyd, "I must have a horse to take me to the railroad. My character is at stake unless I reach Baltimore today."

When Lloyd had gone, and Luther and his father were hauling wood from the distant mountains, Hugh Fenwick came down the stairs like a ghost.

"What ails you, Father Hugh?" sighed Katy.

"Sister, I am *anathema*. Tempted by pride and praise, I claimed to have the right to marry people. It was a wicked assumption, for I am not yet in holy orders."

The dog howled at the threshold.

Katy fell by the fireplace, with her head in the ashes.

"Ah-coo-roo! coo-roo!" spoke the doves in the tree, which had quit the South just in time.

Quantrell reached Baltimore in season to be taken to a meeting called for the purpose of resisting the passage of more troops through the city; some United States artillery and some German companies from Pennsylvania having marched through that afternoon, despite threats, insults, and ruffianism, to protect the national capital. The nature of that meeting was black and insurrectionary, and Quantrell joined his military friends right afterward; and the bottle was the presiding genius there as everywhere.

He could not find his father; but Light Pittson was in the house, and Lloyd told her he was committed to leave for Virginia at call. The girl, unacquainted with more than the spirit of the hour, commended his resolution.

Next day Lloyd arose late, and heard a wild din in the streets.

"The Yankees! The myrmidons! More of them are coming."

He drew on his clothes, and fell in with the mongrel swarm of tatterdemalions and bravoes — the unthinking, the pale, and the fierce — and they swept him toward the harbor of the city, where the flood-tide bore the bowsprits of ships nearly across that street where the one track of a railroad alone connected the capital of the Union with the great States of the North, just risen from the swoon of the news of disunion.

The rioters were marching on that track thousands strong, as if Jones's Falls and its pollution had burst, and were deluging the quays.

Quantrell learned that a portion of a Northern "army" had just been hauled through the town in cars by horses; but that some fragments had remained behind, and that these were now to be murdered. People were already tearing up the track and piling stones and ship-anchors in the streets.

In a few minutes a moving coherence of some kind was seen at a place in the broad street, where a bridge crossed the great open sewer of the city. It seemed like a stone wall moving yet crumbling, and at the head of it waved a sort of color or flag, torn and gay and dirty. The air was mottled with things that seemed to be tossed out of a machine, or revolving like bats or butterflies in the wind.

As the moving disaster drew nearer, there was seen enveloped a little band of men staggering under arms, beaten and bloody, the air and the street spouting stones at them; and at their head a miscreant of destruction was carrying, to insult them, the new piece of finery conceived in the Southern barracoons — the insurgent, separating, or confederated flag.

Quantrell picked up a stone.

He saw at the head of that little, tired soldiery, the mayor of the city, walking by their officer, pale and dusty, but doing his duty at the risk of his life.

The troops came so close that Lloyd could hear them panting. Their tongues were dry, like those of sheep driven without water. Here and there one would be tripped up by some coward and fall beneath his heavy and unwonted accoutrements. Yet the eyes of all were shining at something farther on, and seeing this alone.

"What was it they saw?" Quantrell often asked, afterward, but could never tell. It might have been the unprotected capital of their country, or the presence of death, or the worship of a faithful posterity which could feel for their agony that day.

They numbered less than two hundred; they spoke no more than the ox going to slaughter. The Christian martyrs in the Roman arena were not beset by as many thousands nor by more ravening beasts. Yet all that these men were doing was obeying a proclamation of law and using a peaceable post-road of the country to go to their capital.

Quantrell was fascinated with the scene of duty and of dread. The stone he was holding in his hand was wrested from him, and the villain who seized it hurled it against an old man limping at the soldiery's side, with a face like the dust of battle on the skins of the dead.

"That is my father!" Quantrell gasped, and rushed where the old man fell.

"Go back, sir! This is my place," a woman spoke, rising, with Abel Quantrell in her arms.

Lloyd gazed, and saw the face of Hannah Ritner, stained with his father's blood.

The butchers of the mob had now presumed too far; it had become a question of resistance or death. Hemmed in and blocked fast, stoned and spit upon, prodded with staves and stuck with awls, deserted by police and outlawed in that place of public commerce, the soldiery from near the ancient battlefield of Lexington waited for one word, and it came, at last, with nasal curtness and meaning:

"Ready! — Fire!"

Then rolled through Baltimore the echoes of Fort Sumter, and the streets, all strewed with flying scavengers, ended the war on that spot forever.

The flight of the rioters gave the police room to form in, and the volunteers of Massachusetts were molested no more, save by that local chatter which ever follows in the wake of the brave.

Lloyd's father was dangerously hurt, but the son demanded permission to see him that night.

"Father," said he, "I am going — you must know where. I little thought the first bloodshed would be upon your aged face. Wide as we differ, father, there ought to be love between us. Can you not forget the cause I go to fight for, and bless your son?"

"You will never see me again!" Abel Quantrell spoke, his face with lines of blood upon it, but the mouth firm as the dead Cid's brought from his tomb to fight the Moors. "I can not bless by my finite power. My heart has been warmed of late toward you, and if you could stay here, where Heaven should make you see your duty, affection might grow strong between us. How can I say 'God bless you,' sir, when, blessing you, I dare not ask liberty for your slaves, against whose sorrows you go to war?"

"I have anticipated that, father," Lloyd replied. "You can bless me, sir. Here is a bill of sale of every slave I own, prepared to meet this hour and your consistency. Take it and set them free, and say, 'God bless you, Lloyd!'"

He laid the paper upon the bed.

Abel Quantrell drew his son to his face and kissed him with emotion.

"The blessing of your State go with you, when Maryland is free my son, take my farewell from her shield, *'Crescite et multiplicamini.'"**

Light Pittson kissed him all her approbation.

Hannah Ritner whispered in his ear:

"When thou killest everything,
  Still the turtle-dove will sing."

---

*   "Grow and multiply," the motto of Maryland.

Chapter XXXIV

THE OLD SLAVE COUNTIES

QUANTRELL left Baltimore, with other recruits, for the seceding or insurgent government – the two lads Arnold and O'Laughlin, already referred to as Booth's dependents, and the liquor-dealer Martin, who had business in the peninsulas below the city of Washington, where, also, were situated Quantrell's lands and slaves.

These peninsulas stretch eighty miles south of Baltimore city, and are comprised between two broad sheets of tidal water – the Chesapeake Bay coming up to Baltimore, and the great river Potomac, ceasing its tides at the city of Washington. The general peninsula is divided lengthwise by the river Patuxent, flowing halfway between the two large cities, and further compressing the land for traversable purposes to the breadth of only twenty miles east from Washington. It was forty miles by the railroad from Baltimore to Washington, and Quantrell then had forty miles to go by private conveyance before he should be able to cross into Virginia at Pope's Creek, near the old court-house town of Port Tobacco.

This Pope's Creek suggested to our traveler that the parent country of the Roman Catholic religion in the English colonies was in this old isolated district of Maryland.

While Raleigh was seeking to plant Virginia, a young Tory politician at court cut out from Raleigh's colony the province of Maryland, and introduced the old religion there in its decaying and persecuted times, after the Catholic conspiracy of Guy Fawkes. After a course of fifty years a Protestant revolution arose in Maryland, and for nearly a century the Romish worship was suppressed, or till the American War of Independence released all worships. In that interval the old faith of Queen Mary smoldered and the Lords Baltimore had professed Protestantism; but John Carroll, a priest of Rome and educated on the Continent, gathered his folds together, and brought over refugee priests from the French Revolution; and thus, in eighty years, Maryland had again become the proselytizing province of American Romanism, with its springs in Baltimore and its antiquities in the old Potomac peninsula.

Upon the edge, indeed, within the rim, of this old English Catholicism stood the American capital, and much of its population was of the faith of Calvert and Catesby, while a Jesuit college and the oldest convent in the land overhung the city from the steeps of Georgetown. Hardly fifty thousand people remained in Washington, but soldiers were quartered in the halls of Congress, and all the railroads to the north had been destroyed the night following the riots in Baltimore.

The city of Washington stood, the melancholy monument of slavery incorporated with a democratic system, and extending through that white democracy, to the lowest man, the prejudices not of the democracy, but of the slavery. It had resisted all the efforts of Congress to make it a free district, yet slavery had spoiled its proportions, and, originally a square, it was now only the Maryland side of the square, and gave some force to Abel Quantrell's remark, every time he saw the map of the District of Columbia:

"Cube it!"

There stood a long Grecian Capitol on a nearly naked hill, with the splintered drum of an iron dome, like a broken bundle of *fasces,* unfinished in the middle. A broad, unsightly avenue stretched from its base, between stunted rows of generally mean-looking houses, to a Treasury Department in borrowed architecture, and some other ministerial buildings,, surrounding the sorrowful new President's abode, out of whose official window he could look upon a neglected obelisk of Washington, halting like the pillar of Lot's wife till Sodom and Gomorrah should burn in chastising fire.

The same glance which showed Abraham Lincoln the decivilizing impotence of slavery showed him the new rebel flag hoisted on the Virginia hills — that Virginia whence his forefathers emigrated to the West. Lloyd had the privilege of seeing this man for the only time in his life, when the President walked, the day of Lloyd's arrival, from his white official mansion to the war building.

Lloyd and his three companions encountered a tall man, a small one, and one neither small nor tall, but wearing spectacles.

"I'll swaw," whispered Martin, "if yer ain't the devil himself!"

The other lads looked up and gave room.

The tall man glanced down from a long and peculiar face, and said, with a look of most fatherly tenderness, where sorrow and sweetness seemed mixed in the cup of dignity:

"Good-morning, friends!"

The two others would not have spoken at all but for the tall man's condescension, and he with the spectacles barely noticed our loiterers;

while the little man, with hardly any color about him, smiled at them out of a boyish, old face.

"Who is it?" asked Lloyd, seeing only one face of the three, and that had seemed to shine down into him and through him, like the light of foliage tremulous in water-wells.

"The little fellow is See-ward, their Secretary of State. He un in specticles is the great lawyer in Washington — Stanton."

"But the other man, with that noble voice: who was it? Where have I seen him?"

"Why, on every picture and newspaper for the last year, Lloyd. That's the Yankee President, Abe Lincoln."

Quantrell drew his breath in a woe he might have borrowed from that magistrate's gentle forlornness.

"Oh, boys," said he, "I hoped he was an uglier and a more wicked or degraded man. That is a gentleman, and the truth has not been told us."

A hired carriage took our adventurers to heights of clay and forest overlooking a broad arm of the Potomac, called the Eastern Branch, where were a navy-yard and a bridge, guarded by hastily improvised militia. As they looked down from these hills at the squalid city of the government, basking in blue haze and in the cleft of broad, deserted rivers, Martin, the liquor-dealer, said:

"Boys, we might have give old Abe Lincoln and that abolitionist See-ward a couple of shots, and got out of town easy."

"I was thinking of that," Mike O'Laughlin added. "If Johnny Booth had seen him, I b'leeve he *would* have clipped him. Booth's bitter as death."

"I never could have fired on that face," Lloyd Quantrell spoke. "I told father I would do nothing between the lines."

"Harkee!" Martin interposed; "I want you all to j'ine me, boys, and we'll cut out this steamboat that runs from Balt'mer to P'int Lookout. I'm down yer now to spot her. We'll hide a crew aboard of her, and drive her own crew overboard and take her as a present to Jefferson Davis."

The other two watched Quantrell, to form their opinions from his.

"Martin," said Lloyd, "I'll do no such Indian ambushing. If our cause is right, it wants to be supported by soldiers, and not by robbers and assassins. I shall enlist in the Virginia line."

As subsequent events proved, Mr. Martin did lurk within the government lines, and he gend others seized this steamer; but the military punished the chief offenders, and Mr. Martin ran away to Canada, where he lived a scheming life during the remainder of his days. And yet this man had a certain influence upon the greatest personal crime of that long civil war.

They had loitered away the whole Saturday morning in Washington, and the long, steep hills of clay, still in the pools and ruts of winter, delayed the carriage, so that it was near supper-time when they reached Surratt's tavern, ten miles from the capital.

It was a respectable, white wooden house, with green shutters and two chimneys, and a paling was around its pretty flower-yard and vine-clad porch on the broad-eaved side, while a shed along the northern gable shaded a bar-room and post office; and here were assembled some Negro overseers, woods farmers, and young men, with their horses tied around the fences and in a grassy space.

A locust tree grew in this open area, a small peach-orchard was behind the house, and some bird-cages adorned the roadside. Near and far the melancholy woods of oak and chinquapin and small wild pine enveloped the clearings, and the brown fox-grass blew with a whistling sound, and the tender green of spring made cover and fringes in the forests.

They saw within Surratt, the tavern-keeper, and the lad of the same name who had been at St. Charles College with Hugh Fenwick, distinguished by his long nose, lean chin, and sunken eyes. The elder Surratt was ill, and not long to live; the son grave and uninteresting; and therefore Quantrell was rejoiced to find the ladies of the family in the dwelling part — Mrs. Surratt, a wife of round form and soft complexion, and of hospitable ways, and her young daughter, pretty and chirrupy.

Quantrell had brought Katy's accordion along, and he played and sang to the females in the snug rooms and wide hall-way, while Arnold and O'Laughlin, habitually impecunious, spent Quantrell's money at the bar, and retired to bed tipsy.

Young Herold, whom they had met in Charlestown, came in and sat with the family. He had some married sisters in the peninsula, and was full of talk about "patridges." His little bashful face was a mirror of dimples and blushes, and no subject found him talkative but that of gunning; on snipe and wild ducks, and especially on "patridges," he was eloquent.

Lloyd had the reputation of wealth in this region; and the young-looking mother and pleasing daughter paid him attention — the more, that he was about to volunteer in the armies of secession.

He thought of his child-wife passing her honeymoon in those walled mountains, of the brief bliss of their union and violent sundering, and he was in no mood to indulge in political acerbities.

"Dear Mrs. Surratt," he said, when his ears had been too long harassed by epithets of "Yankee," "despot," "nigger-worshiper," "black republican," "vile abolitionist," and so on, "don't let the women, also, go to the war! Some day we shall cease fighting, I hope, and home will be so grateful without politics. Then the ladies can make peace speedy and easy with their soft ministrations, instead of blowing the coals of war to flame again."

"Never will I live under Abe Lincoln, that vile and nasty abolition President!" said the hostess, with all her dainty temper.

They kissed the young man good-night, with mingled confidence and coquetry; and their boy, who would be a priest, lighted the way for him.

"It must make you feel proud, sir, to go to war for your country!" young Surratt exclaimed, with timid admiration.

"My country," repeated Lloyd, "where is it? Go back to school, my friend, and stay there, and don't loiter here between the lines."

It was long before Quantrell could fall asleep, thinking of the un-natural compulsions which now were driving himself and millions more away from love, home, and law — the despotisms of pride, perversity, and moral cowardice.

He would not be ruled because he had said he would not, and he had said so because others did the same; yet not one grievance had he received except the expression of the lawful majority against the weedy and gypsy instincts of slavery, to go everywhere and spoil good land, and sow arrogance, brutality, and dissension.

That gentle, fatherly face he had seen in Washington, so different from the hard- and cold-faced President just retired, had spoken to him and his fellow-truants the word "friends," with a sensibility inherent, and a smile that was the God's upon the cross.

"Could he," thought Quantrell, "rise in tomorrow's sun with that same countenance and be beheld by all who are breaking up the country, and say 'friends,' as he did to us, would they not submit to his rule? Alas, no! for I can not myself hear the cry of my father nor of my wife. A haughty and cowardly fear to turn back and be right, drives me and all of us to a silly insurrection."

A feeling of indignation possessed him against the original secession-ists; but he could not think of the name of a single one. All secessionists had been secondary ones. If there was one original secessionist, it was not an individual, but a system; and John Brown had tried to kill it with his pikes. Slavery was the only original secessionist.

The nearest Lloyd could come to an evil influence over himself was Booth. Here seemed a man of insurrectionary incentive — headlong as the thunderbolt, yet the child of the cloud — gathering young men together to make them drink and swear; governing them by his dark-eyed will, and lending them his affections to incite their revenges.

That oath by Harper's Ferry, illegal and unbinding as secession ordinances themselves, still lay in Quantrell's mind like a coiled and hissing snake! "If trouble ever comes, to revenge the South; if invasion comes, to invade her invaders — *Sic semper tyrannis!*"

Lloyd wished he had never seen John Wilkes Booth.

Ah! if some woman had only entered where they took that oath and dashed their glasses down — some gentle woman, like her who had kissed Quantrell to bed!

But she, too, was full of political bitterness, and could not stay her tongue from wagging when the deep-mouthed guns were full of shot, and Law and Treason stood on the instant of war.

Quantrell fell asleep, with the spirit of his child-bride in his arms; but he dreamed a horrid dream.

It was the dream identical with Atzerodt's in the night when Lloyd first knew Katy Bosler, and when love came between them on the tremor of superstition.

There was a man of pale and black complexion, like Booth, riding a horse in a wood, and Quantrell had overtaken him there, and drunk with him; and out of the bottle seemed to come other men every time they drank; and "the last man," as Atzerodt had expressed it, "was a woman." That woman was the exact copy of her by whom Quantrell had been kissed, motherly, to his bed!

The man they encountered, as they rode along under that dark and white influence, was the tall President who had called his enemies "friends" but yesterday, and the same deep, feeling tones came from his face in the dream: "Good-evening, friends; we're 'most home." "The devil you are!" answered the voice of Booth.

So the vision proceeded, till the black-and-white rider fomented hate against the tall, unsuspecting gentleman, and called for a show of hands; and when the men were at a tie, the woman in this same tavern gave the casting vote, by calling "Charge!" — and over the precipice went she and all of them, trampling the "long man in black clothes" to the earth in his blood.

Quantrell awoke, all throbbing with excitement. He looked out in the night on woods and pallid moon, and heard the whip-poor-will cry down the cross-roads from Surrattsville.

Back to bed he went, and dreamed the same dream, with variations, over and over, till he fell into a better sleep at dawn, and, when he came down to eat, the ladies were starting for the Catholic church at Piscataway. Quantrell bade them good-bye, saying:

"Dear Mrs. Surratt, I had a bad dream last night. You had become a politician, and felt an evil influence. Pray against it, today and ever: *'Ab insidiis diaboli, libera nos, Jesu!'*"*

That first Sabbath of the war in April time carried Quantrell and his trio, Martin driving, through the woods just tingling with the rising sap, to a little stage station called Tee Bee, and through the deep-washing creeks and their aguish swamps of Piscataway and Mattawoman, till at

---

*　　From the Roman litany: "From the snares of the devil, Jesus deliver us!"

the ruined hamlet of Beantown they turned to the east and saw the congregation dismissing at a roadside Catholic church, whose graveyard adjacent was filled with little tombstones invoking "Jesus, Mary, and Joseph." Here Martin went on with some communicants bound for St. Mary's County, and the other two walked to Bryantown, five miles to the south, while Quantrell went to dine with a country physician, Samuel Mudd, who had a farm and numerous slaves. In this vicinity was Lloyd Quantrell's property; and the country toward Bryantown was the best improved of all in this old tobacco region.

Dr. Sam Mudd lived far back from the road on a wheaty plateau, and, as he preceded Quantrell from church on his horse, he wore a troubled look, asking about the fight in Baltimore, rejoicing at the attack upon the soldiery, and wondering whether his slaves would run away.

An enterprising father had both educated him and left him slave property. In this old region had once existed a high degree of professional cultivation, and two of the physicians hereabout had been cited to the deathbed of General Washington, who lived hardly ten miles from Mrs. Surratt's tavern, but on the opposite side of the Potomac. These old Scotch-graduated surgeons had kept medical students in their houses, and in a land of slaves and few proprietors the doctor continued to be more necessary than the lawyer. So Dr. Mudd had a proprietary and a practitionary interest in slavery.

He was a lean man, of a rather hungry and nervous temperament, with light-red hair, and his complexion easily betrayed his feelings, which were quick to brood and seldom buoyant long. He was married and agreeably surrounded. His white dwelling, with long blank roof, stood high above the surrounding wide swamps, and from its summits the Patuxent might almost be seen, where he shipped his wheat, corn, and tobacco. A peach-orchard showed its warm tints in the front, high trees flanked the gable, and servants' quarters were near by, with the convenient cool spring that Marylanders covet, and a house-yard and garden, making home neat and independent.

He led Quantrell into a hall and office-parlor taking up the front of the dwelling, and there they talked about property matters over a social glass.

"People are going crazy," said Dr. Mudd; "we had to send off one of our leading citizens to a lunatic asylum a month ago. He had manumitted all his niggers, and wanted to rob his family. I gave the certificate to send him to the asylum."

"On that act only, Sam?"

"That was the main thing; yes."

"Then I am a lunatic, Sam; for I have set all mine free."

"You? what's the matter with you?"

"As far as it can be done, with the embarrassments of our laws against manumitting, I have done it. My father is against slavery, and I sold my Negroes to him, giving a blank receipt, and they are as good as free. I shall tell them so today."

Dr. Mudd lost his temper, and looked at Lloyd with incredulity and suspicion.

"What in God's name are you going into the Confederate army for, then?"

"Freedom," answered Quantrell.

"Freedom? You're talking like an Abe Lincoln abolitionist! Don't you know that slavery is the only cause for separation?"

"Why, Sam, your blacks will all run away. They are only a night's walk from Washington city, and every one of them knows that secession was on account of slavery. So I shall help the South to resist invasion; but nobody shall tell me that I have quit my father, my country, and my girl, for no nobler end than to keep my Negroes as slaves."

Quantrell's face shone with something higher than pride — the dawning principle which comes after disinterested sacrifice. Dr. Mudd leaped up and flashed his spiteful blue eyes on his guest.

"Damn you!" he said, "they won't have you in the Confederate army. No man is wanted there who is not a thick-and-thin pro-slavery man. Do you think I would leave the Union to fight for a part of it, if I had to give my niggers away? No, sir! I shall send them to Virginia and sell them to go South, if I can't hold them safe here."

"Don't get mad, Sam. You can't get me mad, because the rotten old interest is off my mind, and I feel, in that quarter, a relief that makes death in battle only half terrible. Perhaps the Federal Government will offer to pay for all the slaves in Maryland."

"I wouldn't accept it, sir!" shrieked Dr. Mudd. "I've got my constitutional rights, and I won't be bought up."

"Sam, you'll drive the Government to emancipation if you don't give them some kind of chance."

Dr. Mudd broke into curses furious and irrational; the Negroes, slipping by, heard the welcome sounds which proved their freedom to be the white man's apprehension.

"Doctor," Lloyd spoke, at last, "are you quite sure the other man should not have given you the certificate for the asylum? Be respectable, at least. Holy Easter was but three weeks ago, when Christ arose; you have just come from church, and I am your guest: here are three reasons not to swear."

"You are welcome to go!" snapped Dr. Mudd; "I never entertain abolitionists."

"Good-bye, then," said Lloyd, rising. "Take care you don't entertain, some time, a man less candid than I am, and with hands less clean! The devil is abroad, watching for people in a passion in such times as these. He was in my dreams last night at Mrs. Surratt's. He may come into this room if a humble spirit does not guard it for you."

The wretched man, cut in his sense of hospitable duty, lay all that day in self-accusation, while Lloyd Quantrell went to his own Negro estate not far away, and dined with the slaves he meant to rejoice.

They were always glad to see him come, and they were all there; and responsibly above them was Ashby, the hostage of John Brown's invasion. When Lloyd had eaten of the toothsome Negro fare he loved so well from childhood's time, he called them close around him, the aged and the babes, the supple girls who had loved him, and the hardy young laborers he had romped and wrestled with.

"My dear old friends," spoke Lloyd, "some of whom knew my dear mother, and combed her long, bright hair —"

The healing springs of Charlotte Hall, near by, flowed not quicker than their tears, to see Lloyd catch his rising sob, and stop and tremble. The little mulatto children came to his knees, the dusky grandmothers groaned and rocked their heads; if Lloyd had never been loved before, there were gentle-hearted women there, and pure as slavery could permit, to nurse his suffering now upon their bosoms, and wipe his eyes with their hairs.

He felt himself as on that day when he wept in Katy's rapt embrace going to the love-feast, and she fought with the angels for his soul!

The angels had yielded then, and now the archangel, with the trump of jubilee, was to let poor Quantrell wind an unpremeditated strain:

"Oh!" he cried, putting down his emotions with a noble confession, "I wish I was the owner of every slave, instead of only this family, that I might set all free as I do you, this Sabbath after Holy Week! I wish I was the President, not of the United States, for he has not the opportunity, but the President of the Confederate States, to call Freedom loud, and ask God's blessing and alliance!"

"Amen!" rolled round the circle. The aged women, with not long to live, shouted for their few days of freedom like the trembling virgins and the honest wives. All faces glowed as if the stone had been rolled a little way from the tomb, and the bright supernal light shone forth of the everlasting Redeemer.

"Hallelujah! Bless God, he's come! God bless young mosster everywhere!"

"I feel so good," cried Lloyd, "I could shout! for today I make you free. Father has the papers; I gave them to him. He can not disappoint you. The sacrifice has not cost me a pang, and my heart is full of more than happiness — of glory!"

"Glory! glory!"

The slave people sprang to their feet; the old forgot their rheumatisms; Methodist and Catholic Negro danced together; Lloyd danced and leaped like a Negro of the tribe. No church in Maryland felt the frenzy of excitement at revival-time like these who had seen their rights, so long denied, come in upon the generous breath of kindness, ungrudging as the blossoms of the spring.

When weary nature ceased to shout, and all lay panting around, the porches and on the earth, some lute-stringed throats of women started melodious tunes, and at the end the patriarch of the family prayed.

Lloyd's time was out. He kissed them all — the children tenderly, the fair ones with pure and brotherly lips; the men, too, in the Dunker fashion, not a bit afraid or dainty.

"Mosster," spoke Ashby, "these yer — all but me — has got friends in Merrylin. I ain't got none but you. Take me, and let me be your servant."

"Not into the slave States, where you have no rights! Not into battle, Ashby!"

"Mosster, I got only one right left — de rest is dead; dat is de right to love and die with you!"

"Come, then," spoke Quantrell; "it is sixteen miles farther to Pope's Creek."

Chapter XXXV

REBELLION

ASHBY was not the only Union volunteer for Lloyd that day; the great dog Fritz, long left at his estate, and now old but valiant, followed the two exiles.

They skirted the rapid running waters of Zekiah Swamp, and crossing a branch, entered Bryantown, three or four miles from Mudd's, a small cross-roads village of later date than most of the peninsular hamlets, with several respectable houses and more wooden cabins, some mechanics' shops, and a double-porched tavern, with dark bar below; from its upper veranda could be seen, on the hills toward the south, a prominent Catholic church.

When they reached the church, Ashby driving, they saw a singular scene on the cedar- and fir-crowned lawn before the airy churchyard.

A large buzzard, or vulture, was settling down in the road, his sable wings scurrying the dust where lay a fine riding horse — such as is native to that country — fallen dead. The stolid black scavenger, undeterred by Lloyd's advancing, had already run its beak into the charger, when Fritz, the dog, darted upon it.

Too gluttonous or too sluggish to know alarm, the carrion-bird held its ground, and stared with dull and drunken eyes upon the dog, as if expressing a willingness to divide the prey. At this the dog drew back, glared at the horrible bird, and ran from it in avoidance worse than fear.

Six miles toward the south, then westward through Zekiah Swamp and six miles westward more, brought Lloyd at nightfall to old Port Tobacco Town, in the miasmas of a deep inlet from the Potomac. It contained a venerable Episcopal church, a court-house which once taxed bachelors to support that church, some law-offices, and two taverns; and around it, on the hills, showed mansions of a once opulent time. Lying in a bowl of the hills, neglect, night-poison, and slavery had come like three witches to grin upon it.

"Don't sleep heah, mosster," the Negro said; "it's death to strangers after sundown!"

Quantrell gazed around on jail and crumbling wall, on public pump and butcher-stall, on gravestones uninclosed, and hollow ruin.

"Think of it," he reflected; "thirty-four miles from the city of Washington! — only an evening's drive!"

The time came when this reflection put into another head an enterprise of desperation. Port Tobacco was on the direct line, as the crow flies, from the city of Baltimore to the city of Richmond, and as directly south from Washington as the plummet could hang. Did the government at Washington forget this when, the very day Lloyd Quantrell arrived in Port Tobacco, he saw a "Home-Guard" to recruit for slavery established in the town? Atzerodt did not forget it, whose home was in Port Tobacco.

He came out to Lloyd's carriage from a large brick edifice with massive forking chimneys built against it, and a long porch on squalid piers — a house of a tenement character, degraded from old stability and pretension to be the offices or lodgings of various people, the office-holder, the lawyer, the doctor; and in the once ornamental garden stood an old stable or shop, where Atzerodt worked at his trade of coach-maker.

"Here is where you wanted to bring Nelly, Andrew. It was good for her she didn't come."

"Py Jing! she proke dat Dunker's heart, Lloyd. She'll preak te next feller's, too. Who is he? Ain't it Pooth?"

"No, no. Nelly loves nobody, Atzerodt. She wants money and admiration."

"Den she'll cry her eyes out for not taking me. Lloyd, py Jing! I'm going to rake money in now easy as rakin' oysters. Nigger-catchin' is done. Te tam apolitionists has stopped kidnappin' and remantin' of slaves. Te Logans is all proke up. But right here, at Port Tobacco Inlet, te plockade-runners will pe comin', and I've got a boat an' crew to run te river to Fergeenia."

"There's a rope spun for you, Andrew! You go to Canada, or this war will catch you; for it's going to be a big one, and you're a poor, chattering coward that I wish no harm to. Where is Father Fenwick?"

"He's down to St. Thomas's Manor, waitin' for you. Put stay here tonight. Yonder's Captain Sam Cox on te porch, te ringleader of Charles County. He's goin' up tomorry or next day, and capture Washington, py Jing! and cut ole Abe Lincoln's head off!"

Quantrell saw Captain Cox, a fierce, consumptive-eyed man, standing at the old tavern.

"Here, Andrew, take my dog, and keep him till you hear from me!"

As Lloyd drove away, Atzerodt put up the dog for drinks at the tavern-bar, and one of the few government or Union men in the county got him and led him home.

Quantrell continued along the high banks of the Port Tobacco River, nearly a mile broad, and lighted by the moon, till at its mouth there stretched below the landing and warehouses of Chapel Point, and, on the heights above, the venerable chapel, mansion, and school of St. Thomas's Manor.

This was the most elegant establishment the Jesuits possessed in Maryland, in those years when they strained the provincial laws to give a private estate ecclesiastical scope and opulence. A church was connected with a refectory and study, in handsome design, of dark-red brick, with Roman arches and heavy chimneys, spire, wide hall, and cool gallery within the hall, and slave quarters; for slavery became more influential than the Jesuits, and it broke their discipline down, till the brethren of him who penetrated through the wilderness to discover the Mississippi yielded by the Potomac to the soft blandishments of master and slave.* Behind the large yet gloomy construction the graves of the Jesuit brothers lay in myrtle-beds; and terraced slopes and garden-walks dropped away to the shores of the mighty Potomac, here contracted to a width of three miles; and in the soft procession of the moon upon the waters the Virginia woods at Mathias Point crept onward, like an ambush of the gunner for the wild duck.

Hugh Fenwick came out and put away Lloyd's horses. He seemed half guest, half assistant there. They talked of Katy before they went to bed.

"Hugh," said Quantrell, "I shall send to you at this place all my letters. In the morning I shall write to Katy, recommending her to your care. My father is too ill to bear the news of my marriage yet."

How deeply was the young priest in religious enthusiasm that night! He would not let Quantrell sleep, without saying over him the prayer of St. Thomas Aquinas — to keep love's torments down.

"Get out, Hugh!" Quantrell said, at last; "don't paw over me so! You seem to be in what they call 'ecstasy' of some kind!"

If he could have peeped into Fenwick's chamber, Quantrell might have known the cause of that ecstasy, as the student upon his knees sighed out:

"Lord, if it pleases thee to continue this war sufficiently long, be bountifully gracious to forgive my sin in marrying this man and woman." And he might have added, "Incline her heart to me!"

Quantrell crossed Pope's Creek and the Potomac next morning, and,

---

*   See a curious book on a residence in Maryland before the American Revolution, by J. F. D. Smyth, loyalist officer. Dublin, 1784.

riding across the Northern Neck, reached old Port Royal on the Rappahannock. The third night he was in Richmond, and falling in with many volunteers he had met at John Brown's scaffold, they took him to a concert-saloon to see a remarkable beauty who had recently turned out.

The place was coarse and without female patrons. Men smoked cigars, and waiters peddled liquors up and down the aisles. After minstrelsy, dancing, and other variety entertainment, a loud howl arose from the motley audience for the fresh favorite that is ever requested and devoured, like fresh babes by the sacred crocodile. The present slave of the mob was announced as "the dazzling Protean Empress in her reigning parts and dresses, Miss Nelly Starr."

The curtain rose, and Nelly Harbaugh was before Lloyd, in evening dress of black silk — superior to the place she stood in, as modesty with beauty well might be. Instead of seeming coarser, she seemed better in every way, more pale, more cold, more superb. She recited in hoarse, crude, deep tones, and with too little good tuition, a ballad Quantrell had heard from John Wilkes Booth.

Quantrell could hardly believe his eyes, as the curtain fell, that this was the mountain weed which had stood by his side in the loft of the Dunker church.

The first piece had been above the taste of the audience, but the second was cried for by whistling and yelling — the yell that often resounded afterward on the field of battle like the Indian war-whoop.

Nelly now appeared in knee-breeches of velvet and a steel corset, with a light sword in her hand. Her long, mountain-exercised limbs and trunk stood nearly of man's height and sinew, and her hair was gathered up. After juggling with the sword awhile to the sound of music, she was confronted by a "professor" of fencing, and, amid the continued yelling of the audience, she crossed rapiers with him, more in main strength and rude pluck than in skill. Her prowess was greeted by expletives low and familiar, and, at the disarming of the professor by the "Empress," Lloyd saw her bosom heave when she bowed her thanks.

"Poor girl!" thought he, "this audience is a sore exchange for an honest husband."

The curtain soon rang up upon Nelly as "Virginia" — the Virginia not of Knowles, but of Jefferson, as depicted on the seal of the State. There stood this fine and powdered woman, in the dress, or want of dress, of an Amazon, with a short tunic, bodice, and sleeves of spangles, and with sandals and helmet, and bare limbs and breast — a wonder in flesh and yellow hair, stalwart and palpitating. Her left hand upheld a spear; from her right hand fell a falchion; and her foot was upon a nondescript figure which lay prostrate and held a broken chain and a slave-whip.

"'*Sic semper tyrannis!*' — ever thus, tyrants!" — exclaimed the girl, in hollow, untrained tones, quoting the motto of the State.

Her strong Roman nose well became the study, and her fine chin and throat and arching eyebrows.

As she drooped her eyes, that had been raised in dramatic apostrophe while the curtain was coming down, they fell upon Lloyd Quantrell, and she started; her foot shook the effigy, her bare knee trembled, and her lips parted.

This impersonation had to be several times made to gratify the Virginians, but every time the actress turned a meaning glance on Lloyd, whose companions finally noticed it, saying:

"Lloyd, the Empress is 'gone' on you. You're lucky, for she has been cold as ice to every devotee of pleasure in the city."

A waiter soon came to Lloyd with a piece of paper on which was written:

"*Do* wait for me at the door! I want to hear from home."

She came out among officious and insinuating men, spurning all their attentions, and saw Lloyd's tall figure, and took his arm.

"Come," she said, "to my lodgings."

They crossed the shady square under the Roman-French portico of the old barnlike Capitol, soon to be the insurgent government's, and saw the great brass statue of Washington and horse ride the moonlight like a wave of electrified cloud. Nelly boarded with a German family from the Valley, and in the little parlor she sat by Lloyd's knee and whispered nervously:

"Luther — is he sick?"

"No."

"Thank God! But does he accuse me?"

"He has never spoken of you since, I hear."

"O Lloyd, I could never have filled the place he would have put me in. Once I might have done so. I had struggled and prayed to be made humble to do my duty as a Christian minister's wife. Just as I thought I had triumphed, the devil appeared to me and made me as treacherous as himself."

"It was not John Booth?"

"Who else? I will not give you any lies. He set his traps for my ambition, and I fell to hell with him! Did he never tell you?"

"Not a word. I was sure it was some other man — or none."

"Ah! Lloyd, he can keep a secret well, especially if it is a dark and tangled one. That he calls honor — to betray and not scandalize his victim — as if a woman would be content to find him false in everything but that!"

"Nelly, you hate him."

"I fear him more. There is not one man in him, but many. Three devils possess him at different times, or all together — pride, drink, and lust. The first and last of these are steadfast; the second is never far off. When he was drunk, I let him strike me. When he was proud and bullying, I flattered him. When he was false to me, I knew him, then, as I shall always know him, like a treacherous mountain stream, shallow but with dark pools until there is a flood, and then it is a terror."

"Are you sure he was untrue?"

"Pah! Everybody knew it. He expected me to nurse him after the fatigues of villainy. At Montgomery, in Alabama, one woman stabbed him, and then he came to me for sympathy, having the cool selfishness to suppose that where he really loved no offense could be taken; for, Lloyd, if that gypsy can love anybody, he loves me."

"God help him, then!" exclaimed Lloyd, ungallantly. "Why do you call him a gypsy?"

"He looks like one. He acts like one. I have seen real gypsies in our mountain country, some of them English gypsies camping there. I think the boast of John Booth, that he was partly Jew, was to conceal the gypsy in his stock. He loves a wandering life, has no social feelings, finds things out to profit by them like gypsy fortune-tellers, and can be still and cunning as a cat."

"You mean he is like Hannah Ritner?"

"No. She is no gypsy, but a wonderful woman. Part of all our fortunes has come true as she told us that peaceful Sunday when I was well beloved —"

The girl stopped and choked down a sob, and walked the room rapidly, till Quantrell said:

"Yes, indeed; all 'the game beneath the sun has risen before me' since — raiders, rioters, soldiers, tumult, and war; Katy has lost her ring; and 'something dark and white has marked you, Nelly, with the dark'; but, blessed be my dear little dove! I have the promise that she shall yet sing for me."

"Go back to her!" Nelly turned and addressed Lloyd with a vigor which made him see that the natural actress was there; "go back out of this South, with its fierce, torrid passions and hopeless and audacious task of destruction! I love you and Katy both, cheated and fallen as I am, and I speak out of the arisen knowledge of good and evil that woman has who has eaten of the forbidden fruit. There is nothing whatever in this Confederacy that is substantial, except courage and ferocity. Forethought, humility, or lawfulness, is left out of its constitution, and it will fight and fail."

"Nelly, that won't do here. I am a soldier of Virginia."

"And I am going back to the Union lines! Haven't we followed this disunion program with our company — I mean Booth's company — wherever it has made a crowd? We saw South Carolina secede and forbid the payment of Northern debts, and steal the government forts. We saw Alabama go next, and refuse to let her people vote on the ordinance of treason. Mississippi, without any public credit in the world, next resolved to fight the United States, which pays rich and poor. They made the Union orator in Georgia drunk at dinner, so that his eloquence, which had been dangerous in the morning, would be silly enough in the afternoon to pass their silly scheme. The first act of Louisiana, after separating, was to steal the money in the mint, and of Texas to depose her President and hero, General Houston. These are the States which expect to raise cotton in the rear and let the border, like Virginia and Maryland, be overrun with their savages. Don't I know it? Haven't I heard them talk it in my presence? This rebel government is nothing but officeholders out of power and slaveholders out of hope, meaning to keep by force the offices the Black Republicans have been elected to; and they will conscript their poor whites to fight for their Negroes, until the hollow bubble breaks to a drop of lye, and then everybody, except the fools, will be glad."

"How could *you* have seen the gentlemen of the South?"

"Oh, an actor is a good deal more, South than North. That is why John Booth is such a Southern patriot. Think of that man being invited into respectable families, with his forked tongue and luring eyes! He cheated me of my promised place in the bills and the casts!" — here Nelly seemed to show a double fury — "but I had my callers and admirers, too — generals, governors, coxcombs, and simperers — and none without a title. The poor old officers of the army and navy they have compelled to resign, told me their real remorse and apprehension, at being made the waiting beggars of an experiment; for in this confederacy all must join the dance of death — all but the niggers, who are the princes of the country, and white men's sons go fight for them!"

"How did you get this fluency of words, Nelly?"

"By the great teachers of unhappy women, Lloyd — Sin and Necessity. I have studied hard, in order not to be dependent on that man Booth. He has made thousands of dollars in this unsettled, feverish time, when towns fill up with crowds, and men grumble, and women lose their souls. By the sharpened wits of the castaway I see my needs, and earn money as I can; for I am going to work hard to be a successful woman, and to marry the man I love. He will fall, somehow, too; we shall both have much to forgive. But when I can earn my thousands in the eminent walks of the drama I shall be worthy of his notice again, and I know — oh, I know! — he loves me dearly!"

Falling upon her knees, the girl grasped Lloyd's hands, and cried again and again:

"Oh, tell me so! Oh, tell me so! I am so lonesome for my love!"

"Nelly, it is a mercy to Luther that you roved away before you married him! He did love you, and he may love you yet, but he sees you now too well to marry you, and he was slow and reluctant to ask you; for I was there, and you said you could obey him with joy, and do your part in toil and saving for his sake."

"I did! I did! If I could be forgiven now, I would leave this life of tinsel and jealousy, where we are homeless, persecuted, and tempted, and fed on hollow praise, to be Luther Bosler's Dunker wife, and ride with him through our native hills and valleys, visiting the sick, praying with the dying, seeking out the poor, and seeing my applause in the softly beaming stars, or feeling it in my peaceful soul and on his tender kiss. Will it ever come, Lloyd?"

"Nelly, I can't see it, but many things are possible to the persevering, and God forbid that I discourage you! for my father says that love can distill its own corruptions and be pure, and that I must not harshly judge love's aberrations."

"God bless his old age for that!" Nelly cried. "There was but one man kind enough to say so before your father, and he was the Lord of heaven and earth."

"My poor girl, it was said by that man, 'Go and sin no more!' Can you obey him?"

She rocked her head, intimating contrition and obedience.

"In my father's spirit," spoke Lloyd, "and not to judge love's many willfulnesses and wandering paths, and because, Nelly, I see in you now a sensibility that interests me in your disposition for the first time, I offer you my friendship and confidence."

He reached out his hand. She drew back and looked at him, saying: "You tempting, too?"

"No, my own dear love forbids! Katy is mourning for me – perhaps, also, as one without hope."

"O brother among sinners! Gentlest of proud and overbearing men! May you, who can see anything good in me, find good in everything!"

She took his hand, and he kissed her as he would have kissed Light Pittson, in tender pity and respect.

Often, while she remained in Virginia, Lloyd consoled this woman, generally taking her home from the variety hall, and all may have misconceived his motive; for it is the despair of an erring woman that none can think of her except in her false relation, and they who treat her otherwise suffer in the same uncharity.

Quantrell had other occasions to refer his conduct to his father's principles.

He was not only tempted to enter independent, partisan, or guerrilla organizations, and assume that Maryland had left the Union, and that he was entitled to carry her flag lawlessly; but the Virginia authorities, to whom he transferred his allegiance, desired him to do a semi-spy business for them on the lower Potomac.

"Not a step will I make," answered Quantrell, "except as a soldier in line! You can have my life in fair war, but my father's last command was, 'Never lurk within the lines in Maryland, and be a spy and a villain.'"

In spite of all attempts to carry Maryland into the great rebellion, the city of Baltimore was occupied by the government, and gave no further trouble except in the way Abel Quantrell feared, of being of an uncertain mind — trying to save the whole of slavery with one hand, a silly consistency with the other, and some of the Union, if that Union could take care of itself. Virginia was cut in twain by her western citizens, never to be repatched, and the western volunteers chased the secession troops across the Alleghanies.

The insurgent President and Congress moved to Richmond, as Nelly Harbaugh had predicted, two months after they commenced the war, and Lloyd heard the former person describe the President at Washington in the polite terms of "an ignorant usurper," and speak of Virginia as "the theater of a great central camp." The theater, indeed, seemed to have become the society. This "President," from one of the Gulf States, closed by saying, "To the enemy we leave the base acts of the assassin and incendiary."

Yet, the next day, Quantrell was sent for and told to go over into Maryland and arrange for a secret mail post, to give the new government the correspondence of its opponents. He refused to go farther than the borders of Virginia, and became a signal-officer opposite Pope's Creek.

There lived on the opposite high mortar bluffs of Maryland a simple farmer, who had been raised in the family of the most energetic rebel in that region — namely, the Captain Cox who was pointed out to Lloyd in Port Tobacco. This Captain Sam Cox lived about six miles north from his humbler neighbor, Jones, in an agreeable residence near the edge of the great Zekiah Swamp, which flowed from springs near Dr. Sam Mudd's retired farm.

The insurgent mail passed to Jones's Bluff in a row-boat every sunset, was sent on to Cox's by wood-paths, and went thence to Bryantown or Sam Mudd's, according to the urgency; and so a secret post-road was made all the way to Canada; the government mails, intended to benefit the humble Marylanders, thus remote from railways, being unscrupulously loaded with treasonable intelligence, and the cabal of plotters in

Montreal and Halifax receiving by this route commands for material to run the blockade, and for incendiaries and pirates to annoy the free States from the rear.

Surratt's tavern and post office often received this surreptitious mail for Washington, and soon after the war opened Mrs. Surratt was left a widow, young, fond, and passing fair, and the young clerical of a son became the head of the family.

None can tell how much a foreign interest, like the great Rebellion, poisons an enterprising society through which may flow one of its secret drains. The liquor-dealer, Martin, who had accompanied Lloyd Quantrell to the lower Potomac, following out the clew of this secret thread to its termination in Canada, soon became a fitter-out of ships there, to run the blockade of the Southern ports; for now the government and people were aroused, and a coil was being slowly drawn around the ambitious slave empire; but the processes of law are ever more scrupulous and gentle than the spasms of insurrection, and it often seemed to Quantrell as if the Federal state meant, like the founder of its era, to be offered up to martyrdom rather than to exert its heavenly powers and overwhelm its enemy.

The character of people, and their errands, who crossed the river in the boats of Jones and others between Port Tobacco and Pope's Creek, tended to confirm Lloyd's appreciation of his father's acumen and advice. Mischief and avarice were their ruling motives, with some incidental devotion or necessity, and frequently nothing more profitable than restless curiosity or assurance.

Some were trimmers and parasites, who desired to make their compliments to the insurgent side in case it finally prevailed, and slip back again and court the other government with timid counsel or interference. Others were speculators — a class just graduated from the lobbies of legislatures, corporations, and exchange, in time to practice their craft in the fluctuations and surprises of a civil war, as wide as the continent, and paid for in notes and currencies issued for the hour.

The contractor, the arms-manufacturer, the peddler, the gold-broker, the insurer, the schemer and hare-brained notoriety-seeker; the Jew, traveling toward gold with the instinct of iron for the loadstone; the broken Northern politician, out of a job, and willing to serve any cause that would let him repay his salary in lip-service or gasconade; the sinister lawyer, seeking to snatch some interest from danger or confiscation; the huckster for cotton or treasonable loans; the military beggar, of ruined habits, hunting a new commission; the foreign mercenary, yesterday in jail, going to demand a generalcy; the newspaper spy, intent on the highest sensation; the adventuress, who had heard that her intimate had become a cabinet minister; the seduced one, braving battle and insult to save her good name, and obtain the marriage-cloak in which to plague society more; the loud-throated woman, who expected to beat the government forces by bellows-power and innuendo; the popinjay, sneaking over to enlist and run away, or not to enlist and take credit for "patriotism"; the aged crank, switching up some vagary on which he had ridden for years and been a bore to his species; the clergyman whose congregation had refused to let him preach disunion and be paid for it — all these swelled the motley tide of rebellion, and made even dull men think how their English ancestors had put treason highest of crimes, because it would supplant the system and order of the million with the wild anarchy of the impatient and ungovernable. A frequent errand of the go-between was to sell slaves on which he had a lien or heritage-right, and then run away from the war, and be sleek and compromising.

The citizens of Maryland soon lost many of their slaves, although the Union army would return these and get no thanks; while some of the slaves remained in nominal bondage in order to enjoy the profits and vices of the contraband trade.

Along the Virginia shore batteries were thrown up to annoy shipping bound for Washington and the army; light gunboats cruised the river, and finally destroyed most of the yawls and skiffs on the Maryland side; but there were women to do the work of spies after the men had been intimidated, and who trusted to the faith of men in women and men's untoward mercy for their safety.

In the residences, standing high on the bluffs below Pope's Creek, a shawl or a dress would appear at a garret-window and be read by Quantrell's telescope to mean — "Danger! Beware!" A woman's hand had stretched it, and perjury had been willful in her soul; for the government administered oaths of allegiance to all who preferred its protection, or sent them within the insurgent lines.

When this signal appeared, no boat would leave Virginia; when it was withdrawn, the rebellion mail-boat darted out in the neutral light between sunset and the hour of setting the night-patrol, and came unobserved to the foot of the bluffs of shell and clay, left the mail in a hollow tree, took the return mail previously put there, and so glided back to Virginia like a water-snake.

The United States never exerted its repressive hand like the fierce enemy; and so the wages of avarice or mischief outbid the mild, occasional punishment of the spy, until one day, when it was too late, and the world was in woe, a single woman paid the penalty of her sex; and the gallows, which should have met Lloyd Quantrell's telescope when he peered out at Maryland, became the solemn conclusion of the war.

Atzerodt went into the trade of running the lines, and became more wretched and blustering than ever; he would also drive spies and strangers toward Washington, stopping at Surratt's tavern.

Nelly Starr and Booth passed the Potomac one day northward, apparently reconciled, and Booth had a new piece of poetry he repeated with admiration, which had been written in Louisiana, to seduce Maryland to take the leap from treason's Tarpeian rock. It was set to the German air of "Tannenbaum," and said:

> "Hark to a wandering son's appeal,
>   Maryland!
>   My mother State! to thee I kneel,
>   Maryland!
>   For life or death, for woe or weal,
>   Thy peerless chivalry reveal,
>   And gird thy beauteous limbs with steel,
>   Maryland! my Maryland!*

> "Dear mother! burst the tyrant's chain,
>   Maryland!
>   Virginia should not call in vain —
>   'Maryland!'
>   She meets her sisters on the plain;
> 'Sic semper,' 'tis the proud refrain
>   That baffles minions back again —
>   Maryland!
>   Arise in majesty again,
>   Maryland! my Maryland!"

Booth had a mind up to the instinctive grade of this poetry, and no higher. He had been in the military lines a very little while, and found discipline too tame for his nature, and so he was leaving the South to fly from its sacrifices, but gorged with the consideration he had received there.

"What are you going to do, John?"

"Lloyd, I'll try the stage in the Yankee States awhile, but they never warmed to my style up there. If I fail, I shall go into some of their speculations and make a stake out of them, and then —"

"John, are you going to take all that money you drew from the Southern people, out of their country? If you are really a brave man, send it to your mother, and come into the ranks!"

Booth bent his face to Quantrell's ear as he stepped into the canoe,

---

*   "O Tannenbaum! O Tannenbaum!
       Wie grün sind deine Blätter!"

and whispered:

"My boy, you'll hear from me before this war is over!"

*L*loyd did hear from John Beall, before the war had well begun. That young man of twenty-six, tortured with apprehensions and by furies, had nearly departed for the Western States to be out of the reach of the war; but, sucked into its Maelstrom, he stood, on the second anniversary of Captain John Brown's invasion, in the vicinity of his home, looking through the Lurlei's gap of Harper's Ferry, where ever sat the siren above the "Suck," and he saw the Union flag advancing, and the wide valley full of bayonets.

"John Brown's re-enforcements have come at last, friend," spoke Quantrell, riding by. Lloyd had been given the congenial place of signal-man to General Joe Johnston, who was now trying to prove to his employers that Harper's Ferry was a hole and not a rampart — but neither government could believe it.

In five minutes more, Mr. Beall, who had been shooting at the "enemy" with the cheerless rage of a Covenanter on Magus Moor, was lying on the ground, with three ribs broken and an air-crack in his right lung. The district attorney, who had prosecuted John Brown to the gallows, picked the young man up and carried him to Charlestown, which was already familiar with another ballad of the war, sung in its streets by advancing and retreating thousands:

"John Brown's knapsack is packed upon his back,
  And his soul's marching on.
    Glory, glory, hallelujah!
  For his soul's marching on."

The general to watch Harper's Ferry and prevent that hole from deserting somewhere, let the insurgent army behind it slip away through the Blue Ridge and swell the army on Manassas plateau; and a battle took place, where three thousand fellow-countrymen gasped or sighed in pain and dissolution.

"John Brown's army has failed once more," thought Quantrell; "but what a scare he gave us, as before!"

The behavior of Lloyd in this battle was so fearless and cool, that he would have been promoted, except for three things — the universal desire for office and commissions; the utility of Lloyd to affect his native State in its peace and seclusion; and a whisper that he was unsound on Slavery as the particular lamb of Christ and main purpose of salvation.

So he was sent back to the lower Potomac, to superintend the chief sally-port of the blockaded hydra, and there he waited to hear from his wife, in love's great thirst and hunger; while Hugh Fenwick, on the opposite shore, sent him reports of her spiritual condition — reminding him of Luther Bosler's hostility to rebels, and Jake Bosler's hatred of all warriors and peace-breakers; and poor Lloyd had promised his father never to enter Maryland, and could verify nothing for himself. At last he did receive a letter in Katy's hand, and with Hugh Fenwick's *adden- dum*:

> LLOYD:
>
> I haf been faithful. Haf you, Lloyd? Sir, I am a poor girl, and I haf no wedding-ring. People and eyes up in heafen, too, looks at me, Lloyd. You haf deceived me; but I bless you, if I must die!
>
> KATY

Quantrell had been playing Katy's accordion, and he took it up and drew a shriek of anguish from it to stifle his own.

Queer pains had been in his head and back all that day, and his ears were buzzing; and as he read what Hugh Fenwick added, his eyes swam and he could not see:

> LLOYD:
>
> Your wife has run away from home and can not be found. They say in the Catoctin Valley that you are the cause of it. She knows that in Richmond your heart and honor were transferred to Nelly Harbaugh, the actress, and it broke her heart. I pray for you and for the cause. Pray for me, who married you in error! You are free from Katy, and she is as your widow. *Christie Eleison!*
>
> † HUGH

"O Abel! my father!" cried Quantrell; "come to me in my desolation! Nothing is left but you — no mother, no country, no wife!"

They said it was the bilious fever of the old Potomac country, which laid him for months on the bed of fire and ice, and raised him to be the shadow of himself.

Chapter XXXVI

CRESCITE ET MULTIPLICAMINI

KATY had grown close to her brother in her desertion, and he, deserted by Nelly, made his sister his idol, and filled her pure soul with spiritual food. Suspecting that the flight of Lloyd had given her pain, Luther, never dreaming of his sister's matronhood, kept her tenderly at his side, and every Dunker congregation along the South and North Mountains, from Virginia to the Susquehanna, knew this constant couple.

Long before day they would be up and away, to attend market at remote old towns like York, Carlisle, and Winchester; or auction-sales, to which the country people loved to repair; or Dunker love-feasts and celebrations. In those still, starlight times, in the hush of mountains and of woods, Luther told Katy of creeds, and heard her prattle of everything but that which made her soul cold with fear.

Little did he know that the miracle was repeated of which he often preached, in that tiny form at his side, or that quickened spirits rode with him, and that they, twain, were not alone together.

She, filled with the agony of a double secret, looked upon her brother as her priest and judge; but she dared not make him her confessor. That place Hugh Fenwick filled, and his consideration for Katy was equal to her brother's.

She inspired love more now than ever, as she bloomed out of the scrawny stem of girlhood to life's accomplishment; and poor Jake Bosler, who had feared her nervous energy and premature passion of love were breaking her down, saw with joy that his child rounded and grew more beautiful, until she almost made him fear.

"Katy leave fader — Bi'm-by," said Jake, thinking of marriage for his girl.

"Fader," said Katy, "I must wait for Lloyd. Will te war last long, fader?"

"Te city mans, Katy, fooled your little heart. Tere's Nelly down in Washington, gone from Luter to pe wicked. My little girl, if you would leave fader like dat, my heart would preak on my olty's grave."

As Jake Bosler kissed her, he did not know the pain he had made. Katy prayed and prayed, and lay awake hearing the rain upon the roof, and walked to the window in the night and saw the valley, in ghostly sheets of fog, fall like a deluge around a nearly submerged world; or saw some red planet burn on the mountain's crest, like shame with leveled eye seeking her out.

She lost her brother, too, when his rising indignation at the secession intrigues, and at repeated raids upon the Dunker valleys, recalled to his warm brain the soldierly prophecy of that singular woman who did not merely tell fortunes, but told, and instigated, character also — Hannah Ritner; and as Luther stood in the Dunker meeting-houses to pray, there would roll through his mind like a drum:

> "Attend the bugle-horn,
> And all thy merit see!"

The influence of Abel Quantrell, that strange, suggestive man, like the prophet Samuel, carrying among the sons of Jesse his anointing horn, was also felt by Luther, and his admonition, "Go, tell your people everywhere that Christ is for liberty," had never ceased to plague the Dunker preacher's conscience.

At last he raised his voice, like Balaam of old, and blessed the Union camps, almost against his will.

The old Dunker conservatives heard him, and muttered together that, since that worldly Nelly had cast him off, his talents and mental disorder had made him a lunatic. In vain did he demonstrate that the German Baptists were the oldest anti-slavery men in the world, saying in Antietam church:

"Te German brethren was te first apolitionists. In German's town, py Philadelphey, when te earliest slaveholding Quakers had only peen six year in tis country, te protest against slavery was writ py Hendricks, Op den Graeff, and Pastorius, saying: 'We are against te traffic in mens-body. Those who steal men, and those who buy or purchase them, are they not all alike? As here is liberty of conscience, which is right and reasonable, here ought to pe likewise liberty of pody, except of evil-doers. This makes an ill report in all those countries of Europe where they hear that "ye Quakers doe here handel men like they there handel ye cattle"; and for that reason some have no mind or inclination to come hither. Have tese negers not as much right to fight for teir freedom as you have to keep tem slaves?'"*

The English secessionists fanned the Dunker hostility to Luther favoring war and resistance, and he realized the marvelous foresight of the prophetess who had counseled:

"Though in the church they censure some,
    Pain and duty keep thee dumb!"

The slaughter of Senator Baker's command at Ball's Bluff — he who had been President Lincoln's neighbor and Broderick's funeral eulogist — aroused the German military nature, as the musketry reverberated on the Maryland hills; and from the town where Booth was born, another Union Governor was selected. The insidious Legislature, which had slipped away to Frederick, was dispersed by the government before it could assume to vote Maryland out of the Union, and the two Maryland regiments drew each other's blood in the Valley of Virginia, fighting under the old and the opposite flags.

Before all this had happened, Luther enacted the part of Muhlenberg of old.

He preached one peaceful autumn Sunday; drew tears by his emotion and eloquence; solemnly suspended himself from the Dunker sect, and rode to old Sandy Hook, where General Banks was collecting an army, and enlisted as a private soldier in the cavalry.

While he was at Charlestown, encamped on the site of John Brown's gallows, his colonel sent for him and gave him a letter. He opened it and found a commission as captain in the quartermaster's department by order of Abraham Lincoln, at the request of Abel Quantrell and Henry Winter Davis. Luther trembled, as he remembered the lines:

"To hollow heart the hollow drum
    Beats peace and victory."

Luther was ordered to repair to the city of Washington, where Mr. Davis — the only Marylander who had voted in either branch of Congress for compensated emancipation, in both the Federal city and his own State — took him by the hand, and led him to the new Secretary of War, saying:

"Mr. Stanton, you wanted an honest man to supervise your quartermasters and buy horses and forage for your armies. Here he is — a Dunker preacher, enlisted in the lines."

"The hour," said Mr. Stanton, looking at Luther with considerate brown eyes through his glasses, "is the test of every true conscience; and that you broke the traditions of your life, to lay that life down for your

---

‡   Pennypacker's "Settlement of Germantown, Pennsylvania."

country, as a humble soldier, recommends you to me, who am of Quaker and of peaceful instincts, too. Go about your duties! Come freely to me, and be my friend, amid all this falsehood and deception. If ever your scruples against war return, tell me so, and you shall be honorably discharged!"

The manly, nervous diction and delicate feeling, smote the young man dumb, but it was the dumbness of worship. In the next minute he heard the same Secretary order a brigadier-general, in tones of thunder, to quit his office and the city, or have his shoulder-straps torn from him in the streets.

From that moment Luther never doubted the success of the government armies, nor that the nation would emerge from the conflict with every false sentiment and sham stamped under the Quakerly Stanton's feet.

*T*he reoccupation of Virginia awakened young Mr. Beall to the truth of John Brown's prediction, made to Lloyd Quantrell on the mountain, that the Great Valley would be the inevitable line of war, and would be the flanking route, to alarm the Government at Washington by marching to its rear. Yet both sides continued to regard Harper's Ferry as the key of every campaign, and, like the Irishman's recipe to make a cannon, they took that round hole and wrapped it about with brass.

John Beall, who had recovered from his wounds, marched down the Valley with Stonewall Jackson, and saw the handwriting of war upon his farm and county, and heard the stave of John Brown's hymn roared in the church where he was vestryman. He resolved to leave Virginia, and settle among his kinsmen in the West.

In that interval of grief and chagrin, of Highland Scotch and Indian rage, there appeared to him one day a lovely vision, as he strolled by the old tan-yard at Charlestown — it was the remembrance of Katy Bosler's great, soft eyes.

"This war has leveled all distinctions," said Beall, who was a self-communer, and had no intimates among men. "I will marry that girl, and take her to Iowa."

He had an impetuous brain, and that evening found him inquiring the way to Bosler's farm. Katy saw him come with joy, hoping he had news of Lloyd.

"Are you engaged to Mr. Quantrell, Kate?" Beall asked.

"Oh no, sir — not engaged."

Katy remembered her secret, and told the truth.

"I thought not; for Quantrell is an honorable young fellow, and he was very attentive, in Richmond, to Miss Nelly Starr, the actress, who is quite a different person. Katy, your home and mine are in the lines of war, and the war will be long, and battle and blood will finally drink our souls in. My blood has been shed already, and I have killed my enemies. I want to go away and live out my days, and escape the dark temptations hanging over me. Will you go, too?"

Katy's soul was full of woe, and she had not heard one sentence between the first and the last. Nelly Starr, with her fervent beauty, had cast her arts upon Lloyd and made him false to his wife as to his country, and the gentleman at her side had asked, "Will you go, too?"

"I *must* go," cried Katy; "I can not stay! Oh, fader loves me so, it preaks my heart! Te little lame man comes efery night to my bed, and says, 'I want your soul, Katy!' Last night he had his hands on my head and feet, at te spring-house, and told me to say, 'All between tese hands pelongs to te divel!' I tried not to say it, but I couldn't help it, and it had 'most come, when Hannah Ritner come riding down to te spring and shouted, 'God! God! she pelongs to God!'"

Katy had thrown herself upon her friend's shoulder in terror and confidence; and he caressed her kindly, his distant and reticent face growing studious of her weakness.

"You do belong to God, my dear child, and can draw me to His will. The day is at hand when every white man must labor, and will need a wife with the spirit of frugality and toil. I will take a mill and a farm in Iowa, and lead you there from the dangers of your native valley, and you will be my wife."

"Oh, no!" cried Katy, shaking herself loose; "I did not unterstant you, John Beall. Pefore you can marry a Union girl, git a Union heart! Then all te troubles you make in your mind will fade away, love will come easy, and friends will pe eferywhere."

"Where is Quantrell?" the young man asked, in Virginia hotness that his condescension had been so sincerely rejected. "Why can't you make *him* one of your Union men?"

"He is in te rebel army, waiting to be winnowed with te good wheat, I pray! If we nefer meet, heaven is all union, and no secession there."

Beall looked at her a moment with pale rage and wonder; her rounder figure swelling with emotions of piety, and her eyes bright with the enthusiasm of the martyr. He resumed his hopeless, pinched expression, saying:

"The women, too, have joined John Brown's gang!"

"Why don't you go py Lloyd in te rebel army?" asked Katy. "It is safer for you, and out of bad temptations."

"Because I have not the spirit of discipline. Because my mind is infested with brooding and impatient purposes. I want revenge; I want to retaliate. The example of old Brown has never left me, and it will make me a hero or a fiend!"

"Say 'Te Words!' cried Katy. "Lloyd said 'Te Words,' and was saved. I'll say tem to you, John Beall, and wickedness will fly away!"

She whispered in his ear the names in the Trinity.

He trembled a moment, and then tossed his head with contempt.

"Poor Dutch superstition!" he exclaimed. "Farewell, Katy of Catoctin!"

"He's drived te Holy Spirit away!" sighed Katy, looking after him with gentle tears. "He's lost!"

With Luther's sound head and strong hand gone from the farm, Jake Bosler was like one without his wits. Luther in soldier-clothes! Luther in the government! Luther a great man of the world! All Dunkerdom was full of visions and backsliding!

Old fellows in short coats would come out of meeting, on the green, to talk about it, and forget the subject in its mightiness, till they would disperse, merely saying, "Well, *luss mohl sae.*"

The blooming Dunker girls, all suffering for Luther's absence, would huddle together before meeting and ask, "Him? How?" and then all would laugh with little sallies and alarms, "He, he, he!"

Katy would come up to these, and some would stare at her and some would say, "How's Lloyd? Is Lloyd a rebel?" Some would also whisper and have decided looks, and follow her to the very horizon with their eyes.

Katy was the sincerest of Dunker devotees. Her tears might have washed her feet; her Lord's supper was eaten every Sabbath; she read the holy book to find her wedding-ring, but nothing could she see there but women's sins, sufferings, and tears.

"Oh, where is te brook I must wade down to find it?" her frightened soul cried. "I'll take off my shoes in this cold, icy weather, and go down te bed of efery brook — only tell me where?"

Did Katy ever think the brook she waded was made by her tears?

As Jake Bosler was drawn by Luther into the government business — buying and fattening steers, selecting mules at Baltimore and searching the mountain counties for horses — his monetary instincts aroused again, and Katy was left much alone, for which she was very grateful, although Gilmore's men and Mosby's spies, and long lines of white deserters and fugitive slaves, traveled northward on the mountains, and replaced the wild beasts of old. She did not fear the face of man, but only the face of woman. When woman goes astray, with men alone she finds equality and refuge — though woman should be kindest.

Hugh Fenwick came sometimes to see Katy from Washington, where he was at present a government clerk, having his quarrels now and then with the priests and conventual people; and, as for his politics, nobody could tell what it was from day to day. He boarded with secessionists and never rebuked them, and he took the government oath. Katy could no more understand him than she could her dog Albion, which was often left alone with her days and nights, and seemed to have a human soul, though a disagreeable one.

When she or any other person was happy, as after a Union victory, or election, or at baptism, or old neighbors' reconciliations, this dog grew surly and unsympathetic, and would dart out and snap at the cat or bite a chicken; but when musketry sometimes sounded in the distant hills, or forests were afire upon the long spines of the mountains, or a quarrel of any kind arose, Albion was like a gymnastic smile, leaping and pointing, unctuous and sinister, possessed of the devil, some said, and yet at such times affectionately insinuating.

When Katy sat in the great mystery and gloom of one abandoned by love and confronting heaven and death, with health superb if only sympathy and honor were by her side, but ignorance and secrecy wrapping her around as thick darkness, and in her house and heart, even in sleep, the knockings and movings of a spirit abroad — this dog would softly creep to her feet, climb upon her lap, and lay his spotted muzzle against her cheek, and his hazel-yellow eyes would burn in the darkness like lamps in mines, seeming to say, "You are lost, and I fill the bridegroom's place."

He never let her disappear, but followed her everywhere. At midnight he was astir if she was looking in the dark. His kid-brown nose would come cold against her hand in the sighs of prayer before dawn. When he heard John Beall say that Lloyd loved Nelly Harbaugh, he fawned upon the relator like an heir-at-law. He hated the doves in the apple tree, and often pulled Katy's gown to go and look at them, and see him strive to leap to their nest and put them in distress.

Katy loved these doves, though they reminded her of Lloyd's killing the dove upon the mountain, and receiving the great old bandit's rebuke. She sang over Job Snowberger's coo-roo song to them, and the old doves knew her well, and left her in the fall with many soft adieus, taking their young away. When they were gone, Katy had nothing left her but Albion, and the mystic guests that came unseen like the wind in the pigeon-cote and the weasel in the nest.

It was nearly Christmas when Hugh Fenwick paid his last visit to Bosler's farm. He brought sunshine with him generally, for he was only clerical in his affectations, but in realities was healthy, blooming, genial, and sympathetic. The church was his fastidious conceit and passport to a rarer society of virtue and respect, and Katy had tested him well to see if a coarser earth was covered by his piety, but found only abiding reverence for herself, with certain peculiarities of the moral weakling and the ecclesiastical prig.

He prevaricated, and was less sincere about essentials than forms; had a conscience which he could quiet by formulas and penance, believed in mild acts of deceit if they pointed to good conclusions, and approached nothing by the bold right line, but had humor and even gayety, and often just and humane impulses.

The mountain girl felt that his affection for her was stronger than friendship, and based upon something like fear of her reprobation; pity, also, controlled her feelings, in that this man had been so weak before her ardent and compelling lover as to open to her the door of happiness and anguish, by marrying her with anticipated authority because caught in the meshes of his own boasting.

Improbable as this act still seemed to Katy, like a dream that must yet pass away, it was no more than Cardinal Wolsey's prevarication — old as America's discovery — by which, against his will, he divorced a wife and remarried a king, and entrapped himself by moral weakness into deeds his conscience shrank from.

In Fenwick were two races seldom mixed — the impulsive, uncertain Irishman, and the colder, formulating German; and these hot and cold currents gave him two natures — the social and the ideal, the effervescent and the mystical. Not quite legible to himself, the estimate Katy Bosler made of him was shrewd up to the limits of her inexperience; no other man was so comforting to her, though she feared he might be her lover, while she desired the better nature in his friendship.

The dog Albion was also extravagant in his friendship, for Fenwick always brought him a present, like a ribbon or decoration of some kind, with which the aristocratic animal performed — taking on a sudden frigidity, being consciously indifferent to the remaining live creation, stalking in the front of the house to bark at all strangers; and the more he was decorated the more he was inhospitable. He licked the priest's hand, while rejecting the bounteous nature in Katy.

"O Father Hugh," the girl said, at last, with will and woe, "am I not married? Is te law so bad I can not get te wedding-ring? Maype Lloyd deceived me, too. I hear he was making love to Nelly in Richmond. Oh, why haf I not had letters from him? Where can I go? You must save me!"

"Katy, he took advantage of me, too, poor fellow! I had boasted a little, for then I expected to be soon a priest; but Lloyd bullied me, and I took pity on you both, knowing how great was your infatuation. Oh, the penance I have done! And the worst is that Lloyd has not been faithful."

"Perhaps you are a false friend!" cried Katy, her eyes fierce with the wisdom in despair. "Where has your friendship left me, sir, while Christmas is pefora me? I am a good woman, put no wife. And now you accuse Lloyd! If you are te devil, I will hit you with Luter's inkstand, like Friar Luter, in te Wartburg!"

She took the ink-bottle up from the eating-table, and the seminarist failed to cross himself, as he had started to do; for he was afraid of this woman — physically afraid!

The dog barked at Katy, snarling all about her feet, vicious as if she had ever been his enemy instead of his only friend on the globe.

The impulse was too mighty in Katy not to give her misery vent, and she turned upon the lesser spirit of evil:

"You?" she cried to the dog. "Ah! it was you who p'inted me, like te mountain dove, te night Lloyd Quantrell come."

She threw the ink-bottle at Albion and beat him with the broom, till, splotched with black and sore of ribs, the creature howled and ran, and Fenwick let him out at the door.

Pale and exhausted with the spasm, and repenting of her treatment of a guest, Katy relapsed to a helpless woman when silence had given Fenwick courage to speak.

"You are sorry you are Mr. Quantrell's wife?"

No," exclaimed Katy, on her remaining breath of spirit. "I won't say that, if he deceifed me. If he has gone away and forgot me, I won't say that. Te priest and te people, te church and te world, may p'int at me like that p'inter-dog, but I am God's child — and, above tem all, I call on God to come, and come quickly!"

"Katy — sister — I have not been your confessor in vain. I am here to assist and save you, and your severity is not of yourself. Come away! You shall see Lloyd; you shall have the protection of the Church's sheltering arms and walls in Washington. There are conventual places under our control open to the wounded — yes, to the betrayed."

"I am not petrayed," cried Katy; "I don't believe it. This war te slaveholders haf got up against te Union of our country has petrayed many a poor man out of home and life, and me out of a wife's name. I will not hide; I will stay here and die!"

She sank into a chair and felt faint and swooning. Fenwiek's impulses broke down his timidity, and he came and knelt at her feet and bathed her eyes with cool water.

"I must be firm, my child. You shall be made happy, and I must take you away. Your father worships you; your brother is in Washington. I will send for Lloyd to come."

The dog whined softly at the door; the wind blew, and snow came down the chimney upon the failing wood-fire.

"Lloyd?" sighed Katy. "How can he get through to lines?"

"Easily. I can have him brought across the Potomac, passed into Washington as one of our priestly refugees from the South, and made your fellow-prisoner in walls of the faith no government can enter."

Katy raised her head. The picture of Lloyd with her so soon, so close, so long, came like the phantom of the arisen Lord to Mary Magdalen, when the angel said: "There shall ye see him; lo, I have told you!"

"I have a carriage here; the night will be cold, but our robes are buffalo and lamb's wool."

The feet of his horses she heard on the frozen ground.

"Decide, Katy! Your father is overdue. Time is precious as your fame in this valley and the peace of this honest house. You can say that you went to find your brother in Washington, that Lloyd is there, and that I came at his request for you."

She stood up and said to herself in simple prayer, "Let me think of eferypody but me!"

The nature of the prayer contains the answer, and this was instant as the glance of love:

"Hugh Fenwick! Lloyd's fader said he would pe a villain to pe coming through te lines, like a spy. I won't tempt Lloyd to come. If God takes his life, let it pe where my brother Luter's life is enlisted — in te honest lines of battle!"

As the neophyte shrank before these words, the chivalric sense of which the true woman perceived as if she had been a military law-giver, Katy also felt admonitions beyond the help of sentiment.

She fell to the floor, and knew no more.

"I must exercise my discretion," Hugh Fenwick spoke, bending nervously over her. "Old Jake, her father, will find her here and go crazy, and she will lose the brightness of her soul, that is to me the only saint I worship. I will carry her to the carriage and start away."

He had lifted her tenderly in his strong arms and reached the door.

The dog outside was fighting desperately with some one, and, as Hugh Fenwick opened the door, this person darted in, kicking Albion off, and exclaiming:

"Katy, *unshuldich! Unshicklich!* I'm come, on one of Shwester Marcellus's errands, and te dog won't let me persewere!"

The breath of the evening revived Katy's senses. She slipped from the grasp of her uncertain friend, and spied a package in Job Snowberger's hand, which she seized with a kiss of joy upon that bashful monk's least obdurate cheek.

A letter in the old German *patois* said:

Dear Child:

I have kept you in mind, but the public enemy in Richmond put me in jail for my attention to our prisoners, and I am just home, at dear old Snow Hill in Pennsylvania. I send you my roan riding-horse to come instantly to me; he is very gentle and sure-footed. If you do not miss the road, it will be only twenty-five miles to ride to Snow Hill. I have often done it in an afternoon on Charlie. Brother Philodulus will come with you, but he is a poor guide and often loses the roads. Come over the mountain, and not around it! I will show you where to wade down the brook and find your wedding-ring.

Hannah Ritner

"God! God!" shouted Katy; "I pelong to God!"

She sat in ecstasy and wrote the letter to Lloyd Quantrell we have seen him receive, and bade her father, in writing, also be of good cheer, and gave the first letter to Hugh Fenwick, to forward.

"Where are you going, insane child?" Fenwick demanded.

"To te one woman in te world, I guess, who is not ashamed of me."

"Goin' to persewere," explained Job Snowberger, as he put Katy on one of the horses and climbed on the other himself, and they dashed northward and away.

Hugh Fenwick stopped superstitiously in the road and muttered a prayer beside his carriage.

"Is it a devil who has carried her from me?" he concluded. "I will recover Saint Kate for the salvation of my soul, or be a monk and leave the world!"

Chapter XXXVII

"TICK-A-TOCK-A!"

IT was very late in the afternoon, and Job Snowberger explained that he had once lost his way in the tangled mountains, and they must ride hard to get anywhere before midnight. Katy felt the incentive of desperation to be clear of her own neighborhood and escape meeting her father, and she gave free rein to the beautiful horse, whose feet on the frozen road went "tick-a-tock-a, tick-a-tock-a, tick-a-tock-a," in that carefully taught gait easier than the pacer's, where the hind feet seem to shuffle and the front feet go on, like the shuttle and the eye of the weaver at the loom. It was the single-footed rack —

"Tick-a-tock-a, tick-a-tock-a, tick-a-tock-a!"

The gentle gelding, compactly built, and his back steady as the seat of a rocking-chair, felt the double instinct of a lady's necessity and his dear mistress awaiting him; and the gallantry of a "gentleman of the old school" rose to his black mane and free head. Bealsville was passed, and, leaving on her left the dear road over which she and Lloyd had ridden to church, she skirried up the creek's side to the north —

"Tick-a-tock-a, tick-a-tock-a, tick-a-tock-a!"

Ah! thought Katy, should she ever again have Lloyd's head upon her breast and see his tears of contrition flow, and his face among the disciples eating the Lord's feast?

"Tick-a-tock-a, tick-a-tock-a, tick-a-tock-a!"

"The Lord sent this horse," Katy thought; "I wish I had my old dog, Fritz, too, so steaty and strong."

The strawberry roan shied and lost his rack, as something growled at his heels and flashed on before like a spotted and bleached will-o'-the-wisp; and then, as Katy recognized Albion in the place she had hoped for Fritz, the racker's black-striped back settled easily down again, and his black tail streamed, and his black feet slid over the ground —

"Tick-a-tock-a, tick-a-tock-a, tick-a-tock-a!"

The snow came down finer and faster as the shades of evening deepened, and over the twinkling lights of Wolfsville Katy looked toward the Black Rock on the mountaintop, where she had been the queen at picnic-parties before the coming of Lloyd Quantrell for his doves. How happy and wistful of love then! How unhappy and thornful of love's fruition and poverty now! How uncertain that she would return and have that simple happiness again if to throw away love's power and dread knowledge!

"Tick-a-tock-a, tick-a-tock-a, tick-a-tock-a!"

The evergreen cedars kept their fresh tints in the snow, but nature in general seemed dead. The woods upon South Mountain seemed bare and open, save where the firs and pines stood together in bunches, like the last of old men. Some crows, hastening home to their rock nests, cawed, up among the snow-flakes, like the poor mountain people going home from work to hungry children. A rabbit ran once or twice, leaving his leap-marks in the snow-sheet, and snow birds came abroad as if the Lord's white tablecloth were spread over the world, and only the very tiny and very cold ones were bid to his feast. Job Snowberger suggested that they could stop all night in Wolfsville; but Katy cried "No!" and dashed across the creek, and on the steep ascent the strawberry roan made bleak music —

"Tick-a-tock-a, tick-a-tock-a, tick-a-lock-a!"

Katy had barely made her decision, when she felt the lonely distance and wild region it implied, with night and winter upon the untraveled mountains where they were wildest, and twelve miles of their fastness, at least, before her, and the snow growing deep. She saw the parallel ridges pinching the valley and lifting it up, and gnarled and naked apple trees marked the few homes and meager farms. Job Snowberger at her side, riding a rougher animal, sighed, and tried to keep up with Katy, and his many groans all took the articulated sound of "persewerin'!" The night came down black, with snow-flakes making the blackness visible, and they saw a light in a field near by.

"I must ask te way," said Job, "or we may freeze to death on te mountain."

She followed him into a kind of lane, and soon there arose above their eyelids an old tumbling house.

"Why, Job," whispered Katy, "tis is Nelly Harbaugh's teserted home; and who can pe in it?"

She rode up to the window and looked within, while Job dismounted and tried the door.

Katy saw a number of men feeding a fire upon the floor. Some she recognized by their blue and gray capes and coats to be deserters from both rebel and Union armies. They were vagrant, thievish men; and some were sleeping, some quarreling, some gambling, while other persons she knew as dealers in contraband things and mountain parasites of the times of war — the man who sold civilian suits of clothes to deserters and bounty-jumpers, the unlicensed whisky-peddler, the army horse-thief, the ruined slave-catcher. Above them all, the firelight showed Nelly Harbaugh's pastings of actors and actresses from the newspapers, with Laura Keene, in "The American Cousin," largest of them all.

Suddenly Katy saw Job Snowberger enter this cabin, unaware of its contents, and ask a question.

Before his mouth was well open, he was surrounded and forced to the floor, and his pockets searched. He shook himself loose, and Katy saw him glance furtively around the bare walls as if for some window or weapon.

"*Unfershamed* (barefaced)! *Unshicklich* (improper)!" Job shouted.

The pointer-dog at Katy's feet barked loudly in the night. Hearing the sound, the tatterdemalions within turned their heads from Job Snowberger, and rushed out to see what else had come.

Katy had just an instant to observe the action of Job Snowberger before they were upon her: he had leaped on a table disordered by refuse food, whisky, and cards, and he brought from over the door, where he knew its place of concealment, the old gun of the sergeant, deserter of the army and of his child.

The thievish gang had seized Job's horse, and, guided by the dog's loud information, had nearly distinguished Katy in the dark, when she, with self-resources never tried before, cried loudly:

"Fire on tem, Union men!"

To Katy's astonishment a gun responded, and a blaze of light, and the agonizing yelp of a dog.

"We're surrounded!" cried the cowards, and vanished in the snowstorm down the mountain gulleys.

"I'm a-persewerin'," sighed Job Snowberger, recovering his horse and carrying the old gun along, "but I'm backshlided, too."

"How, dear Job?" cried Katy, riding after him.

"I've made war — and I reckon my soul's lost," observed the man of peace, very inconsistently adding, "Hooray! *Seech-reich!*"

"Tick-a-tock-a, tick-a-tock-a, tick-a-tock-a!" went Charlie's feet in the snow, and Albion limped after them, still howling fearfully.

"Job," said the girl, unable to see him in the dark, though he was at her side, "I guess you're not very wicked, for you've fired that load all into our dog."

"Hooray!" cried Job again, intoxicated with his personal prowess; "can't you love me some, Katy, for savin' of you?"

"Yes, Job — only keep your hands to yourself and don't pe a fool this awful night! Pray for me — I'm a-growin' blind, and can't set my horse much longer."

"Tick-a-tock-a, tick-a-tock-a, tick-a-tock-a!" — in the bare places of the snow-drift and on the broken stones.

Albion, really wounded by the old flint-lock of earlier wars, defaced by writing-ink, and receiving no pity, must needs go on or perish now, and it was hard traveling for him.

"Poor dog!" called Katy, out of her own misery, to the snarling, squeaking brute.

He snapped at Charlie's heels, and received a side-tip from the shuttle hoof which laid him fairly on his back, howling to all the nations for benignant intervention.

"Coom on!" cried Philodulus, chattering with the cold; "te more we mind dat beast, te less he cares for us!"

"Tick-a-tock-a, tick-a-tock-a, tick-a-tock a!"

The wind now blew on the high staircase of the valley, and the highest rills of Catoctin Creek gurgled away behind them. As the snow ceased to fall, black and wind-bellied clouds moved overhead, giving just light enough to note solitary peaks or knobs in the gullet of the valley, and the ear was smitten by the crash of supernumerary trees resisting not the death-chill of old age. The South Mountain seemed also to have died and to be laid in the valley, that had risen to its stature; for it had disappeared in the west, and all around them was a sort of spongy and stony glade, in which the good gelding, wet with sweat, still made a sound with his feet, like the last American slave picking on his old banjo:

"Tick-a-tock-a, tick-a-tock-a, tick-a-tock-a!"

"We're 'most come to Foxville and to hickle-te-picklety roads," Job Snowberger said, through his great coat-collar; "I don't know which is which, but I'm persewerin'."

A charcoal pit of ignited logs set upright in a circle and covered with earth appeared now in the roadway, giving a little warmth and light, but no person could be seen, although Job hallooed loud; and he noted that there were forks of the road, both going to the north.

"Ich cons hardly du!" groaned Job; "how can one persewere when he comes to two roads, and both p'int right?"

"Go ofer te mountain and not around it, Job, te letter said."

"Te right-hand road seems straightest," Philodulus sighed. "Te left-hand road may take us back agin, on down te mountain, to Cavetown and Beaver Creek."

"O my friend, decide! I am not able to ride much furder; if I git off my horse, I nefer can get up agin."

"Katy, stay here py te fire! Te war I was in tonight has turned my wits. I've shipwracked te faith; and with all my persewerin' — *unshuldich!* — I love you."

His voice trembled, and his bachelor blush was felt in the dark.

"Job," cried Katy, "if I was aple, I'd git off tis horse and slap you! Holt that gun away from your chin, and don't pe leanin' on it; it might haf loaded itself."

"Katy, stay py te warm fire; I'll guard you all night with this wicked musket, and gif you my coat to lay in. We don't know te way."

"Sir," Katy cried, between modesty and despair, "I dare not wait one night, one hour! Go on, some way, any way — or I shall fall in te snow and perish!"

"Let te dog decide, then," Job Snowberger cried, shouting to the dog to go forward.

The dog chose to go to the right.

"Tick-a-tock-a, tick-a-tock-a, tick-a.tock-a!"

They soon heard water trickling, and found themselves following a rill, and the wind began to lull, and the sky parted, letting some moonlight through. The wood-paths divided again near a mountain clearing like a hermit's farm, which lay as in a triangle of gaunt ridges, and showed a ruin but no habitation, and the dog again went to the right, following the stream, perhaps, to bathe his burns and bruises; and this stream was so near the track that in its overflows it had covered the latter with stones, like a road-mender, or rather road-destroyer, showing, by the widening light, a dreary stretch of uncrushed rock, hard sandstone, and other primal stones which would not roll round in the washing of centuries, but remained hard and unshapen like a savage race. Over these infinite stones the good horse picked his way and stumbled, and his knees trembled.

"We must surely pe comin' over te mountain now," Katy thought.

Of this broken stone there seemed miles, and yet the cold brook just beside it had a talk to itself, as if it were gliding comfortably onward among the stunted oaks.

"If Charlie could only wade in there," Katy thought, "he wouldn't bruise me so. Oh, I am sore as if I was full of stones, and every step shook tem! Maype tis is te brook I am to find te book and te wedding-ring in."

There stood a cabin of logs near the road, and Job shouted for people, but only brought out some lean fox-hounds, which chased Albion along the broken stone, and their yelp filled the night. Katy lost the stream awhile; but it returned soon with the power of other affluents, and began to enter the impressive walls of unseen mountains, making themselves felt like dungeon-walls in darkness. There were easier declivities in the road, and again the single-footed racker made a sound like the living spirit of some former water-mill —

"Tick-a tock-a, tick-a-tock-a, tick-a-tock-a!"

"O Shwester Kate!" Job Snowberger exclaimed, "dis love tey talk apout, is te worst of all te Christian's life. Bruder Martin Luter was so persecuted py it that he tried to drown it in te Rhenish wine, and te drunker he got te more he was peteviled, till he had to marry a nun. Maype, if you was to marry me, I could write music like Conrad Beissel and Friar Luter."

Job raised his voice and sang, in high, piping notes, the Christmas-eve hymn of Luther:

"Give heed, my heart, lift up thine eyes!
 Who is it in yon manger lies?
 Who is this child so young and fair?
 The blessed Christ-child lieth there.

"O Lord, who hast created all,
 How hast thou made thee weak and small,
 That thou must choose thy infant bed
 Where ass and ox but lately fed?

"O dearest Jesus – Holy Child!
 Make thee a bed, soft, undefiled,
 Within my heart, that it may be
 A quiet chamber kept for thee."*

Thus the legend of Asia replaced with its songs the owls and katydids of the American forest. Katy listened with awe and consolation.

"Happy could I pe to lie down in a manger, too, Job, and rest my bones; but here is neither ped nor stable; and if it is midnight, we are in Christmas-eve!"

"Tick-a-tock-a, tick-a-tock-a, tick-a-tock-a!"

They could see the enclosing mountains now raise their heads like the Wartburg Castle, where Luther composed and burned, between the dual poles of the human and the divine passion. Pulpits, lofty and cold as Calvin's, on the steep streets of Geneva, those rock-shapes seemed; or, like the papal tiara, they towered above the little stream, or bishops' caps in the narrow alleys of Rome. So runs the rill of human nature through the ramparts of creeds; and travelers, down the brook, want an inn more than heaven; and if the inn is full, a bed in the stable.

Shelter, shelter! how much is it of joy; and what word of pain is like that one of *"shelterless!"* Katy wondered if the infinite millions spent in temples and churches to provide homes for people in heaven, might not afford this world a bare shelter, and straw on every road, like the

---

* Catherine Winkworth's translation.

birth-bed of Mary's untimely-born son in the tavern-stall.

"Tick a-tock-a, tick-a-tock-a, tick-a-tock-a!"

With snowy luster, rocks and bare woods shone, and mountainsides upheld the hemlocks, and in the damper places grew long, open groves of beech trees, as on the bowlder-strewed slopes of the German mountains of Harz. Cedars clung to stones, and spread their roots around them like a hand from the grave, pulling the tombstone in. The little pines leaned against the precipices, starving rather than leap down; the little oaks roved up the desolate ravines, and moonlight shone on a wood-chopper's chips and gleaming axe; the only signs of animal existence. Nothing moved — no rabbit, nor squirrel, nor bird; and the only sound they heard was of the foaming brook, now grown to a fierce torrent, and defying the frost to fasten it more with silver chains. Piled in that torrent, like maledictions from the overtopping cliffs, were mighty rocks flung down and staying the water in cascades — which roared, or boomed, or tingled, according to the resistance; and beneath them were hollow basins in the stones or pools, suspiciously silent after so much conflict. Signs of coal were to be seen in the ledges where the road had delved its way; and down the slopes the horse, with yielding knees, bore Katy, sometimes giving her a shock that seemed to bring an echo, and to make her cry aloud, till poor Job Snowberger, himself nearly dead with chafing and jolting, would cry, pipingly, "O Katy, persevere!"

"Tick-a-tock-a, tick-a-tock-a, tick-a-tock-a!"

The brook was so long, so wild, the road so steep and unknown, that Katy was sure it was the brook she was to wade down to find her wedding-ring, and at every circle of the moonlight on the path she was thrilled with the thought that the magic hoop of gold had been reached.

The dog had become confidential, and trotted at her side, and sometimes the shaggy woods and precipices made a deep, impenetrable shade, beyond which a seeming path would open on the torrent. At one such place the road seemed to end, and a fallen tree appeared to have been felled to notify the travelers. Job called to the dog to go ahead. The animal was soon heard yelping in the bottoms to their left, and there Job Snowberger, in opaque darkness, forced his faltering horse, and Katy followed. The limbs of trees struck them, and thick brush galled their limbs, but still the pointer-dog barked seductively, as if to say, "Hasten and find security!"

They followed along, and there soon appeared light, as from above, upon a smooth place like a trodden way, and in the light the dog was seen at a stand, tail out and muzzle toward them, and foreleg raised.

Job Snowberger pushed along, and the dog bounded before him, and was next seen on a stone amid the deep roar of unseen water — a stone with lichens spotting it, and clay upon its smooth, large face. Albion barked again, and again he came to a "point," as Katy had seen him do so often when congenial mischief was afoot.

"Stop, Job! Te dog never p'ints fair."

Job pulled up suddenly — and he was on the edge of a chasm that would have swallowed him up, at another impulse forward of his horse.

Below him the creek had made its way beneath the bank, leaving the old bed dry and rock-strewed, and its abyss was ragged with sharp stones whetted by the freshets and cataracts which had laid them bare.

"O treacherous hound!" cried Job; "and, Katy, he's persewerin' yet."

As the dog stood on the stone beyond the chasm, revealed in the streaming light through the tree-tops, and still insidiously tempting the travelers on, something seemed hurled at it out of a bow or catapult, and this thing skipped right up the opposite bank like a flying mass of rock with eyes and muscles in it.

Both horses trembled, and seemed to swoon down upon their bellies, and to blow terror through their nostrils.

The opposite steeps and thickets cracked and shook for a few instants, as if with convulsive life.

Then, on a high rock, above the torrent a hundred feet, a beast emerged like a great cat, with ears turned outward and lashing tail, and stripes upon its sides. It bore a parcel in its teeth, and, standing upon that, ripped the object with a jerk of its black-shadowed and shining neck.

The horses turned and rushed back into the woods, and regained the road over the trunk of the fallen tree, and bounded away regardless of descent or obstacle till, under Katy, the good racker found his cultivated gait again of —

"Tick-a-tock-a, tick-a-tock-a, tick-a-tock-a!"

"Gracious! what is it, Job?"

"O Shwester Kate! I ain't seen one on te South Mountain for years. It was a catamount, a painter, and he's killed and eat te dog! I reckon he had prowled te bare mountain for food till he was tesperate."

"He's killed te dog that p'inted me," spoke Katy, shuddering; "but it was Lloyd's dog, and I pity him."

Yes, Albion might have become a favorite on the seacoast, and, as an exotic, have lived several years of luxury; but he fell a victim of the American interior, whence a few animals of the provincial habit and spring still issue forth.

"Tick-a-tock-a, tick-a-tock-a, tick-a-tock-a!"

The single-footed racker soon entered a region with signs of life and improvement; some remains of mills and mill-races were seen, and finally open fields and barns, and at last a town stood huddled in the sheen of moon and frost. Their horses stopped at an old stone tavern on a corner.

"Is dis town Vaynesporo?" piped Job Snowberger, to a man who was shutting up the tavern windows.

"Waynesboro? No; this is Mechanicstown."

"Oh, *unshicklich! Unshuldich!* — Katy, we've come around te mountain, and te kloster is on te furder side."

"I reckon," said the landlord, "you've come down Big Hunting Creek. It's a wonder you tidn't lose your lives. If you'd took the same road the other way, you'd come out at Smithsburg, or Cavetown, and been in the Cumberland Valley; but now you've got the mountains to cross again, and you're fourteen miles, the shortest way, to Waynesboro."

"I couldn't help it. Te dog did it. I was a-persewerin', Katy," Job piped in tears.

A feeling of despair, followed by a resolution of the highest energy, seized upon Katy Bosler. Sending Job peremptorily to bed, Katy took the landlord aside and minutely inquired the way to the Dunker Nunnery of Snow Hill.

"The easiest way is to go to Emmittsburg, eight mile from here, and take the pike. But there you're no nearer Waynesboro than from here. The shortest way is to go up Owen's Creek to Harbaugh's Valley, and turn over the South Mountain and over the short mountain beyond it, and from that view you can see Waynesboro standing out in the plain. Snow Hill is three miles north of that."

"I want my horse fed pefore daylight," whispered Katy — "te strawperry roan, that racks. Please let that man sleep, and wake me without noise. I'll pay you now."

After a night of strange, deep, yet haunted sleep, Katy was awakened and started on her journey. Another creek flowing out of the mountain's mane, gave access to pierce the mountain's head, and by abyss and overhanging height, rock and cascade, narrow pass and cave, the fainting child went on, crossed the South Mountain, and looked back on nature wildly broken and uptilted, and she scaled the next mountain's notch among frozen cascades which she felt to be tributaries of the Antietam.

"Tick-a-tock-a, tick-a-tock-a, tick-a-tock-a!"

From the fissure she descended there suddenly stretched under and away, like a golden scarf, the zone of a prodigious valley in snow and field, stack and large barn, pike and town, miles on miles; soft to the hollow palm of heaven as the young head of David, in its silken curls and rosy blushes to the transparent hand of the prophet, full of shining oil.

The sun was sinking in the west, and as it basked upon the faint gray line of the North Mountain, thirty miles away, it seemed to Katy, this eve of Christmas-day, to be the star of Bethlehem the wise men had followed, and the abundant plain to be the gifts they had brought the newborn baby in the stall — gold, frankincense, and myrrh.

She was delirious now, and only knew the town in the foreground of the great valley to be Waynesboro, and down the mountain tripped her gallant roan —

"Tick-a-tock-a, tick-a-tock-a, tick-a-tock-a!"

Waynesboro has been passed; she knows the old Dunker meeting-house on the Little Antietam, with its ten doors and windows in the low story of stone; she is in the noble woods above the lower road in the valley, and sees the old white Dunker mill; and she has fallen from her horse to the earth at the monastery door and read the notice posted there:

"By order of the trustees of the Snow Hill Society, the undersigned do hereby notify the loafer or vagrant not to call for lodging or otherwise annoy the people, as the law will be used."*

The fainting soul applied the warning to herself: she passed through the long, narrow house by an open hall, passed to the rear and saw no one, and entered the little dairy among the shining pans and tins.

In the water seemed a circle of silver or gold mystically rippled.

"Te ring!" sighed Katy, and sank upon the cold floor.

*W*hen she could see, or recollect, she was in bed and very weak, yet somehow happy. She heard singing of a queer, shrill kind, and looked upon something that shone upon her finger. What could it be that had slid, as if from heaven, upon her slender hand?

"Dear," spoke a voice heavy with music and tenderness, like the bass of Lloyd Quantrell singing, "you have found your wedding-ring."

Hannah Ritner was standing by the bed, as well as Abel Quantrell, both looking at her with interest gracious and mutual.

Katy looked again at the dear-bought ring, and saw that Hannah had nothing like it upon her hand.

"Won't you give her one?" Katy whispered to Abel Quantrell. "It is so comforting! It makes me feel that Lloyd is mine."

"Hannah," said Abel Quantrell, "we always were in love: cube it! Love, multiplied by offspring, and once again by opportunity, make the three times the base. Take the child's ring, and I will put it on your hand and call you 'wife.'"

"No, master. The sacrifice shall be complete: your younger son by this marriage would suffer in his careful sense of honor. *Our* son has become nature's own, and does not need that we should wear a ring."

---

*　　The author copied this from the door of Snow Hill Dunker Nurnery.

"Sho! this child is not married. — Are you, Kate?"

Katy flushed even in her weakness, but, remembering the promise of secrecy made to her lover, she took the ring from her hand and gave it to Hannah Ritner.

"I come a good ways to git it, teacher," she said, "but maype it pelongs to you. Oh, I feel so happy. What is it?"

"This," said Hannah Ritner, holding up a little sleeping babe which she drew from Katy's bed. "Here is Saint Christmas, born in the dairy of them who never marry. — Take the child, master, and look at it awhile — your second grandchild — while I ride for the doctor!"

As the old man looked at himself in the third generation, and Katy wondered what it all could mean, they heard the single-footed racker go out the lane:

"Tick-a-tock-a, tick-a-tock-a, tick a-tock-a!"

Chapter XXXVIII

PURITAN, JESUIT, AND GERMAN

SNOW HILL was a remnant; once a wilderness cloister, or society, which had possessed bright-eyed converts and intellectual piety; but with beauty and youth intellect had also died here, and the old printing-apparatus and printed books, the natural music and mechanical craft, traces of which still continued, only emphasized the dullness and strained devotions of a fragment, which had property enough to make internal contentions, and where Job Snowberger had till now been the beau and baby.

Katy's baby was the first convert Snow Hill had made in many a year, and Job's "nose was out of joint," as the saying goes.

He came half-way in the door to see the baby, got a glimpse of its palpitating head, and went off into the mill to cry and to blush. Had Job been the sole witness of baby's advent into this world, he must needs have left Katy at the roadside and run away. The old belles of the nunnery looked into the mill and made faces at him, saying, *"Dummkup,"* or dunce, and executing little waltzes and jigs quite novel to the holy life.

Some of these silly virgins peeped through the crack of Katy's door, to see the young mother and babe on Christmas-day, and one walked in, looked at the bed a moment, and said *"Kint!"* meaning "brat," and turned up her nose and seemed to blow disgust through her nostrils with her eyes; but all that afternoon this woman scoured the tins in the dairy till they were bright enough to look into, and show her reflected, unexpressive face, the wick of whose experience had never been trimmed and lighted, so that, in the darkness from it, the bridegroom had gone past.

And that night, when all were gone to bed, this queer, roundfaced, sour-looking woman of forty or fifty years, crawled up the stairs and into Katy's room, and reached beneath the quilts to where the baby lay, and, taking it tenderly forth, put it against her breast, and saying, *"Bubbelly, bubbelly, labe goot,"* or *"baby, by-by,"* burst into tears.

Katy looked up in wonder, and reached for her child. The woman turned from her in a kind of quarrelsome pout, sniffed again, and stole away.

"Hannah," said Katy, after she had rested some days and grown strong, "why is love so natural and tangerous?"

"My child, there came into this world a stranger to its nature called Pride, and began to whisper to people till they elected two evil spirits to watch them, called Scandal and Appearances. Since then, no baby has been like the young of other animal life around it, where song and gamboling, innocent delight and no evil-thinking, make nature unceasing Christmas, and every opening bud, or egg, or infant eyelid, a redeeming spirit. Man only, looks beyond life both ways, before and hereafter, for the portion all things, besides, find in living. 'How came you into the world? Where will you go after the world?' These are the questions which man asks alone. The rest of nature sings and loves, and holds to the life that is."

"No, Mootter Hannah; else why is baby-life?"

"Life aspires to life. Death itself, left alone, rejoices in the seed that is dropped into its decay, that it may sprout and bloom. To Nature, the triumphs of intellect and society are nothing, my child. What are all the vanished empires, the social systems, theology, science, literature, and conquest, to the subtle mechanism of your little babe, which eats and sleeps and dreams, which blesses you and drives down the dark stream of time the mirror and spirit of ourselves? The toil of Shakespeare's head is to Nature lost, but a babe, even of Hagar, the desert animals will protect. Seed is the only end of Nature, and the earth is still its garden. God said to Pride, 'I will put enmity between thy seed and woman's seed.'"

"O teacher, how can I tell people that this is my baby and I haf no wedding-ring? Must I pe wicked?"

"To Pride you may be, my child, but not to Nature. Our sins were forgiven by the blessed and unfathered Master, in the great court of the Pharisees, when he wrote upon the ground with his finger in the dust and said, 'Go; sin no more.'"

"*Our* sins. Have you sinned, too, fortune-teller?"

Hannah Ritner looked up and saw Katy's dark eyes shine upon her pale, white face.

"I have had a lover and a son," said the seer.

"Was Lloyd's father your lover?"

"Yes."

As the dark woman faintly blushed, Katy leaned over and kissed her and said:

"Then, Hannah, you're my mother."

"I can be your step-mother, my dear child, and I have tried to be. From the day Lloyd brought you to my cabin I have taken a mother's care of you both. But my son is older than Lloyd; Lloyd's mother wore the wedding-ring, and this babe has society's protection, while mine —"

"Why," cried Katy, "Senator Pittson must pe your son?"

"My son," spoke Hannah Ritner, proudly, "has the protection of the angel which said, 'Thy son will be a wild man, and he shall dwell in the presence of all his brethren.'* He is in the councils of his country; Nature has never marked him with his Egyptian mother's shame, but in the bright blood of the passover, and he does not fear!"

Katy listened with astonishment at the secrets of a society she had esteemed far above her.

"I told you, my child, that you should find your ring by the *book*. Let me open a page of the beautiful book of human nature that is printed in the rose-leaves of my heart! I was a child like you, a woman when scarce in my teens, and inspiring love in the master at whose feet I was his pupil. He was strong and weak as Samson of old. I pulled his justice and resistance down, but never sheared his strength away. I sent him on his course, and let him marry and increase, lest the humble life he would lead with me might rob his country of his services."

"Would he marry you, Mootter Hannah?"

"I would not let him make the sacrifice. I was poor, of influential connections, but romantic and independent like my grandchild, Light. When Abel Quantrell loved me, as I knew, by the intuition which makes me read people's fortunes, I saw his solitude and hunger of heart for my sympathy and companionship, and I knew his poor mother and her large brood were living on his pittance in their distant and rocky New England State. While our Pennsylvania lawyers persecuted him as a stranger, I felt the daring compass of his mind, and saw his infirmities — lame, penniless, tender, and ambitious! I gave his heart rest, and would not add my burden to his back, nor let the fatherhood of his boy rest on his reputation. Men have often been unselfish enough to refuse a woman's hand lest she might be dragged to a lower sphere by them. I found the compensation of my sacrifice in an older friend — one I had refused — who took my son to the West, gave him his name, protected his secret, and gave him education. That true republic, where neither ancestral merits nor sins affect a man's deserts, sent Edgar to the Senate at Washington."

"Mootter Hannah, are you happy?"

"My child, who is? I have my cares; for woman is still a social animal,

---

*   Genesis xvi, 12.

and sensitive to the criticisms of her own sex. My master was not as true as I have been — he married."

Katy kissed her friend upon her great, rich, upturned eyes.

"Forgive him even for that!" the young mother said. "That is why Lloyd lived to come to me."

"My simple dove, I saw in your lover's face the lineaments of his father, and told your fate as it has come — we are both deserted!"

"Oh," cried Katy, "it is te war, not Lloyd!"

"Is the cause Lloyd fights for, against his strong father's will, holy enough to justify the son's selfish anticipation of pleasure in your young life and soul? He could not wait, but let you wait and suffer. His father yielded, too, when the temptations of material life came to him — a lady of beauty, gentleness, and wealth, and family influence in politics. I do not murmur that he forgot me, for I had exacted no terms in the almost maternal passion I felt for his distress; but he forgot his son, and his son has a daughter, who looks into my eyes and rejoices in her noble paternity, while my step-son strikes his own father to the heart as he reflects upon my child!"

Katy could not understand all this refinement of confusions, but she listened on:

"Ah!" cried Hannah Ritner, "there is a taint of self and gainseeking in these Yankees, with all their philanthropy and idealism: Franklin himself was voluptuous and politic, though he loved knowledge and abstract justice. Look at the brother of Abel Quantrell, following him to Maryland, and setting up a slave-pen to earn money! Does Abel wonder that his son, Lloyd, grows up without domestic reverence, is predatory in love and violence, and strikes his country in the face? Give me, after all, our sweet, unselfish, and commonplace life and motive of the Middle States: we profess less, we are slower in public spirit, the outward deifying of morality we are not skillful at doing; we do not hate systems and people from far off, like the Jews of old, sparing neither Philistine nor Amalekite; here persecution never went beyond gossip and back-biting, while yonder it banished, hanged, and whipped."

"Hannah, ain't you an apolitionist?"

"Yes: I gave my enthusiasm when I gave my all, to the proud, obdurate man whose self-love never has conquered his indignations. I recognize his righteous leadership as Miriam, the sister of Moses, prophesied and danced to his law. The great contest with slavery I helped to bring about: John Brown received from me shelter and direction where to strike the vital spot — so close to the free States that Virginia and her slaveholding posterity in the West must needs fall within the seam of war, and slavery everywhere meet a common doom. I must now cherish the soldiery of our cause, and keep watch over the new captain of our hosts, the

President at Washington. He hesitates between mercy and the old statutory gods. He must come to the nature of John Brown, and strike the dragon at the vital point: *slavery* — it must fall!"

Carried away by impulses powerful as those may have been which gave her love's reckless impulsion, Hannah Ritner arose, seeing not Katy nor anything except the lightning-play in her stormy soul, and she planted her feet as upon remembered heights, and looked away, yet inward, as if down at chasms where her life had been banished, and still remained in lonely entanglement with the lines of imperial movement. Her nose was long and hollow, like a bow which shot impressions from without into her brain.

"I believe slavery will fall in these mountains; that its grave is by the Potomac, and that the echoes of its death will die along the South Mountain side. The soul of my friend awaits the reverberation. Yes, he awaits companionship, and I hear the sound of its feet! Who comes, so joyfully, with the whistle of victory, and careless as the happy school-boy's mind on Friday afternoon? Who comes at holiday's brink and bears the sheaves of harvest and does not see the hunter's trap? Oh, linger, linger, gentle friend, for the tyrant hides in wait, his expiring mortality concentered in one blow! It has fallen: I see him reel across the open grave, and the Emancipator is caught up by the Pioneer — Death! Death! but Victory!"

As Hannah Ritner sank down by Katy's bed, a gun went off directly beneath the window of the room, and was followed by a piping cry of —

"Persewerin'! Wictory and te *heilich* life!"

It was soon reported that Job Snowberger had been fooling with the old gun he found in Harbaugh's cabin, and had shot himself, painfully, but probably not fatally.

All sorts of tales were told about Job's accident. Some said that he had become vainglorious since he had fired on the renegades at Harbaugh's, and brought Katy safely across the mountains, and that he had taken to drilling and marching, and had finally shot himself to experience the feelings of the wounded.

Others said he had lost his wits trying to understand the mystery of Katy's baby, and had some way conceived himself to be the undiscovered guilty party.

Others told a queer story about Job being desperately in love with Katy, and tortured between his affections and his vow of monkish celibacy, and that he had resolved to persevere in the holy life if he had to commit suicide.

Whatever the mystery of his act, Job was a changed man when Katy came down from her room after some days, and offered to attend his bed and return his kindness to her.

He was now completely indifferent to her charms and coquetries, and read the great book called "Der blutige Schau-Platz," or "The Baptist Martyr's Looking-Glass," which his father had set up in type at Ephrata, and he composed bits of music under the pages of Conrad Beissel's hymns in the "Turtle-Doves" collection; and toward spring got about, and remained silent, pious, and a little sour till the end of his life.

Some of the bad boys used to call names at Job over the fence, such as *"maidle,"* and *"gowl,"* and *"asle"*; but he was deaf to their tantalizations, and still the warrior spirit revived sometimes in him, as in Narses and other generals of the past; and the next fall, at the love-feast of Snow Hill, when the Seventh-day Baptists were imposed upon by the thousands of disorderly spectators, Job, to use the neighborhood saying, "whipped his weight in wildcats," to the battle-cries of "persewerin'," and "te heilich life."

Relieved of Job's attention, Katy had no other male friend than Hugh Fenwick, who came across from Gettysburg to find her, and a council was held as to the attitude Katy should assume. The novitiate did all the advising. Katy was to await a time when her lover could see her and explain himself, and meantime was to apply her mind to The Book, or, as Hannah Ritner said:

"My darling, the *brook* you are to wade down to find your wedding-ring is your tears of penance and passion; the *book* you are to use for direction may be the Holy Scriptures, or it may be education. Seek which of these — and both may be needed to satisfy you — will fill up the uncertain and contending years till the prodigal lover finds his way back to his father's door."

"Hugh," asked Katy, "maype you had te right te marry me?"

"Katy, I have looked it carefully over. By the law of 1777 no person can perform the marriage rite but established or dissenting ministers, or Romish priests 'appointed or ordained,' and only after three times publishing the names in a meeting-house of the bride's own county. The recent law of marriage is more rigorous yet: 'No persons in Maryland shall marry without a license and triple publication, nor except by some minister of the gospel ordained according to the rites and ceremonies of his or her church.' None of these conditions are answered in your case, and clandestine marriage is forbidden by Rome itself."

Hannah Ritner brushed back her long locks of black and silver, and looked the speaker through and through.

"I am baffled in your character," she said. "Do you understand it yourself?"

"No."

"It may be like the kitten's marks in the snow, gone over and over in her puerile play, till they are without clew or even form. Yet you have had some purpose with this girl. Why did you marry her to Mr. Quantrell? Why do you discourage her now, and see your duty as you disobeyed it? Why are you here again, after your act has driven her from home and made her a mother?"

Fenwick could not withdraw his eyes from her, though his soul was seeking to slide away, like a man from his own deepening shadow.

"Answer!" said Hannah Ritner. "Was it because you loved her?"

"Yes. I saw her suffering. Rather than see her suffer, I married her to another. Everything at that moment seemed excusable to me, and the reparation easy. I thought my superiors would give me indulgence and confirm my presumption. They dare not do it; and I am now in secular occupation, fearing the legal and eternal consequences of my sacrilege."

"Ah!" said Hannah Ritner, "how many a man mistakes his cowardice for religion and evidence of his fitness to be a priest! — Katy, can your simple soul understand why I will not solicit a ceremony to make love and constancy more exalted, when it must come from a frail creature like this man? Yet I think he is no villain. His avowal that he loved you had the touch of nature. Do you love her yet, Fenwick?"

"I do," sighed the neophyte, with downcast eyes.

"Go; trust him!" spoke the seer to Katy. "Love with respect never harmed any woman, and his will not harm you. He is a part of the book you must master. Your husband has deserted you: prepare yourself for life, even if it brings you the wedding-ring from a second husband."

As they turned to go, the babe in Fenwick's arms, Hannah Ritner called him back.

"Do not think, sir, to prevail over Lloyd Quantrell by any trick of deceit! There is a man that Rome itself will stoop to, for the poor privilege of closing his eyes at death, and numbering him among its distinguished converts. He shall compel Rome to do this child justice, if Rome must make you a priest and antedate your ordination to effect it. That man is Abel Quantrell, to whom I am a higher power than Rome to you."

As Katy and Fenwick stepped out upon the lawn, the fruit trees in blossom, and the blue flowers and water-rill stirring in the May, they sat upon a bench at the thick-walled church, and looked back at the nunnery in silence.

"That woman could be a pope," the young man said. "Nature is the widest church. In time it will absorb them all, and God be everywhere."

For months Katy applied herself to The Book. She read much of the fifty books issued from the Ephrata press, wept over the Scriptures, and joined in the devotions of the household. She was of natural piety; but her mind leaped along and over the barriers of this perishing monastery and its dull existence. Hannah Ritner's influence kept her a welcome guest, and her beauty the sour old women deferred to. Her name was changed to "Sister Azuba," or "The Deserted."

Sometimes Hannah Ritner took her away awhile, among the hospitals and on the steamers of the Sanitary Commission, and she saw the bleeding edges of the mighty war that at one baptism immersed the wide continent; but her child called her back, and she learned to love the cove among the Dunker hills, and to hunger for the books of human knowledge.

"Lloyd must not find me ignorant," she said. "And first I must learn the English language!"

So Katy set to work to destroy the old German sounds upon her tongue that had almost grown physiologically into the brain.

The Pennsylvania Dutch speech had no written language nor grammar nor fixed forms of orthography, and was a colloquial language with hardly any literature;* but it was spoken by nearly a million of the American people, less from preference than from one unvaried race intercouse of above a hundred years.

The long *e* where the short one should be used, the use of *oo* for u and of *aw* for the short *o*, the mixing of *t* and *d* and of *p* and *b*, of *j* for *ch* and of *g* for *tsh*, the confusing of the two sounds of *s* and of *th*, and saying *f* for *v* and *w* for *v*, and the leaving out the *h* sound after *w*, were the true labors of the German Augean stable, which required a river of English to purify it; for, under a decaying language, ignorance hides like dust and mice on unused books. Katy was a little of a poet, and she set these defects in verse:

> "*Eggs* are not *aiks, tunes* are not *toons,*
> *Dogs* are not *tawks, spoons* are not *shoons;*
> A *gill* you drink, a *chill* you sweat,
> At *jests* you laugh, in *chests* you get;
> A *gem* you wear on a *chemise,*
> But play no '*zell*' on the *polize;*
> The *vine* you grow, the *wine* you bottle,
> The *which* you whistle, the *witch* you throttle;
> It *iz* a job to chop Jane's chain,
> Not, *iss* a *chop do job Chane's jane.*"

During all such exercise, in which Hugh Fenwick was a teacher to Katy, he received Quantrell's letters by the secret mail and suppressed their tender messages and contents, appeasing his conscience by the arguments that Quantrell was not worthy of his wife, and not entitled to communicate with loyal people. Many a prayer did Hugh Fenwick

---

*   Rev. A. R. Horne, Kutztown, Penmylvania. "German Manual."

make as penance for this deceit, promising to present Katy's soul in conversion at the altar as a brand plucked from heresy and sin; and he also sublimated his patriotism, declining outwardly to speak to a secessionist in Washington, while he was also the guest at Surratt's tavern in the country — until it had been rented to a dissipated Washington policeman — and, after that, a guest at the widow's Washington boarding-house, where occasionally harbored some lodger between Canada and Richmond with a rebel commission in one pocket and the government's oath of allegiance in the other.

Fenwick saw these things while he was in the public service, and cautioned the hostess mildly, but never expressed his indignant sentiments, if, indeed, he had any.

The part he loved to solace himself with, was that of a disinterested mystic, supervising, for authority, and without any earthly prejudice or consideration, the higher relations of the soul.

He had the self-love of a religious amateur who denied to himself the real purposes of his double-dealing, which were to mold Katy to his social likeness, marry her, and in some church or other, it mattered not which, become a comfortable and somewhat sensational ornament.

The mystery of such a being was, that he had a nearly devout respect and love for his friend's wife.

Hugh met both Abel Quantrell and Luther Bosler sometimes, as well as Nelly Harbaugh.

*T*he senior Quantrell and Henry Winter Davis had both antagonized the President, as had the great body of professional abolitionists, partly because the latter were on record against him and their dear intellectual self-love, strengthened by the delights of having been right when only a few, resented the rule of a man who meant to obey the laws first, and, if possible, make the law and not lawlessness destroy slavery. With every personal ambition to emancipate these blacks, the President had even a higher duty — to preserve the republic, for which every aristocracy and court were lying in wait. Emancipation without America, which was nothing but the United States, would be like the voice of Rachel, in Rama, weeping for all her children.

"Cube it!" sternly demanded Abel Quantrell.

"I shall," said President Lincoln; "and, if I understand a cube, it is a solid, and not a sound. We want our country back. You, Uncle Abel, are like a friend I had in Illinois, who had a homemade cherry bounce, bottled up since his childhood, and powerfully heady, of which he used to drink too early in the morning, and it made him see everything in pairs. He was about your age, Uncle Abel — say seventy — when he celebrated his birthday by falling downstairs. He saw two balusters — one was there, and one wasn't there, and he took hold of the one that wasn't there, and fell all the way down."

The tall President had dropped into his chair while speaking, and rested his long feet on his heels, turning up an old pair of carpet slippers; and he now leaned his long arms on his knees, and almost shouted with laughter.

"Cube it, Mr. President!" again said Abel Quantrell, almost pityingly, at such levity.

"Abel," replied the President, "that reminds me of the saying, 'Which of you, by taking thought, can add one cubit to his stature?' It is not ideas now which can win the day, but armies. I want a victory in the field, and after that I may, as a war measure, set a date for the legal termination of slavery. Even then it will be a sound and not a solid, my friend, till our soldier-boys cube it with victory on all four sides of the rebellion at once."

The laugh was on Abel Quantrell, and reformers can not bear to be laughed at.

Mr. Davis considered that the President had not enough personal resentment in his nature. Surrounded by unscrupulous and malignant personal and political enemies, that Congressman wanted aid to smite them in Maryland, but the President was too noble to hate anybody.

The most complete and many-sided man of his day, President Lincoln was too original to have any petty intensity, and his way of meeting intense and narrow people with light jokes and laughter seemed to them the marks of a low mind.

The East was still worshiping appearances and studying European military history, while the West, with an everyday look on its face, was driving the great lines of the rebellion in, and only on the line of the Valley, indicated by John Brown, was the border still vulnerable to the enemy; and he was now to cross it, and invade Maryland.

Hannah Ritner arrived at Snow Hill one day in a hired buggy.

"Katy," said she, "the insurgents have beaten McClellan and Pope, and crossed the Potomac! They are in Frederick City tonight. I was robbed of my single-footed racker on my way to apprise your father, and I came too late — his herd was driven off, and the old farm is a desolation! Catoctin Valley is held by the enemy, and they are investing Harper's Ferry."

"Hurrah!" piped Job Snowberger, coming in with the old Sergeant's gun; "I've persewered as fur as te *heilich* life, and now I'm backshlided and goin' to te *heilich* war!"

Chapter XXXIX

LLOYD'S HUNTING-PARK

*I*T was natural enough that the guide of the insurgent army into
Maryland and Pennsylvania should have been one of the Logans — the
mountain slave-catchers. They knew all the by-roads, and, if the invasion
had succeeded, the blood-hound would have been the next guide,
chasing up fugitive slaves.

The issues to be settled under the South Mountain, and by the
Antietam mill-stream, were the same determined by Charles Martel, on
the plains of Europe — whether women should have souls, and Christians
liberty!

The defeat of the Army of the Potomac there, might have made
slavery the dictator of all future American law and policy; it would next
have compelled Canada and Mexico to remand fugitive slaves, and the
slave-trade would have been opened with Africa and Polynesia, and
Europe forced to consent or fight; for men who would attack the United
States in the proportion of one to three, would not hesitate to attack
any state in Europe; and, in fact, the education of slavery had made the
fiercest white race on the globe since Mohammed and his caliphs — a
democracy practicing slave-driving had all the energy of a popular
society with all the bigotry of Orientalism. The fatalist Presbyterian, to
whom was consigned the capture of Harper's Ferry, as the principal
result of the invasion of Maryland, would have been no unwelcome
general to Abderrahman or Kara Mustapha.

There, under the fatuity of belief that the old mountain hole was
important, the government kept a garrison of twelve thousand men,
while the insurgents also felt annoyed to leave this hollow post in their
rear; and, turning to take it, they lost the great battle of Antietam, and
also learned that their remaining sympathizers in Maryland did not
enlist for open war.

Lloyd Quantrell, like many a one returned to his native State, kissed

the ground, and heard the bands play "Maryland," and read the proclamation of the heir-at-law of Washington, that "freedom of the press has
been supressed"; and next, Lloyd saw the Union newspaper office at
Frederick destroyed. The more honest proclamation was that of the
Maryland rebel brigadier: "Come, all who wish to strike for their
liberties, and each man provide himself with a pair of shoes, a good
blanket, and a tin cup."

The mountain counties had too few slaves to be interested in an
otherwise causeless rebellion.* The false prophet lost nearly as many by
desertion as he took at Harper's Ferry.

There an officer with great consideration for slavery was in command,
and at the head of the government army was another who had rather
instruct his President on the enormity of freedom, than go and strike
the invader and follow him home.

Stonewall Jackson was the John Brown of his cause, and, like Brown,
sat down in Harper's Ferry and paroled his prisoners; and the war was
to continue till every influential officer and civil ruler of the two sides
became fashioned to their likeness — a Union man had to hate slavery,
and a disunionist to fear freedom. Stanton was the one great Unionist
with the intensity of the secessionists themselves; they saw him and
hated their own likeness.

Quantrell served as the staff-officer of a great slaveholder from Georgia, who had seen his political party break up and the Republican party
prevail, rather than let his rival, the opponent of President Lincoln,
receive the Democratic party's leadership. Jealousy, commencing in the
party, had been the widening avenue to treason. This able man, who
had handled the finances of his whole country, now found himself
defending Crampton's Gap, one of two depressions in the long South
Mountain wall; and as the government troops stretched across the
Catoctin Valley to carry the pass, something in their numbers and
deliberation awed his heart. Quantrell was sent along the mountain-crest
to solicit re-enforcements from the greater insurgent wing which held
the pass of the old National road, some miles northward.

Suddenly he heard the strains of a band of music swell up from the
plain behind him, to the air of a Maryland poet of other days:

"Oh, thus be it ever, when freemen shall stand
   Between their loved homes and the war's desolation!
   Blest with victory and peace, may the Heaven-rescued land

---

*   "The section occupied by the Confederate army was inhabited by people
   who had, for the most part, very different views and feelings from those
   of the more southern counties. In the latter, and in Baltimore, thousands
   would have flocked to the standard of Lee," but if, and so forth. —
   Scharf's rebel and official "History of Maryland."

Praise the Power that hath made and preserved us a nation!
Then conquer we must, when our cause it is just,
And this be our motto — 'In God is our trust.'
And the star-spangled banner in triumph shall wave
O'er the land of the free and the home of the brave."

Lloyd's eyes filled with tears as he heard this tender music — plaintive, hopeful, and trustful; like a *Te Deum*, threatening none — execrating none — resting upon the spirit of Heaven in the hearts of the young and devoted.

"Why can not we play that piece?" said he. "I know it is never played in our camps; but why not? Have we lost our State, our flag, our music, too? What have we got in return?"

As he dried his eyes, and looked at his shoes, half unsoled, and his garments and skin dirty, and himself come back, like a gypsy tramp, to the mountains of his childhood, he heard the fifes and drums in Crampton's Gap playing the old, monotonous, drunken-student tune, like a Roundhead drawl sung through the nose to insidious suggestions, to the words —

"Better the fire upon thee roll,
  Better the blade, the shot, the bowl,
  Than crucifixion of the soul,
    Maryland! my Maryland!"

"Nice present for Maryland from her friends," Lloyd reflected — "the torch, the dirk-knife, the assassin's shot, and a bowl, either of poison or turpentine-whisky!"

He drank of the good rye he had purloined at one of the distilleries in Catoctin Valley, the capture of which had appeared yesterday to be the political motive of the whole war.

Suddenly he thought of the Sunday evening when he had left Katy, near Crampton's Gap, and the mysterious music of fife and drum had followed her retreating wheels.

"O prophecy of this desolation!" Quantrell cried; "was it I who brought this war upon my country? Did my coming to these mountains bring ruin to a single heart or shame to any hearth? God help me! What will tomorrow bring them, when every fife screams hate, and every drum beats 'kill'?"

He had stumbled along the mountain-table, when he found himself at the edge of a rock parapet, and identified the spot as that where he had met Isaac Smith and sons under their assumed names, the day he shot the dove.

Looking out upon the rival valleys, Lloyd recognized his hunting-park, somewhat as he had desired it that day, when he said: "I would clean out the whole region like a Norman king; all the wild beasts should return again — none but native American beasts, you bet!"

Every beast was here; every hamlet had become its lair; and from the North Mountain, more than twenty miles away, to Hagerstown and the Pennsylvania vales, stretched the uncoiled insurrection, with one fold only around Harper's Ferry, and the flat head, like the sluggish copper-head snake's, hissing at Baltimore, where lay the government fleet to raze that city if it sought to rise and destroy itself.

The mild, wistful eyes of Abraham Lincoln, whose life would pay the price of his devotion if his army failed, looked out from Washington city — his enemy far in his rear, and hardly a day's march from his person — and he knelt in the agony of his responsibility to the God he had sometimes doubted, and promised, if the battle were favorable, to proclaim slavery the nation's outlaw.

As if Heaven had taken the President at his word, the army charged the South Mountain with a spirit it had never shown. Behind Quantrell, the old statesman's command was torn to pieces, and among the killed were some of his own family; and, in the Gap ahead, the soldiery of the West fought far into the night, and hurled their enemy down the mountain, though he had massed thirty thousand men to keep this rampart. Three thousand fellow-men lay on the mountainside, crying for water and death.

Quantrell was caught up in the tide of flying men and carried on to Sharpsburg — that same little town where he had volunteered to carry the letter to Isaac Smith nearly three years before.

Here, in the dawn, stretched thousands of men upon the bare ground; hundreds more were contending for water at the stone-arched spring.

"The blessings of our Confederacy have been, up to this time," Lloyd thought, "hardly to leave Maryland water to drink."

He went to the commanding general's and asked for a place in the coming battle, and they sent him to the Dunker church near by, where he had plighted troth with Katy; and that night, as Fate would have it, he slept beneath the September stars, in the Dunker grave-yard, where, at the grave of Katy's mother, he had put his own mother's ring upon Katy's hand, and heard a mystic music in the fields.

Now, from the small mountainous ridges, from the fields ribbed with limestone, and the drooping woods of hickory and oak, came the pipes and bands of vast and organized war — not like the handful of John Brown's followers caught in the mountain's jaws, but landscapes of men embroidered between the great quilting-frames of the North and the South Mountains; and the Antietam brook, like a ball of blue yarn, lying on the floor below.

At dawn, next day, the bright needles began their task, and the red and white patches spangled the rich groundwork; like scissors cutting, the shell and shrapnel clipped the air; while smoke of burning rags and flesh went up to God in human sacrifice. It was the domestic quilting-party over domestic slavery.

During that night, thinking of where he might lie the night to follow, Lloyd Quantrell imagined he saw on the South Mountain summit the gaunt form of John Brown demonstrating with a pike upon the great blackboard of the battlefield, and saying, "This, gentlemen, is the inevitable line of war!"

*T*he battle of Antietam may be likened to two leopards lying in a brook, and fighting all day with their heads and teeth, and not till near night remembering the terrible claws upon their hinder feet, when these, also, do ferocious work.

At light of Wednesday morning, the flexile animals began the roar of war, contending for the Dunker church through corn-fields and lanes; and that little temple of the peaceful Dippers, standing on a white turnpike in the edge of beautiful woods, was the only Christian sign to twenty-five thousand dead or bleeding men, who lay that night beneath the breeze that carried the symphony of their wails to the old mill-wheels in the creek, which turned as innocently to blood as to water. These mills had ground out flour for Washington's army, and for the French wars a hundred years before.

The three arched bridges of the creek typified to many a burning man the three heads on Calvary with the hyssop at their lips.

In little villages, like Nazareth or Bethlehem of old, the taxed people crowded to pay Pilate the currency of blood, and many a pale virgin heard Joseph the carpenter's saw all the night working in human bones.

Artillery had been busy as the talk of crows in the standing corn, for a full day's farm-hands' work; the volleys of musketry seemed to rend the intervening mountains, and account for their present partitioning; the old sycamores above the sluggish windings of the creek calmly slept in the tornado of iron, like the Dunkers in their graves.

How many a barn of stone, such as were scattered over that rolling battle plateau, seemed to its fugitives of both armies, who crowded there fraternally, to be the palace of God's abundance, until the missile of Christian chemistry made it burst to flame, and be old Torquemada's sacrifice to the faith!

In grassy cross-lanes, where the sighs of pastoral love had passed in the innocent sight of nibbling sheep, there lay at morn the specters of entangled bodies, swelling, to quick decay, like the hewed trees upon the mountains and the corded wood.

By night, the lamps of good Samaritan and robber moved among the sufferers, hearing the cry of "water," and answering it with rapine; or the cry for "death," and answering it with water and with wine.

The whole world contributed to that last supper to slavery; the multitudinous tribes that had swelled by their mutiny and emigration the, as yet, unwelded American race, dipped in the sop of Antietam, and sighed in all the tongues before the Pentecostal day.

The public enemy, with the Potomac at his back — looped up to his flanks and cinctured by his pontoons — held the horizon line above the creek, and watched the three stone bridges of the Antietam; but only at the far left was battle given for the Union willingly, and it seemed in the moral laws of the world ordained that the commander, who would qualify freedom in his heart, could receive only qualified obedience. The nearest bridge to Sharpsburg was not attacked till afternoon, though ordered to be carried at dawn; and when that town was almost taken, the returning victors from Harper's Ferry appeared and saved it.

Thus one hundred and fifty thousand men had tried a whole day to destroy each other, upon the issue of two nations or one — no other moral point was then at issue.

But the President at Washington had recorded his vow. The day but two after the battle he read to his cabinet the proclamation of emancipation, and the Monday after the battle — washing-day in the State — it was published to mankind.

Before it serfdom went down everywhere. The Russian and Brazilian followed the spirit of old King Frederick, and the American followed the example of Frederick's sword-wearer, Captain John Brown.

These were the words of mercy, born out of the autumn harvest of the Dunker's vale:

"On the first day of January, in the year of our Lord 1863, all persons held as slaves by the people in rebellion against the United States shall be then, thenceforward, and forever, free."

The stream of Dutch immigration moving down the Cumberland valley from the Delaware, had prepared the battlefield of emancipation, and verified the proclamation of Mennonites and Dunkers a century and three quarters before: "We shall doe to all men licke as we will be done ourselves; making no difference in what generation, descent, or color they are."*

In the night the enemy had abandoned Maryland and crossed the river.

---

*   Mennonite protest against slavery to the Pennsylvania Quaker slaveholders, April 18, 1688.

Not long afterward, President Lincoln rode from Frederick City across the mountains, in the month of October, to see these battlefields — the nearest to his fame — and they took him to the mountain-farm of John Brown, whence that outlaw had descended upon Virginia with his Gideonites, nearly three years before, in the same russet month.

The President got down from his carriage in the lane by the old log-hut, and asked the privilege of entering the spot alone.

He looked within the humble stone basement at the bare floor, and peeped into the small, contracted loft.

He sat in John Brown's own room; and the memory of his childhood, in such a hut as this, brought back the recollection of his mother and her barefoot brood.

He thought of his tanned and hazel-eyed mother, crossing the Ohio to a home as bare as this, among the wild pines, and a little clearing of Indian corn, in the bottoms of Indiana. He thought of her dying when he was only nine years old, and the digging of her lonely grave, without a preacher near to see her dear mold go down beneath the October sycamore; and of his desolate father, looking his last upon her with a sound of inarticulate woe and wringing hands. The trees without made the same sound now in the same October weather, saying Indian things in the afternoon light.

"Dear mothers of poor boys!" the President said, "look down in pity on the orphans who have made their way to public life in honor of your characters, and never find the unselfish joy you gave them, even in the solace of such opportunities for good as poor John Brown's and mine! Oh, could you tell me, mother, that I am right, and give me the luxury of that great grief I felt when you were suffering, I would gladly lie down here and surrender to the silence of a grave like yours, the honors and the troubles I am so much envied for!"

Tears bade the President go down to the old spring-house and bathe his eyes. As he reached it, a large, black-haired woman sat there beneath the hooded roof, and looked up at him like one expected, and with compassion like the mother of his youth.

"My son," she said, in deep, indwelling tones, "have you come, also, to the martyr's farm? Shall I see you go out of this lane never to return, however victorious?"

"I know your face," the President said, in pleasant recognition. "You are one of the hospital nurses and Sisters of Dorcas who come sometimes to my office. Did you know John Brown?"

"He was another son of mine," the dark woman said; "I brought him to this barren shrine, near the hut where I had ministered to many escaping slaves. I saw his destiny, and I see yours, President. Let old Hannah Ritner, the witch of Smoketown, look into your hand!"

The President hesitated, still looking at her kindly, and he touched his moist eyes with his hands.

"Be careful, friend," he spoke; "my sensibilities have been a little moved by thinking of some things of childhood, and I derive from my old Dutch ancestry, which lived at both ends of this same valley, a vein of superstition. I hope you will not press me too hard."

"Your fortune has already been told, my gifted son."

"Yes; once it was. When I was a young man I went to New Orleans, and saw a beautiful yellow girl sold on the block, and I wished I might live to see slavery end. That very day a fortune-teller — an old Voudoo — solemnly told me that I would be President, and all the Negroes would be free."*

"It has come to pass, my noble son! I will soon be laid away, obscurely as the patient mother you were just invoking by those tears, and, like the Scripture witch of old, I would connect my intuitions with your fate; for you look down on me like Jonathan, the son of Saul's own stature. Give a poor mourner for the hero who died on the gallows, that hand which executed his unsuccessful purpose with the more merciful pen!"

The President held out his hand. She took it and drew him toward her, and, gathering up her sheet of black and silver hair which had fallen in the spring, she wiped his eyes and scoured his palm with her hairs.

With face bent over his hand, and accents which were low, but made her bosom throb, Hannah Ritner spoke these words"

"The fierce are threatened oft,
    And live life out;
The wolf assails the soft —
    Have thou no doubt!
He whose remaining gun
    At thee takes aim,
Shall save the tenderest one
    All of his fame!"

When the President heard these words, he saw the woman sink to her place upon the stone, by the log spring-house, under the rotting roof.

"Thank you," said he, "for the kindness of your augury. When my time comes, may God find me with no cares upon my face!"

*D*uring the battle for the Dunker church, Lloyd Quantrell, at the head of a detachment from everywhere: conscripts, filibusters, lads taken

---

*   This prediction is recorded in Arnold's "Life of Lincoln," p. 31.

from school to stop bullets, and lads never meant for school at all, but to be "sand-hillers" and "crackers," like all their generations; bright Virginia yeomen and ardent young Carolinians, Irishmen from the wharves of cities, creoles from the levees, with Spanish and St. Domingo blood; fat, chicken-fed Georgians and Alabamans, lean duelists and card-players from Mississippi, men without origin from the spontaneous grass of Texas, and freckled skeletons from Tennessee — fought the ever-recurring advance of the Union army with the business coolness and rallying power he showed in Baltimore in firemen's times. Though Lloyd had reasoned upon the errors and follies of the secession cause, he gave it his full physical loyalty, and on his native soil would surpass his best endeavors, in the sight of all these wild levies.

His gun in hand at times, his pistols at others, his sword at closer quarters, and at times with nothing at all, he made the trembling stand, cheered the young tyro at man-killing, pointed the place of latest danger, and hurried to make it good; and, gigantic in stature, free in humor, forgetful of everything but the pleasure and hotness of the fight, he stood more distinct than a general, with clothes ripped by bullets and hat already ragged, one arm in a sling and his pair of new boots taken from a Federal corpse, his face black with powder and his food an ear of corn, and the dead around and before him unobserved as the limestone ledges which stood also in battle-lines under the beautiful woods.

His Negro, Ashby, brought him water at times, constant but automatic, and once in the lull of battle, when far away the artillery roared like lightning in the mountains, Lloyd raised a laugh among his desperate but discouraged men by saying:

"Ashby, how did you get on *this* side? The Yankees will hang you!"

"I's cornscripted," replied the Negro, "like most of dese yer patriots — cornscripted by my 'fections!"

The blue line of battle came on again through the shot-mowed Indian maize, announced by the skirmishers falling back with reports like pop-corn in the pan.

"Now, boys," cried Quantrell, "we'll blow them out like a candle! We've had a little rest. Lie down behind the stone copings and take aim, and fire low — only when I give the word."

The emaciated, awed, but energized battalion fell down, and awaited the shock of war.

"Great Patapsco!" laughed Quantrell, "how many more Yankees can there be? We've killed a million, and here they come again. This war will last till the Yankees learn to fire low, and then it won't last six months."

He was a great comfort to his men — candid, saucy, satirical, as apt to sing as to swear — and now he, alone, stood up, gnawing a half dry ear of corn, and shaking the cob at the enemy — otherwise unarmed — and daring them to come nearer:

"Come on! Right here, to meeting! Come to love-feast! Come get your feet washed! Come get your hair cut! Come and get some lamb-soup! Come, brethren — come to hell!"

Stalwart and ragged as a pirate, Lloyd's sense of humor even in this moment of intensity rose supreme; for the Federal leader was, like the Dunkers he had described, with straggling beard and shaved lip and long hair.

A blast of flame and lead blew from the Northern rifles, and the old Dunker church cracked like a white slave under the rawhide.

"Hold fast! I'll make him who fires before I speak, eat all this corn-cob! Low, now, and — *fire!*"

The ground burst with smoke, and in the smoke rose the feeble rebel yell, and on before was another yell like women screaming.

"Snuffed out!" exclaimed Quantrell, grimly; "all are dead that have got legs. Give me a fresh ear, somebody!"

His men had hardly congratulated themselves, when the blue line reappeared, decimated, shorter, but steady yet — reformed behind the knoll and the corn — and the bearded figure leading it on, wore his arm also in a sling now, like Lloyd Quantrell.

"That Yankee's almost as saucy as I am," chuckled Lloyd to his men. "Now, down again, and finish them! Not a trigger goes till I call out! — What are you doing here, Ashby? Go to the rear!"

"Don't you want your sword, mosster?"

"No. Give me a drink! — *That* is a cool chap yonder, sure! Now, *low* — fire!"

As the smoke and dust arose from the fields, the same mournful wail and the same rejoicing rebel yell echoed to each other.

"The graveyard's full!" said Lloyd; "I don't see a man!"

As the volleys of musketry went round the circuit of the battlefield, and the hushed and wondering soldiery gazed forth from the Dunker woods, they saw the same man, in beard and long hair, appear at the edge of the corn-field, at the head of a poor and uncertain handful of men in blue. He waved a sword and shook his head, and seemed to be saying, "Forward!"

It was in vain. The waft of death, twice blown from those mysterious woods, had broken the hearts of his followers.

"Come, brother!" shouted Lloyd, "we'll divide the porridge with you. Bring them along! — And you, my men, down there again, and wait for the word!"

The bearded man seemed now making a speech. He threatened his soldiers with a drawn pistol. He stripped his sword-sash from his body and threw it on the ground and stamped upon it.

"They won't come," said Quantrell; "I wouldn't if I was they. But the bully, yonder, is a lion."

The man they looked at now walked right toward them, head up, and the heroism of death in his tension and devotion. He came on, pistol in hand, not to surrender, but to defy, and to set the example of duty, and to die.

"Why," Quantrell said, "if this was his church, and he the preacher of it, he couldn't show more confidence walking up to his pulpit. Don't fire at him. Don't kill that man!"

To the credit of the worst among them, there was no such intention. His personal, unattended valor, and the appreciation of it, encompassed the whole battalion of his enemies. But it became apparent that he must die, lest he kill some one or many among them. His pace never slackened, nor were his features relaxed. He meant to give his life, but to exact life for it.

The whole stooping body peered up to see him; guns were cocked, and his heart seemed to beat visibly in the air where he walked, like the perforated cardboard it was in a moment to be.

"Don't shoot so game a fellow-man!" called Lloyd; "I'll trip him up and take him alive."

As he and they all stared at this effigy, whose breathing they could almost hear as it came at full momentum, like a bull to the Indian ambush, their flank, which they had neglected for this spectacle, flamed and thundered, and Lloyd Quantrell turned his head to see the woods full of blue blouses and charging men, and to hear a wail of anguish at his very feet, and see his battalion rise and rush from his side in the panic of demoralization.

At the same moment a pistol went off at his own ear, and he grappled with a strong man.

Another human body rushed between, and the pistol was again discharged.

Lloyd seemed to be in a burning house, and suffocated.

*H*e awoke in the night, clasped in some one's arms, helpless, athirst, and everywhere in pain. The air smelled of the tons of sulphur shot into it a whole day long, and spasmodic cries or dying wails, the lonely trumps of camps, or random picket guns, ascended to the stars.

"Help! countrymen! Help! Oh, help!"

His wail also had arisen among the rest, for he felt like a sick babe.

The person in his arms relaxed his grasp, and said:

"Mosster?"

"O Ashby! Take me up, my poor old friend!"

The Negro's throat seemed to rattle, and he also sighed.

"God's took me up, Lloyd! I took de las' shot Luther Bosler fired at you. De first hit you and fetched you down. He's lyin' yer, too, wounded wid your sword: I had to run it in him — he was so brave."

The Negro's form seemed to stretch, and his lips to give forth bubbles. Lloyd shouted for help again, and this time not for himself.

"Ashby! Servant! O my friend!"

"Lloyd, good-bye! I'm a pore black man, but I love you. Oh, don't oppress my people. Let whisky alone: it's ruinin' of you. — Daddy — I'm comin'!"

A long suction, a gap, and silence.

Lloyd put out his hand with pain, and the black face was cold with a night dew that awaits no morning sun.

"Help! help! Some water! Oh!"

Voices and a lantern came near, and people were heard speaking in old German. Soon there was a cry of affection, and the words, "Sohn! Bubbelly! O Luter — Bi'm-by."

"Father, attend to te people first here at my right. They're suffering te most. Give them a drink of your water and whiskey: it's good, now."

A man raised Lloyd's head and pressed cold spirits to his lips, and said:

"Drinksht! You was Yasus' man, too."

"Jake, don't you know me?"

The man wiped Lloyd's face and held the lantern to his eyes, and fell back, as in horror or hate.

"You?" he cried. "You robbed me of my heilich dowb, my Katy! We fed you, and you bit us. — Luter, te feind, te difel is py your side! Don't speak mit him. He dies in hell — Bi'm-by!"

Luther did not hear; he had fainted.

W̅hen morning came upon the battlefield, Ashby lay stark upon his back, testifying to the spheres, with eyeballs white as the fading moon.

All day Lloyd lay there in delirium, shouting unconsciously, and at night it seemed that millions of lamps were moving over the battle-plain seeking out the dead. He lost all sense of time or place, or everything but torment, and only heard repeated the old man's bitter words: "He dies in hell bi'm-by!"

He felt a breath of cooler air, and heard a voice say:

"Lloyd!"

He was in a boat upon a sort of bier, crossing a river, and Hugh Fenwick looked down at him, saying:

"*Dominus vobiscum!* Poor friend, I have sent you to your own side of the river!"

"Virginia? Oh, let me stay in Maryland! I want my wife, my father!"

The boat grounded on the pebbles at Shepherdstown, and Quantrell was abandoned to his political environment.

*I*n the long hospital, at Washington, Luther Bosler lay, with his sister and Hannah Ritner by his cot.

Hugh Fenwick came in to these, and took Katy's hand.

"*Benedictus,* my pupil. Lloyd Quantrell is dead!"

Chapter XL

INSTIGATION

JOHN BEALL settled down to milling in Iowa for a few weeks, and saw nothing to his liking. The people were earnest for their country's support and union, and suspected himself and his friends — who came from Missouri and Kentucky, and lived between the lines — to have some incendiary project on foot. The Iowans were not the undecided people who lived in the Eastern provinces, and when they set their fierce regard upon Beall he fled to Canada.*

There sullen imaginings he had indulged in Iowa were re-enforced by the society of escaped prisoners and cowardly fugitives from military duty, who had taken into their confidence certain predatory Canadian Scotch, ready with mechanical suggestions or bloody foray.

Beall had once thought of starting an insurrection among the Confederate prisoners at Chicago, but now was persuaded that Johnson's Island military prison was the place to raid from neutral soil, as it was out in Lake Erie, defended on the water by a small armed boat, and in the line of Canadian steamships going up the lakes.

In Montreal the liquor-dealer, Martin, from Baltimore, had established himself in a small note-shaving and war-supply business. He was a man of Irish stock apparently, bitter against the flag of Irish refuge, and desperately intent on making money.

In a retired room of his lodgings a meeting of conspirators was held around a singular piece of mechanism, called "The Hozological Torpedo" — an instrument to run by weights for a long given time, when it would explode a chemical preparation. A red-haired Scotch merchant present explained that he owed to a refugee college professor from Virginia the secret chemical in the apparatus, while the mechanical work

---

*   "Suspicions being aroused as to his real character, through the imprudence of his friends, he was obliged to flee the country." — Lucas's "Memoir of John Yates Beall," Montreal, 1865.

was English, ordered and imported by him. He wanted to sell the incendiary article to the insurgents, and realize a fortune. John Beall spoke up to this man, whose name was Keith, saying:

"I can't approve of that method of warfare yet. You murder innocent people by it as indifferently as the guilty. It will destroy a vast ocean-ship of thousands of tons burden, you say; but are the innocent passengers – women and babes – to be left out of our prayers? The idea is too monstrous!"

The moral sensibility of the Virginia vestryman divided the sentiment of the party. They were bitter, white-livered men, against whom the war was going hard everywhere but in Virginia, and they burned to carry devastation into the new and intrepid West, which had so recently dawned upon their consciousness as the land of Lincoln, Grant, Burnside, Buell, and the Odins and Thors of the forest.

"You will come to it," said Martin, touching his malt whisky to his lips, "when the West re-elects Lincoln, and pens your whole Confederacy up between the Alleghanies and the Potomac. We considered that one Southerner was equal to three Yankees, but left the West out of our calculation. We have tried it every way, and can make no impression upon it. You, Captain Beall, know that all the Knights of the Golden Circle, Vallandigham movements, and Kentucky neutrality jobs have jailed. Nigger emancipation will be accepted, too. The Union mountaineers in Tennessee, the Carolinas, and Alabama will swell the Western Yankee army. We must blow up all the commerce of the Mississippi Valley and the lakes, set Chicago, Buffalo, Detroit, and Cleveland on fire, and light the flames of death and damnation in their rear!"

Keith, the Halifax Scotchman, arose and toasted this sentiment, exclaiming:

"You think anything's fair, Martin, in war or trade? So do I."

"What we want," spoke Beall, "is a crew of Confederate-line picked men, sent out on a blockade-runner, with a cool man in command, to ship here at Montreal for the Canadian mines. Their light artillery and weapons can be shipped as freight. In Lake Erie they can seize the steamer, point for Johnson's Island, run down the Yankee gunboat there and board her, and open with artillery on the stockade. Eight thousand officers will join us there; we will seize the shipping in Sandusky, and attack every city on the lakes."

These words, spoken in fitful, smothered sentences, out of cold and brooding eyes, filled with gloomy fanaticism, alarmed all the timid majority in the place. The Falstaff of the band looked at the door; the banished statesman breathed quick and rose to go; the cackler and Federal spy in the party reached for liquor, and said "good," in a thin, small voice.

"Where is such a leader to be had?" the medical Satan of the band inquired.

"I know a man whom I shall ask to be commissioned for the work, when I reach Richmond."

The door opened, and Booth, the actor, entered, who had been moving between the new oil-regions about Buffalo and Montreal. His unexpected coming alarmed all but Mr. Beall, who greeted him at first distantly.

"Gentlemen, don't be disturbed," said Booth. — "I want to see you, Martin, about shipping my theatrical wardrobe on your blockade-runner to one of the Southern ports. We have a good many destitute Maryland soldiers in the South, and I have got a scheme to go there and play, to raise them funds."

He sat down and talked about his enlisting against John Brown, and restored the confidence of the band.

"How will you enter the Confederacy, John?" asked Beall. "I must get there some way. I am poor, and broke."

"That's just what I came to see friend Martin about. He knows everybody in the old, lower counties of Maryland, and I want some letters to them. Oil is played out; and I'm going out of it and into land."

Time passed along, and the blockade-running vessel of partners Keith and Martin went down the St. Lawrence River from Quebec, well insured, and with the wardrobe of the actor, Booth, on board. In a few days she was found wrecked in the Canadian gulf, and all souls lost; and Mr. Martin, who was a passenger, perished from the world.

Mr. Keith had taken Mr. Martin at his word, and put a hozological torpedo on the vessel, wound up to explode at the proper time and spot, which would prove his loss and recover the insurance. All had been fair in war and trade.

But Mr. Booth kept the letters of introduction from Mr. Martin to the old families in Maryland.*

Booth relieved the necessities of Mr. Beall, and they went together from Montreal to the United States.

The American civil war had produced on the Canadian boundary a similar demoralization to that already described as latent on the lower Potomac, and Canada was long plagued by raids, and was altered in political character through her jealousy of the great republic, and, perhaps, of the sentiment of President Lincoln, that slavery and the divine right of kings were "the same principle";† and twenty years after

---

*   Related to the author by Marshal John P. Kane, of Baltimore, to whom P.C. Martin gave a letter of introduction to Booth. Ten years later, Keith, under the false name of Thomassen, blew up an ocean-steamship at Bremen in time of peace, to recover insurance, and died of the wounds he received.

the United States came to peace, Canada was hanging her rebellious
Riels and other scions of seventeenth-century superstition.

Beall and Booth were both individual and secretive men, and something mutual on their minds caused them to cross the frontier, without
any conference, at another than the usual route. Booth held the purse,
and he directed the travel, guided into the wilderness of New York by
his gypsy love of wandering.

They came one afternoon to a solemn spot in the Adirondack
Mountains, where a cabin on a hillside looked out upon a mighty
amphitheater of peaks, and in a neighboring gorge the adjacent springs
ran into the river Hudson and the St. Lawrence lakes — systems spanning
in their flow nearly all America that was free.

Near the cottage-door stood a great rock, and beside it was an old
scarred tombstone, dense with inscriptions, of which one said:

JOHN BROWN,
Born May 9, 1800,
Was Executed at Charlestown, Va.,
Dec. 2, 1859.

Three slain sons and the father of John Brown lay here beside him,
in the solitude of the oldest mountains on the globe, at the earliest birth
of human life in the forest, and the pioneers of freedom.

Booth said to Beall, as they read the inscriptions, in silence, of the
Revolutionary father, the executed son, and the devoted grandsons:

"Has this man ever lost his influence over you, John?"

"Never!"

"Nor over me. His proclamation of war has become in Lincoln's act
the law of the land. He reached in a campaign of thirty-three hours a
fame that will last forever, if the slave States are to be beaten."

"All is not lost yet," affirmed Beall, with intensity.

"Lincoln is the tyrant of the South," spoke Booth, returning to his
old dramatic manner. "What is he worth to us?"

"Nothing, I reckon."

"Not as hostage?"

"No. I saw in the West hundreds of men just like him."

"I will take you to see him," said Booth.

They reached the city of Washington in a few days — Beall in the
uniform of a Federal lieutenant; and the actor, his friend, acquainted
with everybody, and vouching for the silent stranger. In that capital of
an enlightening idea, like the new star over Bethlehem's shamble,

---

§   "It is the same spirit that says, 'You work, and toil, and earn bread, and
     I'll eat it.'" — Lincoln's speech at Alton, 1858.

malignant suspicions of strangers did not exist; and, to further protect his friend, Booth put him under the social care of Senator Pittson's family.

"Let me tell you a secret, John," said Booth. "Light Pittson is my affianced wife."

The National Hotel was the center of the new Western society at the capital, and there Booth and the Pittsons had long been boarders; and the fine, impulsive daughter of the senator had attracted the fatal regard of the dark-eyed and insidious actor.

He sometimes appeared upon the stage in Washington to oblige a friend at a benefit, and Light saw his almost glittering face and trim, powerful figure, in classical or melodramatic characters; but she saw him oftener in recitations in the private rooms of the hotel, where he controlled many a wild army blade or family of an absent officer, and was the poetical character of that crowded house.

He caused it to be understood that he had made a fortune speculating in oil lands and wells — a development in American nature contemporaneous with the loss of cotton and slaves — as if abundance and compensation were the returns for doing right.

Booth was universally considered a fortunate and retired man, no longer subject to the imputation of his profession, social and handsome; and if looked upon adversely by prudent mothers, he was the exciting principle in many a daughter's heart, who could not separate artificial from real heroism.

Maidens with fathers at the front of war, and foolish or unprincipled wives whose husbands were in ships on blockading or cruising service, or upon the military staff, felt the dark wizardry of his eyes, his confidential, low tone, and the touch of a hand daring in its mingled respect and familiarity.

He had measured the virtue of the world by the stage, and considered himself of a theatrical and political aristocracy. His father he supposed to have been the relative of lord mayors and great public men, and the noblest figure on the British stage. His pride was greater than his assertion of it; for, like many people in the weaker professions of *belles-lettres,* he had no capacity for facts or affairs, and applied the scale of superficial art to everything. He could no longer study even the plays with conscientious devotion. Too early success in acting, and admiration, flattery, and worldly lusts, had made him one of the most self-contained idiots in Washington.

There stood the powerful fiber of an athlete, the exterior of a gentleman, and the apparent descent of genius, without discipline, humility, or much reality, deceiving himself and everybody.

The fabric was false in everything but headstrong pride, and by his physical exercise he was dangerous. He could whip almost any man he met with his fists; he excelled in arms and the gymnasium; yet he had no conception of the regularity and honor of war, and the brute in his nature did not permit the soldier to enter there. Thus, in the Rome of the New World, he was a mere gladiator under the delusions of a patrician.

He knew nothing of international law and obligations, nor of the moral tone of mankind, and supposed that a boundary-line stopped at once pursuit and public opinion.

How much slavery, and how much an intemperate, possibly insane descent, aggravated this precocity of self-will, may be inferred.

He had attended school with some of the rising young insurgent chiefs, and yearned to rank with them in prominence; and the idea that liberty included black people was atheism to him. Unquestionably a victim of the slave code, whence came his brutal part, he was also derived from the more intemperate and reckless years of a father who had lived upon the consuming fire of an inadequate and unprincipled genius.*

Republican surroundings had given this scion of the English actor a high sensibility as to his descent, intensified by the homage of school-boys and gossips, and obscurer-born actors, and the only liberty he understood was slaveholders' privileges. His political faith was that "all abolitionists ought to be hanged," while yet he howled "liberty" on the stage with such circus feats as cleared the good seats, and finally satisfied the gallery; and once he managed a rude little theater in Washington, playing his father's most violent parts to little advantage.

There was mixed with Booth's cool self-appreciation a derived passion to get along well in the world. He had, therefore, picked up a smattering of speculative talk, and used about six thousand dollars of his savings, from Southern acting, in oil lands and exploitings; but he wasted in country amours the time he had designed for that commerce, and was now thinking of something between acting and speculation to raise money and fame at a sudden bound, for he was growing poor.

Thus he professed to be rich for social influence, and the social influence he exerted upon the managers of theaters, while all these pretenses were fraudulent. He was neither independent, nor an artist, nor a gentleman, nor intelligent enough to pilot himself through those false situations without losing some portion of his coherence.

A treacherous deed of some kind he had in view, and already it began to draw him into abstraction and dissipation. He did not know what it

---

*   "During this tour (1835), the calamity, which seemed to increase in strength and frequency with maturer years, assumed many singular phases. When his habits were the most temperate and abstemious (in youth), we occasionally find those slight aberrations of mind . . . between genius and madness." — The elder Booth's "Life," by his daughter.

might be; but it was to deceive one population and become a hero in another — to take a wife, at least, out of the North, and money out of the South, and be some kind of a Junius Brutus or Claude Duval.

Senator Pittson took Booth and his friend Beall to the President's house; he liked Booth rather the more, that he seemed to solicit nothing.

The President, that morning, was expecting some embassador, foreign general, or prince, and the doors were closed to the public; but the President himself came out in the hall, hearing Senator Pittson's voice, and told him to use the time till it should be required, and to bring his young friends in.

They entered the chamber of emancipation.

"And this is the son of Booth, the actor? My eloquent young friend, I have seen you act: it was a little robust; but artistic progress, I have noticed, is from the robust toward the trained; and if there is nothing strong in a horse, training him seldom comes to much. My robust generals, I think, will get the science of the thing some day; but, ah! — if my scientific generals would only be a little more robust!"

As President Lincoln spoke, he looked out of the window upon the new-made forts encircling his capital, without whose ramparts the insurgents were even now conscripting to make up the losses of Antietam. A look of pain crossed his face, which also wore the age of his responsibility. He was dressed in fine broadcloth, and, standing six feet four, looked dignified in every inch.

"Lieutenant," he said to Beall, "where were you wounded? In Kentucky? Tell me, how does my native State take my proclamation of emancipation?"

"Not favorably, Mr. President."

"So I fear; but its benefits will set the intellect of the South free, and I believe that the Southern head is the best natural head we have. That is the head I carry — one of the poorest specimens, I suspect — but if I could confer a great blessing on my old kin and tribes, it would be to give them some of the free air and joy of looking back at slavery from the other side. Slowly I have progressed that way — perhaps God has led me along — and the mind grows confident in it, like jealousy dismissed from a husband's spirit, when a prejudice against the wife of his bosom has been fully dispelled. The world wants self-restraint; but restraining others in what God gave them breaks all habits down. Sweet will be the scene, some day, of freedom in the cotton as in the corn; but better yet when the reign of intolerance is gone from the ruling mind, and the master's intellect is released to humility, fraternity, and knowledge."

Beall looked up at Mr. Lincoln out of pinched eyes, as if at some social inferior in a pulpit, but Booth remarked:

"Oh! the States in rebellion must lay down their arms, and the abolitionists accept your policy, Mr. President; then we will have the Constitution and Union again."

The President looked at Booth considerately, and said:

"To me it would not matter long if the Union could be restored with slavery still milking at its breast; but you, with many years before you, would receive the benefits of a more complete revolution, and for your sake, and yours, my gallant young friend" (to Beall), "I accept, with a sorrow which is not dissatisfaction, the belief that the war will be long."

His shoulders somewhat stooped, like one receiving a burden for a long up-hill walk; but he looked right onward, with expressive, dark-gray eyes slightly elevated, and the curious, puckered lines around his mouth and chin strengthened, and the square-cut beard of the jaw and chin meeting the square of the temple locks and crown-mane, formed three inflexible sides of a square; and the well-cut nose and angle of the cheekbones receiving the light of his purpose to go on with the geometry, made Senator Pittson say:

"You will live to square it — yes, to cube it."

The President turned to Mr. Booth and put his hand upon his arm, with an open, country look of his substantial mouth, while his stiff, black hair seemed to soften, and his heavily marked eyebrows to take the light of his smile.

"Booth, give me a little Shakespeare! Do you believe Shakespeare wrote his own works? They say Seward writes all my messages."

This last remark was caused by the Secretary of State entering, to be ready to present the expected notabilities. He was introduced to the young men, and joined in the talk with address and merriment shining up a somewhat faded face.

Booth had been studying *Marc Antony,* to make an appearance soon with his two elder actor brothers in New York — of whom the only distinguished one was to vote for President Lincoln's re-election — and John Booth rehearsed:

"I come to bury Caesar, not to praise him. . . .

When that the poor have cried, Cæsar hath wept:
  Ambition should be made of sterner stuff: . . .

But here's a parchment, with the seal of Cæsar: . . .
  Let but the commons hear his testament, . . .
  And they would go and kiss dead Cæsar's wounds,
  And dip their napkins in his sacred blood;
  Yea, beg a hair of him for memory. . . .

Oh, what a fall was there, my countrymen!
  Then I, and you, and all of us fell down,

While bloody treason flourished over us."

Mr. Lincoln clapped his hands, and made Mr. Seward shake hands with the reciter, and cried:

"Ah! Billy wrote Shakespeare. Some say he wasn't educated enough; but there's poor white knowledge in Billy, that Lord Bacon wouldn't have had. Whenever I heard anything original at the Illinois bar, it was from a poor fellow who read his law books under the shade of a tree where he stopped after he had borrowed them. He would give us law and anecdotes, and use as bad law and as good human nature as Portia or Imogen."

The President began from Imogen:

"I see a man's life is a tedious one. . . .

Plenty and peace breed cowards; hardness ever
  Of hardiness is the mother."

The expected guests had been delayed, and the President went on reciting from Shakespeare at many points, seeming to have a knowledge of all his works, and inviting Booth to "come on" with something better.

"Ah, Mr. President," spoke the actor, giving Mr. Lincoln all his rich, dark, beaming face to enjoy, "if I could only commit my parts as you can commit everything!"

"Shakespeare, my eloquent young friend," replied the President, "is always wise and lovely, but Burns was the poet of the people. Shakespeare seems to teach you, but Burns to eat with you and sleep in your bed."

He started Burns with —

"Then let us pray, that come it may,
  (As come it will for a' that),
  That Sense and Worth, o'er a' the earth,
  Shall bear the gree, an' a' that.
  For a' that, an' a' that,
  It's comin' yet for a' that,
  That man to man, the world o'er,
  Shall brothers be for a' that."

"Seward," said the President, "don't you wish a man like Burns was the foreign minister of England? But we have friends wherever that poetry is believed, and, I think, nowhere else — not even here."

The President continued to conduct himself like a boy among boys, showing that he knew Burns "by heart," as he said; and his heart and merriment recited together, until it was announced that the notabilities were coming.

"Before we go, Mr. President," said Senator Pittson, "I want to ask you for a pass for Mr. Beall — it was always pronounced *Bell* — to visit some kin in lower Maryland."

"Oh! the provost can give him that — however, Pittson, here is my card."

The President wrote on it, and spelled the name "Bell." The pass was without limit as to time.

As they arose to go, they saw the strange princes enter with their ministers, and the Secretary of State introduce the President, in the elegant room set for that purpose, and Lincoln wore the dignity and stature of a natural monarch.

At the portal, going out, Booth and Beall stumbled upon two men — one bleached, large-eyed, and walking on a crutch; the other smaller, and wearing spectacles.

"Mr. Stanton, good-morning," said Booth to the last.

"Good-morning Mr. John Booth, and Mr. John Beall," spoke the other tall and invalid man. "When did you, Mr. Beall, lay down your arms?"

"Oh, some time ago, Major Luther Bosler," replied Booth; "he's all right now, and has the President's pass."

"The President's pass," spoke the war minister sternly, "is no pass at all. What right have you, as a good citizen, to take up our kind magistrate's time with giving passes against his own safety and ours? — Major Bosler, have this man report at the war office today!"

He pointed to Beall and passed in.

"We will go to the National Hotel, where we stop, and meet you there — Luther," spoke Booth.

"There are other things I may want to see you for when I come," remarked Luther Bosler, slowly, looking them both gravely over.

He passed into the President's mansion.

Booth stopped a passing cab and bade the driver go hard to his hotel.

"You are in a tight place, John," he said, "but their police system is very loose, and I can get you out."

"I should think so," replied Beall; "why, any assassin could reach Abe Lincoln's side. I believe he could be run out of this city on his own pass and delivered up in Richmond."

Booth sat back in the carriage pale and silent; they were both excited, for the gallows might be very close to Captain Beall and the Old Capitol Prison close to Mr. Booth.

They reached the hotel and passed to Booth's room on an upper floor. He threw out to Beall a suit of countrymen's clothes and a false whisker.

"Actor's wardrobe," explained Booth, carelessly. "Here is Abe Lincoln's pass. What did you think of him?"

"Coarse chuck, but all intellect. That's the way with this North: it isn't much for stock, or manners, or disinterestedness, but it runs to brain like the cauliflower to a head."

"John Beall," said the actor, all flushed and with compressed features, "that man is the most cunning fanatic and hypocrite in the world. See how he read Shakespeare! I want you to lift up your right hand and swear to me that you will never use for yourself, without my knowledge and control, the idea you just now expressed."

"What idea?"

"That old Abe Lincoln can be abducted from Washington and carried to Richmond."

"Pshaw! It was a mere reflection. Nobody would attempt it."

"Swear!" hissed Booth; "swear, or you shall not leave this city!"

"You're mad, I reckon." Beall finished his toilet.

"That's the idea I had at the grave of John Brown, when I asked you what Lincoln would be worth as a hostage. Then I had never seen him in his household as we have today. Your reflection has confirmed my idea and observation, and I want to preempt it here. Swear that you will acknowledge me the author of the proposition to abduct Abraham Lincoln!"

"Why, certainly; and that you're a fool, too."

Beall held up his hand and removed his old white slouched hat.

Booth clasped him in his arms and whispered:

"My fortune's made! I'll carry the Yankee Washington and show him all over the South as a feature of my star engagement. By God! I'll make him recite Shakespeare, and pay him a salary or shares. I want you to make the secret proposition for me to the Confederate President when you reach Richmond. The man I shall ask for to conduct the enterprise is —"

"Not Lloyd Quantrell?"

"The very man!"

"Why that's the man I want sent to Canada to command my expedition."

"Let him choose between us," spoke Booth. "He is under oath to us, since John Brown's raid, to revenge the South, and we'll kill him if he shirks his vow!"

"Come," said Beall, looking with pinched wonder at Booth's demoniac face, as he stood with a great knife unclasped, and blazing eyes, like Shylock starting to cut Antonio's heart's flesh out.

When they descended the stairs, Major Luther Bosler was seen by the front door of the hotel.

"Come by the back way," said Booth. "I'll get you out."

He whispered to a hotel clerk, who conducted them through some kitchen apartments to a large, hollow, stable court, out of which ran two alleys, but not in line with each other. Taking the alley to the left, they entered a quiet street in the rear of the hotel, where two common inns stood among livery-stables.

"This farther tavern," said Booth, "is the stage-office for Port Tobacco and Leonardtown. Go in there and take a room, and leave Washington by the next stage. You have the highest pass in the land. *Remember!*"

Booth went around the corner of the National Hotel, and, entering the front door on Pennsylvania Avenue, met Senator Pittson and Luther Bosler talking in the hotel lobby.

"Mr. Beall has gone to his people in the Valley," Booth said. "Friend Bosler was not too polite with him."

"Mr. Booth," spoke Edgar Pittson, quietly, "I forbid your further visits to my daughter."

Chapter XLI
GRASS WIDOWS

JAKE BOSLER would have been lonely and heart-broken from Katy's loss, but that his son had become a great man about the government, and had given him honest employment in such wide measure that he was growing rich.

Thousands of horses the old man bought among the Dunkers of the East and West and sold them at the regulation price in Baltimore. The mighty war minister gave a few Marylanders his trust absolutely, and of them was John W. Garrett, the railroad president, who shifted armies on his road, and Luther Bosler, the Dunker, who had now sealed his convictions with his blood.

He was to Mr. Stanton like both conscience and an orderly sergeant, a loyal reprover of his errors and the silent dragoon of his secret errands. He was hated, of course, but ambition in him was regulated by religion. He, also, honestly thrived in the opportunities of the time, with his natural genius for business and the clairvoyant power of fair-dealing.

"O Luter, 'tis money is for nopody now," Jake Bosler said. "Nelly is gone; you has no child; I haf no Katy."

The grievous war went on, with the sky in the West always light, and at last the West sent her simple captain to the East, to wrestle with the mutilated hydra's head. He brought a friend to clean up that side-aisle, the Shenandoah Valley, through which the heir of General Washington had carried the army of slavery a second time into the German settlements, to meet his defeat on the sources of the Monocacy among the "nest-hidings" of Hannah Ritner and Abel Quantrell.

The new general in the Valley burned the barns and mills which had supplied the devastating insurrection with food; and in retaliation Chambersburg was raided and burned, greatly to the joy of bandits, who remembered that John Brown had made it his base of supplies.

As Brown had been the pilot of Freedom through these valleys, a

Logan of the slave-catchers was the pilot of a hundred thousand insurgents, through his native scenes about Snow Hill, to Gettysburg.

From that great battlefield Hannah Ritner brought an insurgent prisoner by the name of Powell to Baltimore, and set him to work in the hospitals. He was the same young Floridian whom Booth had encountered at Charlestown.

The last campaign of the enemy across the Potomac was by the slavery candidate for President of the United States;* his adversary was dead, and Mr. Lincoln had become the central character of history. This disappointed man, whose loyal uncle had presided over the convention to renominate Abraham Lincoln in Baltimore, fought a battle near Frederick City, burned houses in the outskirts of Washington, and paraded his troops before one of the forts, and then the rebellion fell back from the Potomac forever, and Richmond was beleaguered amid its ghosts and crimes.

The witnesses of John Brown's deed and death were in their graves: Stuart, killed at Yellow Tavern, Stonewall Jackson at Chancellorsville, General Ashby in the Valley. Booth thought of all this with a lonely, savage soul, when he received Beall's letter by the secret mail.

Dear Sir:

I waited on the Secretary of War at Richmond with your proposition; he was disposed to favor it, but our President set his foot on it. Lincoln, he said, might be killed in the attempt, and that would inflict a permanent stain upon our reputation in the eyes of the world; and, besides, he would not know what to do with Lincoln if he had him, and a worse man would then be President,† and hang everybody he had hated. The Cabinet is nervous about reprisals in case they approve a brigand war near Lincoln's person.

I asked permission to destroy the enemy's commerce, and it was given me with reluctance. I asked Quantrell to be ordered to join me, and discovered him dangerously wounded in a hospital. He wanted to pray with me, and denounced our methods of war.

So I burned a good many vessels on the Eastern Shore of Maryland and made some booty; have been captured, and was threatened with execution as a pirate and a spy; but our government put some of the finest Yankee officers on bread and water, and threatened to execute them all, if I was not exchanged.

I am not appreciated at my true valuation here in Richmond,

---

*   Breckenridge.

†   The son of Albert Sidney Johnston told the author that a relative of Zachary Taylor, who had visited Mr. Lincoln surreptitiously, made the proposition as above, to the insurgent President, and met with the answer in this story.

where self-seeking influence and conservatism prevail, as in all governments, and I am going to desert and return, by the help of Lincoln's pass, through Maryland to Canada, where I shall try to anticipate this government, which, I have reason to believe, means to use my idea about capturing Johnson's Island for its own glory. I will not be robbed of my patent like that! Secret and extraordinary service agrees with my nature, but I can not serve where I am a cipher.

Your idea would be popular with our people if you could carry it to a successful result, which I very much doubt. I shall keep my oath — to revenge the South and invade her invaders.

Beall

Booth read this letter off by a cipher-key he possessed — a cylinder of printed letters from which a pointer, shifted in a frame, selected the letters meant for those written. The same cipher was in the rebel war minister's office. Booth and Beall had obtained models of it in Canada.

The bravo finished the letter with fury. They had not even remembered him in Richmond, where he was so great a favorite. His self-esteem was wounded, and his funds, which he had designed to replenish by this feat of abducting the President, were down to a few hundred dollars.

He must resume acting, much as he hated steady occupation, and he had no *status* in the North.

He locked up his effects, took five hundred dollars in his wallet, and started for Montreal.

As he walked through the ladies' parlor of the National Hotel, in the twilight of evening, a single person sat there by the window, and she looked up and saw his white, fierce face.

"O Mr. Booth, what is the matter?"

"Miss Pittson, excuse me; you can have no interest in me. I am forbid to speak to you."

"Who could have injured you in papa's estimation, sir? You were such a true friend — so generous, with such a sense of romance, that all acting and loving, too, seem tame since you have become a stranger."

"Dear Light, I thought you felt for me. My country is beaten, and here in Maryland, where I am a native, all to whom I am candid upon my political feelings suspect me. It is the Dutch Hessian, Bosler, the tool of that devil, Stanton, who has caused your father to insult me!"

"Surely not; he is so mild. Next to you, I esteemed him my noblest friend."

"Light" — he had taken her hand and drawn her within the darkness of the window-curtains — "can you love a poor rebel, without a country, with no other home than his genius can find, but that home certain if you will fly to it, and be his friend? Oh, I am so much forgotten, so desolate!"

He assumed the tones and hyperbole of the stage, and drew her large, impetuous frame close to his eyes, which seemed to make room by their blackness in the dark.

"I feel for your defeat in battle," she said; "I sympathize with the brave. I will go with you to the ends of the earth!"

The sense of romance had raised her, in truth, to his simulated passion; he touched the lips nothing less than filial affection had kissed, with a mouth which had gone wandering like a jackal's appetite.

"My darling," he sighed, "we will fly to the land of the bonnie blue flag. I am going to Canada to send my wardrobe there. My country will hail you as my Pocahontas, my queen. Oh, there are ardent and hospitable hearts there! My family name is greater in England than in America, and we can cross the ocean and unite my patriotism and your romance in everlasting poetry and passion!"

As she promised to keep his secret and await him, a light foot touched the curtain; a match flashed upon the gas-bracket at their side, and the senator's wife looked scorn upon Booth and anger upon her child.

"Go to your room, miss!" she said, and once more bent on Booth a glance of such loathing that he retorted:

"Madam, I am a gentleman!"

"You are the first that ever said so," answered Mrs. Pittson.

He felt but little rage as he went down the stairs, chuckling to himself:

"Lucky at cards, unlucky in love — not I! There is time before the train for a visit to Nelly."

He took a carriage and was driven toward the Treasury Department. They were lighting the lamps at the National Theater as his carriage turned to the left at Thirteenth Street, and went slowly over the unpaved roads through the Alsatia of the town, where blacks and whites feasted by crime and license upon the wandering habits of war. Dwellings neglected and unpainted stood amid tottering rows of tenements; music and laughter came from low bar-rooms where soldiers treated women; a sinister and suspicious look was over everything.

At the farthest margin of this central pest-place, where the city seemed to stop at a desert of rubbish-fields, upon a desolate avenue never yet occupied or paved, stood a brick structure at a corner, like a wheel-wright's shop, with habitations above it. Booth applied a key and felt his way along a stair to a door in a corridor, at which he knocked.

There seemed to be whispering within.

He knocked again, with the decision of jealousy.

The door opened, and Nelly Harbaugh appeared with a candle. Before she could distinguish him, Booth had seized and kissed her, saying:

"Nell, I am going away, and my heart is full of you!"

"You are?" the girl answered — leaner, fiercer, commonly attired. "Why don't you go jump off the Long Bridge? Nobody cares what becomes of you!"

"O Nelly! I depend on you more than ever, as I grow more estranged from good fortune. Don't break my heart!"

"I would if I could, and let the lies and serpents in it loose! Here am I, making my living by taking little menial parts at the theaters, standing in the chorus and processions, and tempted by a thousand men — yet true to the dismal sin you deceived me to commit. I learned enough of man when I knew you, John Booth. Go, quit my door! the theater is soon to begin, and I must take my stand among the supernumeraries. Not a dollar have you sent me in months!"

"Nell, I have been in a great scheme, waiting on ungrateful friends. Here is money; take what you want."

She put down the candle and took his hand, full of notes, and threw it against his breast.

"Judas!" she said. "Not one of your thirty pieces will I ever take. You have degraded my soul. Nothing but ambition gave you the victory over me. I never loved you. My heart is true to the man I still expect to fall to my experience and forgive me!"

The action and the words raised the brute in him.

"Whispering, were you?" he hissed. "Let me search a minute!"

"Go out!" commanded Nelly Harbaugh. "I don't want to hang you, but every rag in this room is mine, and I will defend my property against the thief who robbed me of my character."

She had cocked a pistol in his face, and aimed behind it, like famine full of recklessness.

With a movement of his foot he tripped her, never ceasing to look into her eyes, and, as she stumbled, he seized the pistol in one hand and her throat with the other. His arms were like swelling bands of steel.

The powerful young woman threw all her weight upon him, but in the wrestle his gymnasium art enabled him to turn her sidewise and to fall above.

Before he could conclude what to do, a cord was thrown around his arms and neck repeatedly, and it entangled his knees. He gasped and fell.

The cord was drawn tighter. Nelly Harbaugh arose, and stood before him with the pistol cocked again. He felt death to be in her eyes, and strangulation from some hidden foe was overtaking him.

"Now, you slave-dog," spoke the fierce woman, "I may as well end you and save innocent souls! My father was a soldier; I am a mountain-girl. Kneel down and pray!"

He sank upon his knees. Death was before him and the cord behind.

"Nelly," exclaimed a deep voice, "don't shoot! Open the window, and you can call for help if we need it. He is tame now."

The girl threw up the broken casement, and stood beside it with the candle.

When Booth recovered strength enough to see, a large woman sat before him, and Nelly Harbaugh was guarding the door with the pistol.

He looked into the strange woman's face. It was the same which had read him the fierce, fateful prophecy at Harper's Ferry with Atzerodt.

"In some such naked place as this," exclaimed Hannah Ritner, slowly, to Booth, "your pride and cruelty will end unless you can repent. Did you not come from a lady's side this night, full of lies and deceit, to glut your unbridled wickedness upon this deserted temple of my sex?"

She pointed to Nelly Harbaugh, in all that actress's unconsciously awakened powers of beauty and expression.

"Witch," spoke Booth, in a spiritless tone, "if you tell fortunes right, you know I love this cruel girl alone, and none besides."

His voice gave way in tears; he was the greater woman now.

"If you love Nelly," asked Hannah Ritner, melting somewhat herself; "what makes you neglect her, and be the disturber of the generous heart of Miss Pittson?"

"Mischief," said Booth. "Ambition and the devil!"

"Rise up and go," commanded Hannah Ritner. "We know you now, and do not fear you. The cord I predicted for you has already been around your neck. Beware next of the eternal fire!"

He staggered up and looked around; they were prepared for him at every point, both watching him with the courage of confederates.

"I know you always carry a pistol, sir," Nelly Harbaugh remarked. "Touch your hand to your hip, and your little brains will be spilt upon this bare floor!"

"Nelly, do you hate me?"

"I do!"

"Then kill me! I came here tonight to designate the leading parts you were to play with me in the West on my return from Canada. Since you do not care for me, my career is done."

"Go!" said Nelly Harbaugh; "you have told lies enough. I am now prepared to play leading parts, and hire such unreliable actors as you to support me."

As his footsteps died on the stairs, Nelly Harbaugh fell at Hannah Ritner's feet.

"Must I forgive him?" she said. "I do hate him, but I want to play so much!"

"Be prepared for what may come, ambitious girl! You may save this man from greater crimes; if he disappoints you, I will see that you have an opening for your talents, if you will be faithful. Then, he *did* see Light Pittson tonight."

"O Hannah!" exclaimed Nelly Harbaugh, "were you only finding out what you professed to know?"

"Come!" concluded the fortune-teller, "it is time you were at the theater. We all act a little. You say Lloyd Quantrell treated you like a gentleman and no oppressor?"

"Hannah, he was a brother to me in Richmond. How different the manly Southern soldier from these low spies between the lines! If poor Lloyd was alive, Katy Bosler would find him a gallant and tender man, I know."

Booth walked along the streets of what was called "Murder Bay," in Washington, with a nature cowed yet treacherous. He yearned for some occasion to excite his prowess again. It came as he passed the intervening corner and heard cries from a small frame cabin where women and men were fighting in a low bar-room. Bending and stealing along like a cat, Booth reached the small box-window, and, peering within, saw the positions of the drunken combatants.

In a moment he was among them, fighting cool and manfully, every blow of his powerful arm felling a man; and before they could determine whether he was officer, or policeman, or an apparition, he had leaped over the threshold and turned the corner; and at the theater, across the avenue, he stopped and drank some brandy.

"Are you going up to see the President?" asked the bar-keeper. "He's got a box here tonight."

"No," answered Booth, with a rolling curse at Mr. Lincoln; "I'll go through under the stage, though."

He passed on to an alley and area in the rear of the theater, used to get in scenery and horses, and afford escape from the stage in case of fire.

As he stood there, the "Star-spangled Banner" was played within, and its high-pitched, swelling strains streamed into the *cul-de-sac* of the alley and empty square, to take the resonance of walls and stables, and echo with a lonely grandeur on the vagabond's solitude. The President was entering the theater. Booth listened with the hate of convicted insignificance to the loud applause of the grateful people.

A woman came out of the theater back door into the area and shut the door behind her.

Booth crouched behind a step and heard her say:

"For this painted life I left a good man and despised a church — God forgive me!"

Nelly Harbaugh threw back her long, yellow hair, drew in the balm of the night and the twinkling childhood of little stars, and reentered the National Theater.

A horse, from one of the stables in the alley, made a great clattering on the stones as he was ridden out of the alley to F Street. Booth walked after the horse, and came out into this thoroughfare between blank house-walls. He stopped in the outlet and looked back.

"I could have killed Abe Lincoln," said he, "and been half-way to Capitol Hill on that horse. These blind alleys behind the theaters have no connection with the audience or the street in front, except by that little postern-door!"

Something in the idea put nerve into his step, and he walked down F Street rapidly three blocks to Tenth. There rose before him, in the soft night, the pediment, pilasters, and many Roman doors of Ford's Theater, with drinking-kennels along its sides. It had once been a Christian church.

Booth turned down a dark alley from F Street running to a large court at right angles with the alley. Only one house had a door upon the alley, and the court contained several stables and no respectable habitation; but, to the right, the great naked gable of the church-theater closed the court, and one small door was low to the ground.

Booth opened this door and stepped into the lighted theater. A man called his name — one Spangler, a Baltimorean, half carpenter, half drudge.

"Hallo, Ned!" said Booth, and advanced with the man toward the corner of the stage. "Which box, Ned, does the President generally occupy here?"

"That upper one, across yonder — they knock them two boxes into one."

Booth looked up, and a woman in the box raised her handkerchief to her lips and smiled at him.

It was Light Pittson, with her father and old Abel Quantrell beside her. How much they all looked alike!

Booth raised his finger to his lips and drew back.

"Ned," said he, as he stepped out into the desolate area behind the theater, "see how much you can rent me one of these old stables for. I may want to keep a horse."

He gave the man a quarter of a dollar. Nothing but a homeless dog roamed the old court as he left it by the alley and regained the street.

He was trembling. To men of his profession, who live by rote and imitation, an original idea often carries all the vanity of authorship. He turned into a large brick inn at the corner of Ninth Street and ordered a cock-tail of brandy.

"Drink with me," he said to the bar-keeper; "I have got an idea for a play I wouldn't sell to President Lincoln's Billy Shakespeare."

Yet that night, as Mr. Booth traveled northward, his sobs were heard from his berth by fellow-passengers.

What was it made him weep?

Not his new idea for a play.

Not his prodigal and precocious life.

Not even Light Pittson, in the ripeness of pure womanhood and the devotion of romance.

It was the loss of Nelly Harbaugh's regard.

Sometimes the deceiver becomes the forsaken; and that, when he can no longer appreciate purity.

As Booth reached Canada, he found great excitement there.

John Beall had seized a small American passenger-steamer plying between Canada and the United States, and with it committed several piratical deeds, but had failed to attack Johnson's Island, where his spy had been detected, and the tardy Canadians were now giving up some of Beall's men, and were searching for him.

Booth had barely arrived in Canada when another gang of bandits, in the name of the insurgent States, crossed the American line and robbed a bank and shed blood, regardless of the hospitality they had solicited or the rights of nations. They returned to Montreal to show their commissions from Richmond, and to make a series of illiterate affidavits rejoicing in their shame.

The Americans, now aroused, turned on Canada and crossed the border. Fear exacted what civilization could not obtain, and the British line was at last policed by the Canadians, but not until a band of felons had endeavored to set fire to the city of New York, one of whom, an escaped prisoner from Johnson's Island, was captured with his combustible in his hand.

Finally, John Beall, the most persistent incendiary the East had produced, was seized at Suspension Bridge, after having led a party into the State of New York to throw trains of flying passenger-cars from the track.

Beall and the other incendiary were condemned to die as pirates and spies.

These nearly simultaneous outrages were all parts of a general purpose to defeat the re-election of President Lincoln, and terrify the free States into selecting the candidates who would let the authors of the war resume their political importance, and let slavery make the terms it had so long rejected.

Inhumanity and treachery never did the best cause any good; a bad cause they could not save. The State of Maryland voted for Abraham Lincoln, and he had half a million majority in the Union.

Luther Bosler's one vote, "sticking all up py itself" at the tail of two hundred and eighty-one, had become more than forty thousand.

Mr. Booth kept his own counsel in Canada, had it understood that he was engaged to be married to the daughter of a Republican statesman, and he bought a bill of exchange for three hundred dollars at a Montreal bank, saying he was going to run the blockade to the South.

Chapter XLII
LEGITIMATE DRAMA

KATY BOSLER was the mistress of Abel Quantrell's house in Baltimore. The old man took a sardonic joy in his grandchild, which he named Winter, in honor of his Congressman friend, and to mark its want of fatherly care. He seemed the prouder of this boy because it was disowned, and the tenderer to Katy because she was abandoned.

He never mentioned Lloyd's name; and once, when Hannah Ritner spoke for the absent boy, declaring that he had never disobeyed his father, but had kept in fact and spirit within the regular lines of the insurrection, the old man took down the writings of Franklin, and pointed to the words:

"Nothing has ever hurt me so much as to find myself deserted in my old age by my only son, and not only deserted, but to find him taking up arms against me in a cause wherein my good fame, fortune, and life were all at stake. . . . The part he acted against me in the war will account for my leaving him no more of an estate he endeavored to deprive me of.

> "'My son is my son till he gets him a wife,
> But my daughter is my daughter all the days of her life.'"

These were the words of Franklin concerning his natural son: Abel Quantrell might have forgiven his natural son for a similar course, but his legitimate son seemed to him in the rights of legitimacy to possess no rights of pathos; by the law he judged Lloyd, like a Jew by his Jewish code, and Edgar Pittson, his natural son, he judged as Paul judged the Gentile Timothy, "my own son in the faith."

He divided his property, while yet alive, between Katy Bosler and Light Pittson.

Lloyd's own property in Maryland was now a confiscated waste, and he possessed nothing but the gun in his hands.

There arose, however, for the absent one a second motherhood. The fervid abolitionist, Hannah Ritner, adopted Lloyd Quantrell in her heart, and clothed him in the panoply of her prayers.

She had nurtured the hope that she might yet find it consistent to marry Abel Quantrell, for the sake of her grandchild Light Pittson, who was innocent of the lapse in her family pride and name; but the obduracy of her lover toward his acknowledged son settled the question in Hannah Ritner's mind.

"Edgar," this strange and homeless woman said, "if I have been unjust to you already, I must be more unjust still. You are abundantly blessed with popularity, public influence, and the right convictions; your brother Lloyd has none of these; he is poor, obscure, and wrong. Shall I take from him the pride of his descent, also? If you are Abel Quantrell's lawful son, Lloyd Quantrell has not even the memory of his mother to inherit. One of you must wear the stain."

"Mother, I am the older. Can you ask how I shall answer?" the senator replied. "I know what is in your heart, and its tenderness is in my veins. No mess of pottage will I cook for my hunter-brother to defraud him of the precious inheritance of his mother's fame and our father's repute. My pedigree shall be from immaculate freedom, working its miracles in you, the purest of loving souls, and blessing my descent with relationship to every detached and fatherless child of God."

Quiet as childhood he kissed her brow, and took her worn and bruised frame into his arms, and sang her the tunes she had never been blessed to sing to him nor rock him to sleep in the cradle of domestic happiness. The pilgrim mother, seeking everywhere to do the penance of duty, sacrifice, and alms in lonely places or on dangerous tasks, closed her eyes upon her tears of enthusiasm and sorrow, and slept in the arms of her consoling son.

The penalty of their integrity was still to be paid.

One day in the Senate the new amendment to the American Constitution — the thirteenth in number, like the number of the English colonies in America — was to be debated. It abolished slavery, and compelled Congress to enforce that emancipation which now existed only in the President's proclamation and as a measure of war.

President Lincoln was deeply interested in the passage of this amendment, and came to the Senate to hear the debate; and a noble audience was there collected of the fashion and public intellect of the country.

Senator Pittson was the debater of whom the reasoning work was expected, to persuade other border-State senators to vote for the bill, like Mr. Reverdy Johnson, who had been sent to the Senate from Maryland by Henry Winter Davis.* But there were some bitter opponents of the measure there, and one of these, claiming some merit of originating justice for his party, was reminded by Edgar Pittson of the person who published some poetry as "original," and when called to task replied that it was marked "original" in the newspaper he took it from.

The opposing senator, intemperate of habits and speech, rose and exclaimed:

"If I were to quote anything from that senator, I should mark it, 'ANONYMOUS.'"

The brutal reference to a mooted illegitimacy or unauthenticity of Edgar Pittson caused a low ripple of laughter and stamping feet to emanate from the more degraded spectators in the galleries.

Booth had heard this story, and he watched Light Pittson and her mother, sitting near him, the latter scarlet and the former laughing with others, unconscious of any imputation.

"Ha!" exclaimed Booth aloud, "he'll feel that, on his daughter's account."

A woman before him turned and said:

"You speak false, sir! He will not feel it at all."

He recognized the face of the dark woman who had bound his arms at Nelly Harbaugh's lodgings.

Looking again, Booth saw the President, the senators, the foreign ministers, and everybody, deeply interested and watching.

A vacant chair on the Senate floor, by Edgar Pittson's side, had been occupied temporarily by Abel Quantrell, who now slowly rose, leaned upon his cane, and put his remaining hand into his bosom, like one standing to be counted in a vote. His face was white as plaster; his under lip was folded upon the upper; he bent his head and looked at his unavowed son.

Then, without a sign of passion, or any deeper expression than contempt for his coarse opponent, the Western senator sketched the sufficiency of slavery to insult the progeny of its own licentiousness. Amendments had been offered that no descendants of Africans should be citizens, and that "no person whose mother or grandmother is or was a Negro shall be a citizen, or eligible to any place of trust or profit."

For the first time, the young senator said, the mothers of the American people had been arraigned in the Senate. The expiring throes of slavery, in the pillory rebellion had brought it to, exemplified its genius in that all who were helpless — innocent sons or aged mothers, dark or white — fell beneath the curse of its drunken rage; like Noah, exposed in his cups, hurling the stigma of his own shame at his grandchild. For half a century the proposition had been maintained that the helplessness

---

¶   Maryland, through Reverdy Johnson, voted for the amendment.

of one race of women was the only security for the virtue of the other; and wherever this spirit saw a woman toiling, it insulted her with a suspicion of her honor, making industry the yoke-fellow of shame, and canonizing sloth among the vestals of religion.

The American senator laid down the broad proposition that there was not an untainted pedigree or descent upon the globe. In every great migration or incursion the women fell to the conqueror, and slavery spared no refinement, but rejoiced in the high-breeding of its victims, until the abuses of Christian women at the hands of a religion which denied all women souls, expelled the Moor and created at once Isabella and Columbus — Europe and the virgin world it came to wed. As long as the African slave-trade prevailed by law, the women of America were subject to capture and degradation by the Moors; in the eye of Heaven the sufferings of the one in the harem and the other in the barracoon were the same. Presuming upon a few generations of putative descent, caste, dating back to the Norman Goth and his villein's unconsulted daughter,* found its nearest imitators in the New World among the weedlings and swamp-flowers of yesterday, the very orthography of whose names was lost, and in whose custody, perhaps, the immemorial princesses of Africa bore them a posterity whose lineage had been older than Moses, till crossed by this alligator, in the serene complacency of his appetites.

The reference was obvious, and, as the unfortunate senator rose to apologize, his opponent held him up by the wand of his subtle finger, and illustrated with him, as Ariel might have lectured upon Caliban.

All saw the relative quality of the two exemplars: Pittson, the son of Mercury: in every globule of light a thought reflected, in every motion some sign of the spherical harmonies, his words the unconscious flakes of an agitation as gentle as the snow-fall, his client the ages of human-kind in their loving evolutions from the one unfailing fountain of every perfect aristocracy — a mother's woes!

Of that rock of origin sure, he had the model of every tribe before him, and the nerve of every noble feeling was in his heart. Honoring his father and his mother, the whole land became his personal heritage according to the promise of God. If the barbarous Crusader, knowing no alphabet, could ride to Palestine to redeem the sepulcher of a lawgiver who was fatherless in the world, the son of two venerable spectators might be a paladin, indeed, in the lists where four million souls were this day to come into the genesis of nations, and be accountable to some

---

*   "Of all princely lines the ducal house of Normandy paid least regard to the canonical laws of marriage, or to the special claims of legitimate birth. William the Norman was emphatically William the Bastard. Throughout the whole of Duke Robert's life she remained in the position of an acknowledged mistress." — Freeman's "Norman Conquest."

parentage.

The other in this bright light — as from the Grail, which administered a holy communion to the nations — felt his rankness and low presumption sting himself, like a nettle shrinking upon the parterre. The man he had imputed dishonor to, shone by him like a knight above a toad.

"Even from that source," said the senator, after a pause, "the little children, white or yellow, cry, *'Heureuse à vivre!'* and thank Nature for the gift of life. To live: it is all we are sure of. So glad of life are we that we would live forever and again. In every tree the birds sing, 'Life!' in every swamp the chorus of life is certain as the night. Give life, my brother; release from the bondage of your prejudices and the oppressions of your laws, and we shall start the world from this hour with every man the Norman conqueror!"

At the conclusion of the debate the whole Senate crowded about the senator; the doors were thrown open, and mothers and daughters entered to shake Mr. Pittson's hand. A generous age, brought slowly to the incentive of a magnanimous deed, felt the touch of nature like a tongue of flame, make all see and speak in the glow of liberty. The great President himself, whose legal authenticity was to be disputed after his fame had become the light of the world,* pressed Mr. Pittson's hand, and said:

"Ah! Eddy, there were great women in Egypt!"

The other senator, who had nursed the scandal like a niggard's gold, to make the most efficient use of it some day, found that he had expelled himself from the family of decent mankind.

Booth was too obtuse to get the spirit of Senator Pittson's reproof. He merely said to himself, as he looked toward Light Pittson in the happy instant of her father's popularity:

"He didn't deny the fact, and there must be folly in the blood."

As Edgar Pittson walked through the public grounds with his parents and family, the birds burst into song, the sun kissed the glad earth and awoke the seed within it, the browsing animals sought pasture with their unaccredited young, and the squirrels skipped wantonly in the poplar trees. Nothing was melancholy for having been brought to life.

Suddenly the air quivered with the sound of a cannon. Another and another took up the reverberation and carried it around the circle of the earthen forts, till the whole land seemed to leap with the roar of artillery, and the broad rivers to be touched by the skipping feet of iron aërolites, vaulting from heaven to dance for man.

They looked back, and saw upon the dome of the great white Capitol

---

*   The marriage certificate of President Lincoln's parents was not discovered till some years after his death, and when its non-production, from an obscure society, had caused inquiries and exclamations from imputative minds.

the head of the unfinished statue of Freedom let down from a crane in the sky, as the sculptor had modeled it when it did not embody a reality. Today it was a dome of history, complete, and mother of a pure, uncertified race.

As he gazed up at the saluted statue, a film shot across Abel Quantrell's eye and his side seemed to leave his body. His son and his son's wife caught him.

It was a stroke of paralysis.

*T*hat evening, Luther Bosler, who knew the reality of Senator Pittson's paternity, hastened to seek Light Pittson before she could suspect the occasion of the debate.

"Miss Pittson," said Luther, "I have the consent of your parents to come to you upon a trembling errand — to tell you that in your family I would make the hearthstone of my own and you the idol there, and over the purity of your impulses would lay the protection of my care."

"Luther," said the girl, "if you had come to me, like a fellow-countryman, instead of courting my parents first, I should have felt the romance of your attachment. Now I must tell you that the means you have used to prejudice a poor Southern patriot in papa's eyes have excited my indignation. My answer is 'No.'"

With a possible idea that she meant Mr. Booth, Luther sought that gentleman at his own room in the hotel.

Mr. Booth was seated at a table in riding-boots, spurs, gauntlets, and slouched, corded hat. A map was before him, kept in its place by a bowie knife and a revolving pistol. He leaped up and confronted Luther with a look of frenzy.

"Sit down, Mr. Booth," said Luther; "we have broken bread together at my father's table. I am still a man of peace, and my errand is a cordial one. I want you to go with me to call on Miss Nelly Harbaugh."

"What business have you with that lady?"

"Nothing but assistance: to reconcile you to her, Mr. Booth, and disabuse your mind of any jealousy of me. That is why I choose to call with you. Do you love the lady?"

Luther's words had the soft authority of a priest's. Booth glared at him, and then set out a bottle of brandy.

"I have been poor," said he, "and unable to be just to Nelly. She has treated me like an enemy. If you can reconcile us, it will be a friendly act; she has so much genius and application that if we were to work together we might make a fortune."

Luther took the bottle and said:

"Mr. Booth, put this away, with your other dangerous weapons. It is the armorer of them all. You know I have been your friend ever since you brought the spy, Beall, to the President's chamber: I was the only witness who recognized him. He is now under sentence of death for willful perseverance in acts covered in no land by military protection."

"You can save him," said Booth. "You are a good fellow, and will do it."

"No, nothing can save him. The President would pardon every guilty man if he could, but Beall has aroused military and public opinion, and civilization is against him. As this government hanged but one slaver in all its history,* it hopes to close the warning by the death of one pirate. You know him to deserve it!"

Booth looked down and ground his teeth.

They walked to the purlieu where Nelly lived. Booth said:

"I am not sure of my reception. I will trust you, major, to make my peace, and will be within call from the window. Do your best for me! I love the poor girl with all my soul!"

Luther entered the old brick tenement and knocked at the designated door. A voice cried, "Come!" which awoke remembered echoes in his heart. He lifted the latch, and there stood before him the goddess of his youth, Nelly, in the white, sleeveless robe of a Roman girl.

She was standing before an old, cracked mirror, in the act of reciting. Her splendid hair seemed to be one sheet of golden brown from the low forehead backward almost to her feet, and her Roman nose, as strong in character as the lines of her throat were gentle and womanly, parted eyes of power and of pain. She was thinner and worn, and the place was bare as a prison.

Giving a scream of agony and joy, she threw herself at Luther's knees, crying:

"Oh, I knew you would come! I have seen you passing, and hid myself in doorways. I have read your name in papers, and have cried with pride. You love me still!"

He looked down at her tenderly, but silent; some tears were in his eyes. She reached up with her own eyes, almost blind, until she could touch his face. Its expression made her scream again.

"Not love me!" she sobbed. "Why do you wear these worldly clothes? Why have you left your Dunker cloth? If not to follow me down through my sins to seek my side, why have you fallen so?"

"Nelly, I came to be your friend — to put you on your way, and say with Him who came to lift up sinners, 'Go, sin no more!'"

---

*   Gordon, hanged February 21, 1862, for bringing eight hundred and ninety-two blacks from Africa. President Lincoln's son died the morning Gordon's mother and wife went to Washington to ask for a pardon, and they could not therefore see the President.

The girl looked at him, with her long, serpent-flowing arms extended to wipe her eyes of moisture, and to see him well. As she looked, she shrank away.

"Not stained in thought or act?" she whispered. "Not changed at all? Not worldly; and not even tempted? O my God!"

She fell upon her knees and next upon her face, and stretched her white arms wide, and moaned:

"I have lost him!"

"Nelly," spoke Luther, not rejoicing in this proof of his supremacy in his first mistress's soul, "you loved ambition more than me. You were right to be candid. I have interested myself to give your genius an opportunity, and, as the last proof of my friendship, before we part, here is a little bank-book, with a deposit to your name, on which you can draw these checks."

He raised her up and put the book into her hand, and kissed her brow respectfully.

She looked at the book and saw written there, opposite her name, the sum of four thousand dollars.

"Nelly, the President is one of the subscribers to this endowment. Now, give Mr. Booth a chance to redeem himself! He says he loves you. Let him prove it by the act of honor, and make you his wife."

He stood at the window, and made a sign. A foot bounded upon the stairs, and a dark form knelt at Nelly's feet.

The girl stood cold and worldly between them.

"I am rewarded in my own coin," she said; "gold instead of love, career instead of home. Oh, thank you, sir, for your manly help, when I betrayed you so falsely at this man's bribe of making me the mistress of his counterfeit world! Let him now fulfill the promise!"

She exhibited to Booth the deposit in the book. His eyes flashed between shame and avarice.

"I give you for doing my ruin," said Nelly Harbaugh to Booth, "a benefit! I am capable of sustaining you, and will play the leading female part. I will not remember the paltry parts you gave me to play when you employed the company."

She looked very unlike forgetfulness, however.

"May I hope you can love me, Nelly?"

"Not unless you can assist my career. My heart is dead. You broke it through my ambition, and can only win it again when you have proved yourself an actor."

Booth set to work to study, and with unthinking selfishness he chose Richard III, his father's old part, where Nelly had nothing strong to do; but she had improved the time of his negligence by diligence and observation. She repulsed his caresses, prepared herself with the courage of the castaway, wherein the genius of acting often lies; and, the day before the benefit, he began to drink, like his father of old.

The theater was not one of the fashionable pair in the city, but an audience of notables gathered there. Booth was inflamed with brandy: he ranted and leaped for three acts, exciting more laughter than admiration; while the beautiful amateur, announced as his pupil, played with power and discretion, and became the "rage" of every gallant in the city.

In the fourth act John Wilkes Booth found he could not articulate at all. As sometimes had happened to his father, after a fellow-actor had broken his nose in a drunken bout, the wanton son was dumb as a pantomimist. The most he could do was to speak in a whisper.

In the last act he had to fight the Earl of Richmond, who was represented by an actor out of the Union army.

Desperate from the failure of his voice, and his head full of crazed illusions, Booth looked upon this man as a proper person to kill.

The rival actor knew the quality of his opponent in drink, and was too brave to decline the combat. At the morning's rehearsal Booth's attack had been observed to be fierce and wicked, and his superior height and length of arm were plain to his antagonist, who stood, at night, prepared for the worst. The wings were thronged to see the broadsword encounter, by carpenters and supers, hot for a real fight.

The two began with single-hand exercise, and the earl scratched Booth's cheek. He whispered to Booth to pause and end it there.

Booth objected, and, in the stage phrase, "led up with two hands." The manager and ladies now hurried to the entrances to see a combat of real blood.

Booth rushed forward with both hands grasping his weapon, and there was a short series of clashings and sparks, when down came Richmond's temperate and accurate sword, severing Booth's eyebrow and clipping the cheek.

"My God! I've killed you!" said the earl, in an undertone.

Booth staggered, bleeding and stunned, and sought the support of the tree-bough that, in the tradition of his father, he always nailed to the wing in "Richard," and there, with sparkling eyes and white, glistening teeth, and blood-stained countenance, he sought to renew the fight.

The manager ordered the curtain to be rung down.

Booth was led, faint and blind, to his dressing-kennel.

"That's all right, old fellow," he said to Richmond's apologies; "that was splendid!"*

---

*   Nearly literal transcript from an observer's reminiscence of Booth.

*J*ohn Beall was fighting the last enemy not long thereafter. A little procession in the morning of a wintry day, with music playing a dead-march, brought him, with pinioned arms, beneath the same gallows that the only slaver had been hanged on. He looked out on the sparkling waters of New York Bay, and the mountains of New Jersey touched with snow — so like the Blue Ridge by his home, near Harper's Ferry — and the fate he had labored so hard for, came with the severing of a cord and the dropping of a weight.

The incendiary,* who was also executed in time, danced a jig under the gallows and sang a stave.

Irregular warfare, though it long followed the civil war, in the form of mail-robberies and many bloody crimes, was to have but one other exemplification in America.

*M*r. Booth called on Nelly Harbaugh when he was again presentable.

"John," said she, "you are of no service to me. I have passed you in the profession. It is time I looked out for myself, and there are several rich men ardent to put up money to establish me. I love nobody. Money is what I want, and you have not got it. You will have to drop out of my life."

Cold as what he had made her — an adventuress with the acting talent — she bowed him formally from her presence.

He turned, all stung and insulted, on Light Pittson, whom he met at his hotel.

"I have none but you," he spoke, with real tears. "They are tearing up my country with armies, and have plowed my heart with a golden plowshare. Will you fly with me?"

"Yes!"

"Be ready, then; for I am desperate."

---

*   Kennedy.

Chapter XLIII

THE ABDUCTION PLOT

MR. BOOTH had rented a stable in the rear of Ford's theater, and Ned Spangler, the scene-shifter, who slept in the theater, groomed his horse.

Spangler was a typical product of slavery in its influence on the poor mechanic whites around it, making them the unacquisitive admirers of those of the social grade above them. He worked for mere subsistence, had no home, drank as much liquor as he could get, and his summer holidays were spent in catching crabs off the wharves and spits about Baltimore. He had a blunted, obeying face, with thin beard all round its long, heavy chin, and Booth was his idea of an educated gentleman.

For the first time Mr. Booth ranged the old slave counties below Washington upon an October Saturday, and on Sunday morning persons to whom he delivered the letters of introduction from Canada took him to the Catholic church in sight of Bryantown.

He had probably arranged his visit with reference to the Sabbath attendance at this church, where the substantial planters of the deepest slavery prejudices in the peninsulas gathered to hear the news, and most of these had sons or kinfolk in the insurgent army.

The church was of brick, in a moldy tint, with low gallery-windows above, the taller windows below them, and its end pointed to the road and upheld a cross, cupola, and bell above the notched gable. The graveyard spread around, and the priest's house was close by, and the cedars and firs on the airy church hill were haltering-posts for the small, freckled horses which the soft climate nurtured all winter in the open air.

The handsome stranger with an historic name, now thrown upon his own resources, attracted general attention. It was already said that he had come down from Washington to buy the old lands for improvement, as he had made money by buying oil-lands in another State. He was introduced to everybody of consideration, but seemed most attracted to Dr. Samuel Mudd, the red haired person whom we have already seen, and who considered his family's grievances the greatest in the State; there was, of course, only one grievance in the country, namely, the legs upon the "nigger" which let him walk away from his master, who was shocked that the obdurate government did not let go of its enemy in the trenches, and bestow its whole military force upon catching the "nigger."

Here was a man after Booth's own heart, and he distinguished Dr. Mudd by accepting his invitation to go home to dinner.

Another person at worship that day was David Herold, the little apothecary's clerk from Washington, whose passion for "patridge" shooting obtained his periodical discharge by successive employers; and he loved the vicinity of the old academy he had attended at Charlotte Hall, which was some six miles distant from Bryantown church. He came up to the distinguished arrival and said:

"Mr. Booth, I met you at Harper's Ferry in the times of ole John Brown."

"Why, Dave," replied the actor, remembering the little simpering face — in which, however, the eyes had become more set and furtive, from gypsy ways and wandering — "how queer that I should see you here! Where's Andrew Atzerodt?"

"Down yer to Port Tobakker, makin' carriages and runnin' the blockade."

The two pursuits thus oddly conjoined — carriages and boats — touched the stranger's seductive dark eyes to emit a little soft flame.

"Dave," said he, "are you very busy now? Could you take me to see Atzerodt?"

"Oh, yes, Mr. Booth, I can always borrey a horse down yer in Charles, and I like to hunt and ride. Don't you want to shoot some patridges?"

"That's just it," replied Booth; "don't tell anybody we are going, but meet me tomorrow noon at Bryantown tavern."

The people remarked that there must be something dead in the vicinity, from the large number of vultures soaring over the church.

Booth entered this church with the others; in the three galleries were Negro communicants; four rows of pews, divided by two aisles, filled the body of the church; the arching altar at the head, flanked by banners, already showed the good priest at work with boys and bell and mystic tapers, amid the humble ornaments of crucifix, image, and shining metal.

Booth touched the holy water at the door, but did not make the pious signs upon his breast, and he took a place in a family pew, half folded his arms, and pulled with one released hand the ends of his black mustache, watching the ceremony of the dying Son of man.

He knew the significance of most of the high mass from school-days, and heard again the wailing words of Saint Leonard: *"Behold, my God, the traitor who has so often rebelled against thee! . . . The blood of Jesus cries for mercy; and my sorrowful heart also implores mercy."*

The little bell, to recall the wandering minds of communicants from their distractions, rang again and again, like an alarm-watch, set for this hour, on the ear of Booth, but he did not notice it.

The priest put on the vestments of the Savior's torture — the amice to blindfold him, the girdle for his cords, the chasuble to mock him as a king — and bowed to the linen cloths upon the altar representing the innocent victim's winding-sheet. Booth watched it all, and stole glances at the more comely women reading their books of prayer; but all the while he thought of another victim to blindfold, to bind, to mock, and to deliver up, and gritted his teeth when he imagined some disappointment in his plan, and smiled, looking straight at the altar cerements; and as the alternative of murder filled with its necessity the distended caverns of his soul, he put out his hand mechanically and took from the sacramental bread and ate.

So had the political forefathers of some in that church eaten the sacrament twelve generations before with Spanish-made assassins who meant to blow up Parliament.

A man came up the road from the Potomac while the sermon was following the mass. He rode an old country horse, and wore a faded gray suit whose color could hardly be told, but in it were some signs of a military life and rank. He was of great stature, but his hair was gray and thin, and his shoulders stooped with troubles, and he rode mechanically. Who could have guessed that this broken and dissolute-looking man was the former pride of the county he rode in, Lloyd Quantrell?

As he came opposite the church, which stood higher up on the knoll to the east, the traveler saw sitting along the panels of the crooked fence, so close that he could strike them, at least a hundred vultures, breathing through their slender bills, balancing with difficulty on their weak toes, and emitting a foul odor from their dull, raw necks. Quantrell looked for some sign of a carcass to attract them, but only saw the picked bones of a horse, long bleached by rain.

Turning his head, he saw the cedars and other trees, in a thicket between him and the church, black with other scores of these great turkey-birds, roosting in the branches. Suddenly, while he was in their midst, these buzzards uttered in concert a loud, hissing noise, and the fence beneath their weight broke down. The rough, poor animal Quantrell was riding took flight, and did not stop till it had passed a running brook that crossed the road.

"Three years and a half ago I saw a saucy buzzard at that spot," said Quantrell; "is it an omen of my capture and execution as a spy? No; I wear my uniform, and do not come disguised."

He remembered that a dog, which he recognized as Katy's faithful Fritz, had assailed him desperately in the road as he landed on Port Tobacco River, from Virginia, that morning, and that no kind recognition or petting could conciliate the animal.

"What a reception," reflected Quantrell; "when I remember that it was the boast of Charles County to have had only seven Union men in it!"

One of these was standing at his gate as Quantrell entered Bryantown — a physician of the same surname and family as the other Dr. Mudd. He looked up and bowed, and, after dropping his eyes, looked again and cried, "Is not that Lloyd Quantrell?"

"Yes, doctor."

"Why, come in! If we differ, we are not personal enemies. Lloyd, stay this Sunday with me, for your mother's sake!"

"Thank God," spoke Quantrell, with a tear, "one man remembers me! No, doctor, I am here under orders, as a soldier. Unless they capture me, I shall be gone this night to my own lines."

"I am for my country," said the unpopular Unionist, "but I wish you no harm, my boy. A few months will bring you home a willing captive!"

Quantrell entered the hotel, ordered a bottle of whisky, and lay down in a bedroom opening on the upper porch. He drank, and opened again two curious letters he had received. The first said:

Washington City

My dear old friend and sworn avenger of the South, I call upon you by your sacred oath, made with me and one other, five years ago, to cross the river and meet me at Bryantown tavern, next Sunday, the ——. I will surely be there, and the business is important. You are as near Bryantown as I am, in Washington. Remember, *'Sic semper tyrannis!'*

J.W. Booth

It was not this letter which Quantrell was obeying, but a dearer one, that he read again with feelings aroused and wondering:

Baltimore

Captain Lloyd Quantrell:

Your father commands you to obey the letter you will receive with this. For this time only, he removes his injunction that you shall not come into our lines. Abel Quantrell is now a paralytic, and can not use his pen. The person who is his secretary is your friend and your faithful wife's.

Hannah Ritner

"What can it be?" the poor fellow sighed. "My father and Booth at work together? Hannah Ritner my father's secretary? Poor father! And O my wife; what a wreck I shall bring to her!"

He looked at the glass, and it told the story: exposure, men's company alone, and the ravages of drink.

"O that I were in the grave with the poor black fellow who died for me!" thought Lloyd, and he lay upon the bed and slept.

It was nearly evening when he was awakened by Booth and Dr. Mudd entering the room, and the former apologized for having left him alone so long, saying:

"I had a letter to deliver to the doctor from your old friend Martin, in Canada, and to make with it, Lloyd, a proposition which required tact, and which I am now about to make to you."

He took the candle and went out of the door and examined the rooms, porch, and stairway. Then he came in and set the candle down and opened a bottle of brandy. As Lloyd Quantroll drank of the pure French liquor, with almost religious ecstasy, after the raw alcohol he had swallowed for years, Booth looked him over with satisfaction; he was wrecked enough, demonized enough, fierce enough by wolfish war and killing, to meet the actor's approval.

"Now, bully," said Quantrell, as the liquor warmed his chilled system, and he looked at Booth over a great navy revolver he put upon the table, "I am ready to listen to whatever dream you are tempting that fool with."

He pointed to Dr. Mudd, and looked at Booth without the least affection or confidence of old times.

"Lloyd," said the actor, leaning forward and speaking low, "I have formed a plan to give the Southern cause a great advantage. Dr. Mudd approves of it, and is my first recruit; you will be the second. It is to capture Abe Lincoln alive in Washington and convey him by swift relays to the Potomac and immediately send him to Virginia. I know all his goings and comings, am in the inner circle of his friends, and have studied all the ground over except this route, which I have selected through lower Maryland, because of the safe crossing we have maintained here at the river since our independence."

"Plan large," said Quantrell, unexcited, and taking a drink. "Now, how?"

"Lincoln is unsuspecting as an idiot; rides to his Soldiers' Home retreat and other lonely country places in a large carriage with no one but a driver, and has neither a guard nor even a weapon. My proposition is that you and I, with a few confederates, shall waylay him, shoot the driver, and get on the carriage, and, by threat of death, make Lincoln, by showing his face and bowing his assent, be our passport out of the city. All the guards know his countenance, and the Eastern Branch is the only guarded place we have to pass; there are two bridges across this stream, and I have tried them both, and have been allowed to go and come repeatedly without any pass whatever."

"I am to drive, I suppose," said Quantrell. "and you are to kill him if he is not tractable? Now finish!"

"Dr. Mudd says that one Surratt, who has a tavern ten miles out of town and keeps the secret post office, can be got to establish the first relay of horses at his tavern, or at Tee Bee, just below. There we have a choice of three roads to come to Port Tobacco, and all those roads have gates upon them, dividing the private fields. For us the gates will all be open; for our pursuers all closed.* Either at Beantown or near Piscataway we will have a second relay and, if necessary, another carriage, well greased. If it is more expeditious, we will tie Lincoln on a horse, like Mazeppa, and make him ride. In four hours, by hellish speed, we can make Port Tobacco River, where we will have a boat all ready and men at the oars, and in a moment they will be out on the dark water, and Virginia flashing us her signals in the night across the Potomac!"

Dr. Mudd listened, with his blue eyes twinkling on pallid cheeks, and leaned forward to receive some emboldening from Quantrell.

"What is the recompense for this, provided it can be done?"

"Why, Lloyd, our fame and fortune are made. We will demand the release of every Confederate officer as fair exchange for Lincoln, and Yankee money to boot for the heroes of the enterprise. They would give us hundreds of thousands of dollars!"

"It is plain to be seen," said Quantrell, "that you see everything with an actor's eyes. What actors call 'effects' seem to you, John Booth, common sense. You are looking on Lincoln as some kind of a king, without whom the state can not go on. Do you suppose the great Yankee people, whom we expected to lick in six months, and who are just beginning to fight, care a straw about who is their President? We have taken away from our President at Richmond the control of affairs, and Lincoln, too, has been wise enough to let Grant have absolute military control; and all the fierce radicals, like Winter Davis, think they are smarter than Lincoln. The Yankees wouldn't give you a dollar nor a prisoner of war to return him. After the first sensation the rebels wouldn't approve of the feat. There are kind men as well as brave men in the South, and gentlemen! Behind Lincoln are ten thousand Presi-

---

*   Until about 1876 these private gates were lawful and continuous on all the roads leading south from Washington city.

dents among the Yankee people, and he is probably the superior of the least of them only in a lawful tenderness and the yearning desire to make emancipation pay the cost of the war."

"There!" said Dr. Mudd, starting up, "I told you he was unreliable, because he set his niggers free."

"Turn that man out," said Quantrell, taking more brandy, "after he hears my answer. *No!* I wear the gray uniform; there is no stain on it but battle-blood. Some day I shall want to come home in honor, and be trusted of my fellow-men. The mighty arms of this Union, in chastising love, are squeezing the life out of our mutiny, and the end can not be far off. I would not, for all the applause you expect to get for this boyish freak, John Booth, injure the poor fellows who have fought with me, and make the terms of submission hard for them!"

Booth, with twitching lips and looks sweeping the floor, turned once, to see the door shut behind Dr. Mudd escaping, and next his eyes seemed to leap upon the table where the pistol had been.

"You don't find it there," observed Quantrell, dryly, raising the huge weapon from his side and leveling it at Booth. "Hold up your hands, or I'll kill you where you stand! Turn your back here!"

He reached his left hand out and took a Derringer pistol from the actor's rear pocket, and drew the cartridge from it, and threw it back to him. He also corked the brandy, and put it in his pocket.

"This is for the protection of both of us," added Quantrell, with a more polite inflection. "Brandy always makes you crazy, John, and you have no business with a pistol unless you want to be an assassin. I have lived beyond fear, am shot all to pieces, and to kill a man is hardly an event to me."

The faded, swollen, giant mold of the soldier with his warped eyes carried an awe to Booth's brain.

"Lloyd," he faltered, "what have I done?"

"Nothing, because I anticipated you, John. You were going to remind me of a foolish oath that you, who administered it, have never kept, while I am a ragged monument of my fidelity. You meant to threaten me by that oath. Three times I have invaded the North. You never invaded anything more hostile than my brother Bosler's confidence and took his girl away."

"Nelly Harbaugh? Oh, she is a lizard, cold and ungrateful, and has thrown us both off."

"I met her in Richmond," said Lloyd, "and know all the story. It has changed my estimate of you. For that reason I had Senator Pittson advised, by an exchanged Yankee officer, to cut off your intimacy with his daughter."

"You did that?" cried Booth, rising; "I thought it was Bosler himself.

He has proposed to her, and been refused; while I —"

"Stop!" said Quantrell; "I won't hear you, for I might call you a liar. That girl is pure and free as an Indian maid from her native lakes and forests in the West. At one glimpse of your polluted life she would fly from you. Her father is not a play-actor, but a statesman, with faculties pure as his daughter's romance."

"Pooh! It was only lately that he was exposed in the Senate as somebody's bastard son, and never denied it — but rather gloried in it."

"He is my father's friend: I seek to know no more. Have you, John, a descent so unspotted that you rejoice in scandals like that?"

"My descent?" cried Booth proudly; "the world knows my name and pedigree!"

Quantrell looked at him gravely through his weather-beaten eyes.

"It is time you respected better-derived men, John Booth. All your life you have been under the glamour of a delusion, and your contempt for a lady like Miss Light Pittson — your using, also, Miss Harbaugh's ambition to destroy her happiness — impress me that the hour has come to disenchant you."

He drew from his pocket a small gold ring and handed it to Booth. The actor read:

"*J.B.B., TO HIS WIFE, CHRISTINE, 1815.*"

Quantrell's great hand closed around the ring before Booth could raise it from near the candle-flame.

"That ring," pursued Quantrell, in stern but respectful tones, "your father wed his wife with. Your father had a wife, whom he deserted in London, to fly to America with your mother. She was a simple Belgian-French child, but was his wife for thirty-six years; he lived with her six years, and never was divorced from her until you were my playmate, ten years before this civil war and all your brethren born. Then, the day she forced from your father, in the courts of Baltimore, a confession of these facts, the real marriage of your parents could be celebrated for the first time. It was so celebrated, and that poor foreign woman, sent to America for justice by the actors of London, died only the year before we met again at John Brown's scaffold!"

"How came you by this discovery and this ring, sir?"

"Your half-brother, your father's eldest son, came to me, starving, to sell it! I proved his tale by the records of the courts, and sent him to Europe, that he might not annoy your father's family and you, my early friend."

Quantrell arose, and said, in appeasing tones:

"John, don't commit any act to make men hate your name and bring these buried ghosts to life again! Go to the tomb of Mary Christine Adelaide Delannoy, in the old Cathedral Cemetery at Baltimore — the poor, abandoned woman died at sixty-six — and make your vow to live a modest life, and spare your mother and her better offspring the scandals you but now rejoiced in!"*

He rose to go. Booth made a constrained effort to detain him, saying: "You will eat with me?"

"Here," replied Quantrell, taking an old haversack from his side, and showing its contents of corn-bread and bacon, "is the ration common now to Negroes and heroes. Your brandy I will confiscate; that's always contraband. But Bob Lee's orders in Maryland are to take no private property. I'm off for Virginia."

"Very well," said Booth, smarting under the exposure of his *amour propre.* "The next time you preach to me, don't forget that you have abandoned Katy of Catoctin, and that if your own father don't marry her, that young snipe of a priest, Hugh Fenwick, will soon carry off your wife!"

The soldier was already gone, but Booth's words stung his heart to strange suspicions. He had sent all his letters to Katy in Fenwick's care. His father had never sent him a word or a line since his expatriation. The instinct was fierce in his soul to desert the Confederacy, and return to Baltimore and meet Fenwick face to face.

"No," said he; "they would send me to a military jail. If Hugh Fenwick has been false, I will have his life! Something tells me that I have only one friend — that sorceress, Hannah Ritner."

Herold and Booth went next day to Port Tobacco, and found Atzerodt in his retired wheelwright's shed, asleep in an old family carriage that was tumbling to pieces. His business had been neglected for blockade-running, and his domestic life was concubinage with a poor widow near by.

---

*   Inscription in the Catholic Cemetery, Baltimore:

"Jesus, Mary, Joseph,
Pray for the soul of
Mary Christine Adelaide Delannoy,
Wife of Junius Brutus Booth, Tragedian.
She died in Baltimore, March the 9th, 1858," etc.

Colonel Frank A. Burr possesses the marital correspondence between J.B. Booth, Sr., and his first wife. His cruelty in leaving her and his child in London, without bread, suggests the heartlessness of the assassin Booth, who killed an inoffensive man among ladies and by his wife's side. As this matter has been fully exploited in the daily papers, I make no apology for producing it here, among other preludes to the chief crime upon our continent. Edmund Dean contributed to send the deserted wife to America.

"Py Jing!" said he, when the proposition was mooted to him, "I know shoost te boat. I can make a wagon to run like a shtreak of greased lightnin', and I want money pad."

They rode together down the west side of Port Tobacco River, and on the way Atzerodt slipped behind the others furtively, saying:

"Tere's a tog here at Carpenter's dat I believe knows a rebel from a Union man. He comes for me efery time, although I sold him to tis feller."

As they spoke, a large fierce dog came down to the road, bounding, looked at them an instant and leaped the fence, and, hardly barking at all, vaulted in the air at Booth's knee. Atzerodt slipped past and whipped his horse, and the other horses fled behind him, the dog still rushing at Booth's stirrup, and so they got off with the first impressions of real war.

Three or four miles below Port Tobacco, where they could see St. Thomas's Manor-house and Chapel Point beyond the broad ocean inlet which cut into Charles County like the cleft of a human heart, was a house near the water, and in a ravined cope near it Atzerodt uncovered a large boat on low wheels and axles.

"I made tese wheels," said he. "Te Yankee navy has proke efery boat afloat to stop te running of te blockade; so we haul tis one up an' hide it. Abe Lincoln will git to Fergeenia so soon in dat boat he won't know it from Marylin."

"How far to Washington from this spot?" asked Booth.

"T'irty-six mile. If you git dat old Abe at four o'clock in te afternoon, you can make dis boat-landing at half-past eight, and haf him in Fergeenia py ten."

"I'm going to ride it tonight through Piscataway," said Booth.

As they approached the Unionist's dwelling, the alert dog came out again, like a faithful sentinel.

"I'll settle with him now!" the actor remarked, between his teeth, and stopped and balanced his pistol.

The dog, which seemed to be setter and mastiff, and old for his variety, ran along the inside of the worm-fence till opposite them, and there vaulted high; as he rose in the air, Booth's pistol was discharged, and the dog came rolling down the slope dead as a stone.[*]

If every Union sentinel had been like this poor Fritz, whom John Brown had also left to guard his cabin, the road which spies and assassins traveled so long might now have a sweet and peaceful name.

"So Abe Lincoln shall die by this pistol," exclaimed Booth, "if other measures fail to bring him! And now, both of you" — he slipped another

---

[*]   Related to the author by Thomas A. Harbin, who was in the abduction
       secret.

cartridge in the Derringer, and held the pistol up in his right hand —
"hold up your hands and say what I shall say, and swear. Which of you
refuses, dies like that dog, and his life I will have at any time he dares
to disobey me or betray me! You both possess my secret — you both
know what the 'oil-business' means."

The smoking weapon in his hand, his pale face and obdurate expression, and deep tragedy voice, made Atzerodt's stomach grow faint, and
he hardly had the strength to raise his arm.

Herold was rather seized with admiration, and a blushing grin
marked his countenance as he held his hand up.

"You swear," said Booth, "never to leave this enterprise, never to tell
of it, to live and die in it, under the penalty of death in this world and
hell in the next, for which you entreat — so help you God!"

The mastery of Booth over both of them he felt to be complete. All
the way back to Port Tobacco they were nearly silent, and there he
dismissed them, with instructions to call on him in the capital city, at
the National Hotel, and turned his horse toward Washington.

Over this same road, but sixty-five years before, a galloping servant
had come to get a doctor for the dying Father of his Country, and Booth
could see Dr. Brown's old house overhanging the Port Tobacco River;
and, as he approached Piscataway in the shades of evening, he saw
Mount Vernon across the wide water of the Potomac, and fancied he
could almost hear the steamers on the river toll their passing bells. Not
the smallest idea entered his head that the man he meant to pursue
would subdue the heart of the whole world by his love, as Washington
had done by his dignity.

As he passed out of the ruined town of Piscataway, whose old brick
chimneys stood houseless, like the widowers of many wives, he noted
the long, red-brick Catholic church, with green shutters and yellow
cupola, and under the wooden cross in its gable the words:

*"Come unto me all you that labor and are heavy laden, and I will refresh
you."*

Two ladies came out of the churchyard with the priest, and drove
away in a country carriage. Booth looked respectfully at them, and said
to the priest:

"Father, who are those pleasing ladies?"

"That is Mrs. Surratt and her daughter, sir, who formerly lived close
by, but have removed to Washington."

"Isn't there a son in that family?"

"Oh, yes, sir, Mr. John. He's the widow's only stay now. His brother
is in Texas — perhaps in the Confederate army."

As Booth took the straight river road, he thought of the inscription
over the old church many times: "Come unto me, and I will refresh

you"; or, as the Protestants have it, "I will give you rest." "Ah!" he said — as in the night, at quite ten o'clock, he saw from the Insane Hospital slope the lights of Washington flash across the Eastern Branch — "I don't like this abduction plan as well as my hint about the back of the theater. I must have the performance actable!"

"What is your name?" asked the guard at the bridge. "You are coming back pretty late."

"Lloyd Quantrell," answered Booth.

The guard took down the name in a book, and said:

"Pass over, sir."

Chapter XLIV

THE BAND

*A*S Abel Quantrell and Katy, his ward, were playing cards at the window in Old Town — money invariably staked, for Abel gambled as he battled, for realities — John W. Booth went past with two slouchy, inferior men.

"Sam Arnold and Michael O'Laughlin!" reflected Hannah Ritner, aloud. "O'Laughlin deserted from the rebel army at South Mountain to escape fighting at Antietam. He was Booth's school-mate and Booth's mother's tenant. That Arnold also went to the war for loot, and his name is a common one in mountain Maryland. But what companions!"

"The square of his father," said Abel Quantrell, speaking with difficulty — "who was, Hannah, a man of soft whims, but his delight was to be the Hector of low and boozing inferiors. He would wait at a three-cent liquor-saloon for the police station to discharge its vagrant lodgers — men, often, of some social past, but ruined by drink and the habits of slavery — and there he would set the brandy up and inveigh, recite, and squander the gifts of beauty and temperament upon those swine by the hour and the day."*

"Aunt Hannah," said Hugh Fenwick, "the soldier who calls himself Payne, or Powell, has been here, asking for you. He has again deserted from Mosby's or Gilmore's band, and taken the oath."

"I can not help him," said Hannah Ritner; "for a while I thought he had a modest heart, but the murderer was there, although he had a preacher for his father. He beat the poor colored woman where he lodged in Baltimore, and was compelled by the provost to go north of the city. He stamped upon her like a demon because she would not clean his room in an instant. I fear that so many of these whipped but not penitent men, between the lines — this city is full of them — will become fire for some evil tinder. Who is this Mrs. Surratt you visit, Fenwick?"

---

*   Mr. William Wilkison's recollections of Booth, the elder.

"A widow, with a fairer daughter. She is not very deep, had an old husband, and may not be averse to a young one."

"There is her danger," Hannah Ritner mused; "conspiracy can hide beneath love like the copper-snake under the blueberry-bush. Do you believe Lloyd Quantrell has entered Washington?"

"The guard took that name down as he crossed the bridge."

"It was not Lloyd," spoke Katy Bosler. Her German accent was all gone now, and only the beaming eyes expressed a discomposure. Lovely and refined by study and society she had grown. Her lover's father looked at her and said:

"Do you maintain that traitor to be true to anything?"

"Yes, to his father, if not to me."

"Look at this young man who has waited upon you almost four years — sedate, religious, tender as a girl — what comparison does your betrayer bear to him? Give him your hand, while still the fugitive holds out against every natural affection, and let him return to find love sealed forever against his claims."

The old man had staggered up and sustained himself on Fenwick's broad shoulder, and the coarse lines returned to his fallen mouth as he strove to close it hard. The divinity-student looked at Katy in modest reverence and respect, his red and white colors healthy as the peach-skin — his habits adapted to all degrees and sects.

"Miss Kate," said Fenwick, "I broke my heart to unite you to another one. It has healed under your forgiveness and confidence. We have pursued our studies together, and grown in unison of mind — I hope, of soul. When will you let me restore you to your father as my wife?"

Katy stood with quiet grace, hearing this speech, and all watching her closely.

"I want the truth," she said. "I have heard you, Hugh, tell one falsehood. Lloyd Quantrell never has. His going to the war against his father's wishes shows the rude sincerity of the man. Why he never writes to me I can't tell. Maybe he's tired of a child's love, or is waiting for the war to end, and to see me again with eyes of understanding. I have tried to raise myself to his mind. He may come back, unworthy of my troubles, and leave me free to enjoy, as your pupil still, the world of intellect displayed by the tenderest friendship."

A slight movement of her head toward him indicated a preference for his society.

"The test shall be," spoke Hannah Ritner, "to set you, Fenwick, and Lloyd Quantrell, face to face!"

"I never can fear that test," the demi-clerical spoke, with cheeks where the roses had suddenly flown. — "Brother Abel, your friends, the nuns, are at the door."

A trio of nuns came in and made themselves sociable, and Abel Quantrell allowed prayers to be offered for him in his afflicted state. He liked women better than men, but liked his indignations best of all; and among these last was a hatred of the Napoleons — singularly enough, for their treatment of their wives — and the pope had refused to divorce the brother of Napoleon from his Baltimore wife at the emperor's demand. So Abel Quantrell, with a swerving against power everywhere, had become a favorite and patron of the Sisters of Charity, and the less ascetic monastic orders, like the Visitation Nuns, who were now engaged in the gradual work of converting him — the more desirously, because his political opinions had come to rule the land. He, resisting authority, and they, sheltering under it, proved that extremes often meet.

It was Hugh Fenwick, in pursuance of his amateur diversions, who set on this conversion; but the old man, in his enfeebling age, grasped only the worldly part of the proposition — that he, or somebody, might convert the pope to proclaim for The People everywhere. For the heaven of blessedness they promised him he did not care, nor greatly for his worldly fame; but the idea of taking the most reactionary engine in the world, as he esteemed it, and running it forward, gave to his own mind a light of satyr joy. If Pepin and Rienzi and Hildebrand had seized Rome, why could not a Yankee do the same, and batter aristocracies down with a crozier?

Thus they prayed together, unavowedly, for the trophies of this world — the ecclesiastics to add an important radical to their pantheon, and, perhaps, get their share of appropriations; the old agitator, to reverse Rome, and use it on this earth for democracy.

Katy, alone, prayed to God for justice and mercy, kneeling among the rest.

When Abel Quantrell had received the kisses and benedictions of the gratified Sisters, and all had gone, he turned to his ward and said:

"What did you pray?"

"To give God your soul, and let it eat the bread of love."

"Through whom?"

"Father, I tried to say through God's Son; but into my mouth kept coming the words and the face of your own son, Lloyd. Oh! yield your heart to forgiveness of our poor wanderer, and the Son of Heaven will come there too, like Jesus and the dove to the water of John's baptism."

As she looked, a tear came down his cheek, that all the pursing and folding of his lips could not retard.

With a scream of joy, Katy kissed the old man's eyes.

"My prayer is answered!" she cried. "You love your boy!"

"Let him stand the rest of the test," old Abel Quantrell said; "the war is nearly done."

Mr. Booth, meantime, had been demonstrating his social and business resources to create a band of abductors. He sounded two or three actors of Maryland stock; but they imputed any war scheme of his to the drink he was taking so freely, and Ned Spangler was the nearest he could come to a convert.

While this poor, imbruted carpenter worked at Ford's Theater, Booth would slip in and study the situation of afternoons, try the lighting apparatus, to plunge the auditorium in profound darkness or blazing light, pace the length of the stage and of the aisles to the back door, and sometimes come leaping down from the upper box to the stage-floor, like a trapeze-performer.

This leap might have been made by many a lad for a wager or exercise, and a gymnast would esteem it no hard matter; the gymnasium had prepared Booth for some great public exhibition of this kind of prowess in which he excelled all actors, though many of these kept up their physical training for the death-scenes, wrestles, and combats so rife in the dramas of a sword-wearing age; but "the jump" was Booth's monopoly, he being light and flexible in the ankles and knees, and with a bow-legged tendency, which enabled him to drop akimbo after he had stepped limberly.

How much of his ultimate black deed is traceable to his passion for strength for brutal ends a prize-fighter might guess. The fact that he could so leap from a high place invested his purpose with a public ambition he never could shake off, and materially weakened his interest in the original abduction design.

The theater would give him an audience which a highway assault could not afford; it was really the safer place of the two, from the entire novelty of its selection and his superior knowledge of its exits, and the ignorance of the public of there being any rear avenue from a theater, or conversance with such a purely professional path; and, more than this, to abduct the President from the theater would make but one hero of the act. Booth was jealous of giving other men fame by his idea.

The miserable parcel of country tools he had assembled would do to drive the vehicle from the back of the theater, and could be kept unseen over the foot-lights. He had the full run of Ford's Theater by intimacy with nearly all its people; the man was found in Spangler to do his more sneaking work within it; where could he get an actor, filling a part at the moment, to catch the President when Booth should throw him from the upper box and leap down after him and drag him down the dark aisles to the back door?*

---

*   "Booth urged that the part I would have to play would be a very easy affair and was sure to succeed, but needed some one connected or ac-

There was manifestly no such ruffian, with intelligence enough to be an actor, except this man himself.

No sense of his hospitality as an actor, and the son and brother of actors, ever occurred to him, when considering how to earn a mean distinction by thus brutalizing the theater of his friends and dragging an elderly magistrate across its boards though an invited guest. The hospitality of the Bedouin Arab this gypsy could not feel in his native tent.

The tatterdemalions he assembled came easily enough. Dr. Mudd brought him the widow Surratt's son, originally a modest country boy, now inflated by some experience as a civilian spy and secret-mail carrier, and who had known no other employment in all the multiform opportunities on either side of that war, except in the little tavern and bar of his mother, ten miles from Washington.

Through this son of twenty-two, Booth gained access to the widow's little boarding-house in an obscure yet central part of Mr. Lincoln's capital, only six street blocks from Ford's Theater and six from Booth's hotel.

It may have been the only respectable house the actor visited in that full city; and the only friends of the family were some country farmers, and priests, and people off the courses of public life.

Fenwick alone among the visitors there could have exposed Booth's insidious relations to the softer sex. He knew the two or three boarders there who were all of his religious profession, and who gave a scanty living to the family, where the actor's advent was the sensation of its dull existence.

There was the widow, older than Booth, but in full health and bright color; and the widow's daughter, agreeable to the eye and the mind; and the actor seemed to be rich, influential, manly, and even beautiful. Booth took the son, by the mother's help, from his first occupation, in an express-office, where he had just entered upon an honest livelihood, and sent him to obtain persons for the abduction scheme in the vicinity of Port Tobacco; some of these the government afterward considered beneath responsibility and let them go, or never discovered them.

The plot at one time had quite a show of names in it, but the contingent was always the largest at the distant end, where running instead of fighting was to be the task; for no person higher endowed than a ruffian or tramp cared to earn the precarious livelihood of Booth's bounty and be scouting in the army-mired lanes of a pleasant city in the winter at the behoof of a theatrical speculator.

---

quainted with the theater." — S.K. Chester, actor.

"I asked Arnold what his part was to be; he said he was to catch the President when he was thrown out of the box at the theater." — E.G. Horner's testimony.

Generally speaking, all who were in the contraband mail and carrying business, on both sides of the Potomac, knew that something sensational was coming.

The manager of this motley company was alarmed lest his copyright should be invaded by some other adventurer, and on one occasion his hirelings reported that a plot had been overheard in a hotel, nearly like that of his abduction. He swore his men by oaths, at once theatrical and practical, only after he had awakened their cupidity by often-postponed explanations: the part of the oath they kept in mind was that they would be pursued for life and assassinated if found false; and he at times observed to them that they were in his power, and had already done enough to be justly hanged by the army within whose lines they spied and confederated.

Booth, in fact, saw that the President's death was a very probable incident of the abduction, and he labored to draw the courage of his satellites up to that philosophy. But one of his Baltimore recruits, Arnold, who had the only good countenance in the party, reflecting on the matter more and more, finally took the position, in a meeting of the band, six or seven in number, that if Booth meant to play fair, he should go ahead and capture the President, or release them all from their obligations. This was the only man steady enough to earn a living, and, although Booth turned on him and swore he ought to die, the man maintained his point, and soon after got away.

The *morale* of all the band would have broken early but for their absolute dependence on the actor for mental occupation, employment, and drink. He had bought two or three horses, and went riding among them, spying out the President's ways and experimenting with parts of the route of flight, and at least twice again he went down to Mudd's, exciting that weak, bitter person with golden prospects or alarms. Money, indeed, was the object of everybody taken into Booth's confidence; and he, after arousing that hope, marveled that it was the only vitality his enterprise had. Nobody seemed heartily to hate Mr. Lincoln but himself, and he did so because the President's mildness had laid him open to an animal's passions.

As the beast hates the lamb, attacking the weakest after observing it, Booth's carnal appetite had fallen on Lincoln because he was the softest enemy in nature and speech, and had sought the moral pathways through the physical warfare, to ends beyond the lusts of victory. Booth could not formulate this, though he felt it; the bully always detects the magistrate by something above the common in him: Mr. Lincoln's tender strains, used in the affirmation of human brotherhood and final rights, had affected Booth like a woman's hymns heard by the painted, ambushed savage; to his doctrines and qualities they seemed atheistical;

they involved consideration for a "nigger," and touched the core of the war.

Besides, Mr. Lincoln was the ruling foe and name to the scornful thousands and the illiterate millions who contended against him, and Booth had once been a favorite among these, and would be again a hero. He knew their impulses, but he could not foresee their education, and he did not know that the calamities of war bring resignation, in which a better humanity is born.

The young Surratt, a long, sunken-eyed youth, grew also doubtful about the public reward from the insurgent side for the contemplated outrage, and was perhaps dissatisfied with Booth's influence under his mother's roof. That house was being used too much by the conspirators not to awaken there the wonder of a government clerk or two, who saw the well-dressed actor, mature in all his bearing, call often in the little parlor at the top of a high ladder of wooden steps, and next in the hostess's private room, and have long, confidential talks with her; and, as the son worked out of the original plot, the mother was taken in, and proved the sincerest recruit.

The hand that touched hers expressed a confidence, the eyes which drew so near her beamed an interest, the tone lowered to her ear sounded so much will and half-filial, half-passionate respect, that she obeyed with almost the joy of the affianced. She at first had feared and objected to any perilous adventure for her boy; but he was not as scrupulous of her mighty hazard; although many a female spy had been sent to the prisons, to be exploited and released, until, in the blind belief that the American Government was too gentle to punish a woman, these knights and squires from the gutter played a woman's life against the ruler's, and ran away and left her with all the evidence piled around her.

Into this little house Booth sent his fellow-assassin to call upon the son, and have the mother find him lodgings in Ford's Theater block — a giant brute entering there by the name of Woods, tried under the name of Payne, but really named Powell. He was hardly twenty years old, the son of a slave-owning preacher in the Gulf States, and dyed in civil war since his boyhood, at first in regular warfare — till Hannah Ritner found him at Gettysburg — and after that a partisan horseman among the Potomac valleys, learning guerrilla feats. He deserted and returned to Baltimore, and, tortured for money to meet his expenses, he brutally beat his chambermaid, and was sent to the provost-marshal as a misbehaving prisoner, and ordered to live north of Baltimore.

In that instant of despair, a deserter from one side, a "suspect" upon the other, without money, clothes, or address, he heard his name called at twilight by a beautiful-faced man on the steps of Barnum's Hotel, past which this Payne was dragging himself, a homeless tramp.

"Booth, is that you? I want bread; I am starving!"

"You are the very man I want. I'll give you money, to go into business with me, if you'll swear to stick; it's in the oil-business."[*]

This butcher of twenty was what Booth needed to conclude or intensify his project; and in that man, of weak cultivation and easily frenzied brain, he poured his subtlest distillations, awoke the subsided sentiment of revenge, carried him up and down Washington and Alexandria to see lost or gutted dwellings deserted by their former owners in the fell suicide of party or sectional passion, and pointed out the houses of the President and Cabinet as the authors of the war. The barbarian aroused himself, like the gladiator to whom Nero gave the torch while accusing the Christians. Payne trembled and raged, and Booth adjured him never to let such men be victorious.

As has been said, Booth was the first, perhaps the only, actor Payne had seen at Richmond before hostilities, while the slave States were arming; and, after that play, with proud self-confidence, he had sought the actor out, and found him easily won by his inferiors; and now, after four years of separation, the intimacy is renewed, when the reckless soldier is Booth's pupil and pauper, eating the bread of him who gives him also a stone.

At last the intentions of Booth were revealed, and the murderer, long glutted with blood, yearns for more.

"Now," said Booth, "that I have seduced a soldier, I'll take Abe Lincoln as it suits me, and let these country louts and lunch-fiends quit, or make them obey."

Something mysterious was happening in the great victim's favor. By prying into the circle of his grooms, Herold, who had been an apothecary's clerk where the President's family bought medicine,[†] several times anticipated the times and routes of Mr. Lincoln's driving excursions, and the band started out with horses, arms, and cords supplied by Booth, but never found the President where they went. Again and again this information was obtained, only to prove false. The weaker spirits began to feel superstitious on the subject, and Surratt discovered that the government was building a stockade at the bridge to lower Maryland, menacing an attack from outside, and he wanted to withdraw.

Booth observed that Major Luther Bosler was often riding on the roads he and his tools took at such times, and the thought of treachery somewhere, other than his own, discomposed his mind.

Besides, the abduction plot was too expensive, and the coincidence of an opportunity and of the relays and boats to be set for the event

---

[*]   Argument of Payne's counsel, W. E. Doster.

[†]   Thompson's drug-store, one square east of the President's mansion; Herold there discharged, July 4, 1863.

was very unreliable. His character was running down, from the public observation of his low companions and of the low mail-stage inns and saloons he frequented with them, and by the alcohol he drank while evolving a mathematical problem from an empty mind. The season that winter and spring was severe, and the clay roads of lower Maryland were almost impassable, so that, when the band seemed ready above, word would come from below to postpone the deed.

But nothing was retarding the magnificent campaign of Liberty. On January 31, 1865, the lower House of Congress, after more than two years' debate and delay, passed the amendment abolishing slavery, Maryland giving it four votes out of five, led by Mr. Davis, and ended by the Congressman from Booth's own native town;* and after that the rebellion lived only four months — Savannah, Columbia, Charleston, Wilmington falling, as the great scythe of Sherman moved like the rainbow of a comet onward — and meantime Abraham Lincoln stood before his countrymen to be inaugurated again.

A brilliant star stood at midday in the sky, following clouds and rain,† as the great procession went up to the Capitol. In the train of the President hung Booth and his band on horseback, with a scheme to hitch to the President's carriage and gallop away with it, but a single glimpse of the actual scene had destroyed this theory.

The President, before the grand assemblage of his sovereigns — the now equal and consistent people — stood lofty and history-wrinkled, confronted by thousands of his maimed and crutched soldiery, shedding tears before his face, as the knights of the Crusade wept at the sight of Jerusalem and its shrine. He kissed the Bible, after the roar of voices, at the words —

"Whose arrows are sharp, and all their bows bent; their horses' hoofs shall be counted like flint."‡ The President spoke as words can never speak without a great event behind them, or a destiny following near.

"Each side," said he, "looked four years ago for an easier triumph, and a result less fundamental and astounding. . . . With high hopes for the future, no prediction in regard to it is ventured. . . . With malice toward none, with charity for all, with firmness in the right as God gives us to see the right, let us finish the work we are in, to bind up the nation's wounds, to care for him who shall have borne the battle, and for his widow and his orphans, to do all which may achieve and cherish a just and lasting peace among ourselves and with all nations."

These words, the last preceding his solemn oath, enemies might have felt the nobleness of; but as the President walked back through the

---

*   Edwin H. Webster, of Belair. The only Marylander to oppose it came from the counties below Washington.

†   Arnold's "Lincoln," page 401.

‡   Marked by Mrs. Lincoln, where his lips touched the book.

Rotunda of the Capitol a man stood in his path dressed in a rowdy imitation of an officer's clothes, and striving hard to get to the front of a cordon of people who themselves opened an avenue for their Chief Magistrate.

It was Booth, full of brandy and self-comparison, moody under the expenses of his band, and suddenly seized with the idea that he could also inaugurate himself this day and take the first page in history.[*]

In his long boot-leg was a knife; in his overcoat-pocket a pistol, covered by his right hand.

He pressed along and had broken through the front line amid some confusion and resistance, and his white face, with black jewels in it and cruel teeth sparkling, expressed a sinister purpose.

The President came along in cloak, and cordial countenance under his tall hat, between the glow of good-will and the celestial melancholy which plays around the immortal times of man.

As the President looked into the young man's intense and undergazing eyes, he seemed to recognize an acquaintance, and lifted his left hand to his hat, uncovering his heart.

At this moment a large woman rushed across the President's path, and threw herself upon the actor, crying:

"You shall not crowd me out of my place twice!"

"Shame! shame!" from the people, thus disturbed in expecting to see their ruler, eye to eye.

The woman's velocity was like her weight and will; she bore the actor far back, and faced him with an inflamed and hostile face, and cried:

"What woman will you push next out of her place?"

The President had gone through the small, guarded door toward the Supreme Court.

The man gritted his teeth, paid no heed to his assailant, and rushed down the dusky, hidden stairs in the shell of the old Capitol.

Hannah Ritner was also heedless of the people who gaped at her and her wild hair and mien. She who had thus made a tumult before the President, went down Pennsylvania Avenue, and turned into Nelly Harbaugh's quarters.

"Nelly, are you ready to show Miss Pittson the character of the man who wants her to elope with him?"

"No. She is a proud creature, and let her be unfriended as I was. Who advised *me?*"

The strange woman listlessly picked up the girl's hand and looked it

---

[*]   "He exclaimed, striking the table, 'What an excellent chance I had to kill the President, if I had wished, on Inauguration-day!' He said he was as near the President on that day as he was to me. This he said on Friday, the 7th of April, one week previous to the assassination." — Testimony of S.K. Chester, actor.

over, while Nelly felt a sense of superstition come over her jealous cruelty.

"Go to her," sighed Hannah Ritner, "and you shall find the *red bird.*"

She repeated from the old Dutch prediction she had made sixty-five months before:

> "Gaed der roth-fogel uf'n reis',
>   Dann waersht net dunkel or net weiss!"

"Hannah," exclaimed the actress, "do you see fortunes with your mind or your witchcraft?"

"How can I know, girl? She who wills to be a mother might receive, by widening love of all mankind, the genesis of them all who came in strong contact with her. Your beauty and will impressed me. I saw you would fall by climbing, and still the hand that shook you from purity would have to be a treacherous, fierce one, and in time would kill. Now, go and learn who the red bird is."

"I know," said Nelly; "I have used my old lover Atzerodt to discover that John Booth is in some rebel plot. But Atzerodt does not know himself just what it is to be. Booth may not know."

"Go to Light Pittson, my girl! What shall happen there, will put you in Booth's heart again, and you shall read it for me."

"Then I will not go, to be the menial of that man again."

"You must," said Hannah Ritner, rising and showing the latent power she employed with such self-suffering; her bosom heaved and her eyes conveyed deep night and lightnings, and her hair seemed to fall, unshaken, like a great black serpent uncoiling from a tree.

"Oh, mercy! Hannah, do not look at me like that!"

"Awake — the woman is dying in you! Did Pilate's wife not send him word, 'Have thou nothing to do with that just man, for I have suffered in my dreams of him'? The high priest's house-maids challenged Peter's treachery. And Jewish women followed Christ when every man turned from him — a magdalen, a fallen one, that day, the purest, bravest, in the world! What now can save the just man at our side but women? He is a man himself and will not fear! Let woman only waken, and he is saved!"

As she hesitated, like an oracle seeking to be remedial to its own harsh prophecy, Nelly Harbaugh threw herself at Hannah's feet and cried:

"Teacher, I will go!"

Hannah Ritner staggered like a drunken woman as she reached the street, and some in that evil quarter might have laughed at her. As she reached the avenue, the bands and bugles, dispersing, filled the sky with sweetness like the angel choirs.

"Mother!" spoke a gentleman.

"O Edgar, my son, I have been all night guarding the President as he sat from midnight to the morn, signing bills at the Capitol in the last night of the session. They would not let me see him. He will not admit me anymore. And yet that Booth and parcels of his band were lurking there: I saw them, Edgar!"*

"Mother, since your strange behavior in the Capitol today, there is talk of confining you at the insane asylum. Your presence here threatens your grandchild, Light, with some exposure, before a good man can marry her. Let me tell you that the President is in no danger, among ten thousand friends, and if he were, his duty is above his life."

"Send him away, I implore you!"

"There is no place he will go but to the army."

"Then send him there! Go with him. I am not mad, my boy."

"No, mother. You do affect my sensibilities; for you are so often right. He shall go."

Hannah Ritner next sought Hugh Fenwick in the old Catholic Church of St. Patrick, where he was enjoying the day in congenial mysticism among the tapers and altar matters.

"By yonder Host," she said, pointing to the wafer's place, "go this day to Mrs. Surratt's, and in your holiest relation, whatever that may be, tell her that her new friend is fatal, and will splash with righteous blood the woman's century!"

"Is her house being watched?" asked Fenwick, with well-bred surprise.

"Yes, by me and the stars!"

The novitiate crossed himself.

"I will go and tell her," he said.

"Then every woman will have been warned," lisped Hannah Ritner, hastening away.

Had she been one moment earlier, she might have seen Booth and two of his men ride up the alley right opposite this church, behind Ford's Theater.

"I guess it's none of my business to become unpopular with 'Mrs. Surratt," mused Fenwick to himself, after she had gone. "What can I do, if Quantrell ever returns? I hope he is in this, or some other, treason scheme."

A few days afterward the band was called together, and all were mounted, Booth at the head. The information was positive that the President would go that afternoon to visit the wounded soldiers in a suburban hospital.

---

*   The testimony of the intelligent witness Louis J. Weichman is that Booth and Surratt went to the Capitol the night of March 3d, and Surratt had been all day after the procession on horseback.

He was now to be forced, by the plan, at the pistol's point to get upon a horse and ride; and at Surratt's tavern carbines, and rope to tie him, had been concealed only a few days before his second inauguration.

He did ride out, but some cavalrymen were beside his carriage, put there by the Secretary of War; and he went, not to the hospital, but down to the river and to the army, to stay away several days.

Booth sent Payne to the army with a pass, to assassinate him, but the President was kept upon a steamboat in the James River, and the strange man was repulsed when he tried to board.*

"Ah!" said Booth to Payne, when the latter returned to Baltimore, "had you been there on the 4th of March, I would have killed him like Caesar in the Capitol."

Young Surratt, who had been fishing a long time for the confidence of the insurgent government, now got a job to take a female spy from his mother's house in Washington to Richmond, and there he was paid to go with dispatches to Canada. He left his mother, never to see her again. The day he left Richmond the American army broke the thickest shell of the rebellion in, and President Lincoln entered Richmond amid the joys of a mighty race set free. He was in no danger there, where the people had lived behind their own lines.

Upon the 9th of April, 1865, Virginia and her valiant army surrendered to the government.

There still remained a large insurgent army in North Carolina, and other smaller armies in more remote States.

President Lincoln addressed the people from his mansion in Washington on the night of April 11th, saying:

"If universal amnesty is granted to the insurgents, I can not see how I can avoid exacting in return universal suffrage, or at least suffrage on the basis of intelligence and military service."

There were then hundreds of thousands of colored soldiery, and the insurgent President had demanded the right to arm the slaves.

Booth was standing before Mr. Lincoln on the outskirts of the large assemblage.

"That means nigger citizenship," he said to little Herold, by his side. "Now, by God! I'll put him through."†

---

* President Lincoln's son, at the trial of John Surratt, gave testimony as above, that a tall man, rather of Surratt's appearance, tried at City Point to see the President.

† Frederick Stone, counsel for Herold after Booth's death, told the author that this was the occasion of the deliberate murder being resolved upon by Booth, and in the words above.

Chapter XLV

ASSASSINATION

WHEN a man has once let murder enter his mind, it will drive out all the lesser passions. Booth had recovered Nelly Harbaugh, and raised the flame of love in her again, but it did not satisfy. His voice had returned, and he had played at Ford's Theater with Nelly in the cast, to their mutual credit; but he now wanted to act murder, and his diabolical part, Pescara, was of itself an explanation of the assassin's mind.

Pescara hates the Moors because they are of a different race and views from his, and resolves to exterminate them, forces the noblest of their wives, though she is white, and stretches her husband and his aged friends upon the rack of the Inquisition, crying aloud as he stabs:

> "Ha! ha! a Moor —
> One of that race that we have trodden down
> From empire's height and crushed — a damned Morisco!
>   What if I rush,
> And with a blow, strike life from out his heart?
>   Come forth, my sword!
> Be true as fate to me. Rise, Spaniards, rise!
> Rush on the slaves, and revel in their blood!"

Fifty years before this — the last play-part acted by John Wilkes Booth — an Irish lawyer had made the character of Pescara, from a close study of Booth's father's rendering of types of hideous cruelty and revenge. The piece was no longer allowed to be played in England, but the father had played it in America, and this son now demanded to play it at a fellow-actor's benefit.*

By another promise he had made, to play for the benefit of the chief

---

*   John McCullough. This piece was played March 18, 1865, by Booth, in the presence of Surratt, Herold, and Atzerodt, and probably Arnold and O'Loughlin — some of whom were in the President's box.

officer of that theater, his access to the building had become nearly like a proprietor's, and there Spangler was Booth's man and sworn confederate.

The day before Good Friday, April 14th, Booth, seeking to decoy the President to a theater, went also to the National Theater and suggested to the proprietor to invite Mr. Lincoln the next night, which was to be the celebration of raising the public flag again upon Fort Sumter. Both theaters were therefore tendered to the President; but his wife accepted Ford's Theater, since "The American Cousin" was to be played there — a piece of the humor flavored to Mr. Lincoln's cares.

Although Booth had sold one of his horses, he could hire others less expensively; for he meant to steal them at the livery-stables. All the band still hung around him except two. He sold his buggy the day after he resolved to murder. The bills of exchange he had bought on Canada constituted nearly all his means, and he meant to spend the rest on this bloody spree, to which liquor was now giving demoniac ferocity.

He designed to kill the President himself, and to kill Mr. Seward — the founder of the Republican party — by the hands of Payne; for Booth was an exemplification of bigotry in general, in that he chiefly hated the thinkers and writers among his opponents. There is something of Booth in every narrow, domineering intellect, and five months before this murder he began to be a literary man himself, and keep a diary like his grandfather.*

Payne was not told of his particular task until evening, when it was plain that General Grant would not come to the theater; but, had it been otherwise, Booth reserved Payne for a bloody part in the theater-box.

O'Loughlin came over from Baltimore to be made the assassin of Secretary Stanton and General Grant; but, after taking a look at them, he wisely concluded to finish out his spree, and, in this case, wine was wit.

The new Vice-President, a Southern man, and hardly an opponent of

---

*   In November, 1864, Booth deposited with his brother-in-law, J.S. Clark, a long composition, extenuating some crime he meant to commit, of which the following is pertinent to the motive of this book:

"When I aided in the capture and execution of John Brown (who was a murderer on our Western border, and who was fairly tried and convicted before an impartial judge and jury of treason, and who, by the way, has since been made God), I was proud of my little share in the transaction, for I deemed it my duty that I was helping our common country to perform an act of justice. But what was a crime in poor Brown is now considered (by themselves) as the greatest and only virtue of the whole Republican party. Strange transmigration! Vice so became a virtue simply because more indulged in. I thought then, as now, that the abolitionists were the only traitors in the land, and that the entire party deserved the same fate of poor John Brown."

slavery, Booth desired to kill because he was a "renegade" and the successor, and he concluded to put this task on Atzerodt.

Little Herold was to guide Payne to Mr. Seward's door, and then show him, by an upper bridge over the Eastern Branch, the road to meet Booth at Surratt's.

Booth's reliance on Atzerodt lay not in the latter's courage, but his despair, at being left behind, the accomplice in a great crime, and penniless in Washington, while his safety would lie in escaping to his own district and using his own transportation there to Virginia.

Booth, drinking at intervals all Friday, fed this hideous scheme, the logical outcome of himself, his courses, and his former plot, with whisky, which hardened his purpose and shut out all moral abstractions.

He set Spangler to work upon making him a bar for the private box after it was prepared for the President — by taking out a partition, and decorating the double box with flags; and, seeing the position of the President's chair, Booth took a small gimlet he had bought and bored an eyelet-hole through the thin box-door, and cut it clean with his pen-knife; while in a short private passage behind the box, used to reach the inner box without passing through the first, he made in the cheap theater plastering a hole to fit the wooden bar, so as to bar out the audience, forcing the other end of the stick against a little door opening inward from the second or dress circle.

If a trap had been invented to catch the victim, it could not have been more complete or economical than these united boxes, the little blind passage behind them, and the narrow wicket opening obliquely to the side-wall. Once within there, the murderer could take breath, be unseen by any, fix the bar behind him, peep through the eyelet-hole at the President in his box, open the box-door, and fire.

The key to his own escape Booth had been forging at a gymnasium for years — the cat-leap — and this day he tried it again and again in the darkness of the deserted theater, while his man was loosening the screws of the bolt-catch on the door toward the audience, so that it might open to the murderer's push.

The bait to this trap was the American flag, the cheese of comedy, and the sympathy between the glad people and their well-acquitted servant. Coming to that theater, the President would bring revenue, in a crowded house, for its sullen scullions, some of whom cursed him as they were fixing the colors.

The carpenter and scene-pusher, who had been taken into the plot long before, was, like accomplices generally in murder, of dead self-respect, no ambition, no particular wickedness; and, while hating the great emancipator, had sold himself to be a slave. Booth owned him, fed him on drink, shillings, and familiarity, and meant to leave him behind, as other adventurers in war had lost their slaves — no loss when lost.*

In the stable that Spangler attended behind the theater, for Booth, was a one-eyed racking horse, which Booth had bought on his second visit to Dr. Mudd, from one of Mudd's neighbors, and in his presence; it was a brownish bay, a stout work-horse, with heavy fetlocks down to the feet. Beside this heavy animal, intended for Payne, Booth put on Friday afternoon a small bay mare he had hired on C Street, in the rear of his hotel, of a city livery-man from lower Maryland; for, with highwayman's impartiality, he took both the horses he afterward sacrificed, from his Southern friends.

Spangler had fitted up that old sable with two stalls for Booth, and thus was his carpenter, hostler, and door-keeper.

Had this insignificant man been of honest poverty-proof, the greatest of poor white men might have been saved; for Spangler made Booth's plan possible, as, without a confederate on that stage, Booth's leap from the box would have been as reckless as Harlequin's leap through a flying trap without any assistant beneath.

The door at the rear of the theater opened inward; the horse beyond it had to be held; from the baited and barred box, through the juggling shifts of scenery, to the ready-made exit and the rear door closing in the face of pursuit, the saddled horse, and the convenient stable — this fellow Spangler was like a clothes-pin, of no incentive in himself, but taking hold everywhere.

As Booth gave Spangler the bay mare, he handed him a tie-rein to hitch her. The mare had black legs, mane, and tail, a spotted "off" fore-foot, and a white star in the forehead.

Soon afterward, Herold and Atzerodt separately appeared at a stable, masked, from the head of Pennsylvania Avenue, by a small square of trees — the livery-keeper thereof having been the messenger between Richmond and Washington at Nat Turner's slave insurrection in 1831.† There Atzerodt left a small bay mare, to be kept till called for; with difficulty, on his bad face, he had obtained it of a livery-man.

When Herold afterward came, he asked to pre-empt a lady's saddle-horse for that afternoon.

"Here," said the clerk, "is the easiest-moving horse in the stable. He is a single-footed racker."

He brought out a light roan, with black legs, tail, and mane, a little

---

*   Mr. Harbin, who was in the abduction plot with Mudd and Booth, related to the author that Spangler understood Booth's design from an early period.

†   A. Nailor, Sr. — That insurrection almost led to the voluntary abandonment of slavery by Virginia, because it cost sixty-one white people's lives. The messenger in question lived to hire a horse to the emancipator's murderer, after the sacrifice of more lives than Virginia had people.

worn on the back by ladies' saddles. As the horse was chased along the stable's length, his feet came down —

"Tick-a-tock-a, tick-a-tock-a!"

"Now, le' me see yer saddles and bridles!" said Herold, with country-jockey slyness; and, walking into the harness-room, he picked out for himself, indifferent to advice, an English saddle with steel stirrups, and a double-reined and double-bitted bridle.

This boy, as he was generally called, was twenty-three years old, not ill-connected, and a natural product of Washington city as it was in slave-times — without any fixed place or tone, unaffected by any of the subjects or men of government; his bias toward the South, but not stable enough to reason or argue that, or any other subject; and, while they had no outward resemblance, Booth and Herold belonged to each other by the frequent tie of nothing-to-do — the same which brings dogs together unassorted. Their highest trait was mutual — restless exercise — Herold's maggot toward sporting, Booth's toward physical and fierce adventure. Herold had been as high as hospital assistant and as low as the monkey of a quack doctor who practiced upon the vices of the town.

By Booth's combination of low tastes and high mental ferocity he was able to sleep with Herold and dream with President Lincoln, and the explanation is easy: his self-assertion met no resistance from his mindless followers, and with them he basked in grateful amiability, or ruled them with tyrannic effervescence. That was the condition of all masters' sons among their slave playfellows: Booth's father left him no slaves, so he went and found white ones, to love and admire him like the others, in the catching pride of slavery's contact.

Strange that, amid this studied guilt, Booth believed he had the heart of love and the manner of chivalry!

When moral resistance gives completely away, the reasoning safety merely flutters. Mrs. Surratt sometimes borrowed the horses Booth but recently owned for his abduction scheme, and, on the day he declared he should now kill the President, she sent to Booth to borrow his horse and buggy again; he hired another for her, and she went to Surrattsville, and on the way she saw her tenant who kept the inn, and told him, at Booth's request, that the "shooting-irons" would soon be called for. By the obligation thus created, and ripened confidence, Booth concluded, on the day of the murder, to send her to Surrattsville again. She had no adviser, and considered that woman's part in war and politics did not count. On this occasion she had private business, and paid for her own buggy before he came.

Those horses, which Booth long owned — one of them, like its rider, to come home to her door — had been liveried nearly in the rear of her house, on the parallel street — an alley running through — by her own son. To that same stable she sent on this Good Friday, whereupon the crucifix she worshiped had been reared. Her messenger was a boarder who had been a schoolmate of her son, and who had seen nearly every person in the plot come to her house, and ride these and other horses before it, and display pistols, bowie-knives, bits of disguise, and fancy riding accoutrements about the son's bedroom, until his curiosity had reached the point of wonder.

As the boarder went to the stable, there was Atzerodt, being refused a horse; and as he went to her door with the buggy, there was Booth again, in close conversation with Mrs. Surratt, and Booth gave her a tied package to carry. It was then almost three o'clock. The murder had been shaped by Booth in every part for that night, and at a time only seven hours distant. He did not tell her how he was allying her with his crime.

Where was Hugh Fenwick, with his delicate consideration for women — he who had accepted the duty of giving this widow some warning to stand upon, and revive her thinking parts?

Where was her son — a voter, a man subject to draft, and mature enough, in his own esteem, to outwit and capture the ruler of the whole land?

He had gone from Richmond to Canada, and — fateful now to remember! — she had gone part of the way to Richmond with him, and a female spy was in the carriage at her side.

So the widow drove that Good Friday the long and hilly ten miles to her spy-haunted tavern, that for four years had done its evil, sinister part, and three years and a half of that time was her own abode — post office of the government, as well as custodian of the insurgent mail. Her heart was light, for her son had received three hundred dollars at Richmond.*

All care had been thrown aside, in view of the virtual conclusion of the war. A little picket on the wayside spoke to her with courtesy as the cavalrymen turned their horses toward Washington. She reached her tavern half an hour before sundown, and rested in the dwelling part, and dictated a business letter till her tenant came home. She went out to him at his wood-pile, and handed him Booth's package, and said:

"Mr. Lloyd, put this with the other things of John's you've got hid

---

*   "Next Tuesday, and the jig's up. Good-bye, Sutrattsville! Good-bye, God-
       forsaken country! Old Abe, the good old soul, may the devil take pity on
       him!" — Letter sworn to be John Surratt's, dated at leaving his tavern to
       live in Washington, November 12, 1864 — five months before the assassi-
       nation. — (Surratt's trial.)

away."

"What things?" asked the man, fuddled by drink, He had been that day at his county court, to prosecute a customer who had stabbed him.

"Why, you know well enough. The shooting-irons, ammunition, and so on, hid over the store-room. They will be called for by parties tonight — late tonight. Give them to the men who ask for them, and have two bottles of whisky ready, too."

As the man took the package upstairs, curiosity tempted him to open it. It contained a field-glass, such as military officers used to observe a distant enemy. His visitor's buggy was hardly out of sight when he reached far under the rafters of his main hotel, from a small hidden loft connected with his bar, and brought out two fine Spencer breech-loading carbines, in canvas covers, a box of ammunition for them, a coil of rope, and a monkey-wrench, such as might be used to screw up the nuts of carriage-wheels. He brought these out and put them upon his own bed, to be ready when called for that night.

"These things has troubled my mind ever sence John Surratt left 'em yer," mused the landlord, tipsily. "He and Dave Herold and Port Tebakker Atzerodt come together, just before ole Abe's inogeration, and sence John's been to Richmond this house has been on the p'int of bein' s'arched. Well, I'll git rid of 'em now!"*

Twenty miles down and back brought Mrs. Surratt, at almost nine o'clock, to the descent of a hill overlooking Washington. The city was illuminated, and the young man at her side expressed some mild glow of satisfaction at Peace.

"I am afraid that all this rejoicing will be turned into mourning," she said; "this is a proud and licentious people, and God will punish them."

Her violent hostilities in the war, she felt to have been in vain, and the scene humiliated her. The horse shied in the city — at the torches of a glad procession going to serenade the President.

They were tired when they reached the little steep-staired house; but hardly had they supped, when the bell rang.

---

*　How well the government treated this family and tavern may be inferred from the following boastful paragraph in John Surratt's public lecture on his military campaigns, delivered at Rockville, Maryland, December, 1870: "We ran a regularly established line from Washington to the Potomac, and I being the only unmarried man on the route, I had most of the hard riding to do. I devised various ways to carry the dispatches, sometimes in the heels of my boots, sometimes between the planks of the buggy. Never in my life did I come across a more stupid set of detectives than those generally employed by the United States Government. They seemed to have no idea whatever how to search men. . . . It was a fascinating life to me. It seemed as if I could not do too much or run too great a risk." On one occasion, it is Weichmann's testimony that John Surratt told him he was going on the stage with Booth to play at Richmond.

Booth appeared before her, stern and intense with the excitement and stimulation of the day. Drink changed his nature, but keyed up his physical system and made him positive as the intoxication of tyranny.

"The devil and his hour have concurred at last!" he said. "I'm going to kill him, and as many more as my few braves can reach tonight!"

"Lincoln?"

"Yes!"

He seemed insane between the bloody purpose and the vagrant yet deeply preoccupied day.

"O John, friend, pet — oh, sir, think how you will bring me in! Here I am just home, and have done your errand with my own."

"Fear not," said Booth; "your tavern tenant is with us in feeling, and he'll never betray you. I have closed up every leak and written my confession, and shall show myself to Lincoln's thousands, among whom I mean to strike him!"

She endeavored to affect him, but it was too late. The mark of the drink was in his brow, deep as the brain. He talked strong and with dramatic accent, broke down her feeble plaint, and made her see, the instant he had left her, the injury she had done her family by mixing in the war between the lines and suffering the daring conspiracy of abduction to enter her household and get possession of her son. Oh, for this son tonight, to rush upon an errand and arrest the madman's hand!

She had no son: the insurrection had swallowed them both up, and the last, willful fugitive, and restless, but once meek and pious boy, had received the Confederacy's employment only the moment before its fall, and might now be hastening home from Canada in time to perish!

She thought of the youth who had driven her that afternoon, as one to send and give the alarm. Alas! he was a clerk under the stern Carnot of the War Department, Mr. Stanton.

Finally, she thought of Hugh Fenwick, and of his intimacy with Secretary Stanton's brown-eyed friend, Major Bosler; but him it seemed impossible to find tonight in the peace-celebrating and holiday-taking city. The door opened, and her late escort came in, and found her running over her prayer-beads nervously.

"Pray! pray!" she said, "for my intentions."

"Ah!" said he, "I thought you were a Christian, and wanted peace to come, even if we must have our Union back."

The hall and parlor filled with the laughter of young women, her daughter among them, and the hostess chased them to bed. Then she sat down and said:

"Oh, he's an actor! He won't do anything like that, fierce as he has often talked."

Ten o'clock came sounding from the city bells.

As she stepped into her room and finished her toilet to retire for the night, the hoofs of horses — two of them, as it seemed — went past the door loudly.

"How that cavalry tears along tonight!" she said, and put out the light.

*T*urning the great Doric Interior Department of marble, Booth, after leaving Mrs. Surratt, paused under a hotel and bought at a drug-store a vial of medicine. In the inn above, Payne had been kept caged, like a beast before the performance, for two weeks, his room previously secured by the Surratts, and he was visited there by Mrs. Surratt, and that dusk he had received his instructions.

Booth turned into the hotel block a few steps farther on, by the dark theater alley, and clicked his key in his low stable-door.

"Lew, wake up!" he whispered.

"I haven't been asleep, John," from a voice in the straw.

"This is the vial you are to take to Seward's: remember, the doctor's name is Verdi. Herold will see you pass Nailor's stable and follow you, and be your guide. Take out *your* horse first! Good-bye, and make yourself a great man!"

They shook hands in the dark, and the horse, bought by Dr. Mudd, went out of the narrow alley with that powerful column of a youth on his back — the youngest of the band.

When the horse's feet had died away, Booth led out his bay mare and pulled her up the dingy theater area to the low stage-door, beside which was a bench. One or possibly two poor tenements were now inhabited in this court of stables, and a colored woman in one heard the call of "Ned," and it was repeated at a stage-window above.

Spangler appeared and held the animal until some one within had summoned a lad of the foundling order, by the name of "Peanuts," who distributed the theater-bills. He took the horse and lay down upon the bench, and there in the solitude, the moon being not yet up, the horse stamped for almost an hour, and the boy dozed in the chilly night.

Booth had passed in, whispered to Spangler, and had come out at the theater front, on Tenth Street. Just as he reached there, the President's carriage drove up, and the tall form of Mr. Lincoln was seen, behind an officer and a young lady, coming forward with his wife upon his arm. These four, assisted by ushers, passed into one of the round doors of the theater.

Booth felt a quivering and a gloating together pass like a cold and a

warm current to his heart. The man so long hunted was in his den; he
rather rejoiced that there were women with him, to lull apprehensions
and reduce the area of resistance. He knew the accompanying officer
carried no arms where ladies went, as only the ill-bred do. Yet there was
a nervous void in his breast as he muttered, under the blowing alcove
lamp:

"This time I think I've got him!"

He went into one of the three saloons girding the theater, and drank,
and rushed out.

"Do I regret that I am in it?" he asked. "No, I'll go through with it!
I've sent my friends in there, and told them they would see great acting."

He walked rapidly — the spurs rattling a little on his feet — to the
avenue, and turned into the Kirkwood Hotel, and mounted some flights
and knocked at a door.

A cry and a shivering chatter followed, and a voice asked:

"Who's — where?"

"I — open!" the actor's bass rolled low.

"O Mister Boot! I tought it might pe, maype — somepodies. He! he!"

The coachmaker of Port Tobacco was there, Andrew Atzerodt, a little
boozy, but more ashen pale under his dirty skin and low-crowned hat.

"Why ain't you ready? All are out but you. If you fail to do your
work, remember! Your name goes in the hands of the authorities, and
they'll hang you without a trial. Where's your knife?"

"Tere, Mr. Boot!"

He pulled up the mattress of the hotel bed, and showed a large bowie
knife, and under his pillow was a revolver, loaded and capped.

"You have got Herold's overcoat on the peg," said Booth, "with my
bank-book and tooth-brush in it. It may turn cold. I can't do my job
with an overcoat on, and depend on you to fetch it. We all move on
our men at five minutes after ten, sharp! Andy Johnson's room is right
under you. Go at him and finish him — or he'll raise the alarm on you!
Then, as I told you, mount your horse at the door and ride fast for
Benning's Bridge, where Payne will meet you. Your only hope for life is
to obey!"

He was gone, and Atzerodt fell on the bed, and sobbed and panted
in the terror of the grave.

"Where can I go now?" he moaned. "I don't know. Maype I can go
up-country where I got a gal and a cousin. I reckon tey won't haf me.
Te witch at Shmoketown said I would pe hanged and Boot pe burnt.
My God! my God! Tat is a pad man — tat Boot. I tought he was shoost
braggin', like me, and now he's got drunk, and maype he'll kill somepodies. Oh, let me prays some!"

He dropped upon his knees and set up what he thought was a prayer, but it came to him, after he had grown very fervent, that it was a piece of a song he was saying.

"I don't know none," he exclaimed. "I'm gone up. If I shteal dat horse, I'll pe sent to te penitentiary. I wish I was tere now! I reckon I'll go down and tell Andy Johnson I was put on him to kill him, and won't do it. Then I won't pe hanged."

He leaped to his feet, put on his hat, felt confident and plausible, and went down to the Vice-President's room. A soldier had been guarding it in the earlier evening; he was now gone, and no response came from Atzerodt's knock.

The wretch hastened out, disconsolate, and up the avenue to Nailor's stable to get his mare.

He saw Herold and Payne turn the corner of the avenue around the Treasury Department façade, riding steadily.

Atzerodt spurred his horse down the obscure streets of Murder Bay, behind the stable, and rode along the stinking ditch of the old Tiber Canal, and wondered where he could go.

"I been goin' to te devil efer sence John Brown's times," he said. "Nigger-ketchin' got me to plockade-runnin', and dat got me to know Surratt and Boot, and I reckon I'll shoost go take a drink at some dive and git hanged."

He dismounted, all incongruous and weeping, at the settled city line, seeing there the red light of a bar. A woman came past him and called his name —

"Andrew?"

"Why — Nelly! Don't you know I told you I should hang for you some day? Go stop dat Boot: he's at te theater, and old Abe Lincoln's there, and tere'll pe murder!"

The woman checked a short scream, and ran through the next cross-street to the avenue, and up to Ford's Theater, where she had the *entrée*:

"I can give you, Miss Starr, a seat, if you can get it emptied, right opposite the President's box," said the ticket-seller.

She hastened through the lobby and past the parquet, and up the dress-circle stairs, and gave an usher whom she knew her ticket, whispering:

"Has John Booth been here tonight?"

"I saw him over yonder just now, near the State box. — Please give this lady her seat, sir!"

As the usher spoke, a report came from somewhere, startling and loud. Nelly glanced at the President's box.

There sat the President, with his head dropped, as if glancing away from the piece into the parquet, sleepily, while his wife had turned her head toward the young lady at her side, each looking at the other, and the officer behind the ladies had risen.

Smoke next curled curiously, slowly, at last strong out of the box, and in the smoke it seemed that the officer and some other one there were fighting. A voice came out of the short *mêlée* like a command given on a ship, with the word "revenge" in it, and a flash of steel or glass followed; and then, while the play seemed to halt, and part of the audience to be observing the box, a bare-headed man in black, with pallid face and large eyes, came right to the box-railing, parted the flags, set his left hand on the rail, passed his right hand up with a knife flashing below the palm, and vaulted lightly over to the stage, fourteen feet below. There came trailing down with him a strip of the starry corner of a flag caught upon his foot. He fell to one knee, faltered, slowly rose and turned his face toward the people, and uttered, in a sepulchral, enforced tone, *"Sic semper tyrannis!"* and raised the knife again. Then stooping, like one with his belly yearning for the ground, he made awkwardly the skipping strides of actors who run off in combat-scenes, and disappeared beneath Nelly's eyes toward the prompter's hidden desk.

Everything had been done — from the firing of the pistol to the disappearance — in hardly one minute.

There passed over the audience electric waves of wonder, inquiry, movement, and sound. As they wavered to understand it all, the piece also stopped upon the stage, and people there came running from behind the painted scenes; the orchestra rose, and a wild scream came down from the upper box, through the festooned flags, and the portrait of Washington. The President sat as before, quiet, as if the pleasant farce were going on, and smiles had brought him near to sleep, like babies' dreams.

Now, all the audience was up, and people were pushing at the little door behind the President, and against the dress-circle wall. They could not for a moment get in there, and began to scale the posts and gilded pilasters of the box; while other people clambered over the orchestra tins and wire-nettings, and ran across the stage — some hither, some thither — in a maze that plain wayfarers never had explored. Actors and actresses came out in their fancy attires, powder, and rouge; and some wanted to faint, some to help, and everybody pointed, explained, and shouted.

There stood upon the mimic stage a dairy scene — like that where the President's fate had been foretold on John's Brown's farm — partly flanked by a toy fence, and masked by a wing of other scenery, with a bird-house and bench before the dairy, the front scene now torn open in the spasmodic actions of some thirty people employed upon that stage.

God had called the emancipator home when there were "no cares upon his face."

As the President was carried down the stairs, Nelly followed, being among the last to leave, and she saw his body enter a dwelling opposite, where Booth had at one time lodged with a fellow-actor.

At this moment the fellow-actor, in another lodging, was burning Mr. Booth's labored confession, in the terror of one on whom had been pilloried a deadly secret.

"I know the red-bird now," sighed Nelly Harbaugh, "and he has marked me with the dark! In the morning they will find me neither dark nor white, but where poor Lincoln is, asking Him to try my cause."

Chapter XLVI
FLIGHT OF SPIES

ABEL QUANTRELL sat on Good-Friday night in his house, preparing to antagonize the President; and Katy was reading from Lincoln's speech on the third anniversary of the Baltimore riots:

"Calling to mind that we are in Baltimore, we can not fail to note that the world moves. Three years ago, those soldiers could not pass through Baltimore. I would say blessings upon the men who have wrought these changes, and the women who have assisted them!"

"That means you and Davis here," said Senator Pittson, "and here you are 'blessing' the President up and down hill."

"Oh, what a scene was that!" spoke Hannah Ritner. "The old Negroes and the children, the fair girls and the new-married pairs, weeping, and singing, and praising God, when the tall, tender man came past — and they say it has been the same in Washington and Richmond. Oh, why be so impatient with him, friends, when these poor slaves have waited for him trustfully these hundred years?"

"Lincoln is a fine politician," said Mr. Davis, who now had two Maryland senators, and nearly all the delegation in Congress, but considered that he was no politician at all; "I wish he would move in here, and show me how to let all the returning rebels vote, and yet not break him down. I see the same soured element returning, and they will wheedle our Presidents away, and we shall always be thirty years behind the North and West — afraid to say 'Liberty' loud, singing the old pine tree Maryland whine, and rather rejoicing that we are wrong."

"Cube it," said old Abel Quantrell, looking like the face of Moses carved on his broken tablets. "Liberty is not a gift, but the returning of a right. The gift is the ballot. Freedom itself is a counterfeit without civil rights. Put me to sleep among the blacks, and let Gabriel call me when Africa is white!"

Senator Pittson observed that Winter Davis a little flinched at this, though with grim admiration.

"O friends!" said Lloyd's halt-brother, "all true legislation is for the present. See how we have got along; and the greatest man on the globe this day, in popular faith, is Uncle Abraham. I tremble for his perfectness of fame."

The door opened, and Light Pittson entered on the arm of Luther Bosler. Light's father looked up with a quick interest.

"Senator," said Luther, "this lady is to be my wife."

They all started up except Abel Quantrell, whose limbs would no longer bear him, and he made a motion to Hannah Ritner, who came and kissed him, while Katy and Light's father alternately embraced the affianced couple.

As Mr. Davis departed, the old radical spoke from his wheeled chair, bringing it forward:

"Bosler, in this house we pretend nothing. Do you know that I am the father of this boy, and that this saint should be my wife?"

He pointed to the senator and to Hannah Ritner. They looked at the lover calmly, yet both were anxious for his response.

"I have known it long," replied Luther Bosler. "To give this lady my name has been my purpose, since I first discovered the possibility of a misapprehension."

He reached his hand to Abel Quantrell's grandchild, but she was gone from his side, and now stood with flashing and indignant eyes, comprehending a situation she had never anticipated.

"Spare yourself, sir," said Light Pittson, "an act of charity! It was for this you professed to love me! I know the blemish in my nature now, and it points me where to fly. The man who is all romance, and against whom I have been so hypocritically warned because he was not pure enough for me, implored me to leave Washington with him this night. I will not return there, but will follow him to where my friend, my uncle Lloyd, fights in Virginia, and I shall be the wife of Mr. Booth!"

"O Light!" spoke Katy Bosler, seeing the trouble of the senator and his parents. "Am I so wicked? Yet where is my wedding ring?"

The door-bell rang as the town clocks sounded midnight. Hugh Fenwick, entering, exclaimed:

"It is too true — Wilkes Booth has killed the President! The Secretary of State has been butchered! The assassin's companion, following him across the navy-yard bridge, gave the name of Lloyd Quantrell!"

At this appalling information the silence was long, till broken by Light Pittson's asseveration:

"I will marry Mr. Booth, if at the foot of the scaffold!"

Abel Quantrell looked up at Hannah Ritner with a hard but ghastly face.

"Three times the base is the cube," said he. "Am I not happy in my posterity?"

"I don't believe it was Lloyd!" cried Katy Bosler.

"No, child," spoke Abel Quantrell, upon the inward breath of a groan, "for both my sons had honest mothers."

"Fenwick," exclaimed Hannah Ritner, "did you warn that woman Surratt, as you swore to do under the altar of your church? I see you did not! I arrest you, sir, as one of the assassins!"

Before he could reply, she had taken hold of him with a grasp of man's strength, and drawn a bunch of keys from his clothing.

"Major Bosler, take these; arrest this man, and search his room and trunk. If he has done Lloyd Quantrell an injury, they shall settle it, man to man!"

Old Abel Quantrell's head fell down. The second stroke of paralysis had come to him.

*T*he interview between Nelly Harbaugh and Light Pittson had commenced in hostility, and ended in good influence; for behind it had been Hannah Ritner, her object a double one — to reveal Booth's impurity to Light, and have her awaken in Nelly's nature a new interest in the actor, that his dangerous character might be under Nelly's control.

Booth had now fallen entirely under the malignant influence of his contemplated crime, and he deceived both women: secretive as the grave to Nelly while daily in her chamber, and though forbidden by Light to see her again, his pen was at work vainly seeking to have her meet him in Virginia. He desired to enter there with the double trophy of a "Yankee" senator's daughter and the President's death. Light Pittson attracted his lower nature, and her sympathy with the misfortunes of the Southern people, of late unreservedly expressed, caused her name to be more closely linked with Booth's than the facts warranted, and gave her parents many apprehensions, who now knew the unprincipled relations of that worthless person in many an unguarded woman's life!

Booth was piqued that Nelly Starr, as she was called, valued Luther's love, while he, her injurer, had never gained her heart; and he had a grudge against Senator Pittson for ruling him out of Light's society. On the other hand, Nelly relieved Luther Bosler from any suspicion of having prejudiced Booth, and showed Light that Lloyd Quantrell had taken that pains. She exceeded her own intentions when she found the excellences of Miss Pittson's nature, and freely implored her to see the gentleness and merit of the soldier Nelly had sacrificed and lost.

It was from this advice, and from loathing evil, that Light accepted the officer in time to hear that her own family had been throwing stones at others from a house of glass. Their trouble was the deeper, that now the world would mention Light's name as connected with Booth in a tender passion.

If she would only marry Luther Bosler before the scandal could get well abroad!

Nelly Starr had undertaken, from both ambition and loneliness, to remodel Booth's education, to study his parts with him, and get out of his mind the rant and fustian of his old father's example.

She found him headstrong and incurable. With profound belief in himself, and enamored of his one bloody idea — the wickedest in the land, but he thought it the greatest — he already lived in the satisfaction of one famed and great. He was like the man in the tale, who had tried to discover where the unforgiven sin was, and thrilled with the conceit that it was monopolized in his own breast.*

The intuition that there was something too deep for her in Booth's thought and intention, rallied all the energies of Nelly's nature, and Hannah Ritner kept the motive alive. Nelly sounded him about the President, and he even complimented Mr. Lincoln. She inquired about his prospects.

"Why," said he, "I was always popular South, and now we shall have peace, and I will be the first to enter there, and you and I will draw great houses, Nelly."

On the day of the murder he came to her again, renewed the protestations and endearments of deceitful love, and bade her go to Ford's Theater that night, as he had requested many others, in the egotism of his bloody patent-right. Later on, he sent her word that he would call for her, but, finding his time spent, she heard by accident from Atzerodt the explanation of his mystery, and hastened to the theater, forever too late!

When the officers came to seek the assassin's mistress, as the papers related, they found her insensible, and an empty bottle of chloroform at her side.†

Liquor crazed the Booths, but made them "letter-perfect," as the actors would relate, in their parts: so Wilkes Booth had an unnatural brightening of his faculties all that day, and when the moment approached to carry out his threat, he merely drank more often and more regularly, and his last act in front of the theater was to drink alone, at a bar; next he stepped into the lobby and noted the time, and then he

---

*   Hawthorne, "Ethan Brand."

†   "The detectives proceeded to the house at the corner of Thirteenth Street and Ohio Avenue, where Booth spent much of his time, Ella Starr, the woman who attempted suicide, being his mistress." — "Washington Star," April 17, 1865.

climbed the dress-circle stairs and made his way, with spurs upon his feet, along the wall to the right, behind the stools and chairs packed there, asking one person to move, or bowing to another, until he was within a few steps of the little door entering the box passage.

There he paused, put his low-crowned, slouched hat behind his back, and inclined his head forward, with a large seal ring on his little finger raised to his chin.

His head was broad, the forehead large, and the black hair, parted behind, had a curling tendency; and the nearly straight, heavy, black eyebrows shaded black eyes which wore a look between modesty and obduracy, and, in conjunction with the decisiveness of the mouth, conveyed the idea of dangerous equipoise, needing only a breath from the willful soul within to overturn the whole fabric of the man.

His nose was thin and not prominent, rather subordinate to the brow. In his expression could be felt the influence of both alcohol and self-consciousness. His chin was small, and the rich black mustache around the mouth hid a commonness there, and his neck was scarred just above the collar by both a tumor and a wound.

He weighed one hundred and sixty pounds, was hardly five feet eight, and unusually compactly set, the child of a large, healthy English-woman, who survived him more than twenty years, and of a small, Jewish-marked, and acutely organized English father.

The lower portion of this young man's face was almost generic in Baltimore. His clothes were dark, bound with silk trimmings, and he was not unobserved by many, most of whom saw only the fine, sparkling contrasts of his face and did not know his name. He had avoided the company of the average stock actors as beneath his notice, to shower time and favors upon ignorant dependents.

He now pushed the last chair aside, took a card from a case, and handed it to a messenger of the President, who read the name and hesitated.

"He has just sent for me," said Booth, "and is expecting me."

The messenger heard the words, looked into the serious, respectful countenance, and said no more.

Booth stepped down one step, as the circles inclined, and pressed the door at once with his hand and knee: the loosened screws came out, and he entered the passage and closed the door behind him. He took the wooden stick from a corner and barred the door against the audience.

He then bent his eye from that darkness to the eyelet-hole, and saw the President, with his head a little turned from the stage, exposing his neck and the lower portion of his brain to the assassin.

Mr. Lincoln was seated in a cushioned and arm-furnished rocking-chair at the angle of the box nearest the audience, and immediately before the door Booth had bored; in placing his seat there the confederate had allowed for a space between him and the next chair, for the assassin to escape by.

Booth saw to the buttoning of his coat, drew the Derringer pistol from his pocket, opened the door, and fired the powerful slug into the President's brain, his weapon nearly against Mr. Lincoln's skull. The sting and smoke produced a kind of paralysis among all in the box.

He immediately dropped the Derringer upon the floor of the private box and drew a large bowie knife, and, rushing to the front of the box, shouted in the deepest tragedy tones:

"Revenge for the South!"

The officer in that box was the step-son of a senator, and the young lady there was his espoused wife. He came forward and took hold of Booth, uncertain what the intrusion meant, when the assassin, in the frenzy between desperation and drink, endeavored to stab him to the heart; but the officer's left arm was interposed, and the sharp blade ripped it from the elbow almost to the shoulder.

As the inmates of the box recoiled, and the wife of the President screamed, the murderer, whose victim sat unmoved and unprotesting, rushed between Mr. Lincoln and his wife to the railing, cleared away a festooning flag with a motion of his clinched hand and the knife-handle, and by his unemployed left hand vaulted over to the stage below. Every motion had been rehearsed again and again.

The matter of these exterior ornaments — there being three different flags upon the broad united box — he could not provide as perfectly for, and in descending more than twice his own stature his spur was caught by a ravished blue ensign, and he was thrown out of his adjustment and struck the stage upon the opposite foot, and came down with a swooning feeling that, for an instant, threatened to detain him there until he could be seized.

In the leg of a man are two long bones, the thinner one, called the *fibula*, or splinter-bone, being on the outside, and serving to keep the ankle from turning outward. It lies there somewhat like a ramrod on the outside of a gun. By the unexpected shock of falling on this foot only, the rather unusual accident resulted of the immediate fracture of this bone alone, and not of the accompanying stock, or larger bone; but it produced a momentary nervous shock in the assassin's whole system.

Booth rallied his powers, exclaimed, *"Sic semper tyrannis!"* according to rote, and limped across the stage to the opposite wing, more sobered than he had been at any stage of the tragedy.*

---

*　　Booth said to Thomas Harbin, in Virginia, that if he had not been a very courageous man he would have given up and have been taken right there, as he for an instant seemed about to faint.

As he proceeded, between pain and ferocity, he resolved to slash and kill anybody who came in his way. His confederate had cleared him a lane to escape down — the scenery piled against the wall; and when Booth, who had dropped his hat as he entered the box, had nearly reached the back door, he met the orchestra leader and cut twice at him and kicked him, and the back door mysteriously swinging open in his face, he passed out, and it shut behind him.

The boy "Peanuts" stood there holding his horse, as Spangler had ordered him to do, and weary, after being exposed a whole hour in the lonely night in that passive task, he had been aroused from his orphan meditations by the firing of the pistol; and suddenly a man ran upon him, cursing and shouting:

"Give me that horse!"

With one foot in the stirrup, Booth turned and struck the boy savagely with the butt of the knife, and knocked him down upon the cobble-stones and kicked him there.

Then, digging his spurs into his horse, he turned out of the narrow alley and spurred again, so that the animal ran up on the opposite pavement under St. Patrick's old brick church.

"Ride hard!" cried Booth to Herold, waiting there; "the devil is to pay!"

They turned at Ninth Street, and went two blocks behind the Patent-Office, and passed Mrs. Surratt's door at a full run; and, crossing the naked judiciary Square, between the Court-House and the old jail, descended the next street beyond the City Hall, and crossed the little Tiber on the Avenue.

The moon came out as they galloped up the slopes of Capitol Hill, and a few people passing there turned to see such fierce riding.

"Walk your horse, Dave," said Booth to Herold, "and let me get over the navy-yard bridge before you come. I want you to give the name there of Quantrell. I'll fix that fellow as I have fixed Sam Arnold, who deserted me; for I have left his letters to me in my trunk at the hotel, and they'll hang him, sure!"

When Herold reached the bridge, a few minutes after Booth, he added to Quantrell's name the information that he had been on a low female carouse in the city. The sergeant, in the kindly glow of restored peace, passed both these murderers. After they crossed the bridge, Booth got with difficulty and pain on Herold's easier riding-horse — the same once owned by Hannah Ritner.

*I*n the meantime Herold had ridden with Payne to the door of the

Secretary of State, in an old tall brick house, on a secluded side of the President's green square. At the next corner below, in a brick dwelling, was the headquarters of the commander of the city of Washington, where generally orderlies and horses were to be found ready to take dispatches; but these murderers had chosen a late hour of the night, when the military business was done, and while peace was so far insured that discipline was much relaxed.

Leaping from his horse, Payne handed the bridle to Herold, who sat there with a foolish smirk of dread.

The tall brigand, with perfectly beardless face, and something of an Indian in bearing and in straight black hair, and with a powerful columnar neck and broad chest, walked up to the bell and rang it.

He wore the heaviest cast-off boots of Wilkes Booth, black cloth trousers, an overcoat of white and brown, conspicuous in the night, a dark-gray undercoat, and a slouched brown hat. He was familiar with saber and knife exercise, and had been kept sober until just before this essay, when he was toned up to his bloody work by drink.

He had disappeared within the hall-way, perhaps five to seven minutes, when Herold, sitting on the horse in morbid apprehension, heard cries and shouts within the old gloomy house, and the sound of blows and of failing bodies.

The horses raised their ears, and moved around their halters uneasily.

"Murder! Murder! Murder!" came in a half-stifled outburst from the mysterious interior, and was followed by the same terrible word in a piercing scream from a lifted window at the eaves.

Herold let go of the halter of the other horse, and stuck his spurs into his own fleet roan.

"Tick-a-tock-a, tick-a-tock-a!" came the single-footed racking echoes out of the old cobble-stones, and the horse turned the military head-quarters and skipped down the softer avenue, until, at Willard's Hotel corner, a man rushed out at Herold, crying:

"Here, now! Get off that horse! I didn't hire him to you to ride all night!"

Seeing the livery-man, but not recognizing him in the terror of the moment, Herold wheeled up Fourteenth Street, past the newspaper correspondents' offices, and, turning down F Street, had barely paused at the outlet of the alley, when Booth burst out, and they joined in fierce, wild flight, as has been seen.

Chapter XLVII
PAYNE

*T*HE Secretary of State was a man almost sixty-four, of slight and delicate structure, and without any personal enemies except those whose unjust interests felt the silver arrows of his argument. In youth he had been a tutor in a slave State, and formed the opinion that the systems of free and slave labor were irreconcilable. As Governor and senator of the most powerful State in the Union, he nurtured freedom among the young men and made it captivating, and now was triumphantly closing the greatest career of any foreign secretary from the New World. The same hand which sealed the Proclamation of Emancipation had foiled Europe in its attempts to divide the raiment of the republic, and was yet to settle with the crowned puppet in Mexico, and also to terminate Russian rule in America.

Ten days previous to this Good Friday Mr. Seward had been thrown from his carriage and his jaw and arm broken, and he was now lying helpless in his bed. With cruel indifference, Booth considered that these disabilities made it the easier to dispatch him, and used the package of medicine to procure for Payne admittance to his chamber of sickness.

The ruffian entered, and was dressed as neatly as Booth could afford. He stated to a colored boy in the hall that the doctor had sent verbal instructions by him about taking the medicine, and spoke awhile plausibly in a soft, fine voice through his thin lips; but, as the black boy protested that Payne could not go upstairs, Payne thrust his right hand in his white-overcoat pocket and said he *should* go up, with a menacing air, somewhat considering whether he should not dispatch the door-keeper on the spot.

Finally, he started up the stairs alone, the uncertain boy preceding him, and at the top of the house — the third story — the eldest son of the invalid, who was the Assistant Secretary of State, came out to see what was the matter.

The man, holding up the package, repeated that the doctor had sent him to make a personal communication to Mr. Seward.

At this the son unwittingly entered his father's room, thus laying bare its location to the murderer; but, coming back in an instant, he said:

"Father is asleep now; give me the medicine, and I will repeat the doctor's instructions to him."

Payne said that would not do, and kept insisting with rising aggressiveness that he must go in, until peremptorily told to retire. He muttered an assent of disappointment, turned a step down the stairway, and then leaped back with his heavy pistol in his hand, and proceeded, cavalryman-fashion, to beat in young Mr. Seward's skull, merely saying in a low, vengeful tone:

"I'm mad! I'm mad!"

His temper was a fierce paroxysm, indiscriminate, and bent on massacre.

The upper floor of that lonely house had been for some time a kind of hospital; the aged Secretary's wife also lying maimed and ill in an adjacent room, and she was to expire, her death accelerated by this night's events, within a few weeks.* The Sewards were an affectionately domestic family, and their daughter Fanny — who also died before many months — and their eldest son's wife, occupied this remote upper floor, with the two sons — the Assistant Secretary aforesaid and Major Seward — and a wounded soldier-nurse detailed from one of the hospitals.

The helpless statesman had been unable to sleep all day, with fever and debilitation, and had just dropped into repose when the solid, decisive tread of a man was heard on the stairs, and Fanny Seward said to the soldier — a lad from the forests of Maine, named Robinson: "I wonder who that is? Some one not used to approaching sick-rooms, I should think!"

The same tread called Assistant Secretary Frederick Seward from his wife's room, in the front of the house; and he, confronting this stranger with the package, only observed that the man was rather dull in understanding, and imputed his obstinacy to his fidelity to the doctor.

Payne, indeed, was of a low order of intelligence, approximating to the family slaves he had been overseer of, and his mental organization was both inharmonious and deficient; his eyes without the radiance of mind, the two sides of his head unsymmetrical, his memory slow, and his moral distinctions weak. Education might have disciplined and aroused his mind, but the instinctive habits of the Alabama plantation, and the school of war, had made him only a machine of his savage temper. The obstacles he encountered aroused this to the highest pitch

---

*   Mrs. Seward died June 21, 1865, surviving the assassination about seven weeks, and departing two weeks before the execution of Mary E. Surratt.

before he had struck a blow. Booth had set his mechanism like a clock to this hour, and the alarm-spring was now released.

Frederick Seward had closed the sick-chamber door behind him when he returned, but Fanny Seward, his sister, opened it to see what the messenger wanted, and left it partly open. Therefore, when the assassin turned back, and with all his strength beat his great navy revolver on Frederick's head, he also rushed for the door ajar; but the stunned man, with affection almost stronger than life — his head open to the brain — slipped before the assassin, blindly groping against the wall, and pulled the door fast and staggered before it, so that Payne could not reach the knob, but continued to beat his frail obstructor, and again fractured his skull with the pistol.

The gas in this landing-hall burned bright, and Frederick Seward's wife came out, wondering, in time to see her husband and a giant, in a great white coat, fall into the sick-room through the burst-open door.

For months this son was speechless, and between life and death.

The sick-room had a single gas-light turned low, and on the farther side, near the front window, was the statesman's bed, in which he was raised to an inclined position by a skeleton hospital apparatus, and was leaning over the farther side of the bed so as to let his broken right arm, in the bandages, be free of the bed-frame.*

The assassin in the dim light discovered his victim, and drew his knife. His hat had fallen off, and, as he bounded toward the bed, the soldier-nurse interposed, and was felled to the floor by a downward thrust of the knife in the scalp; and the daughter of Mr. Seward also coming between, Payne with his left hand hurled her aside and threw himself across the bed, holding the sick man down with one hand, and stabbing him with the other.

The eldest son's interference had deranged the assassin's sight or nerves, and, aiming to cut Mr. Seward's throat, he merely cut his cheek nearly off, and wounded his neck. The bowie knife had an upper edge and sharp upturned point, and, hastening to complete his work, Payne drew it backward, and also slashed the lower side of the secretary's neck.

As Payne was about to complete his work, the soldier-nurse, still suffering from a battle-wound in the leg, leaped upon his back in the bed and seized his upraised arm, while Miss Fanny Seward cried, "Don't let them carry father off!" and she threw up a side-window overlooking the near President's mansion, and screamed "Murder!"

The house was now alarmed, but not a weapon was at hand for defense, while the murderer still had a revolver full of balls and his blood-dyed knife. The colored boy had run down the two flights of stairs

---

* How like the wounded Coligni's assassination on St. Bartholomew's night!

to hunt assistance at the avenue; the eldest son lay insensible in his own blood; three women were there, but Mr. Seward's wife, dangerously ill, required the assistance of the other two.

The Secretary's younger son, in deep sleep, was now slowly aroused by the noise, and groped into the hall in his shirt and drawers.

Nothing meantime had saved the great Secretary's life but the common soldier and his own astute action.

As soon as the soldier seized his assailant, Mr. Seward rolled himself up in the bedclothes, dropped out on the farther side, and rolled under the shelter of the bedstead.

The soldier from the forests of Maine now grappled with the soldier from the forests of Florida — pine tree against pine — the one gigantic, hardly of man's age, armed, and in a premeditated task, to which his Seminolelike temper had now fully aroused;* the other, surprised, stabbed in the head, confused, unarmed, and barely convalescent. Yet Robinson clung to Payne as if he had been the last resistant in the last ditch of disunion. Both had been private soldiers, and they fought with the desperation of an ordeal by single combat.

The Floridian — longer, stronger, and padded in an overcoat — brought his knife right over his shoulder-blade backward and drove it into private Robinson's shoulder twice, to the bone.

The man still held to Payne's arms, and pulled him off the public man's bed and rolled with him on the floor. In the oversetting, Payne slipped his knife into his pocket and gripped his heavy pistol there again by the barrel, and, with the frenzy of a tiger, struck Robinson, with his right hand released below the elbow, time and again and under the left ear, the heavy pistol-butt seeming to split the soldier's spinal column. But Payne could not shake the man off, who clung to him like a sheriff to a highwayman, and held him closer, so that he could not fully command his weapons.

The assassin then dropped his pistol, which was found in pieces on the floor, the pine-knot cranium of Maine having been too hard for it; but there was left the bloody knife, and this Payne produced again, and attempted the favorite feat with bowie knife, of disemboweling his detainer as they had both leaped to their feet.

The agile soldier hugged him from behind, slipping sidewise as the

---

* Payne was from Florida, of Alabama birth, his family named Powell, and it is a curious suggestion that he may have been related to the Seminole Osceola, for which see Benton's "Thirty Years," vol. ii, chap. xix: "The prime mover in all this mischief, and the leading agent in the most atrocious scene of it, was a half-blooded Indian, of little note before that time, and of no consequence in the councils of his tribe. His name is not to be seen in the treaty of *Payne's* Landing; we call him Powell; by his tribe he was called Osceola." — Benton's speech, 1838.

knife was pulled upward; and also avoiding the lift-strokes against his breast — for the murderer, with lightninglike rapidity, cut upward and downward, toward groin and bowels below, and head and lungs above. In dodging these strokes, Robinson worked his way to the unknown maniac's front, and they clutched now, eye to eye, and only one man armed.

Robinson seized Payne's wrist, pinned the knife to his side, and streaming blood, while the other was uninjured, even unbruised, tripped his knee to throw him, Northern fashion, over his hip to the floor.

The soldier's wounded leg would not support him in the effort to lift this gladiator, whose weight was nearly two hundred pounds, and all of it brawn; as he raised the great column up, his leg began to give way.

"I'm mad! I'm mad!" the assassin gasped between his teeth in the dim room, feeling that he was finding his match.

Both men now worked for each other's throats, and Robinson was the quickest. His idea was to edge the man over the threshold and work him against the banisters of the stairs, and throw him down the well thereof. Intelligence, growing by steadiness and moral consciousness, was compensating for his loss of blood and many wounds; for this man had come from the land of wild beasts, and had fought the winter, freezing at his vitals in the roaring torrents of the Aroostook. His alligator opponent was already sliding out, worried and broken-spirited, and his heart in his legs, when the fresh son of the Secretary, almost undressed, entered the room and took hold of the assassin.

Major Augustus Seward had leaped to the conclusion that his father was delirious, seeing a man in the imperfect light firmly held by another; but taking hold of this former person, he became conscious of a frantic strength and extraordinary size, and his next idea was that it was the military nurse — a stranger to most of the household — who had gone crazy and attacked his father; for the sick man's bed was empty.

"I'm mad! I'm mad!" repeated this stranger in a low voice, as if by rote, the vehemence in it gone, and this suggestion he derived from Booth, who had told him to pass for a lunatic after beginning the combat, and throw the sick man's attendants off their guard.

"Major, for God's sake, let go of me!" said the nurse, all bloody, and now somewhat held, too, by the son.

The major pushed both men toward the chamber-door.

"Take his knife from this hand I am holding and cut his throat!" the nearly breathless attendant said.

The major still pushed the enclasped pair toward the door, and there Payne let go of Robinson, and with his left fist knocked him down, while drawing the released knife upon Major Seward and cutting him with spent strength in the forehead and hand.

The assassin now sprang with the terror of death toward the stairs, and bounded down them. The whole combat, in all its involutions, had hardly occupied five minutes.

As he was going down he overtook a messenger of the State Department escaping also, and Payne, by a forward blow, stabbed him between the spine and the rib, and felled him there.

At the street the dark-brown horse was just making off. Payne pursued him, and mounted with the ease of one long in the irregular cavalry, and plunged into the miry ground of Vermont Avenue, and disappeared in the darkness of the scantily settled suburbs there. In mounting the horse he had dropped his bloody knife in the street.

He had wounded five men in that encounter, but failed to take the life of anyone, and they all recovered, while his own sluggish yet torrid temperament had been deranged by the courage and pertinacity of the only and the accidental *soldier* encountered by any of these spies.

With the scant drilling Payne had received in the byways of Washington, he now lost his way. Herold had been placed at the door by Booth to work upon the pride of Payne, and make him go through with his part; but now Herold had run away, and Payne was reduced to a mere boy in spirit, and he forgot the roads.

He aimed to strike the old Bladensburg toll-gate, which stood at the corner of the road to Benning's Bridge. Even in our day the inlet to this by-road from the turnpike is narrow, like a private lane, and, though Booth had repeatedly shown it to his band,* Payne failed to recognize it.

He rode through the northeastern suburbs skirting the boundary, took the old Bladensburg pike, and followed it farther than the Eastern Branch should be, and then got into an army-road leading between two of the forts. Movements in those earthworks struck consternation to him; he heard horses come out from the city, and the picket called. So he rode into a piece of woods, and, as the moon came out of the horizon, beheld his nearly white overcoat soaked in blood.

With a shudder he removed it, and threw it upon the ground.

He saw his shadow in the woods, and he had no hat upon his head.

In despair he took off his undercoat, and cut the sleeve from his woolen shirt over the muscular arm, and made himself a sort of cap of it.

Then he rode his horse across the fields and back into the eastern skirts of the city, and finally felt his way down toward a brook in the

---

* 　　John McCullough told me that Booth put him on a horse and took him to Benning's Bridge, months before the murder, saying, "If a man was in a scrape, here would be a good lane to get out."

red-clay soil, and saw broad water open before him: he recognized the Eastern Branch he was to cross.

As Payne picked his way toward the environing marshes to find the bridge, cavalry dashed down the crossing road, and he heard the guard doubled and set, and the order given to let no man pass alive. The bells from the city struck twelve o'clock.

He turned back and urged his horse with fury, until he saw the Poor-House at the river's brink, and thought how glad he would be of a refuge there. As he looked up, a meteor trailed across the sky, and filled his heart with superstition.

He rode down along a strand before naked bluffs of clay, and turned up a dismal ravine from the chill river, on whose summits were some poor people's houses. In these he heard animated talk, and distinguished the words:

"Nobody knows who did it. It seemed like de devil hopped down all black and said —"

"What did he say?"

"'He's sick! Sing fur hosannas'!"

"What's dat?"

The door opened, and heads appeared.

"It's him — de devil!"

Payne spurred his horse away, and before he could recover self-possession had been stopped by a great yellow hospital on a plateau, and not far away the dome of the Capitol was seen, sailing through soft, fleecy clouds, like Columbus's egg upright under a setting swan.

He saw people ride out. The town was alarmed. Slipping from his sweating horse, he left it forever, and crept away across the moorlike April commons until he saw a large cemetery rise under the trees, with monuments and vaults.

It occurred to him that at the old Virginia churches he had sometimes found an empty vault above the ground to bivouac in, and he tried the slabs upon several of these Washington vaults until one gave way, and he removed it far enough to creep within and lift the slab back by his back and shoulders.

He then lay down in the cold stone walls, felt the glutinous blood on his coat-sleeve at the wrist, and knew that he was spotted everywhere. He was splashed with mud, bruised, wrenched, thirsty, and abandoned; unacquainted with any family in Washington except Mrs. Surratt's, and he had no hat to wear, so that it would be suspicious for him to walk abroad, and had no money to equip or move himself.

He lay there all night without blanket or overcoat, chilly and miserable. It occurred to him to attack and kill any man who might approach, but the next day the cemetery was deserted, as the murder had called everybody in marveling groups to the city.

He lay still all day Saturday, and on Easter-Sunday, when Christ arose, a funeral came near him, and a person dropped a newspaper, which Payne reached out and took, after all were gone. Near it lay a pick for digging graves, and this also he drew within the vault.

The paper contained a proclamation from the stern yet tender Secretary of War, saying:

"One hundred thousand dollars reward!

"The murderer of our late beloved President, Abraham Lincoln, is still at large!

"Fifty thousand dollars will be paid by this department for his apprehension.

"Twenty-five thousand dollars reward for A. Atzerodt, sometimes called 'Port Tobacco.'

"Twenty-five thousand dollars reward for David E. Herold.

"All persons harboring or secreting the said persons, or either of them, or aiding or assisting their concealment or escape, will be treated as accomplices, subject to trial before a military commission and the punishment of death.

"Let the stain of innocent blood be removed from the land!"

As Payne read this with horror, he observed that his own name was not printed, probably not known, and that none of his victims were dead. In a revulsion of gratitude and tears, he fell upon his face in the stone vault, and said a prayer his Baptist father had taught him.

The fourth night following the crime fell upon the old graveyard and the monuments of senators, vice-presidents, state ministers, and jurists. Payne, nearly dead with hunger, crawled forth that drizzling, chilly, Monday night among the low cedar trees to execute the only device he could mature: to visit Mrs. Surratt, with the pick upon his shoulder and in the guise of a sewer-digger, and obtain a hat and clothes and money.

He left the cemetery after ten o'clock, and came over Capitol Hill, avoiding the Avenue, and, ascending the widow's high wooden steps, he rang the hall-bell. In a moment the door opened with a quick twist, and an alert and searching-eyed man confronted the starving wretch, but not before Payne had walked right into the hall pursuant to his plan and from his fears. The man shut the door behind him, and locked it.

"I guess I am mistaken," faltered Payne.

"Whom do you want to see?"

"Mrs. Surratt."

"This is right; walk in!"

The Nemesis that punishes by man's delays had brought the assassin to the headquarters of the band at the very moment when the family there were being arrested. Payne was taken before them, all surrounded by their personal effects, and waiting for a carriage. His prevarications had aroused the officer's suspicions, and a cocked pistol was held at his body, and he was made to lay the pick down.

Mrs. Surratt had just requested permission to fall on her knees and pray. As she arose, making the sign of the cross, the officer said:

"Mrs. Surratt, do you know this man?"

She looked, and saw the man, above all others, she had most to fear. Raising her hands, fresh from making the holy sign, the wretched woman swore:

"Before God, sir, I do not know this man — I never saw him before!"

Yet he had been her guest, had sat in the very box where the murder was to be done, with her son and family, and had been secreted in the hotel in the theater-block by her request.

The circle of the crime was now completely closed. On Payne's feet were Booth's boots, marked with his initials; Payne's horse was afterward identified as purchased by Booth in Dr. Mudd's presence, a quarter of a mile from the latter's house. In Booth's vest at the hotel had been found — with the handcuffs befitting a slave-buyer, but intended to bind the martyr President's hands — the card of Mrs. Surratt's son. And Mrs. Surratt's daughter bore unwilling testimony that Payne had lodged in her brother's bed.

The photographs of insurgent chiefs in the house, a card with *"Sic semper tyrannis!"* upon it, the testimony of the family and boarders, and the flight of the son back to Canada, indicated too well the character of the house, and the most responsible person there: the only one with claims to religion and family ties was this spiteful-hearted woman, on whom the heavy hand of the state had fallen when the blood of its chief cried aloud that mercy to woman had been abused.

A Baltimore actor in New York, to whom Booth had proposed to take a place at Ford's Theater, and there turn off the gas while he committed the crime, came and testified; and the evidence around Spangler, the carpenter, gathered tight. O'Laughlin was arrested, and Arnold's letter, found in Booth's trunk, incriminated them all. Arnold made a full confession, as did Atzerodt, but the Government would admit neither as its witness. Vengeance, postponed for years on cowards and lurking spies, was to fall at last!

Atzerodt had spent a miserable night at the stage-tavern behind Booth's hotel, and in the morning he struck out for the mountain country, selling his pistol in Georgetown, and he was arrested half-way to the Catoctin Valley, hiding in bed and endeavoring to disguise himself in the German dialect — a thin disguise, but the only honest garment he had left. He immediately informed upon Herold, whose coat, he said, and bowie knife were to be found in the room at the Kirkwood Hotel, where Atzerodt came on the morning of the assassination-day. They found there a silly mixing of arms, cartridges, spurs, and licorice; the latter designated Herold's tastes as an apothecary's boy, and Booth's Montreal bank-book was in his pocket. The Government now meant to promote Mr. Herold to a position more worthy of his years, and teach him dignity by elevating him.

The fact was apparent to the Government that, next to Booth, the active genius of evil had been the widow Surratt's son, who paid no more attention to the obligations of his protection than had Payne, who displayed at the moment of his arrest the military safeguard and solemn oath of amnesty.

But this son had been absent from Washington, on messenger spy-service, for three weeks prior to the assassination, and the deliberate murder of the President, Vice-President, General, and ministers had been resolved upon after the son disappeared; therefore some other person in the house of the Surratts would have to bear the responsibility of complicity in this later plot.

There was none but Mrs. Surratt, and she had been the tool of Booth; her message to the country tavern that day, her silence after the crimes, her denying of Payne, and the continued absence of her son, as well as the testimony concerning her violent talk for years, led the Government to conclude that she might have been the unwomaned spirit of the whole plot.

Atzerodt met her at the prison, looking up at her window, and exclaimed:

"'Te last man was a womans.' Look tere! I see my dreams. And te black man with te white face, will hang us all!"

Chapter XLVIII

IN THE SHORT PINES

WHEN the assassin passed over the navy-yard bridge from the city he gave his own name — "Booth." In his years of premeditating some deep act of treachery he had cultivated police officers and detectives, and observed that they were governed by their suspicions and always distrusted candor. So, when he had given the name of Booth, the earliest professional officers who arrived at the bridge exclaimed: "This must have been the dummy, to make us a false scent. The real Booth has gone another way."

Meantime, Booth, leading Herold in the ride, spurred his racking horse fiercely, and they both rode without mercy until they reached Surratt's, standing out against the old fields and woods like Endymion's bower in the kiss of moonlight.

"Get off," said Booth," and wake the man up! I've got a toothache in the foot. We must find a doctor to set this broken bone, which moves and scrapes."

Herold, raised by the exercise from his fears, went in and shook up the drunken landlord, a besotted creature, who had once been on the police force in Washington, but had dropped down to keep this low country bar. He set the whisky-bottles ordered by Mrs. Surratt, that very sunset, before Herold, who said, "For God's sake, Lloyd, go get them things!" And, while Mr. Lloyd was bringing down one carbine, and the cartridges for it, and the field-glass the lady had fetched, Herold gave Booth, sitting on his goaded roan, a bottle of whisky. He was already drunk,* but drank more than half the bottle, and sat on his horse

---

* Lloyd's testimony in the Surratt trial: "The man talked as if he was drunk; he was drunk, in fact."

between sleepiness and recklessness, now stiff, now swaying. He boasted aloud of murdering the President himself, and of having killed Mr. Seward, at least, of the Cabinet; and nothing of this import affected the landlord at all, who had, in six months, heard so many atrocious hopes and wishes expressed there against the public authorities that he rather congratulated the assassins.

"I can't take my carbine," said Booth; "I can't manage it with this leg. Where is the nearest doctor?"

"There's a ole Doctaw Hoxton nigh by, but he won't practice no mo'. You must git down Beantown way, to find any doctaw tonight. There's Doctaw Mudd! Don't you want t'other carbine, and the rope and wrench?"

"No. We want a splint and a crutch. Put down that carbine, Dave!"

"John, I can't do without my gun," replied Herold. "I reckon Payne and Atzerodt ain't a-coming."

"Dr. Mudd's the man," exclaimed Booth, spurring the roan horse Herold had watered, and the soft road gave the sucking sounds —

"Tick-a-tock-a, tick-a-tock-a!"

*T*he next day, when a parcel of officers reached Surratt's tavern, some of them friendly in former years with Mr. Lloyd, he affected not to have seen anybody that night, and gave them the wrong hint for pursuit; yet in their company was the young boarder who had driven Mrs. Surratt there, and had seen her privately speak to this, her tenant, and in the tavern was even now the remaining carbine and the rope designed to bind Mr. Lincoln. In a few days more, when things were looking serious, Mr. Lloyd told the truth, and the son's coil of rope became the deserted mother's punishment.

Thousands of times in that tavern had it been wished aloud that "somebody would kill Abe Lincoln," and these curses were flying home to roost.

*T*he night-ride on that lonely road was marked by neither coherent talk nor thinking, liquor having imbruted both the fugitives, and Herold gave forth some drug-store knowledge about remedies for fractures and bone-fevers, and Booth indulged in some jargonry about tyrants and fate.

Before daylight the house of Dr. Mudd, remote from the highroad, was entered by this pair, who had probably intended, but for the fracture of the leg, to leave his house to the east, although this was not certain to themselves, for it was a convenient breakfast-place for them, and on a more retired route to Pope's Creek.

At the first announcement of their deed and errand, Mudd was rather rejoiced, but, as the day wore on, he took the reflections incident to his weak moral quality, became afraid of his Negroes, and, after he had completed a crutch for Booth, Dr. Mudd and Herold started out to see if Bryantown had heard the news, leaving Booth to doze off his liquor and pain.

As Herold came to a brook within sight of Bryantown hollow, he observed blue-coated soldiers in the public roads of that hamlet, and shrank back into the brush, while Mudd went on, and learned at the store and tavern confirmation of the assassin's tales, that the ruler and his chief secretary had been killed. Proclamations were being put up, and Mudd saw the terrible situation he was in, as a harborer of outlaws and the first convert in that whole country to Booth's mad theatrical schemes, of abducting the man since killed; the introducer of Booth to Surratt, and known to every resident of that district to have been visited by Booth in the previous fall.

He saw the floating vultures over the heights about Bryantown church, with a pathetic sense of being the next carcass, perhaps, to draw them to the ground. There was his cousin and medical preceptor in the village, to whom he had long been inimical as the solitary Union white man there. How strong and clear that kinsman seemed today in the eyes of the restless man who wanted, above all things in this world, an honorable and loyal adviser now — one who had kept his heart generous and faithful to the dead ruler! The towns-people had not yet got the idea of Booth as the assassin, and considered that word — pronounced among the Negroes "Booze" — to probably apply to a local assassin named Boyle, who had some time before killed a provost-marshal.

Mudd hastened home to urge his visitors to depart, and, entering his main room, saw the desperate man asleep, snatching at sighs in his bandit dreams, and pistol, knife, and carbine in his reach. He had shaved off his mustache. Mudd thought of Lloyd Quantrell's warning, bitterly: "Take care you don't entertain, some time, a man less candid than I am, and who may come into this room, unless you guard it with a humble spirit!" He pressed Herold to play on Booth's fears, and they were mounted at early dusk, Booth being in dreadful pain and lifted upon his horse. Martial law had been declared at Bryantown.

Where next were these two vagrants to go?

Unerringly along the returning thread of that dark spy and secret mail system, which had been maintained since the war began for universal slavery.

The chief post station on it between Mudd's and the river was Captain

Sam Cox's, almost twenty miles away, by the roundabout road to avoid Bryantown and the soldiery. A Negro was paid to guide them there, and they arrived at Cox's near Saturday midnight.

Sorrow had struck the household of this earliest taker-up of the sword. His adopted son had returned from Richmond, with the news of another nephew's death; and barely had the news of President Lincoln's taking-off been received, when here were the assassin and his pilot, both probably known to Cox, and Herold certainly known to him — for Herold, as has been said, had gone to a school near by — and he now came in and awakened the family, while Booth sat on his horse in an outer barn-yard, awaiting a reply.

Captain Cox we have already had a glimpse of at Port Tobacco, drilling his company at the outset of the war. A ringleader, with the force of a consumptive, he had done his best for the insurgents and lost the stake; and now that he was ready to meet the new situation and strengthen his considerable property by free application, the hidden paths of his record were traced backward, by this insensate theatrical fool, mimicking war, until, like the barber monkey in the tragedy, Booth had cut an innocent throat.

There was nothing to do but get the men away: Herold was directed to send off the Negro and to hide Booth, and be his guard in a thicket of nearly impenetrable short pines about a mile from Cox's house and four or five miles from the Potomac, and Cox was to have them fed until his henchman, Jones, could slip them over the river.

In the drizzling night of that open spring, the dawn of Easter-Sunday and the arisen Savior, the gratuitous murderer entered the pine-thicket, not to arise from the ground for six nights and days. An overseer, a white man, was sent to bed them, and on Sunday, Jones, the Charon who long had kept the ferry to the Confederacy, was directed to seek them out.

Every hour made the situation of all who harbored them more perilous, as every new development more firmly located the conspiracy in this peninsula of swamp-bottom hill and wilderness. The Government, misled by Dr. Mudd, began to beat up the swamps, though the pines had always been the hiding places of go-betweens; and from their covert, where the little tree-stems were so close that sunlight could not pierce to the earth, Booth and Herold heard the scouting cavalry tread past on the roads with jingling sabers and bridles and neighing animals. Said Booth to Herold, "They can also hear our horses if they can not see them."

When Jones came in on Sunday morning, he found Booth's bay mare loose in the more open woods, nibbling, with the saddle upon her. He whistled, according to a signal conveyed to him by Cox's nephew, and was met by Herold with the cocked carbine, mounting guard like a little sneak spaniel, barking watch.

Booth lay on the ground, pale, with his foot tied and supported, and blankets around him. His broken fibula now exclaimed against his pride of strength, and like a needle in the bone sewed and sewed into his flesh and nerves, as if the heart was the thimble to drive it with every industrious pulsation. He felt the nimble enterprise of this heart as it rose and returned to the seamstress task, while, at times, it seemed that the sewing-spirit with one hand lifted his flesh up like a fabric from the floor and threw it against the shuttle; and then the long, quivering shaft of bone drew a groan of agony, as it seemed to pull a strand of lockjaw through the being of the wretch.

"Oh, a doctor! Can't I have a doctor?" exclaimed Booth to Jones.

"No, my young friend. Not a doctor in the country dare come to you. We can't trust anybody, and our own lives depend on getting you away from us. The best we can do for you is to feed you, and, if we can, to send you to Virginia. Every Negro in the land is wailing for Lincoln and watching us. Your horses must be killed, or they will betray you; nobody dares keep them, as they will both be advertised by age, size, and spot. There is no doubt, I reckon, about your being Booth?"

Jones was an old, cool river-scout, whose face concealed in mournful Maryland lines the amiable craft and fortitude of a Daniel Boone. He was uneducated, and had been raised with Captain Cox as the poor boy companion.

Booth raised his hand at this query and showed the initials "J.W.B." pricked into his wrist in boyhood.

"I want a doctor. I want to get to Virginia, where I can have a doctor. And I want the newspapers!"

Jones left them common Negro and country fare, and next day brought the papers of Baltimore and Washington. The whole land was mourning for the President, and the assassin found that every Southern and conservative interest sought to repudiate him.

He now appreciated, for the first time in his life, discipline. His crime he did not regret, but the world seemed to have become ungrateful. How had men lost pride in him who only had treasured up and executed their threats and hates of years! Did they not see his courage, devotion, and stratagem?

Alas! he who is the executioner of base and frivolous popular resentments, only realizes for himself their infamy, being instantly deserted by his instigators; for no man thinks any man is wicked enough to wreak in cruelty the passing political intentions of the heart. But women and non-combatants will be politicians, and, as they talk, some men will do.

Booth read the papers every day, as once and only once in the day his humble steward came with the meat and brought them.

"Dave," he said, "do you know I feel, some way, as if I was a fugitive slave, like one of them John Brown had, who had got away, and only one poor man had the humanity to feed him?"

But his heart sank deeper after this suggestion, when he thought how he had gloated for nearly six years upon his implacability to any abolitionist; and here he wanted life and freedom, the dearer to him every hour.

No relief the papers gave — some of them the very papers which had assisted to mold and arm his mind for murder; papers which had represented the war for the Union of the country as tyranny and malice, and were edited by renegade or mercenary or unspiritual men, to lead communities deeper and deeper into sullenness and self-abasement. And now they named *him,* the Junius Brutus Booth of the age and famous Tarquin-killer, a crazy man and a drunkard, and, what was still worse, said he was a circus-jumper, and never could act!

At this he would have started up and killed somebody, but only his wounded ankle felt the bone take a great hem in it, and his heart pushed the bone-needle in, and with the chill sweat of anguish on his pale and working face he said over, to drown the pain, the words he had often recited to others from Tom Hood:

> "Stitch — stitch — stitch,
>   In poverty, hunger, and dirt,
>   Sewing at once, with a double thread,
>   A shroud, as well as a shirt!"

He must needs run on to the next stanza a little and say:

> "But why do I talk of death,
>   That phantom of grisly bone?
>   I hardly fear his terrible shape,
>   It seems so like my own —
>   It seems so like my own
>   Because of the fasts I keep;
>   O God, that bread should be so dear,
>   And flesh and blood so cheap!"

"Who ever thought that any man would live to remember that 'Song of the Shirt' in the middle of these gloomy little pines, or that death should grow visible to me on the end of my favorite rhyme? My foot, that I was so proud of, turned traitor to my performance, and now even my recitations bring ghosts to me."

He threw himself out of position, and nearly howled with pain, to hear at a distance the firing of a pistol or carbine. It was the horses Herold was killing in a ravine of Zekiah Swamp.

These animals, no more than the theater where Lincoln died, would ever again be used for men's low purposes. The great genius of war, Secretary Stanton, notified the Baltimore showmen who would have opened the theater while yet it might "draw," like a museum of horrors, that they never should prostitute the blood of Lincoln; and to this day its walls contain the curious wounds and operations of the war, out of whose great opera of groans and agony this tender air of healing mercy and science still lulls the place where the emancipator died.

The horses had been led down a narrow gully, deepening as it was descended from the pine summits to an arm of the great Zekiah Swamp, until the sky above seemed far withdrawn and the smell of decay, some said, was absorbed by the rank vegetation and the shell-lime in the cliffs. There, if the wandering buzzards did feast upon the flesh of those steeds which Herold shot, they did so undiscovered, like familiars in the Inquisition, and picked white the humble and unoffending bones; and in the legends of that country the slain animals alone are thought to have had souls and were ridden by the brutes. Hannah Ritner's racking steed the Negro hears, as he waits at Cox's Station — where the railroad has rifted the little pines, like a beam of education from the moon — go past on Good-Friday and on Easter nights, sounding —

"Tick-a-tock-a, tick-a-tock-a, tick-a-tock-a!"

So does the flight of old barbarisms continue, in the remembrance of martyrs' days and deaths and benefactions.

Day came and night spread round its solemn gloom, all divine with infinite life of waking insects, and in the mornings sang the mysterious birds, each with its secret and its praise, its living purpose and its joy of species. There was a red bird over Booth's head, with a single note like a melted berry or cherry, so lush and full, like "Cheery! cheery! cheery!" and saying it impatiently, like a bride to be kissed again and again.

Another little bird, like a ball of wool with a bit of beak in it, and on a little twig — some of the wren or sparrow tribe, perhaps — whistled:

"Coo-choo — chilly-chilly!"

House-martins came near, but flew away again, and one bird cried, "Hoo-e! hoo-e!" and then softly added, "Hooch! hooch!"

Far overhead, like the police upon false scents, the crows or rooks went straight in pairs only, the bird ahead crying, "Hack! hack!" — the following bird adding "Hock!"

All these sounds the actor heard, wondering how Nature could take her outlawry with such joy; and the cocks and turkey-gobblers in farms of unknown location crowed and clucked, like the sounds of a world drifting away in Noah's ark.

When the sun rose at morning, all the tree-tops seemed to steal toward blossoming, and the moon remained with its inner lamp gone out, like love repulsed yet duteous. No tree could the assassin see but the little pines, though Herold, who could walk, and strayed away a little, reported that he had seen prickly pears or cactus growing in the marl sand, and that the swamps were full of maples already budding red, of fox-grape vines like the cables of great, unseen ships, and birch and beech, oak, poplar, and sycamore; while on the upland, in the stiff white soil or gray clay, among the red and white oaks grew the green holly, deep, cool cedar, and liberty-loving pine.*

Booth had to threaten Herold that if he ever forgot their mutual danger, and shot at a bird or wild animal, he would kill him; for Herold was continually gunning in his mind, and the highest flight Booth could take in bathos or invective never carried Herold above "pa'tridges." Sometimes, when Booth's mind was full of grisly things, and the chill of horror dampened his brow, he would hear the boy near by whistling "Bob White, Bob White," softly, and looking with his shy blue eyes at his carbine, like a child denied the shooting of its gun on Christmas Sunday. When Booth talked about eagles and Caesar, Herold told a story of losing a canvas-back duck and being kicked over by his shot-gun.

"Ah, Dave," said Booth, "you are Nimrod, a mighty hunter before the Lord."

Before the Lord! The idea remained in Booth's mind. Why any hunter before the Lord? Brought before the Lord for killing? Or killing where the Lord would save? What did it mean? And must the mighty all stand before the Lord?

Up to this time Booth's title for preachers had been "Biblethumpers,"† and he despised religious reflections; but he began to fear his mind might run that way. He grew tired of the newspapers, as they all stamped upon his name and act. He read of the arrest of his eldest brother, "June," for having been the custodian of his abduction secret; of Payne's capture; Mrs. Surratt's arrest; Arnold, O'Laughlin, and Atzerodt hunted down; and of his own trunk found with a colonel's military dress-coat in it and two pairs of handcuffs.

Ah! the illustrious man he had sentenced to wear those shackles, like the last remaining slave, was now the theme of poetry and eulogy everywhere, while Booth's labored confession never appeared, and no man spoke for him.

For two days and nights he anticipated some visitation from his victim's spirit, like the dead Caesar entering the tent of Brutus; but it

---

*	The author made this study April 15, 1884, at Cox's Station, on the site of Booth's concealment.

†	John Matthews, actor; story related by him of Booth.

did not come. The third night, when all mental anxiety seemed allayed, and his mind was dozing, the President and he sat quietly reciting Shakespeare together in the woods. Again the tall, loving man called him "my eloquent young friend," and challenged him to follow, passage by passage, from the bard of Avon. Again he gave the speech of Antony, and the President replied from Imogen, and led the way down all the plays, to Robert Burns, at last.

Booth wondered he did not speak of being killed, and make some accusation, and finally expressed an apology, more rhetorical than repentant, to the President's face.

"Don't mind it," said the President; "we lived in a period of misunderstanding. I got well and came to see you, thinking you wanted a little company. Good-night, Johnny!"

As he took the President's offered hand, it was so cold that he awoke, shouting, in the midnight chilliness of the pines.

"I've seen it!" he faltered to Herold, who had waked and was wondering.

"A pa'tridge," asked Herold, "or a fox?"

"That long-lived fox, Dave — Abe Lincoln. Don't sleep! Come, talk awhile!"

And then the ankle began to knead with itching and shooting pains, the heart to do needlework with the bone, the quilting-party to start, and the hot fever sizz in the night's rainless drizzle.

Night after night he sat in the woods with Lincoln, hearing parts of Shakespeare long studied and forgotten, and seeking to explain matters, and only the dread settled in his soul that the victim would soon go, and at last would come that cold hand, and Booth would wake shouting again.

It is the going of apparitions and not their coming that we often dread; they come like life's own semblance, and they leave death's desertion behind them. Booth, left alone, was haunted, for nothing but this spirit did him the benevolence of society.

Three ideas became the new construction of his life: To enter a warm house and feel a fire; to get to Virginia and the sure sympathy and doctoring for him there; and to have the appreciation or forgiveness of his mother. Already the sun of glory was set in his heart, and the world was like an empty theater when company, lights, and audience are gone.

He sat in the woods as in that theater, seeing the dead man in the box, and he with a broken leg transfixed to the stage. There were but two of them, guarded by the poor, boyish scullion Herold, and they must face each other out.

"Oh, let me smell your fire," he said to Jones, "and drink my coffee warm! These woods are like a damp tomb to me."

When life seemed only dear from its eternity and intensity, and despair made a solid wall of the pine poles, Jones appeared in the night of Friday, a week following the assassination, and bade them instantly depart.

"It is your only chance," said he; "the cavalry has gone on a false clew to St. Mary's County, and tomorrow they will be back to beat up these pines."

He and Herold lifted Booth on Jones's own horse, and Herold led him, while Jones preceded to guide by a whistle agreed upon.

For nearly one hundred and fifty hours Booth had lain on the ground unmoved, and his bones seemed now collected from a vault and put together cold. Yet he clutched his revolver as they gained the high-road, on which they had quite a space to go in impenetrable darkness; for life grew more precious as it ran down, like the final sands which shine crystal in the hour-glass. Suffering the death of apprehension, of bodily thorns, and of bone-coldness, Booth saw, at last, a gleam of warming light in an old, decayed house.

"My God!" he said, "there's fire. Coffee, too! Take me in!"

The weather-beaten and poverty-ground guide shed some tears at the anguish in the plaint.

"No, friend! There's my Negro in the kitchen. He's faithful to me, whatever I do. But you —"

He had killed the freedom-giver, and murdered the prince of peace!

In the dripping fog of an old pear tree Booth ate and drank, sitting on the horse, and saw that the last man he knew in Maryland trembled to shove him forever from her shores.

He paid for the little boat he was to take, at the bottom of the long gully — his ready money was nearly gone — and, looking at a little compass by the aid of an end of candle, he was rowed by Herold out on the mysterious river.

For hours they pulled in currents and tides, the boat aleak, Booth's foot on blades of fire, conferring, quarreling, apologizing, cursing, sighing. His scullion and pilot was becoming a tyrant, the thin veneering of Herold's modesty wearing off in the friction of beasts' life.

At morn they were grounded in a marsh under a bluff of clay, and Herold landed, while Booth nodded over his clutched carbine.

"Here was Virginia, thank God!" he said again and again, "and his patron State would not forget her champion."

Herold returned. "We're lost," he said. "This is Maryland yit — ole Nanjemoy! I've shot pa'tridges on this farm."

The proprietor, beside himself with dread, had sent Herold away with food; and now all day they hid among the brush at the water's marge, miserable, impatient, waiting for night and another endeavor.

The Sabbath rose upon a low strand with raveled banks of clay and copse before, and the Potomac plashing under the boat.

"Virginia!" cried Herold. "John, you're going crazy! Come, hobble along. The gunboats are watching every rod of landing now."

Booth struggled up, carrying his cross beneath his arm in an old oar made by a bowie knife into a crutch, and with imprecations he climbed the ruined land and reached at last old Bryan's hut — the other Charon, opposite Jones of Maryland.

Bryan lived with a Negro woman, and had no other wife, and was illiterate, mercenary, and suspicious. He heard that Booth was a Confederate officer, whose horse had thrown him and broken his leg, but had his doubts. He had horses, but no vehicle, so Herold sallied out to seek some method of conveyance to the Rappahannock crossing, half a day distant.

Beneath an oak tree, in the field before Bryan's naked abode, Booth reflected that this was the Virginia of his idolatry — this slave of a Negro woman Virginia's embassy to him. But the real Virginians were not far off; there was consolation in that!

His wandering visions were wholly of his mother now — that poor exile from her native land to a home of logs and dry clay woodlands like this. He remembered the story of her coming hither, cheated, perhaps, dogged by her predecessor, set in a doubtful light, yet blessed by beauteous children, and bound, as in bonds, by them, to the everlasting banishment of a false position, unless they should bring honor out of misunderstanding, and crown her patient age with their manly virtues and the healing of charity.

Had *he* respected his mother, whose only hope was in this generation, whose marriage had been a dish of herbs served in a theater's pewter silver, yet whose pride in her sons had been all the consolations of religion?

At slow, deliberate pains, unauthorized, uncommissioned, untimely, he had done this great, gratuitous murder, and set the light of Lincoln's life against the cottage where his mother hid, and invited the world's inquisition and comparison.

Yet even there, all stricken by his crime, she seemed his mother still, and pitying him who had not where to lay his head — refused by hearths and refusing the grave.

The President was by his side, calling him "Johnny," and saying, "Never mind"; that it had been an age of misunderstanding, and now he was well again; and so that strange, cheerful man went on reciting to Booth the wail of King Edward's widow for her sons, Prince Arthur's plaint to Hubert, Jane Shore's appeal for Christian shelter, Macduff's despair at his children slain, and Portia's lines to Mercy. Again the

President's cold hand awoke him, and he cried:

"Mother, I thought it was my country. I thought it was for the best!"

"John Booth," said a voice of grave, sad pity, "you have set up the corpse of the Confederate cause and assassinated it! Joe Johnston surrendered to General Sherman last Tuesday. There is no place to hide you now this side of Mexico!"

Booth looked up — an old, old man he was, all overgrown with ragged beard, uncombed and dirty, and like a city tramp feeding from the garbage-barrels, as he hobbles on in faded, crumpled raiment; and so he seemed to Lloyd Quantrell, who now gazed at him in Virginia.

Chapter XLIX

THE RETURN

WHEN Lloyd Quantrell said there was no place for Booth to hide, short of Mexico, he spoke from locality. Herold had found Lloyd on the farm of Iturbide's aunt, and Iturbide was to become Emperor of Mexico if Maximilian lived.*

It was to protect the ladies there that Lloyd went to seek Booth and compromise himself. When he reached Booth, the woe-worn plight of that bravo touched his heart, and smothered the indignations he meant to express. He exerted himself to procure from Bryan horses to carry them away, and he concealed their identity. Proclamations and descriptions had not been posted up in this part of Virginia. Quantrell, however, said to Booth as the latter indulged in some boasting on his feat:

"They will take you before you get far. I feel for you, John!"

"I will never be taken," said Booth, "to be paraded over Washington. If the worst comes, I'll put a ball from this through my head!"

He showed an elaborately mounted pistol.

Quantrell always believed, in the sequel, that Booth shot himself.

When Mr. Booth reached the summer dwelling of a rich Virginian, some eight miles distant, that evening, it was lighted and merry for the close of war and the return of soldier friends; but the proprietor had adopted a rule to entertain no spies or suspicious persons, and the assassin and his uninteresting friend had to sleep in a colored woman's

---

*   At the moment in the text the clerical Emperor, Maximilian, had adopted young Iturbide, whose father had married Miss Green, of Georgetown, D.C. Her sister, Mrs. Quesenberry, lived on the farm near Booth's landing-place. In two years more, Mr. Seward, reviving from his wound, was to see that government "by the people and for the people" did not perish even from Mexico. In spite of the appeals of our Government, Maximilian was executed — "one of the most solemn scenes ever witnessed, save the murder and burial of Abraham Lincoln," says the Hapsburger's law-officer and biographer, Fred Hall.

cabin on the farm. Cut to the heart, and hereafter dropping Virginia and gratitude from his mind, Booth wrote next morning to the proprietor:

"I have some little pride. I can not blame you for want of hospitality. You know your own affairs. I was sick, tired, with a broken limb, and in need of medical advice. I would not have turned a dog from my door in such a plight. However, you were kind enough to give us something to eat. . . . 'The sauce to meat is ceremony; meeting were bare without it.' Be kind enough to accept the enclosed five dollars (although hard to spare) for what I have received."*

A Negro was hired to take them in a cart to Port Conway, across the weary hills and hollows — twelve miles' journey — where they arrived early Monday morning, and some disbanded rebel cavalry were picked up by Herold and used to procure Booth ferriage across the Rappahannock. He rode on a young officer's horse along the skirt of old Port Royal town, and was left at a retired farmhouse three miles south of it — a wretch without a plan, a friend, or a country!

Let man hereafter hesitate who issues himself a commission, creates himself a state, and expects alliances for nothing but a crime!

*P*resident Lincoln died in a plain room, opposite the theater, after breathing unconscious for nine hours, his chief officials around him, and his wife and son in another room. The bed was cheap and humble, the prints horses and sheep, but the wise men were there, and the spirit he exhaled freshened the world and made Cæsars piteous.

His death was the woman's spikenard-ointment that perfumed his weary feet and diffused his balm wherever humanity had wounds. He had been his own precursor, and the faculties and moralizers felt ashamed that he had come, instead of another; but his wisdom put their words to better than shame — to contrition. They said he had no model, but they had not seen the poor; for in the clay of which God made men are left many models for Jove or Jesus.

Mr. Lincoln was composite of every humble, natural, and unaffected feeling; one touch of pretension would have slain him more than the assassin's ball. He was one of the rare great men who could live without quarreling, envy, or even indignations. The man who killed him was replete with all the virtues of the self-complacent.

Men reflected that the theater and slavery put together were the

---

*   Letter from Booth to Dr. Stewart, composed in his diary found on his dead body — the date April 23 or 24, 1865. Booth had outlawed himself, and his mere lodging at this man's house cost the host captivity and great mental anxiety.

combination in Herodias and in Nero; that the purest reproof was written on the ground, and that spittle which cured the blind man could cure a blind age.

Lincoln's power was in his philosophy: to be gentle with infirmity, like the Creator, and to hold humor to be man's golden book of law. The piece he lost his life to see had seemed to the critics vulgar enough, yet it proved, in time, to contain more humor than any actor ever made, and its subject was his native land, however imperfectly described.* The great war hardened, but could not construct this man; he was made out of the trials of little causes and in the competitions of popular politics, and his patience was tested at every point before Heaven would trust him with its sword or pen. New discoveries in morals he never felicitated himself upon, but found perennial comfort in human nature. Living in a fiery transport of human faith to break away from fettering bondages of body and of mind, he succeeded greatest because he was richest in love and mightiest in trust.

The farm of Jake Bosler looked almost princely in the spring, as the masons and carpenters had improved and enlarged the buildings, and art had arranged the grounds; but the old man, with his fair possessions, had a hunger that neither wealth nor heaven could satisfy, till, one morning, he came down from bed, and saw that strangers had entered his house in the night, taking advantage of a latch never secured by any bolt.

A child of fair hair and large dark eyes, like his missing daughter's, sat playing upon the floor.

"Why, *bubelly,*" exclaimed Jake, stammering, "whose is te baby?"

"Danpa's," lisped the child, arising; "we's tum home."

"We?" articulated Jake; "I dinks I hear my olty. Is it te shpook of death?"

He sank trembling into a seat and stared at the child, as if his hour had come.

"Don't you know Winter, danpa?" asked the child, coming up and leaning on his knee.

"Winter?" the old man said. "It was winter when my Katy went away. Winter nefer has been gone since then. It will pe winter in my heart till — Bi'm-by."

Tears dimmed his eyes, but through them came a vision of a woman in the Dunker dress entering the door, and the early sunshine from the crest of the Catoctin Mountain followed her along the floor, giving her the golden halo of the martyrs in the Baptist book.

"Fader," said the apparition, kneeling down, "I waited till the war was

---

*　　"The American Cousin" made, in the subordinate part of *Dundreary,* the fortune of Mr. Sothern, who played it till his death.

ended for the father of my boy to come and put the ring upon my finger. I trusted him, and still will trust, and here, it has been predicted by the good witch, that he will come today to do me right. May we stay here, fader?"

She took the boy into her arms, and waited like one afraid.

"Stay with fader?" the old man said, tottering up, "where can you stay but here? I feel te summer in my old heart, and all my prayers is answered. Te only ring I'f looked for is my child's arms around my neck, where Gott unites us and noting can efer diwide."

They were kneeling, and they entered into prayer. The old man used his native Dutch, and thanked the Lord, not for the gift of honor, nor even purity, but for the gift of child; and as he prayed, the door being open, the unaccredited creation came in — chickens without pedigree, ducks without a family tree, the peacock without other primogeniture than a spangled tail, Guinea-hens fearing to forget their name of species, and conning over "buckwheat-buckwheat," and the capon, most indifferent of all.

The child — also uncertified in the herd-book of mankind — left the prayer, and ran and raced among these, his silken ringlets bounding from his shoulders, and in his large eyes the mountain landscapes seemed to stand reflected like Narcissus in the well.

"Fader, forgive my ingratitude," spoke Katy, as she and the old man walked forth upon the new veranda in the soft spring air; "I longed to see you, but I did not come for that: love for *his* father brought me here."

She pointed to her boy.

"I know, my child," said Jake, "how te young must leave fader and modder and cleaf to a young man, and nater led you away and back to home ag'in. Te Lord be thanked for nater, dat makes te lost sheep find home. But *his* fader has peen a rebel, and Fader Abe is killed! How can Luter, your bruder — poor Lincoln made him a cheneral te day he died — meet te man dat wounded him and took his sister's goot name?"

As they spoke, there was a sound of hoarse and broken singing in the road, and three men approached the gate, staggering drunkenly, but one of them had music in his windpipe, though he was the drunkest of the three, and with arms across the gate, sweeping the house with his dazed, unseeing eyes, he let the deep notes roar to the sound of an accordion he played:

> "My country! 'Tis of thee,
>   Sweet land of liberty,
>   Of thee I sing!"

His great stature and weight, unmanageable against the frail lattice gate, broke it down, and he fell on his face in Bosler's lawn, the accordion flying from his hand and breaking to pieces.

His companions looked at him with tipsy grins, and hands in idiotic flowing gestures, and laughed a loud and hollow —

"Ha! ha! ha! ha!"

The mocking sound seemed to roll between the parallel mountains, and echo and echo, like the mourning-guns from Harper's Ferry.

"The slave-catchers have got my Lloyd!" shouted Katy. "The Logans have brought him back!"

She started down the path with winged feet, pursued by her boy.

The ragged, ruined, wind-beaten man turned up his dry, bleared eyes and muttered:

"I'm for she Gover'ment! I'm true blue. Hurrah for she ole flag!"

"O Lloyd, my love," cried Katy, "there is one battle more that you and I must fight — for your poor soul!"

"My love," the great giant looked up and spoke, with humor in his beggary, "we shelebrated she peash lash night at Harper's Ferry. We shwore allegiensh on honor bright. It'll be all right in she morning when we go shee my father — God blesh him!"

"Ha! ha! ha! ha!" went up the laughter of Lloyd's retreating comrades, pursued by echoes from bridge and barn and dwelling.

"I am promised this conversion," spoke Katy, kissing her child as she held him in her arms, and looked to the skies with streaming eyes; "God, who has given me his father's penitence, will not deny me my husband's soul!"

"Paptize him in te spring-house where we found him," cried Jake Bosler; "he'll come to — Bi'm-by."

With this, Jake poured on the drunkard's head cold water from the dairy, and Katy rubbed his temples; and while they worked at him in dread and pity, people stole in the gate and stood around them.

"That is your man," spoke one of these at last. "Put your irons on him while you can! He is strong and dangerous."

As Katy saw bracelets with chains slipped over her lover's wrists, she screamed and leaped from the ground.

Strange men were standing there, and, shrinking in their rear, was Hugh Fenwick.

The cold water and the woman's scream brought Quantrell, also, to his senses, and he stood up in his rags, and looked at his hands thus manacled, and asked:

"What's this? I took the parole!"

"We arrest you," said one of the strangers, pistol in hand, "as one of the assassins of Abraham Lincoln, and you are wanted in Washington."

"My God!" exclaimed Lloyd; "who has suspected me of such a crime as that?"

"Mr. Fenwick, here, saw you in Washington the day of the murder. Your name was given at the bridge. You met Booth in Bryantown last fall, and met him again last Sunday in Virginia. You made an oath with him and Beall, the pirate, to be revenged on the Government."

"Take hold of him," cried Fenwick, edging away. "See how he looks at me!"

"If I am guilty of this crime," spoke Quantrell, humbly, "I shall not ask to live. If I am innocent, I will rid the world of that man who has accused me!"

Katy threw herself upon her husband, all shackled and dishonored as he was.

"No, no," Jake Bosler spoke; "te blood of te President must first pe washed from his hands."

Lloyd put back his wife with gentle strength.

"Katy, your father is right. If that is my boy, let him never see me again — till I am dead or exonerated."

Lloyd had come home by way of Harper's Ferry, and his one bad habit, following him through the war, had now brought him to the stage that he could not drink without becoming drunk. A popular companion and honorable soldier, his song and accordion had been known through the camps, and his counsel had always been tranquilizing and just, so that many of his army friends felt their sense of country and freedom return, until, when the physical war ended, the moral rebellion was also worn to a thin shell wherever men were gentle-natured.

Put in a military prison, Quantrell was allowed to see nobody, and his old father said:

"That boy is not guilty. Though I shall not see him, I know that his obedience to me and to his poor cause never would allow him to be an assassin. I can say, with Admiral Penn, when they thrust his son William into a prison, 'This is the reward I have from the government my services restored.'"

In another direction the old man was more successful — to have his son's wife righted by the Roman Church.

In that body was an historical passion to defend marriage, and Abel Quantrell's wishes were sent to Rome itself.

His views had prevailed in the land, and the indifferent moral assistance they had received from a church long identified with slavery, created there a greater desire to conciliate the powerful political party of which he was a rather popular oddity.

The candor and extremeness of his views, his kindness to individual insurgents and his high political influence, and also his chivalry to women, for whose weakness he made every allowance, created an enthusiasm for him among the Sisters of Charity and poorer monastic orders — especially the Irish — and they worked upon the higher clergy until a dispensation, or other species of concession, was made, somewhat in these words:

"The sacrilegious person who presumed to administer the marriage ordinance in name of Holy Church may be taken into orders, and his ordaining can date from a time anterior to his sin, provided that he take the vows of the most rigorous monastic life and disappear from the world."

"I like a church that can do anything," Abel Quantrell said, sardonically; "here the marriage-ring is taken out of solution, and the circle squared; but how are you going to catch the bird, to put the salt on his tail?"

The Sisters of the Church resolved to have the secular law punish Fenwick for personating a priest, if he refused to be a monk.

That individual was, indeed, in deep waters; but he put all his amateur versatility in motion, and had made himself a useful auxiliary to the Government in detecting the assassins. The escaped Surratt had been hidden in Canada by the mistaken zeal of priests there, who could not see that they were taking his mother's life, as well as violating the law of nations. Ultimately, when it was too late to save the woman, the shallow son was tracked to Rome, and found in the Papal Guard, where another American recruit from Maryland* knew him and gave him away for the reward, and then the Papal Government ordered him delivered up.

The church hostility to Fenwick, however, was the greater, because of his prying cognizance of certain family facts, in making use of which, for the ends of justice, he was doing the principal good of his life. Nothing showed the legal and worldly incapacity of neophytes and priests more than the behavior of both Fenwick and his enemies in this matter, and proved that while denouncing secret societies the Church forgot its own tendency that way.

Fenwick had a fine smattering of doctrinal lore and the church institutes, and he fought for his life with an adroitness worthy of those other Bohemians, Huss or Jerome, before councils armed with fire.

The woman he dreaded and depended on, with nearly equal anxiety, was Hannah Ritner. In the demoralization of his mind between cunning and devoteeism, self-love and superstition, he consulted this strange seer, who was worthy of being the mother abbess of the whole nation.

She looked at him with a weary touch of humor in her grand face, and wrote him some lines, and dismissed him. He read them with a great sense of fear in his heart; for of all things living or dead, he feared

---

*   St. Marie.

Lloyd Quantrell most:

> "Little mousey in mishap,
>   Choose the dog, or choose the trap!
>   Death is in the mastiff's yell,
>   Life's remainder in the cell.
>   Mice as foolish thou may'st tease
>   In the trap, and eat the cheese."

Fenwick was taken to Nelly Harbaugh by Hannah Ritner while he was in this state of apprehension, and told to co-operate with that actress, who now was preparing for a *début* as a "star" with her own company, and while keeping refuge in the ragged house at the edge of the purlieu, she discussed with him the basis of a social play, and Fenwick outlined several themes. He had no other than assisting literary talents, while she, by pains and application, had ransacked the Library of Congress for foreign models of some drama which should display her personal charms.

Nelly saw that the hideous old pieces out of the Gunpowder-Plot age — the butchering Richards and mouthing Brutuses — had survived their day to end with this murderer, and that the French and other Continentals had recreated the stage and made the heart's woes and the inconsistency of human environment the drama of the present. Fenwick was a good literary milliner, and Nelly was a wonderful head and bust to hang his subtleties upon.

In the course of their experiments they found a topic near home, so inspiring to them both, that an interest of opposites kindled in their natures, and while the subject they mutually labored upon was of Fenwick's eavesdropping in people's houses, Nelly Harbaugh saw in it a chance to repay a noble favor at the sacrifice of her own idolatry.

The Government had released her, finding her clear at every point of complicity in the President's murder; and now, with her stage name changed again, she was prepared with a dry, seared, but still ambitious heart, to run the actress's career and draw upon mankind for her outfit and advertisement.

Luther Bosler entered one day, when she was sitting among new dresses, ornaments, and properties for her *début*, and he said:

"Nelly, joy and misfortune have come together. My old Dunker brethren have made me a preacher again, taking the view I did, that *this* war was a sacred duty; but Lloyd, my poor prodigal brother, is in the toils of hard evidence, and my lady — you know it was Miss Pittson — has rejected me and offended Abel Quantrell, and still adheres to the subjects of her romantic sympathy, Booth, the assassin, and Lloyd Quantrell, who is in chains."

While they spoke, the voices of newsboys in the streets were heard approaching, roaring as they came almost breathless:

"Capture of Boot', de assassin! Capture of David E. Herold! Death of Wilkes Boot' in Virginia! De 'Evening Staw!'"

Nelly had started up, the roses gone from her face, and she threw out her hands for something to take hold of, but only found the broad shoulders of General Bosler, and there she leaned, not coming nearer, while some tears ran from her eyes.

"Pardon me, Luther," she said. "You know what he was to me — my greatest injurer — but it was in the wiles of love, and for my account I pray God to forgive him."

"Live to do mercy, my sister!" spoke Luther with his palm above her golden-yellow tresses; "to set at rest the misunderstandings of other hearts, and to be of the peace-makers who shall be called the children of God!"

"I will, Luther, I will! I see within my hands, let down to me from angels, the cords of many compassions, and pray for me, O brother! that I shall have the wisdom and assistance, even in this false art of playing life, to set the innocent free, to save the foolish one, and let love and not blood be the law!"

*A*t the farm overhanging the sunken road which wound behind it, and was screened by trees and thickets partly in bloom, Booth had awaited the unknown with a broken heart. Nobody in Port Royal town would take him in; at his identity with the assassin — which Herold had blabbed — and at his own showing of the inked initials under his skin, "J.W.B.," the soldier had shrunk away and hid him, and gone ahead, not to return, except with his takers.

Herold, too, was growing restive under his confinement to this crippled outlaw, and high words had passed between them; for Booth was nearly destitute, and Herold was a hireling as well as a vagrant, and now Booth could give him neither adventure nor money.

After Captain Jett, the Virginian, had left Booth at Garrett's farm, Herold rode nearly to Bowling Green, fifteen miles away, with the disbanded insurgents, and the next day, Tuesday, he went quite to Bowling Green and back; and hardly had he returned, when blue-clad cavalry went around the farm-gate and down into the swamp-crossing, and could be seen filing up the southern slope, carbines all ready, and their sabers, like sleighing-bells jingling, to kill the last enemy, and go to Northern homes.

Booth did not know that they were riding to get Captain Jett and find where he had hidden that broken-legged man; but Booth did know that the blue-coats were now south of him, and Virginia unthankful to him.

The Garretts, who owned the farm, became distrustful of their two quarreling guests, though Booth had used all his tender talk to get their confidence, and played with their child, and breathed domestic sentiment. He felt that he must have lost his art since this blood had smeared him.

A neighbor or two dropped in and sounded the stranger, as he lay out in the yard under the trees, and went away suspectful. At last the men of the family said: "We can not accommodate you another night; our house is full."

They had no idea that here were the murderers whose capture would make them rich; but they felt that something was not honest.

This man, all armed, yet not in uniform; this boy, so unworthy of the man, and so sniveling and fugitive; their inquiry about roads and distances, and want of innocence or location — could they be horse-thieves?

"We can sleep in the barn," said Booth. "Allow us to go in there!"

His pleading eyes, in which some of the humility and light of childhood had returned, procured a wavering assent; but after they had entered the small barn, the eldest son of Garrett, considering that they might steal the horses, slipped out and locked them in.

They were at last enjailed; but the assassin had a repeating carbine and a pair of pistols, and kept his tone of confidence up, to Herold, as they made their beds in the straw.

They would reach the mountains, and go through Tennessee to the Gulf, and Herold should yet have rambling.

Herold fell asleep, but Booth would never sleep again!

Chapter L

DEATH OF BOOTH

*T*HERE are three crimes hard to excel in wickedness: the robbing of woman of her innocence, of a good magistrate of his life, and of a race of brother-men of simple, humble rights. All these were now to settle with John Wilkes Booth.

Negroes, of the race he would deprive of freedom, informed upon the disappearance of Jones's boat in Maryland, and described two armed and suspicious men adrift.

The man whose affianced virgin Booth had taken away, General Luther Bosler, received upon the army telegraph-wire from Chapel Point this information in the War-Office at Washington, and he drew down a Coast-Survey chart and looked it over with Secretary Stanton. "Here is the route they must take," said Luther, "through King George County to Port Royal, the usual route of spies. By putting some cavalry on a steamboat, they can be landed at Bell Plain and intercept the murderer!"

The great Secretary, who grieved for the good magistrate, his friend, replied, "Take that action at once, and send two of my police-officers along!"

So, as Booth lay down in the barn, the cavalry had scoured the country behind him and gone past, receiving his description from the Negro ferryman at the Rappahannock River.

Death is a ghastly presence at the end of long sickness and the wearing out of nature; but to him who is well, robust, and superstitious, and who has inflicted Death's embrace upon another, and is sneaking away from Nemesis, Death is the King of Terrors. How slight had seemed death-giving to this young man, who preferred cruelty for his pastime; but how vast and inconsolable was death-taking to him, even when life had lost its meanest relations!

He forgot his burning foot in the clammy sweat of fear and the craving of the appalled heart. The barn seemed full of witnesses, the straws to be musket-barrels, the night-sounds to be accusations, the roof of the shamble to be high as black heaven, and all the interval the throne of Death!

He thought of each particular of every pertinent subject, and, still the sequel of each would be Death. It seemed unreasonable that Death should not allow any matter whatever to be considered without thrusting in its horrible demand, and he proceeded softly, cunningly, to head off that grisly guardsman and get past, "running like a cat," as he had expressed it, and taking the byways of joy and love — thinking over his finest love-sentence with Light Pittson, when he stole her first resisting kiss; of his soft, prolonged amours against the mountain-maid; of the many humble suburban coquettes entrapped at theaters, and the yielding of women of station to his untiring wiles; and still Death closed the reminiscence and seemed to say, "Cold to the bone forever is *my* assignation, and neither audience nor applause will ever be there!"

With this fear of the black fate was a care and oppression he could not understand — an old man's feeling, haunting him and abiding, mixed with the dread little boys have of being lost by their parents in great cities, or wandering far away from home penniless and without lodging. Between the two — the old pauper's dread and the child's desertion — Booth's anxiety roved the whole earth, and lived for ages in those few hours.

Where were New Guinea, Kamchatka, Patagonia — and could the newspapers go so far and make him known? Where was Crusoe's Island, or the Florida of the Young Marooners, or the pirates' Isle of Pines? He felt his geographical ignorance, and, the more, that he had never admitted it before in his blind, headstrong folly.

He also felt the cowardice which attends upon money spent and gone.

Would he have dared to kill the President if Booth had always been a poor, unprodigal young man? Or, rather, was not his deadly vanity the offspring of the fool's money and the dupe's gaming?

He thought of the dollars wasted on bowie-knives, revolving pistols, spurs, pocket-compasses, horses, and livery-men; on drinks, loans, clothing, lodging, fire, and concubines for the parcel of tramps and roustabouts, who were soon to be paraded, beside himself, before the fashion and society of Washington, like Falstaff's band with him, for Prince Hal in the midst. How the officers of the army court-martial — men of courage too well ingrained to be conscious of it — would despise the skulking and treacherous gypsy they were to foul their minds with! He had not even an overcoat, and his bank-book was left in Atzerodt's room with Herold's outfit.

And all this he had given his mental dignity and powers to bring about, unasked, untempted, unabused, in evil and gratuitous self-seeking, like the beaten politicians who had made war upon the Union from the groveling yet soaring spirit of the vulture — to pick the eyes and vitals from the dead republic, expecting to reproduce them in that sable image of the Prometheus-eating bird.

Booth felt that he was also part of that blind trap, and a statesman of the thinly scenic government whose civil *dramatis personæ* were now, like strolling players, wandering toward the Gulf. Even State-rights was a mockery, and the unavowed John Brown was more the hero of Virginia than he who had killed a commander-in-chief, shouting the motto of the State.

He groaned again, *"Sic semper tyrannis!"*

The circling furies in the sound began to repeat, *"Sic — Semper — sic — Tyrannis.* At him, dogs!"

The old barn echoed with the hissing sound of *"Sic, sic,"* as used to blood-hounds on the scent, and fiery dogs went round his brain, all fever-filled, and their eyes and teeth were gnashing.

"Herold! Dave Herold! some water, for God's sake — I'm afire!"

The boy slept peacefully, having, of himself, premeditated no crime.

Then the prediction of the old Quaker witch at Harper's Ferry, that he should cry "Water, water, Lord!" came to mind. He burst into another chilly sweat, between terror and malaria, to think he had already verified this prophecy.

"Never mind, my eloquent young friend," said the tall President, sitting there in the barn upon the straw, "don't mention your misunderstanding of me! You know I recovered, and bear no malice. Now — that pretty piece from 'King John,' where Constance mourns! Oh, if you had really killed me, think of how my wife and children would have cried! How pleasant to think it was all a mistake!"

With faltering tongue he tried to match Shakespearean passages with his victim again, who laughed and laughed at his discomfiture, and put out his cold, cold hand, and this time it shot a pang of chilliness to the outlaw's heart.

"O mother!" he cried, "save me — oh, pray for me! 'Pray! pray! pray!'"

As he stirred the straw he lay in, there seemed animal footsteps outside, and whispering, and then the ringing of accoutrements. A fear greater than he could ever have imagined came upon him, and an oppression like the removal of every living organ from the encasements of the body.

"Dave! Dave!" he whispered, and his hair seemed to stand, as the noises proceeded upon the sward. He thought they might be spirit-sounds, like those the bandit Stevens heard at Harper's Ferry, and, for an instant, was relieved to hear a human voice speak aloud in the night:

"To the persons who are in this barn! We call upon you to surrender your arms to the man who will come in for them. We notify you that you are surrounded, and had better give up."

A neighing of horses came on the night air, and a sound like the cocking of gun-locks went round the barn, from side to side, from end to end. Herold heard it, and was up, with sniveling in his cry:

"John, we're tuk! Le's us give in. I don't want to be shot!"

"Get down, you coward! They may be our friends."

Booth had roused up, and stood upon his crutch, with the carbine in his hand. The night was so dark that the many cracks in the barn afforded no view of forms outside, now mysteriously still, as if their fire-arms were intently aiming next unlocked, and a man entered, saying:

"They were going to hang father and me if we hadn't told them you had gone to the barn. If you don't come out, they'll burn our property."

Booth swore, while trembling, that he would kill the man for betraying him.

"'Tain't worth while," said the son of Garrett, "to kill me. It won't save you. If you hain't done nothing wrong, you can come out safe."

Booth damned his soul in impotent profanity, and only the greater fear of what was coming restrained his hand from brutality. The young man cowered and backed out of the door, and then Herold said:

"I want to surrender. I'm afraid! I want to see my sister!"

"Will you leave me, too?" cried Booth — "the last follower I have, the last friend?"

"I'm a coward," said Herold. "You can tell them I didn't kill nobody. Oh, do, and let me go!"

Booth cursed him also, and fought for a little parley; so precious is life to those who take it from others wantonly!

He indulged the hope that these might be insurgent soldiery, with his ignorance of news and an obtuseness of general perception which steadily diminished his mental reputation, until his brain, at last, seemed a mere glittering pin-head, like one of the beads sown upon an actor's royalty.

"Perhaps I am taken by my friends," he shouted, and the interval seemed a year before the cool, thief-taker's voice outside replied:

"Come and see! Your life will not be taken by us if you surrender."

He asked whom he was thought to be, and another silence so long as if to answer, "You are nameless; you are nothing; you are annihilation" — was followed by a dry response to come out, or take the consequences.

There was a cricket, or katydid, or strong-throated animal in the barn, which all the while counted its accorded measure of prayers during this term of agony, till the assassin's ears seemed bursting; but Herold hardly noticed it, he said, though hearing in the distant night the baying of coon-hunters' dogs, where the freedmen celebrated their deliverance in the rolling country.

"Oh, let me go, and say, John, I didn't kill the President, before we part; it'll save your soul, maybe, to let up on me."

The assassin had already put his hand around his crutch and taken hold of his revolver, with the action, rather than the meaning, of killing himself; but at the word "soul" he dropped the pistol in the straw and shouted greedily:

"There's a man here who wants to surrender. Take him out! He is innocent of any crime."

Without saying good-bye, so much was he afraid of the enemy before and behind, Herold put out his hands through the door opened for him, and they were handcuffed before he stepped across the sill. The two detective officers searched him and then handcuffed him around a small tree near by, and one of them, disappointed in the small and pusillanimous object he had found, kicked Herold's posterior with an interjection of contempt.

"I don't know that man in there," sniffled Herold; "I met him on the road by Port Tebakker, and he hired me to be his nuss, with his leg broke."

"Here! here!" spoke the same unfeeling voice beside the barn, nearly at Booth's side, yet shifting, as if the possessor had a stealthy foot, "surrender, or we'll burn you like a rat in this barn! If you have any gratitude to the man who sheltered you, save his property! We are men of business, and this is your last chance."

A low word of "Be ready!" in another voice, showed that the death-vise was being screwed close.

How now to die was Booth's soul-strained option — by suicide, fire, or in combat?

The cricket sang indifferent to his ordeal; the sounds of the midnight hunting seemed musical as heaven, and made the world stretch wide and dear to all who could still possess it. He alone was to let go of life, and the muffled familiars of death seemed gliding up to him like sheriffs' men, and from the invisible beams of the barn seemed to droop the hangman's cord.

He rallied every desperate ambition, and breathed a prayer to Nature in her generosity that he might have the courage to be a soldier for one moment, as he had never been since John Brown's time.

At the suggestion of John Brown, his wandering powers took coherence and example, and he remembered the manner in which old Brown had faced his fate, and Booth tried to be his pupil.

"Captain," called Booth, assuming a hollow, theatrical voice, "give me a living chance: withdraw your men a hundred paces from the barn, and I'll come out and fight you!"

This had been John Brown's request, when entrapped in his engine-house, and Booth aspired to die like Brown.

He repeated the request, and thought it quite unmerciful that he was not accorded a little stage-space to die effectively in.

"We'll waste no more time," the civil officer, without, spoke in a tone of disgust.

The katydid or cricket never ceased to call its resounding beads, and "Pray, pray, pray."

Booth searched the heavens and the world for some intercessor, and fetched from weakness his mother's name. By that saint he asked for fifty yards and for a little more time.

Everything was refused.

"Now, then, my brave boys," he declaimed, in the tones of the stage again, "prepare a stretcher for me!"

"Stretchers" were the canvas biers to carry out of battle wounded men. Booth — assuming to the end — would appear to be a veteran entitled to the honors of war.

He raised his carbine, feebly resolving to kill some one, or to fire it off, at least, and as he stepped, on foot and crutch, toward the center of the barn, to be farthest from men's aiming, a friction-match was scratched behind him as if his broken bones had rasped each other, and sent a cold chill up his spine.

He turned, and saw the barn on fire!

A lighted wisp of straw, twisted by some one without, had fallen into loose hay, and some brush, piled against the outside of the barn, was also afire. The warm flame for a single instant carried the odor and crackle of his father's log-cabin to his heart, and he shouted, as his crutch fell from under his arm and left him helpless:

"Captain, do it quick! Now shoot me through the heart!"

The cricket ceased to sing, though everything besides came forth in the bright light, till what had been the throne of gloom stood revealed in the blessed implements and yield of husbandry, and there were wasps flying around their nests in the roof, scenting flame, and in the litter of the floor ran rats in single file, all slyly, as from a sinking ship, and one squealed as it crossed his shadow like an old witch in an incantation scene.

The plow and harrow-teeth took a ruddy gleam; some swallows in the timbers flew round and round, blinded by the fire, and the pegs for tobacco and the burning tobacco-leaves grew to be ferns and scallops of gold, as they hung, like gilded scenes in spectacles, around the desperate man.

He had seen fires upon the stage and helped to stamp them out, and he limped toward the greater flame near a corner; but suddenly a great tongue of fire licked him and singed him as if Cerberus at hell's door had fondled on him with a furnace-tongue!

Fear seized him, and he ran toward the door on misfitting bones — the door held open as by some invisible angel — and as he ran, the ponderous beams and trees in the structure seemed to fall upon his skull and mash it like an egg.

*B*ooth next felt water in his face, and two men were holding him up and searching his body and putting their fingers in his brain.

"It's here," said one, "right where he shot the President, behind the ear, and on the same side, and here it's come through!"

In gagging torments he discerned before him two men in Confederate dress, all shown by the light of the burning barn, which was reflected in the homestead porch he lay upon.

"Did — he — betray — me?" sighed Booth, pointing to one of these, the officer who had brought him to the house.

He did not hear the answer, but he made it himself:

"Tell — mother — I thought — I did — best — rights — a country — till — I died. Kill me! Kill me!"

Herold, tied to the tree in the little flat lawn, saw them turn Booth, to make him comfortable, and heard him gasp and groan, and Herold shed the only tears.

Booth could not swallow, and his words were measured like dew in the honeysuckle's cup, that drooped above his eyes and opened to the fire.

He saw them, in his paralysis, hold up the arsenal of things he had carried so long — a great, fierce knife, with rust of blood upon it; two pistols with revolving cylinders thick as his riven ankle, and loaded in every chamber; a seven-shotted carbine; a candle-spotted pocket compass; his diary full of protestations and despair, and holding Light Pittson's name; his pipe and scarf-pin, and the likenesses of ladies; and a little Catholic medal. He sighed:

"Tongue!"

The detective opened his mouth and said:

"Booth, no blood is on your tongue."

He started at his name, which seemed a century since it had been mentioned, and gasped:

"Hands!"

The officer raised his hand and moistened it with a piece of ice, and lifted it all limp to Booth's face. It fell uncontrollable, like his broken foot.

He feebly moved his eyeballs through an arc which swept all nature and exhaled the closing words:

"Useless — 'sless!"

His face now expressed the unseen agony for which there was no word, and his cherished pride of strength pushed Death away that mercifully drew near again and again, but ever was repelled by the flushing rose and pulse of life, till the fine countenance of the actor and athlete seemed a battleground of wounds and spasms, growing hollower with each contention, and ready at the cock's crow, like the wandering ghost, to fade into the morn.

A carbineer had killed him in the barn; and, long afterward, was found in the ashes there the field-glass delivered to him at Surratt's — its leather case found uninjured in a distant farmhouse.

The cocks began to crow. The morn awaked with sullen eye. A doctor had come, but it was too late.

The assassin's body was put into a Negro's cart and hauled to the Potomac, and on the way the captors read to the thrilled Negro's ears, from Booth's diary, such words as these:

"Hunted like a dog through swamps and woods — wet, cold, and starving, with every man's hand against me — behold the cold hand *they* extend to me — God can not pardon me if I have done wrong — serving a degenerate people — so ends all — that makes life sweet and holy — misery upon my family — no pardon in the heaven for me, since man condemns me so — bless my mother — the curse of Cain upon me!"[*]

When the body was brought to the city of Washington, Senator Pittson and his daughter with others identified it.

There was one great scar upon his neck, made long before by a tumor from a pistol-ball which had been accidentally shot into his side, and had worked its way out to his neck, and the tumor had been torn open by a jealous woman before healing.

"Here, Light, my daughter," said the senator, "is a symbol of what should turn you from the spurious to the good romance. Old shows and showmen try to stop the world and kill its real actors. Theatricals in government are doomed."

"Miss Light," said Luther Bosler, drawing the beautiful woman from the awful scene, "let us reflect that, perhaps, in John Brown's illegal act to do good, this boy, Booth, found his example; and so violence is a poor ally of justice everywhere. I am a Dunker yet, in the belief that peace is the only good result of war."

"Thank you for your charity to that poor Absalom," said Light. "I

---

[*]   These entries are to be found beginning *"Te amo,"* and the first date "Friday, the Ides," in Lieutenant-Colonel Conger's testimony in Surratt's trial, vol. i, p. 310. The testimony of different persons naturally differs very much.

fear that I have wronged, in you, a gentleman."

"I am earnestly waiting," said Luther, "to forgive you, and with all my heart!"

Chapter LI
EMIGRAVIT

*T*HE judge-advocate, who was to arraign the prisoners before a court-martial of nine accomplished officers, made up his case in advance. Lloyd Quantrell was brought from prison and privately examined. The state of public feeling made it difficult to separate what men imagined from what they knew; but the military attorneys were the coolest of the people, and the civil attorney-general had settled the propriety of their jurisdiction.

"This is a crime," said the judge-advocate, "which has been committed in the midst of a great civil war, in the capital of the country, in the camp of the commander-in-chief of our armies; and if the common law of war can not he enforced against criminals of that character, then I think such a code is in vain in the world."

The only excuse of moment for the eight culprits arraigned, was that the court could not have jurisdiction; and the blood of the President might have smoked for justice in vain had his slayers been turned over to the common courts of Washington, where the virus of slavery, like a deadly alkali, long survived in the soil; and more than two years afterward a jury failed to punish a principal in the conspiracy.

Quantrell had nearly abandoned hope as he saw the case close around him — Booth dead, and Fenwick testifying that he had seen Lloyd in Washington.

Hannah Ritner appeared, before the findings were determined, and with her came Lloyd's wife, and Luther Bosler, and all the Pittsons.

"What is the power that woman exercises over me?" said Lloyd to his wife. "Has she come here to destroy me?"

Hannah had grown very gray, and, since the death of the President, her flesh and bearing were both reduced.

"I have but one labor in this life to do," the gaunt and weary woman said, "and my strength is just enough to finish it. It has been testified by General Bosler that this man" (pointing to Lloyd) "swore on oath with Booth to revenge the South. He has been a Southern soldier to the last — no more, no less.

"Again, he visited Booth at Bryantown. Gentlemen, I sent him there, claiming to have his father's commands, whom he so revered, and here is the letter he sent to that father, which I have never shown to any man before this day. Read it, and behold with what scorn he rejected the assassin's advances and discouraged his plot!

"There was another vow this young man made, and he has kept it in the faithfulness of hunger and love's temptation — he made it to his father in the bitter sundering of civil war — never to play the spy, nor cross the lines of war. I set one oath against the other, and they become consistent."

Lloyd's eyes were flowing as he heard his father's name, and had found an advocate in this incomprehensible being, who had long ago predicted his career.

"Gentlemen," continued Hannah Ritner, "it is of record that Lloyd Quantrell manumitted his slaves; and here is the bill of sale to his father, that the act might be effected. Would that manumitter hate the President for the act of emancipation, and desire to have his blood?"

"How came she by all my father's private papers?" asked Quantrell of himself. "Is she a soothsayer indeed?"

"And still there lies the charge that Mr. Quantrell was in Washington. Twice his name was given at the bridge. In the first case he has no witness; for Booth, who gave his name, in mean revenge, can never speak again; but in the other case, where the companion of the assassin, on Good-Friday night, passed for Major Quantrell, I read your mind, Mr. Assistant Advocate, and charge that Herold has admitted already that *he* gave the name of Quantrell at Booth's direction!"

Something of the old fire and spiritual frenzy was in her manner now, and an exclamation of wonder and fear went round the apartment when the attorney bowed his head, saying:

"Yes, Herold has relieved the prisoner of that charge, but Fenwick *saw* him here."

"Call Fenwick in!" said Hannah Ritner. "He is confined in this prison, and I dare the prediction that he will say he was mistaken."

The Old Capitol Prison it was — once the seat of government when the British invader destroyed the Capitol edifice, and from its shades the gloomy spirit of Calhoun, brooding over beleaguered slavery, had floated away like a soul upon the river Styx.

Fenwick appeared and glanced around the room, and Lloyd Quantrell rose and looked at him, relentless and avaricious of his life as some highwayman, and his port was like the executioner's.

"Look at these letters, Fenwick," said Hannah Ritner, "and see if you identify the writer of them in this presence!"

She gave him a bundle, and he turned them over once, and became pale and seemed to swoon for an instant. Hannah Ritner took the letters back and spoke:

"Give him that Bible and cross, and let him swear that Quantrell was the man he saw!"

Fenwick took the book and cast a look of imploration on Hannah Ritner and of terror upon Quantrell, and faltered:

"I see I was mistaken. That was not the man I supposed to be my old friend Lloyd Quantrell."

As Katy embraced her husband with the rapture of relief, the Government's lawyer exclaimed:

"Mr. Fenwick, you have barely saved yourself. We have been looking for some one to make an example of for perjury, and we had already obtained a clear alibi for Major Quantrell. — There remains, major, but one undisproved imputation against you: did you see the fugitives, Booth and Herold, in Virginia?"

Quantrell had remained standing, still looking the speechless fury of an injured friendship upon Fenwick.

"I did see Booth," said he, "and gave him the commonest offices of mercy. If he had been strong, reckless, and my equal for an encounter, I might have treated him far differently; but he was helpless, disappointed, so changed in all the attributes of man, that I saw remorse was working out a penance worse than death, and that death also was close before him. My situation made me morally weak: I did not know what to do, and I let my impulses decide me. I thought of him in better times, the playmate of my childhood — and of his mother's sorrow. Something is due, gentlemen, to our weakness at the close of such a war, and the lingering tyranny of hospitality we may have extended, even to those whose crime we abhorred; and perhaps the great victim of that crime, overlooking our exposure and temptation, guided our hands to mercy, or forgave the little charity in which we sinned!"

Prompt, soldierly, manfully, as Quantrell spoke, the justice-seekers weighed his manner and his words, and the plea he made saved life and captivity to many; for the Government was now possessed of every person's name and act of abetting, in the course of that long, mysterious crime — the original parties to the abduction plot, all of whom were guilty of the consequences of that beginning; the shelterers of Booth from point to point, to some of whom he went, relying upon their implication in past misdeeds; and some who made his cause their own.

It was determined to let those go, in time, who had merely done humane offices to the fugitives, or who had not been active in the plot.

Captain Cox, and Jones, who sold Booth his boat, and the Brawners and Smoots, who had been leagued with Atzerodt and Surratt to row the captive President over the river, escaped the court-martial, as did several aiders and abettors in Virginia, to whom the assassin disclosed his name, and who had read the public proclamations.

Yet, with low, abiding party malice, the kindly discriminating military men, who punished only the grossest of those offenders, were traduced for years!

The judge-advocates shook Quantrell's hand, and the benignity and greatness of the Government, as Lloyd's palms thrilled beneath the grasp of soldierly opponents, he felt like more than pardon — like fatherhood.

"Never," said he to Luther Bosler, "shall my father find me sullen to his ideas of freedom and of nationality again. As I am for the Government now, I shall be among those who have ever been for it, and who look not to the past."

In a few days Quantrell was paroled, but ordered not to leave the city, and Fenwick was imprisoned as a slippery witness.

"Quantrell," said Hannah Ritner, "I am going to see your father, who is in the mountains, to escape the heat of Baltimore. He is very ill, but I trust you may see him once more. When you are permitted, come to my old cabin, where I read your fortunes by the light of a great personal experience. And here, my children, are letters taken from poor Fenwick's trunk, full of the music of the turtle-dove."

When she had gone, Lloyd and Katy found every letter Lloyd had written to his wife through the long war and separation, breathing love and devotion and brave trust in Heaven and time.

"O husband," said Katy, "you need but one thing more to wash your spirit white — humility."

"Where can I find it, my darling?"

"Where I have found my wedding-ring again — in the water-brook of my tears. Lloyd, you must be baptized among the Dunkers, who are people of peace and worldly rest, and have no wars nor idle passions. Liquor and tumult wait to consume you in the city. Come into our mountains and be wrapped in their soft arms of shelter and of love!"

"Katy, the man who denied you these letters of assurance, and let you think me all these years a villain and seducer, ought not to live."

"Hush, Lloyd! he was false to you — because he loved your wife."

*T*he pains ecclesiasticism was at to make the most of Abel Quantrell's conversion and to rectify his son's matrimonial irregularity, gave slight concern to Lloyd and his wife, who were well understood to have been married as legitimately as was usual, and to have been unusually faithful; and when it was found that Katy would be nobody's convert, and that Quantrell would probably become come a Dunkard, the Church set about ordaining and disciplining Hugh Fenwick, who was meek as a sheep.

There being no strictly monastic institution for American men, Fenwick's captivity lay between the old novitiate block in Frederick City and the convent at Georgetown. Beneath the convent slept an assassin who had once been a soldier and a priest, and before Abraham Lincoln's birth this person had sacrificed fifty-two human lives by an infernal machine he exploded, to kill First-Consul Napoleon Bonaparte. Escaping to America, he was used awhile, with his aristocratic notions, to put down "usurpations of the laity,"* and finally he died director of the Georgetown convent.

At this Limoelan's tomb, in the middle of the Sisters' vault, where politics lay dead amid disappointed love or immolated sensibility, Lloyd Quantrell and his wife were led to witness the penance and hear the confession of *Father* Fenwick at last.

It distressed them both to see the plight of this overtaken fox as he paraded in the gloomy place with sandals on his feet, in a long shirt, with a shaved head, and carrying a ponderous candle.

"Katy," said the monk, "the fasting and the tasks I must do for the remainder of my days, will not be hard compared to the pain of losing you forever; and I can not blame my imperfect nature that, having drunk once at the wells of your soft eyes, I should have been always athirst to see my image reflected there. But your husband was my friend, and the injury I did to him will weigh upon my soul in the solitude of my cell, unless he fully forgives me and takes my hand."

"Take it, Lloyd," said Katy. "He always was respectful to me, and was the best of teachers. We are blessed so much that we can not hate anybody."

"Fenwick," said Lloyd Quantrell, "I fear if we had met elsewhere than in these mysterious shades, I should have given you my hand in more than cordiality. But since the world is to close upon you, my spirit shall not stay here to give you any trouble. I tempted you, being myself under love's sore temptation, and I ask you to forgive me for the infliction our clandestine marriage has brought upon you."

"Do you forgive me unreservedly, Lloyd?"

"Without reserve. If we ever meet in this world, it shall not be as enemies."

As the receding footsteps of the happy pair were lost on Fenwick's ear, he murmured to himself:

---

*   De Courcy's "History of the Catholic Church in the United States."

"I feared that live fellow more than all these unmuscular ghosts. Since he is no longer dangerous, I'll make my way to Nelly's soon, and she has promised to marry me. How true it is that —

'When the devil was sick, the devil a monk would be;
 When the devil got well, the devil a monk was he!'"

As Lloyd Quantrell reached the city, the drums of the two great disbanding armies of the Union thrilled his ears. For two days they had been passing in procession before the President's house, and he looked with astonishment at the resources of the state, unending, it almost seemed, like the corn-fields of the New World. More than one million men were marching back to private life, and, alas! of fellow-countrymen, more than half a million had lost their lives, and, last of all, the magistrate of all.

General Bosler called to Lloyd that they would go to the theater that night and see Nelly Harbaugh bring out her new piece. A private box just accommodated the Pittson family of three, and Luther, Lloyd, and Katy.

"I have never before been in a theater," said Luther, "but this poor girl needs our assistance, and presented me with this box."

Lloyd thought there was an appearance of constraint on Mrs. Pittson's face; for he had no knowledge of the close ties which bound him to the senator, and these had embarrassed Mrs. Pittson from the instant when her daughter met Lloyd at Harper's Ferry.

As Light and Katy sat together at the front of the box, with their contrasts of bright and night, many a returned veteran of the war looked at them in almost trembling homage, as the wonders of a beauty perfected during the war. Light was still excited on the painful subject of her father's parentage; but its discovery had done much to bring domestic humility to her heart, and this night she was to relinquish or accept Luther Bosler, who had arranged to settle in Kansas with other Dunker emigrants, and to take Jake his father along — the old place having been sold to Katy, who was to live in Catoctin Valley with her husband.

The curtain rose upon a school scene in the old Dutch country, and Nelly Harbaugh was a pupil. The teacher, a lame youth, full of animal life and with beauty in spite of his lameness, betrays a rough favor for this pupil, who weaves around his strength and susceptibility the coquetries of love and willfulness; and with some humorous display of German habits and *patois* the girl is ordered to be "kept in" after school and set to a task, for punishment. When all the lads and maidens go, and the teacher is alone with his tormentor, he asks why he is persecuted, and betrays the deep feelings of his heart, and avows the love she has fully understood. But he is poor, hated as a Yankee trespasser, an abolitionist, and worse than infidel. His loneliness, however, has been his greatest charm to her; for he is loved through pity.

While they all praised the acting, and felt the native inspiration in the tale, the curtain rose upon the teacher's home in the Green hills of Vermont: a little mother, hardly to be distinguished from her large brood, sewing shoes for livelihood, and the flour gone in the barrel. Poverty and struggle are revealed, and nothing is left but one son, whose education has taken the last cent of the patrimony, and whose pittance as a teacher is the widow's stay. And now this son has felt the pangs of love himself, and would be married where there is family pride and high connections, but no fortune. The teacher has sent his favorite pupil to his mother, and at the widow's tale of woe and ceaseless dependence the pitying maid resigns her hopes, and hears the widow's gratitude.

"Why, this is the tale my father has often told me of his own life," said Lloyd. "How beautiful is Nelly in her dark wig and false tresses, and I seem to be reading a story I already know!"

He looked at Light Pittson, and saw her face full of emotion, as she said:

"There is surely romance here, and, Lloyd, it concerns us both."

Now the scene showed the teacher discharged and in a bare law-office, desperate for occupation, but deeper hurt in love's involvements; for his pupil is promised by her guardian to a man of rising station who is to be the Governor of a new American Territory, and has already gone there to prepare her home. His absence is prolonged, and love reenters the hearts of the twain behind him. A strong, remorseless, mighty power impels the lover to demand what nature ever would concede him — the possession of his idol; and in his burning zeal her weakness melts like wax.

The actress and the man played passion to the life, as only in rare, dauntless breasts its fires burn and heave; and when the tardy lover comes, he finds — his rival's child.

The father offers the amends of honor and the marriage rite, but is refused by his lady, because there are hungrier mouths to feed at his mother's hearth.

In admiration of the woman's spirit, the rival becomes her gallant friend, and asks the gift of her child as the solace of his Western home.

The scene where the parents relinquish to the behests of society the offspring of their passion, touched multitudes to tears, and Nelly was called before the curtain and made the heroine of the city.

"Lloyd," said Luther Bosler, gravely, "could any heart be so hard as to impute evil to that little child?"

"None but a coward's," Lloyd replied.

He looked at Edgar Pittson, who smiled at all this tale, as one of life's kindly trifles.

The last scene of the play shows that fortune has turned in the lame lover's favor, and he has secured clients, following, and gold, and seeks the image he had worshiped, to become the companion of his maturity.

She has made for her penance austerity, and exposure for philanthropy's sake, and taken vows to Heaven holier than enthusiasm's; and she haunts the wilderness of the hills.

He is a man, and the social instincts draw him hard; and so, while the music of a lighted church woos him to his bridal with another, the lady of his youth stands in the winter snows outside, resigning him in the extremest woe of expiation.

"What is this tale?" Lloyd Quantrell whispered; "it seems to me I know that teacher, and that suffering woman, too."

"Lloyd," said Nelly Harbaugh, to whom they had gone, in her dressing-room, to give her congratulations, "I chose that part to play, because none could render it by deeper experience than mine; and I also heard there was an old misunderstanding in your father's life, hard to be explained and better to be represented. Do you understand it now?"

"I? Why, I thought I felt my father through it all. That woman, then, who suffered all too nobly — she was who?"

"Lloyd, I think it was meant for my mother," Edgar Pittson said, without the least excitement of manner. "The old were once young, and romance blazed in their lives and made fantastic shadows and similitudes, such as they see who live by country hearths and stir the embers to an occasional glow. I was the child they parted from. Your father was my father also; and now, I hope, your German brother will be my son."

He looked where Luther Bosler stretched his hand to Light Pittson, and saw the roses climb to her cheeks as she accepted it, and Katy kissed her fondly.

"Lloyd," said Light, "do you remember when you kissed me in the train that night at Harper's Ferry? Something purer than love made you do it — the romance of old times flowing in our related veins. I want you to kiss me again; and to kiss my mother's dread of you away, also."

"I am all confused again," said Lloyd, tenderly kissing all the ladies, and his wife at last. "How came this play to be made?"

"Why," said Edgar Pittson, "1 found that jesuitical fellow, Fenwick, knew something of it, and I freely told him the rest, and I suppose he made the piece for Nelly."

"Don't abuse him," cried Nelly Harbaugh. "I am to try the remainder of life with him, and he will have enough lies to tell, as my husband and traveling agent, to keep me well advertised."

"But the lady who is your mother, brother Edgar," said Lloyd, "do I know her?"

"Thank God, she still lives," spoke the senator, in fervent respect, "and is at this moment with your father! Lloyd, she has fulfilled a mother's part with you, and is worthy of your tenderest care. She has genius, that may have been developed by her misfortune into nearly double sight, and a heart as loving as universal humanity."

"I have not wandered from my father's house for years," said Lloyd, "to return with mean uncharity. Now I can see, in his wounded heart, the reasons for his suffering, and his spirit of resistance to all forms of oppression. I might, also, have returned and found Katy another's, or been parted from her by my own error — and even she has been pointed at, with all her purity, as one wooed and flung aside. He who gave me the precious gift of life transmitted his warm affections to me also, and I long to throw myself at my father's feet and assure him that nothing in his youth could keep me from honoring him forever."

"That has been my feeling, Lloyd," said Edgar Pittson, "and in honoring our parents we are promised long life in our land. Our father's apparent preference for me over you was another proof of his generous nature, for he thought you possessed the greater share of worldly acknowledgment. There are men who hate the offspring of their mistakes and banish them to unaccredited obscurity, but I have possessed my father's love and given him all my confidence, and I have worked in his heart an equal love for you, my brother. Your wife has been his daughter, and is possessed of half his estate. Thus religion can be brought out of what might have been dishonor, if we had let nature be our shame. I have used the disadvantage of my birth to incline my heart toward other willful or weak fellow-creatures, and make the allowances of charity for them, and a faith that is never ashamed goes with me; and when you took your side, Lloyd, with the slave States, in arms, I gave you my sympathy, all the more, that I felt you were in error; and I knew, if your life was spared, that you would come back to your father's house a noble man."

As these tones of strength and gentleness came down like a shower in sunshine, and love looked out at Lloyd from every eye, he tried to speak, but could not. His tongue grew thick, and a sob came up from his deep chest that moved all to tears.

"Let me sit awhile alone here," he said at last; "I want to cry a little."

They kissed his forehead, one after another, and stole away.

*A*nd there, as in the theaters, where the apostles preached of old in the colonies of the Greeks, the spirit of conversion came upon Lloyd Quantrell; the birth of peace in his soul, and the alighting of the heavenly dove.

A religious instinct, derived from his mother, took root in his contrite heart like a rose-bush, and her prayers were answered as by the singing of a bird from its thorns. The desires of duty and of rest overcame him, and he went out changed, like the bright spirit that was seen going from the fiery furnace of Nebuchadnezzar.

*I*t was a Sunday laden with blossoms and dove-warblings when Quantrell sat again in the old Dunker meeting under the azure bar of the South Mountain, and heard Luther speak the gospel of peace and forgiveness.

Lloyd thought how he had been spared where so many fell — some by the sword, and some by the flesh; some by their weakness, and some by their strength; some shipwrecked upon the world; some brought home, like the ark of Noah, to the mountaintops; and the soft, illimitable bar of the mountain gave him rest to look upon it as if it were the rainbow of God's covenant brought down to be his barrier against the consuming fires of human rage.

As he walked toward the flowing stream to kneel and be dipped into the Pietist brotherhood, Katy looked at him with the sense of an old belief now assured, and Jake Bosler murmured:

"Nefer mind! — Bi'm-by is come, Katy!"

Then they went on to the inclination of the mountain, where Smoketown stood like something lost and sprinkled along the highway. The jaws of the sundered hillocks drank them in, and the witch's wild lawn stood in rank strength and flower, around her little cabin, while the clear torrent gurgled around the fruit tree roots, and near the door two doves were sitting side by side on an apple-bough, and in a low tone were saying:

"Coo-roo! — ah, coo-roo!"

"Go in, my brother," Edgar Pittson said; "your father is expecting you. Tread lightly, for he is very low today!"

There, in the little home the lonely woman had kept so many years in danger and the terror of bad laws, sat Hannah Ritner beside a bed lighted round by tapers; and on the bed was a face closed in a smile of plaintive obduracy, as if regarding the ceremonial of his death indulgently, because women had pleased to arrange it.

"We have taken him into holy church, and sprinkled him with holy water," said one of the nuns of Emmitsburg.

"Father," Lloyd whispered, bending to kiss the sleeper; but the coldness of the lips made him start. — "O Edgar," he cried, "come here!"

The elder son entered and touched the old man's brow.

"Lloyd, we are equals now. We have no father."

"I thank God, Edgar, that the blood I saw on his face when we parted, is there no more. He told me we should never meet again; but I know there is a land where all tears are wiped away. And now, where is our mother — she who suffered with him all those years?"

"Here, friends," spoke Luther Bosler, "and she has not survived him long. See! she is not yet cold. The last poor fugitive to take shelter in her cabin, has passed on with her. No bloodhounds can follow them."

Lloyd and his wife knelt down at Hannah Ritner's feet, and still the turtles at the door were heard to murmur together, as she had foretold.

"Pray!" said Edgar Pittson to his new son.

Luther raised his hands above the aged sister of the Magdalen, and spoke what came upon his lips:

"Thou shalt be called by a new name, which the mouth of the Lord shall name. Thou shalt no more be termed Forsaken; neither shall thy land anymore be termed Desolate; but thou shalt be called Hephzi-bah, and thy land Beulah: for the Lord delighteth in thee, and thy land shall be married. For as a young man marrieth a virgin, so shall thy sons marry thee."